399

One of the Best Novels of 1999:

Best Fiction: Borders.com
(Top Ten Fiction Titles of 1999)

Best Book/Editor's Pick: Amazon.com
(Top Ten SF/Fantasy Titles of 1999)

A Best Book of the Year in SF/Fantasy:
BarnesandNoble.com

The Readers' Choice List: SF Site
(Top Ten SF/Fantasy Titles of 1999)

P9-DMJ-382

"Elizabeth Haydon makes a magnificent fantasy debut. Her voice is warm, often humorous, and sure, her world a richly realized place of myth and magic, and her characters complex and utterly compelling." —Mary Jo Putney

"A well-worked out backdrop of impressive depth and appeal." —*Kirkus Reviews*

"A powerful novel. It is lucid, interesting, well paced, well organized, adventurous, magical, and with characters who are original yet consistent to themselves. There are sequences of considerable power. This author will surely go far.

"I am amazed by the growing number of strong new voices in fantasy, hitherto mostly male. Elizabeth Haydon is sure to change that." —Piers Anthony

"Combine the witty banter of Shakespeare's *Taming of the Shrew* with the star-crossed soulmates of his *Romeo and Juliet*, add a little dash of modern fairy tale à la *Star Wars*, and you'll get a hint of the fantastic new world created by first-time novelist Elizabeth Haydon."
—*Romantic Times* (4½ stars out of 5)

"In a genre choking with predictable worlds and characters, Haydon blows in on the fresh air of new insights and talents. A very auspicious beginning!" —Jennifer Roberson

"*Rhapsody* provides readers with a different heroine and the kind of action and interplay that proves the art of storytelling is alive and well." —L. E. Modesitt, Jr.

"Prepare to lose a weekend. Elizabeth Haydon's *Rhapsody* is filled with wit, adventure, and delightful characters. Pick up this book at your own risk—of neglecting your family, friends, and chores—while under the enchanted spell of *Rhapsody*." —Kathi Kamen Goldmark

Rhapsody

CHILD OF BLOOD

Elizabeth Haydon

TOR®
fantasy

A TOM DOHERTY ASSOCIATES BOOK
NEW YORK

This is a work of fiction. All the characters and events portrayed in this book are either products of the author's imagination or are used fictitiously.

RHAPSODY

Edited by James Minz
Maps by Ed Gazsi

A Tor Book
Published by Tom Doherty Associates, LLC
175 Fifth Avenue
New York, NY 10010

www.tor.com

Tor® is a registered trademark of Tom Doherty Associates, LLC.

ISBN: 0-812-57081-2
Library of Congress Catalog Card Number: 99-31360

First edition: September 1999
First mass market edition: June 2000

Printed in the United States of America

0 9 8 7 6 5

To

November, October, and September

the three best months of the year

with love and appreciation

for all they have given me

ACKNOWLEDGMENTS

The strength of a musical rhapsody is in the variety of inspiration that brought it into being, and the talents of the musicians who make it come alive. Please take a moment to acknowledge the orchestra:

Richard Curtis, agent, artist, and music aficionado extraordinaire, who believed in my song before anyone else, even I, did. Without him there would be no book.

My excellent editor, James Minz, the conductor who knows the tune better than I do, and all the wonderful people at Tor.

The concertmasters, T. L. Evans and W. J. Ralbovsky, for their help and friendship at the very beginning, the most trying of rehearsal periods.

The reviewers, Rebecca Mayr, Sharon Harris, Jennifer Roberson, and Anne McCaffrey, who listened in on dress rehearsal and pointed out some rough passages before opening night.

Robert J. Becker, for his cartogeographic calculations and geological expertise.

Norma J. Coney, for her knowledge of all things herbal and floral.

Luis Royo, for his extraordinary cover art, and Ed Gazsi, for his beautiful maps.

Helen M. Kahny, for her expert understanding of medieval music in general and the Guido scale in particular, as well as everything else she has given me.

Professor Wilhelm Nicolaisen, for expanding my love of folklore and showing me how to read its secrets.

And last, and most, my husband and children, my unflaggingly loyal patrons and captive audience.

Heartfelt thanks and appreciation to you, one and all. Please take a bow.

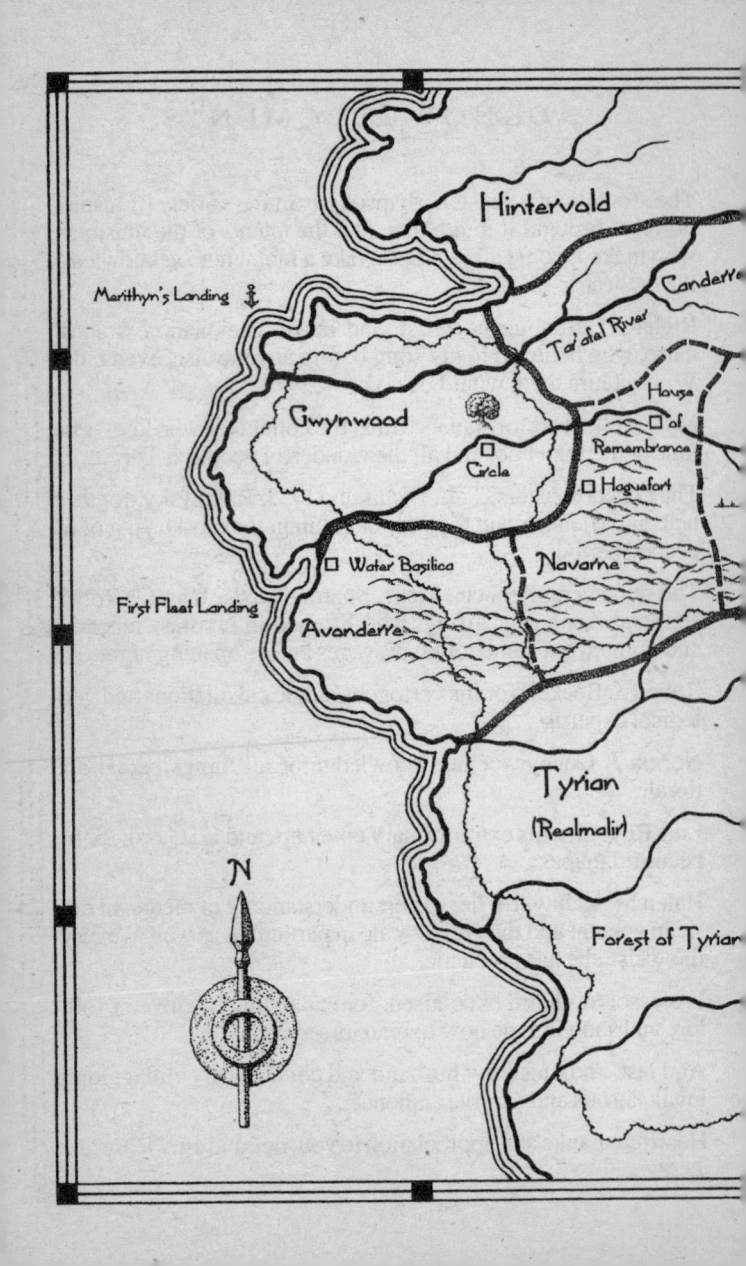

Ylorc
(Canrif)
Yarim
Roland
Bethe
Corbair
Krevensfield
Plain
Fira Basilica
Wind Basilica
Bethany
The Moot
The Cauldron
Sepulvarta
Ethar Basilica
The Teeth
(Manteids)
Night Mountain
Earth Basilica
Desert
Sorbold

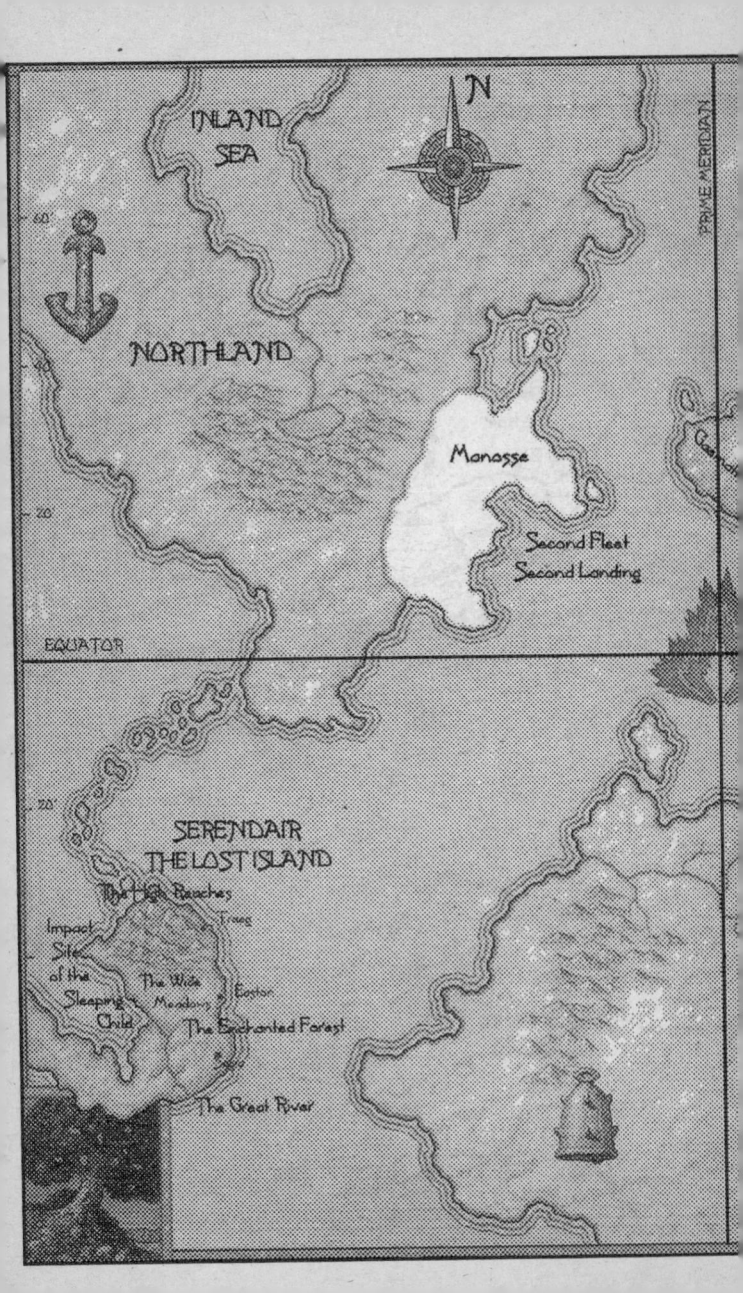

Hinterwold

Explorer's Landing

Tor'alet River

Gwynwood

Roland

Great White Tree

First Fleet Landing

Forest
of Tyrian

Second Fleet
First Landing

Tyrian
(Realmalir)

Montaids
(The Teeth)

Firbolg
Conrif

Sorbold

non aligned

Third Fleet Landing

THE FIERY RIM

THE GREAT OVERWARD

40°

20°

20°

40°

60°

THE PROPHECY OF THE THREE

The Three shall come, leaving early, arriving late,
The lifestages of all men:
Child of Blood, Child of Earth, Child of the Sky.

Each man, formed in blood and born in it,
Walks the Earth and sustained by it,
Reaching to the sky, and sheltered beneath it,
He ascends there only in his ending, becoming part
    of the stars.
Blood gives new beginning, Earth gives sustenance,
The Sky gives dreams in life—eternity in death.
Thus shall the Three be, one to the other.

THE PROPHECY OF THE UNINVITED GUEST

Among the last to leave, among the first to come,
Seeking a new host, uninvited, in a new place.
The power gained being the first,
Was lost in being the last.
Hosts shall nurture it, unknowing,
Like the guest wreathed in smiles
While secretly poisoning the larder.
Jealously guarded of its own power,
Ne'er has, nor ever shall its host bear or sire
    children,
Yet ever it seeks to procreate.

Overture

Meridion

Meridion sat down at the Time Editor and began to work. He adjusted the lenses and checked the spools of diaphanous strands, ranging in density from the thick, clear film of the Past to the foggy, wisp-thin threads of the Future. He gave the slender tools a final cleansing wipe and spun out the thick thread he had identified off the Past spool, drawing it over the frame of the machine and positioning it under the lens. Separating carefully, he picked apart each timeline, working through centuries and years down to days and moments until he found the precise point of entry that he needed.

He smiled to himself as he watched the gait of the boy, cocksure and unguarded, as he wended his way along the forest road. The gait was very different from the one he was used to seeing. The scenery surrounding the boy was achingly bright and fresh, a glistening summer morning that begged appreciation, but he seemed oblivious of it. Meridion stopped the frame.

From the prismatic disc hovering in the air beside the Editor he took a tiny flask, dense black stone molded carefully into a spill-resistant phial. Upon uncorking it, Meridion recoiled slightly; the harsh odor was always more intensely astringent than he was prepared for it to be. He blinked several times, unwilling to use his hands to clear the water welling in his eyes, knowing the risk of even an infinitesimal droplet being accidentally applied or, worse, wasted.

When his vision cleared again he carefully drew forth the hair-thin brush and waited while the tiny bead of glimmering liquid elongated into an oval tear, then reabsorbed back up the miniature bristle. Finally satisfied, he meticulously dabbed the liquid onto the eyes of the boy in the now-frozen image and waited to see that the solution had spread across the sapphire-blue irises to the corners of each canthus. The window of opportunity would be small and final; it was important that the boy be given every chance to see things clearly and quickly. When he was done he recorked the phial and set it back on the gleaming disk.

Meridion removed the spool from the Time Editor and replaced it with a different one, another Past, even older. This he spun out with even more care, owing to its extreme age and the nature of the place from which it had come, now vanished beneath the waves. It took a great deal longer to find the right point on this thread, but Meridion was patient. It was important to do this correctly; much depended on it.

When he finally found the right place he stopped the frame again and picked up a different tool. With a practiced hand he made a smooth, circular slice, plucked the image from the first strand, and placed it gently into the second. He looked through the lens to check his work.

The boy had not lost consciousness, as he had expected, but instead lay writhing facedown on the ground with his head cradled in his hands, frantically rubbing his eyes. Meridion was both amused and sorry. *I should have known he would fight it,* he thought. He sat back and turned the viewing screen onto the wall to watch the outcome of his work and wait for the moment of meeting, and of exit.

The Lost Island

1139, THIRD AGE

The pain subsided as quickly as it had come. Gwydion spat out the dust from the road and rolled onto his back, allowing himself a deep groan. He glanced at the sky above him and was instantly aware of the shift not only in location but in time of day. A moment ago it had been early morning, and now it was afternoon, winding toward evening. That he had been removed from where he had been was clear to him; he had no idea where he was.

Gwydion had been blessed with a pragmatic nature, and after a moment of adjusting to the new surroundings he stood and began calculating what to do next. How or why this had happened to him was not an issue for the moment.

The air of this place was thinner than the air of home, and Gwydion knew it would take some time for him to acclimate to it. Glancing around, he spied a small copse of trees a short jog away, and he hastily made for it.

Upon reaching the shelter he sank to the ground and began to inhale in short, shallow breaths, slowing and expanding each one until his lungs began to assimilate, shielding his watering eyes to give them a chance to adjust. Then he felt for the items he had brought with him on his way to town: his dagger and pouch were still there, as well as his waterskin and the apple. He took a quick drink. As he was capping the skin he felt faint vibrations in the ground below him. A cart, or something like it, must be approaching.

Gwydion sank lower to the ground as the ever-thickening dust cloud signaled the arrival of the group. He could see three men walking beside the cart, which was pulled by two oxen with a calf following along behind. It was laden with barrels of grain and loose straw, and a fourth man was driving it. The dress of the men was unfamiliar to him, although it was apparent that they were peasants, probably farmers.

Gwydion listened as carefully as he could over the rumbling din of the cart's wheels. His eyes throbbed slightly and then were drawn to the farmers' lips, strangely accentuated in the haze that filled his view. Suddenly his vision became intensely clear; it was if he could see the words as they were formed in the men's mouths, and could hear them as if they were being spoken directly into his ear. When he recognized the language pattern, his head began to spin.

They were speaking Old Cymrian. *It isn't possible*, he thought. Old Cymrian was essentially a dead language, used rarely in the holy-day ceremonies of religions other than his own, or as a vanity language among those of Cymrian lineage. But it was being spoken here, between peasants, as common vernacular on an average day in farmlands. It wasn't possible, unless—

Gwydion shuddered. Serendair, the Cymrian homeland, had been gone for more than a thousand years now, vanished into the sea in the cataclysm that swallowed the Island and some of its neighbors in volcanic fire.

His ancestors had come from there, as had those of a few

of his friends, but by and large the refugees of that land were a dispersed people, the casualties of wars they visited upon the lands of their hosts. Could there still be an untouched pocket of them here, wherever he was, living as they had thirteen centuries before?

As the cart and its accompanying dust cloud rumbled out of sight, Gwydion's head emerged from the patch of trees and brush to watch it go. He saw it make a laborious climb up a graded hill to the west and disappear over the summit. He waited until he knew that he could reach the top of the hill with them in sight while remaining unseen, checked to be sure there was no one else on the road, and then made for the summit himself.

The countryside was hilly, and when he got to the top he paused a moment to take in the sight of the late-afternoon sun favoring certain pastures with blankets of gold. This rolling land was beautiful, and he knew he had never been through these parts before, or he would have remembered it. It was verdant in the heat of summer, the green earth filling the air with the rich scent of life.

The farmlands stretched out as far as he could see in an endless expanse of field and meadow dotted with trees but no real forests. There was no sign of any major waterway either, except for small streams that crossed the pastures, and the wind held no scent of the sea.

Gwydion had no time to wonder where he was; the light was beginning to leave the sky, and the cart was almost out of sight. Its destination was probably the small village he could see past the next valley. Between here and there were several small farms and one large one. He decided to stop at the first small farm and see if he might find lodging and, with any luck, answers.

Gwydion removed the gold crest ring from his hand and tucked it quickly into his pouch. He took one last look around the hilly vista, and drew in a deep breath. His lungs had gotten used to the air here; there was a sweetness to it, mixed with the scent of pastureland and barns, a richness that spoke of a happiness he had never known in his short life.

A sense of calm overtook him. There was no time to wonder how he had gotten here, and no need. Whatever the reason, he was here now, and he meant to make an adventure of it. He took off in a dead run for the farmhouse at the dip in the road, where candlelight was just beginning to shine in the windows.

$\mathcal{A}$ number of men were finishing the day's chores when he reached the first small farm, bringing the plows and animals back into the barn and making ready for the night. The sunset was a brilliant one, and it bathed the farmhouse and the surrounding pens with gentle streaks of crimson and pink.

The farmhands were laughing and joking; there was a festive mood in the air for the end of such a long day. Gwydion located the man he thought was the farmer. He was distinctly older than the others, with a shock of silver hair crowning a body still strong and muscular, and he directed the others with a soft voice that belied his great height.

Gwydion moved to the end of the carriage path next to the house, hoping to catch the attention of the farmer without seeming threatening. He stood there for a moment, but the men were hurrying to be finished and didn't see him.

"Partch!" A woman's voice called out over his head, and Gwydion turned around. An older woman, most likely the farmer's wife, was standing under the eaves of the house, pointing at him, and calling to the tall man. "Looks like you've got a new hand." She smiled at Gwydion, and he returned her grin. This was easier than he had thought.

The farmer gave the reins of the last of the horses to another of the men and came over, brushing his hands on his shirt. "Hello there, Sam," he said, offering his hand to Gwydion. "Looking for work?"

"Yes, sir," Gwydion answered, shaking hands. He hoped his pronunciation was correct. That the language was not his mother tongue was instantly apparent to the farmer, who slowed his words in an effort to be more easily understood. He gestured to one of the men, who came over, wiping his hands on a rag.

"Asa, show Sam here the shed. You can get settled; I'm afraid you missed supper, boy. But the foreharvest dance is in town tonight, and these young fellas are goin'. Why don't you ride along? There's bound to be food there if you're hungry."

The woman clucked at her husband. "We have scraps he can have now, Partch. Here, young man, come with me." She turned and went into the farmhouse.

Gwydion followed her, taking in the sight with amazement. The walls were stone with a wood interior, and the furniture was simple but well crafted; it bore the hallmarks of Cymrian artistry. The spindles on the chairs and staircases were turned in the exact manner of the railings on the altar of the basilica in Sepulvarta, the holy city of his homeland, the tables fashioned similarly to ones he had seen in the Great Hall in Tyrian.

"Here you are, dear," she said, handing him a plate of leftovers. "Why don't you take this with you out to the shed and clean up a bit? The foreharvest dance is a big thing in these parts—do they have one where you come from?"

Gwydion accepted the plate with a smile. "No, ma'am," he said respectfully.

"Well, I'm sure you'll enjoy it; it's the last dance before the marriage lottery, so you best have fun while you can." She winked at him, then set about finishing her work.

"Marriage lottery?"

"You don't have one at home?"

"No," said Gwydion, following her to the door. She swung it open for him and walked back toward the two men, who were washing with the others at the well.

"You must not come from a farm community, then."

"No, ma'am," said Gwydion. He thought of the place he lived and hid his smile.

"Well, you better get ready. It looks like the others are almost ready to leave."

"Thank you," Gwydion said to her gratefully. He took a scrap of the bread and ate it hurriedly, then followed Asa to the shed where the hired hands slept.

Gwydion leapt from the wagon as soon as it came to a stop. The ride had been rocky, but pleasant, and the farmhands agreeable, if not talkative. He had sensed a reserve from the beginning, and he wasn't sure if they were distant because he was unfamiliar or because of his mixed bloodline. Without exception the men were human, as were the farmer and his wife and everyone else he had seen thus far. The pure, homogeneous makeup of this place was so unlike the rest of the world, where half bloods dominated.

The village was ablaze with light, lanterns set on barrels and strung in trees, making for a festive mood. The community was obviously not a wealthy one, but the farms seemed substantial and the people reasonably fed and clothed for the most part.

Noticeable was an absolute lack of luxury, and Gwydion's eyes took in the details of decoration that had been fashioned out of simplicity—fresh-cut boughs of evergreen trees and fragrant flowers festooned the main hall that apparently served the community as house of worship, meeting place, grange, and school. Long tables laden with baked goods and harvest foods were set to the sides of the large open room with a dirt floor, and muslin love knots were tacked everywhere.

Despite being used to a far more wealthy and sophisticated life, Gwydion found himself taking in the homespun celebration with delight. There was a simplicity here that felt easy on his shoulders; it stood in marked contrast to the dull and ponderous ceremonies of festivity he was used to.

Excitement was starting to fill the air as people began to arrive, young women in pale-colored broadcloth dresses, young men in clean muslin shirts. There was a musician with a stringed instrument he didn't recognize and two others with minarellos, sometimes called groan-boxes back home. They were dragging barrels over to a place behind the food table. The village was making ready to celebrate the upcoming harvest, both of crops and of marriageable young people.

As the room started to fill, Gwydion began to sense that he was not going unnoticed. More than once a group of young women passed in front of him, looking him up and down, then whispering to each other in excitement and young laughter. This made him quite uncomfortable, but it was momentary; the group would disperse quickly or move on, to be joined by others or by some of the young men. He gauged the girls to be about his age, fourteen or so, while the boys seemed four or five years older, although there were a few that were younger.

Gwydion went to the refreshment table and was encouraged by an older woman to help himself, which he did gladly. No one asked him who he was, despite notice being taken that he was not local. Many others were apparently here from outside the village as well. When addressed by the villagers, an unknown young man was generally referred to as Sam or Jack; now he understood the farmer's greeting earlier.

An older man came into the room carrying a large wooden box, and a swirl of excitement rose up from the crowd. He made his way to the table and the woman behind it began clearing an empty spot for the contents of the box, which turned out to be a large number of small parchment sheets and several inkpots with quills and writing reeds.

Here the crowd began to separate by gender, with the young women continuing to mill about while the men hurried to the table, searching through the papers for specific ones, and, upon finding what they sought, scribbling on them with the quills. Gwydion was familiar with the concept of dance cards, and it seemed to him that perhaps that was what these were. He decided that this would be a good time to get some air.

The night had come while he was inside, and now the sky was totally dark. The lanterns and candles illuminated the area, and people continued to arrive, amid laughter and arguments and other sounds of excitement. They jostled past Gwydion as if he weren't there.

He was aware as he watched them of the seriousness of this festive ritual. Despite the light mood there was an undertone of solemnity, of portent, that was palpable. In a community such as this, mating and the propagation of families was essential to its survival.

Gwydion left the area around the meeting hall, looking to find a dark place where the stars were visible. He was well versed in astronomy, and suspected that he would be able to discern where he was once he got a clear look at the night sky.

The lanternlight played havoc with the visibility, and he

needed to get a good ways away before he was able to see anything. When he finally could, it didn't help much. He didn't recognize any of the constellations, or even a single star. A very bright one hung deep in the sky by the horizon, but even that was unknown to him.

He felt a cold wave of fear wash over him. Until now he had expected that it would be relatively simple to navigate home once he had ascertained where he was. But if even the stars were foreign, he was much farther away than he had originally thought, though the season was certainly the same as the one where he had been. Nothing was making sense. Gwydion sat down on a bank of barrels and fought the panic that was rising in his throat.

Across the road a slight movement caught his attention, and he turned to look. Someone was moving behind the identical bank of barrels that lined the roadway, crouching low and peering over the tops of them toward the meeting hall. Gwydion decided to investigate. He had left much of his gear back at the farmhouse, but he still had his dagger, and he drew it now and ran silently across the road, circling around behind the line of barrels.

When he was in position he rose carefully and rested one hand on a barrel, looking around it to spot the intruder. To his surprise it was a young woman, hiding behind the line of barrels and watching the comings and goings of the crowd.

He couldn't see her face. She had long straight hair with just a hint of a wave to it, and it hung like a silken sheet down her back. In the dark it appeared to be the color of pale flax, and Gwydion was struck by the desire to run his hand down it.

He reached out and instead tapped her on the shoulder. She started and gasped, reeling around to face him and nearly toppling the empty barrels into the road.

The look of shock on her face did nothing to diminish his instantaneous impression that she was undoubtedly the fairest thing he had ever seen. Her face was delicately formed, with large, dark eyes fringed with black lashes and an upper lip shaped like a longbow. Unlike the other young women at the party, she was clearly of mixed blood, as he was, and thin. As she backed up toward the barrels her hair fell over her shoulders, obscuring much of her upper body and the corsage of flowers that adorned her breast.

"Don't be frightened," Gwydion said as gently as he could. "I'm sorry if I startled you."

The girl took a deep breath, and her enormous eyes ran rapidly over his face. She blinked abruptly, as if trying to clear away sudden stinging tears. It took a long moment for her to be able to respond, and when she did the wonder in her voice made his stomach tighten with excitement.

"You're Lirin," she said. The words held as much awe as he had ever heard uttered before.

"Yes, partly; you are, too?"

She nodded slowly.

Gwydion coughed to cover the flush he felt creeping into his face. "Uhm, are there many of **you**, I mean, Lirin, around here?"

"No," she said, and the amazement was still in her voice. "Except for my mother and brothers, you are the first I have ever seen. Who are you?"

Gwydion thought about how to answer her. He wanted more than anything to tell her the truth, but he wasn't sure himself what that was.

"I'm called Sam," he said simply. "What about you?"

The young woman smiled for the first time, and Gwydion felt a strange stirring he had never experienced before. It was heady, and frightening, and dizzying all at once, and he was not sure that the control he normally had over his face or voice was still in place.

"Emily," she said, and then she looked behind her. Two young men were approaching, bantering between themselves, and looking around the area. The young woman backed up, almost into him, and then ducked quickly behind the barrels again. Gwydion sat down next to her, hidden from view as well.

Together they watched as the men searched around, looking down the dry dirt road and over the neighboring fields. Just then the music started, amid a swelling of laughter and applause from inside, and the men turned back toward the hall. Emily waited until they were out of sight, then let loose a long sigh.

"Do you know them?" Gwydion asked, wondering what he had missed.

"Yes," she said curtly. She rose up onto her knees to see better. Catching sight of no one else, she relaxed, then stood once more and brushed the dirt off her skirt.

Gwydion stood as well. In general he had little use for women, young or old; being motherless, he had little experience with any. But this girl was different somehow. There was an innate intelligence in her eyes, as well as something indescribable, and he was fascinated by her. Perhaps it was that she was the singular example of her race whom he had seen so far. Or it might have been the mild humming in his eyes and his utter inability to break his gaze away and stop looking at her. Whatever the reason, he wanted to make sure she didn't walk away.

"Why are you hiding? Don't you like to dance?"

She turned to face him again, and Gwydion felt the strange sensation once more. It began in his groin, but rushed rapidly to his head and hands, leaving those areas weak and perspiring a little. "I love to dance," she said. Her tone was wistful.

"Well, then, shall we? I mean, would you like to?" His voice sounded inane to his ears.

Emily's eyes filled with regret, and she shook her head. "I can't," she said sadly. "Not yet. I'm sorry."

"What's the matter?"

She looked behind her again. Seeing nothing that bothered her, she turned back around. She gave him a direct look. "Doesn't this all seem, well, barbaric to you?"

Gwydion stared at her in astonishment, then let out a laugh. "Yes, actually," he said, trying not to be rude at the same time he was being honest. "Yes, it does."

"Well, then, imagine how I feel."

Gwydion felt his liking of her instantly increase. He put his hand out to her. "Come out of there," he said.

Emily gave a backward glance, then took his hand and allowed him to assist her over the debris around the barrels. They walked a little farther down the road, then looked back toward the hall. The dance was in full swing, with merry music issuing forth and the sound of excited voices filling the night air. It was warm, with a soft breeze; a perfect night.

Gwydion had so many questions that he didn't know where to start, but he was sure that he did not want to frighten her off by overwhelming her with his need for information. He pointed to the corsage.

"Are you here with someone?"

Emily's brows furrowed; then her eyes followed his finger. Rapidly, understanding crossed her face.

"No," she said, smiling slightly. "These are a gift from my father. You don't come to the foreharvest dance with anyone, that would be counterproductive."

"I see," Gwydion said. Now that she was out in the lanternlight he took the opportunity to study her more. Her dress was velvet, probably a dark blue, and it was cut with a deep, curving neckline. Underneath it at the throat was a modesty piece that matched the lace at the hem, studded with a line of small silver buttons of simple manufacture. A tiny matching ribbon pulled two of the front strands of her pale hair off her face, securing them at the back of her head.

Her Lirin blood was obvious in her slim build and delicate features, but she was only three or four inches shorter than he was, probably just over five feet. Despite the calluses on her hands, and a small scar on her wrist, she had an absence of the coarseness that some of the other farmgirls had, and there was an air of dignity about her that belied her age. He wished he could tell more about the colors of her complexion and beautiful dark eyes, but the light was too weak.

He was suddenly grateful for the first time to his own father for the years of intense insistence regarding Cymrian language study. "Well, what are you going to do now? Since you obviously don't want to go in."

Emily looked back at the hall. "I think I'll just wait here until my brother comes to fetch me at midnight," she said, sounding a little disheartened.

"Seems like a pretty miserable way to spend a summer evening."

"Well, there are varying degrees of misery. It could be worse."

Gwydion nodded sympathetically. He could see that her family must be somewhat better off than most to afford her the trimmings on her dress, though in his family's circles she would still be seen as a very poor peasant, or at most a common landowner. Her family's relative wealth, coupled with her appearance, had obviously made her a prime target for the young hunters inside. Unlike the other young women, however, she was unwilling quarry, and he respected her for it.

"I have an idea," he said, casting a glance around. "There's a clear, flat area over there near the meeting hall, but not too near. I'm sure we can hear the music from there. Why don't we have a dance or two there? If you're willing, of course." All his years of etiquette training stumbled over his tongue and he screeched to an awkward halt.

Emily's face brightened, and Gwydion's heart rose. "What a wonderful idea," she said happily. "I would love to. Thank you."

He offered her his hand once more, and led her across the road and over the fields to the small clearing he had seen. They ducked quickly to the side of the building when more people came through the door, but managed to avoid being seen.

A mazurka was ending just as they reached the field. They stood, facing each other in awkward silence, until the next dance began. Gwydion put his hand on her waist, and was almost unbalanced by the thrill that shot from his fingers up his arm to his head. He took her hand as she lifted the edge of her skirt, and they followed the rhythm of the music across the field, turning in time.

Almost immediately there was a problem. Though the dance was a simple two-step, Gwydion's training had been in classical military style, and as a result, the unsophisticated step Emily used caught his foot on the fourth pass. She trod lightly on his toe, and embarrassment flooded her face. He ignored it, going on, but at the same point in the next set of passes it happened again. She stopped, looking humiliated, and turned away quickly.

"I'm terribly sorry, Sam," she said. "You must think I have all the grace of a farm animal. Maybe you should go back inside."

Gwydion took hold of her shoulders and turned her around. "What are you talking about? I'm the one who doesn't know the dance. Please don't do that."

"Do what?"

"Start acting like I'm one of them." He gestured at the hall. "I'm enjoying your company, Emily, and I can't think of anything you resemble less than a farm animal. Do you know what the next dance will be?"

Emily's smile returned. "Probably a courting twirl."

"Well, can I have another go of it? I think I can handle that."

She nodded. Gwydion noticed that he had not released her hand, and she had not pulled it away, so he held it as they stood, waiting for the waltz to begin. When it finally did he was careful to stick to the basic steps and not add any of the flourishes that he had been taught for use at court.

This time they meshed perfectly, and he could see exhilaration take her as they waltzed across the field in time to the diminished music. When she was excited her eyes caught the light, or perhaps they generated it themselves. Either way, by the time the dance was finished they were sparkling brighter than the illumination from any lantern.

"Emmy, what are you doing out here? Are you coming in?"

She whirled around. Gwydion looked over her head to see a small group standing at the edge of the field, staring at them. The speaker was a dark-haired young man of mixed race; he concluded that this must be her brother. In addition there were two young women and one of the boys who had been out looking for her earlier. All wore expressions containing varying degrees of displeasure.

"Everyone's waiting for you, Emmy. You've missed three dances already and your suitor card is messed up completely. Come on."

Emily straightened her shoulders. "I'll be in eventually, Ben," she answered with an annoyed tone. "And I couldn't care less about the suitor card. I didn't put one in the basket, so I shouldn't have one anyway."

"Everyone has a suitor card," said the other young man,

his annoyance a match for hers. "And I had the first dance. Now get in here."

Gwydion watched Emily's back go rigid. "Don't you dare speak to me like that, Sylvus," she said coldly. "I'll be in when I'm damned good and ready." He swallowed a laugh at the look of horror on the faces of the young women, and the astonishment of her brother and Sylvus. Ben smiled slightly, and turned to the other boy.

"See, didn't I tell you? Are you sure you want to risk ending up with *that* for the rest of your life?" He winked at her and went back inside, followed by the girls. Sylvus stared at her. Finally he spoke.

"Hurry up, Emily, I'm waiting." He went back inside, with a backward glare at Gwydion.

He heard her mutter under her breath. "Yes, and you're insufferable, too."

Gwydion leaned his head down near her ear. "Good for you," he said encouragingly. "Want to take a walk?"

Emily gave his question no thought at all. "I'd love to. Come, I'll show you my favorite place in all the world."

The moon was just beginning to rise as they ran down the road and cut across the field, heading up the slope of a rolling hill and leaving the noise and light of the party behind them.

Ꮐwydion had always been happier outdoors than inside, and as a result spent much time running and walking out in the world. Despite that training it was difficult to keep up with Emily, who, her dress and sensibly laced shoes notwithstanding, climbed the hill without even breathing hard, running most of the way.

Gwydion had still not completely adjusted to the thin, warm air, and found himself struggling up hills and steep grades, trying to stay beside her, but more often lagging behind. Occasionally she would remember he was there, and slow her steps, or turn and offer him her hand. Finally he decided not to release it when her excitement spurred her to hurry again, and she got the message. They climbed the rest of the way together, hand in hand, at a speedy but reasonable pace.

Just before the summit she stopped in a shaft of moonlight that made her hair look silver. "We're almost there," she said, and he could see her eyes sparkle again in the dark. "Close your eyes."

Gwydion complied, and followed her blindly up to the top of the grade. She turned a little to the right, and gently led him behind her.

"Watch your foot, there's a hole here."

He stepped around it, and felt her come to a stop. He could hear the intake of her breath as she released his hand.

"All right, you can open your eyes now."

His vision adjusted automatically, but his breath was taken even further away by the sight. The valley stretched out below at his feet, bathed in moonlight, as far as he could see. A variety of fields made it up, some tilled, some fallow, with a great willow tree in the middle bending down over a stream that bisected the land. Even in the dark Gwydion could feel the beauty of the place, made somehow more intense by Emily's love of it.

"Where are we?"

Emily sank to the ground and he followed her lead gratefully. "This is one of the hills that overlook our farm," she said. "My dowry lands are the fields in the middle by the stream, where the willow stands. I call this place the Patchworks, because in the light it looks like the quilt on my bed, with the different textures and colors of the fields."

Gwydion looked at her face shining in the moonlight, and heard a door in his heart open. There was something much more than the alien chemical excitement that had been coursing through him from the moment he laid eyes on her, leaving him feeling giddy and stupid. Deep inside him he felt a need more intense than he had ever felt before.

It was as if he had known her his whole life, or perhaps merely that his life had really started when he met her. Either way, and for whatever reason he was here, he knew he couldn't bear to be away from her for even a moment now. And there was something in her eyes that told him she was examining these same strange and wonderful feelings within her own heart.

She turned and looked into the valley again. "Well, do you like it?" she asked, a little anxiously.

He knew her meaning, and added his own to it. "It's the most beautiful sight I have ever beheld."

Awkwardly he leaned toward her, hoping that his lips would find her willing. He had never kissed anyone except in gestures of respect, and so moved with agonizing slowness, his extremities going cold in the expectation that she might dart out of the way in horror.

Instead, when his intentions became clear to her she smiled, closed her eyes, and leaned into his kiss quickly and with eagerness. He had not anticipated the softness of her mouth, or its warmth, and the sensation sent cold shivers through him, even on this hot night. She touched his face before their lips parted, and the gesture went straight to his heart.

Then, as the happiness he was discovering began to envelop him, an icier feeling rose up to meet it. He looked over the valley and the picture in front of his eyes began to shift, the luminescence turned from moonlit silver to the flat gray of caustic smoke.

In his mind's eye he could see the valley in the aftermath of a devastating fire, the pastureland smoldering, the farmhouses and outbuildings in ashes. The ground was razed, and the fields swam in rivers of blood that seeped through the whole of the pastureland. Gwydion started to tremble violently as the red tide began to surge up the side of the valley below them, coming their way with an unstoppable insistence.

"Sam?" Emily's voice was filled with alarm. "Are you all right? What's the matter?"

Gwydion snapped out of his reverie, and as he did the vision vanished, returning the valley to peaceful silver again. A look of consternation had taken up residence on Emily's face. Her fingers still rested on his cheek, and he took her hand. His own was shaking uncontrollably.

"Sam?" Emily's eyes grew darker, and worry flooded her face.

"Emily, where are we? I mean, what is the name of this village?"

"Merryfield."

His stomach began to cramp. Merryfield was a common enough name; it could be anywhere. But on the ancient maps he remembered there was a village by that name, somewhere in the midst of the Wide Meadows, the great expanse of open plains that made up a large part of mideastern Serendair. The Meadows had been devastated in the war; none of the human villages had survived. And even when peace was restored, the villages were only beginning to be rebuilt when the Island was destroyed.

"What are the nearest towns? Cities?"

Emily's concern was growing as each moment passed. "There are no towns or cities around here, Sam, not for more than a hundred leagues. My father only goes into the city once a year, and he's gone for more than a month when he does."

"What's the name of the city, Emily? Do you know?"

She squeezed his hand in an effort to calm him, though he could see she had no understanding of his panic. "We're in the middle of two. To the west, on the other side of the great river, is Hope's Landing, and to the southeast is Easton. That's the biggest city in the land, I think."

Gwydion's eyes began to sting. *It can't be*, he thought desperately, *it can't be*. Both of the names she had mentioned were cities in Serendair.

"Sam?" His panic was beginning to take Emily over, too. Gwydion looked into her face. His eyes cleared suddenly, his vision became intensely acute again, and from the depths of his despair his pragmatic nature reemerged.

Of course, he thought, his fear subsiding instantaneously. He was here to save her from the destruction of the Island. He knew how, and to whom to go, and when they would need to leave. Some beneficent Fate must have sent him back in Time, given him this chance, though he had no idea why.

He looked at her again, and smiled, and that realization came to him as well. This must be his soulmate; he knew it more certainly than he knew his own name. He could *see* it. With the clarity of the knowledge came a sense of calm assurance and growing joy. Emily was his soulmate. It was easy to believe, given how much he knew he loved her already.

Gwydion took her face in his hands, and pulled her into

another kiss. "I'm sorry, I didn't mean to scare you," he said when he released her. "I need to tell you something."

She moved back from him a little. "What?"

He tried to keep his voice from cracking, as it occasionally did when he was excited or anxious. "We have to leave as soon as we can, and go east to the Meadows. If anything happens to me, or if we get separated for any reason, you must promise me you will find someone named MacQuieth, or Farrest, or Garael. Please, promise me."

Emily stared at him in amazement. "What are you talking about?"

Gwydion thought about how to explain, and then realized he couldn't. How could she possibly understand now? No one knew this was coming; the war had not even reached here, and the death of the Island was centuries after the war. Then a sadder thought occurred to him. Perhaps he wasn't destined to go back, either. Perhaps instead he was to live, and die, here, in the Past.

He took her face in his hands again and studied it carefully. Despite his irrational behavior, she seemed to understand his distress, and she wanted to soothe it. Her eyes sought answers in his face. They were dark with concern; their sympathy had no visible bottom to its depth. It was a face he could look at forever and still not tire of, or even fully know everything about. Tenderness welled up inside him, choking him, and he decided, without a second thought, that dying here with her was infinitely better than going back to living without her.

The moonlight shifted and filled her eyes, and she smiled. When she did, his fear of the situation evaporated, and he kissed her once more, lingering longer this time. The wonderful, queasy feeling returned to his stomach as he felt her lips part slightly and her breath filled his mouth. The intimacy was more than he could handle without losing control completely.

He drew back, and found a look of wonder on her face. "I can't believe you really came," she whispered. "Where are you from?"

Gwydion was astonished. "What do you mean?"

Emily took his hands, her excitement spilling over from her eyes to her body, which began to quiver happily. "You were my wish, weren't you? Have you come to save me from the lottery, to take me away?"

Gwydion swallowed. "You could say that. Why do you think I'm your wish?"

Her face held no shyness, no awkwardness. "I wished for you to come last night on my star, right after midnight, and here you are. You don't know where you are, do you? Did I bring you from a long way off?"

Gwydion's eyes grew larger, and he gave her a silly smile. "Yes, definitely."

She sighed. "I can't believe it. I waited for almost a year for the right night, and it worked. You've finally come. You're finally here." A single tear formed in her eye and rolled rapidly down her face, making the intensity of her smile even brighter. There was magic in her, he decided. Maybe magic strong enough to really have brought him here over the waves of Time.

She stood and offered him a hand. "Come on," she said. "Let me show you the fairy fort."

They walked down the face of the valley, slowly this time, toward the stream that wound through the pasturelands. As they descended the hillside Gwydion watched the unfamiliar stars move farther away, and the black sky stretch out above them, filled with endless promise.

When they reached the stream Emily stopped, then looked around in dismay. The water was moving more rapidly than she had expected, and the banks were marshy; one of her shoes sank in and stuck tight. Gwydion helped her pull it free, but when it emerged it was covered with mud. She looked helplessly over to the willow tree where she hoped to take him, and then down at the intricately laced shoes.

"I'm sorry, Sam," she said, disappointment clotting her voice. "I don't think I can make it, and I can't really take my shoes off—they take hours to put on as it is. You should still go, though. The view from under the willow tree is amazing."

"There really wouldn't be any point in going without you," Gwydion said. He looked around for an easier place to ford the stream, but found none. A thought occurred to him, but he didn't know if he could bring himself to suggest it.

"Well, you could carry me," she said, as though reading his mind. "That is, if you don't mind."

"No, not at all," he said in relief. His voice cracked at the first word, and he hid his embarrassment by tying up the ends of his cloak to keep them from dangling in the river. When the heat in his face had subsided he put his arms out. He had never carried anyone before, and he swore to himself that if he dropped her he would find the nearest poisonous plant and put himself out of his humiliation.

Emily came to him without a hint of caution. She wrapped one arm around his neck, and then, as if guiding him, took his arm and placed it behind her knees. He lifted her with little difficulty and carried her carefully to the stream, and then across it. He kept walking once out of the water, wending his way through the soggy grass to the willow tree, where he put her down gently.

It was a magnificent one, with many trunks surrounding a main shaft wider than he could have reached his arms around three times. The tree had grown enormously tall with its ready supply of water, and the delicate leaves cast lacy moonshadows on the ground, like summer snowflakes.

Emily patted the willow lovingly. "Farmers believe that a solitary tree in the middle of pasturelands is the home of all the fairies that live in the fields," she said, looking up at the tallest branches and smiling. "That means this tree is very magical. It's terrible luck to lose a fairy fort to lightning or fire, and no farmer would ever cut one down."

Gwydion thought back to his vision, the pasturelands burned and desolate. He had seen the willow then, blackened and dead, and he shuddered involuntarily at the memory. He turned back to Emily. She was walking around the tree, her hand resting on the branches above her, speaking to it softly in a language he didn't understand.

When she came back around to him she smiled. "So, now that you've seen it, what would you like to do next? Do you want to go back?"

"Not yet," he said, returning her smile. "Do you know anything about the stars?"

"Yes; why?"

"Will you teach me?"

"If you'd like." She started to sit on the ground under the tree, but he stopped her. He loosed the drawstring of his cloak from around his neck and spread it out on the ground for her.

Her grin of approval made him shiver. "Sam?"

"Yes?"

"Would it bother you if I took off my dress?"

Gwydion felt all the blood drain from his face. A moment later, he was painfully aware of the place to which it had decided to run. Before he could speak she interrupted him, embarrassment in her voice.

"I'm sorry; I should have been more specific. I mean this part." She touched the blue velvet overdress awkwardly. "I assure you, I am quite modestly attired beneath it. It's just that this is my only fancy dress, and if I spoil it, it will break my mother's heart. Would you mind?"

Many answers ran through Gwydion's head, and the corresponding expressions all passed over his face in an instant.

"No," he said.

Emily turned her back and walked over to the tree again. He watched her unlace the bodice of the velvet overdress and slide it over her shoulders; it was off before he had a chance to realize that his blatant stare was rude. She stepped out of it and hung it carefully over a tree branch, then turned to face him once more. She now wore a sleeveless gown of white lace. The modesty piece he had seen before was part of the bodice, and the crinoline was long and full, like the skirt of a summer dress.

She sat down on his cloak, and he took his place beside her. "What do you want to know about the stars?" she asked, looking up into the night sky. Her hair hung down over her shoulders, and it was all Gwydion could do to keep his hands off it.

"Anything. Everything. I don't recognize any of them, so whatever you can tell me would be a help. The stars are different where I come from." It seemed a simple, factual statement to him, but Emily's face shone with wonder at the thought. She settled back on the ground, stretching out with her head resting against the green moss that slanted up against the base of the willow tree.

"Well, first and foremost, that's Seren, the star that the

Island is named for. Most nights in the spring and summer it is directly overhead at midnight."

Gwydion settled down beside her. He stretched out his arm behind her, trying to avoid touching her too soon. As she had several other times that night, she read his mind and took hold of his arm, pulling it around behind her shoulders. The movement didn't even stop the astronomy lesson she was imparting.

She continued to point out stars and constellations, telling him a little of the lore and whatever history she knew. She seemed to have an impressive background in it, some of which was navigational. Gwydion made note of that odd fact, but after a moment he was no longer watching the heavens, as she was, but had relocated his gaze to her face. It was glowing with its own celestial light, and he felt he was learning far more by watching the stars in her eyes than by looking into the sky. He rolled onto his side and bent his arm behind his head, grinning like an idiot.

After a long time Emily looked up, as if awakening, and saw the silly look on his face. She blushed in embarrassment and sat up quickly.

"I'm sorry. I didn't mean to blather on."

"You weren't," he said hastily. "I was listening very carefully." He held his arm out straight. "Tell me some more."

She lay back down again, staring straight up at the sky. This time her face was solemn, and she said nothing for a moment. When she finally spoke her voice contained a note of sadness.

"You know, ever since I can remember I have dreamed about this place," she said softly. "Until recently I had the same dream almost every night—I was out here in the dark, under the stars, holding out my hands to them. And in my dream the stars would fall from the sky and into my hands, and I could hold them fast; I would make a fist, and see them glimmer in between my fingers. Then I would wake up, and when I did, I always had an extraordinary feeling of happiness that would last through the morning at least.

"And then my dream changed. I think it was when I was officially entered in the marriage lottery. I was eligible for it last year, but my father said it was too soon. This year it was unavoidable, and, despite my wishes, and theirs, my parents gave in to tradition and town practice and put me in like a horse on the auction block. My whole life is changing now, and my dream changed with it. Now, it comes much less frequently, and when it does it's not the same."

"How is it different?" His voice was sympathetic.

"Well, the beginning is similar. I'm here in the pasture, in the dark, and the stars are just as intensely bright as before, but when they fall into my hands they fall right through them; I can't hold on to them, and they tumble into the stream instead. I find myself looking down into the water, and the stars are lying there at the bottom of the stream, shining up at me."

Gwydion felt the sadness in her voice seep into his heart. "Do you have any idea what it means, if anything?"

"Yes, I think so," Emily replied. "I think I finally came to understand that all the things I had dreamed of seeing, and of doing, are not going to come to pass. That instead of seeing the world, and going off to study, and all the other marvelous adventures I had hoped to have when I was young, what actually will be my fate is what all my friends dream about—marrying someone of my father's choice, settling down and raising a family here in the valley. In a way, I had hoped to do that, too, eventually; I love this land, and I could be happy here. But—I thought—" Her words slowed and she fell silent.

"Thought what?"

"I thought there was going to be more for me. I know that's selfish and childish, but I had hoped that I would one day see the things and places that come to me in my dreams.

"I think the change reflects my acceptance that this is never going to happen. That in a few days I will give up those silly hopes. I'll marry someone chosen from the lottery who, with any luck, will be kind to me, or at least not cruel, as some farm men are, and I will live and die here, never setting foot outside the valley. I guess I have known all along that would be the case. The dreams come even less frequently now. Soon I expect they will stop all together, and then I will forget them and get on with my life."

Her words made his stomach turn. "No."

"No?"

Once again the pragmatism descended, and the answer was inordinately clear to him. Gwydion sat up, cross-legged, and pulled her up with him. "Emily, what are the courting customs here? What protocol do I follow to avoid the lottery and ask your father directly for your hand?"

Emily's eyes sparkled, then almost immediately darkened again. "Oh, Sam," she said sadly. "He'll never let me go with you. He has saved for my dowry since I was a baby, kept these middle pasturelands for it, just to assure that whoever I married kept me here in the bosom of the family. He'd never consent to you taking me away."

Gwydion felt as if he would vomit. He couldn't explain to her in words the urgency to get away from this place. "Then will you come anyway, Emily? Will you run away with me?"

She looked down at her hands. His throat tightened and his shoulders began to tremble as he waited for the answer. Finally she looked up, and the expression in her eyes was direct.

"Yes," she said simply. "It would be a real waste of a wish not to, don't you think?"

Relief broke over him like a spray of cold water. "Yes; yes I do." He pulled her into a tight embrace, resting his hot cheek on hers. "Is there someone who can marry us in this village?"

Emily sighed in his arms. "There will be in a few days, after the lottery. Everyone will be marrying then."

Gwydion pulled her even closer. He had no idea how long they could delay leaving, but the risk would be worth it. He resolved to wait, and not frighten her unnecessarily.

"Sam?"

He released her reluctantly, and sat back, looking at her with new eyes. When the sun had risen that morning, he had been totally free, and utterly alone; his life was that of other boys his age, with little thought of the Future, and little belief in it.

And now he was looking at his wife. He had always wondered what the other half of his soul looked like, and was delighted, and humbled, to see it was so incredible; he was actually amazed to know he even had one. The prospect of living by her side for the rest of his life filled him with a heady, if terrifying, feeling. In years to come, as he mourned her death over the endlessly passing days of his lifetime, he would think back to this moment and remember the way she had looked when he first saw her with his new eyes, eyes that still believed that life held a great measure of love for him.

"Yes?"

"Do you think we might see the ocean? Someday, I mean."

At that moment he would have truthfully promised her anything she asked of him. "Of course. We can even live there if you want. Haven't you ever seen it?"

"I've never left the farmlands, Sam, never in my whole life." A faraway look came into her eyes. "I've always longed to see the ocean, though. My grandfather is a sailor, and all my life he has promised me that he would take me to sea one day. Until recently I believed it." She looked into his eyes and saw a trace of sadness there, and quickly looked away. Innately he could see that the sorrow he felt for her made her sad for him instead. When she looked back, her eyes were shining as though she had thought of a way to make him feel better. She leaned near him, and whispered as if imparting a great secret. "But I've seen his ship."

Gwydion was astonished. "How can that be, if you've never seen the sea?"

She smiled at him in the dark. "Well, when he's in port, it's actually very tiny—about as big as my hand. And he keeps it on his mantel, in a bottle. He showed it to me once when he came to visit."

Tears stung his eyes. For all the famous and special people he had met in his life, he was sure that the purity of their collective souls couldn't hold a candle to hers. He was unable to speak for a moment. When he did, he said exactly what his heart was thinking.

"You are the most wonderful girl in the world."

She looked at him seriously. "No, Sam, just the luckiest. And the happiest."

His hands trembled as he touched her bare arms. Their kiss was deep, and held all the promise of a nuptial blessing. For the first time it was easy for him, and the difficult part was bringing it to an end.

"Sam?" Her beautiful eyes were glistening in the light of the moon.

"Yes?"

"I have two things I need to tell you."

He could tell from the smile on her face that neither would be difficult to hear.

"Yes?"

Emily looked down for a moment. "Well, the first is that if you kiss me again, I think we will end up consummating our marriage here, tonight."

His trembling grew to an uncontrollable level. "And the second?"

She ran her hand down his face until it came to a stop on his shoulder. "I really want you to kiss me again."

As if in a trance, Gwydion smoothed his cloak out on the ground, and Emily lay down on it. He sat back on his heels, looking at her for a moment, until she put her arms out to him. With a catch in his throat he eased down next to her and came into her embrace, hugging her as tightly as he could without hurting her. He held her like that for what seemed like a very long time, until her hair brushed the tips of his fingers, and he gave in to the desire he had had all night to touch it.

His hands ran down her hair over and over again, relishing the cool, smooth feel of it, like polished satin. Gwydion felt her hands slip into the circle his arms made as he held her, and begin to loosen the tie that bound his shirt closed. He shivered as she gently pulled the shirt loose from his trousers and slid her hands up his abdomen to his chest, where they came lightly to rest. The gesture gave him courage, and he closed his eyes as his lips sought, and found, hers. He could feel them trembling as much as his were.

The warm night wind blew over them, caressing their hair. Gwydion released her with one arm and leaned back, taking in the sight of her. There was no fear or embarrassment on Emily's face, just a look of loving approval.

His eyes didn't leave her face as his hand went to the bodice of her garment, taking the first tiny heart-shaped button between fingers that shook as though the wind were a wintry blast. As the material came apart beneath them his hands shook even more, until on the fifth button they lurched in a spasm of nerves and tore the button loose from the lace.

Gwydion stared down at his hand in horror. "Emily, I'm so sorry," he gasped, embarrassment flooding him and turning his face red as the setting sun had been. His panicked glance returned to her face to find her smiling in amusement. She took the button from him for a moment, turning it over in her hand.

"Aren't they pretty?" she said, almost as if musing to herself. "My father brought them back for me from the city on his last trip as a birthday gift. I'm sure they cost far too much money."

"Emily—" She stopped him by putting two fingers of her other hand on his lips. She replaced the button in his hand, closing his fingers around it.

"Keep it, Sam," she said. "As a memento of the night when I gave you my heart." She felt hot tears fall on the bare skin below her neck, and she wrapped her arms around him and pulled him to her chest. "It's all right, Sam," she said. "You won't hurt me. Really. It will be all right."

She was reading his mind again. Gwydion felt a wave of sureness crest over him, and he brushed the flimsy fabric out of the way, lowering his lips to the hollow between her breasts. With all the tenderness his young soul could muster he kissed her soft skin while his free hand gently slid the top of her frock off her shoulders and onto the ground beneath her.

His hand returned to the swell of her small breast, and with the slightest touch, his fingers caressed the pink nipple, followed by his mouth. As his lips touched the delicate skin she began to shiver, and the sensation swept through him, leaving him cold and burning at the same time.

Wonder filled his heart as the moonlight came to rest on her beneath the tree, illuminating her face that had been shining already without it. Her eyes glittered in the light, and he saw tears in them that matched his own. The look in those beautiful eyes was so certain, so sure, that to question what they were doing would have been to scoff at the magic they were both undeniably feeling. Gwydion's lips returned to the breast he had laid bare, and his hands moved beneath the crinkly skirt. When they made contact with the warm skin of her legs he was afraid his excitement would give way there and then.

In turn she pulled awkwardly on the laces of his trousers, and then made some calculated adjustments. As the waistband came loose she pushed them down, freeing him from the restrictions that had been keeping him in check, and exposing him briefly to the wind. Gwydion shivered violently and moved closer to her, seeking her warmth. He leaned up over her and looked down. The expression in her eyes broke his heart.

"I love you, Sam," she said. "I've been waiting for you for so long. I always knew you would come to me if I wished for you."

Then slowly he was inside her, moving as gently as he could, trying not to lose control as he began to gasp in the throes of unimaginable pleasure.

Emily trembled beneath him, and her hands moved up his back, pulling him closer, drawing him in. He could hear her breath grow shorter; she tilted her head back and as she did his lips moved to her throat, kissing it gratefully. He was bathing her neck with tears, and he felt one of her hands leave his shoulder and move to her head, caressing it with a comforting motion.

When they were finally completely joined he lay above her, within her, motionless for a moment, afraid that if he moved or took a breath he would awake to find that this was only a dream. Even if it was, he was unwilling to let it end yet.

Emily's other hand came to rest on the side of his head and she kissed him, imparting a wordless, loving encouragement. Then she began to move slowly, rocking him from below, wrapping one of her legs around his.

From the bottom of his toes Gwydion felt a exquisite heat rise, and with it came an insistent movement that matched hers, building the fire he felt in his stomach into a raging inferno that swelled within him and consumed his entire body. He lost touch with his thoughts and let them drift away on the warm night wind, concentrating instead on the rhythm of her heart beating beneath him and the delicate sounds she was emitting.

She whispered his name, or what she thought was his name, and the thrill of hearing it drove his excitement higher. The word became a cadence she repeated, spoken softly over and over as she began to grow warm and sigh with pleasure. The sound reached down into his heart, pushing him past the gates of control, and as the thunder rolled up within him he felt her begin to cry out, gripping him as an anchor as she was swept away by the same wave he was riding.

Time became suspended; how long he made love to her he couldn't realistically gauge, having nothing to compare it with, but it seemed to last an eternity. With each passing second he felt the love in his heart for her expand until he was sure it had outgrown his body. He had expected this event to come much later in his life, and to be far less meaningful, so the shuddering sobs that consumed him when it was over took him completely by surprise.

"Sam?" Emily's voice was alarmed as she pulled him nearer.

"Gods, did I hurt you, Emily? Are you all right?"

She kissed him tenderly, and then pulled back to look into his eyes. "Are you kidding? Did it feel like I was hurt?" She laughed, and the feeling shot through him like a hot bolt of lightning, running up his spine and resonating in his forehead.

He bent his head down over her shoulder, weak with relief. "Emily, I would never, never hurt you on purpose; I hope you know that."

She look him straight on the eye. "Of course I do. Why would you ever hurt something that belongs to you? Because I do, Sam. I'm yours."

He sighed. "Thank the gods."

"No," she said seriously, "thank the stars. It was them that brought you to me."

Gwydion lifted his head with great effort and stared into the moonlit sky above him, sprinkled with grains of light like sand from a diamond beach.

"Thank you!" he shouted. Emily giggled, then sighed as he moved regretfully away and began to put himself back together. She adjusted her clothing as well, and as they finished dressing a look of disappointment came over her face. She turned toward the village, then back to him.

"That's the Lorana waltz. We had best get back, the dance will be ending soon."

Gwydion sighed. He would have been happy to stay in this field with her forever.

"Oh, all right," he said.

He took her hand and pulled her up, then drew her into his arms and kissed her once more. When he looked at her face he saw no trace of regret, or second thought, just blissful contentment.

He put his cloak back on and lifted Emily off the ground, carrying her across the stream again, knowing that they were crossing the threshold of the place she loved, the place she thought of as home. He felt a twinge of sadness at the knowledge that their hasty exit would mean this was the last time he would ever carry her over that threshold.

They crossed the fields hand in hand, walking more slowly than they had coming here. When they crested the face of the hill, the grip of Emily's hand tightened suddenly.

He turned to her anxiously. "Are you all right?"

"Yes, but I need to sit down for a moment."

Gwydion took hold of her other hand and helped her to the ground, then sank worriedly down beside her. "Emily, what's wrong?"

She gave him a reassuring smile. "Nothing is wrong, Sam. I just need to rest a minute."

"Are you sure?"

"Yes. Can I ask you something?"

"Of course, anything."

"How old are you?"

"Fourteen. How old are you?"

She thought for a moment. "What time do you think it is?"

"About eleven o'clock, I would say."

"Then I'm thirteen."

Gwydion looked at her, puzzled. "Why does the time matter?"

"Because in an hour I'll be fourteen, too, like you."

Now he understood. "It's your birthday?"

"Well, tomorrow."

He pulled her into his arms. "Happy birthday, Emily."

"Thank you." She grew very excited. "Wait; I have an idea! Do you want to come to supper tomorrow?"

Gwydion hugged her tighter. "That would be wonderful."

She pushed out of his embrace, and he smiled at the eagerness on her face. "You can meet my parents and my brothers. Maybe if my father sees how happy I am with you he will give his consent."

"What time?"

"Why don't you come about five—we eat at six."

He looked down at his dusty clothes regretfully. "This is all I have to wear, I'm afraid."

Emily touched the material of his shirt. It was woven of a fabric finer than she had ever seen before, and the craftsmanship of all the garments was superior to even the needlework of the best seamstresses in the village. "This is fine," she said simply. "I'll show you my house on the way past."

Gwydion was rummaging around in his pockets. He pulled out his pouch, and looked inside it. There was nothing that would make a suitable gift, and he doubted there would be any merchant in the village from which to purchase one. He took out the five gold coins he had brought with him on his way to the market, and put them in her hand.

"This is all I have; it's not much of a gift, but I want you to have something from me tonight." Tomorrow he would search the pasturelands for the most beautiful flowers he could find.

Emily's eyes widened in amazement, and a look of horror came over her face.

"I can't take this, Sam—this is as much as half my dowry." She turned one of the coins over and stared at it. The face minted on it was that of the prince of Roland, a land that would not exist for another seven centuries. She took his hand and opened the palm, returning the coins. "Besides, if I come home with that, my parents will think I've been doing something terribly wrong."

His face flared crimson in understanding. Then a different thought occurred to him. He rummaged in the pouch again, and pulled out another coin, copper this time. It was small and oddly shaped, with thirteen sides, and he opened her hand and put it in. Then he pulled out another just like it.

"As far as I know, there are only two of these in all the world. They have no real value other than that, but they're very special to me. I can't think of anyone better to give one to."

She examined the coin for a moment; then she smiled and drew him close. "Thank you, Sam; I'll treasure it. Now, we better get going."

He helped her stand and brushed the loose grass off the back of her velvet dress. "I wish I had a better gift for you." They began to walk down the hill leading to the village and the meeting hall.

"You couldn't give me a better gift than what you've given me tonight. You came here from far away in answer to my wish. Who could ask for more than that?"

He put his arm around her. "But it's your birthday."

"Do you really want to give me something special?"

"More than anything."

She smiled, and slid out from under his arm, taking his hand instead. "Tell me about the places you've been, the wonderful things that you've seen," she said, her eyes gleaming in excitement. "Talk to me about where we will go, what we will see someday."

"Well, since you've never seen the ocean, we could begin with the tall ships that will carry us across the wide Central Sea."

He told her of the masts and the riggings and the woven net beds called hammocks that the sailors slept in, of the great port of Kesel Tai, where ships from around the world sought the trade and wisdom of the Sea Mages. He told her of Port Fallon on the shores of his own lands, where a great lighthouse stood a hundred feet tall, illuminating the way for lost mariners. And lastly he told her of the Lirin port of Tallono, whose exposed bay had been turned from an open mooring to a sheltering harbor with the aid of a woman who held the wisdom and power of dragons.

Emily listened in rapt excitement, drinking in his words. She broke loose from her reverie long enough to show him her family's farm. It was the large one he had seen from the summit of the first hill. Warm carriage lights burned out in front of the pasture gate in welcome.

There was so much Gwydion would have told her—of the river so cold and wide in some places that its opposite bank could barely be seen through the heavy morning mist, the river that led up to the Lands of the Gorllewinolo Lirin, where she could meet many of her mother's people, and even as half-caste she would be welcomed.

He would have told her of the Oracle of Yarim, with its mad prophetess, and of the great city of Sepulvarta, where the priests held their temples and the people were ruled by the Patriarch. And he most certainly would have told her of the Great White Tree, but before he could they were back in the village, approaching the entrance of the meeting hall. He promised himself, as their steps slowed, that one day he would show her all the things he knew she wanted to see.

When they came to the place he had found her hiding, she turned quickly to him as a thought occurred to her. "Do we have a patronymic? A family name?"

Gwydion felt a shiver of delight pass through him at the thought of her sharing it, but was at a loss to explain the nomenclature to her. "Yes, sort of. It's complicated. And my name is different as well. You see, the way—"

"Emmy, there you are! Where the blazes have you been? Justin is here, and he's looking everywhere for you, as are a few other people." Ben's voice was filled with relief as well as anger.

Emily ignored the question, pulling Gwydion over to where her brother stood. "Hello, Ben. Did you enjoy the dance? This is Sam; Sam, this is my brother Ben."

Gwydion put out his hand, and Ben looked at him for a second, shifting his focus. He shook Gwydion's hand, then turned to Emily again. "You're going to catch it when Father finds out."

"Finds out what?"

"That you didn't go to the dance."

"I most certainly did go to the dance, and I had a wonderful time."

Ben was turning red with annoyance. "You didn't dance once, Emmy. There are an awful lot of upset fellows in there."

Emily started to laugh. "I did so dance, just not inside. You even saw me. Let it go, Ben; I had a lovely evening."

"Emmy?" The new voice was deeper, and Gwydion turned to see a much older youth hurrying toward them. He also had dark hair, and he was a head taller than Emily. She ran to meet him and he lifted her off the ground in a wide embrace.

"Happy Birthday, Ugly," he said affectionately, kissing her cheek. "Did you have fun? Was the dance nice?"

"The best ever," she answered, grinning. She introduced her oldest brother, Justin, to Gwydion as well, and he walked with them to the wagon Justin had brought to drive her home in.

As her brothers hitched the horses, Emily turned to him again. "Thank you, Sam," she said softly. "I'll see you to-morrow."

"At five on the nose. Happy birthday, Emily. I'll be thinking about you every moment until I see you again."

She gave him a quick kiss on the cheek and ran to the wagon. Pain welled up inside him; he had no idea how much truth was in the last words she heard from his lips.

"I love you," he called after her as the horses began to pull away. She put her hand to her ear, signifying she hadn't heard him. He watched the wagon rumble off into the darkness, Emily waving until she was out of sight.

The next morning Gwydion rose before dawn with the other farmhands, preparing to work as the other men did, bare-chested in the summer heat. He wrapped his waterskin and dagger, along with his shirt, in his cloak and stowed it beneath the cot he had slept on.

As he was putting it away he noticed three small, dark spots on the lining of the cloak. He pulled it back out and looked at it again; they were tiny bloodstains.

Gwydion checked his back to see if he had been injured without his knowledge, but could find nothing. He stuffed it beneath the cot again and set to work on the day's chores. As a new hand he was given some of the lighter, but dirty, tasks, and he watched in dismay the inevitable and increasing soil on his trousers.

When the farmhands took a break for breakfast at sunrise he went out to the pastureland, looking for flowers to give her. He spied a patch of wild columbines growing amid clouds of nymph's hair and decided they would be perfect flowers for Emily's birthday bouquet. Then he went to the well and washed his pants clean with a rag, hoping to remain somewhat presentable. It would not do to meet her father and ask for her hand smelling like the inside of a barn, although many years later it occurred to him that the scent would not have been unfamiliar to the man.

In the hope that breakfast or scraps from it might still be available, he headed toward the farmhouse. The heat of the morning made his head swim a little, and as he approached the porch he felt dizzier than he ever remembered feeling before.

$\mathcal{M}$eridion had stopped the frame. He checked the tools once more, then gently pried the image loose from the delicate thread. It stuck for a moment, and he smiled in amusement; it was almost as if the boy's force of will were holding it fast. Carefully he slid the first strand forward to the exact place from which he had removed the piece, and replaced it, wiping the strand to cement it back in place. Then he looked through the lens again.

$\mathcal{G}$wydion appeared in midstep on his way down the forest road. Everything was exactly as it had been on that achingly fresh morning, everything except his memory.

He whirled around on the path. The sun was rising in the sky, as before; the birds were calling to each other in trees that glistened in its light. He felt a faint chill as the warm wind blew across his naked chest. Otherwise all things were as they had been.

Panic coursed through him, and his heart began to pound as he darted wildly up the path, then back, trying to deny where he now was. His hands clutched at the air, trying to reach back to the other reality, but his efforts only resulted in stirring the wind around him and raising a bit of dust from the road.

His stomach roiled in agony at the thoughts that were pounding in his head: had he been hallucinating? Was he going insane? The prospect that it had not been real was better than the belief that it was, but he knew in his heart that the events had happened. He never in his wildest imagination could have made up something as wonderful as Emily.

Emily. The implications threw a cold, gangrenous feeling into his stomach and legs. Where was she? What had happened to her? He remembered his warning to her about being separated, and winced in anguish at her look of confusion that had followed it. Did she understand him, understand the urgency of his admonition? Had she survived?

He felt for the items he had brought with him, but they weren't there; the waterskin and dagger, his shirt and cloak. His chest tightened at the thought of the cloak, rolled around his gear under the cot, and he went cold as the realization hit him of what the bloodstains were. They had made love on it, and the blood must have been Emily's, the sign of the loss of their mutual virginity, the consummation of what felt like a marriage.

Despair began to consume him as he searched his pockets, and then he felt a sense of calm descend. He reached deeper and pulled forth his pouch, the one possession he hadn't left in the shed.

With shaking hands he pulled open the drawstring and felt carefully inside it. A smile touched the corner of his mouth when his fingers brushed it, hidden at first in the corner of the bag. Carefully he drew the tiny object out; it was the button she had given him the night before. Proof of his sanity, proof that his memories were not hallucinations.

He sighed deeply as immeasurable sadness overwhelmed him. He thought of the cloak, and the other possessions, and the shed, and the farm, all reduced centuries before to cinders, only to be scattered over the ocean on the other side of the world where the Island had its grave. The thought that her ashes blew about in the fair sea wind as well was not to be contemplated; Gwydion knew that would be enough to make the possibility of his insanity real.

His father would know what to do. She surely had lived, and had found the leaders of the Cymrian refugees he had told her about in the Patchworks. She must have come on one of the great ships. His heart rose in the hope that she had, for it would have been her first opportunity to sail the ocean she wanted so desperately to see.

All of the other terrible possibilities—that she had been killed in the war, that she had survived the war but had died before the Cymrians left, that she had boarded one of the ships but hadn't survived the voyage that had taken the lives of so many, that she had landed but had died since—all were relegated to an unopened room in his mind. First he had to go home and talk with his father. His father would know how to find her.

Gwydion turned and started for home. The day had lost its shine; to his eyes, if no others, dark and foreboding clouds were rolling in. He took five steps before the loss overwhelmed him and he fell to the ground, lying facedown in the road as he had the day before. A tremendous, racking sob tore from his throat, a scream of pain that frightened the wildlife for miles around. And then he bent his head over the dust of the path and wept.

On the morning of her birthday Emily took advantage of the offer to be excused from her chores and slept in past sunrise. Her dreams were sweet, if intense, and she was deep in the middle of a particularly poignant one when she felt, rather than heard, a high, heartrending cry.

Noooooooooooo.

She bolted upright in bed, trembling. The sunlight was pouring through the curtains and the birds were singing; it was a perfectly beautiful day. She rubbed her hands up and down her arms to shake off the feeling of deep fear that had settled on her like a cold mist.

The memory of Sam and the night before flooded back into her cheeks, and the bad feelings vanished like a dream. She leapt from her bed, singing, and waltzed across the room in her white muslin nightgown, counting the moments until she would see him again.

The day dragged by. Emily busied herself by helping her mother make the supper preparations, sharing as much of the story as she was willing to. As evening came she grew more and more excited, until her father remarked that if she grew any happier he could light the carriage path with her.

As the appointed time for his arrival came and went, Emily stood at the window in her best white blouse and a pink broadcloth skirt, watching intensely. The supper hour came and went as well, leaving the lovingly prepared repast cold and uninviting by the time her mother gently drew her away from the window and made her eat. It was a quiet, sad affair with little talking; the look in Emily's eyes swallowed any hope for cheerful conversation.

After supper her brothers and parents gave her gifts, which she smiled on and praised as best she could, even though her heart wasn't in it. As the night came and deepened she went back to the window again, certain in her belief that he would come eventually.

Finally, long past midnight, her father took her gently by the arm and suggested she needed her sleep. Emily nodded and headed numbly for the stairs. As she started to climb she looked back at her parents, and was brought out of her trance momentarily by the sadness on their faces. She knew they ached for her, and she couldn't stand the thought.

She gave them both as bright a smile as she could muster, and made her voice sound confident.

"Don't worry, Father," she said. "There will be lots of other boys in the lottery I can fall in love with." She watched as they both drew sighs of relief, and her mother's eyes lost their worried look.

"That's right, honey; there certainly will be."

She blew them both a kiss as she ascended the stairs. She spoke the rest of the thought to herself.

"But I never will."

*Y*ears later, after the same amount of time of fruitless search, Emily came across MacQuieth, one of the people the boy had mentioned to her that night in the Patchworks. It was completely by accident, on the streets of an immense city, and though he was a warrior of great renown, and she was no one, she summoned her courage and asked him about the boy. MacQuieth initially was annoyed, then kinder when he saw the look of intense hope in her eyes, a look that spoke of a soul that was clutching the last vestige of belief in life.

"I'm terribly sorry," he said, wincing as he watched her face absorb his words. "But I never saw anyone like that, nor have I ever heard of anyone by those names." And the warrior stood, his attention successfully diverted from his task for perhaps the first time ever, watching as she walked away and into anonymity, her shoulders lower than a moment before. MacQuieth was not prescient, but even he knew he was watching a human soul as the life went out of it, blending with the throng of the great unwashed, beginning the descent into the meaningless existence of those who only marked the days until death came for them.

Gwydion waited for the Seer's answer as patiently as he could, but his desperation and pain would have been obvious to anyone. That the Seer was also his grandmother could only help, he reasoned.

Anwyn studied his face, a look of profound curiosity in her searing blue eyes, the color of which was more intense even than Gwydion's. How her grandson had managed to elude the stoic nature that was inbred in the family was of great interest to her. Though the realm that was her gift to see into was the Past, she felt enough of the Future to know that one day Gwydion would be a powerful man, as was each person in the family, and that he had more potential than any of the others to bring the line into its dynastic glory again. That made him a valuable asset to control.

My soulmate, he had insisted, his voice breaking. *I'm certain of it, Grandmother. Please.* The liquid that glinted in his eyes obviously came from a wellspring deep within him; the Eye-Clear would have worn off long before he had thought to come to her for answers. Anwyn could not see even a residual trace of it, but was certain of its use nonetheless.

Who had used it on him was another matter; the formula for the elixir had gone to the depths of the sea with Serendair a thousand years before. And though she had a partial answer to his question, some of the events Gwydion described—the stinging eyes, the transportation across Time itself—were hidden from her sight into the Past. Anwyn shook off the disturbing thought and focused on her trembling grandson once again.

He had climbed at great risk to see her, braving the biting wind that screamed with fury around and within the rockwalls of her cavernous castle, high in the darkest of the isolated crags of the pale northern mountains. His hands still bled from where he had gripped the rocks in his cold ascent to her lair. He clearly had been quite driven to see her and she so rarely had visitors, especially these days. Even in his preoccupation and despair it was good to have company again, especially the company of one who could be of use to her someday.

She thought about his question, and a distant look came over her face as she realized the implications of what she had to say to him. It would take careful thought to deliver this news appropriately. She took his hands in hers and began to wrap his bloodied knuckles with a soft cloth. Her smile was almost sad as she spoke.

"She did not land—she did not come. I am sorry, child. She did not set foot in these lands, nor in Manosse. If she was Lirin, the stars of this land would know her had she been anywhere beneath them, and they do not. She went to no other land. And she was not among those to leave on the ships from the Island before its destruction."

"Are you certain? There must be a mistake. Please, Grandmother, look again. Are you sure she didn't go off course with the Second Fleet?"

Anwyn hid her smile, and went back to the altar where the tarnished spyglass lay. It was the second most ancient artifact in the land, the scrying instrument that her father had used to behold this land for the first time. She picked it up and held it for a moment, feeling the warmth of its power. Then she walked to the great window that faced the sea a thousand miles away, and put the glass to her eye once again. She watched for a long time, then lowered the spyglass, turning back to her anxious grandson once more.

"Well, child, I'm sorry to disappoint you, but no one by that name or description was among those to leave on the ships from the Island before its destruction. She did not land; she did not come."

Anwyn watched as he began to sink to the ground, collapsing under the weight of his grief and her pronouncement, his body heaving with the force of his sobbing. She turned slowly back to the altar, smiling as she replaced the artifact.

"Well, then, how about some lunch?"

1

He moved like the shadow of a passing cloud, unseen, unnoticed, even by the wind that blew around him as if he were not there. He crept up the rise to the crest of the hill, his mismatched eyes scanning the fields below. It was partially in shadow, the scorched grass bent from the wind that rippled across the valley. Aside from the wind, nothing disturbed the silence.

As darkness covered the land he rose to a stand. The Brother turned and looked over his shoulder. He nodded and returned to his reconnaissance.

A moment later an enormous shadow joined him on the summit of the hill. In the remaining light of the setting sun the hilts of the weapons that jutted out from behind the giant's back resembled the armored claws of a gargantuan crab. The Sergeant matched the angle of his vision to the Brother's, then spoke.

" 'Ow long we got?"

The figure in black paused before answering, his hooded head angled as if listening to a distant conversation.

"They are a quarter of an hour behind us. They are not what concerns me."

"Oi know." The heavily armed giant sighed. "We ain't gonna make it, are we?"

The Brother's eyes did not leave the horizon. "Ultimately, probably not." After a moment he looked up at his seven-foot companion. "You might, if you leave now, head elsewhere."

"No, sir," the giant replied, a wry grin revealing a carnivorous smile. "Oi've come this far; 'twould be a pity to turn back now. Besides, it'd only be a matter o' time before they caught up with me. If it's all the same to you, sir, Oi'd rather buy it 'ere with you."

The Brother nodded, and his gaze returned to the horizon once more. "Well, then, I'd rather not be caught with the hunters behind us." With a shrug of his shoulder the large, crossbow-like weapon the Brother carried across his back swung into his hands, and he was off down the face of the hill.

"Oi suppose not," said the giant to the wind, the only thing that remained with him on the hilltop.

The descent of darkness was heavier than the footfalls of the Brother, whose passing was unnoticed even by the small creatures of the field. Unseen as well; black weapons on black cloak, he was as tall and thin as one of the fading shadows to which he now clung. He made no sound, left no tracks; there was no way to tell he was there unless one happened to be keen-sighted enough to pick him out of the darkness in which he was wrapped. And that would have been most unfortunate for the witness, for, no doubt, his pulse would have quickened, his heart would have hesitated for a split second, and that would have been enough. The Brother would have sensed it, and the witness would have died before his next heartbeat.

The Brother slipped through the gusts of the wind, avoiding disturbing in any way the myriad vibrations of the world that few beside himself could sense. His targets were formidable, the signatures of their personal power strong; his former master had spared no expense in the hunt. The Brother had expected no less.

He dropped to one knee and positioned his weapon. Beneath his veils a grim smile took up residence. His targets were now in range.

He could not see them, not yet, but he didn't need to. In the distance he could feel the tread of their footsteps, the beating of their hearts. Like a shark in the water he could smell their blood, sense their movements. It was the reward of his inhuman inheritance, though he was more sensitive to these things than even Dhracians of full blood. He was the Brother; this was his gift.

He closed his eyes and sensed the movement of the air, the changes in the wind, the subtle currents that might alter the shot. Then he released his breath and gently squeezed the trigger of the weapon in his hands.

No bolt or quarrel was fired from the bow. Three whisper-thin metal disks, each the size of a maple leaf, were hurled from the three-foot-long weapon, projected by the force of recoil. They cut through the air, their course altered slightly by the strong breeze, but the marksman had accounted for those changes. Long before the projectiles had reached their target the Brother had reloaded and fired again, and again, sending volley after volley into the foreheads and eyes of his victims nearly a quarter-mile away.

Then the Brother was off, even as the first three disks sliced into the left eye socket of his first target, each one driving the other deeper into his skull before erupting through the other side and into the throat of the next victim. Four more of his predators died before they even noticed anything.

Only the commander had a moment to turn his head and look into the face of his own death before it met him. In the distance, already at the summit of the hill from which he had listened, the Brother paused and spared a backward glance.

"The commander was fast," he said to the giant, who nodded.

"Not fast enough, though, eh, sir?"

"Not this time."

The Brother's patrol of the area surrounding their campsite that night had assured him there was no one to witness their fire. Nonetheless, Grunthor placed three metal sheets in a barricade around it to block out the light. Extraordinary precautions were what kept them alive.

The giant Bolg looked questioningly at the heavy sack that contained their rations, and the Brother nodded. Grunthor sat down before the fire and opened the sack, dragging forth the haunch of a hind they had killed two days earlier.

Using one of its long bones as a spit, he positioned the meat on two small notches in the metal sheets, turning it over the low flames. The two sat in silence until the outside of the meat was charred, the Brother keeping his ear to the wind. Grunthor paid no attention; he knew the routine. If something was wrong, he would be told.

After a while the giant Bolg took the meat from the fire and ripped off a palm-sized piece. He handed it, still dripping with juice, to his companion, taking the remainder for himself. The Brother watched as Grunthor sheared the flesh from the bone with his teeth. Then he sliced his own piece with his dagger and began to eat. It had a foul, slightly fishy taste to it. He swallowed.

"This is pretty close to rotten."

The giant Bolg nodded. "Well, guv, we could start in on the dry goods."

"No. We need those for the trip along the Root."

"Oi know, but this is all we got left."

"What about the coney?"

"We ate it yestaday."

The Brother put down the rest of the meat. "Then tomorrow I'll hunt."

They returned to their accustomed silence. After a moment Grunthor stretched out downwind of the fire. The Brother watched the giant as he fell asleep. He let his mind wander, and was lost in the memories that had brought them to this place in time.

He recalled how he had walked across the devouring blackness that was the Deep Chamber of the F'dor. He could not stop his boots from sounding loudly on the polished obsidian floor.

The walls of the chamber were so distant that even if the room had been lit, he would still have had a poor view of the black volcanic-glass surfaces, intricately carved with obscene patterns. Despite the braziers burning with black fire, there was no illumination within the cavernous chapel except the circle of light that the Dhracian assassin had approached.

Within the circle stood the figure of a man clad in the crimson robes of the demonic priesthood, the man who had summoned him here, once human, now the human host of a demonic spirit, blended into one obscene entity. A man he would never have accepted voluntarily as a client.

The Brother had clenched his teeth as he fought against his instinctual reaction to the place, and to the creature he approached. Needles seemed to run in his veins as he repressed his natural response to the perversions of nature that were conducted here. His ancestral hatred, born of generations of racial crusades by the Dhracians against all F'dor, revolted at being in the place his race's enemies had made their home.

Both sides of his bloodline—the vibrationally sensitive Dhracian inheritance of his mother and the Bolg's love of the deep earth bequeathed to him by his unknown father—rebelled at the defilement of what had once been a holy site. Strongest of all was the disgust he felt towards the demonic spirit clinging to the no-longer-human figure that stood before him now. The Lord of a Thousand Eyes. The F'dor. Tsoltan. His master.

When he stepped into the circle of light he heard a soft voice speak, warm as honey.

"I have a job for you."

The dark priest's red-rimmed eyes searched the Brother for a reaction. The Dhracian's sensitive nerves screamed at the intrusion, a sensation similar to the prodding examination of a butcher searching for the best cut. The Brother did not answer. He was doing all he could to keep from breathing the same air.

"Your hand," said the demon-priest.

The Brother unclenched his fist and slightly extended his left palm.

The F'dor chuckled in the darkness. "Your resistance amuses me still," it said. "By now you've learned there is no way to reclaim your true name. Your service is too valuable to me. There is no price for which I would ransom it back to you, nor will I reveal how I obtained it."

Directly in front of the Brother a vine grew up from the glass floor. It seemed made of glass itself, spiked with obsidian thorns. A key was wrapped in its highest tendril.

"Take it."

With a decisive motion the Brother plucked the key from the vine. The obsidian tendril shattered like the stem of a fragile wineglass.

He held the key up before his half-Bolg eyes, the night eyes of a people who had risen up from the caves, smiling inwardly at the increase in the rhythm of the demon's formerly human heart, the only outward sign of its consternation at his defiance. The key itself was unremarkable except that it was made from a dark bone, its shaft curving as a rib might.

"You will take this key to the base of the failed land bridge to the northern islands. The foundation of this bridge contains a gateway unlike any even you have ever passed through. The fabric of the Earth is worn thin there; you may experience some discomfort. If you have passed through correctly, you will find yourself in a vast desert.

"You will know the direction to go, and an old friend of mine will come to meet you. Once there, you will agree to the time and date when you shall serve as his guide through the gateway to this side. My only concern is that it be as soon as possible. Return to me, and I shall prepare you as his guide. Is this clear?"

"Yes."

"You will tell me of the arrangement, and carry any message he might send."

"I am not a page."

"How right you are. You are but a footnote." The talisman around the neck of the demon caught the light from a distant brazier and glinted, black, in the darkness. Within the golden circle of flame was a pattern of red stones that spiraled into the center of the amulet, in which was carved the image of a solitary eye. It bore the same piercing stare that now met the Brother's own.

The F'dor approached him, and the Brother's nose wrinkled from the reek of burnt flesh on the demon's person, and especially its breath. It was a stench that accompanied all those of its race, but his master's malodor was particularly strong.

"I want this done quickly. It will make whatever trivial catalogue of death you think yourself responsible for a mere jot, an afterthought of inconsequence. I am the true master, and you will be my thrall until you follow me willingly, or are swept away in my victory."

He had done as the demon demanded.

The Brother had no compunction about death, did not shirk in the presence of evil, but what he had encountered in the wasteland beyond the horizon defied any horrific description of which his mind might be capable. In the face of the destruction that would ensue, the devastation that would come over the world, he decided instead, for the first time in his life, to run, to abandon all he had, to risk an eternity of something worse than death. Even for him, anything else would have been unthinkable.

The Brother shook off his thoughts at the stirring in the distance that had alerted his senses. The key was in his hand, glimmering slightly in the darkness, and he slipped it quickly back into the pocket where he carried it.

He looked in the direction of the vibrations and felt the presence of approaching wolves. They were a long way off, but they were on the prowl. A discordant vibration indicated they were not ordinary wolves, but animals used as eyes by the F'dor.

He made a soft clicking sound. Grunthor's eyes opened at once, and his hand went immediately to his weapons belt. He turned in the direction of the Brother without making a sound.

The Brother made a few fast hand signals: *six wolves, three on each flank*. Grunthor nodded, and with one hand drew his great bow. With the other he placed a large metal lid on top of the fire, smothering it without allowing the smoke to escape. The Brother held his own odd weapon, the cwellan, at the ready, while Grunthor positioned his pike close at hand. They waited.

The Dhracian's head tilted to one side as he concentrated on the animals. The wolves didn't even slow down. They continued on their prowl until they had passed over the horizon and beyond his senses. They had not noticed the small camp in the hidden dell. When they were well away, the Brother nodded and took a breath, exhaling deeply. Grunthor did the same.

"They're getting closer," the Brother said.

"No surprise really, is it, sir? They've got our scent, and we've got that key. They can probably feel it."

"I know. We have to make haste to another city. Get lost in the crowd."

"Lovely. Oi know how much you like cities."

When the deepest part of the night had passed and the summer rain began, the two broke camp and headed for Easton ahead of the approaching thunderstorm.

2

"More soup, love?"

"No, thanks, Barney." The young woman glanced up at the barkeeper hovering over her and smiled. "It was good, though." She returned her attention to the messy pile of parchment pages and odd objects that littered the table in front of her, scratching away furiously with a quill and humming softly to herself.

Barney sighed and brought the soup tureen back to the bar, enjoying the physical thrill that always resulted from being the recipient of that smile. Then he glanced furtively about, hoping Dee hadn't seen him grinning like a fool. Dee loved the girl too, but it was best not to rock the marital boat.

Under the pretense of wiping clean the ale-spattered surface, he indulged in another look. The girl brushed a loose strand of golden hair out of her eyes and touched her throat absently, untangling a simple gold locket that hung from a delicate chain around her neck.

She was still writing away at an intense pace, pausing every now and again to examine one of the assorted small things on the table before her, or to pluck a few strings of the shepherd's harp resting on her lap beneath the table. She was glowing with quiet excitement, and despite her being tucked away at her favorite table near the back of the bar, that excitement was radiating through the crowd of regulars and generating quite a din. Generally the middle of the day was a dismally quiet time at the Hat and Feathers; today it was as loud as a holiday night. *No wonder Dee loves her*, Barney thought, chuckling to himself. *She's good for business*.

Few noticed the stranger enter over the clamor of voices and clinking of tankards. He made his way impatiently through the crowd, searching the tables until he came to hers. The man stood over her, waiting for her to look up, but she ignored him and continued with her writing, frowning as she scratched out the occasional mistake.

Finally he spoke. "You're Rhapsody."

She did not look up, but moved a few of the papers into a neater pile and drew forth a fresh sheet of parchment.

"Well?"

She still did not favor him with a glance. "Oh, sorry. Thank you for reminding me." There was a pause, and then she spoke again. "If you'll excuse me, I'm rather busy."

The man swallowed, choking back the anger her dismissive tone raised in his gullet. He could feel the eyes of some of the patrons shift to him, and he attempted to keep his voice calm.

"I am here representing a gentleman friend of yours."

There was no break in her concentration or the focus of her attention. "Really? And who might that be?"

"Michael, the Wind of Death."

The hubbub in the Hat and Feathers died away, but the young woman didn't seem to notice or care. "Either they have redefined the words *gentleman* and *friend* in this language, or you're making very sloppy use of it," she said. "What does he want?"

"Your services, naturally."

"I'm not in the business anymore."

"I don't think your professional status is of much interest to him."

For the first time she stopped writing and looked up at the stranger. The eyes that met his contained no hint of fear and were such a startling green that he took a step backward. "Well, what he wants is not of much interest to me," she said evenly. "Now, if you will kindly excuse me, as I said, I'm very busy." She returned to her work once again.

It took a moment for the man to recover his composure. As the look of rage spread over his grizzled features, the bar patrons began to exit or at least move to safer corners. His hand slammed down on the table, fingers spread wide to crumple the pile of parchment.

He stopped in the nick of time, the blade of her dagger pressing between his middle and index fingers just before the point of drawing blood. The motion that had put it there was so quick and fluid that he hadn't even seen it.

Rhapsody looked up at him for only the second time.

"Now, I believe I've been polite, but you don't seem to be

listening. If you have smudged one note of my work you will
henceforth only be able to count to six, and you will need to
drop your pants to do so. Now please, go and leave me in
peace." With all eyes now on her she reinked her quill and
returned to her work, her hand still on the dagger.

The stranger glared at her, removed his hand gingerly from
the table, and left the tavern, jostling past a few of the remaining patrons and slamming the heavy wooden door behind
him. Barney watched him go, and then came to Rhapsody's
table, a look of concern wrinkling his kindly face.

"Don't you know who he works for, darlin'?" he asked
anxiously, watching Dee begin to gather the plates and debris
left on the hastily vacated tables.

Rhapsody was methodically stacking the parchment leaves
and rolling them into scrolls. "Of course. Michael, the Waste
of Breath. What a ridiculous name."

"I wouldn't be talking so disrespectfully, love. He's become a lot more dangerous of late. And he has a lot more
ears than he used to."

"Oh dear. And he wasn't all that attractive to begin with."
Rhapsody stuffed the roll of papers into her oilcloth satchel,
and began to pack up the small items on the table, leaving
out only a wilted primrose and a scrap of vellum.

She corked the inkwell and tied it carefully into the pocket
she had sewn within the sack, wrapped her harp in its burlap
cover and placed it in on top. Then she began to write again
on the vellum scrap, methodically and slowly this time.

"On second thought, Barney, I will have some more of that
soup."

𝒯he others were already breaking camp when Gammon
reached the outpost outside the northwestern wall of Easton.
He could tell by the tone of Michael's voice, barking commands to his henchman and berating the men-at-arms, that
this was not safe news to deliver. His only hope was that the
wild instability that had plagued their leader of late might
cause him to forget the errand that Gammon had been sent
out on. That hope was dashed with one look at Michael's
face.

"Where is she?" he demanded, striding to Gammon and

shoving aside the lackey he had been abusing.

"She's apparently out of the business, sir."

Michael's eyes opened wide and Gammon saw within them a battle for self-control raging. "You couldn't find her? How could you miss her?"

Gammon hesitated, then plunged ahead. "I found her, m'lord. She refused to come."

Michael blinked, and it seemed to Gammon that his eyes darkened and grew calm again.

"Refused. She refused?"

"Yes, sir."

Michael turned and watched the men packing up the horses and the weapons.

"Perhaps you misunderstood my order, Gammon," he said calmly as the sour black smoke from the doused campfires billowed toward them and over the wide meadow, where it hung like dirty wool in the air. "I didn't want you to ask the wench if she would like to accompany us. I expected you to bring her back."

"Yes, m'lord."

"Now go back to town and get her. Gods, she barely comes up to your shoulder. Drag her by that beautiful golden hair, if necessary. Did you see her hair, Gammon?"

"Yes, sir."

"I have thought about that hair for a long time, Gammon. Can you imagine what that hair feels like in your hands?"

"Yes m'lord."

"No, you can't, Gammon," Michael said, his voice cold and emotionless. "You can't because the pouch between your legs is empty. You have never had her, have you? I thought not. It is not something one such as you would survive.

"Now I, Gammon, I have had her, and I have never experienced the equal of it. She's part Lirin, did you notice that? Lirin women have an especially sweet taste, did you know that, Gammon? Hers is particularly fine. And—well, let us just say that her hair is only the beginning of her charms, charms you could not even begin to imagine.

"Perhaps, though, Gammon, if you remain in my good favor, I will let you try her out a little. Just enough to make your wretched life worth something while keeping you from

any major damage, hmmm? Once I've had my fill of her—
or should I say she's had her fill of me? What say you, Gammon? Would you like that?"

Gammon knew this trap. "I'll go get her, m'lord," he said.

"Good man," said Michael, and he returned to the field.

ℜhapsody had just finished the last penstroke on the
scrap of vellum and was blotting it dry when Gammon returned to the Hat and Feathers. The tavern was now empty
save for Barney and Dee, and they watched in dread as he
strode to her table again and stood across from her. As before,
Rhapsody did not look up at him as she finished her work.

"You will come with me," Gammon said.

"Can't today. Sorry."

"Enough of this," Gammon snarled. He grabbed with one
hand for the long fall of golden hair held in place by a simple
black ribbon; with the other he drew a short sword.

The tavernkeepers watched him double over in pain as
Rhapsody slammed the table forward into his groin and
pushed him up against the wall with it. He gasped as she
ground the corner of the table into his genitals, and his head
bobbed down over the table board. She knocked his sword
onto the floor next to him, retrieved it, and then leaned forward over the table and spoke directly into his ear.

"You are a very rude man. Go and tell your commander
that I said what he was planning to do to me he should do to
himself. Do you understand?"

Gammon glared at her, and she put her dagger to his throat
before moving the table for him to pass.

"One more thing," she said as she backed him toward the
door. "I will be leaving right after you, and I won't be back.
Either you and the other thugs you will undoubtedly summon
to help you can bother these people, or you can try to catch
me. I wouldn't waste the time here if I were you." She threw
his sword into the filth of the street.

Gammon spat at her as he left the tavern for a second time.

"A very rude man," Rhapsody repeated to Barney and Dee.
She dropped a handful of coins onto the table, then gave Dee
a quick hug. "I'll go out the front door. You should probably

close up until suppertime. I'm sorry for any trouble I've caused you."

"Be careful now, dear," said Dee, fighting back tears.

Rhapsody pulled her cloak from the peg by the entrance and donned it quickly. She slung her satchel over her shoulder and onto her back, and made for the door. As she passed him she gave Barney the scrap of vellum along with one last smile.

"Good luck to you, Barney," she said, kissing his cheek. "And if you should ever come upon a troubadour, get him to play this for you."

Barney look down at the scrap in his hand. On it were graphed five straight lines and a series of musical notes. "What is this, darlin'?" he asked.

"Your name," she said, and she left.

Dee went to the table, pocketed the coins, and picked up the soup bowl and spoon, and the discarded quill. "Barney," she said, "come have a look at this."

There on the table lay a primrose, fresh and fragrant as the moment it was picked.

𝒯he back streets of Easton were dark and cool, a haven from the scorching sun. The two men traveled silently over the cobblestones, past bickering merchants and domestic squabbling, unnoticed in the shadows. That Grunthor could pass without being seen attested to the blinding heat of the day and the depth of the shade in the streets. Normally his sheer size and mass stopped conversation and traffic on the rare occasions he entered a city.

The Brother could sense the more crowded streets long before they got to them, the deafening vibration of the heartbeats of the unwashed masses throbbing in his ears and skin. Whenever a large group of people were present in an upcoming street they would circumvent it, taking an alternate route, adding time to their journey but increasing their chances of going unnoticed.

They picked their way down a deserted section, avoiding scattered refuse and the human garbage that was sleeping off the last night's binge, belching and muttering at the cobblestones beneath their faces. Neither man looked down as they stepped over the drunkards and piles of rubbish, dodging the obstacles with a practiced gait.

The upcoming alley was empty, the Brother knew, and it was a feeder street to the external thoroughfares of the southeastern section. A few streetcorners more and they would be within reach of the wharf, and the surrounding bustle would swallow them up into anonymity.

The Brother and Grunthor had traversed most of the alley, were within fifty yards of its end, when a commotion spilled into it. A handful of clumsy town guards rounded the corner and came into the alley, chasing a street wench. The two men came to an involuntary stop in the shadow of the buildings.

Rhapsody stepped into the street in front of the Hat and Feathers, scanning the area for any of the miscreants and lowlifes she remembered from Michael's ragtag band of followers.

The pub was on the Kingsway, one of the busiest of Easton's thoroughfares near the northwestern gate, and the street was teeming with human and animal traffic, pounding with noise and stench. Not seeing anyone she recognized as one of his ruffians, she crossed the muddy road, avoiding as best she could the puddles of muck left over from the last night's thunderstorm.

At the center of the Kingsway she met up with Pilam the baker, attempting to navigate a heavy wheeled pushcart covered in burlap through the bemired street. Like a stone breaking the flow of a river, he was causing the stream of people to part and pass around him, sometimes narrowly missing him. His bald pate was red with exertion and shiny with sweat, but his face broke out in a wide grin when he saw her.

"Rhapsody! How are you this fine afternoon?"

"Hello, Pilam. Here, let me give you a hand with that."

Rhapsody scanned the street again, dodged some merchants who were skittering around the obstacle, then took hold of the near side of the cart and raised it out of the rut that was preventing it from moving. Pilam gave it another push and the cart lurched forward, scattering a pile of flat loaves of bread from under the cloth covering. He caught one as it fell, then offered it to her as they again joined the traffic propelling down the muddy street.

"Well, thank you, dear. Please, take this, with my thanks."

"Pilam, you are so gallant. Thank you," Rhapsody said, tossing her head in a manner that made the golden fall of hair catch the light and flashing him a smile that made him weak in the knees.

She stuffed the bread into her pack, then looked around again. Her exaggerated movements had caught the eyes of a number of passersby, which was her intention; the more witnesses who saw her away from the Hat and Feathers, the safer Barney and Dee would be.

As she came to the cross street, she noticed a familiar-looking man engaged in an intense conversation with a town guard. Quickly pulling up the hood of her cloak, she stepped behind a line of barrels in front of the bowyer's shop and watched as a second guard joined the conversation. Then the three of them made their way rapidly down the street toward the Hat and Feathers.

Rhapsody looked on anxiously as the men approached the tavern, stopping passing townsfolk on their way. After having no apparent luck with the first three or four people they asked, a woman nodded in answer to their questions and pointed up the street in her general direction. She sighed in relief as they turned and ran back toward her, the opposite way from the Hat and Feathers. She put her hood down again and rounded the corner onto the cross street.

Leaving the Kingsway put her out of the mercantile district and into the narrower, alleyed streets of residential buildings. Rhapsody knew this area well; it was easy to find alcoves and porticos in this section of town in which to hide. She was almost to the end of the first block when she heard shouting behind her.

She wheeled around to see about a dozen men, several of whom were town guards, running at full tilt toward her, drawing weapons. Rhapsody was amazed. Michael had never been able to count the town guard among his lackeys when she had been unfortunate enough to have commerce with him, but that was almost three years ago. Apparently Barney was right about his growing influence. This was going to be more difficult than she had thought.

Rhapsody ducked around the corner and pulled up her hood once again. She hurried across the street and made for the second alley, which ran between a one-story shack with a thatched roof and a building with two floors fashioned out of mudbrick. The shack had a root cellar, and she was able to squeeze along the side of the hole and under some thatch fallen from the roof. She made herself as comfortable as she could, listening to gauge the guards' approach.

She could hear them for some time before they came into her line of sight, checking the alleys across the street. From the sound of it they had broken into smaller groups and were splitting up to comb the area more quickly. It also seemed to her that there were many more of them than before.

A group of three came around the corner and walked past her head. She took a deep breath and held it while they looked around, kicking over broken crates and boards, cursing.

She felt like cursing herself—how could she have missed Michael's ascent to importance? Her general loathing of him had won out over her common sense, and her miscalculation could cause her problems she was not prepared to deal with. *But,* she reminded herself, *it's not like I had another choice.* To have gone with Gammon obediently would have been unthinkable.

Rhapsody watched as one of the three guards scattered a pile of lump coal next to another mudbrick building a few blocks up. A man in a leather apron ran out into the street, cursing and shouting. As the argument grew heated she used the distraction to slip out of her hiding place and dashed around the corner, back toward the cross street that led to the Kingsway. She was almost to the first corner when a cry went up behind her.

There was no way to make it back to the Kingsway now. There was also no hope of taking shelter in a house—even if the residents let her in, she might be responsible for bringing disaster upon them. Rhapsody fled, breaking into a run that took her up the first alley and three blocks deeper into the back streets before the guards rounded the corner. They were shouting, and as they pursued her up the alley two more appeared from a street just in front of her. She was trapped in the middle.

Rhapsody tried to run for a side alley, but she was brought to the ground almost immediately. The guard who seized her rolled her over onto her back and slapped her full across the face; she returned the favor by booting him in the testicles. As he hunched over in pain she scrambled to her feet and broke away from his grip, only to be grabbed by the second guard. He pulled her arms roughly behind her back, lifted her off the ground, kicking and struggling, and carried her back into the main alley.

"My, you certainly are a lot of trouble," he said into her ear as he jerked her down the street. "But I'm sure you'll make it worth his while, won't you? When he's rammin' it in you, darlin', think of me." His mouth closed on her neck, and his free hand groped her breast.

With great effort Rhapsody twisted one of her arms free, sending a stabbing pain from her shoulder to her fingers. Fighting to overcome the wave of nausea that followed the pain, she flicked her wrist to bring her dagger forth, twisting her fingers to make it slide into her palm.

She slashed over her head and behind her, aiming for his eyes. The speed with which she hit the ground as he dropped her and doubled over assured her she had struck her target. His screams shocked the three guards who had been following behind her and had stopped where they stood when they saw her captured.

Before they could move she had taken off again, running at breakneck speed down the main alley and into the darker parts of the back streets. When they recovered their composure the three gave chase, while the other tried to tend to his hemorrhaging companion. They saw her dart past two women carrying baskets of clothes and slip down yet another corridor in the street.

Rhapsody entered the alley and stopped, looking around for a place to hide. There was none. She ran forward again, then stopped abruptly when she saw two shapes approaching her from the other end of the street.

The first was a man of gigantic proportion in metal-banded

leather armor wearing a helmet with a pointed spike on the top. The second figure was cloaked and hooded, his face covered with what appeared to be a form of veil, and though he appeared diminutive next to the giant, she knew he was tall as well. He moved with an agility that startled her; when he saw her he stopped immediately, about three steps sooner than the giant was able to.

Rhapsody looked behind her again. The three guards had rounded the corner and had closed the distance between them to about thirty feet. She was trapped between the strangers and the guards. Given what she knew about the guards, she decided to appeal to the strangers for assistance.

She turned to the two odd travelers. "Please help me," she gasped, puffing from exertion. "Let me pass." The strangers looked to each other, but did not move.

The guards slowed their steps but continued forward, walking three abreast. Rhapsody turned to face them again. She would need to convince them these strangers were her allies, powerful allies. She did her best to smile at the odd-looking men.

"Pardon me, but would you be willing to adopt me for a moment? I'd be grateful."

The man next to the giant nodded slightly.

"Thank you," Rhapsody gasped again. She turned back to the town guard. "What an extraordinary coincidence," she panted, a smile of false bravado on her exquisite, sweating face. "You gentlemen are just in time to meet my brother. Brother, these are the town guards. Gentlemen, this is my brother—Achmed—the Snake."

For a moment it was as though time expanded all around Rhapsody. Heat flushed her face and she heard, and felt, a distant but audible *crack,* followed by a *puff,* like a spark exploding, or smoke dissipating.

A strange feeling washed over her, unlike any she had ever felt; light-headedness from all the running, perhaps. She winced internally at the idiotic name that had come to her on the spot, but it seemed to have done the trick, because the town guards were now staring over her head in abject fear.

A series of soft *thoop* sounds whispered behind her and whistled past her. Faster than her eyes could track them shining projectiles, thin as butterfly wings, struck the throats of all three, toppling them over in rapid succession. The guards fell heavily into the mud of the alley, not moving.

Rhapsody looked down at the bodies, amazed. She turned to the strangers again. The smaller of the two was slinging a strange-looking weapon, shaped somewhat like a crossbow but with an asymmetrical curved arm, over his shoulder and under his cloak again. She looked at him in blank admiration.

"Nice work," she said. "Thank you."

The two strangers looked at each other, then around the alley. The cloaked one put out his hand to her. It was slender in its leather sheath, but the grip looked deadly.

"Come with us if you want to live," he said.

His voice was dry with an unnatural rasp to it; it was a percussive sound that widened Rhapsody's eyes with interest.

She looked quickly over her shoulder, hearing the approach of more guards, and then turned to the stranger once more and took his gloved hand. Together the three of them bolted from the alley and into the shadows cast by the afternoon sun setting over the back streets of Easton.

3

$\mathcal{T}$he walls of the vast city could no longer be seen and darkness was swallowing the meadows that surrounded Easton long before the three travelers stopped to make camp. They had left the city by the eastern gate, down by the docks.

Easton was a port city, a thriving relic left over from the days of the racial campaigns in the Second Age. Though its original planning, and recent attempts at restoration, saw it as a great center of art and culture at the crux of the trade routes, during the wars it had been refitted for defense, as a walled fortress, surrounded on three sides by great stone bulwarks eighteen feet thick leading down to the wharf. The bustle of the seafaring traffic made handy cover for their escape.

Rhapsody had run through the back streets of Easton before, had even been dragged once or twice, but never as purposefully as with these two who half-led, half-carried her through the yards and cobbled alleys. She was able to keep up with them only because of her knowledge of the city.

When they cut through two abandoned buildings well after the point where she was sure they were out of tracking range, however, she lost her bearings. Certainly they had also lost anyone who might have identified them at the scene of the crime. In front of a busy portside tavern, the slighter man stopped.

"These will do," he said, then stole two horses in broad daylight.

The giant lifted Rhapsody onto one of the horses, and they walked a few blocks before the men mounted and rode quickly out of town, across the fields south and along the sea.

The giant rode slightly behind, and Rhapsody could hear the horse working hard to keep up with the pace set by the man with thin hands. In fact, even though she rode in front of him, in the same saddle, she could not hear his breath. It felt only as if she were wearing a modestly heavy cloak instead of sitting in front of a person intent on escape, guiding the horse from behind her. The vibrations from the galloping horse hid her trembling.

They rode the entire afternoon. Rhapsody had never been outside of Easton's southern wall before, and kept casting mournful backward glances at the great gray vista of mud-and-thatch buildings, decaying marble temples, ramshackle stone houses, and towering statuary receding more and more into the twilight with each moment. At dusk she could barely make out the high, twisting wall that led down to the harbor, where distant lights were twinkling; it was nothing more than a faint black line in the approaching darkness.

Once they were out of sight of the city, they slowed their pace, but it was clear that the two men intended to put as much distance between themselves and Easton as possible. Even as night fell and Rhapsody had to acknowledge to herself that she was lost, and might have been kidnapped, not rescued as she first thought, they pressed on.

For a while Rhapsody had felt it was dangerous to the horses to keep moving when no one could possibly see a safe path. Then, without a sign or warning, they stopped. The night had come into itself, and the riders were surrounded by darkness.

"Get down." The voice seemed to come from the air.

Before she could react the smaller man quickly moved her from the saddle. He was down himself in an instant, and with a swift motion threw the reins to the other man.

"Grunthor, lose the horses." The veiled man vanished into the night.

Rhapsody lost sight of him almost immediately. She turned to the shape that the darkness made even more huge, simultaneously backpedaling a step and reaching quietly for the knife in her wrist sheath.

Grunthor did not look at her, but dismounted, tied up the reins on each horse, and stepped back.

"Get on with ya," he said, but the animals were so spent that they hardly reacted. As if he had anticipated this, the giant removed his helmet and moved to a spot directly in front of the horses, where both of them could see him clearly, even with all trace of twilight faded from the sky. He spread his arms and roared.

The sound rumbled and echoed through the horseflesh and through Rhapsody. For a moment the mounts were frozen, but after a breath they were reanimated and fled in the panic of prey in sight of the predator, wild-eyed and screaming.

Grunthor replaced his helmet and turned to Rhapsody. He took one look at the expression on her face and roared with laughter.

" 'Allo, darlin'. Oi'm so glad to see it's love at first sight for you, too. Come along." He walked away into the night.

Rhapsody was not sure that it was wise to follow the giant, but was sure it was even less so to make him angry, so she took off after him. She struggled to keep up, trying to sort things out in her head. "Where are we going? Are we walking all the way?"

"Doubtful. We already been on forced march today."

At the edge of the horizon the full moon appeared and began to rise, golden, blanketed in the fog at the edge of the sea. Its light did nothing to illuminate the darkness; impenetrable blackness hung, heavy as pitch, in the summer air.

Rhapsody thought she had good night vision, but she was still moving along more by touch and sound than sight.

She trailed after the giant as he followed a path that was apparently only visible to him until she nearly stepped into a small fire. Grunthor had sidestepped at the last second and had to put his arm in front of her to keep her from putting her boot directly into the flames.

A camp was already made. She was not sure if she didn't see it because he was in the way, blocking her view, or because of the darkness of the night, or the way the camp had been placed.

Grunthor moved to a spot upwind of the fire, took off his helmet, and drew a long breath before sitting down. He had paid little attention to her so far, and even though it would put her directly into his line of vision, Rhapsody went to the opposite side, keeping the fire between them, and dropped her pack to the ground. She wasn't bothered by smoke, and thought the flames might provide at least a small barrier if necessary.

In the firelight she took a good look at the giant across from her. Sitting on the ground, he was easily still eye to eye with her, which meant that he was a minimum of seven feet tall and at least as wide as a dray horse.

Beneath his heavy military greatcoat she caught a glint of metal. His armor was foreign to her, and better-made than she would have guessed. It looked like a kind of reptile-scale leather banded by support joints of metal plate, but she had not heard any scrape or other resonance from it the whole time. She was slightly alarmed that she had not heard much from his many weapons, either. He wore an extremely large ax and several wicked-looking blades, and had a number of hilts and handles jutting out from behind his armor.

His face was even more frightening. At least one tooth protruded past his lips, and it was difficult to tell what color his hidelike skin was in the inconstant light. His eyes, ears, and nose were exaggeratedly large on his face, and Rhapsody guessed that he was able to see, hear, and smell her much better than she could him. At the ends of his massive hands were talonlike nails that more accurately resembled claws. He was the stuff of an adult's nightmare. At the moment he was pulling food and something to cook it in from his pack, still ignoring her.

"Let me guess; you've heard of Firbolg but you never met one before, right?"

The sandy voice of the other man spoke directly behind her and Rhapsody jumped. She had not sensed his presence at all.

She stared across the crackling flames at the giant. "You're Firbolg? You don't seem it."

"And just what do ya mean by that?"

"I'm sorry, I didn't mean to be rude," she said, her face turning red in the light of the campfire. "It's just that, well, in my limited experience, Firbolg are thought of as monsters."

"And in my not-so-limited experience, Lirin are thought of as appetizers," Grunthor replied breezily, without rancor.

"I assume it's your preference not to adopt either of those assumptions," said the cloaked figure.

"Absolutely," Rhapsody said, smiling and shuddering at the same time. She had a feeling the giant wasn't kidding.

The thin man dropped a pile of rabbit carcasses near the giant.

"Who are you?"

"My name is Rhapsody. I'm a student of music. A Singer."

"Why was the town guard chasing you?"

"Much to my surprise, and chagrin, they were in the service of an imbecile who was looking to have me brought to him."

"Brought to him for what?"

"I assume for entertainment purposes."

"Does this imbecile have a name?"

"He calls himself Michael, the Wind of Death. Many of us call him similar, if less flattering, things behind his back."

The two men exchanged a glance, then the man in the cloak looked back at her again. "How do you know him?"

"I'm sorry to say he was a customer of mine three years ago when I was working as a prostitute," Rhapsody answered frankly. "It wasn't really by choice, but not much is when that's your profession. Unfortunately, he became a bit obsessed with me, and he told me at the time he would return for me, but he was such a pompous windbag that I never was much concerned about it. The first of several miscalculations on my part. The second occurred today, when he sent one of his slimy minions to fetch me, and I refused to come. If it had been his regular lackeys, I could have eluded them, but he's managed to enlist the aid of the town guard since I last saw him."

"Why didn't you just agree to meet 'im, and then go into 'iding?"

"That would be lying."

"So?" said the cloaked one. "That would be living."

"I never lie. I can't."

Grunthor chuckled. "What a convenient memory ya got there, sister. Oi seem to remember you tellin' them town guards that you and we was related. Oi think you might look a bit out o' place at our family gatherin's."

"No," interjected the sandy-voiced man. His eyes were full of clear comprehension as they stared at her. "That's why you asked us to adopt you first."

Rhapsody nodded. "Right. My attempt to dissuade them from bothering me wouldn't have worked if it wasn't the truth, at least on some level."

"Why not?"

"Lying is forbidden in the profession I have chosen; if you don't speak the truth, you can't be a Namer, the highest form of Singer. You have to keep the music in your speech on-key and attuned to the world around you. Lying corrupts those vibrations, and sullies what you have to say. It's not an exact science, since truth is partially influenced by perspective.

"That's the academic reason. As a more personal philosophy, my parents always told me deceit was wrong. More recently, it's because once I broke free of my old, uh, line of work, the thing I treasured most was the truth. There really isn't any in being a whore—you are always someone else's lie. And you have to bite your tongue and participate in other people's fantasies, many of which you can't stomach.

"So now that I am free of that life, I couldn't contain my loathing of Michael for one minute more. It was probably a mistake, but I'm not sure I could have done anything differently and still have lived with myself."

"Well, there's no 'arm done."

"Yes there is. I just exiled myself from Easton. I probably

blinded one of the town guards in my attempt to escape, and now I can't go back."

The smaller man laughed. "I doubt there are any eyewitnesses."

"Maybe not that saw you," said Rhapsody. "There were many more that saw me—they chased me for eight street-corners."

"Then you have a problem." The cloaked man sat back, surveying the field as the smoke from the fire formed a twisted tendril that pointed to the stars. "You could simply choose not to go back. Have you a family you would leave behind, or perhaps one elsewhere on which you can rely?"

The utter indifference in his voice gave Rhapsody the feeling that this was an interrogation, not an attempt at friendly advice. She was fairly sure she had been able to persuade them that she was harmless and relatively valueless, but the fatigue of the flight and uncertainty of her situation was beginning to take its toll.

By now the giant Firbolg had skinned the rabbits and arranged the fire to cook them. Rhapsody did not know whether to expect them to offer her anything, but she would hardly have been surprised to see the game eaten raw. When she first undertook to become a Singer, one of the earliest lessons was an epic song of Firbolg history that had left a grisly impression on her, and her two rescuers had done little to change it.

The men moved as though they had traveled together for a long time. There was a routine to the tasks of preparing the meal that spoke of practice and mutual respect. The thin man had killed the rabbits; the giant skinned them. The giant arranged the fire; the other man found fuel. The entire meal, from the meat to some root that also required cooking, was accomplished and the campsite laid out without a word, one to the other. They behaved almost as if she were not there at all. Grunthor did motion at her once, across the fire, with a skewer heavy with sizzling meat, but she shook her head.

"No, thank you."

For her part, she rationed out a small portion of the bread Pilam had given her, and stored it in a pocket of her cloak rather than return it to her pack. She was feeling more and more uneasy about her companions by the minute, and wanted to be ready to flee if necessary. Her pack was not within easy reach. Normally she would never have considered leaving her instruments, but when he stopped to eat, Rhapsody had caught sight of the thin man's face.

She tried to look at first without appearing to look, but as horrifying as the giant was, she was unprepared for the shock of the slightly more human face.

In the whole expanse of skin on the front of his head there was not a single smooth spot. It was not lumpy, but scarred, pocked, and it was marked with traceries of exposed veins. She had seen diseased faces, and faces marred by time and weapons and other scourges, drink and worse, but here it looked as if the entire army of Destiny's Horsemen had run roughshod over his face, sharply clipping flesh from his nose, thrusting the rest around with the force of their riding.

What truly caught her, though, were his eyes. As if plucked from two different heads, neither size, nor color, nor shape were matched in them, and their placement in this remarkable and terrifying face was not even symmetrical. He looked as if he were sighting down a weapon. Just then she became aware that he was staring back at her.

Rhapsody had been in the city long enough and was a quick enough reader of people to seldom be caught looking. Her recovery was swift, if fumbling: "So where are you headed next?"

"Off Island."

She smiled uncertainly. "You must have irritated someone really important, too."

A cloud passed over the moon. Rhapsody could vaguely tell that she should be aware of something.

She continued to stare at him through the fire, which seemed to have changed ever-so-slightly, and as she watched the thin man chewing, she saw the fire roar up and reflect in his eyes. She imagined that he was staring at her while chewing on her answers instead of the roasted rabbit she now felt foolish to have refused. *Everyone deserves a last meal,* she thought ruefully.

Somewhere in the deepest part of her, the part of her that was a Namer, a storysinger, she heard her own musical note ring through the roaring of the fire, through the silence of the men. The clarity of her Naming note, her touchstone of truth, told her that this was a trap, a trick of the fire. Then she saw the thin hands and the battlefield face step through the fire itself, and she knew it was too late to escape. She blinked with eyelids made heavy by more than exhaustion; the smoke must have contained a hypnotic herb with which she was not familiar.

He was angry, but he did not touch her. Instead, he grabbed her pack from the ground next to her and began rifling through it.

"Who are you?" the cloaked man demanded. His voice was a fricative hissing, his cloak still smoky from his leap over the flames. He waited for an answer.

"Hey, put that down." She tried to stand but satisfied herself with shaking off the trance.

The giant stood up. "Oi wouldn't do that if Oi were you, miss. Just answer the question."

"I already told you; my name is Rhapsody. Now put that down before you break something."

"I never break anything unless I mean to. Now, try again. Who are you?"

"I thought I got it right the first time. Let's see; I'll try again. Rhapsody. Isn't that what I said before?" Her head was swimming, her answers seemed fuzzy. "What did you put in the fire?"

"I'm about to put your hair in it. How did you know who I am?" He grabbed her injured arm with fingers that behaved more like shears, cutting off feeling to her wrist and hand. Without moving, her muscles began to spasm. There was a small shock of painful interrupted bloodflow at each heartbeat.

Rhapsody did not react. One advantage she had always had was that she could stand a little abuse. She had also learned that hiding her pain and fear could keep her alive.

"I have no idea what you're talking about. I have no idea who you are. Now let go."

"In the alley you named me before those guards."

Even though her fingers were going numb, Rhapsody remained steady. *You gentlemen are just in time to meet my brother. Brother, these are the town guard. Gentlemen, this is my brother—Achmed—the Snake.* Despite her drugged state, she felt embarrassment.

"I needed an ally at that moment, and you just happened to be there," she said. "It was the first scary name that came into my head, even if in hindsight it was rather, well—I'm sorry. I didn't mean to presume."

"That's not the part 'e's talkin' about," said Grunthor. " 'Ow did you know 'e's the Brother?"

"Whose brother?"

For a moment, Rhapsody thought it had gone too far, that she was going to pass out. With each question the sensation that he was severing her arm with his grip grew more urgent. Suddenly, he relaxed his hold on her and looked across the fire at his partner, then back at her.

"I certainly hope you're only pretending to be this stupid."

"No, I'm afraid not. I have no idea what you are talking about. Is your name supposed to mean something to me?"

"No."

"Then could you let go?"

Grunthor moved to help her stand as the man with the nightmare face released her and returned to searching her bag.

"What 'e's sayin' is, those troops after you were nothing next to what's chasin' us. This is a serious business, miss. My friend wants to know 'ow you knew 'e is the Brother."

"I'm sorry, but I've never heard of the Brother, if that's your name. I was trying to convince them that you were *my* brother. That's why I asked if you would adopt me, so that it would be true. I guess this was an unfortunate coincidence. But I've already told you I never lie. So either believe me, or kill me, but do *not* break my instruments."

"I'll smash every one here if you do not tell me the whole truth. Perhaps you had well-meaning parents. Perhaps you were once a professional whore, perhaps you took a vow. Perhaps you now are the consort of some holier-than-unholy man who gets his jollies from your candor. Tell me now who you really are and how you knew to name me."

"First, tell me who you both are, and what you intend to do with me."

The piercing eyes regarded her sharply. "This is Grunthor. No one has concealed that."

The giant glanced at her quickly. "Although you can always call me 'The Ultimate Authority, to Be Obeyed at All Costs,' " he said lightly. "My troops always does."

The joke had its intended effect. The robed man exchanged a look with the giant, then seemed to relax somewhat.

"At the moment, Achmed is as apt an appellation as anything for me, since that is what you chose to call me," he said sullenly. "As to who I am, and your fate, both of those are yet to be determined. You spoke my name and then changed it. Normally this would only be an annoyance, but those who are hunting us can make the dead speak, and surely will if they feel they can learn something. Those dead idiots heard what you said. What is a trollop doing with expensive instruments?"

Rhapsody rubbed her shoulder, feeling the pain begin to abate.

"I am not a trollop. As I told you before, I am a student of music, and I have achieved the status of Singer of Lirin lore; our word for it is Enwr. My goal was to go on to become a Namer, a Canwr; it is a rare accomplishment but the skills are useful.

"Four years ago I was accepted as an apprentice. I studied for three of those years with Heiles, a Namer of great renown who lived in Easton, but a year or so ago he vanished without a trace, and I was left to finish my studies on my own. I was completing my final research just this morning."

"What can you do?"

Rhapsody shrugged, then held her throbbing hands closer to the fire.

"Assorted things. The main thing Singers study is lore. Sometimes lore consists of old tales or the history of a race or a culture. Sometimes it's the knowledge of a particular discipline, like herbalism or astronomy. Sometimes it's a collection of songs that tell an important story which would otherwise be lost."

The man now known as Achmed stared at her. "And sometimes it's the knowledge of ancient powers."

Rhapsody swallowed nervously. The subject of lore was more akin to a religious belief than a science. It was the way in which the people of her race and profession derived wisdom and power from the vibrations in the life around them. Since in the Lirin creed Life and God were the same thing, the use of lore was a form of prayer, a kind of communion with the Infinite. It was hardly something she wanted to be discussing with a stranger, and especially not this one.

She looked up to meet his gaze and found an intensity in his eyes that stung her own. It was compelling her to speak, silently demanding an answer.

"Sometimes, yes, but that generally is something known to Namers and Singers of great experience. Even then, the reason a Namer can draw on the power of a primordial element, like fire or wind, or on a lesser element, like time, is that they have intimate knowledge of it; they know its story, in a sense. That's another reason for the need for the vow of truth among Namers: if you should interject falsity into lore it dilutes its story, makes it weaker for everyone."

The hooded man stuffed her burlap-wrapped harp back into her pack and cinched the drawstring savagely. "So I'll ask you again, Singer; what can *you* do?"

Rhapsody hesitated. The man who had once been known as the Brother lifted her pack off the ground, balancing it precariously on one finger over the fire. It was as subtle a threat as she had ever seen.

"Not very much, outside of singing a rather extensive collection of historical ballads and epics. I can find herbs to throw into the fire to mesmerize people. Obviously that isn't going to impress you much since you can, too. I can bring sleep to the restless, or prolong the slumber of someone who is already asleep, an especially useful talent for new parents of fussy babies.

"I can ease pain of the body and the heart, heal minor wounds, and comfort the dying, making their passage easier. Sometimes I can see their souls as they leave for the light. I can tell a story from a few bits of fact and a good dollop of audience reaction. I can tell the absolute truth as I know it. And when I do that I can change things."

Rhapsody pointed to her pack, and he handed it over. She

reached inside without looking, and took out a shriveled flower from her morning study session. Gently, to avoid crumbling what was left of the dried petals, she placed the blossom on her open palm and spoke the name of the flower as it might be said in the humid summer day of its glory.

Slowly, but strongly, the petals drank life into themselves and, as long as she whispered the words, bloomed again. Grunthor touched the flower with the tip of one claw, and it bounced a little, as it might if it were fresh. Then Rhapsody fell silent, and the life evaporated into the darkness.

"In theory, I could also kill a whole field of these by speaking the name of their death, if I knew it. So, I suppose the explanation of this afternoon's events goes something like this: we came upon each other in the circumstances you know. By happenstance I spoke your true name, for which I apologize most humbly, but it was, after all, an accident. And then I renamed you; now you really *are* Achmed the Snake, it's your identity on the deepest possible level. I'm sorry if that was presumptuous. I had no idea I could actually do it yet. I suppose that makes you my first."

"How ironic," said the man she had called Achmed, with a sneer. "I wonder how many other men have heard you use those very words."

"Only one," she retorted without a hint of offense in her voice. "As I said before, and am tired of repeating, I don't lie. Not knowingly, anyway."

"Everyone lies, don't be naive. I don't know whether your party trick has shortened the time we have, or covered the trail."

"Will you at least tell me who you are running from? I have told you all about what I was up to and who was chasing me, and here you have stranded me in the middle of gods-know-where, without a clue about who you are or where you're going or whether you're worse than what I left. I want to know if I should stay or take my chances back with the guards."

"This presumes you will be given a choice." Achmed turned his back on her and conferred quietly with Grunthor. For a very long moment she was stalled in her frustration and confusion. As her head cleared from the intoxicants she began to plot out how she might escape, and, if successful, find her way to somewhere she could survive. As she rearranged the displaced contents of her pack, Grunthor approached her. She turned quickly, but the other man was gone again.

"Miss, you should come with us."

"Why? Where?"

"To return to Easton is death. If the Waste o' Breath don't get you, then our particular problem will. You won't 'ave any chance to say you weren't with us, and they'll torture you until you tell what you know or die, whatever comes second."

"I could go to another town. There are plenty of places to hide. I'll be fine on my own, thank you."

"Your choice, my dear, but leavin' is better than stayin'."

"Where did the other one go?"

"Oh, you mean 'Uchmed'? Oi believe 'e went to scout for Michael, to make sure 'e ain't picked up our trail yet."

Rhapsody's eyes widened in horror. "Michael? Michael is following us?"

"Could be; it's 'ard to say. 'E was camped outside the nort'western wall when we left, so 'e probably ain't too nearby yet unless 'e is particularly intent on findin' you. Michael ain't got no trouble with us."

Rhapsody looked around in the darkness nervously. "Where are you going?"

"You can follow us as far as the forest, if you'd like."

"The Lirin wood? The Enchanted Forest?"

"Yeah, that's the one."

"I thought you said you were headed off Island."

The giant rubbed his jutting chin. "Oh, we are, believe me. But we're goin' to the forest first."

"What business do you have in the Lirin wood?"

"Actually, we're on a bit o' a pilgrimage, miss. We're gonna go see the Great Tree."

A look of awe came over Rhapsody's face. "Sagia? You're going to Sagia?"

"Yeah, that's right. We're gonna pay our respects to the great Lirin Tree."

Her eyes narrowed. "You aren't going to harm it, are you? It would be a tremendous mistake on your part."

Grunthor looked offended. "O' course not," he said indignantly. "We intend to do a bit o' prayin' there."

Rhapsody was mollified. "All right," she said, lifting her pack. "I'll go with you, at least to the wood."

" 'Ow many miles you got left in you today, miss?"

"Whatever I need to have, I guess."

"Well, Oi'm afraid that makes you the only one. We been on the road all day, and we're campin' 'ere. Why don't you get some sleep, darlin'? We'll wake you in time to leave before daylight."

"Will we be safe? From Michael, I mean."

A look of utter amusement crossed the giant's face. "Oh, very safe, my dear. Not to worry."

"I can sit a watch," Rhapsody offered. "I have a dagger."

Achmed's voice came from behind her in the darkness. "Well, I for one will sleep much better now knowing you're protecting us, Rhapsody. Try not to hurt any small animals that might attack unless they're edible."

Deep in the foothills of the High Reaches, within the Spire, the silent vault of obsidian that was its hidden seat of power, the red-rimmed eyes of the F'dor's human host broke open in the darkness.

The chain had snapped.

Slowly Tsoltan sat up on the smoothly polished catafalque where he customarily took his repose. He passed his hands through the darkness, grasping futilely for the invisible ends of the metaphysical restraint that had held his greatest trophy in servitude. Nothing; not even a frayed thread of his former absolute control.

The Brother had slipped his leash.

As his anger mounted, the air around the demon-priest grew suddenly dry and thin, on the verge of tangibly cracking. Tsoltan rose quickly and strode down the long hallways to the Deep Chamber.

Sparks ignited behind him, combusting tapestries, altar cloths, and the robes of a few unfortunate priests along the way. His minions gasped for breath in the smothering air and shivered in the black light of the flames, recognizing the fire for what it was—the prelude to the venting of the demon's wrath.

In fury he ascended the red-veined marble steps to the highest altar, his place of blood sacrifice. A solid block of obsidian, mined in the Second Age by the Nain of the Northern Mountains, it had once been the cornerstone of a temple to the All-God, the Deity of Life, built by the united races.

Now it rested at the top of the enormous staircase of concentric marble circles reaching to the unseen ceiling of the Spire, its leather limb restraints and metal collection vessels amusing testimony to how times had changed. It had seemed a fitting place to store the true name of the Brother, the Dhracian whose birthright had bequeathed him a link to the life's blood of the populace of Serendair. The Child of Blood, as he was known in some circles.

Vast ceremonial braziers, standing cold and silent, roared to hideous life in a wide, screaming circle of black fire as he raged past. The smoky flames threw grisly shadows on the distant walls, twisting and writhing in grim anticipation.

Upon reaching the sacrificial altar, Tsoltan hesitated for a moment. He extended a shaking hand and gently caressed the symbols of hatred exquisitely carved into the polished surface, tracing the crusted black channels that laced the smooth top, curving downward into a brass well in the center.

Through this metal mouth he had fed the assassin's captive soul the blood of the Brother's own race, and, when the Dhracians were largely exterminated, that of other innocents, by way of keeping his prize's unique blood bond alive even in slavery.

It had been especially effective in ensuring the Brother's cooperation in his master plan, though he had no illusions about the assassin's allegiance. It would have been a coup just to secure his services; the Brother had a reputation, prior to the capture of his true name, for taking only those assignments that he selected himself. His enslavement changed all that. It had made him Tsoltan's most effective weapon and his primary agent in the completion of the plan's final steps.

The F'dor's hands gripped the altar table more firmly now. He muttered the words of Opening in the ancient language of the Before-Time, perverse countersigns of power tied directly to the birth of fire, the element from which all of his race had sprung. The black stone altar glimmered for a moment, then glowed red as the fire within the obsidian burned, liquefying the stone into molten glass. With a hissing snap, the altar split in two.

Tsoltan tore through the layers of aqueous stone inside and reached into the hollow reliquary within the belly of the altar where the Brother's name had been entombed. When the name had first been brought to the altar to be sealed in the coffer it had been the most singular moment of satisfaction the F'dor had ever experienced, at least in this lifetime.

It was the culmination of great search and great expense, first in obtaining the name, and then capturing it. Finally, the greatest Namer in all of Serendair had been persuaded, after months of torture so excruciating that it bordered on artistry, to write the name in musical script on a scroll of ancient silk. Tsoltan himself had taken the scroll from the man's lifeless hand and surrounded it lovingly with a whirling sphere of protective power, born of firelight and held in place by the spinning of the Earth itself. It had been a thing of great beauty, and securing it within the altar had left him strangely sad, almost bereft of the joy its capture had brought him.

Not, however, as bereft as he felt now. The reliquary held no radiant globe, no Namer's scroll, only the fragments and crumbs of silk left over from what seemed to have been a small explosion. Feverishly Tsoltan gathered the pieces, searching for the musical script, but what few shreds remained were blank.

A howl of fury echoed through the mammoth chamber, cracking many of the obsidian walls. Tsoltan's servants waited in dread to be called in, but heard no further sound. A moment later, their apprehension expanded into full-fledged horror. They could feel the darkness fall about them, palpable and cold as a mist on their shoulders.

Tsoltan was summoning the Shing.

4

Rhapsody was already in the throes of a nightmare when the enormous leathery hand cupped her mouth, snapping her eyes open. Her heart, thrown into feverish racing, pounded so loudly she feared it would rip forth from her chest, but like the scream Grunthor's hand had stifled, it remained in place for the moment, unable to escape, careening off her ribs in panic.

"Sshhh, miss. Don't move. Stay 'ere, darlin', and don't make any noise, eh?" The giant's voice was soft. Rhapsody nodded slightly. Grunthor removed his hand and moved away.

Beneath her back she could feel the ground rumble. She strained to hear over the whine of the night wind, and after a moment thought she could make out the sound of distant horses, many of them, galloping hard.

With great effort she twisted onto her side, taking care not to rise above the grassy scrub where she had fallen into her troubled sleep. The fire was gone without a trace.

Grunthor knelt beside her in a shaft of moonlight, his enormous shape obliterating any other view she might have had. He was gleefully pulling weapons from his back and boot scabbards, fondly examining each blade in the muted light, humming softly to himself. Then, with surprising alacrity and silence, he was gone.

"You don't follow directions particularly well, Rhapsody." The silty voice came from directly over her. Rhapsody choked back a gasp and quickly lay flat again. Above her was nothing but darkness. "Grunthor told you not to move. It was for your own good."

Near her head she felt a slight movement of air, and the darkness twisted before her eyes. Achmed crouched beside her. "Of course, you're welcome to make yourself a target if you'd like. After all, these idiots coming momentarily are friends of yours."

"Michael?" Even in a whisper, the crack in her voice was clear.

From within the veiled hood, mismatched eyes stared down at her thoughtfully for a long moment, then looked up in the direction Grunthor had gone. She was aware of a faint hum, an almost insectlike buzzing; then Achmed looked down at her again. When he spoke his voice was soft and vaguely hoarse.

"His men. He's not with them."

"How can you know that?"

A low, distinct sound of irritation came from above her. "You're right. Why don't you stand up, wave your arms, and call out to him? I'm sure he'll be glad to see you if he's there."

"I'm—I'm sorry," she whispered, swallowing the choking knot of fear that had risen in her throat. There was no response. She waited a moment longer, then squinted. She could no longer see him. "Achmed?"

The warm night wind blew over her, whipping loose tendrils of golden hair and a few dried blades of long grass over her face. Rhapsody closed her eyes as the rumbling in the ground grew louder; the horsemen were coming nearer. She tried to keep them shut, but found herself involuntarily searching for stars in the sky above her, its blackness muted in the blistering light of the full moon. There was nothing she could do now but wait and listen.

Karvolt, Michael's lieutenant, reined his horse to a slow walk, signaling the others to caution. The scorched meadow grass was high in the peak of summer and undulated gently in the night wind; otherwise, there was nothing in sight for miles around, nor had there been since they left Easton.

Nonetheless he had sensed a hesitancy in his mount, an unwillingness in the gelding that usually signaled danger, although it might just as easily be the animal's exhaustion instead. They had been riding at a ridiculous pace, inspired by the ferocity of their leader's reaction to the discovery that his quarry had escaped. Each of the nineteen other men in the hunting party reined his mount to a stop in response.

Karvolt's black eyes scanned the dips and swales of the Wide Meadows again, listening to the clamor of the overheated horses coming to halt over the labored breathing and muttering of his men. The night wind blew through his matted hair, caressing his neck, but instead of drying the pouring sweat it only served to throw a chill through him. He shook it off; there was nothing in sight, just the waving highgrass and the billowing shadows cast by the moon.

Absently he wedged his forefinger into the collar of his mail to ease the chafed welt that was rising there. His glance shifted to the men, some wearily leaning against the necks of their mounts, others uncapping their waterskins and drinking gratefully. He patted the gelding and felt it trembling still. Karvolt looked around once again at the wide panorama of darkness. Nothing.

"Careful," he instructed in a low, clipped tone; Karvolt was a man for whom words came at great mental expense. "My horse's actin' afright. Anybody else's?"

As if in response, from the ground in their midst came an earsplitting, heart-exploding roar, a war scream that was equal parts anger and mirth, triumph and savagery. Ascending with it, equally fast, came its source.

The flickering shadows of the midsummer moon only illuminated part of the man-monster, a hideous mountain of snarling claws, tusks, and muscle wrapped in hidelike armor, both worn on his body and, worse, an intrinsic part of it. The beast was whetting two gleaming blades, one against the other. As it reached its full height it threw back its head and laughed uproariously, a sound even more gruesome than its initial roar.

To a one the horses reared, screaming, tossing and trampling their shocked riders in their fright. A maelstrom of panicking horseflesh swirled in the windy meadow, a few resorting to rolling on the ground or bucking the soldiers off like stinging flies, amid the shouts and cries of terror.

After a few initial seconds of snorting misdirection the animals broke free and dashed off, in a loose, frightened herd, to the west. One unlucky soldier, unable to disengage from his stirrups, was dragged along with them, his screams echoing for only a moment, choking off abruptly long before the horses were out of sight.

"I think that's a unanimous yes."

Karvolt, who had managed to rise to one knee after disengaging from his fleeing mount, turned slowly and looked behind him, panting.

Coming toward him was what appeared to be a moving slice of the night. As it got closer he could make out that it was a man, swathed in a cloak with a deep, veiled hood, whispering across the field like an ill wind, coming his way unhurriedly. Karvolt scrambled backward over the broken body of one of his men, grasping at the hilt of his weapon with a shaking, sweaty hand.

He glanced quickly over his shoulder and then ahead again, judging the distance of the fallen saddle and saddlebags behind him to be just a few paces too far to serve as cover. Off to his left he could hear the sickening ring of metal and the subsequent thudding of falling heads and bodies as the giant lopped away, still laughing aloud.

Karvolt backed away, trembling, struggling to hang on to his composure and balance. Around him, men who had lost the fight against panic were bolting, only to be decapitated or impaled with something thrown by the chuckling giant. In his darkest nightmares, and all his bloody campaigns with the Wind of Death, he could never have imagined this. He rose to an unsteady stance and drew.

The other soldiers, some motionless in injury, others in fear, were bringing forth their weapons as well. Karvolt limped slowly back, his eyes all the while on the moving shadow, its cloak dancing smoothly in the warm wind.

The man was coming rapidly, fluidly, stopping before each of the fallen soldiers, swiftly removing their weapons from their hands, deflecting their final charges, with a patient, almost professional air. Though he knew they were attacking to the best of their remaining ability, it seemed to Karvolt that the soldiers were almost handing over their weapons to him. The shadow-man moved faster than his strained eyes could follow, slitting a throat, inserting a dagger into an ear, respectfully, almost kindly.

He passed between each of the remaining soldiers on the ground, gliding from man to man like an angelic spirit, offering a hand to one as to a long-lost kinsman, then moving the blade from the soldier's grasp to his own and returning it, with one near-invisible motion, into the pit beneath the man's arm. With an air that was almost gentle he held down a hand to leave a neck exposed, dispensing death more swiftly and efficiently than Karvolt had ever seen, switching hands freely, never pausing, but never pushing. For all that Michael might call himself the Wind of Death, this truly was seeing the wind itself.

Time slowed for Karvolt as the realization came upon him, like a comforting mantle, of the imminence of his own death. Detachedly he was aware of the tightness of the skin around his eyes and across his brow. He knew his face was fixed in the skull-like expression of utter terror he had seen so often in the faces of his own victims, though he felt little of the actual fear it must be displaying.

As the hooded man finished with the last of his remaining comrades and started on the final approach toward him, Karvolt wondered with the last of his abilities of supposition how all the mothers he had put to the sword over the years had managed to fight until the end, as they invariably had. All his years of training and experience in murderous slaughter and the reactions that came with them had deserted him utterly in the face of death.

Summoning the last of his will, Karvolt swung the triatine that had been his father's before him, knowing that it was in vain, and fell back. The man stood over him now. Karvolt was sure he was being looked at from within the dark hood with sympathy. His weapon was gripped by a thin, iron-strong hand that closed over his own trembling one. The voice that spoke in his ear was courteous, almost courtly.

"Allow me."

As even deeper darkness surrounded him, Karvolt was vaguely aware of the subtle twist that repositioned the triatine, then thrust the thin, triple-bladed sword through his chest.

In his last moment he noted the surprising lack of pain, and the absence of effort that the shadow before him expended on withdrawing the weapon; the weight of his own body falling away drew him off it quite cleanly. His vision closed in on him, starting at the outer edges of his eyes. He only heard fragments of the words the giant exchanged with his executioner.

"You certainly took your time gettin' to 'im, sir."

"He had an interesting blade. Add it to your collection."

When Grunthor returned he found Rhapsody exactly where he had left her, motionless, staring directly above her. He pushed aside the body of one of Michael's soldiers who had fallen within a hairbreadth of her, extended an enormous hand, and dragged her gently to her feet.

"Ya all right, miss?" The Bolg followed behind her, watching her expressionless face as she surveyed the carnage in the field. Rhapsody nodded slightly, continuing her examination. She shivered in the wind and ran her hands over her arms as if chilled, but otherwise betrayed no outward sign of emotion.

"Quite a testimony to your charms," Achmed said, a grim half-smile visible even under his veiled hood. "I guess they were just dying to see you again."

Rhapsody stopped before Karvolt's body. The men watched as her slender back went rigid. She crouched down and took the corpse by the shoulder, turning it slightly to better see the face. Then, like a rolling wave, hate swam visibly through her muscles.

She leapt to her feet and aimed an impressively savage kick squarely at the corpse's head, then another, and another, with growing intensity. Between shallow breaths she began to mutter a string of inspired curses more vile than either of the men remembered hearing, much to Grunthor's delight.

"Balls! Not bad for a little sparker! She could teach me an oath or two, eh, sir? Figger she knows 'im?"

Achmed smiled. "What gave you such a notion? Give her another shot or two, then see if you can pull her off. We need to be heading on."

Smoke from the breakfast fire hung low in the heavy morning air, blending with the rising fog of dawn, as Achmed had intended. The girl was not back yet, having excused herself a few moments before and walked a short distance away, to the other side of a deep swale in the field, out of sight. He could feel her anyway, her heartbeat slow and steady, not as it would be had she been preparing to run. He stirred the fire and the clumping stew in the pot that hung over it.

Her words of courteous leaving were the first she had uttered all night, though she had not been given to speaking much before that, anyway. Grunthor had inquired several times in the course of their march if she was all right, and each time she had nodded politely, staring straight ahead as they walked. He knew that the giant felt her to be traumatized, but Achmed was more inclined to believe that she was traveling down old roads in her mind, roads much rougher than the rocky fields they were now crossing. It didn't matter to him in either case.

They would need to bring her along. It had been his belief and position from the first discussion with Grunthor after their exit from Easton, but he was even more sure of it now. Her safety was not of concern; her problems with the Waste of Breath were her own matter. Far more important was the insurance that having her alive would provide until he could determine what exactly had happened with his name.

The collar of his servitude, the invisible chokehold that he had worn since the F'dor had come into possession of his identity, was gone, broken from his neck as certainly as anything he had ever known. From the moment she had uttered her inane comment in the cool darkness of Easton's back alley he had been free of it, and more: he had actually become a different man. She had changed not only what he was called, but who he was, a dangerous power to be entrusted to one whose actions characterized her as idiotic. That power must be substantial, colossal, in fact, to subvert the will of the F'dor. A powerful idiot; *marvelous*. Achmed snorted in irritation.

The name change had not seemed to affect his birthright. He was still assailed by the pounding of the heartbeats of millions, drumming in his dreams and each waking moment as they had from the moment of his birth.

But the details of this new arrangement of identity remained to be seen. He would need to retain her, at least until they arrived at their destination, to ensure that there was no unfinished business, no detail in the situation that he had not accounted for. The Brother, before his enslavement, had been the master of not only his own destiny, but the destiny of anyone else he chose. This Namer's actions might have returned him to that state, or might not have; he now knew nothing about himself whatsoever. Another man might have been grateful for the salvation. Achmed was merely annoyed.

In the distance he could hear a soft, bright tone rising on the morning wind, a sound that eased the age-old pounding in his blood and cleared his mind; the girl was singing. An orange ray of dusty sunlight had pierced the blue gloom of morning, illuminating the smoky haze around them. He turned quickly to look at Grunthor, who had just awakened and was staring off in the direction she had gone as if entranced. The giant then shook his head, as if shaking off sleep, and turned to meet his glance.

"What's that?"

The man now known as Achmed the Snake gave the pungent stew another stir.

"Devotions."

"Eh?"

He banged the metal spoon savagely against the side of the pot. "She's Liringlas, a Skysinger. The kind of Lirin that mark the rising and setting of the sun and stars with song."

The giant broke into a wide, pasty grin. "Lovely. And just 'ow do you know that lit'le bit o' fact?" Achmed shrugged but said nothing. Dhracians and Lirin had ancestral ties, but he deemed it a piece of information not worthy of explanation.

A moment later the sweet music ended, taking with it the fragile sense of well-being it had brought a moment before. By the time Rhapsody returned to camp, Achmed's hidden face was wrapped in a scowl again. By contrast, the grim expression that had beset her features the night before was gone, replaced by a placid, almost cheerful mien.

"Good morning," she said. She smiled, and the giant smiled in return.

"Mornin', miss. Ya feelin' better?"

"Yes, thank you. Good morning, Achmed." She didn't wait for a reply, but sat down next to her gear and began tightening the leather bindings on her pack. "Thank you for your—assistance last night."

The sun cracked the horizon behind her, bathing her in a shaft of rosy golden light, causing her hair to gleam brightly. She pulled a crust of bread out of the pocket of her vest, then brushed the crumbs from the long sleeves of her white muslin shirt, stained with grass and dirt. She held out the bread, offering to share. When the men ignored her, she took a bite, wiping her mud-brown wool trousers free of debris.

"Eat quickly," Achmed said, ladling the stew into two battered steel mugs. "We have a lot of distance to cover today."

Rhapsody stopped in midchew, then swallowed painfully. "We? Today? What do you mean?" The Dhracian handed Grunthor a mug, then raised one to his own lips, saying nothing. "I thought—Michael's men are dead."

Achmed lowered his mug. "Are all Namers given to such rash leaps of assumption? He has many men. That was only one contingent. Do you really think it was the only one he sent?" He ignored Grunthor's glance and raised the mug to his lips once more.

Rhapsody's face went white for a moment, then hardened into a considered, calm expression. "How far to the Tree?"

"Less than a fortnight, if the weather holds and field conditions don't worsen."

The Singer nodded again. "And are you still willing to let me come with you?"

Achmed finished his stew, wiped the remaining droplets out of the depths of the mug with his forefinger, and shook it out, upside down, over the fire. He tossed grass into the other utensils, spun them out as well, and stowed them away, her question hanging heavy in the air. Finally, when the equipment was packed, he shouldered his weapon and gear, slipping both beneath the black cloak.

"If you can keep up, and keep your mouth shut, I'll consider it."

They made their way at a brutal overland speed, traveling in long stretches, for a dozen nightmarish days, stopping rarely, barely pausing before moving on. Traveling time was not limited to either day or night, but rather to Achmed's scouting. It seemed to Rhapsody that he had some sense of inner warning about the presence of other beings, man or animal, that stood between them and the wood.

They might hide for hours, waiting for a group of unknowing travelers to move out of their path. When this happened, she would take the opportunity to doze, not knowing when it would come again. Or they might go for an entire day at a forced-march clip if the way was clear. The men were used to the pace, and she could keep up fairly well, only needing to stop when she found the sun in the same place it had been once more without a rest break. After a week she was able to match their pace, and they traveled quickly, and in silence.

Finally, at noon on the twelfth day, Achmed pointed directly south and stopped. The two exchanged soft words in a language Rhapsody had never heard except between them; then Grunthor turned to her.

"Well, miss, you up for a good ten-mile run?"

"Run? We haven't stopped for the night yet. I don't think I can do it."

"Oi was afraid you might say that. 'Ere, then." He crouched down and patted his shoulder. Rhapsody stared at him, exhaustion making her confused, then realized foggily that he wanted to carry her on his back, a prospect she particularly loathed. She shuddered at the sight of the many hilts and blade handles protruding from various moorings and bandoliers that crossed his shoulders. It would be like lying down in a field of swords.

"No. I'm sorry, I can't."

The cloaked figure turned to her, and beneath the hood she could see the irritation in his eyes.

"We're almost there. Choose now: shall we abandon you here, or are you going to be gracious about Grunthor's offer of help? The woods are in sight; those that defend them are not. These are bad days; they take no risks with wanderers strolling near their outposts."

Rhapsody looked around. She had no idea where she was, nor could she see the forest. As she had several times since beginning the journey, she considered staying put, hoping that whatever she encountered after the two moved on would be safer company. But, also as she had decided before, her traveling companions rescued her, had not tried to harm her, and looked out for her in their own way. So she swallowed her displeasure and agreed.

"Very well, I'll walk as long as I can first, all right?"

"Fine, miss, just let me know when you're tired."

She rolled her eyes. "I've been tired for days. I'll let you know when I can't go on."

"Fair enough," said the giant.

*T*he moon was on the wane. It hung low in the sky, trimmed with blood-red mist, a silent observer of the answer to the F'dor's summons.

From deep within the dark temple the call had come, channeled out through the massive stone steeple above, standing black against the night sky.

The towering obelisk was an architectural marvel, a joint masterpiece of man and of nature. Thousands of tons of basalt base and obsidian shaft reached up into the darkness that surrounded its well-hidden cavern in the High Reaches, Serendair's forbidding northern mountain range. The actual spire of the mammoth fortress a mile below the ground, the shadowy monolith pierced the racing clouds, thrusting skyward proudly, almost insolently, tapering to a point in which was carved the image of a single eye. As the chant began, the scraps of vaporous mist that hovered in the humid air around the Spire dissipated instantly; the eye was clearing, readying itself.

The ancient words of Summoning, spoken by the dark priest at the altar of blood sacrifice, were not known in the language of this Age, or even the two Ages previous to it. They came from the Before-Time, the primordial era when the elements of the universe were being born, and symbolized the most ancient and essential of all ties: the link between the element of fire and the race that sprang from it, the F'dor.

Twisted, avaricious beings with a deceptive, jealous nature, the few surviving F'dor shared a common longing to consume the world around them, much like the fire from which they came. Also like fire, F'dor had no corporeal form, but rather fed off a more solid host, the way fire grows by consuming fuel, destroying it in the process.

The demon-spirit that clung to Tsoltan, high priest to the Goddess of Void in the world of men, had made its way to power slowly, patiently, over time. From the moment of its birth in the Earth's fiery belly it had taken a long worldview, planning its steps carefully, willingly attaching itself to hosts who were weak or inconsequential in order to give itself the time to grow into the fullness of its potential.

Even as it passed, through death or conquest, to increasingly powerful hosts, it held back, reserved the time of its revelation, to ensure that nothing compromised its ultimate goal. The possession of Tsoltan had been an inspired one, achieved willingly, early in his priesthood. The duality of his nature served to make him doubly strong, lent a strategic composure to his innate desire to devour. Living at one moment in the world of men, the next in the dark domain of black fire, Tsoltan existed on two levels, both as man and as demon.

And neither of them had the power he needed over the Brother.

From the ground around the Spire dew began to rise, steamy mist ascending into the scorching air of the summer night. Hot vapors twisted and danced, forming clouds that in the light of the just-past-full moon grew longer, taller, then began to hold a human shape.

First one, then several, then many, then a multitude of glistening figures formed beneath the unblinking eye of the obelisk, robed like the Brother himself, but with utter darkness within their hoods where a face would be. The bodily frames on which the mist-cloth hung began as thin and skeletal, but as the chant continued they took on the appearance of flesh, of a sinewy musculature, of fire-tipped claws, unseen indications of the demon's substantial investment of power expended in bringing them into being. The thousand eyes of the F'dor. The Shing.

In the great vault below, Tsoltan watched them assemble through the obelisk's eye, trembling with strain and joy. They lingered motionless in the air, absorbing more and more of the heat their master had committed to them, stripping it from himself, growing stronger as his power ebbed.

Within their empty hoods a glimmer could occasionally be

seen, perhaps a moonbeam reflecting off the mist, but more likely the reflection of the lens of the immense eye which they now formed. In the world of living men one moment, in the spirit world the next, flitting back and forth between the two domains, much like their master himself, the Shing waited. They were as ephemeral as the wind, but not as fleeting: when sent forth to seek their quarry, they were as relentless as Time, as unforgiving as death.

Tsoltan clutched the altar, his strength waning like the moon on the fields above. In a moment his thousand eyes would set forth, resolutely combing each pocket of air, each step of the wide world, searching endlessly until they found their prey. When they finally came upon him, the results would be horrific.

The demon-priest trembled as weakness washed over him. The Shing would be taking virtually all of his life force with them, a heavy risk. As one knee, then the other, crumbled out from under him, Tsoltan wondered if the Brother would appreciate the compliment. His head struck the polished obsidian floor as he fell, splitting his brow and staining the stone with blood, an appropriate sign.

"The Brother. Find him," he whispered hollowly.

Tsoltan, high-priest, man and symbiotic demon-spirit, rolled onto his back and stared into the blackness overhead. A mile above, a thousand Shing turned and set forth on the wind, under the unblinking gaze of one solitary eye.

5

On the rare occasions that Achmed deemed a campfire safe, Rhapsody made sure to sleep as near to it as possible. Despite the blistering heat of midsummer, which lingered on well into the night, she found the crackle and smoke comforting, a reminder of the home she hadn't seen in so long.

Near the fire the voices in her dreams changed. They no longer repeated the jeering words of Michael and his ilk, but rather harked back to a deeper, farther Past, earlier, sweeter days near a different fire, drawing those days, if only for a moment, into the Present. Wrapped as she was in the fitful sleep of the outdoors, memories in the dark brought warmth, instead of fear, to her soul.

"Mama, tell me about the great forest."

"Get into the tub first. Here, hold my hand." Soap bubbles glistening in firelight, spinning in round whirling prisms, hovering for a moment, then disappearing before her mother's smile.

Warmth closing in with the water and the hot air from the hearth. "What did you put in the water this time?"

"Sit all the way down. Lavender, lemon verbena, rose hips, snow fern—"

"Snow fern? We *eat* that!"

"Exactly. Why do you think the water is so warm? I'm not bathing you, I'm making soup."

"Mama, stop teasing. Please tell me about the forest. Are the Lirin that live there like us?"

Her mother sitting back on her heels, crossing arms with rolled-up sleeves, leaning on the edge of the metal washtub. Her face was serene, but her eyes clouded over with memory, as they always had when thinking about the Past.

"In some ways, yes. They look like us, at least more than the humans do, but their coloring is different."

"Different how?"

"Their coloring matches the forest more. Ours is a reflection of the open sky and the fields where our people, the Liringlas, live." The hair ribbon pulling free with a gentle tug. "Now, for instance, if you were of the forest, this beautiful golden hair that your father is so fond of would probably be brown or russet-colored; those green eyes might be as well. Your skin would be darker, less rosy; that way you could blend in, walk the greenwood unseen, as they do." A cascade of warm water; sputtering, blinking.

"Mama!"

"I'm sorry; I didn't expect you'd turn like that. Hold still for a moment."

"Do the forest Lirin have little girls, too?"

"Of course. And little boys. And women and men, and houses and cities; they're just different from the ones we live in."

"Will I see them someday, too? Will I have a Blossoming Year and go to the forest like you did?"

A gentle caress on her cheek, the sadness in her mother's eyes growing deeper. "We'll see. We live among the humans, child; this is our home. Your father may not want you following the customs of my family, especially if it means you would leave for such a long time. And who can blame him? Why, what would we do without our girl?"

"I'd be safe among the Lirin, Mama—wouldn't I? They wouldn't hate me because I'm part human?"

Her mother had looked away. "No one will hate you. No one." The opening of a wide drying cloth. "Here, stand up, little one, and step out carefully." The harsh chill of the air, the rough fabric rubbing briskly on her wet skin. The soft warmth of her nightgown closing around her along with her mother's arms. "Sit in my lap, and I'll comb your hair."

"Tell me about the forest, please."

A deep, musical sigh. "It's as wide as your eyes can see—bigger than you can possibly imagine—and full of the scent and sound of life. The trees within it grow in more colors than you have ever seen, even in your dreams. You can feel the song of the wood itself, humming in every living thing there. The humans call it the Enchanted Forest because many of the things that grow and live there are unfamiliar to them, but the Lirin know it by its true name: Yliessan, the holy place. If you are ever lost, the wood will welcome you because of your Lirin blood."

The crackle of the fire, its flickering light on her hair, so like her mother's. "Tell me about Windershins Stream, and the Pool of the Heart's Desire, and Grayrock. And the Tree—Mama, tell me about Sagia."

"You know these stories better than I do."

"Please?"

A gentle hand running smoothly down her hair, the bite of the comb. "All right, I'll tell you of Sagia, and then it will be time for devotions.

"The Great Tree grows in the heart of the forest Yliessan, on the northern crescent. It is so tall you can barely see the bottom branches. You could never see the top unless you were a bird, because those branches touch the sky.

"The legends say it grows at one of the places where Time began, where the light of the stars first touched the Earth. Sagia is as old as the ages, and its power is tied to Time itself. It is sometimes called the Oak of Deep Roots, because those roots reach out to the other places on Earth where Time began.

"It is said that its trunk root runs along the Axis Mundi, the centerline of the Earth, and its smaller roots spread throughout the Island, tying it to all things that grow. I know this is at least true in the great forest—it is the power of Sagia that creates Yliessan's song, keeps the forest safe. Now, come; the sun is setting."

The chill of the evening wind, the smudges of inky clouds lining the horizon on the final edge of the pale-blue sky. The glow of the bright star, appearing over the fields and valleys of the wide, rolling land. The sweet clarity of her mother's voice, her own awkward attempts to match the tone. The single tear on her mother's translucent cheek.

"That was very good, little one; you're learning. Can you name the bright star?"

"Of course, Mama; that's Seren, the name-star of our land."

Her mother's embrace, warm, strong. "That is also *your* star, child; you were born beneath it. Do you remember how to say 'my guiding star' in our tongue?"

"*Aria?*"

"Good, very good. Remember, though you live in the human world, though you have a human name, you are also descended of another proud and noble people, you have a Lirin name as well. The music of the sky is in you; you are one of its children, as are all Lirin. Seren hangs in the southern sky over the forest Yliessan. When all else fails, you will be welcome there. If you watch the sky and can find your guiding star, you will never be lost, never."

The grip of the huge, taloned hand, the caustic smoke of the campfire. The sting of the morning air. The deep voice ringing in her ears, drowning out the sweet one in her memory.

"Miss? Ya 'wake?"

If you watch the sky and can find your guiding star, you will never be lost, never.

Rhapsody sat up, clutching at the air in one last attempt to retain the memory. It was of little use; the dream was gone. She choked on the loss that welled up from inside her, then rose to a stand, brushing grass and twigs off her cloak.

"Yes. I'm ready to go now."

They had been in sight of the Lirin forest for several days before Rhapsody realized what it was.

Initially when she saw it, across the Wide Meadows at the edge of her vision, she was certain they must have inadvertently traveled east, that the broad, dark expanse in the distance was the shoreline of the sea. Like the sea it radiated a shimmering, undulating pattern of heat above it, lending it a mystical air, even from tremendously far away. Her mother's teachings notwithstanding, she was unprepared for the immensity of the forest, and the power that vibrated in the air around it.

They were hiding in a grassy thicket at midday in the endless meadow when the realization of what the dark panorama really was first occurred to her. Without thinking she stood, as if enchanted, and looked in the direction of the vast wood. Immediately Grunthor's enormous hand grasped the back of her vest and dragged her down into the brush again.

"What's the matter with you? Get down."

Angrily she twisted free and cuffed his hand away. "Let go. What's the matter with *you*? There's no one in sight, and I want to see the forest."

"Settle," whispered the sandy voice next to her. Rhapsody's protest died in her mouth, her words choked off by the authority in Achmed's tone. He was staring off to the west, crouched low behind the highgrass, his palm open to the air, the forefinger raised at an angle. "They've seen you."

There was the slight rustle of the wind in the distance ahead, then nothing more. After several long moments Rhapsody glanced to her side and saw Achmed still frozen in his crouch, his eyes closed, listening intently. She looked west again and saw the highgrass of the field ripple beneath the hot breeze. Still nothing.

Then, closer than she possibly could have imagined, off to the southwest she saw a face rise infinitesimally out of the scrub, its colors matching the dry brush so completely as to be almost indiscernible. The brown-gold hair crowning its head flowed in crimped waves that blended into the highgrass, the face itself almost the same color, shaped in the slender planes and angles that made her throat tighten with memory.

The large, almond-shaped eyes, the high cheekbones, the translucent skin, the slight build of the body hidden within the scrub, long of limb and muscle—Lirin. Darker somewhat than her mother had been, and than the Liringlas she had met the one and only time she had ventured into the meadows west of Easton. Perhaps these were the people known as Lir-inved, the In-between, nomads that were at home in either the forest or the fields, settling in neither.

Suddenly she was aware of many others, not too far behind the scout, spread out through the billowing highgrass of the meadow to the west. A cloud passed in front of the sun overhead, casting a shadow onto the field, and in that brief moment of darkness she saw the glitter from two score or so eyes. Then it was gone.

Unwilling to look away even for a moment, Rhapsody could see out of the corner of her vision a glint of metal in the grass beside her. Achmed had drawn the cwellan as silently as the cloud had passed; it rested in his thin hands, ready but not yet aimed.

Grunthor's grip on her had eased and disappeared. Rhapsody's heart sank in the knowledge that the giant Firbolg was undoubtedly armed as well. Panic coursed through her, though she was only aware of it when she felt her cheeks redden; she was too busy trying to think of a way back from the abyss on which they now found themselves.

The hooded man had held his fire, which she took as a hopeful sign that Achmed didn't want the bloodbath that she knew was looming before them. That notwithstanding, having witnessed her two companions dispense with Michael's men, she had no doubt that they were capable of surviving being outnumbered, and were intent on doing so. This was the Lirin's land, however. She had no idea what advantage they had because of it.

In addition, Rhapsody was not sure on which side of the impending conflict she was safer. Though her two traveling companions had rescued her and had not tried to harm her, she did not trust them. The slaughter of Michael's soldiers had instilled in her a deep sense of apprehension, bordering on dread.

The Lirin were, in a sense, her own people with whom she felt a soul-deep bond, but to them she was a stranger, possibly an enemy. *The woods are in sight,* Achmed had said. *Those that defend them are not. These are bad days; they take no risks with wanderers strolling near their outposts.* Either way, she knew she was expendable. She felt a silent click on her neck as the cwellan disks were loaded next to her.

A stalk of dry scrub slapped her face, buffeted by the wind. Rhapsody closed her eyes against the onslaught of tiny grains she knew would be released by the bleached seedpod; she had studied highgrass in her training as a Namer. *Hymialacia,* her mentor had called it. Meadow grass, the fodder of the open spaces of the world. Its true name.

Its true name. The sense of danger vanished in the clarity of the answer. Rhapsody cleared her throat, parched by the heat and the fear she had been holding within it, and began to whisper.

Hymialacia, she said, speaking in the musical language of her profession. *Hymialacia. Hymialacia. Hymialacia.* Her skin hummed as the vibration she emitted naturally altered into a new pattern, pulsating, reverberating in the air around her.

Beside her Achmed reached out and touched her back; there was a tenuousness to the contact that told her he couldn't see her. She had blended as smoothly into the meadow grass as the Lirin; more so—for all intents and purposes, she *was* the meadow grass.

Rhapsody reached a trembling hand behind her and felt for Achmed's hand. Carefully she slid her fingers into the thinly gloved fist, whispering the song of the grass all the while. It had become a roundelay, a repetitive melody.

I am the Hymialacia. Achmed the Snake is the Hymialacia. Over and over she whispered their names, blending into the roundelay the song of the wind, the clouds passing overhead, the name of silence. The grip tightened and pulsed like a heartbeat. Achmed was signaling his understanding.

A moment later he whispered something in a language she didn't recognize, and Grunthor turned his head to look at her. This would be harder: she did not know Grunthor's true name.

A rustle in the grass a few dozen feet ahead almost broke her concentration. The Lirin had closed the gap, were almost upon them, spread thinly but resolutely through the meadows, approaching silently, relentlessly. Rhapsody closed her eyes and touched the giant's shoulder.

Hummock, she sang softly. It was a word she had learned early in her training when studying herbal lore, a word she had known from her childhood treks with her father through the wide open fields, over the swales and hillocks of her homeland. A knoll, a clumped elevation rising above the ground like a mound of soil. *Hummock.*

Rhapsody opened her eyes, still chanting her namesong over and over. Before her where Grunthor had been crouched appeared to be a small grassy hillock, with thin saplings of scrub trees sprouting from the ground atop it. She ran her hand over the brush on the knoll. *Hummock. Hymialacia. The wind. The clouds above. Nothing here but the meadow grass.*

Through the brush in front of her she could see legs clad in fawn-colored leather boots and trousers, close enough to feel her breath. *Hummock*, she whispered, trying to keep her voice steady. *Obstacle. Dangerous footing. Pit. Hummock.*

The gait of the approaching legs slowed, never stopping, then stepped smoothly to the south, circumventing the place where she knew Achmed was. She could see nothing there herself but the waving grass of the meadow, hear nothing above her own chant but the rhythmic buzz of hovering insects, the faint crack of the ground beneath Lirin feet, feel nothing near her but the heat of the blistering sun, the whipping of her brittle hair in the dry wind. *Hymialacia.*

She chanted the roundelay over and over until the angle of the sun changed and moved into her eyes. Rhapsody blinked; midday had given way to afternoon, shafts of light now bathing the rippling fields of gold and amber grass. The namesong faltered to a stop, her voice dry and swollen from exertion.

On her left side the grass parted. Achmed released her hand and rose to a stand.

"They're gone, out of range," he said.

Rhapsody looked to her right. The small hummock in front of her flexed and uncoiled, growing tall before her eyes again. What had appeared as the saplings of brush trees took on a more solid form as Grunthor's myriad weapons rose with him, still jutting out from the bandoliers and scabbards on his back. The former hill turned and smiled at her broadly.

"Well, miss, that was impressif."

"Indeed," said Achmed wryly. "Are you going to tell us that was another 'first' for you?"

As Rhapsody opened her mouth to reply, the clouds lurched overhead and the sky tilted at a strange angle. Achmed's hand shot out and grabbed her elbow, assisting her shaking descent to the ground. Once down she lay on her back and stared at the pinnacle of the sky above her, noting the swimming blue circles that hovered in the air. "Water, please," she croaked, then slipped into throbbing unconsciousness.

Dusk settled over the field like a gray mist, and still Rhapsody had not awakened. She lay silent, without moving, in a state of deep sleep the men had rarely seen. The girl was given to nightmares, and over the course of their journey they had become grudgingly accustomed to her fretful whispering and the occasional moans, as she tossed and trembled in the grip of night terrors that sometimes ended in her bolting upright with a heart-stopping gasp.

"No wonder she gave up the bizness," Grunthor had commented after one particularly wrenching performance. "Oi imagine 'er customers didn't get much sleep one way t'other." Achmed had just smiled.

Now she shifted slightly on her side, then lay quiet. The sun disappeared beyond the world's far rim, and the night watch passed from Achmed to Grunthor, who had been busy tallying and repacking the remaining supplies they had pilfered from the saddlebags of Michael's soldiers.

The Dhracian handed the Bolg Sergeant the waterskin from which he had been giving occasional drops to the unconscious Singer, then lay down on the northern side of the camp to sleep.

As the twilight deepened, Grunthor squinted for a moment, then strained to look harder into the distant horizon. After a moment he shook his head and settled back into his watch, only to sit forward again. He extended a foot and nudged the sleeping Dhracian, who did not move but opened his eyes.

"Oi see somethin'."

Achmed rolled to his side and sat up, looking off in the same direction as Grunthor. His vision was generally superior to his companion's, especially in the open air, but he saw nothing. After a moment's concentration he could sense no heartbeat drumming in the distance, a more certain sign that they were alone. He shook his head.

Grunthor shrugged, and Achmed started to lie down again, only to freeze as the Bolg quickly stood up.

"There it is again, sir. Oi'm sure. Far off, but somethin's there."

Achmed rose to a stand as well and walked to the top of a grassy swale, the crest of a rolling wave of earth. He stared off northward into the night, still seeing nothing. He waited.

Then a moment later he saw it too, a host of flickering lights, barely visible in the gray half-dark. In a heartbeat they glimmered, then disappeared again. There were hundreds, perhaps a thousand of them, crossing the distant meadows, spread uniformly out in a endless, near-invisible line, moving slowly south. *A search party?* he wondered. But for what? Who or what might be so important that so many men were sent out in the dark to find it, guided only by lanternlight, here in the middle of nowhere?

Achmed closed his eyes and threw back his hood to better allow the vibrations of the oncoming heartbeats to impact his skin. He held his hand aloft, one finger in the air, tasting the wind in his open mouth to try and ascertain the source of the thousand different rhythms coming toward him. But there was nothing on the wind, no taste, no rhythm, no heartbeat. Only silence and evening breeze.

Once more he opened his eyes and stared, and saw it again, an infinitesimal flicker a thousand times over, moving steadily toward them, still far away but closer than a moment before. Movement, a twinkling light, repeated a thousand times, then darkness. Nothing on the wind.

Now the heartbeat that filled his ears, bristled on his skin, was his own.

"Gods," he whispered. Shing.

Like crows before the coming storm they gathered up the sleeping Singer and their gear and fled blindly in the direction of the great Lirin forest.

6

ℜhapsody awoke in darkness. The moon was gone, having all but vanished the night before into dormancy, and the sky was overcast with racing clouds. Woozily she tried to sit up, then reconsidered as the pain that encircled her head stabbed her violently behind the eyes. She settled for rolling slowly onto one side and propping her head up with her hand, her elbow resting on the stony ground. The groan that wheezed forth from her chest came from a voice she didn't recognize.

Immediately Grunthor was there with the waterskin, his hand behind her neck. Rhapsody drank gratefully, holding on to the skin with a shaking grip. When finally her thirst was slaked she sat up carefully and looked around her. Where before there had been nothing but open sky and highgrass all around them, now they were hiding within a thin copse of trees. A patch of night thicker than the rest of the air around her blotted out the dark horizon not far away.

"What's that?" she asked. All she could manage was a whisper.

Achmed looked up from behind his hood. "The forest." He smiled and looked away, but the Singer's reaction was unmistakable anyway. Her heartbeat intensified angrily; he could feel the blood rise to her face in fury.

"You carried me? All this way? How dare you."

"Yeah, she says that now. 'Ow come you didn't protest at the time, eh?" Grunthor's smile disappeared in the face of her building wrath. "Come on, miss, you didn't think we could stay out in the fields, did you? Oi didn't want to just leave ya there."

A thin hand with a grip like iron clasped her mouth, the scratchy voice low and deadly.

"Bad call on your end, Grunthor. Now listen carefully, Singer, and rest your throat; it will be to your advantage on many levels. We are alone for the moment, but not for long. We are in the scrub-tree line, almost at the outskirts of the Lirin forest. This barrier is far more heavily guarded than the fields.

"Once inside the forest proper it is imperative that we get to the Tree as quickly as possible. Past the first major stand of trees to the southeast there is an outpost of twenty-four border guards. Being Lirindarc, forest Lirin, they are even more difficult to discern in daylight than the ones we met before you decided to take your little nap. What can you do to aid our avoidance of them and getting to the Tree?" He removed his hand, ignoring her withering stare.

"How do you know these things?" she spat. "Michael was not with the hunting party, which you knew somehow beforehand. The Lirinved—the In-between, if that's what they were—saw me, and you knew it. You knew they were there from hundreds of yards away. Now you know the number of Lirindarc and where they are within the wood? How do you know this? And why on Earth would you need me to help you at all?"

The strange eyes regarded her coolly; then Achmed looked off into the distance, considering his reply. He had no intention of answering her question; his gift of blood lore, the ability to sense and track any heartbeat of his choosing, was something that only one friend and a few enemies knew of, although his prowess as an unerring assassin was legendary among the seedier element in the eastern lands. He was trying to determine how to craft his response to achieve both his goals: gaining her cooperation while returning her to a more placid state.

Under normal circumstances the anger or dismay of a hostage would mean nothing to him, but this one was decidedly different. In addition to her obvious power and potential, there was something soothing about her when she was calm, an almost pleasant rhythm to the vibrations she emitted. It had an agreeable effect on his skin. Perhaps it was the result of her musical training. He took a deep breath and measured his words.

"We don't need you to help us at all. The Lirindarc do."

Her face went slack in shock. "Why?"

"Because you may be the one thing that can guarantee their safety if they come upon us."

Rhapsody's eyes narrowed. "What does that mean?"

The piercing gaze fixed on her again. "We have no need to harm these people. They, unlike the rest of the complacent fools in this land, are not asleep. The Lirin we met in the fields and the Lirindarc are attuned to the world around them. They know what is coming, or at least that something is."

Even in the dark Achmed could see her go cold. "What's coming? What do you mean?"

An ugly laugh came from beneath the veils. "How can a Singer not feel it, not hear it? Was it all the noise of Easton that drowned it out, kept you innocent, Rhapsody? Ironic; an innocent whore. Or are you just oblivious?"

Even in the dark Achmed saw her green eyes clear, and a hard, resolute look come into them. "Tell me."

"No, Rhapsody; *you* tell *me*. The Lirindarc from the eastern outpost are making their way here now; they'll be upon us shortly. Grunthor and I need to get to the Tree, and get there in all due haste. We will allow nothing—and I assume you know what I mean by this—to get in the way. Now, what can you do to ensure that no harm comes to them?"

The staunch expression on her face crumbled. "I—nothing. I've never been here before, I don't know where I am. How can you expect me to ensure anything?"

Achmed turned east and sighted his cwellan. "I suppose I can't. Grunthor, ready your bow."

Horror replaced the confusion. "No, please! Don't do this. Please."

The robed figure turned and looked at her without dropping his weapon. "Once more, then, I'll ask you: what can you do? After this afternoon, I would think you'd have a less pathetic answer."

A large hand came to rest on her shoulder. "Come on, now, miss, surely you can think o' somethin'. Think 'ard, now."

Rhapsody took a deep breath and cleared her thoughts, one of the earliest techniques Heiles, her first mentor in the science of Naming, had taught her. After a moment she heard a voice in her mind, a voice that had told her the only tales of these woods she had ever heard.

Mama, tell me about the great forest.

It's as wide as your eyes can see—bigger than you can possibly imagine—and full of the scent and sound of life. The trees within it grow in more colors than you have ever seen, even in your dreams. You can feel the song of the wood itself, humming in every living thing there. The humans call it the Enchanted Forest because many of the things that grow and live there are unfamiliar to them, but the Lirin know it by its true name: Yliessan, the holy place.

Achmed could see the change come over her face. "Well?"

The Lirin know it by its true name: Yliessan.

Rhapsody looked up at the stars. "Its name," she said softly. "I know the name of the forest." Her eyes cleared, and when she looked back at the two men her face was calm, the expression in her eyes deadly. "But let us be very clear, as we will be parting company shortly: I use it for their protection, not for yours."

"Fair enough," said Grunthor, grinning.

When the Lirindarc patrol passed directly in front of the three strangers a few moments later, they saw nothing unusual, heard only the sound of the wind singing in the trees of Yliessan, and continued on their way into the night.

By morning they had arrived at the outskirts of the Lirin forest. A gentle wind had picked up with the dawn, and Rhapsody loosed the black velvet ribbon in her hair, letting the breeze blow through it, cleansing her mind of the painful memories that lingered from the day before.

She stood before the unbroken wall of trees, her eyes trying to penetrate the forest edge and look into the greenwood, where in the distance she could see verdant leaves of every hue, dark and cool as the night even in daylight.

Her mother's image was with her still. Rhapsody felt a catch in her heart as she tried to imagine her as a young woman, a girl really, at the beginning of her Blossoming Year, standing at the threshold of the forest where she was standing now.

Slight; neither Rhapsody nor her mother was particularly tall, perhaps her mother's golden hair twined in the intricate patterns plaited by the Lirin for practicality and ornamentation. Dressed in a billowing tunic and borilla leggings made in accord with the old ways, the traditional woven leather mekva at her waist. Eyes gleaming in quiet excitement. *Had she been happy then?* Rhapsody wondered, knowing that if she had been, it did not last.

Her mother had spoken rarely of that time. Her pilgrimage to Sagia was made, in the tradition of her race, just as she was coming into adulthood. The time she had spent in the forest, learning its secrets, was a mystery to Rhapsody, as her mother had been loath to talk about it. It was only when Rhapsody was entering her teen years that she learned why.

Upon the completion of her Year of Bloom, the second year of her pilgrimage, her mother had returned to the fields to find her longhouse decimated, her family gone. It was only her absence that had saved her, and for many years thereafter she had mourned, wishing she had not been the sole survivor, the only one spared.

Had she been able to turn back Time, she would never have left the longhouse, would have preferred to die with them all, rather than face the world alone. Any happiness that she had found afterward had come in the wake of that memory, leaving Rhapsody to wonder if her mother had ever really gotten over it.

Now Rhapsody stood in the same place, feeling the same awe, the same anticipation that she supposed her mother had felt. Her Lirin ancestry had lain dormant in her for her entire life, though in recent years she had seen and come to know more full- and half-caste Lirin than she had in childhood.

Easton was the thoroughfare of the eastern seaboard, so in her time there she had seen travelers of many different races and backgrounds. Perhaps now that she had come to Yliessan she would finally find welcome and acceptance among her mother's people. Perhaps she would finally find the strength to return home.

* * *

By sunset they had come to the forest proper, the exterior copses of trees and thickets becoming dense in the transition to the greenwood. The three travelers waited until the night was in full flower before venturing in, watching intently for eyes glittering in the dark.

Many times in the course of coming this far Rhapsody had whispered the namesong of the forest, singing the roundelay over and over again: *Yliessan. Yliessan. Yliessan.* It had seemed to her that the branches had moved aside in answer, that the brambles and scrub of the forest floor had not sought to hamper them in any way, allowing them to pass quickly, silently, in the dark.

All around her, in the sound of the wind through the leaves and the birds in the tree branches above them, she felt the greenwood answer back, as if calling her to itself. *Yliessan.* A sense of welcome, innate and primal.

There was a richness to the air in the forest that Rhapsody had never felt before; she drank it in eagerly, filling her lungs and finding them cleaner upon exhaling. She wished they had been able to arrive in light, because she would have loved to see what the forest really looked like. Though it was a sacred place to the Lirin, and only the Lirin knew its name, the legends of the enchanted woods and the Tree were common even hundreds of miles away in Easton among people who would never see a forest in their lives.

Unlike the exhaustion that had consumed her after she had hidden herself and the two men within the highgrass, the sensation she felt during their disguise as part of the forest was invigorating. From the first moment she had matched their vibrations to the signature of the forest, Rhapsody had been filled with a bright, calm sense of home, a cool serenity that cleared her mind and spoke in gentle tones to her half-Lirin heart. *Yliessan. Welcome, Child of the Sky. Yliessan.*

"Any ideas?" The words, spoken softly by the still-unfamiliar voice, caused Rhapsody to jump a little. Achmed was speaking into her ear, though a moment before he was nowhere near her.

"What do you mean?" she whispered back.

"The Tree; do you feel where it might be?" The tone held a strong tinge of disgust.

She closed her eyes and let the night wind brush over her face, and listened again to the music it made as it passed through the branches and leaves all around them. The rustling was not unlike the sound of the sea down the coast of the city, far enough away from the port to be free of its noise.

After a moment of careful attention Rhapsody could hear a low, deep tone resonating through the ground and hanging in the air above it. It was clear and singular, with a faint harmonic around it, and the more she concentrated the more she could hear its voice. She had no doubt that it came from the Tree.

She pointed southwest. "There," she said.

Achmed nodded; he had felt the tone as well. Silently they passed through the underbrush, making their way carefully in the dark. Eventually she found she was leading, but it was not a problem for her, as the tone was growing deeper and louder; she could now feel it through her feet.

The forest was vast. Rhapsody had assumed that they would not come to their destination before dawn, or perhaps even in that cycle of the moon. She was surprised to find the song of the Tree so nearby.

Finally, she began to see a pattern in the trees to the east, a thicker, darker line of evergreens forming an almost impenetrable barrier. The song was strong and clear, emanating from behind the treewall. Without a word both she and Achmed turned instinctually toward the sound and increased their pace. A few muttered curses were heard behind them, as Grunthor had to suddenly correct his course without warning. Apparently he could not hear or feel the song as they could.

The three crept to the tree line, feeling a presence of people in the distance around them, but seeing no one. Finally they reached it and stepped between the dark pines, trees thick with old needles and tall trunks, stretching up into the darkness so that it was impossible to see their summits. They passed between them with some difficulty; Grunthor in particular was hard-pressed to fit between the guardian trees. When they got around to the other side they stopped.

The leafy mulch of the forest floor gave way to pristine

grass that even in darkness could be seen as neat and uniform; the light of the crescent moon reflected off it, touching the pale green carpet with silver. The lawn that began at the tree line stretched for a great distance, ending in another tree line, thicker than the first and composed of ancient, twisting oak trees.

As Rhapsody started forward across the smooth, open lawn she felt a light tug on the back of her vest.

"Wait."

Achmed and Grunthor had fallen back against the tree line, and were conferring softly in their common tongue.

Rhapsody felt her feet begin to itch, her body protesting the halt. The song of the Tree was calling her now, filling her with an intense need to hurry, to come, an almost magnetic pull that was painful to resist.

"I thought you wanted to make haste and get to the Tree," she whispered fiercely.

Achmed held up a hand to silence her and took one more look around. He was uncomfortable at the thought of crossing the wide lawn, open and unprotected by any tree cover or brush, but he and Grunthor could determine no way around it.

The grassy plain was a dry moat to the Tree, positioned between the two treewalls. He could see the immense branches hovering above them, forming a pale, unbroken canopy over this forest meadow.

Carefully he drew the cwellan out from behind his back and nodded. He could discern no heartbeats in the vicinity other than their own. The three travelers checked east to west as though about to cross the Kingsway, then broke into a brisk trot across the open lawn.

Past the next tree line they could see a deep vale, a glen filled with air even richer and sweeter than that in the rest of the Lirin woods. The noise of night in the forest died away as they crept through the oak trees into the glen; the stillness was palpable. Rhapsody looked before her but saw nothing for a moment.

An enormous shaft of moonlight had filled the glen past the oak-tree line, making even the air before them seem white and solid. Then her eyes adjusted and she realized that what she was seeing was the Tree itself, the sacred white oak: Sagia, the Oak of Deep Roots.

Veins deep as rivers scored the surface of silvery-white bark, smooth as a pebble at the bottom of a riverbed. Rhapsody could see no branches, because the trunk of the Great Tree was so tall that the first limbs were high in the air out of sight in the darkness. Fallen leaves littered the ground, however, green and lush, with veins of gold running through them.

Her eyes could not behold all of the Tree at once, it was too mammoth. Its girth was such that she was not sure that should the three of them stand around it in different positions and shout they would even hear each other; eye contact would be out of the question. It would easily have filled the town square in Easton, a place where hundreds gathered for public events. Its sheer size held Rhapsody in awe, so much so that when she became aware again she no longer knew where her two traveling companions were.

She looked around for the giant and his cloaked partner, but they were nowhere in sight. The early symptoms of panic began to swell in her ears and fingers; her hands grew cold in the knowledge that she was no longer sure of their intentions. But the deep calm of the glen stilled the cramping in her stomach as a soothing, resonant hum filled her mind. It was the song of the Tree again, deep and abiding, and Rhapsody could feel the wisdom of ages past in its simple melody. She closed her eyes and listened, memorizing the sound. It was the most enchanting song she had ever heard.

As she stood, breathing in the song of the Tree, the knotting in her forehead and neck muscles that had been present for a fortnight since Gammon had come to the Hat and Feathers melted away. A sense of peace and rightness filled her, calling to parts of her soul that she had long forgotten.

She could hear her mother's voice again as she had in her dream, speaking to her in the Lirin language of her birth, telling her old tales and singing the ritual songs that celebrated the wonders of nature, wonders like this immense Tree.

She did not know how long she stood, eyes closed, listening with her heart to the hypnotic melody, but she came harshly to awareness when she felt a hand grasp her shoulder roughly and a voice speak softly into her ear.

"Where have you been? Come, we're waiting."

Rhapsody turned in surprise. "Waiting for what? I thought we were here to pay our respects to the Tree. That's what I'm doing."

"Come around this side. I've found the main trunk root."

Rhapsody shook off his arm. "So?"

"I am reluctant to shed blood here." There was warning in his voice.

The panic returned, and Rhapsody went cold again, then grew hotly furious. "What does that mean? Is that a threat?"

Achmed held something up; she had to look away as the light it flashed seared her eyes. When she was able to look again she saw it was a key, made of something like bone but gleaming like burnished gold, and filmy, as though it was made of captured sunlight reflecting in the dark.

"Want to see how it works? Or are you just going to stand there like an idiot?"

"No, I suppose I'm going to have to follow you like an idiot."

Angrily she trailed after Achmed around the side of the enormous tree. She looked up into its limbs again but could not even begin to gauge the top for the dark and the immense height of it.

When she came around it farther she could see a little of the first canopy of leafy branches in the vast reflecting pool that mirrored the Tree on the south side. Sagia's song reverberated in the water, sending silvery chills through Rhapsody's soul.

She tarried for a moment to drink in more of the beauty of the sight, and when she looked up Achmed was gone again. Hurriedly she ran around the southwestern side to where he had been headed, and saw him bent over in the shadows. She caught up with him and looked over his shoulder. He was reaching around near the ground, the key seemingly buried up to the handle in the base of the Tree.

"Watch," he said.

With a violent twist, Achmed turned the key, sending a

shower of iridescent sparks in a slender stream skyward from the ground. A thin outline of red light, the size and shape of a small passageway, gleamed for a moment, then disappeared.

Rhapsody backed away, her eyes wide. She continued to stare as Grunthor wrenched a huge rectangular section of the root up and away from the ground. Within the hole that remained was a darkness so complete that she felt it was about to spill out at their feet.

"What are you doing?" she cried before Achmed could cover her mouth.

"Shhhh; listen, and I will tell you. This Tree is the sign that this is one of the places where Time itself began. Its roots lead to everywhere the power of this Island touches." He released her and turned her to face him. "We have to leave. We need to escape to a place of deeper power than even the demon who is chasing us—"

"Demon?"

"—all right; perhaps demon is an understatement—the monster who gave me this key, has access to. This Tree holds immense magic; it is tied to the fabric of the world. It's a metaphysical corridor. We need to go where the Tree's roots will take us."

Rhapsody glared at him. "So go."

Achmed held out his hand. "You too; come on."

"I can't go; I don't want to go," she said, her voice beginning to shake. "Why on Earth would you think I'd go with you?"

"How would you like to see the beginning of Time? You could see the heart of the Tree, or of the world. What would any Lirin give to feel the beating heart of this tree?"

"No."

Grunthor, who had peeled away a section of the Tree so that it looked like a doorway, looked up at her and grinned. "Tell ya what, miss. Come now, and you'll be able to stop us from damagin' the root. Leave us to our own devices and—"

Rhapsody gasped in horror. "You wouldn't dare! This is a sacred oak, the seat of wisdom of the entire Lirin population, not just the ones that live in the forest. To injure it in any way—"

"—would not be too difficult, miss." Rhapsody's eyes opened even wider as Grunthor disappeared into the dark hole. Achmed moved to the Tree and watched as the giant descended, blocking her view.

"Don't you want to see what it looks like inside?"

Rhapsody did, despite her revulsion at what seemed a desecration, but the thought that these two marauders were entering Sagia made her stomach turn. Having seen their prowess in a fight she knew she had little chance to prevent it, but knew just as surely that she would gladly die trying.

"Stop," she demanded, and drew her dagger. "Get out of there."

"Last chance," said the strange, dry voice as the cloaked man disappeared. "Good luck explaining the damage to the Lirindarc guards who will doubtless arrive any minute. I wouldn't wait around here if I were you. Grunthor, you did bring your ax, didn't you?" The question, obviously meant to prod her into compliance, echoed up from the darkness.

Rhapsody looked around. In the distance she thought she did in fact hear the sound of people approaching. Worse, Sagia's song had changed, as if the sacred oak was in pain.

She ran to the place where the two men had entered to observe the damage herself, anxiously running a hand over the silvery bark and feeling the vibration in her fingers that she had felt before in her heart. As she was examining the Tree a hand shot out from the dark hole and seized her, dragging her inside.

Rhapsody screamed for help as Achmed passed her down to Grunthor and grabbed the key. He gave it a firm pull from the ground and spun to face her. As he did, the wall of bark closed behind him silently; then, with a final pulse of light, the key disappeared from his hand, plunging them all into total darkness.

7

When the darkness swallowed them, Rhapsody went absolutely silent. She gave the gloom a moment to settle, then tried to rip free from Grunthor's hands. It was a futile effort; she could hear the giant chuckle as he tightened his grip slightly on her. Instantly she knew that she was mired to the waist in tepid liquid, something more viscous than water, with tensile strands running through it, supporting her weight.

Seconds later she saw a tiny flame appear, and Achmed's nightmarish face came into the light; it was a sight that caused her to gasp again. Grunthor let go of her with one hand and reached behind him over his head, pulled out a small torch, and gave it to his partner. The smaller man lit it, and held it out to look around.

Above them, disappearing into the darkness, was a tapered shaft, the passage through which they had descended. The shadows from the torch leapt off its black sides.

Around them was a wide, irregular cylinder of softly translucent walls, striated in hues of sunless green, pale yellow, and mottled white. As the light from the weak flame passed over the walls she could see they were thick and fibrous, damming in the murky liquid of similar color which surrounded their legs and hips. Ropy strands twisted through the glutinous muck.

It seemed clear that once long ago the opening in which they now stood had been a tunnel of a sort, an irregular corridor descending through the vast root. Time and nature had filled in the base of the shaft with thick new growth, a crazily woven system of branchlike strands that crisscrossed the air around them and formed the netlike floor on which they now were balanced. The thick liquid had been displaced with the opening of the doorway, but ebbed and surged slightly, rising back through the network of vines below them.

Droplets of water from the dank, vapor-rich air came to rest on her skin, leaving it clammy and cold. Rhapsody looked back up from where they had come. In the torchlight she could see no opening. The walls of the tree trunk were as smooth as if they had never been opened.

She squirmed away from Grunthor—he released her when he saw Achmed nod—reached up, and ran her hands over the smooth wooden surface, looking for the break. There was none.

A knotted fiber close to her hip offered a higher ledge. With great effort she extricated a leg from the gelatinous liquid and brought her foot to rest on the strand. It seemed firm enough to bear her weight, so she felt around for a handhold, then lifted herself out of the fleshy slime.

Her head and shoulders ascended into the shaft, but still she could see no break in the wood of the Tree's core. Rhapsody's hands trembled as she ran them frantically over the shaft around and above her. There was no break, no hole, no tunnel in the Tree. The surface was solid as death.

"Where's the door?" she demanded, trying to keep the panic she felt out of her voice. "What have you done?"

"Closed it," Achmed answered without sarcasm.

Grunthor's hand came to rest on her back as she teetered on her fibrous perch. She was almost on eye level with him, and within those amber eyes, remarkable in their humanity above the rest of the monstrous face, there was a distinct look of sympathy.

"The door is gone, miss; Oi'm sorry. We 'ave to press on, we can't go back."

Rhapsody whirled around and glared down at Achmed, her eyes blazing green in the light of the torch. "What do you mean, we can't go back? We have to go back—you have to let me out."

"We can't. You're stuck. You may as well accept it and come along. We're not going to wait for you."

The air in her lungs grew heavier with each breath. "Come along? You're insane. There's nowhere to go but back through there." She jabbed a finger into the tapering shaft above her.

"You really are given to some amazingly incorrect assumptions." The man she had renamed Achmed the Snake shoved aside some hanging branchlike strands, pushed past her legs, and waded to the farthest side of the cylindrical wall, where the flesh seemed thinnest.

He removed his leather gloves and slowly ran his hands along the surface, probing the semi-flaccid barrier carefully, until he found the weakest spot. He glanced back at Grunthor, who nodded and drew from his back scabbard the strangely sharp, three-bladed weapon he had taken from Karvolt.

The giant assumed the same stance he would if throwing a spear. The muscles of his massive back recoiled, and with a single thrust he drove the triatine deep into the fleshy wall. Then he dragged the weapon down, bringing the bulk of his weight to bear on it, tearing loose a hand-sized piece of semi-solid fiber the consistency of melon. The musical vibration of the Tree, muted once they had entered the passageway in the root, surged around her in a frightening crescendo.

"Gods. Stop," Rhapsody whispered, stepping down off her foothold and back into the mire. "Sagia. You're hurting Sagia." She stumbled blindly toward Grunthor, only to be brought to a halt by the grip of a iron hand.

"Nonsense. This is a trunk root; the Tree has thousands of them." Grunthor ripped away a larger section of the fibrous wall, causing Rhapsody to shudder. "The hole in the root wall will close up once we're outside; this corridor is filling in as we speak. Or hadn't you noticed?" Achmed pointed to the viscous liquid in which they stood. Where once it had leveled off at her waist, the muck now reached almost to her breasts.

Once more the giant twisted the three-bladed weapon. The ripping sound reverberated off the liquid in which they stood. Then Grunthor looked back at them.

"Oi'm through, sir."

Achmed nodded, then turned Rhapsody to face him as Grunthor backed into the hole he had just made.

"Listen carefully; I'm only going to explain this once. We need to leave the inside of this root and follow it along the outside. There is a tunnel of sorts that sheathes the root because its flesh expands and contracts, depending on how much water it is holding. That tunnel will serve as our corridor; we'll find water and air there. With a good deal of luck it will lead us to a new place, somewhere safe from those who pursue us. Somewhere where Michael can never find you. But that is up to you.

"Now, you can come with us, or you can wait in here and drown inside the Tree when the root fills in. Your choice."

Dazed, Rhapsody pulled free of his hands and waded to the hole Grunthor had torn in the root wall. The giant moved aside slightly as she leaned into the rip and stared down. All she could see was endless darkness below. She looked up. Above her was more of the same. The shaft ran, with no visible limit, along the pale root that reached down into the abyss beneath them.

Achmed was checking the bindings on his gear.

"Well? Are you coming?"

The enormity of her situation fell on Rhapsody like an avalanche of mud. She was trapped inside the Tree, with no way out, and nowhere to go but into the endless hole below her; where it led to, the gods only knew. It was bad enough to be exiled from Easton, but the realization of what else she would be leaving behind made Rhapsody break into a cold sweat.

Rhapsody shoved Achmed aside, waded back to where the shaft had been, and pounded wildly on the tree wall above her. As her panic broke loose she began to shout for help, crying out as loudly as she could, hoping the Lirin who guarded the sacred Tree would hear her and pry her free. She waited, listening frantically for the sound of help coming, but heard nothing.

Achmed and Grunthor looked at each other, then returned to watching her. When a few moments passed Rhapsody tried calling out again. She repeated this effort four times before Achmed finally lost patience. He reached out and tapped her shoulder in annoyance.

"If you're done with your temper tantrum, I suggest you come with us. We're leaving now. Your alternative is to spend the rest of your short life screaming at a wall of solid wood; not very productive, but your choice nonetheless, at least until the root fills in the hole."

The finality of his words caused Rhapsody to dissolve into tears. It was not something she did very often; anyone who knew her would recognize it as a sign of utter despair. Achmed's eyelids and skin rippled with searing pain as the vibration of her lamentation passed over him. He grasped her arm, his voice unsympathetic.

"Stop that immediately," he ordered harshly. "I forbid you to do that. If you want to come with us, you had best understand that you are never to do that again. Weeping and wailing is banned from here on out. Now decide. Come if you want to—if you can refrain from that noise."

He stepped through the hole, ignoring the hard look Grunthor cast his way after his tirade. The giant Bolg turned to her and gave her what she had come over the last two weeks to recognize as a smile.

"Aw, come on, miss, it won't be that bad. Think of it as an adventure. 'Oo knows what we're gonna find, and besides, ya won't never have to see the Waste o' Breath again." He and Achmed exchanged a glance and a nod before the smaller man began to climb down the trunk root.

"Nor my family, nor my friends," Rhapsody said, choking back tears.

"Not necessarily, darlin'. Just because ol' Uchmed and Oi don't plan to return to Serendair don't mean *you* can't. But you can't get back from nowhere if you're not there yet, can you?"

Rhapsody almost smiled in spite of herself. The giant monster was trying to comfort her, while the allegedly more human of the two treated her, as always, with consummate indifference. This whole event was taking on a surreal quality that made her wonder if she was, in fact, only dreaming. She rubbed the tears out of her eyes and sighed in exhaustion.

"Very well," she said to Grunthor. "I guess there's really no choice. There must be a way out somewhere, some place where the root comes up. Let's go."

"Atta girl," said Grunthor approvingly. "You follow me, sweet'eart. Oi wouldn't wanna take the chance o' fallin' on you." He grabbed hold of the trunk root and began to lower himself into the black hole, which had already swallowed up his companion.

Rhapsody shuddered. "No, we certainly wouldn't want that." She stepped through the rip in the root wall and found the fibrous outgrowth that the two men were using as a rope to lower themselves down, then took hold of it herself. Carefully she began her descent into the flickering darkness of the vast hole that sheathed one of the main lifelines of the Oak of Deep Roots. She was about to discover just how aptly the Tree was named.

Michael walked among the bodies of his men, staring down at a scene of savagery he had never been able to match. True, he had been capable of deeper depravity; there had been no torture or ritual dismemberment in the course of this slaughter, just a ferocious efficiency that rippled the hair on his arms with electricity.

Gammon walked silently behind him, keeping his eyes to the ground. He was afraid to speak, afraid to even meet his leader's glance because his own terror would be readily evident. Gammon had seen greater desolation, larger numbers of broken bodies beneath smoldering skies, but he had never seen so many men dispatched with such obvious indifference. At least Michael enjoyed his work. There was something far more frightening about this brutal nonchalance.

Finally Michael stopped. With a curt nod he directed Gammon to help the others, who were stacking the bodies neatly on the burial mound, then turned in a full circle, surveying the vast meadow where his hunting party had fallen.

He raised a hand to his brow and shielded his eyes, sensitive in their bright blueness, from the hazy afternoon light. There was no cover here, no place that the trap could have been easily laid. As far as his eyes could discern there was nothing but highgrass, brittle in the summer heat, waving silently as the warm breeze whipped through again, bowing in supplication before the sun.

There was only one answer. The Brother.

As the back of his throat tightened dryly, Michael thought about the girl. The sunlit meadow grass rippling in the wind reminded him of her hair, long tresses of golden silk entwined in his hands. How he had loved the feel of it on his chest in the darkness as she lay beneath him. He had carried the sensation with him even as he struggled to put other more erotic thoughts of her out of his mind, fearing the distraction might endanger him.

And now that she was gone, the highgrass would serve as a constant, nagging reminder of what he would never have again. For surely if the Brother had taken her, she was lost to him; the Dhracian had undoubtedly killed her and tossed her body in the sea even before leaving Easton. Not much was known about the mythic assassin, but it was common knowledge that he had no heart, and no vices of the flesh. Those were the only things that would have given Rhapsody a chance.

"Burn the bodies," he directed. "Gather whatever gear is left and saddle up. We're finished here."

8

Immediately there had been a problem.

Just below the rip Grunthor had torn in the wall of the root was a tiny ledge. It was more than likely a lichenous growth of a size that matched the mammoth proportions of the Tree, jutting out from the root wall. Rhapsody had lowered herself onto it without difficulty and peered over into the tunnel below, where the two men were rapidly disappearing, along with the weak, flickering light of the torch.

"Wait," she called, her voice shaking a little. "You're going too fast." Shadows danced on the tunnel walls around and above her, leaving her dizzy and sweating.

"Funny," replied the sandy voice from below, exaggerated and echoing. "One might rather think you're not going fast enough."

"Please," she called again, choking back the panic that was filling her throat.

There was silence, then the ledge shivered. Two enormous hands appeared at the edge of the bulbous growth, and Grunthor hoisted his upper body into view, his face damp from the moisture of the root. Even in the dark Rhapsody could see him grin.

"What's the matter, Yer Ladyship?"

"I don't think I can do this," she whispered, hating herself for the admission of weakness.

"O' course you can, darlin'. Just take your time."

"I'm Lirin—"

The Firbolg giant chuckled. " 'Ey, don't remind me. Oi ain't eaten recently."

"—we don't do well underground."

"Oi can see that. Well, 'ow about Oi give you a lit'le lesson 'ere? Come on, Oi'll show you." He beckoned her forward with the wave of one hand while maintaining his hold on the fibrous rope with the other.

Tentatively Rhapsody crept to the rim of the ledge, swallowed hard, and peered over the side again.

"Now, there's your first mistake. Don't look down. Close your eyes and turn around." Awkwardly she obeyed. The vambraces of Grunthor's armor squeaked as a thick, muscular arm encircled her waist and drew her backward off the ledge. Rhapsody stifled a gasp.

"Right. Now, keep your eyes closed, spread your arms wide, and hug the root. When you're full around it, feel for an 'and'old."

Within the circle of Grunthor's arms Rhapsody reached both hands forward, running them along the surface of the root wall until her chest almost rested against the skin of the root itself. She shuddered as Grunthor shifted his weight to bring her even closer to it, the heavy, metallic odor of armor and sweat and the humid, earthy smell of the root filling her nostrils. After a moment she found a small indentation beneath her left hand, a thick root branch with her right. She gripped both firmly.

"Now the feet. Good. All right, now, open your eyes."

Rhapsody obeyed. Before her loomed the exterior skin of the trunk root, a thick, mottled hide scarred with rhizomes and lichenous growths, as jagged and rough as the interior had been smooth. She rested her ear against it and inhaled, breathing in the rich, sharp scent of it, listening to the humming pulse that vibrated in her skin and the edge of her scalp. There was solace in its song, even here within the dark tomb of earth.

"Ya all right?"

Rhapsody nodded, still resting her head against the root's sunless skin, ghostly pale in the blackness. The last of the feeble shadows fluttered, and the torch in the tunnel below flared out with a hiss.

"Now, ya see, you're doin' just fine. Don't look down, and take your time. Oi'll most likely catch you if you slip." The giant patted her awkwardly, then began to descend once again.

"Thank you," Rhapsody murmured. Carefully she felt for more handholds below. Upon finding them, she cautiously slid her foot down until she found another knot on the root. Her shoulders were on fire, her hands stung, her knees already felt the strain—and she hadn't even started yet.

*H*ow long they climbed down into the darkness was impossible to tell—hours, certainly, though it seemed more like days. Each time Rhapsody found another large growth or rhizome on the trunk root's fleshy skin she took the opportunity to stop and rest, allowing the screaming muscles in her shoulders and legs a moment's respite from the grueling routine.

She could no longer see her companions for the darkness and the distance between them. Achmed had staggered the climb so that each of them could take advantage of the resting spots. As he came to each outcropping he called out its location, and she and Grunthor would hang in place, waiting for their turns to descend onto the new ledge.

It was during one of these momentary rests, with her feet wedged into a scarred crevice in the root, her arms entwined in a desperate embrace about it, that the panic resurged.

The tunnel that sheathed the root had been wide at the Tree's base, stretching to unseen edges in the darkness around it. It had been carved out over centuries of the Tree's growth and the swollen rains from hundreds of springtimes, and as a result had seemed a vast and endless cave when they first began the long climb down.

The farther along the root they went, however, the more narrow the tunnel became. The body of the root itself had grown thinner, with more radix and branch rootlets sprouting from it. The Earth itself was closing in around them, and the closer the tunnel walls came in, the louder Rhapsody's heart pounded. She was part Lirin, a child of the sky and open spaces of the world, not made to travel deep within the earth as the Firbolg, Grunthor's race, were. Each breath was bringing dirty heaviness to her lungs and torment to her soul.

Her head began to spin. Separated from the sky, she was buried alive within the Earth, in a living grave so far down that she could never be found. Even in death, Lirin never entombed one of their race within the ground, but rather committed their bodies to the wind and stars through the fire of the funeral pyre. The awareness of the depths to which they had tunneled dawned on her, leaving her terrified. Deep; they had gone so deep. Too deep.

Suddenly it was as if every grain of dirt, every clod of clay in the ground above her had settled on her shoulders, dragging the air from her lungs. Her grip on the trunk root tightened as she grew dizzy and hot.

The song of the Tree, so comforting and ever-present at the onset of the climb, had dwindled to a bare whisper, taking what little courage she had left with it. The sound of her breathing and the painful thudding of her heart filled her ears, making her feel as if she were drowning. She began to gasp for breath. *Too deep. It's too deep.*

In her memory she heard her father's voice, stern but not angry.

Stop flailing.

Rhapsody closed her eyes, concentrating with the last of her will on her Naming note. *Ela,* the sixth note of the scale. It was among the first things she had learned when studying to be a Singer, the mental tuning fork that helped her discern the truth of a given vibration. It would help her remember clearly, even in her terror. She took a deep breath and began to softly hum the note.

The water of the pond had been cold and green scum floated on the surface. She could not see the bottom.

Father?

I'm here, child. Move your arms slowly. That's better.

It's so cold, Father. I can't stay above it. It's too deep. Help me.

Be at ease. I'll hold you up.

Rhapsody took another breath, and felt the tightness in her lungs slacken a little. The memory of her father's smiling face, his beard and eyebrows dripping, rivulets of water rolling down his cheeks, rose up before her mind's eye as it had from the surface of the pond so long ago.

The water won't hurt you, it's the panic that will. Stay calm.

She nodded, as she had that day, and could feel the droplets of anxious sweat shake off her hair, much like the pond water had.

It's so deep, Father.

A spray of water as he spat it out. *Depth doesn't matter, as long as your head is above it. Can you breathe?*

Ye-e-ss.

Then never mind how deep it is. Concentrate on breathing; you'll be fine. And don't panic. Panic will kill you, even when nothing else wants to.

The next breath was even easier. *Memories are the first stories you learn*, Heiles, her mentor, had said. *They are your own lore. There is more power in them than you will ever find in all your studies, because you wrote them. Draw on them first.* Twice now she had reached back into the Past, and it had given her exactly what she needed.

Depth doesn't matter. Concentrate on breathing; you'll be fine. And don't panic. Slowly Rhapsody opened her eyes.

"Miss?"

The voice from below caught her by surprise, and the fear roared back. Rhapsody started, then lost her footing. She made a wild grab for the bark again and stumbled, sliding without purchase along the pale, slippery flesh of the root.

Rootlets and branches snapped beneath her arms as she slid, bruising her body and slapping against her face. The bark of the root's skin bit deep into her neck and hands as she fell along it, plunging down until she was suddenly, violently stopped by Grunthor's enormous mass. His body absorbed the shock of the impact without moving. Rhapsody looked up, her neck throbbing sickeningly, to see the great gray-green face wreathed in a cheerful smile.

"Well, 'allo, Duchess! Oi was 'opin you'd drop in! Care for a spot o' tea?"

The tension she had been lugging with her for a fortnight shattered, and, in spite of herself, Rhapsody laughed. The giant joined in.

"Grunthor." The dry voice from below choked off the merriment. The giant looked down into the darkness. "We'll be changing course here, following a different path."

"Wait 'ere, darlin', eh?" Rhapsody nodded. Grunthor helped her find purchase on the root skin again, after which he took out a small flask and gave her a drink. Then he climbed down to confer with Achmed. A moment later he was back.

"There's a fairly wide shelf in the root down a lit'le ways," he said. "We'll sleep there. If you want to hold on, Oi can carry you down."

Rhapsody shook her head. "No, thank you. If it's not too far I think I can make it."

"Suit yourself," replied the giant. "It's enough just to know that you fell for me." He descended the root, Rhapsody's soft laughter following him out of sight.

They ate their meal in silence and demi-light. Achmed had lit another torch and stuck it into a shallow fissure above them. Rhapsody basked in the illumination and warmth of the small flame. She had been too busy fighting the feeling of the walls caving in to notice the dark and the cold.

Achmed had gathered a number of different mold spores and growths from the skin of the root, and was testing their use as a source of fuel and light. One type of dense, sponge-like fungi held the flame well, and would glow for some time after being extinguished. Satisfied, he harvested a substantial number of them from the skin of the giant root and stored them in his pack.

"Got the light source," he said to Grunthor. "Should provide some minimal heat as well." The Firbolg looked up over a piece of the dried meat he had found in the provisions of Michael's men and nodded. "Water is no problem, obviously." In illustration, he wrung out a corner of his cloak, sodden from the climb along the damp root. A tiny stream of liquid splashed his boot.

Rhapsody finished her rations in silence. Suspended here, safe for the moment, she had had time to think about what they had undertaken. It was taking all of her concentration just to keep from losing the battle against the panic that lurked, ever-present, at the edges of her consciousness. She had not noticed when Achmed held out a sliver of green vegetable matter. He shook it closer to her face, finally drawing her attention.

"Eat."

Rhapsody accepted the food with a withering stare, then took several deep breaths, focusing on staying calm. She took a bite, then made a face. The vegetable was bland, with tough fibers running through it. Rhapsody chewed, then swallowed hard.

"Bleah. What was that?"

"The root." Achmed smiled, then looked away in amusement at the sight of the expression on her face.

"The *root*? You're *eating* Sagia?"

"Actually, *you're* eating Sagia." He held out his forearm to stop her from rising. "Before you vomit it up, consider again. We are down here indefinitely. We don't have enough food to last nearly that long. When the supplies run out, what do you suggest we eat?" He ignored the furious glance that had replaced the first expression in her eyes. "Or would you prefer I put that question to Grunthor?"

"Not to worry, miss," said the Firbolg giant, chewing on his supper. "Oi don't think you'd make much of a meal. You're on the bony side, if you don't mind my sayin' so. Apt to be tough and gamy."

"The amount of root we will take for food in any given place won't even be noticed by the Tree's parasites, let alone the Tree. You won't be doing it any damage, and you may actually live as a result. You'll just be taking that allegory of the Tree being the nurturer of the Lirin a little farther than most."

Rhapsody had opened her mouth to try and explain to the miscreant before her that Sagia was a living entity, it had a soul, but one word choked off her diatribe.

"Parasites?"

Grunthor snorted. "Come on, now, 'aven't you noticed the 'oles?"

Rhapsody's eyes darted around the darkness. She had been too busy trying to keep from plummeting down into the abyss below her to look for details in the scenery, and even now all she saw was the great, shaggy green-white wall behind them and the rocky tunnel around them. The size of the root and the cavern that sheathed it was monstrous, and had succeeded in intimidating her completely.

"No."

"You're in the ground, Rhapsody," said Achmed, his voice unnaturally patient. "Worms and insects live in the ground as well. They feed off roots—you have managed to notice that there are roots here, haven't you?" He saw the panic glazing her intense green eyes once more, and took her by the shoulders.

"Listen to me. Grunthor and I know what we are doing, at least for the most part. If you stay up with us, and follow directions, you may make it out of here. If you panic, you'll die. Do you understand?" She nodded. "Well, that's a start. Now, if I recall, one of the things you told us you could do as a Singer was to prolong sleep, is that correct?"

"Sometimes."

"That may prove to be important. Now, after we've rested, we're changing course. The root branches out on the other side, goes horizontal for a bit. We'll be following that. Get some sleep." He settled back against the root wall, his pocked face disappearing into the darkness of his hood.

Rhapsody moved closer to the torch, hoping the light would last at least until she fell asleep. She closed her eyes, but still could not escape the image of being covered with the unseen vermin that fed off Sagia's root.

The song of the Tree, so distant while they were traveling, swelled in the silence and filled her ears, then her heart, gently lulling her to sleep. With her last conscious thought, she hummed her Naming note, attuning herself to Sagia's song. It would sustain her in this place of living nightmares.

Far away, in a realm even deeper than Rhapsody had fallen in her darkest dreams, the great sleeping serpent stretched infinitesimally, immense coils unspooling in its slumber. Wound around the vestigial roots of the great Tree within ancient tunnels from the Before-Time, the beast lay in frozen darkness in the bowels of the Earth, awaiting the call. Soon war would rage, the door to the upworld would be opened, and its long-awaited feed would begin.

9

$\mathcal{A}$chmed awoke in the darkness, shaking off the fragments of the dream that had been invading his repose. He knew instinctively, upon regaining consciousness, that Grunthor was already awake. The Sergeant was staring down at the girl, a look of consternation on his broad face, watching her toss and whimper in the throes of a nightmare.

"Poor thing," The Bolg leaned back against the root. "Think we should wake 'er?"

Achmed shook his head. "Definitely not. She's a Singer; she may be prescient."

"She certainly is, cute lit'le thing. Oi like 'er."

Within his hood Achmed smiled slightly. "She may have the gift of prescience, the ability to see into the Future, or the Past. Some Singers do, being in tune with the vibrations of the world. The nightmares may hold important knowledge."

Rhapsody began to sob in her sleep, and Grunthor shook his head. "Not much of a gift, if you ask me. She ought to give it back."

Achmed closed his eyes, trying to discern the heartbeats around him. There was his own, of course, and Grunthor's, the strong, steady thudding he knew almost as well. Then there was the girl's, flickering and racing anxiously. And all around them was the beating heart of the Earth, rich and vibrant, calling from far away but pulsing in its veins, the roots of the Great Tree. In his mind he set these rhythms aside, looking past them for something else. Something slower, and deeper. Something ancient.

After a moment he still could feel nothing solid. The hum from the Tree was loud enough to drown out everything but their three heartbeats. The Earth itself was masking all other sound except for the occasional dripping of water, the cracking of the tunnel walls as they crumbled imperceptibly. He couldn't hear it yet, but he would.

His musings at an end, he looked back up and studied his friend. Grunthor was still watching the Singer keenly, interposing his foot between her and the end of the ledge.

"We're going to have to lash her to the root with a rope when we start climbing, especially when she's asleep." Grunthor nodded, and Achmed rose smoothly to a stand, then looked over the deep ledge into the endless chasm below. It was growing narrower as the root tapered away to thin hairs. Achmed folded his arms and turned around again.

"How noble are you feeling, Grunthor?"

The Bolg looked up questioningly, then smiled. "Oi'm always noble, sir; it's in my blood. 'As been ever since Oi ate that knight a few years back. Why?"

"I think we're going to make a bit of a side trip."

*T*he sensation of warmth on her face drew Rhapsody out of the dream that had been plaguing her. As the nightmare evaporated she opened her eyes.

Achmed crouched before her, a burning spore in his hand. His face was hidden deep within his hood. In the back of her mind, Rhapsody pondered sleepily if this was the first time she could definitely assign an act of kindness to him. He had roused her in the light, and had sought to keep his frightening face from being the first thing she saw upon awakening. She choked back the seething dislike she had felt for him ever since he had dragged her into the Tree.

"Good morning," she said.

The cloaked figure shrugged. "If you say so. It still looks like night to me." He offered her a hand and pulled her to her feet.

Rhapsody shuddered as she looked past him to the edge of their makeshift landing on the giant fungus. Tall shadows whispered across the face of the vast tunnel above them. The giant was nowhere in sight.

"Where's Grunthor?"

"On the other side of the root. We're going to be taking a different path. You may like this a little more; we have to make a short climb up, but then it should be a horizontal journey, at least for a while."

She handed him back the rough camp blanket she had woken beneath, trying to keep her voice under control. "How do you know this path will lead us out of here? What if you are just getting us lost deeper within the Earth?"

Achmed ignored her question. He went to the root wall and grasped the rope that Grunthor had secured, then began to inch around to the far side of the root.

"This way."

It was more difficult navigating the root sideways than it had been to climb down. Grunthor had secured a rope to the root on his way around it, pegging it in place. Rhapsody clung to the guideline and struggled not to look down as the muscles in her legs and arms shuddered from the new strain. The endless darkness below her loomed, frigid and menacing. The air was growing colder.

"Come on, miss, Oi got the rope. Take your time."

Rhapsody took in a deep breath. She knew the giant still could not see her; he had been calling out routinely since she had started around, encouraging her. There was a note of uncertainty in the rich bass voice this time. The musical fluctuation told her that she hadn't moved recently, and the Bolg was wondering if she had fallen. She steadied herself.

"I'm coming," she called, amazed at how fragile her voice sounded. The weakness annoyed her, strengthening her resolve. She cleared her throat, and shouted.

"I'm almost to the bend, Grunthor."

A few moments later she crested the edge and looked around. The giant was standing there, grinning, his hand outstretched, at the mouth of a small horizontal tunnel. The root itself branched off, like a many-tubered vegetable, into the walls of the main shaft they had been descending, some above her, some below.

"Don't 'urry," warned Grunthor. "Take your time."

Rhapsody nodded, and closed her eyes. She clutched the rope and concentrated on finding the last footholds, listening to the rhythm of her racing heart. One by one, slowly. As she had the night before, she began to whisper her musical name in tune with the song of the Tree, and felt its music fill her, sustaining her, giving her strength.

After what seemed like an eternity she felt the grip of massive hands on her arm and waist, and the sickening rush of air as she was torn loose from the rope, then placed gently on solid ground. Rhapsody opened her eyes to find herself in a tunnel not much taller than Grunthor, the root's tributary running horizontally next to her. A choked laugh escaped her as she fell to her knees, reveling in the feel of firm earth. The giant laughed in turn.

"You like that, do you?" He offered her a hand. "Well, then, shall we be on our way, Duchess? We gotta catch up."

The exhaustion she had been fighting every moment since the climb began claimed her. Rhapsody shook her head, lay down and stretched out on her back. "I can't. I need to rest. I'm sorry." She ran her hand up the side of the narrow tunnel wall, staring at the crumbling ceiling above her.

The Bolg Sergeant's face lost its smile. "Oi'll give you a moment, Duchess, but then we're gone. You don't want to be where the ceilin' can cave in one bit longer than you have to be." His voice carried the quiet ring of authority that commanded armies.

Rhapsody sighed, then took his hand. "All right," she acquiesced. "Let's go."

They walked erect until the tunnel grew smaller, then squeezed through the small opening that sheathed the now-horizontal root. The ceiling was too low for Grunthor even to crouch, so they crawled along for some distance until the earth-tunnel widened into a broader vertical space once again. In the distance there was light, and Rhapsody's heart leapt. They must be near the surface.

Finally they came to the opening, struggling to hurry. When she emerged from the tunnel and stood upright, Rhapsody gasped.

They were standing next to a vast bulbous tower that loomed above them, with spidery flaccid branches sprouting from it, long thin trails of radix hanging next to it from the darkness above. By comparison, the root they had descended was nothing more than a branch of this one.

The giant root reached up into the vertical tunnel high above them out of sight. Unlike the absolute darkness of their descent, there was a faint red glow within this shaft, a darklight that held no radiance, just heat. There were no other horizontal tunnels, just more of this new root twisting into the chasm below.

The strangling disappointment of not being at the surface gave way to fearful amazement. "Gods, what is this?" Rhapsody said, thinking aloud.

"Oi believe it's the taproot, the one what connects the tree to the main line," Grunthor offered.

"Main line? What are you talking about?"

A disgusted snort came from the darkness in front of her, and her weary eyes made out Achmed at the edge of the tunnel. Until that moment she had not seen him; he had blended completely into the darkness.

"One would think you would know your Lirin lore a little better. Had you thought this was the end? We haven't even made it to the real Root yet."

Fighting the devastation that threatened to consume her, Rhapsody thought back to the stories her mother had told her about Sagia. *It is the Oak of Deep Roots*, she had said, *its veins and arteries are lifelines that spread throughout the earth and are shared by other holy trees, called Root Twins, around the world.* She had spoken of its massive girth, but the outsize impressions of childhood perspective had led Rhapsody to expect a trunk of great heft, not a tree the size of the town square.

The main roots of the holy trees ran along something her mother had called the Axis Mundi, the centerline of the Earth, which the Lirin people believed to be round, contrary to the opinions of their neighbors. This main axle on which the Earth spun, reputed to be an invisible line of power, and the root of Sagia had melded together. That was the reason the Tree resonated with the wisdom of the ages, that it had grown to such an unbelievable height and breadth. It was tied into the very soul of the world, her mother had said. That might be the main line to which Grunthor had referred.

"You mean the Axis Mundi?"

"The one and only." Achmed spat on his hands, then took hold of one of the flaccid vestigial roots, called a radix. He pulled himself awkwardly off the ground, swinging slightly as the radix flexed, then positioned his foot in the crotch where an outsize knob was attached to the giant root.

He was able to scale the taproot slowly, compensating for the weakness in the smaller roots by keeping one arm wrapped around the vast green-white flesh of the main trunk. When he was ten or so feet from the ground in the tunnel he looked down.

"Saddle up, Grunthor," he said in the strange, fricative voice that had first caught Rhapsody's attention in the market. He looked at her now with an expression that hovered between contempt and indifference. "Are you coming?"

"How far up does it go?"

"No telling. There's nothing but this for as far as I can see, and my underground sight is good. What's your alternative?"

She was without one, and he knew it. Rhapsody was still unsure as to whether Achmed had been her deliverer or her kidnapper, but whatever he had intended, he was now her captor. He had dragged her in here, trapping her inside the Tree with no exit except through the root, and even that was looking more and more unlikely. She tried to keep the seething hatred out of her voice.

"Thanks to you, I have none. I'm coming."

$\mathcal{T}$he climb was arduous, with repeated episodes of slipping and a few almost-tragic falls. Initially it had been a little like climbing a ladder, and almost as easy. There were more knobs and lichenous growths on the taproot to serve as foot-and handholds than there had been on the first root they had descended, the root of Sagia's trunk.

But as the first few minutes passed into an hour, the dull ache in Rhapsody's shoulders roared into full-blown agony. She tried to make better use of her legs to give her arms some respite, but even that did little to ease the searing pain and bone-deep exhaustion. The men had quickly outdistanced her, having far greater strength in their arms and upper bodies than she did, but even they were slowing slightly, remaining in view above her. At least Grunthor was; she could see nothing past him, except for the never-ending pale wall of the root.

Once they had been climbing for more than an hour Rhapsody could no longer see anything that even vaguely resembled the ground below them, just perpetual darkness. It was like being suspended in the sky among the stars, hovering above the world miles below.

The thought of the stars made her choke up, but she held back the tears, remembering her abductor's harsh warning about crying. Her mother's race, the Liringlas, the Skysingers, believed that all of life was part of their God. They held the heavens to be holy, the sheltering sky that touched its children, making them part of the collective soul of the universe. This was the reason they greeted the daily celestial changes with song, honoring the rising and setting of the sun, as well as the appearance of the stars, with chanted devotions.

The pain she had suffered in her life was her own fault. She had run away, abandoned her family as a teenager, but still had longed for the day when she might return, repentant, to the fold. The daily devotions, particularly the songs to the stars, were her way of comforting herself until that occurred. She would faithfully sing her morning aubades and evening vespers each day, thinking of her mother, knowing she, too, was chanting the ancient tunes of her people, thinking of the child she had lost. And now that child was trapped in the Earth, miles below the surface, possibly never to see the sky again.

"Ya all right down there, miss?" Grunthor's deep voice shattered her thoughts; the other two were many yards above her. The Sergeant was leaning away from the taproot, trying to discern what was delaying her in the darkness.

Rhapsody sighed. "I'm fine," she called, then began the laborious task of hauling herself up the towering root once more.

Finally Achmed found a ledge large enough for the two men to rest, with a smaller indentation in the root below it for her. Rhapsody settled into the pit, her body numb from the pain and exertion. Grunthor leaned over the ledge and handed her down a flask of water he had collected from the radix around him while he was waiting for her to catch up.

" 'Ere ya go, Yer Ladyship. Ya all right?"

Too tired to answer, she managed a weak smile and a nod, then drank gratefully. A moment later Achmed's rope landed in her lap.

"Tie yourself to that outcropping of branches there," he directed from above. "We're going to sleep here. You should make sure you never sleep without it." Rhapsody looked up and met his glance, and in the fog of her exhaustion understanding came over her. There was no end in sight. There might never be.

They continued to climb. Any sense of time vanished. There seemed to be nothing at all in time or space but the root, the three of them, and the endless climb. How long it had been was impossible to tell; Rhapsody was rarely hungry, and the other two felt compelled to eat even less frequently than she did, so keeping track of the passing of hours or meals or breaths they took didn't serve to mark the passage of time. Eventually they gave up altogether, becoming resigned to the eternal journey, with the ever-dwindling hope that there would one day be an end to it.

Achmed and Grunthor had become accustomed to traveling with their hostage. She never complained, and rarely spoke, though she had some trouble staying on the root. She was small, and the trunk was too vast for her arms to gain any purchase, so as a result she slipped more frequently than they did, on occasion necessitating that Grunthor make an adjustment in pace to keep from losing her.

The most troublesome aspect to her company was the nightmares. The three companions endeavored to find sleeping places as close to each other as possible, Achmed in the lead, Grunthor next, and the girl bringing up the rear. Rhapsody never passed a sleeping session in peace, always awakening in a cold sweat or a panic, gasping wildly.

Being within the Earth intensified her dreams, changing them dramatically. They now began as distant visions, inexplicable sights that had no bearing on any real experience. Rhapsody dreamt often of Sagia, sometimes walking around it in the darkness of the silent glade, touching its gleaming bark in wonder, unable to find the hole through which they'd entered.

One night, in a particularly disturbing dream, she saw a star fall into the sea, and the waves around it erupting in fire, swirling into a towering wall of water that enveloped the Island, swallowing it. She saw Sagia, its boughs filled with thousands of Lirin singers, dressed in green, chains of wild-flowers entwined in their hair and about their necks, singing sweetly as it vanished beneath the ocean surface.

She had moaned in her sleep, turning over in the ropes by which she had bound herself to the root. Achmed had been on watch, and tore off one of the millions of bulbous growths that disfigured the root, dropping it on her from above in hope of making her stop whining. It had the desired effect; she grew quiet again as her dream changed into an old one, one that recalled her past.

It was a dream of the bordello she had worked in a few years back. She could see the bedchamber again clearly in her mind's eye, the tawdry red furniture that was the deco-rating staple of every brothel, the extra-large bed. She shud-dered in her sleep at the memory that unspooled itself against her best efforts to keep it in check.

Michael had been sprawled lazily across the bed, the mud from his boots soiling the linens.

"Well, there you are, Rhapsody, my dear," he said, his eyes opening wide in delight. "I was beginning to think you weren't coming."

"I wasn't," she answered tersely. "Why are you here? What did you say to Nana? Why does she look so upset?"

"I merely requested an appointment with my favorite girl. Surely there's no harm in that?"

"And surely she told you that I have declined to accept any more appointments with you, Michael. So why, then, are you still here?"

Michael sat up, the dirty boots shoving the bedspread onto the floor as they stepped down. "I was hoping you would change your mind, darling, when you saw how truly devas-tated your rebuff has made me." He took off his boots and nodded to one of his henchmen. The man closed the door behind her.

Her eyes narrowed, and her face set in anger. "You don't look too upset to me, Michael. Please leave. I don't want you here."

Michael looked at her in obvious admiration. She was tiny, but powerful, and he could feel her spirit coursing through his veins. She was the only one who not only stood up to him, but seemed to have no fear in doing so. While fear was arousing to him, this was even more so, especially when he knew he would win.

"Now, now, don't be so hasty, Rhapsody. I've come a very long way. Can't you at least let me tell you what I want?"

"No. I don't care what you want. Now get out."

"Ouch," he said, clutching his chest as though wounded. "You are so insolent, my dear. That's not something I tolerate in my men, but in you it's strangely stirring. And speaking of things that ought to be stirring in you, why don't you just come and sit down over here." He patted the bed next to him, and then began to unlace his trousers.

Rhapsody turned to leave. "I'm sorry, Michael. As I've told you, I'm not interested. I'm sure there are any number of others who are more than happy to serve you."

"You are so right," he said, as the henchman stepped in front of the door. "Though I am crushed by your lack of interest, I am prepared in case you are unwilling to change your mind. Would you like to meet her?"

"No," Rhapsody said, glaring at the grinning lackey. She was not intimidated in the least by the presence of the henchmen; surely Michael was aware that Nana's guards were the best in Easton, and far outnumbered these two. Nana had an arrangement with the town guard as well.

She could feel the frost in Michael's smile even behind her back. "All right, Rhapsody. Have it your way. I'm sorry we couldn't come to an understanding. Let her pass, Karvolt." The guard opened the door and made a sweeping gesture toward it, the cruel smile growing a little more radiant.

As the door opened, a third guard came into the room, bringing with him a child of no more than seven, trembling violently. She was Liringlas, like Rhapsody's mother, and the shawl that was draped around her shoulders had obviously belonged at one time to an adult. It was dirty and blood-stained, and as she came into the room the child's eyes went immediately to Rhapsody. The look of abject terror was barely held in check by the stoic face that the race naturally granted its members.

Rhapsody's eyes opened wide in horror, and she turned

back to Michael, who was smiling broadly as he removed his pants.

"What's she doing here?"

"Nothing yet, obviously," he answered smugly, and the guards exchanged amused glances. "Goodbye, my dear."

"Wait," Rhapsody said, as Michael pulled his shirt over his head and settled back, naked, onto the bed. "What do you think you're doing, Michael? Where did this girl come from?"

"Oh, you mean her?" he asked innocently, pointing at the child. "That's Petunia, my dear ward. A very sad story, really. Her entire family perished when an unfortunate accident befell their longhouse. Tragic. But don't worry, Rhapsody; I plan to take very good care of her. You can leave now, darling."

Rhapsody pulled loose from the grip of the guard who had taken her arm and crouched down, opening her arms to the child. The little girl ran to her and buried her face in Rhapsody's shoulder.

"No, Michael. You can't do this. Gods, you really are the most repulsive thing I have ever encountered."

Michael laughed in amusement, his arousal becoming more intense. "No? And why not, Rhapsody? She belongs to me; she doesn't work here. We're just staying here tonight. I don't want the guests at the inn to be kept up too late tonight by any, er, noises; now, isn't that considerate of me? No one will notice here. In fact, it may even excite some of your customers more."

Rhapsody stared into his crystalline blue eyes; she saw no sign of a soul in them. The smile on his face was triumphant; he knew he had her. She looked back into the face of the little girl. Tears were brimming in the child's eyes. She trembled with fear and clutched Rhapsody tighter. Rhapsody closed her eyes and sighed.

"Let her go."

"Don't be ridiculous, she needs me."

Rhapsody cursed him in her mother's tongue. "Let her go," she repeated.

"Why, Rhapsody, what are you saying? You're jealous! Have you had a change of heart suddenly? Whatever brought that on? Was it, perhaps, the sight of me in all my splendor?"

"Hardly," she replied angrily, running her hand down the child's hair, whispering words of comfort into her ear in their common language. "All right, Michael, what exactly do you want?"

"Well, first I would like some privacy."

"I can certainly accommodate that request," Rhapsody replied, rising and taking the child's hand. "We will be more than happy to leave you alone."

Michael's eyes narrowed. "Don't waste my time, Rhapsody; this game is only fun for a short while. I will send the men away as soon as I have your word that you will meet my wishes upon delivering the child to Nana. I'm sure that's what you had in mind, isn't it? And I know I can trust you, darling. Your reputation precedes you."

"Well, that's one thing we have in common," she retorted. "All right, you sick bastard. I'll be back momentarily." She turned and led the child to the door.

"Wait," said Michael, and his tone had a frightening ring of victory to it that caused her to look at him again. "We haven't discussed my terms yet."

"Terms? Are you expecting something different this time, Michael? Sewing lessons, perhaps?"

He laughed. "You really are amazing, my dear. Impertinent even in the face of very real danger." He rolled onto his belly and crawled to the end of the bed, his muscles moving like those of a cat stalking its prey.

"Karvolt, take the child into the hall." His eyes glittered as the guard obeyed. Rhapsody patted the little girl comfortingly as she released her hand.

"Now listen, my dear. Here is the bargain: my men and I are here for a fortnight, after which we will be leaving for the foreseeable future. I will miss you very much while I'm gone; it will probably be years before we see each other again, though I promise I will come back for you. You're in my blood, Rhapsody. I dream about you almost every night. And I know you feel the same way about me." He smiled at the look of disgust that came over her face.

"Now, this is the first of the terms: I will have you to myself, whenever I want you, until I leave. Nana has graciously agreed to let me rent this room for the entire time. If you perform up to my expectations, which you always do, I will leave the child with you when I go. If you make this difficult, I will take her with me, and you will be left to imagine what is happening to her for the rest of your life.

"Now, the second term. You will want me, too, and tell me so. I expect you to be very demonstrative of the affection and desire I know is pounding through you right now."

"Well, desire anyway," Rhapsody said, trying not to let the seething anger she felt take over her voice. "I would be more than happy to demonstrate what I desire to do to you right now. Give me your belt."

"Karvolt? Is Petunia well?" An anguished cry of pain issued forth from the hallway, turning Rhapsody's blood to ice. "I'm sorry, dear, I didn't hear you. Now, what was it you were saying?" Michael laughed aloud at the murderous rage that burned in her eyes. "Why, Rhapsody, I do believe you're angry. Whatever is wrong?" His own eyes became wild, and the calm amusement that had been playing there moments before vanished before the oncoming storm.

"Now, back to the terms. You will not only meet my needs, you will engage in their succor willingly, with relish. You will make love to me with your words, as well as all your other attributes. I expect to leave here with your heart in my pocket, having placed one of my organs in yours repeatedly. Now, can you do that? Can you promise me a reciprocal situation?"

"No. I'm sorry. I agree to the first condition, but, as you've already said, my reputation precedes me. I can't lie about this, Michael. You would know it was false anyway."

Michael pushed up on his strong forearms. "Karvolt, bring Petunia back in here and put her directly under me."

Rhapsody wheeled as the guard dragged the little girl back into the room. "No, Michael, please. *Please*."

The child began to sob, and Rhapsody stepped in front of the guard, positioning herself between them and the bed. The guard lifted the little girl off the floor, and as she began to scream Rhapsody grabbed her, pulling her away. She turned and looked at Michael again. His eyes were gleaming with a frightening intensity.

"All right, Michael, I'll say whatever you want. Let her go."

"Show me, Rhapsody. Show me why I should believe you."

Rhapsody glared at the guards, whose smiles glittered brighter than the flickering light from the candelabra. Quickly she walked the child to the door, and bustled her into the hallway.

"Nana," she called down over the balcony railing, "please take her out of here and get her something to eat." She gave the child a brave smile and pointed down the stairs, where Nana and the others were waiting. After the girl had descended, Rhapsody sighed and went back into the room.

Michael was plumping the pillows when she returned.

"Well, Rhapsody? Tell me what you want." His voice dropped to a warm whisper, erotic, threatening.

Rhapsody met his gaze. Then, with a practiced hand, she slid her fingers into her shirt and, ever so slowly, began to unbutton it.

"Leave us," she said to the guards. "We want to be alone."

His smile broadened. "Yes, leave us," he echoed. "This beautiful woman wants to be left alone to pleasure her lover. Isn't that right, Rhapsody?"

Rhapsody's eyes never dropped. "Yes," she said, staring at him. She removed her blouse and let it fall to the floor, causing his pulse to beat faster and his breathing to quicken. "Leave me alone with my lover."

Rhapsody's forehead furrowed, and she lurched to one side in the throes of the nightmare. She began to mutter in her sleep, and Achmed, perched on a trunk root higher up, tapped Grunthor with his foot.

Grunthor stirred and woke without a sound to full awareness. He followed the downward angle of Achmed's glance and saw the girl, eyes closed, murmuring, swearing epithets softly under her breath. Then she began to whimper, and her body rocked back and forth, trying to loose the bonds of the rope that bound her to the root.

Grunthor took hold of a long vine and rappelled backward,

leaning out to reach the girl, who was now sweating, crying in her sleep. She struggled to break free, and just as Grunthor came within reach of her, she did.

Rhapsody began to fall into the endless darkness, waking as the world rushed by above her. She gasped and clutched wildly at the root, feeling her hands burn as they stripped along the radix. A huge hand grabbed her around the waist and hoisted her aloft, disorienting her totally.

"There, now, Yer Ladyship, plannin' to drop in on someone else now, are ya?"

Rhapsody fought for purchase, then to regain her perspective, and found herself upright against Grunthor's chest, his enormous arm wrapped tightly around her torso. She leaned back and looked up at him. His grisly features spread into a broad grin.

"Thank you," she said, her brows knitting together. She looked around the endless tunnel in the darklight, then back to his face. "Thank you very much."

"My pleasure, darlin'. If Oi might be so bold as to suggest it, you best sleep on the root between us, eh?"

"Bad idea," came the voice from above. "You can't be certain that a falling body, even one that small, wouldn't catch you off guard and unbalance you, Grunthor."

" 'E's right, miss; sorry," Grunthor said, looking at Rhapsody with what she swore was sympathy.

"I understand," she replied, taking hold of the root once more. She started to climb down, but her foot slipped against the slime on the main vine. Grunthor's hand shot out to steady her again.

" 'Ere, missy, come on up 'ere," he said as he lifted her effortlessly from below him. He carried her like a child back up to his perch, then stretched out again, positioning himself horizontally between the trunk root and its tributary branch. Gently he pulled her down onto his chest and slung an enormous arm around her.

"Why don't you just sleep 'ere, Yer Ladyship?" he asked, patting her awkwardly on the head. "Oi'll keep you safe, darlin'."

Rhapsody looked up into the monstrous face, and decided that what she saw there was kindness, not appetite. Despite his monstrous appearance, and what she knew he was capable of, he had been kind to her. She could trust him, at least.

"Thank you," she said softly, giving him a shy smile. "I will." She put her head down on his chest and closed her eyes.

Grunthor shivered. "Oooooh. Beware the smile, sir; it's a killer."

"Thanks for the warning," came the voice from the root above. "Somehow I think I'll manage."

10

"I see a break in the tunnel."

Rhapsody and Grunthor awoke to the strange voice echoing slightly in the tunnel around them. The earth generally absorbed the sound, so the reverberation caught them off guard. Rhapsody sat up, her hair blanketing the wide chest of the Firbolg Sergeant whom she had been using as a mattress.

Grunthor looked up. High above, barely in sight, he could see an infinitesimal change in the red glow, as if there was airspace above it. He nodded in agreement.

"Right, then, let's make for it in all due 'aste," he said, helping Rhapsody back onto the root above him.

They resumed their climb. It seemed to Rhapsody that the journey was less difficult now that the end might be in sight. She found new strength in her limbs and a more sure footing in her step just imagining being above the ground in the air again. She had tried hard to suppress thoughts of escape while climbing in the endless darkness; it caused feelings of panic and frustration to set in, making her abandon hope and crushing her spirit. Even now she exercised caution about being too excited.

It proved to be a wise move. Even with them climbing as long as they could without stopping to rest, the break in the tunnel seemed no closer. They made a sleeping camp, as was their custom when they had exhausted their ability to climb, and doled out the remains of the stores Achmed carried.

As she swallowed the dried beans and the pieces of Sagia's

root Achmed had harvested, followed by a cup of water droplets collected from one of the tiny, hairlike rootlets that were
the tributaries of the taproot, Rhapsody felt a sense of desolation creep over her. She had been able to avoid thinking
about her dream from the previous night, distracted by the
prospect of the end being near and comforting herself with
the knowledge that Michael would never find her now. Unbidden, her mind wandered back to the horrible memory.

The most disturbing thing about Michael's behavior during
those nightmarish two weeks was not the depth of its depravity, but its wild unpredictability. He would go for days sometimes, locking her alone in the room with him, refusing to let
her leave, demanding constant attention. Then, for no apparent reason, he would drag her down to the dining room and
take her on the breakfast table amid the cutlery and startled
expressions of his lieutenants, who had little option but to
watch or look away while their meal grew cold and con-
gealed.

Sometimes his jealousy ruled him. She had seen him
bloody one of his lackeys for looking in her direction. On
other occasions he would force her to service as many of his
men as he could find, one after another. She had wished for
death, but it had not come, and instead she comforted herself
with the thought that at least the child was safe.

Finally the day had come when he was to leave. Rhapsody
stood and watched him pack his horse; his mood was surprisingly jovial for once. His smile was broad as he took her
face in his hands, kissing her goodbye with great care.

"Well, now, Rhapsody, it certainly has been wonderful to
see you again. I can't wait until this assignment is over. Will
you miss me?"

"Of course," she had said. The lies no longer made her
choke.

"That's my girl. All right, then, Karvolt, get Petunia and
let's be on our way, shall we?"

Rhapsody had felt shock ripple through her. "What? No,
Michael, she's mine; that was the bargain."

"Yours? Don't be ridiculous. I promised her dear father,
right after I sliced his head through, that I would take care of
her myself. You can't expect me to go back on my word,

now, can you?" Screams could be heard inside the house, and Karvolt emerged, carrying the girl.

Rhapsody began to panic. She knew it was certainly within the makeup of Michael's character to have abused her under the terms of the agreement, and then break his word; the prospect was too awful to bear. He was grinning from ear to ear, watching the tears run down her face as he blocked her attempts to reach the girl. Finally, against her will, she gave in to sobbing.

"Please, Michael, no. Don't break your word. Give her to me. Please."

"Why should I, my dear? I have just had the most satisfying two weeks of my life; in fact, I think all the pleasure I have ever had put together could not compare to this time. I'm used to regular sexual exercise now; someone has to satisfy me. Petunia will do as a temporary substitute."

Rhapsody grabbed his arm as he turned. "Take me, then, Michael; leave the girl." She knew what his last words meant: the child was expendable. He would use her horribly and then kill her.

Michael's face glowed with triumph. "How touching. Now, who would have believed you are the same girl that refused me before my men a fortnight ago? I guess my attention was enough to change your mind, eh, my dear?"

"Yes." Rhapsody thought bitterly how true this was. Many things she had believed in had died in the intervening time.

"Well, what do you know? I'm even better than I thought. I'm sorry, Rhapsody, but I can't help you. I doubt you will wait for me in the meantime, so I can't very well be expected to wait for you. Saddle up, Karvolt." He turned to go.

In a last act of desperation, Rhapsody pulled him back into her arms and kissed him. She could feel his heart beat faster as his surprise wore off, and he began to grope her enthusiastically. She drew him as near as she could stomach to and whispered into his ear.

"Please, Michael; would you do this to a woman who loved you?" She knew he would take her words as she meant him to, even though there was none of that meaning in them for her. It was a purely rhetorical question.

Michael pushed her away and looked into her face. "You

love me? You, Rhapsody? Swear it, and I will leave her with you." Behind him she could see Karvolt watching her with interest from the saddle, the screaming child tied roughly behind him.

"Take her down first, and give her to Nana, and I will swear it."

"It will need to be a sincere oath, Rhapsody. I don't intend to be toyed with."

"It will be, I swear it."

Michael motioned to Karvolt, and he untied the girl, swung her down, and led her to Nana, who rushed her back inside. Michael watched until they were out of sight, then turned to Rhapsody again.

"All right, my dear, what was it you wanted to say?"

Rhapsody took a deep breath. "I swear by the Star, that my heart will love no other man until this world comes to an end. There; is that enough for you now, Michael?" His smile of victory made her sick. Michael bent and kissed her gently.

"Yes," he said quietly. "I love you as well, and there will be no other in my heart either; my bed, perhaps, but not my heart. I will be back for you, Rhapsody, and when I return we will be together always."

She nodded dumbly, knowing that what she had just sacrificed had meant less than he thought. She had no heart to compromise, anyway. She had given it away long before, and it had died with the one who took it.

Rhapsody watched, her arms clutching her waist, as the contingent rode off, Michael's broad smile glinting brilliantly in the sun as he waved to her. She waited until they were out of sight, then went behind the bushes and retched.

Vermin."

Rhapsody sat up in shock. Achmed must have been reading her mind. *My sentiments exactly*, she thought ruefully. Then she followed his extended finger in the direction he was pointing and gasped. Spilling down the root above them was a moving wall of pale, wriggling shapes, larger than her forearm, making their way toward the heat exuded by the three of them.

Trembling, Rhapsody flicked her wrist to draw forth her

dagger. The length of the blade was only as long as her palm, with a hilt of half the size. These wormlike creatures were easily three times as long, which would mean that even while she was attacking them they would be on her.

Suddenly the wind was knocked out of her by a tight grip around her waist. Grunthor seized her around the middle and dragged her off the root, lowering her down to a position behind him. Then he climbed a little higher until he found a spot with a wide crevice in the root shaft where he could perch. Rhapsody followed his lead, locating a patch of thin roots that formed an outcropping sufficient to secure herself.

Above her she could hear the air being rent with the whispering sound of the disks from Achmed's cwellan. She prayed he didn't misfire; the missiles would fall on her or Grunthor.

"Draw," he said in a warning voice to Grunthor. The vermin had moved at an astonishing speed, slithering down the root, over every surface and irregularity without a perceptible delay. They swarmed over him, covering his robes. As his hands slashed, lightning-fast, with a blade she could not see, the bodies began to fall, some of them contacting her as they pitched into the darkness below.

The vermin were larvae the color of the pale root, but with thin purple veins that scored their surfaces, and similarly colored heads engorged with blood. One fell into her hair, biting at her scalp with small, sharp teeth that were set in rows within its head. It was all she could do to refrain from screaming.

Grunthor had drawn an enormous sword, thin and long with a pointed tip, and was knocking scores of them off the root above him, precipitating another shower of writhing bodies.

With her reaction speed, born and nurtured on the streets of Easton, she quickly parried the falling larvae and turned her attention to the sluglike vermin that had swelled past Grunthor and were coming down the root at her. There were scores of them; she knew if this many had made it to her, the men above her must be engaging hundreds, if not thousands of them.

In between delivering sweeping blows to the tide of parasites, Grunthor cast a glance her way.

" 'Ere, you can't fight with that lit'le thing," he said, kicking an enormous mound of wriggling flesh off the root next to him. Rhapsody barely had time to dodge out of the way of the falling lump. " 'Elp yourself to one o' my long weapons." He shifted his body slightly to allow her to grab any one of the many handles that jutted out from behind his pack.

Rhapsody shook her head, attacking the two worms that were clinging to the root above her. "I don't know how to use anything but a dagger," she said, slashing off their heads and pushing their bodies off the taproot with two swipes of the knife. A third larva sank its teeth into her upper arm, causing her to cry out in surprise. She shook her arm violently, trying to dislodge it.

"Turn," Grunthor ordered. Rhapsody obeyed. The giant Bolg leaned back and stretched his arm down, skewering the larva on the tip of his sword. He wrenched it off her with a twist of the weapon and she cried out in pain again as it took a small piece of flesh with it into the tunnel below. "We'll 'ave to give you some lessons after all this, miss," he said as he turned back to the larvae on him.

"If I live through this," she muttered, striking the next batch of vermin off the root.

"All mine are dead," called Achmed from above, turning and rappelling down the root to where Grunthor was perched.

"Oi only got this patch o' little buggers; 'elp 'Er Ladyship," said Grunthor, stabbing at the last mass above him.

"Lie flat," Achmed ordered. Rhapsody complied, pressing herself against the root, squashing a larva beneath her chest in the process. She closed her eyes as the cwellan disks whizzed by her, slicing through the vermin around her.

"You can open them now," the voice, thin and sandy as river silt, said from above. She did, and drew in a breath at the face staring at her in the dark.

It had been a very long time since she had seen Achmed's face. He generally traveled in the lead, while she took up the rear, and so she had forgotten how startling his visage was, especially in the dark.

"Thank you," she whispered, her voice coming out like the croak of a crone. Then she noticed his forearm. "You're bleeding," she said.

Achmed didn't look at the wound. "I suppose." He looked up at Grunthor. The Sergeant nodded. Achmed started to climb back up into his position at the lead.

"Well, let me dress it before you go. Who knows if they have some sort of venom." She spoke steadily, her voice belying the pounding of her heart as the reality of the attack caught up with her. Rhapsody had always found that in situations of great danger she was able to function calmly, almost detachedly, until the danger had passed. It was afterward that the symptoms of panic set in.

"I'll live," the robed man responded. Grunthor shook his head.

"She might be right, Sir. 'Oo knows where them worms came from. They might be servants of our lit'le friend."

Achmed seemed to consider for a moment, then slid back down the root until he was positioned across from her in the outcropping. "All right, but don't take forever about it."

"You're late for an appointment?" Rhapsody retorted as she opened her pack and drew forth her waterskin. She took Achmed's forearm and turned it over in her hand. The wound was deep and bloody. Gently she poured some water onto it, feeling him tense but observing no reaction on his face.

Grunthor moved closer to watch as she opened a phial with a pungent smell of spice and vinegar. Rhapsody soaked a clean linen handkerchief with the witch-hazel-and-thyme mixture and applied it directly to the wound, wrapping it in filmy wool. Achmed twisted away.

"Hold still; I've never done this before," she chided.

"Well, that's reassuring." He winced as the spice-soaked bandage began to drench the wound with its vile-smelling liquid, a dismal burning sensation beginning under the skin. "I hope you realize I don't need both hands to kill you, if it was your intent to deprive me of one."

Rhapsody looked up at him and smiled. Her face was bruised and bloody from the fight, but her eyes sparkled in the darkness. She was beginning to take to his sense of humor, and against his will Achmed felt an inner tug. Grunthor was right; she had a powerful smile. He made note of it for future reference.

She returned to her work, humming a tune that made his

ears buzz. He imagined that the slight vibrating sensation was mirrored on his wounded wrist, which no longer stung.

"Stop that noise," he instructed harshly. "You're making my ears ring."

She laughed. "It won't work if I stop the noise, that's the most important part. It's a song of healing."

Achmed looked her over as she continued to hum, and after a moment the wordless tune grew into a song. She sang in words he didn't recognize.

"Oh, 'ow pretty," said Grunthor from behind her. "Well, sir, if we can't find work when we get out o' this stinkin' 'ole, maybe 'Er Ladyship 'ere will teach us some tunes and we can go on the road as a team of wanderin' troubadours. Oi can see it now: Doctor Uchmed's Travelin' Snake Show."

"Great idea," Rhapsody said as the song came to the end. "Let me guess: you sing tenor, Achmed." She received a surly look in response. Slowly she began unwrapping his wrist. "You know, you both really ought to have more respect for music. It can be a very powerful weapon, as well as whatever else you need it to be."

"That's true; my singin' voice can be quite good at inflictin' pain. At least that's what the troops use ta tell me."

Rhapsody's smile grew a little brighter. "Go ahead, scoff if you want to. But music of one form or another will probably be what gets us out of this place."

"Only if you annoy me so much with your singing that I use your body as an auger and drill us out of here."

She laughed. "Music is nothing more than the maps through the vibrations that make up all the world. If you have the right map, it will take you wherever you want to go. Here." She stopped unwrapping Achmed's arm and opened her pack, pulling out a dried blossom.

"Remember this? You thought it was a parlor trick, but that was because you don't understand how it works. Even now, after all this time, it can be made new again." She ignored the sarcastic glance that passed between them, and put the flower into Achmed's palm. Quietly she sang its name, and went back to unwrapping his bandage as she waited for his reaction with amusement.

Grunthor leaned over her shoulder and watched as the petals began to swell with moisture and uncurl, stretching to their full length again. Even in the acrid tunnel, the faint fragrance of the primrose was discernible over the stench of stagnant water and the sweat of their bodies.

"But it only works with flowers?"

"No, it works with anything." She pulled the bandage away, and surveyed her handiwork. The wound was closed, and almost gone. What had a moment before been a deep, jagged gash was now a thin line of raised pink skin, and after a moment even that had vanished, leaving the forearm as it had been before the combat.

Even Achmed seemed somewhat impressed. "How does it work?"

"It's part of what a Namer can do. There is no thing, no concept, no law as strong as the power of a given thing's name. Our identities are bound to it. It is the essence of what we are, our own individual story, and sometimes it can even make us what we are again, no matter how much we have been altered."

Achmed gave her a sour look. "That must be profitable in your line of work—how many times have you sold your own virginity? Does it bring a better price each time?" He watched her wince, and felt a twinge of regret. He didn't like his own reaction, and so filled his voice with sarcasm. "Oh, I'm terribly sorry. Have I offended you?"

"No," she said shortly. "There is very little you could say that I haven't heard before. I'm used to men making jackasses out of themselves."

" 'Ey!" said Grunthor in mock offense. "Watch it, sweet'eart, I haven't 'ad a good meal in a good long time."

"Another example," she said patiently. "You see, men have the upper hand in size and strength, and many of them have little compunction about using it when they can't win with their wits. Who do you think came up with the idea of prostitution in the first place—women? Do you think we enjoy being degraded on a daily basis? I find it incredibly ironic; it is a service in great demand, and one that I can assure you few women go into unless they have to." She dabbed a little of the healing tonic onto her own cuts and vermin bites, then offered the phial to Grunthor, who shook his head.

"Men are the ones who want it," she continued. "They often go to great lengths and great expense to obtain it, and then turn around and insult the women who provide the salve for this overwhelming, insistent need of theirs. Then the men act as though such women are somehow to be ashamed for their actions, when it was the man's idea in the first place; that's what I cannot fathom.

"Anyone can understand a starving person resorting to stealing in order to feed his family, but somehow a woman who is forced into that life by the same threat, or that of violence, is less than a person. Never mind the man who is making use of the service. He has nothing to regret, and in fact it is usually he who expects her to accept the scorn and derision as something she deserves. I say all of you can blow in the wind. I'm going to remain celibate."

"Right," Grunthor chuckled, "sell a bit here, sell a bit there—"

Rhapsody spoke another word, and the giant's leering commentary was choked off in midword. The giant continued to move his mouth, but no sound emerged for a moment. His eyes widened with surprise, and he looked over at Achmed.

Achmed reached over and roughly took hold of her collar. "What did you do to him? Whatever spell you cast, take it off *now*."

Rhapsody didn't blink. "He's under no spell; he can speak if he wants."

"Oi doubt it—oh, Oi guess Oi can at that, now. Sorry, miss. Oi didn't mean to be offensif."

"No offense taken. As I told you, there's very little you can say to insult me that I haven't heard before."

"Well, no one here will sit in judgment of you. We have sort of a 'live and let live' philosophy, wouldn't you say, Grunthor?"

Grunthor snickered, then nodded. "Oh, yes, miss. Live and let live. Or, pe'raps 'kill and eat' might be more like it. You got to remember, Oi'm a Sergeant Major by trade; Oi kills and eats folks as part of my job. Well, actually, just kills 'em; the eatin' part is actually what you might call a side benefit. Countin' coo, as it were." Rhapsody just nodded and went back to rewrapping the bandages.

"So how did you take away his voice, then, if it wasn't a spell?"

"I spoke the name of silence," she said, "and it came, for a moment, anyway. It was the most powerful thing in this, well, this space, because it was in the presence of its name. How's your wrist feeling?"

"Fine. Thank you."

"You're more than welcome."

"Oi 'ate to break up this lit'le love festival, but we ought to get movin', eh?"

"You're right," said Achmed, rising from the taproot and brushing off the dead vermin that remained around them. "I'm running out of disks. We'll have to make the best use we can of them from here on out if the vermin return."

Rhapsody shuddered as the carcasses fell around her, covering her head to keep the pieces out of her hair. She repacked the flower and healing herbs, and followed Achmed back off of the outcropping and onto the root, to begin once more the seemingly endless climb to nowhere.

11

You're the dirt of the ground Oi walk on,
You're pond scum under my heel.
Just try disobeyin' my orders,
Oi'll feed ya three feet o' black steel.

It's a crime to despise the Sergeant,
No matter what 'e thinks o' you
Be sure not to spread your opinion
Or you'll wind up for sure in the stew.

Rhapsody smiled to herself as Grunthor's ringing bass died away below her. The Bolg Sergeant clearly missed the troops that had been under his command, though he had not elaborated much about who they were, or what had happened to them. His marching cadences helped him pass the time, and gave her an interesting window into Bolg military life. More than anything, it made her appreciate that she had not yet become part of the menu.

A small thicket of rootlets offered a moment's respite from the climb, and she took the opportunity to stop, trying to find warmth. As she rubbed her hands furiously up and down her arms, Rhapsody endeavored to stop her heart from pounding in the anticipation she could not control. The sickening feeling in her stomach from too many disappointments did little to quash the hope that was now lodged in her throat.

Finally, after an interminable amount of time, they were almost to the tunnel's break. Above them in the darkness stretched a vast ceiling, too far to see the top, where Rhapsody hoped they might soon see sky. *Perhaps it's dark outside*, she thought, but in the pit of her stomach she knew they had been traveling for far more than the span of a single night since the opening had come into view.

"Wait there," Achmed called down to them as he approached the opening. Grunthor came to a halt as well and waited as the dark figure climbed the rest of the distance up the thickening root tower.

As the taproot grew closer to the opening of the tunnel it widened dramatically, and seeing the outside edges became impossible. Grunthor and Rhapsody watched as Achmed faded from view, scaling the enormous root trunk above them and disappearing over its edge.

While they waited, Rhapsody looked over at Grunthor. During their interminable journey she had grown quite fond of him, and grudgingly friendly with his comrade as well, though she still had not forgiven him or determined his motives. Now that it seemed as if they might be near the end, she had come to realize how the giant Bolg was more a man than many she had met, not at all the monster she had been told of in childhood horror stories.

"Grunthor?"

The amber-eyed Sergeant looked over at her. "Yes, miss?"

"In case I don't get a chance to thank you after we get out, I want you to know how much I've appreciated your kindness, in spite of, well, the way we ended up together."

Grunthor looked up to where Achmed had disappeared and smiled. "Don't mention it, Duchess."

"And I apologize if I hurt your feelings in any way, back in the meadows when we first met, by my comments about thinking of Firbolg as monsters."

Grunthor's smile brightened noticeably. "Well, that's awful nice o' you, Yer Ladyship, but Oi got a pretty thick 'ide; Oi didn't take no offense by it. And you're not so bad yourself, you know, for one o' them glass-Lirin. They're the worst-tastin' o' the lot."

Rhapsody laughed. "What kinds of Lirin have you known, besides Liringlas?"

"Oh, all kinds. Oi've seen Lirin from the cities, and Lirin that live in the dark 'ills, and Lirin from the sea. They all look somethin' the same, you know, all angles, skinny lit'le buggers with pointy faces and big wide eyes. Come in all different colors, mind you. You're not a full-blood, are ya?"

She shook her head. "No, half. I guess I'm a mongrel among Lirin."

"Aw, well, mutts make the best dogs, they say, miss. Don't feel bad. It makes for a nicer appearance, Oi think. You're a pretty lit'le thing, as Lirin go, not so sharp-lookin' and frag-ile."

"Thank you." She smiled at the odd compliment. "You're the nicest Firbolg I've ever met, but, as you noted, I've only ever met one."

"Two." The voice from the root above her caused her to jump a little. Achmed had returned.

"No, I've never met any but Grunthor."

Achmed's expression turned into something more resembling a sneer than a smile. "Well, far be it from me to correct the facts of the All-Knowledgeable, but you've met *two*."

Rhapsody looked puzzled. "Are you saying you are also Firbolg?"

"Perhaps we shouldn't use her for food, Grunthor; she shows a glimmer of intelligence." The giant made a mock sound of disappointment.

She looked from one to the other, vastly different in appearance. Grunthor was at least a foot taller than Achmed, and where the giant was broad and muscular, with massive arms and hands that ended in claws, Achmed, from what she could see beneath the covering of robes, was wiry and of

thinner build, with bony human hands. She turned to the giant.

"Are you a full-blooded Firbolg?"

"Naw."

The robed man snorted. "Did you think you're the only
half-breed in the world?"

Color flooded Rhapsody's face, visible even in the darklight. "Of course not. I just thought Grunthor was Firbolg."

"Grunthor is half Bengard."

Rhapsody nodded. The Bengardian race was a little-known
tribal one, reputedly from a distant desert. They were said to
be monstrously tall and covered with a snakelike hide. She
knew a bit of their lore, and a few of their songs. "And you?"

The two men looked at each other for a moment before
Achmed spoke. "I'm half Dhracian. So you see, we're all
mongrels. Shall we be on our way?"

She had never heard of the race he mentioned, but had been
around the two of them long enough to know when it was
better not to ask. "Certainly," she replied. "I don't want to
stay here for one moment more than I have to." She stood,
stretching the cramp from her leg as she did, then secured her
belongings and followed the two Bolg up the vast root once
more.

'Ere, miss, give me your 'and and Oi'll pull ya up."

Rhapsody gratefully took hold of the massive paw and allowed Grunthor to hoist her off the ridge of the taproot up
into the opening in which he stood. Against all hope she
closed her eyes, praying that what waited above her was the
darkness of the night air, beneath the glimmering firmament
sprinkled with stars. When she opened them again, all she
saw above her was darkness, a void extending as high above
as she could see and beyond.

Before her stretched a remarkable sight. The ground below
their feet was pale like the root they had climbed, but glowing
faintly, with a humming pulse she could feel behind her eyes
and through her entire being. Just as the taproot had dwarfed
the trunk root of Sagia, by comparison, the size of the taproot
was minuscule in contrast to this.

Grunthor whistled. The endless glowing ground that

gleamed with pulsating energy stretched forth wider than the mighty river that bisected the Island of Serendair. This colossal roadway branched out in many directions, each of which was crossed by a network of rootlike veins and radix, hanging and sprouting from the main pathway.

Rhapsody struggled to contain her disappointment. "Gods, what is this?"

"It's the main line; this is the real Root. What we climbed was just a small tributary, probably the trunk that connected Sagia with the Axis Mundi. You didn't think we were at the end, did you? We've barely begun."

She fought back the tears she had been forbidden to shed. "I can't go any further," she said, her voice coming out in a whisper.

The robed figure took her by the shoulders and shook her slightly. "Listen! Can't you hear the music around you? How can a Singer, a Namer, particularly a Lirin one, not be awed by the music of this place? Even I can hear it, I can feel it in my skin. *Listen.*"

Over the beating of her sorrowful heart Rhapsody could hear the hum, a great vibration modulating in the endless cavern around them. Against her will she closed her eyes and drank it in. It was a rich sound, full of wisdom and power, unlike any she had ever heard. Achmed was right, as much as she hated to admit it. There was something magical here, something unique in all the world, a melody that moved slowly, changing tones almost infinitesimally, unhurried by the need to keep pace with anything. It was the voice of the Earth, singing from its soul.

Rhapsody let the music flow through her, washing over the pain and the anger, healing the wounds from their combat with the vermin. She attuned her own note, the tone that was her musical name, to the voice of the Root, as once she had to the song of Sagia, and felt it fill her with its power. A moment later she opened her eyes to see the men conferring, pointing to the different pathways that extended out from this juncture. It was as if they were at a crossroads, trying to decide which way to go.

Finally Achmed turned to her. "Well, are you over your crisis? Are you coming, or are you staying here forever?"

She shot him a look of hatred. "I'm coming. And don't speak to me in that tone. It wasn't exactly my idea to come in the first place." She rubbed her hands, beaded with moisture. At first she thought it was from her anxiety, but a moment later noticed that she was similarly damp on her clothes and boots. The moisture in the air hung heavy here; it was a dank place.

"At least we don't have to climb anymore, darlin', eh? That's for the better, anyway." Grunthor winked at her as he shouldered his pack.

"This way," Achmed said, pointing to a path leading off the left side of the Root.

"Why?"

"Because it feels right," he said without rancor. "You, however, are welcome to go whichever way you please." He and Grunthor climbed over a thick rise in the ground and began following the enormously wide, glowing path into the darkness of the cavern. Rhapsody sighed, shouldered her gear, and followed them.

They made camp when they could walk no longer. The ceiling of the cavern was now in sight, visible in the darklight as they approached the place where the Root seemed to pass through a tunnel in the Earth.

"Since this Root runs through the Earth, there will probably be extremes in the space around it," Achmed observed as they made ready to eat and get some sleep. "Right now we're in a cavernous place, probably because so many of the Root's tributaries meet here. Soon I fear we will be in very close quarters. That tunnel ahead may be the normal space the Root has around it, and if that's the case I think we will be doing a good deal of crawling. In addition, the air is unlikely to be very pleasant. Perhaps if Grunthor is going to train you in the sword, he'd be best do it here, while we still have some space. After we've had a rest, of course."

"You think he needs to?" Rhapsody asked anxiously.

"No, I think you have need for him to," said Achmed tersely. "Those worms came from somewhere. I doubt they were just on the taproot. I would guess we will see them again. It's your choice."

Rhapsody turned to the grinning Firbolg giant. "If you're willing to train me, I would be grateful," she said, "but I don't have a sword."

"Oi can loan you one, darlin'. Actually, it's just a longknife for me, but for you it'll serve as a sword." Grunthor plucked a long dagger from behind the small of his back and presented it to her with a deep bow.

Rhapsody took it shyly. The blade was longer than her thigh, and sharp. It made her nervous even to hold it.

"I'm not sure," she said hesitantly.

"Listen, miss, them worms are gonna eventually get you if you don't keep a better distance," the Bolg Sergeant said. "Ol' Lucy there will 'elp ya."

"Lucy?"

"Yep, that's 'er name."

Rhapsody looked down at the short sword. "Hello, Lucy. Do you name all your weapons, Grunthor?"

"O' course. It's tradition."

Rhapsody nodded, understanding coming into her eyes. "That makes perfect sense. Do you find that you fight better with a weapon you've named?"

"Yep."

Her eyes began to sparkle with excitement. "Why, Grunthor, in a way, you're a Namer, too!"

The giant broke into a pleased grin. "Well, whaddaya know. Should Oi sing a lit'le song?"

"No," said Rhapsody and Achmed in unison.

"Get on with the lessons," added Achmed. "I'm only willing to wait for so long before pressing on."

Grunthor was feeling about his back, trying to decide on a weapon with which to spar. He pulled two more of his blades out. The first one was a long thin sword he called Lopper. Rhapsody shuddered at the imagery, remembering the night in the fields with Michael's men. The other was a thick, three-sided spike he introduced as the Friendmaker. He must have decided to use this one, because a moment later he slid Lopper back into its place behind him.

"Why do you call it 'the Friendmaker'?" Rhapsody asked nervously.

"Well, you may 'ave somethin' there, with all that name

and power stuff," said Grunthor as he took his position. "Take the Friendmaker, for instance. Oi called 'im that, and now, when people see 'im, they instantly want to be my friend. Those that live, o' course."

"Of course." Rhapsody smiled sickly. "I know I do."

"Well, that goes without sayin', miss. Oi should 'ope we're friends, we been sleepin' together and all."

Rhapsody smiled in spite of herself. "All right, friend. Let's have at it."

The sound of clashing steel rang through the cavern around the Root. The giant Firbolg had swept Rhapsody off her feet repeatedly. She was beginning to tire of getting up, only to find herself on her back a few moments later. Most disheartening was that she knew he was holding back, taking it easy on her as a beginner.

Grunthor had left many openings for her that she had tried to follow through on, only to find herself disarmed or compromised in some other way. Finally she took to seeking the openings he had not made obvious, and his approval was growing.

"That's it, Duchess, keep at it, now." He parried her blow. She stripped Lucy the sword down the side of the Friendmaker, only to find him in defensive position again. "Come on, don't give in, sweet'eart. Oi know you can do it. Knock me off the bloody Root. Do it."

Rhapsody swung twice more, futilely. Grunthor was too fast for her. She stepped back and took a deep breath.

"STRIKE!" Grunthor bellowed, causing her to jump away even farther. "Get your pretty 'ead out o' yer arse and pay attention, or Oi'll rip it off and stick it on my poleax!" Rhapsody stared at him in astonishment. The giant's eyes opened in surprise as well. He regarded her sheepishly.

"Sorry, miss, sometimes Oi slip back into my Sergeant Major role."

Rhapsody bent over at the waist, trying to catch her breath. When she stood back up she was still laughing.

"I'm sorry, Grunthor. I guess I just wasn't cut out to fight with a sword."

"Perhaps," came Achmed's dry voice behind her. "But you

should learn anyway. What you need to change is your attitude."

Rhapsody regarded him between breaths. "Really? And what new attitude do you suggest I adopt?"

The robed man came and stood beside her, taking her hand and turning it over. "First, however you initially grasp the sword, change your grip a little, so that you focus on how you're holding it. Don't take your weapon for granted. Second, and far more important: tuck your chin. You're going to get hurt, so expect it and be ready. You may as well see it coming.

"You're spending too much time trying to avoid the pain instead of minimizing it and taking out the source of what will injure you further or kill you. If Grunthor weren't holding back you would have been dead in the first exchange of blows. You should accept that you will be injured and decide to pay him back in spades. Learn to hate; it will keep you alive."

Rhapsody threw her sword onto the Root. "I'd rather not live at all than live that way."

"Well, if that's your attitude, you won't have to worry long."

"I don't want to act like that. I like Grunthor."

The giant Bolg rubbed the back of his neck. "Well, the feelin's mutual, miss, but if you don't learn to take care of yourself, you're worm-meat."

The sense of irony that came over Rhapsody she had felt before, each time she considered her situation and realized that she was indeed in the company of two strange men of monster lineage, stuck within the Earth, crawling along a giant root. The sweet one, the one that looked at her from time to time in a wistful manner she could only interpret as thwarted appetite, was trying to convince her to attack him in order to save herself. The more human of the two, proving the deception of looks, was still treating her with consummate indifference. She picked up Lucy again.

"All right, Grunthor, let's give it a few more passes and then we'll stop."

The Sergeant broke into a wide grin. "That's it, miss, 'it me just once, and make it a good clean blow, now."

* * *

When Grunthor was finally satisfied with her performance Rhapsody sank down to the ground, bruised, disheveled, and hungry. She rummaged through her pack, looking for the small sack in which she kept the remains of the loaf of bread Pilam had given her. She gripped the bag a little tighter and began to sing, chanting the name of the bread, as she had since the day the baker had given it to her. In her song she described it in music the best she could, *flat bread, barley loaf, soft.*

When the namesong was over she opened the sack and took out the bread, breaking off a sizable piece for herself, then offering the remainder to the men. After all this time there was still not a speck of mold on it, even in this humid place, and it was still able to be chewed. By rights it should be harder than a lump of coal by now.

"What was that, now, miss, a blessin' o' some sort?" asked Grunthor, taking the piece she held out to him.

"In a way. I called it by its name." Rhapsody smiled at him, then proceeded to eat her portion. Achmed said nothing.

"And is that 'ow you got it to stay fresh?"

"Yes. It remains as it was when it was first baked."

Achmed stretched out on the thick smooth flesh of the enormous Root. "Well, when we wake up, why don't you call it something else? I've always liked the name 'Sausage and Biscuits,' " he said. It was the first joke Rhapsody ever remembered him making.

"I can recall its original state, but I can't change its nature," she said, chewing her bread. "If I had that power, you would be a good deal more pleasant, and I would be home."

Perhaps it was the pulsing power of the Axis Mundi beneath her head as she slept, but Rhapsody was now plagued incessantly with even more vivid nightmares.

The dreams that night were especially intense. Clearest among them were repeated visions of a man, drowning in darkness, smothering in endless pain. All around him was a blanket of mist. She tried to brush the vapor away, but it hung in the air, unwilling to be dismissed. Rhapsody struggled to wake, but the exhaustion was too great.

She moaned and wrenched from side to side, falling off Grunthor's massive chest as the image changed. It was the picture of another man, his face formless except for eyes, rimmed in the color of blood. He was digging about in the darkness, passing his hands through the air, grasping after something that he could not find. Words formed in her mind, and unconsciously she whispered them aloud.

The chain has snapped, she said.

Achmed, lying on his back and staring into the darkness above him, heard her and sat up. He looked down at her face, contorted in the struggle with the torturous dreams; she looked like she was losing the fight. He tapped Grunthor, who sat up as well.

The man with the blood-rimmed eyes looked up at her, and the image of his amorphous face filled her mind. The eyes, the only identifiable feature, stared at her as though memorizing her face. She knew she should look away, but something held her in an iron-fast grip. Then, as she watched in horror, each of the eyes began to divide, replicating itself, multiplying over and over, until there were dozens, then scores, then hundreds in the formless face. All staring at her.

The Lord of a Thousand Eyes, she whispered.

One by one the eyes broke off the misty face, independent but identical. A cold wind blew in, catching each of them, carrying them across the wide world. And still they stared, unblinking, focused on her.

On the surface of the world above, war is raging, she murmured.

"What's she on about?" Grunthor asked softly.

Achmed waved him into silence. He had heard her name the F'dor.

In her dream a handsome face appeared, gleaming with the patina of youth and moonlight. His cheek grazed her own as he embraced her, nuzzling her ear.

This is all I have; it's not much of a gift, but I want you to have something from me tonight, he said. Then the gentle hands tightened their grip, and muscular legs forced hers apart as the soft breathing turned to the heightened panting of lust.

No, she moaned. *Stop. It's all a lie.*

He laughed, and the clutching hands on her arms squeezed

painfully. *I would never, never hurt you on purpose; I hope you know that.*

Stop, she sobbed. *I want to go home.*

Home? You have no home. You gave all that up, remember? You gave it up for me. Everything. Everything you loved. And I never even told you I loved you.

Gasping in the throes of the nightmare, Rhapsody began to choke on her tears. Grunthor, who had grown visibly more upset with each passing moment, reached over to help her. Achmed caught his arm.

"She might be prescient," he said warningly. "She may be seeing the Future, or the Past. The information might be important."

"Don't you think keepin' 'er from a fatal fit might be a lit'le more so, sir?" Achmed saw the angry look in the giant's eye, and moved aside. Gently Grunthor took her arm and shook her awake.

"Miss?"

With a violent lurch Rhapsody sat up; then she recoiled and belted him in the eye. It was a beautiful shot, innately aimed, with her entire weight behind it, and carried with it the impact of a blow from a man twice her size. Grunthor fell back on his rump with a thud.

Achmed chuckled. "See what being a considerate fellow buys you?"

Rhapsody, now awake, blinked back the tears and stumbled over to the giant, who was gingerly touching his eye as it began to swell.

"Gods, Grunthor, I'm sorry," she gasped. "I didn't know it was you."

The Bolg looked up at her and grimaced with an expression that might, under different circumstances, have been a smile.

"That's all right, miss. Quite a nice right cross you got there. Where'd you learn it?"

She was rummaging in her pack for her waterskin. "My brothers."

"Oi see. Well, Oi guess since we adopted you, perhaps you would do me the favor of thinkin' o' me as one o' your brothers, and don't 'it me with that lovely right cross again, eh?"

A hint of a smile crossed her face as she dabbed his eye. "Who do you think I used it on the most?"

"Oh."

"I'm so sorry."

"No need to be, darlin'. 'Ere, put that away. Oi'm all right. Come and lie back down, and perhaps we can get a lit'le more rest." Rhapsody obeyed sheepishly.

When they woke they gathered their gear and moved into the endless low tunnel before them.

12

Rhapsody had become so accustomed to crawling through cold, wet rock, had been chilled for so long, that she had forgotten what it was like to be dry, not to shiver. The musty smell of the earth and the stale water that pooled within it permeated everything.

Her clothes were constantly damp, and had been for as long as she could remember. At times it seemed as if there had been no other life but this, that her memories of the Past had only been dreams. This was the reality, this never-ending trek along the Axis Mundi.

They had been climbing, walking, and crawling on their hands and knees for so long now that they knew nothing else. Time had passed endlessly, and still they woke after each session of uncomfortable sleep to the same nightmarish reality.

Unlike the two Bolg, who seemed to have no fear of the depths of the Earth or enclosed spaces, Rhapsody still spent a good part of her waking hours silently battling her thoughts of suffocation and enclosure. Part of her routine consisted of driving out the realization of how far below the surface of the Earth they were, how precarious their air and space was, especially during the frequent cave-ins.

She was grateful that they avoided too much hands-and-knees crawling. Most of the time they were able to stand erect, or occasionally walk stooped over, which was barely better than crawling. Every part of her body, and especially her back and knees, ached with each step, each moment they moved along the sandy, rocky floor of the endless tunnel. There was little respite from the torture, even in sleep.

She still failed to understand how Grunthor was able to force his enormous body through the tiny crevasses by which she felt crushed. When Achmed finally declared they were stopping, usually once they had made it out of a tight, wet enclosure, she would sink gratefully into exhausted sleep, only to be wakened by her nightmares.

They grew in intensity the farther they traveled within the Earth, causing Achmed once to threaten to push her off the Root. When room allowed, she slept on Grunthor, finding some comfort in the strength of the massive arms, although waking to the grinning greenish face had taken some getting used to at first.

Achmed's demeanor had changed. Once they had reached the Axis Mundi itself he became more reserved than usual, distracted even, as if he was listening for something just outside the range of sound. His voice had dropped to a near-whisper, though he had not opposed speaking or being spoken to, at least any more than he had before. His preoccupation was apparent to Rhapsody, so she tried not to disturb him, and instead directed most of her conversation to Grunthor.

When space allowed enough air to converse while traveling, the two men taught Rhapsody the Firbolg language, known as Bolgish, more to be polite than anything else. It was their common tongue, and to converse in it made it seem as if they were trying to exclude her. In return, in the rare moments when light permitted, she taught Grunthor to read. The lessons never lasted long.

Once Rhapsody had awakened from her sleep to find Achmed himself pale and clammy, muttering under his breath, much as she routinely did. The tunnel had been narrow for some time, through several stretches of travel, without respite, and several cave-ins had recently occurred.

Grunthor, who had cleared a large blockage of rock from their path a few hours before, slept through his friend's nightmare undisturbed. She raised her head off the giant Bolg's chest and watched for a moment, then rose slowly, and carefully climbed over her sleeping partner to the lookout spot where Achmed generally made camp for himself.

When she reached him she felt her own pulse quicken in concern. His eyelids were twitching rapidly; he was breathing shallowly and moaning intermittently. Gently she stroked his forehead and whispered to him.

"Achmed?"

The Dhracian struggled a moment more, and then his eyes snapped open, cleared from sleep.

"Yes?" His voice had an even drier edge than usual to it.

"Are you all right?"

"Yes."

She caressed the side of his cheek as she would that of a child in the night. "You seemed to be having a nightmare."

The mismatched eyes glared at her. "You think you have an exclusive right to bad dreams?"

Rhapsody fell back as if slapped. His eyes had shot sparks at her the same way his cwellan flung forth its disklike missiles.

"No, of course not," she stammered. "I'm sorry, I was just—never mind." She crawled back over Grunthor, now awake, and settled back down against the absurdly muscular chest. She had planned to ask what he was dreaming about, but realized upon seeing his reaction that she did not want to imagine something that could frighten Achmed.

Beneath her, Grunthor closed his eyes and drove the thoughts from his mind. He already knew.

ℱinally Achmed seemed to find what he was looking for. They had followed the Root into a voluminous cavern, with walls so distant as to be indiscernible in the dark. The robed figure had slowed, then come to a stop.

"Wait here, and try to be quiet," he said softly. "If I'm not back by the time you wake, go on without me." Before Rhapsody could question him, he was gone.

When she turned around and looked to Grunthor for an explanation, she shuddered. The expression on the broad face was grimmer than she had ever seen.

"What's he doing?" she whispered nervously.

The giant reached out a hand to her, pulling her silently down to the floor. The air was chillier than usual, and he opened his coat, offering her his shoulder for a pillow. Rhapsody lay down and he drew the great mantle around her. Slowly he let out a deep sigh, his eyes staring into the darkness at the distant ceiling overhead.

"Rest now, miss."

 $\mathcal{A}$ chmed cast a final look around the immense cavern before he began his climb across the Root to the passage he had finally seen. Unlike the other tunnels, it carried no branch of the Root but lay empty and silent, undisturbed in the darkness.

He had been following the low, flickering heartbeat for a long time. He had caught the first whispers of it just after they had climbed off the taproot onto the Axis Mundi. Swelling intermittently through the loud hum of the Tree, it was the echo of a low and distant thudding in the earth beneath his feet.

It had been his intention, when he and Grunthor first laid their plans of escape from Serendair, to avoid this place at all costs. What lay within the tunnel, coiled within the belly of the Earth itself, was the horrific destiny of the Island. The knowledge of its existence, and the plans for its awakening, had been part of the reason he had sought to leave, though he knew that something even more cataclysmic was waiting for its time to come forth as well. Something he had seen with his own eyes in the desert beyond the failed land bridge.

That he had been able to find its pulse at all was still of some surprise to him. His blood-gift, his tie to men's heartbeats, was a legacy granted to him as the first of his elder race to be born on the Island. This thing preceded him; it was from the Before-Time. And it was not a man. Perhaps the inadvertent choice of names that Rhapsody made that afternoon in the streets of Easton had something to do with it, had given him entry into its blood, access he would not normally have had.

The pulse was almost imperceptible, slow in the frozen depths below, but it was definitely there. By the volume of the blood that ran through its veins, there could be no mistaking that this was what he sought.

He stopped. For the first time that he could remember, Achmed felt paralyzing fear.

His own death was not a concern to him now, nor had it ever been. Death was his partner, something he had dispensed as the consummate master of his trade. The incessant vibrations of the world that irritated his physiology on a daily basis, that which others defined as life, was not something to be cherished, but often just endured.

Occasionally upon dispatching victims he had seen a kind of peace come over their faces, a sense of imminent rest that intrigued him. Certainly he knew that many deaths he delivered came as a relief to those who hired him.

Part of his birthright had been his judgment, his discretion. He was not a ravager, like a pestilence or a war. The death sentences he bestowed were, in fact, often the only sense, the only justice in the tangled strife of the world. He was not afraid to meet death himself. It owed him.

What frightened him was the breathtaking, mindless, incomprehensible scope with which that grim entity was looming. The devastation that would be visited upon the land was absolute; once the wyrm had extricated itself from the earth in which it hibernated it would devour everything it could find. It would eclipse him a million times over as the master of dispensing death. It would be worse than an eclipse, a dark sun of ultimate ruin, not making death the shadow, but bathing the world in itself.

He and Grunthor would buy time by leaving now, escaping to another part of the world. They could probably live out the remainder of their lives and die in bed before it came for them. It had been their original plan.

And yet here he was, on the doorstep of its sanctuary, trying to find the antidote to a poison far more virulent than he could ever negate, something older than the Earth itself.

There was something ironic in the need he felt, heartless killer that he was, to try and preserve the lives of those innocents left behind, the unwitting populace of the Island, and eventually, the Earth. He was now physically unable to pass this chance by, not to intervene.

He stood at the edge of the chamber, breathing the bitter chill. Something about having been the intended agent of the wyrm's release, or the bait, or his loathing of the demon who had tried to command him, or all of these things, made him plan against all better instincts to keep this monstrous force asleep, hidden.

Try as he might to shrug it off, the need to act had clutched at him mercilessly, refusing to let go. He didn't understand its genesis, but he knew it had something to do with Rhapsody.

Somehow she was bound to this as well. He would need her if he was going to make the attempt, would have to convince her that she was capable of this immense undertaking. She would benefit from the confidence he displayed in her, even if, in the depths of his heart, that faith was uncertain. The consequences of a misstep were dire. The consequences of not making the attempt were more so.

ℜhapsody was dreaming of darkness. The light of the candleflame had flickered as the door of her bedroom creaked open. The rustle of the bedclothes as her father sat down beside her.

Are you all right, child?

In her sleep Rhapsody shifted to move away from the root now beneath her ear. She nodded.

Dark, she whispered now, as she had then. *I'm afraid, Father.*

He had wrapped her in the bedclothes as he lifted her from her bed and carried her outdoors, under the star-sprinkled sky.

I used to do this with your mother when she first came here, when she was afraid.

Mama was afraid of the dark, too?

The scratchy roughness of her father's beard against her cheek as his arms encircled her, forming a wall of protection that would keep her safe.

Of course not. She's Lirin, a child of the sky. Much of the time the sky is dark. She was afraid of being away from it, of being enclosed. And of the darkness within.

In her sleep Rhapsody folded her cold hands and buried them between her knees.

Is that why you made the window in the roof?

Yes. Now, look into the sky, child. Can you see the stars?

Yes, Father. They're beautiful.

She could still see his smile gleam in the blackness around them.

And would you be able to see them but for the dark?

No.

You cannot see the beauty without facing the darkness. Remember this.

She thought she knew what he meant. *Like when you first brought Mama to live here, and the people of the village were unkind to her?*

The smile had disappeared, along with its light.

Yes, like that.

How did the village come to change its mind about our family, Father? If they despised Mama so when you first married, why did you stay?

She could see his face in her memory, wrinkles pocketing around his eyes as he smiled at her again.

We needed to face that darkness. And we did, together. I will tell you something that I want you to remember. If you forget all my other words, remember these: when you find the one thing in your life you believe in above anything else, you owe it to yourself to stand by it—it will never come again, child. And if you believe in it unwaveringly, the world has no other choice but to see it as you do, eventually. For who knows it better than you? Don't be afraid to take a difficult stand, darling. Find the one thing that matters—everything else will resolve itself.

Tears fell onto the glowing Root below her. She had listened, had remembered, had taken his words to heart. And, in doing what he said, she had lost everything. Even him.

"Rhapsody?"

The word was spoken so softly she thought she was only hearing it in her mind. Rhapsody opened her eyes and found herself staring up into the darkness of Achmed's hood, the gleam of his gaze fixed on her. She nodded silently.

"I have a story for you. Its ending isn't written yet. Do you wish to hear it?"

Slowly she sat up and took the hand he offered her. As on the day she had first accepted it, the grasp was firm and claw-like, but now his hands were bare, the leather gloves gone.

She thought for a moment that this was still a dream, but the clarity and openness of his gaze and words was something she knew she could never have imagined. He pulled her carefully to a stand and led her from the sleeping giant to a sheltered spot some distance away. He pointed into the darkness.

"Over there is a tunnel unlike the others we have followed. There have been many like it, but I doubt you've noticed them. The tunnels were not carved by the Tree's roots, but have been here since long before its acorn was ever planted.

"Deep within that tunnel is a beating heart. You have asked repeatedly how I know where I am going. The answer is that I can sense almost any pulse in my skin. I know that what I am saying frightens you, because even though your outward expression has not changed, your heartbeat has quickened. If you become lost within this place, if you fall down a root shaft or are buried alive by a cave-in, I can find you, because I know the sound of your heart."

Rhapsody rubbed her eyes in an effort to clear her mind. The words, spoken softly in the now-familiar dry tone, bore no resemblance to anything Achmed had ever said to her before. She concentrated on the music in his tone, and found empathy there. And concern. And fear. She shook her head to clear the lingering cobwebs of sleep; she must still not be thinking clearly. Her skull was pounding.

"Listen to me. I've been following a pulse. First it was that of the Tree itself, but once we found the Axis Mundi it changed; now I have been following that other heartbeat to this place. Something terrible rests in there, something more powerful and more horrifying than you can imagine, something I dare not even name. What sleeps within that tunnel, deep in the belly of the Earth, must not awake. Not ever. Do you understand me? You once said that you could prolong slumber—"

"Sometimes."

"Yes. I understand. This must be one of those times."

Achmed's eyes searched the Singer's face as she struggled to wake more fully. He wasn't doing very well with his explanation. He needed her to understand what he was asking of her.

She had been as uncertain of her abilities as he now was, from the moment she had renamed him by accident to her shielding of their presence from the Lirin of the fields and forests. He had come to realize that this was at least in part because she had finished her studies alone; her mentor had disappeared with but a year left in her training.

His blood ran cold at the thought. Tsoltan had once made a casual reference to a Namer in his thrall. Perhaps there had been an earlier connection between Rhapsody and himself than he had realized.

She had been consuming the flesh of the Root, as he planned, almost from the very beginning. There was no question that it had affected her, as it had Grunthor and himself. They had passed a lifetime or more, or so it seemed, down here in the depths of the world, and had not aged a moment, at least by the vibrations he had been able to sense. The Tree tied to Time itself had prevented its ravages. If anything, they were healthier, stronger, even younger than they had been upon entering Sagia.

But there was also another change in her, an inner strength that he had not felt when they first met. Whether it had come from long hours of practice or as a gift from the flesh of the Tree, Rhapsody was becoming a Namer of great power. He hoped it would be enough.

"I need to know what it is if you want me to try to make its sleep last longer," Rhapsody said softly. "You're talking in riddles, or avoiding the whole story, which is a minor form of deception. I told you long ago that power is in the truth. I can't help you if you keep me in the dark."

Achmed exhaled slowly. He stared at her for a moment, as if gauging her soul. "You named me Achmed the Snake because it sounded frightening to you, didn't you?"

"Yes. I told you that a long time ago. And I've been embarrassed about it ever since."

"Perhaps you shouldn't be. It may have been the only thing that allowed me to find the tunnel. When I was the Brother,

I was tied only to the blood of men and women. It may have been the serpent name you gave me that helped me hear this beating heart.

"In the Before-Time, when the Earth and seas were being born, an egg was stolen from the progenitor of the race of dragons, the Primal Wyrm. If we live to get out of here I will one day tell you its name, though it would not be wise to do so now." Rhapsody nodded in agreement.

"That egg was secreted here, within the Earth, by the race of demonic beings born of elemental fire. My former master was one of them."

"The one who gave you the key?"

"Shhh. Yes." His voice dropped even lower. "The infant wyrm which came from that egg has lived here, deep in the frozen wastes of the Earth's interior, growing, until its coils have wound around the very heart of the world. It is an innate part of the Earth itself; its body is a large part of the world's mass. It sleeps now, but soon that demon wishes to summon it, and will visit it upon the land. Rhapsody, I can't explain its size to you, except to say that Sagia's trunk root was a mere piece of twine in comparison with the taproot, yes?"

"Yes."

"And the taproot was a thread compared with the Axis Mundi. The Axis Mundi is like one of your hairs in comparison with this creature. It has the power to consume the Earth; that was the intent of the thieves who put it here. It awaits the demon's call, which I know for certain is intended to come soon." He blinked, and Rhapsody could no longer see his face. "I know this, because he planned to use me to help bring this about."

"And that's why you ran?"

"Partly."

Rhapsody sat back, and looked at him with new eyes. Hithertofore it had been obvious that her two companions had histories that were nefarious; it was impossible to conclude anything else after the slaughter of Michael's men. And yet despite their pasts there was a nobility to both of them.

Grunthor's she had seen right away. He had been her protector from the beginning, advocating for her with his partner, assisting her in her climb, protecting her from her dreams. It was this other one in whom she had seen no good until now.

You cannot see the beauty without facing the darkness. Remember this.

"And rather than circumventing this place you have brought us here in the hope that we can help contain it."

"Yes, if possible." The mismatched eyes glittered in the darkness. "And even then, Rhapsody, you will only be buying time. You will never have the power to destroy it completely, nor I, nor any living soul."

She rested her throbbing head in her hand. "I can sing it a song of slumber, but I don't have any idea if it will work. And I will have to be very close to it to ensure it hears me."

Within his hood she heard a sigh. "I had suspected that. Grunthor and I discussed that possibility."

"And he objected, which is why you waited until he was asleep to talk to me."

"Careful, Rhapsody, you sound almost astute. You're going to ruin my opinion of you."

"I have an idea, but I'll need my pack," she said, hiding her smile. "You are more likely to be able to get it without waking Grunthor."

*B*efore you do anything foolish, why don't you tell me what you are planning?" Achmed handed her the pack, remembering a night long ago by the light of a hidden campfire in the fields outside Easton's wall.

So I'll ask you again, Singer; what can you do?

I can tell the absolute truth as I know it. And when I do that I can change things.

When the thought passed he looked up again. Rhapsody was untying the rawhide strings that held the burlap cover over her shepherd's harp.

"Thanks for your confidence in me." She pulled the ragged cloth loose and uncovered the instrument. It had not been damaged by its time within the Earth, much like Pilam's bread. "You said that at some point this beast will be summoned."

"Yes."

"What if it didn't hear the call?" Achmed stared at her blankly. She tried again. "In order to summon something, you need to know its true name. Of course, I don't know this thing's name. But if we could obscure the call, keep the beast from hearing it properly, or feeling it, perhaps it would just stay asleep and not answer. At least for a little while."

A fragment of a grin crawled over Achmed's face. "And how would you achieve this?"

"I'm not sure yet. But I'll have thought of something by the time we get to the tunnel."

With great care they crept across the vast, glowing Root, taking their time to ensure silence. Eventually they came to its edge and stepped off it for the first time onto the black basalt rock through which the Axis Mundi ran. In the shadows not far from the Root's edge was an immense tunnel, so huge that it faded into the darkness of the stone around it, its edges barely visible.

The closer they came to the tunnel, the colder Rhapsody felt. When they were close enough for her to see it, she knew why.

An icy wind was rising from the depth of the vast circular cavern. Her ears and fingers stung as it blasted through, freezing the wet clothing to her skin.

"Gods," she whispered. "Why is it so cold?"

Achmed slowly turned to her. When he spoke his words were measured.

"The demonic spirits that secreted the egg here took the element of fire with them when they went upworld to keep the wyrm in hibernation. They wanted it to grow to its greatest possible size before setting it free. I think that's why the vermin are attracted to heat and light." The natural percussion in his voice seemed stronger, as if his teeth were chattering.

"Are you all right?"

Achmed smiled through the ice that was forming on his lips. "I'm pondering hibernation myself."

"What do you mean?"

He leaned slowly over so she could catch his whisper. "You're the one who named me Achmed the Snake."

Concern filled her eyes as Rhapsody reached out and brushed the frost off of his face. His movements were now so slow as to be almost imperceptible. "Gods," she whispered again. He was trapped, living up to the reptilian name she had given him.

What have I done? she thought miserably, watching him freeze where he stood. *If I fail and wake the serpent, he will be unable to escape. He'll be its first victim. No; its second.*

"I'm going to take you back first," she said, taking his frigid hand. "You can't stay here."

With the last of his remaining mobility, Achmed shook his head. His eyes, still piercing, sought hers and stared down at her.

"Rhapsody," he said with great effort, "you do this. I will wait." His words had the ring of finality to them.

She looked down the tunnel into the icy darkness. "Can you still sense its heartbeat?" He blinked twice. "Good. All right, then, I'm going to set up right here. You need to tell me if it reacts to anything I'm doing, if it starts to wake. I'm going to begin softly, so we can stop if we have to. Give me a moment to gauge the direction of the tunnel."

Quietly she put down the harp and tiptoed into the vast opening. Its walls were wider than she could see in the dark, its ceiling higher, so once inside she was blind. She rested her hand on the wall and leaned forward slightly to try and estimate the angle of descent, but could see very little. The dirt beneath her hand was sandy and cold. The tunnel sloped downward, curling into the distance. Rhapsody returned to where Achmed waited.

"The wyrm must be very far away," she whispered. "I can't see an end to the tunnel."

Achmed struggled to speak. "The tunnel—wall—"

She moved nearer to hear him. "What about the tunnel wall?"

"—is—a scale in—the—skin of—the wyrm."

$\mathcal{F}$rost ran through her veins as she realized what he meant. He had said that the body of the serpent was a large part of the Earth's mass, but she hadn't realized that it was part of the cavern around them. If the immense tunnel wall was a tiny piece of one of its coils while its heart was far away, deeper within the belly of the Earth, then surely there was nothing in the known world that could contain a beast of this size should it arise. And she had touched it.

Fighting nausea and panic Rhapsody sat on the ground and took up her harp. She cleared her mind and attuned herself to the diffuse music in the air around her. After a moment, its low, smooth tone began to fill her ears. There was little fluctuation, just the occasional variation in the monotone up or down a half-step. A sign of deep sleep.

Softly she began the simplest slumber song she knew in the same key as the music around her. She looked to Achmed's face, looking for signs that the heartbeat of the wyrm had increased, but his eyes remained steady, watching her intently within the frozen prison of his body.

The melody wove through the music in the air, matching its tune. Slowly Rhapsody added a harmonic element, and noted a slight increase of warmth in the air around her. She looked up at Achmed, questioningly, and he blinked once. Still no change.

A stray thought knocked on the door of her mind, and Rhapsody shook her head to drive it out again. The import of what she was doing, and its potential consequences, was something that had to remain in abeyance until she was finished. Otherwise it would have buried her in its weight.

When the demon summoned the wyrm he would be using its true name, something that would match exactly the musical vibration it was attuned to. She needed to change that vibration subtlely, needed to wrap it in a slightly discordant song.

When using music to cause pain, it is better to be slightly sharp or flat than either of those things in the extreme, her mentor had said. If she did it slowly enough, took it up a degree at a time, perhaps the wyrm would not notice the subtle change, but it would still be enough to interfere with the call of its name.

Rhapsody breathed in time to the song, focusing all the rhythms of her body. All sense of time melted away as it had in the Wide Meadows. She had no idea how long she played, repeating the monotonous refrain over and over again, varying its tone infinitesimally. She shaped it as a roundelay, singing the repetitive melody again and again, over and over.

She added a slightly different beat to the rhythm. Suddenly

Achmed's eyes opened wide; the heartbeat had leapt, the ocean of serpentine blood had begun to pump. He blinked furiously.

Rhapsody scarcely noticed. She was attuned to the song herself; it had become part of the fiber of her being. She continued to play, raising the key a half-step.

The wall of the tunnel vibrated as the great beast stretched slightly, then settled back into sleep. The air cooled imperceptibly, the heartbeat slowed. Achmed closed his eyes and sighed, willing the dangerous game to end.

Hours later, Rhapsody finally rose, exhausted, still playing, and walked back to the entrance of the tunnel.

"*Samoht,*" she said to the instrument. *Play on endlessly.*

The harp continued the lullabye, even as her fingers left the strings. Over and over the roundelay played, repeating the same complex melody. Rhapsody set the instrument carefully on the floor of the tunnel near the entrance, then stepped back. On it played, endlessly. *Samoht.*

She turned and went quickly back to Achmed, whose eyes were now closed. Fighting fatigue, Rhapsody stood on tiptoe and sang his name into his ear.

"Achmed the Snake, warm; come." Achmed blinked but didn't move. The command in the song had not worked.

Exhaustion roared through her, consuming the last of her strength. She fought back tears with the effort to remain standing, and grasped his arms, pulling with all her might.

"Come *on*. Please."

Still there was no response. Rhapsody pulled harder, trying to drag him from the tunnel's maw, but her strength failed her and she only succeeded in knocking his frozen body to the ground, where it lay unmoving.

Tears began to flow, and even the act of crying made her too tired to think. Grunthor. She had to get Grunthor.

Blindly she stumbled back toward the Root where they had left him. She got to the edge of the Root before she fell and landed, sprawling, on the glowing surface of the Axis Mundi.

For a moment she lay, too spent to go any farther, her ear resting against the humming floor beneath her. The song of the Root filled her head again, bringing with it ease, solace.

Rhapsody took a deep breath. The music of the Root had

sustained her before. Perhaps, even in her utter exhaustion, there was strength she could tap. She began to sing her Naming note, *ela*, trying to match the tonal modulations of the Tree.

After a moment she felt a fragile spark of energy enter her legs, and she stood slowly. Grunthor was here somewhere. She had to find him. She had the strength to find him.

Concentrating on the Root's song she pushed on, step after agonizing step, keeping her head down, breathing slowly, until she was stopped in her tracks by the grip of huge hands.

"Miss! Are ya all right?"

"Achmed," she choked, looking up into the face of the Bolg. He was trembling. "Help me get him out of there."

Without a word the giant swept her up in his arms and ran back to where she had come from.

Achmed was still lying on the ground, motionless, when they reached the spot where he had fallen. While Grunthor took off his greatcoat Rhapsody patted the Dhracian's face to check for signs of awareness and was overjoyed to see the familiar scowl radiating up at her from the frozen features.

With an efficient sweep the Bolg Sergeant swathed him in the greatcoat, then lifted him to a stand. Grunthor hoisted Achmed's body, too stiff even to bend, against his chest and shoulder. He turned to Rhapsody.

"Can you walk on your own, miss?"

Rhapsody nodded, watching Achmed carefully. Color was returning to his face, and he flexed his limbs slightly. Rhapsody smiled. She took his hand and gave his arm a solid pull, and was not surprised to find resistance in the muscles. He bent forward slightly and whispered in her ear.

"Look."

She turned and stared back at the tunnel. Slowly it was filling with slender threads of light, like the gossamer of a spider's web. Each new repetition of the melody had formed a new strand, attaching itself in a circular pattern to the cavernous walls of the tunnel.

"The song is freezing in place," she murmured, fascinated.

With each new round the threads grew thicker, the sound of the song louder. Its key was now up three notes from where it had been when she started, different enough, with any luck, to jangle the namesong when the demon eventually spoke it. The roundelay, something Singers learned early in their training in order to be able to sing harmony with themselves, continued on, creating more strands of glowing spider-silk. Each strand hummed, repeating its simple melody, vibrating like the strings of her harp, each song beginning a few seconds apart.

"After a while it's going to be cacophony," Rhapsody said.

Grunthor nodded. Already the vibrations were in pleasant discord, like a band of musicians without a conductor, each playing at his own speed.

"Come on, miss, let's get out of 'ere," he said.

13

Once they left the wyrm's tunnel Achmed's strength returned rapidly. He was able to walk almost immediately and insisted on being allowed to do so, listening, as before, for the sound of the thudding pulse. It was unchanged.

They fell back into the business of finding an exit from the earth, traveling in their accustomed silence for the most part. Achmed had not spoken about the incident with the wyrm, and Rhapsody avoided mentioning it, hoping that one day they would be able to talk about it openly. She understood that there were many battles still to be fought and won in Achmed's memory before he would be able to do so.

For a while the root tunnel ran fairly straight. It didn't tend to twist much, though it often varied its elevation, winding up or down at will, undoubtedly following whatever water source had once allowed the Tree to grow roots this deep, probably the father of what was now the sea. The deeper within the Earth they seemed to burrow, the more often they seemed to encounter slightly wider tunnels, allowing them to walk upright for longer before crouching or crawling again.

Occasionally they would come to great open spaces, places where the ceiling of the tunnel arched high above them, giving them room to breathe freely. Grunthor had speculated that these tunnels were places where the Root had once taken on great quantities of water, swelling in response, then shrinking again as it grew longer. These places were often the most dangerous of all. Cave-ins were common, and it was here that the infestation of vermin was oftentimes the worst.

"They're coming." Achmed's voice roused Rhapsody from her fitful sleep. She swallowed dryly and drew Lucy. They had camped in a cavernous place and there was sufficient room to use the weapon.

Despite becoming accustomed to the endless task of destroying the vermin, she never really had been able to overcome the horror those words always struck in her soul. Her years in the streets had given her the fortitude to face many abhorrent tasks, however, so she brushed the hair off her forehead and looked up into the darkness above her.

Will this never end? she thought as the wriggling worms came into view. They had learned to fight them in the dark, since light made the vermin more excited, causing them to move more quickly and attack more ferociously. *How many times have we done this now?*

The dim light of the glowing lichen in the cavern allowed her to see them coming along the Root. Like a blanket of creeping decay, they swarmed forward, falling from the branches of the Root above them.

The three companions lined up on the Root surface, Grunthor with Lopper at the ready, Achmed drawing the thin silvery sword he hadn't deigned to give a name. The vermin began to drop from above, at first one by one, then in swarms like leaves in autumn.

As was always their unspoken custom, the three formed a circle, slashing at the vermin as they fell. Only Achmed could match the speed of the worms; Rhapsody and Grunthor instead had learned their patterns of movement. The giant Bolg and the Lirin Singer had become accustomed to predicting when they would strike, dodging their painful bites with a twisting motion which at once they turned into a cutting strike. It didn't always work—at times they would miss—but most of the time they would cleave the vermin and be ready for the next attack.

The crawling mass was coming closer; soon she and Grunthor would have to deal with the devouring carpet instead of the strays dropping from above. They left it to Achmed to guard them from the overhead assault while they began their rhythmic slaughter of the oncoming crawlers.

Rhapsody took the left, Grunthor the right, as they hacked wildly at the creatures, Achmed swinging above them to swipe the dropping parasites out of the air.

It often occurred to Rhapsody while they were engaged in this vile activity that this, more than any other action, demonstrated the trust that had grown between the three of them over time. Achmed's weapon whistled past their ears and scalps, diverting the painful attacks of needle-like teeth and insidious venom that caused an insatiable burning itch and occasional fevers.

He left himself completely open to the attack of the encroaching mass, relying on the efforts of the other two to fend off the majority of the creatures. Occasionally in the thick of the fight Rhapsody would find herself musing about how the unequal contributions of all three had grown into an impressive display of synchronized fighting, one in which she had eventually come to feel an equal partner.

The hideous popping of the creatures' flesh as they were severed with the sword, the repulsive smell that their fluids left on clothes for days afterward—it had all the qualities of a full-fledged nightmare each time the task was undertaken. Finally she would look up to see one or the other of the Bolg giving the all-clear signal, as Grunthor was doing now, and she collapsed in exhaustion after kicking a space on the ground clear of the worm bodies.

Now came the cleanup, the crucial act of checking every crevice of their bodies and clothing for the smallest creatures that would hide, attaching themselves to their skin. Generally the vermin were able to wait, without moving, until their host was asleep, before burying their purple heads in the skin like a tick and feasting on blood, leaving behind illness and stinging pain.

Rhapsody was grateful to Grunthor for showing her the old Bolg trick of keeping at least one thumbnail long so that it could be pressed down the seams of their clothes to kill the parasites. This was, she discovered, the real reason why Bolg kept their nails long enough to be claws: it allowed them the tool to cleanse themselves of nits and lice.

"I'm sorry," she had told him, "I thought it was to maul your opponent with."

"It works well enough for that, too, miss," he had replied with a smile.

Now she completed her checkover and looked up to see Achmed staring off into the distance.

"What's the matter?"

He turned to Grunthor. "Have you noticed an increase in their numbers of late?"

"Yep."

"Perhaps it's the heat."

"What heat?" Rhapsody asked, bewildered.

Achmed looked at her in mild surprise. "You can't feel it?"

She concentrated on the air around her. It did seem a little warmer. "I guess so," she said uncertainly.

"There's fire near 'ere; Oi can feel it, too," added Grunthor.

Fear darkened Rhapsody's eyes. "Why would there be fire on the Root? Could it be from mines, or a volcano?"

"Perhaps," said Achmed casually. "Or perhaps we're near the center. Legend has it there is fire at the core of the Earth."

A faint choking sound escaped Rhapsody's throat. She knew of the legend as well, and the thought made her heart sink. If they were only now nearing the center, they had come less than halfway. Additionally, the fire at the center of the Earth would surely be an obstacle they were unlikely to overcome, leaving them trapped deep within the world.

"Are you coming?" Achmed's voice broke her reverie.

She rose slowly, stretching the cramped muscles of her legs and back, feeling the bitter sting of the bites that had pierced her defenses. "I suppose," she said. She slid Lucy back into its sheath over her shoulder and took up her place on the Root again.

Before long they knew they were in trouble. There was still no fire in sight, but they could feel the increase in heat, like an inferno or the flames of a forge, growing hotter in the distance ahead of them.

Rhapsody's hair, which had been wet and stringy for as long as she could remember, now dried into clumped patches the consistency of straw. The heat from whatever fire source lay ahead also dried out the fragmented remains of her clothes, which were now little more than tatters after all this time and distance. With the warmth came both pain and comfort. Her skin cracked in the heat, but her bones and joints welcomed it, as the constant aches abated a little.

In addition, there was a change in the song of the Earth here. One of the only pleasant parts of this experience had been the occasions when she could lie flat on her back or stomach and feel the deep, modulating vibration that she had heard early on, the sound of the Root singing with life, echoing with the vast collective wisdom of time. There was more life to the sound now, a faster change in the tonal melody.

"I wonder if the Root feels healthier in the absence of the vermin," she said.

"Wouldn't you?" Grunthor said, poking her.

"Our efforts have undoubtedly put a substantial dent in the pest population," Achmed said, looking at the basalt walls around him.

"Not substantial enough—you're both still here," Rhapsody joked. Achmed smiled; it was an expression she wasn't sure if she had ever seen before. Like the Root, their moods seemed healthier as well.

The fire took its time to come into sight. They had lost all tools to gauge time below the surface, so it was impossible to know how long they had sensed the heat without it coming into view, but Rhapsody had long been proficient in the Bolgish tongue, and Grunthor had mastered not only the written word but calligraphy and musical graphing as well.

How long has it been—a year? More? Rhapsody thought one night. *Surely we have been feeling the heat for that long, still without finding the source.* She began to doubt they would live to do so.

They became aware of it first as a distant glow, the rocks at the edge of the tunnel glimmering red in the dark. The heat increased; they had felt it for as long as they could recall. The memory of the cold, wet crawling had been almost forgotten, although there was a great deal of water still around them. The earth itself was dry, purged of its moisture by the climate of heat.

The newfound warmth made for easier traveling, but it held its share of perils as well. Occasionally clothing or other dry-goods would burst into flames unexpectedly, metal weaponry would become too hot to touch. Finding drinking water became more difficult, and more a cause for concern.

Finally Achmed stopped, and the other two followed his lead as he peered off into the distance. "Fire," he said simply. Grunthor squinted, then shook his head. Rhapsody gave it a halfhearted try, but saw nothing. She had learned ages ago that her vision was no match for Achmed's, especially in the dark.

They walked on, growing ever closer, until even Rhapsody could make out the flickering flames that filled the tunnel ahead of them. The Root itself, the ground below them, cracked occasionally under the pressure of their steps. The cavern ceiling above them became enormously high. As they approached, even at their seemingly snail-like pace, it became evident that the entire passageway was engulfed in flames.

The fire at the Earth's core burned in myriad colors, more darkly than fires in the open air. Flames twisted and danced within the incandescent wall, blue and purple and white in harmony with the fiery shades that Rhapsody was accustomed to. There was no space around it; the inferno reached to all edges of the passageway, forcing its light and liquid heat over and through every opening and crevice. She stood, enraptured by the sight, her eyes stinging from the intensity of the furious light. She closed her eyes.

"Bloody *hrekin*," Grunthor swore behind her. "We're trapped. We might as well 'ave stayed in Easton." Achmed said nothing.

From behind her eyelids Rhapsody was listening, not to her dismayed companions, but to the fire's song. Unlike the low, slow tone of the Earth, the firesong roared and crackled with life, singing a melody more exquisite than any she ever remembered hearing.

The sound drew from her soul memories almost painful in their sweetness, nights before the hearth where her mother brushed her hair, harvest bonfires ripe with the sounds of dancing and celebration, her first kiss by the light of a campfire in autumn. The brilliance illuminated her face, shining off her tangled hair, making her glow with its radiance. There was a call in the sound of the flames, an invitation to the dance, and she longed to accept. Involuntarily she took a step forward.

Strong, bony hands seized her shoulders and spun her swiftly around. She opened her eyes in astonishment to the sound of Grunthor's shocked roar.

"What do you think you're doin'?"

Achmed, who still held her by the shoulders, studied her face. "Where are you going, Rhapsody?"

The word fell out of her mouth before she had a chance to stop it.

"Forward," she said.

14

"I'm going through," she said simply. Grunthor laughed aloud.

"If you wanted to commit suicide, Oi would o' been glad to 'elp you in a way that wouldn't damage the meat," he said. "Come on, miss, shake it off."

"Look," Rhapsody said, losing patience, "I'm not going back. I can't. None of us can. Remember those cave-ins? The path is blocked. We'll never get out that way. The only way to go is forward."

"Exactly how do you propose we do that?" Achmed asked. His tone was sincere, or at least as full of sincerity as he was capable.

Rhapsody took a deep breath, knowing that what she was about to say would sound inane, at best. "Do you remember what I said about names, and how they can make us what we once were?"

"Vaguely."

"Well, I've been thinking about it ever since this possibility arose. I think the only way to broach the fire is to wrap ourselves in the song of our names and hope that we are remade on the other side."

"You first, my dear," chuckled Grunthor.

"Of course," she said hastily. "I wouldn't have it any other way."

"You really are desperate to get out of this tunnel," said Achmed. His tone was the cross between sympathy and sarcasm that Rhapsody referred to as sympacastic.

"Have you got any better ideas?"

She sat down on the root and unslung her ragged satchel, removing her higen, a palm-sized stringed instrument resembling a tiny harp. "If I make it through, I'll come back for you if I can." She brushed the dirt from the fragments of her cloak and stood again. "If I don't come back, at least you'll know to try something else."

Grunthor shook his head, staring at the inferno before them. "Oi know that without you tossin' your life away."

"Let her go," said Achmed quietly.

Rhapsody smiled. "Thank you. At least if I don't make it you'll finally be rid of me."

Grunthor was growing visibly upset. "If Oi'd wanted to be rid o' ya, Oi'da done it ages ago. I could o' snapped your neck with one 'and and been done with you."

She put her arms around the trembling giant. "Well, maybe you could have back then. I've had some pretty good sword training since." She pulled him tighter, and he bent to embrace her. "Goodbye, Grunthor. Don't worry. I'll be back."

He pulled away and looked down at her, mustering a smile. "Oi thought you always had to tell the truth."

Rhapsody patted his cheek. "I am," she said softly. She turned to the robed man who had vexed her so much, had trapped her within the Earth in the first place.

"Goodbye, Achmed."

"Hurry up," he said. "We're not going to wait long for you."

Rhapsody laughed aloud. "Well, that's incentive." She shouldered her pack and walked away toward the inferno. The two Bolg watched as her tiny black shadow grew longer against the roaring flames, then disappeared in the wall of billowing heat and light.

* * *

When she got as close as she could endure, Rhapsody closed her eyes, resting her higen against her chest. The tiny strings were hot to the touch; her fingers burned as she plucked them, trying to discern the right song, a song of herself.

She knew the single note that reverberated in her soul, *ela*, the sixth and final note of the scale. *Each person is attuned to a certain musical note*, her instructor had said. Rhapsody had been highly amused upon discovering her own: She was the sixth and final child in her family. The note fit her easily; it made sense to her. She sang it now, feeling the familiar vibration. The melody that would capture her essence was more elusive. Her true name, set to music, was easy enough; she started with that.

From the simple melody line she built another refrain, a tune that resonated inside her and made her skin tingle. Note by note, measure by measure, she constructed the song, adding her voice to the composition she played on the higen. Then, gathering her courage, she walked into the fire.

As she reached the edges of the roaring inferno her eyes began to sting from the intensity of the light. Pain seared them shut. She kept walking, still singing, praying that if she was wrong she would be engulfed quickly, and not suffer too long.

There was a natural wind to the fire, and it blew her blond tresses around her, illuminating her hair like a torch. It was becoming harder and harder to breathe. Rhapsody opened her eyes to find herself within the fire's walls.

The innate song of the fire was louder now and she matched her own namesong to it, singing in harmony. Instantly her eyes ceased to sting; she found, upon opening them, a realm of glorious color, whipping around her like meadow grass in a high wind. A sense of peace and safety washed over her. The fire knew her. It would not harm her.

The gleaming hues, sapphire blues twisting through sheets of blazing red-orange and tongues of yellow, billowed around her. Rhapsody felt the pain in her joints and bones melt away. Vaguely she wondered if she was being immolated, consumed in the fire's maw. It was a sensation akin, in a way, to joy, a feeling of being surrounded by ultimate acceptance. She sang loudly, turning the melded tunes of the fire and herself into a song of celebration.

The way before her grew clearer, patches of darkness appearing for a moment, only to vanish without a trace. She steeled her nerve and kept walking; it took all her strength to leave the core. If she gave in to the sweetness of the place she knew she would stay forever, happily absorbing the song of the fire until it took her as part of itself.

Suddenly the delicious heat left her face; it was like being slapped with a cold ocean wave. Rhapsody opened her eyes and saw darkness before her, though the fire walls were still flickering at the periphery of her vision. Before her stretched a tunnel similar to the one she had just left, but with slightly different features. Though she was still within the fire's embrace, she felt a shiver run through her. She had made it to the other side of the core.

She spun around quickly and hurried back through the fire, singing all the way.

On the other side of the core Grunthor waited anxiously, staring into the blinding conflagration, sweating visibly through the pores of his gray-green hide. After what seemed an endless delay he squinted, then pointed into the flames.

"Oi see 'er, sir!"

Achmed was nodding. He had spied her shadow a moment before, tall as the cavern ceiling, flickering in between the waves of fire and disappearing again.

The woman who walked out of the blaze vaguely resembled Rhapsody, but was very different in appearance. Her hair was no longer the color of pale gold, but had been burnished in the fire to the shade of warm, clear honey. She waved to them from the fire's edge.

"Come on," she urged, her voice swallowed by the roar of the flames. "I don't know how long the pathway will stay open."

The two Firbolg ran to the edge of the core, shielding their eyes from the heat. Rhapsody held up her hand to stop them too late. The hood of Achmed's robe ignited, ripping into flame. She watched in horror as Grunthor threw him to the ground and smothered the fire, rolling him in the white-hot ash of the floor.

Achmed's name she knew; she had given it to him. She chanted it now, over and over. Grunthor helped the stunned man rise, and assisted him to the edge of the fire wall. Rhapsody held up her palm to the Sergeant, signaling him to wait, and took the Dhracian's hands in hers. His eyes were clearing as he heard the song of his name. It must be causing the same sense of well-being in him that she had experienced.

When she was sure he could stand erect, Rhapsody transferred the tune to the higen, playing as Achmed stood at the edge of the fire. She began weaving a song for him, based around the melody that was his name.

"Can you feel the song tingling on the surface of your skin?"

"No." The tatters of his hood crumbled and fell to the ground, exposing the terrible burn that now marred his forehead and eyes; Achmed was blind. Rhapsody's own eyes stung at the sight of it. The wound looked excruciating.

She thought quickly. "Tell me something about yourself I can add to make it reflect you better," she said. She added the musical notes to the melody that spelled out *Firbolg* and *Dhracian*. "Shall I rename you back to your old name, the Brother?"

Achmed shook his head violently, spattering droplets of sweat into the flames that dispersed into mist on impact. His face reflected the rippling light of the fire behind her.

"What child were you in the family?"

With great effort he spoke. "Firstborn."

Rhapsody nodded and wove the word into the melody. From the look on his face she could tell that he had felt some sort of additional sensation with its inclusion.

"Just one more trait, Achmed, anything that is part of your identity. What is your profession?"

Achmed began to shake as the shock of his injury overcame him. He bent as close to her as he could, trying to allow her to hear the word.

"Assassin," he whispered.

Rhapsody blinked. *Of course*, she thought. She began to

sing the song again, adding the new dimension.

Achmed's scarred eyes opened wider, and he nodded sightlessly as he felt the song surround him, as she had. In the next instant a memory flickered behind Rhapsody's eyes. It was the image of Achmed at the twisting nexus where thousands of differing paths along the Root met, nonchalantly choosing their course through the belly of the world. He had been unconcerned, had seemed so sure of his choices that there had never been a breath of hesitation as to whether they were heading in the correct direction.

Once Grunthor had whispered in her ear that the Dhracian was following the beating heart of the Earth, feeling its pulse, being guided along its veins and humming pathways the way he had once sought his prey in the realm of the air, the world above.

Unerring tracker. The pathfinder, she sang. Achmed's body grew translucent and began, like his face a moment before, to reflect the light of the Great Fire. Rhapsody reached out and pulled him into the flames. She hurried him through to the other side, singing with all her ability as a Namer. She deposited him just outside the wall of the fire and ran back to get Grunthor.

The sight of the trembling giant standing in the reflected brilliance of the billowing fire's edge squeezed Rhapsody's heart. The amber eyes, transfixed in a look she recognized as stark terror, relaxed somewhat upon seeing her, but his face was still contorted with obvious worry.

"Where is 'e, darlin'? Is 'e all right?"

"Come on!" she shouted over the pounding roar of the flames, waving him on wildly.

Grunthor ran to her, grabbing her by the shoulders. "Is 'e all right?"

"Don't be afraid, we're going to make it—"

A snarling howl issued forth. It rumbled through the massive muscles down through the clawed hands that gripped her upper arms, choking off her assurances and turning her words into a gasp of pain. "Where is 'e?!"

Rhapsody clutched his hands and pulled free of them. "He's on the other side. He's blind, but he's alive." She saw relief temper the ferocious expression on his face, noticed his mighty jaw unclench ever-so-slightly, and she felt another twist of her heart. She knew the fear that held sway over him, and knew also that none of it had been for himself. With a hand that shook she reached up and patted his monstrous cheek.

"What is your Firbolg name?" The giant opened his mouth, and a serious of whistling snarls came out, followed by a clicking glottal stop. Rhapsody exhaled, then closed her eyes. "Tell me again," she said, fighting the panic welling inside her.

Listening carefully to the sounds above the noise of the flames, she matched her voice as best she could to Grunthor's. After several tries she could feel a hum in return emanating from in front of her. When she opened her eyes again, Rhapsody could see a halo of light gleaming around the Sergeant.

"And you're Bengard as well?" Grunthor nodded. *Child of sand and open sky, son of the caves and lands of darkness,* she sang. *Bengard, Firbolg. The Sergeant Major. My trainer, my protector. The Lord of Deadly Weapons. The Ultimate Authority, to Be Obeyed at All Costs.* The electric hum grew louder.

Grunthor broke into a toothy grin. "That's it, miss. Oi feel positively a-tingle. Now let's get to 'im, eh?"

Rhapsody smiled in return. "Grunthor, you're such a faithful friend, strong and reliable as the Earth itself. Here, hold my hands."

She led the towering Bolg through the flames, chanting his name and the characteristics she had ascribed to him, singing the namesong over and over, until the shadows that were dancing off the walls of fire swallowed them.

She blinked and looked around. They were on the other side, out of the flames, surrounded by darkness. Rhapsody buried her face in Grunthor's chest, trying to absorb the sudden, stinging absence of the fire's warmth without bursting into tears of loss.

The giant watched in the dark as Rhapsody began to remove the bandages. They were deep in the tunnel now, the light of the fire still reflecting off them from a distance. She had dressed Achmed's eyes with some of her healing herbs, over the Dhracian's sustained protests.

Achmed lay with his head in her lap, muttering impatiently as she unwound the linen strips.

"I told you this was unnecessary. I can see."

"Well, why didn't you say so before I wrapped you up?"

"I was unconscious," he said indignantly.

Rhapsody chuckled. "Oh, yes, that's it; I thought you seemed unnaturally cooperative." She pulled the second of the layers off. "Now, this was just a palliative treatment to ease the pain—"

"I'm not in pain," he interrupted angrily.

"—and we'll need to treat the wound once we get to a safe—" Rhapsody stopped her thought again, staring blankly at the Dhracian's face. Achmed's wound had vanished.

"Gods," she whispered.

Achmed ripped the remaining bandage off his head. "I told you I was healed."

Grunthor was staring at him as well. "Uh, sir, you're a lit'le more 'ealed than you think."

"What's that supposed to mean?"

Grunthor drew his poleax forward, a long spearlike weapon with a hatchet head on one side that he called Salutations, or Sal for short. "Have a look. That wound you got in that knife fight in Kingston a few years back?"

"Yes?"

"Gone, sir. See for yourself."

Achmed seized the blade with both hands and stared into it deeply. A moment later he grasped the waist of his shirt and examined his abdomen.

"My scars are gone."

"Mine too," Grunthor added, looking over to Rhapsody, who was looking at her wrist. She met his gaze, then nodded.

"All our wounds are gone, and our scars have vanished. Why would that be?"

Rhapsody smiled. "Think about what I told you all that time ago."

Achmed sat up and thought back to their first fight with the vermin, the time when she sang her first healing song and mended the wound on his forearm.

Go ahead, scoff if you want to. But music of one form or another will probably be what gets us out of this place.

Only if you annoy me so much with your singing that I use your body as an auger and drill us out of here.

It's part of what a Namer can do; there is no thing, no concept, no law as strong as the power of a given thing's name. Our identities are bound to it. It is the essence of what we are, and sometimes it can even make us what we are again, no matter how much we have been altered.

"Are you saying that we have been remade?"

Rhapsody shrugged. "I don't know, I think so. I was sure the first time I walked through the fire I could feel my body burn away, almost like I was being immolated. Because I sang each of our true names through it all, I think whatever damage life or circumstance inflicted on our bodies was not mirrored on our new ones. Are there any other manifestations that we might be able to check?"

Achmed slowly ran his hand around the base of his throat. The invisible chain that the demon had once controlled him with had snapped when she renamed him in the alleys of Easton, and had been gone for so long that it was impossible to tell. Bones that had once been broken felt as strong and healthy as if they never had sustained injury, but he was not certain they had shown any indication of it before the fire, either.

"I don't know; is your virginity restored?"

Rhapsody turned away as if stung. Normally she ignored jokes of that sort, but the cleansing, horrifying, ecstatic experience of passing through the fire had exhausted her ability to absorb the jest. Grunthor saw the look on her face and glared at Achmed angrily. The giant looked back over at her again, then found his mouth open in amazement.

"Darlin', turn around a minute 'ere."

"Leave me alone," Rhapsody answered. "I'm not in the mood for any more teasing."

"No, miss, please," Grunthor insisted. "Oi want to 'ave a look at your face."

Slowly Rhapsody turned back toward him, though her eyes remained averted.

"Criton," Grunthor murmured. Achmed looked up and felt his jaw go slack as well.

Rhapsody had been a beautiful woman before her walk through the fire, though time and soil had diminished her appearance somewhat in their endless trek along the Root. That had changed considerably; the walk through the core had burned away any imperfection, leaving a creature they hardly recognized in front of them.

The long golden hair was sparkling in the light of the distant fire, gleaming like liquid gold. Her complexion had been purged of any flaw, leaving skin the color and consistency of a rose petal, glistening in the darkness. When, a moment later, she turned to look at them in annoyance, her emerald eyes flashed, clearer than gemstones, and caught the rays of illumination in the tunnel around them. She had been comely; now she was more than magnificent. Even to Firbolg eyes the aura of unnatural beauty was evident.

"What?" she asked, irritation evident in her voice.

It took Grunthor a moment to find his voice. "Gods, Yer Ladyship, you're beau'iful."

Rhapsody's newly gorgeous face softened, and the expression that crossed it caused both men to flush warm and experience a sudden swelling below the belt. "You're more than welcome, Grunthor. I was happy to help," she said gently. "It was the least I could do to pay you both back for the times you've helped me."

"That's not what Oi meant," Grunthor said. "You're different."

Rhapsody's brows drew together. "What do you mean?"

"He means," came Achmed's thin voice, "that if you were back in your old line of work you could ask any price and get it, just for the opportunity for a man to look at you."

Rhapsody shook her head in annoyance. "I wish you'd stop going on about my old profession," she said. "I don't torment you about your past sins. And believe me, no one pays just to look."

Achmed sighed. They would now. "Rhapsody, you look better than you did. You're stunning."

Rhapsody looked over at his face in the light of the distant fire of the Earth's core. Achmed had always made a point of remaining cloaked and hooded whenever possible, behaving in many subtle ways like a man who felt his appearance to be unpleasant to behold, even freakish. Now, seeing his countenance unguarded in the light, she couldn't understand why he had. He wasn't ugly, at least in her estimation. There was a strange beauty to his face, in fact; instead of a face that reflected atrocity, she saw a distracted god's unfinished work.

It was easy to imagine the rendering that had created him, the unfinished head of a sculpture placed on its body, all full of kneadings and excess clay, unrefined, with just a small crimp to approximate a nose, some uneven thumb marks where the eyes might one day be, another swipe of the thumb to make a half-smiling, half-grimacing, lipless mouth.

The mismatched eyes, the fine scoring of vessels beneath the surface of the skin, had come together to form a work of art, not attractive in the classical sense, but fascinating and rare. Perhaps he was seeing something much the same in her.

"You know, you're not so bad yourself," she said, smiling slightly.

Achmed looked at Grunthor, and they both shook their heads and looked away. She didn't understand. It was becoming obvious that was she wasn't going to.

15

The exhilaration of passing through the fire diminished quickly as the three travelers repeated the steps they had made, trudging and crawling over the Root that seemed to stretch into Time itself, endless and unyielding. The journey was only slightly less arduous because of the knowledge that they had passed through the center, and now were at least more than halfway to the potential end.

Perhaps the despair, bordering on insanity, from the first part of the journey had been a factor of the pulling away from the old life. Now, though the trek was every bit as endless, though time passed with same agonizing lethargy, there was hope at the end of the tunnel, at least most of the time. As the wall of fire receded into distant memory the light had gone with it, and now they walked in darkness again, talking occasionally if only to stave off madness.

Their clothes and leather goods were ragged and worn, their boots gone, the knees of their trousers nothing but holes in tattered fabric. Grunthor had sacrificed the caplet of his cloak and Rhapsody the spare strings for her harp to make new footwear for them. They tied the cloth around their feet and legs to protect them from the jagged stone of the basalt tunnel, buttressing the soles with strips of leather cut from what had once been their boots. Even with the improvised footgear, by the end of a traveling session their feet were often bloody and bruised.

Rhapsody had taken to singing her devotions to the stars again, though day and night had lost their meaning, and she was as far away from the sunrise and the night sky as it was possible to be.

She began to interpret dawn as the time of their rising from sleep, and sang the aubade, the morning love song, as she dressed and attempted to comb the snarls out of her gleaming tresses. When they stopped, worn out, and made camp, she would sing her nightly vespers, sometimes falling asleep from exhaustion in the middle of the song.

Grunthor and Achmed had taken to listening to her, silent in the dark, never speaking until she had finished. Often they would pass a few more moments in dismal conversation, making plans they knew might upset her were she awake.

Strangely enough, time had exhibited no physical manifestation on any of them. The fire had taken away their scars, and some of the wrinkles and lines the men had achieved as hallmarks of battle and a difficult life. If anything, the three of them looked younger than they had when entering Sagia an eternity before.

Rhapsody seemed to glow more as each day passed. An aura of attraction, almost like a magnetic field, was evident around her even in the darkness, though generally her face was not visible. The perpetuity of their mutual youth seemed to belie the endlessness of their journey. The thick coating of mud that covered them made their actual appearances hard to discern, anyway.

Eventually it became clear that they were traveling closer

to the surface of the Earth. They had climbed and crawled through consistently uphill passageways, scaling another towering taproot like the one they had first ascended.

The tunnel had become horrendously wet and slippery again. The chill had returned to Rhapsody's bones, along with the aches in her joints. It became a matter of routine for them to struggle through waist-deep patches of water or mud. On more than one occasion they had been besieged by a flash flood that almost drowned them all.

Finally they entered a horizontal cavern, drier than the previous tunnels had been. The ceiling was higher here, and they could walk erect amid the dripping stalactites that hung ominously from the ceiling above them. Stalagmites had formed as well, jutting up from the tunnel floor like the lower jaw of a great beast within whose grisly mouth they were traveling.

They walked with great care beneath the rocky outcroppings. Grunthor had sustained several wounds from bumping into them, rubbing against them, or having the vibration of their footsteps occasionally jar one loose.

They entered one section of cavern where a long, thin stalactite hung at an odd angle, jutting down from the side of the passageway wall near the ceiling. Owing to its precarious position, Achmed had walked by it cautiously, taking pains not to disturb it.

As Rhapsody passed beneath it a sudden brightness filled the tunnel. The glow was muted by the earth that surrounded the stalactite; nonetheless, the three travelers squinted in unison. Their eyes, used to an eternity of darkness, were unaccustomed to the brightness that even the dim glow produced. Grunthor muttered curses in the language of the Bolg—his head had been closest to the rock outcropping when it began to shine.

Rhapsody reached up and touched the glowing formation. It was just barely within her reach, hanging at a slanted angle from the wall, unlike the millions of other stalactites they had passed. As she did, some of the rock crumbled from the point and fell to the bottom of the tunnel. A blazing beam of light and flame broke forth from the rock, causing all three travelers to cry out in pain and shield their eyes.

"What *is* that?" snarled the harsh voice in the lead.

Rhapsody peered through her fingers. The tip of the stalactite was burning, tiny flames licking up the shaft of the formation. She stared at it in wonder, then put her hand out to it again. As her fingers neared the flames they intensified and the light grew radiant. When she pulled back, the fire returned to its former state, burning quietly inside the rock.

With the same certainty that led her through the fiery core, she carefully began brushing away the crumbling outside of the stalactite. The rocky matter fell away easily in one piece that tumbled to the ground, leaving a gleaming shaft of burning light, flames traveling up it while the base glowed ethereally. Rhapsody caught her breath.

"It's a sword," she said softly.

The Firbolg looked at each other. She was right; emerging from the slime-covered wall was a flaming sword blade, its shaft beneath the flickering fire glowing intensely blue-white and engraved in intricate patterns.

"Can you pull it out, miss?" Grunthor urged.

"Do you think she should?" asked Achmed.

"I don't think I can reach it," Rhapsody replied, looking at the ground for some sort of natural elevation. Grunthor bent down on one knee and patted his thigh.

"Up ya go," he said, grinning at her.

Rhapsody returned his grin. She rested one hand on the enormous shoulder and climbed up onto the ledge he had made with his leg.

The top part of the stalactite was now in reach. She grabbed it where it met the rockwall and gave it a wrenching pull. The sword came loose with no more resistance than if it had been hanging by a thread. Rhapsody would have lost her balance and fallen on her back had Grunthor's massive hand not shot out and steadied her.

She climbed off his knee and sat down on it instead, holding the sword by the blade despite the flames that ran up and down it, so her companions could see it. It was made of something that resembled silver, though its sheen was different. Beneath the glowing light and the flickering flames the blade was slender and lightweight, with intricate runes adorning it.

The hilt was made of the same white-silver metal, beautifully fashioned, with a crosspiece that, along with the pommel at the base, was made to look like a star. Within the hilt was a setting from which a gem, or something like it, had been pried; it was empty now, the prongs bent outward uniformly. It rested in her hands, burning brightly, without harming her at all. Achmed removed a glove and held his own finger near it, withdrawing it quickly.

"Oi think it likes 'er, sir," Grunthor said.

"No accounting for taste," muttered Achmed. Rhapsody laughed. There was a look on his face that almost resembled a smile.

"Kinda makes you wish we'd slapped a few o' these pointy things down, don't it, just to see what's inside. Oh well, looks like you got yourself a fine sword, Yer Ladyship. Oi hope you can use it with some credit to your instructor."

"I'll practice next time the tunnel widens," Rhapsody promised, handing Grunthor back the sword he had loaned her. "Thanks for letting me borrow Lucy."

"It may be unwise to say so, but I believe we're coming to the end of the Root," Achmed said quietly. "What do you think, Grunthor?"

"Well, we're nearer the surface than we 'ave been since we started down this stinkin' 'ole," the giant replied, looking around. " 'Oo knows, we might be only a few miles away from the air."

"That's comforting," said Rhapsody. She was still staring at the sword. Fragments of distant images tugged at the outskirts of her consciousness, but nothing she understood. She blinked, and the fragments vanished.

Achmed bent down and picked up the black piece of the rock cylinder in which the sword had been encased.

"This might do for a scabbard until you find something else. I don't think leather or anything like it would work." He took a small broken piece of the rock and dropped it in the top of the makeshift scabbard, plugging the hole that she had made in the bottom.

Rhapsody resheathed the sword, plunging the tunnel into darklight again. "Did you want me to keep it out for light?"

"Not until we have a need of something brighter than we have," said Achmed. "Let's press on. I want to see where this trunk root goes."

Rhapsody and Grunthor brushed off the sediment from the stalactite. Once their eyes had adjusted, they followed him into the never-ending passageway yet again.

"We're very near the surface; I know it."

They had been crawling for an agonizingly long time, the fissures in the rock growing smaller and smaller, leaving them nothing more than a burrow tunnel sized for a large animal to squeeze through. Grunthor had gotten stuck several times, requiring him to be dug out.

Rhapsody felt her heart leap at Achmed's words. She had been fighting the feeling of suffocation for so long that she feared she might lose what slight grip she still had on reality.

She came to a halt behind Achmed, who had stopped in his tracks, rolled over onto his back, and pulled off one of his thin gloves. He ran his hand over the rockwall above and around him in the silence of an ancient memory.

The fabric of the Earth is worn thin there.

He craned his neck and turned back to Rhapsody. "Draw that thing; I need some light."

She complied, lying on her back as well and pulling the sword out of its makeshift scabbard. Carefully she handed it to him by the hilt.

Achmed held the sword above his head and up to the wall like a blazing torch, feeling his way, using his heels to move himself along. Suddenly he pulled the weapon back in front of his face. In the flickering firelight he examined the handle, his eyes glittering as he turned the weapon over in his hands.

"Gods," he whispered.

"What's the matter?" Rhapsody asked in alarm. She felt Grunthor squeeze forward and press his head up to above her knee, balancing on his palms, which he had positioned on the ground to either side of her thigh.

"Daystar Clarion," Achmed said, his voice a little louder. Grunthor made a sound of disbelief.

"What?" Rhapsody asked, panic beginning to set in. "What does that mean?"

"Are you sure, sir?" asked Grunthor.

"No question."

"What are you talking about?" Rhapsody shrieked. The sound of her own voice frightened her; it was past the edge of rationality.

Achmed tossed the sword onto the tunnel floor past him and clutched his head with his hands, muttering obscenities in Bolgish. Grunthor exhaled in resignation and moved away a little. He patted her leg awkwardly.

"It's a famous sword from the Island, Duchess," the Sergeant said despondently.

"From the Island? From Serendair? Are you sure?"

"Yes," Achmed snarled. "It's unmistakable, though I don't know why it's on fire. The gleam of the starlight is still there, as are the runes on the hilt. It's definitely Daystar Clarion."

"So that means—"

"We're back where we started. We may as well have never left."

Rhapsody tried to absorb the sense of despair that filled the tunnel. Unlike her Bolg companions, her heart leapt in joy. They were home. It hardly seemed to make sense, but, nonetheless, they had managed to take a wrong turn somewhere and end up where they had begun. The excitement that was welling up within her beat down the fury she felt at having spent so much time in agony, separated from her loved ones, only to wind up here again. She was home.

"We have to get out of here," she said. "Keep going."

Achmed sighed. "This is the end of the tunnel. The trunk root's tunnel is too small to go any further."

Rhapsody's heart froze. "How are we going to get out?"

"With the key, I guess."

Cold waves of panic washed over her. "We don't have the key, remember? It vanished when the door in Sagia closed."

"You know, you really are gullible." Achmed pulled his hand out from behind his back and gesticulated; in it appeared a black bone key, no longer glowing as it had.

Rhapsody's face went blank with shock.

"You bastard."

Grunthor's hands shot out and grabbed her by the shoulders, correctly anticipating her furious lunge at Achmed. She struggled violently, futilely, to break free of the giant's grip, clawing at the air between them.

"You bastard. You lying, scum-sucking, manipulative *bastard*!"

"Technically true, but there's no real need to insult my mother." Achmed ran his hand over the ceiling again, ignoring the heat that was beginning to radiate from the white-hot rage building in the tunnel behind him. His fingers sensed the rip in the fabric of the universe, a thin metaphysical opening, directly above him.

He inserted the key, or tried to. Nothing happened. A resounding *clink* echoed through the tunnel as he met with solid rock. He tried once more and still met with no success. In disgust he threw it to the ground, lay back, and cursed again.

Rhapsody's anger vanished. "What's wrong?"

"It doesn't work."

"Excuse me?"

"It doesn't work," he repeated softly. "I guess we weren't the only things remade by the fire."

His hand returned to the ceiling, and as he did a vision formed in his mind. It was related to the sense of direction he had had all along, a rapid soaring through the rock, through layers of earth and clay and dry grass and snow until his mind's sight burst into the sunlight. He gasped aloud and closed his eyes in pain.

Rhapsody reached for him. "Are you all right?"

Achmed shrugged her away. "Leave me alone. I'm fine, except that I'm back where I started and trapped at the only place we can get out. The gods must be laughing themselves sick right now."

" 'Ow far to the surface, sir?"

"I don't know. Several hundred feet."

Grunthor stretched his massive frame along the floor of the tunnel, sighing as his cramped muscles uncoiled. "Is that all, then? 'Ave out o' there, if you please, sir, and Oi'll start diggin'."

Rhapsody tucked her knees under her and twisted to look at him. "Grunthor, didn't you hear him? He said we're still several hundred feet underground."

"Then we better get to it, eh? You got somethin' better to

do, Yer Ladyship? 'Ere, move out o' there." Rhapsody stared at him as he pulled out a small retrenching tool, known unimpressively as Digga. She picked up her sword and did as he asked, followed a moment later by Achmed.

"Do you know what you're doing, Grunthor?" she asked nervously as she crouched in an indentation in the tunnel.

"Nope."

She blinked, then looked to Achmed, who shrugged. "All right," she said finally, "I suppose there's something to be said for winging it."

Grunthor lay down at the head of the tunnel. Taking the small shovel in both hands, he coiled and then thrust it into the wall with all his weight and might. There were sparks, but no visible impact on the stone. He repeated the motion, and a few chips of stone flew. Then again. And again.

Soon he slipped into a rhythm, smashing the tiny tool into the rock over and over. The iron began to bend, but he continued relentlessly. Rhapsody and Achmed set up in the tunnel behind him, passing back the debris from his digging, shoving it behind them to avoid blocking the passageway.

"Isn't this an excellent way to bring the ceiling down on our heads?" she asked the Dhracian as he handed her a good-sized rock. She had to raise her voice to be heard over the sound of Grunthor's strikes.

"Not really," he replied, turning away to gather more stone shards. "If you want him to accomplish that, I'll ask him to dig straight up."

"No, thanks," she replied hurriedly. Achmed had a look of quiet anger in his eyes; she wasn't sure if he was being sarcastic or sincere. The latter was far more frightening.

As the hours passed, several things became clear to the two companions who crawled behind Grunthor as he chiseled his way out of the earth. The first, and most obvious, was that there was no longer any way to stop him; the giant Bolg was unresponsive to their calls to slow down, to rest. It was as if he had taken on a life-and-death struggle with the Earth itself, refusing to give in, even if it would mean his demise.

That prospect seemed somehow unlikely. Another conclusion the two others had come to was that Grunthor was more

than a man possessed, he was becoming part of the Earth as
he worked.

He now aimed unerringly for the tiny fissures and faults in
the granite, sending large chips flying off the rockface. Each
crack, each weakness made itself apparent to him in a way
that filled the tunnel with the sound of ringing metal and
crumbling stone.

Rhapsody watched him work with a smile of wonder on
her face. *Grunthor, strong and reliable as the Earth itself*,
she had called him in his namesong, among other descriptions. She was seeing the truth in her words before her.

The last revelation they had mutually come to was that, for
better or worse, they would either succeed here or die now.
The tunnel behind them was filling with the rubble from
Grunthor's efforts, blocking any escape back down the way
they had come.

The understanding of this had been exchanged wordlessly.
Rhapsody had looked back at the wreckage to find Achmed
staring in the same direction. Their eyes had met, and both
had smiled with the look of shipmates clinging to the last
piece of a storm-ruined ship.

Grunthor stopped only once, long enough to turn Digga at
a different angle. Then he began shearing sheets of rock off
the wall before them, his trajectory changing slightly.

He was as a gemcutter, seeing intrinsically the perfect place
to strike the stone. The more he dug, the more refined became
whatever gift of sight into itself the Earth had given him. He
seemed to see not only the cracks in the wall but how those
cracks stretched into the surrounding bedrock, and where the
bedrock eroded away into the soil far above it. He now had
to break the debris he was passing back to Rhapsody and
Achmed into smaller pieces, as it was growing too large for
them to move.

His sense of conscious thought receded; he fell deeper and
deeper into himself. Whatever awareness of the world around
him that remained vanished, along with dreams of the Future
and the memory of the Past. There was only Grunthor and
the Earth, and then just the Earth. He could feel the element
as if it were his own body. It was all that remained of the

universe, and he was part of it, just the soil, and the clay, and the rock. And then there was no more rock.

Grunthor stumbled out into the air in shock. The wind around him stung his eyes and nose with its freshness, making him feel strangely morose. The blood that had been pumping in great volume from his racing heart slowed suddenly, leaving him faint. He staggered into the new darkness and pitched forward on his face. The earth that a moment ago was entwined around him with a lover's warmth bit painfully, coldly into his eyes.

Immediately behind him Rhapsody and Achmed emerged into the freezing night air. The Singer was on him a moment later, clutching his shoulders in alarm.

"Grunthor! Are you all right?"

He nodded numbly; it was only nominally true. The sensation of being ripped from the bosom of the Earth, expelled from the warmth into the icy wind, was worse than the separation of birth, worse than the pain of death. Grunthor raised himself up onto his hands and knees. His palms and fingertips stung in the snow.

Rhapsody watched him stand and exhaled in relief. Then, her mind assured of her giant friend's safety, she looked around her and stopped, thunderstruck.

She stepped all the way out of the hole in the ground as if she were stepping into paradise. The air around her was clean and bright in the light of a waxing moon; they were in a forest clearing at night, in winter. She laughed shortly, and turned around as Achmed emerged fully from the tunnel. Another giggle escaped her; then she was overcome with shuddering sobs and fell to the ground, at once crying, laughing, rolling in the snow.

Achmed helped Grunthor rise, then walked off to the edge of the clearing, taking in the sights around him. His compatriot stared blankly into the distance, the amber eyes clearing as he returned, piece by piece, to the realm of himself.

Their hostage, the woman they had brought along and kept

alive only because he had not been certain if she would be necessary to recall his old name, having been the vehicle herself of its change, gibbered like a lunatic, digging her hands into the snow beneath her.

Sour bile rose in the back of his throat. If they were back, if this was Serendair, then he had forfeited his birthright. Instead of the beating of a million hearts on the wind, the sound he had known all his life, the air was strangely quiet. The only rhythm came from the slowing pulse of Grunthor and the quickening one of Rhapsody. It was as if no one else in the world was still alive but the three of them.

Rhapsody began to gasp, still in the throes of her tearful laughter. The sound echoed through the forest. Achmed looked suddenly around them. Then he strode to the giddy Singer and grasped her by the arm, hauling her roughly to her feet with a jolt. The look of ecstasy vanished from her face, replaced by one of stunned amazement.

"If your orgasm is over, do you think you might be quiet?" he barked. Rhapsody stared at him, then pulled her arm free, her face hardening into a glare.

"Shut up," she said angrily. She walked away from him and looked up into the heavy canopy of forest branches where a sprinkling of stars glimmered down at her. Her rage melted away instantly at the sight, and she glanced above, looking for a break in the tree limbs where she might be able to see them without obstruction. She started to make for the clearing's edge when Achmed's firm grip closed on her shoulder.

"Hold up."

She twisted furiously away. "Don't touch me."

He ignored her command. "Don't go running off until we make some plans. We have no idea where we are, and who lives here."

Rhapsody pulled her arm free, but already she was beginning to see the wisdom of his statement. "I'm not going far," she said sullenly. "I need to see the stars. Don't try to stop me."

Achmed's eyes ran over her face. It was very different in the dark night air than it had been an eternity ago when they had entered the primeval forest of the Lirin. In addition to the strange physical perfection that had seemed to come over her in the fire, there was a commanding air, a charisma unlike anything he had ever seen or experienced. He looked back to Grunthor, who was walking back to the hole from which they had come.

"All right; be careful," he said, then turned and jogged to catch up with their companion.

Rhapsody waited until Achmed was out of the area, then cleared her mind as best as she could from the jangled cobwebs that the horror of the trip along the Root had woven into it. The stars gleamed above her, shining like the scattered pieces of the soul of the sky. She was vaguely aware of forbidden tears that welled up, only to freeze, unspilled, at the edges of her eyes.

Slowly, as if in a dream, she drew forth the ancient sword she had found within the Earth. Its flames billowed up the blade, licking the glowing steel but conducting no heat through the hilt; the weapon's handle remained cool and dry in her grip. Then, as if directed by a voice only her hands could hear, she held the weapon aloft.

Instead of her view of the stars diminishing in the light of the flames, they seemed to grow brighter, though perhaps it was the blurring of her unshed tears that made it seem so. Rhapsody opened her mouth but no song came forth. She swallowed, fighting down the pain that had risen from her depths. Then she tried again, singing the vespers of the evening star, the song of Seren, for which the Island had been named, the star of her birthplace.

The sweet notes rose slowly up into the sky, captured by the wind that was blowing tattered clouds around the stars.

Far off to the south, in the heart of different forest, another woman woke from sleep to a vibration hidden from her by the passing of many years. *The sword has returned*, she thought, but there was more than that on the wind. It was a longing she didn't understand but thought she had felt before, a sorrow that clung to the outer edge of remembrance. Like a shadow on the face on the moon it passed over her, then was gone. A frown touched the ancient Lirin face.

* * *

Grunthor looked back down the tunnel. He was slowly returning to himself, though the bond with the Earth remained, solid and reassuring, resonating up through his feet.

Every sinew was on fire, every muscle ached with a weariness he had never known before, not even as he and Achmed had made their desperate escape from the hand of the demon. He shook his limbs. He had one more task to perform before he could give in to sleep.

Grunthor closed his eyes and leaned on the edge of the earth-hewn tunnel. His hand ran along the entrance lovingly, sensing, as he had while digging, each strength, each flaw in the ground. He steeled his resolve and struck the ground with all his might at the precise points of greatest weakness. The exit from the Earth collapsed in a rising cloud of fine dirt and crystals of snow. The giant sank to his knees on the ground.

"No exit now." Achmed's voice came from behind him.

Grunthor raised his head at Achmed and grinned, an action that took the last of his remaining strength. "We knew that 'ad to be when we came," he said. "We knew we weren't goin' back."

Achmed chuckled sardonically. "Back? We never left."

Grunthor laid his head down on the snow-carpeted earth, feeling the comforting rhythm of its beating heart beneath his ear. "Not so, sir," he muttered. "This ain't where we came from. We're on the other side o' the world now." Exhaustion took him and he fell into a dreamless sleep that brought him a deeper knowledge of the land born of his bond with the Earth.

Achmed didn't need to confirm what the giant had said; a moment later he heard a deep sob from the edge of the glen. Rhapsody had seen the stars. She knew.

16

The breeze picked up just before dawn, blowing a shower of fine ice crystals across Rhapsody's face.

She woke with a start and sat up, shaking off her dream to find that she hadn't been dreaming. The air had gained a bitter edge in the night, and the sky was now perfectly clear, the stars beginning to fade but still glimmering, as if reluctant to leave. The dawn was coming, bringing with it a wash of violet light barely visible through the trees.

One of the crude camp blankets they had used for warmth, with minimal success, on the Root had been placed over her. She had been sleeping beside Grunthor, who was still unconscious. They were in a sheltered copse of thick brambles. A small fire crackled a few feet away, overhung with a spitted rabbit, roasting in the flames.

Achmed sat across from her under the bare branches of a forsythia bush, watching her silently. He nodded to her as she pulled off the blanket. Involuntarily she smiled at him in return. Then she turned to the sleeping mountain snoring beside her and checked him over. Grunthor seemed none the worse for his heroic undertaking.

"He's fine," Achmed said over the sounds of the fire.

"Good," she replied, and stood slowly. Her muscles had stiffened in the night, leaving her sore and feeling her age, whatever it now was. "Excuse me a moment."

She walked toward the east, grateful for the ability to sense direction again, and found a clearing from which she could view the coming dawn.

As she had the night before she drew the sword, marveling at the coolness of the hilt below the flames that rippled up the blade, burning more intensely than the campfire. Faint tones of purple and rose touched the fiery weapon, turning the flames the color of the sunrise. Rhapsody could feel the heat on her face as she stared at the sword, entranced by its beauty.

Daystar Clarion, Achmed had called it. It had a musical ring to it, like the sound of a trumpet call at dawn. She held the weapon aloft, closed her eyes, and began her morning song to the sunrise, the aubade with which the people of her mother's family had bade the stars farewell with the coming of day. She sang softly, not wanting to call attention to herself.

Her thoughts cleared; she could see the blazing weapon hovering before her in her mind's eye, could hear its song, and noted in amazement that it changed its pitch, its vibration, to match hers. A surge of power swept through her unlike anything she had ever felt and she panicked, dropping the sword in the snow.

Rhapsody opened her eyes and gasped, sweeping the weapon from the ground. The fire had not been extinguished by its brief contact with the cold, wet earth; in fact, it was glistening even more brilliantly when it came back into her hand. She shuddered and sheathed it quickly, then walked back to the camp, where Grunthor was just coming to consciousness.

Achmed had been watching Rhapsody carefully. She cast a small, lithe shadow, standing at the rise in the clearing, her eyes searching the sky in the east. When the first ray of light crested the horizon it caught in her hair and set it aglow, gleaming brighter than the sun itself would a moment later.

The shimmering gold of her hair crowned her face, rosy in the dawn, emerald eyes sparkling in the morning light. She was sending forth vibrations like nothing he had ever felt before, radiating the intense purity of the fire through which she had walked. It seemed clear that she had absorbed some of that element in the course of passing through it, tying it to herself in song. The compelling call of the flames burned in her now; she was mesmerizing, hypnotic to behold. All imperfections of the flesh now burned away, she had become beautiful beyond compare by human standards. The prospect fascinated him, as did all opportunities to tap or harness power.

After she had finished her devotions she came and bent down next to Grunthor, who was stretching in obvious pain and fighting off wakening. Rhapsody rested her hand lightly on his shoulder and sang softly into his ear.

Wake, Little Man,
Let the sun fill your eyes,
The day beckons you to come and play.

Eyes still closed, Grunthor broke into a vast, pasty grin at the sound of the Seren children's song. He rubbed his crusted eyelids with his thumb and forefinger, sitting up with a groan.

"Oi smell food," he said, wrapping an arm around Rhapsody.

"I hope you're referring to the coney," Rhapsody said, looking over at the fire.

"O' course."

"Well, one can never be certain with you, especially in your grasp. How are you feeling?"

"On top o' the world, miss," he said with a laugh. "Oi certainly likes it a lot better up 'ere than down in its bowels." His enormous eyes took her in. "Duchess, 'ave you done somethin' with your 'air?"

Rhapsody laughed. "Yes. I've smeared it with mudfilth and grime and left it unbrushed for time undetermined. Do you like it?" She jokingly pulled at the edges of a mass of tangles, a flirtatious look of humor on her face.

"Actually, yeah. Oi guess grime suits you, miss. Maybe more women ought to try it."

She gave him a playful shove and walked over to the fire, where the rabbit flesh was cooking. As she approached, the embers leapt into new flames, charring the outside of the meat.

"I think this is done, Achmed; if we don't get it out of there it will be ashes. Here, Grunthor, can I have the Friend-maker for a moment?" Grunthor drew forth the wicked-looking spike and handed it to her. Without a thought she reached into the fire and plucked the meat from the spit with it, then pulled her arm out of the flames and gave the spike to Achmed.

Grunthor whistled. "That was nice."

"What?"

"How does your arm feel?" Achmed asked her. She was looking at Grunthor in confusion.

"Fine. How is it supposed to feel?"

"Well, judging by what you just did, I'd say charred."

Rhapsody shrugged. "The fire's not that hot; I was only in there for a moment. Well, come on, are you going to share? Grunthor's hungry, and I have a vested interest in seeing him fed."

Achmed slid the rabbit off the skewer and tore it asunder, handing half to Grunthor, then dividing the remainder between himself and Rhapsody.

They ate in silence, the men watching in amazement as Rhapsody devoured her portion. She had rarely eaten meat in the time they had known her. Perhaps the endless slivers of the Root had given her an appetite for something a little more substantial, or just different.

When the meal was over and the gear repacked, Achmed threw snow onto the fire. Rhapsody stood and cast a glance around, then shouldered her pack.

"What's the plan?"

Achmed looked up at her from the ground and smirked. "You seem to have an idea of where you're going."

"Well, I certainly don't want to stay here. I have to find whatever settlement there is in these parts and make my way to the nearest port city."

"You're heading back, then?"

"Of course. I wouldn't have left if I'd had a choice." Her jaw set, but both of the men noticed the flicker of a muscle in her cheek. The journey on the Root had left them with no sense of how much time had passed. It seemed almost as if a century had gone by, though that was not possible given their apparent lack of aging.

The prospect that her friends and members of her family might have died in the intervening time had always been a real one for Rhapsody, but she had not allowed herself to think about it while crawling along the endless tunnel. To contemplate it would have been to become unable to go on.

"All right," said Achmed, "I suppose that's fair enough. Grunthor and I will see you as far as the nearest major town. Then you can determine if you need our help in getting to the port. We owe you that at least."

"Thank you," Rhapsody said sincerely. "I feel safer knowing you'll be traveling with me for a while."

"But if you're going to travel with us, you have to observe the same rules we do. Bolg generally have to abide by a higher standard of caution." She nodded in agreement. "Then let's start with language. We'll speak only in Bolgish. You're proficient in it now. Serendair had some major ports, and the language of men and the Lirin that lived there undoubtedly was used in sea trade, but no one except the Bolg speak Bolgish."

"Very well," Rhapsody said in the language. Grunthor laughed.

"You just told 'im he did a good job," the Sergeant said.

Rhapsody shrugged. "It takes a while to get the usage issues of a language, and to learn the idioms if it isn't your native tongue. Most languages are easy to pick up the basics in, if they have a consistent base, which most do. It's like a musical pattern."

"Well, if we're agreed on the language, let's talk strategy. We have no idea where we are, or what lives here. We are obviously not at the base of whatever Root Twin was connected to Sagia; we must have left the main trunk root when we started digging. That's probably a good thing, since we know Sagia was guarded. It's a fairly safe bet that there are people somewhere around here and we don't want to meet them, at least not yet. We want to know as much as possible about them and the area before they even know we're here."

"Agreed," Rhapsody said. Grunthor nodded as well.

"And when we do make contact, let's keep as much information as possible among ourselves until we agree to share any of it. It's safer for all of us that way." The Singer nodded quickly. "Oh, and one more thing: Rhapsody, I suggest you keep that sword of yours under wraps until and unless you really need to draw it, or at least try to be sure no one sees it who doesn't need to. It's a powerful artifact; I don't have any idea how it came to be here, on the other side of the world, wedged in the Earth. I doubt it's a good sign."

"All right. Can we go now? The sooner we get on the road the sooner we'll get to port." Rhapsody danced with impatience.

Achmed and Grunthor exchanged a look. They had nothing but time. It was a heady feeling.

After an hour of brisk marching Rhapsody began to shiver. When they left Easton it had been the height of summer, and she had been dressed for it. Now the rags that had once been her clothes were worn thin and full of holes. Even in prime condition they had not been adequate for wintry weather.

Rhapsody had hoped the pace of the walk would keep her warm, but the bitter wind that blew through the forest chilled her as the dampness of the tunnel never had. Despite its continuous state of sogginess, the heart of the Earth was warm for the most part. Here, above, outside its skin, the cold was debilitating.

" 'Ere, missy, 'old up," Grunthor commanded.

He unbound two of the wool blankets they had slept beneath the night before, prized possessions they had dragged with them along the Root. Then he drew Lucy, and with a quick slash ripped a hole in the center of each blanket. He tossed one to Achmed, who pulled his head through the hole and draped the blanket around him like a tunic. Then he gave the other to Rhapsody as he sheathed the sword.

Grunthor smirked as she put it on. The makeshift covering was much larger on her, hanging down over her wrists.

"I hope you don't have to fight anything like that," Achmed said in amusement.

"I hope so, too," she said. "Given the sword I'm using, I'd probably light myself on fire."

"Well, then, you wouldn't be cold no more, would ya?" said Grunthor as they took up the trek again.

The snow was deep in places, but Achmed seemed to be able to tell just by looking at the lay of the land what path to take to avoid the drifts. It was almost as if he was following a map laid out in his mind.

Grunthor also seemed to have a natural understanding of the land. He knew where the drifts were unstable, where creeks were hidden under the blanket of snow, and where, far from view, they would find walls of thorns or deadfalls that they needed to avoid. From time to time he would point these things out to Achmed, who would immediately adjust their course. For men who were in unfamiliar territory, Rhapsody noted, they seemed to know the land as if they had traveled it before.

Midafternoon the sky began to darken. The day seemed to have been too short, even for the dead of winter. Rhapsody had heard that in the southernmost parts of the Island of Serendair the sky darkened very early and that dawn came quite late during the winter. As a child, she had been told by her grandfather that out at sea, on the few small islands that lay even farther south, the nights were even longer. She began to wonder if in fact they were in some southern land, where the winter nights seemed endless but the summers were blessed with long days.

She was about to comment about this when Grunthor suggested a quick course change due east, which brought them to a narrow roadway that ran north-south. Its age was hinted at by the size of the great oaks and ashes that lined the edge of the road and formed an arch of branches high above, giving it the look of an ancient basilica. It was well maintained, with slight ruts on its rocky surface from wheels of wagons and carts. The snow along the route had been tramped into icy brown mush. They stared in silence at the road for several moments.

"Well, I guess we're not alone," Achmed said at last. Rhapsody felt a momentary glimmer of exhilaration at the realization that a road like this might lead to a city, and that even if it were not a port city, she could likely find her way to one from there. But her excitement was held in check by the understanding that the road also might belong to hostile people, or might be thousands of miles from the sea. Still, it was a start, and would eventually be the first step in finding passage back to Serendair.

After some hours Achmed stopped short.

"What's going on?" Rhapsody asked, only to be silenced by a curt hand motion.

He had heard a noise, a sound that was outside his range of hearing. Unbidden, a picture of the place they stood formed in his mind's eye; a moment later, the scene was moving. His vision was racing down the road at an incredible speed, accelerating. The trees became a blinding blur; the swiftest of the turns and bends in the roadway sent his balance spinning.

He had always been blessed with an unnatural sense of direction, which he had utilized on the Root to find the way through the Earth. The fact that Daystar Clarion, something from Serendair, had been waiting for them on the other side was a paradox he had yet to fathom. But now, since he had passed through the fire, seeking the right passage or path had become the dizzying experience that was now occurring. Grunthor's hand shot out and grasped him by the shoulder, steadying him.

"Ya all right, sir?" Achmed nodded, bending over and resting his hands on his knees, hanging his head down to regain his balance. "Was it like it was on the Root?" He nodded again.

"There's a herd of animals coming, and a thatched hut down a bit. The road itself forks after that, but then the vision faded. This new ability I seem to have been blessed with will probably prove useful, but it's going to take some getting used to."

The sound of braying could now be heard in the distance. The three travelers scanned the horizon. Grunthor pointed and led them to a well-hidden gully below a deep snowbank that provided good cover and a clear view. They crouched down behind an ice-covered log and waited.

Achmed shrugged the cwellan from his back into his hands and held it at the ready. As his vision had sped down the road he had seen a child traveling with the beasts; now he tried to lock his heartbeat on to the boy's. Like a wild shot, a misspent arrow, he sought in vain, finding nothing. The world darkened in his mind for a moment. He had lost his bond to blood, just as he had feared.

The thought of the lost gift struck him like a missile from his own weapon. His abilities to hit targets at ridiculous distances, to feel the changes in the rhythms of the world were still there, but no longer as intense as they had been.

Where once he had heard the deafening sound of millions of hearts beating, now all he heard was relative silence punctuated by the sound of Grunthor's ferocious, thudding pulse and the slow, steady rhythm of Rhapsody's. His unique ability, his lock on the heartbeat of his prey, had been the price of his freedom. The loss of it was worse than being blinded, being maimed. The implications of his deprivation began to take hold, making him weak with nausea.

The herd came into view on the roadway. Shaggy, thickly

built cattle with great arching horns, they plodded the ground with a sound not unlike thunder.

Driving them with a long, flexible stick was a young boy, in his teen years undoubtedly, wearing the simple clothes of any Seren farmboy. He was whistling an odd tune that Rhapsody had never heard before. By his side was a black-and-white herding dog, much like the ones her father had owned while she was growing up.

She turned to Grunthor and nodded at the young man, but the giant shook his head. She returned to watching the child and the animals until they were out of sight.

Once the roadway was clear again, she looked to Achmed. Even with his face partially hidden, she could still see what resembled devastation in his eyes.

"What's the matter?"

The Dhracian said nothing, but Grunthor seemed to know at once what was wrong. The two Firbolg had discussed the possible effects leaving the Island might have on Achmed.

When he was the Brother, his gift had been tied to the Island, as the first of his race born there. *Child of Blood*, the Dhracian sage had said, *Brother to all men, akin to none.* By the look on his face Grunthor knew what they had feared had come to pass. The bond was broken, the blood lore gone. Brother to none. He rested a hand on Achmed's shoulder. The assassin merely shrugged and, after checking the road again, climbed over the log and back onto the path.

They made their way down the road to the farm Achmed had seen in his vision, an animal barn and a simple hut with a small garden cleared from the forest.

The larger of the two buildings, where the cattle were housed, was little more than a roofed kraal, but the farmhouse was much better built, a design that utilized the least amount of material possible to the greatest effect.

Set above the doorway was a hex sign similar to the ones Rhapsody had seen her whole life. If the pattern of this one was the same as those in Serendair, to which it was strikingly similar, it was set to ward off fire and disease. She passed this information along to the others in a whisper. Again they hid and watched.

A man came out of the house as the boy approached it, and greetings were passed, but none of them understood the words. The two farmers carried on a pleasant exchange as they penned the animals, returning finally to the farmhouse. Once they had gone inside, the three companions relaxed.

"Did you recognize the language?" Rhapsody asked.

"No, but some of the words sounded familiar," Achmed said. Grunthor shrugged. "Did you?"

"No. I don't know how to explain it, but it seems to have the same cadence as our own tongue, only with slightly different rhythms and word patterns."

Grunthor chuckled. "Maybe all you 'umans talk alike," he said.

"Maybe. What do we do now? Shall we knock and ask for shelter?"

The two Firbolg laughed simultaneously.

"Oi don't think so, Yer Ladyship."

Rhapsody looked indignant. "And why is that such a stupid idea?"

Achmed sighed. "Well, in our experience, Firbolg don't generally get the best of receptions when we knock on doors. *You* might be welcomed. In fact, I'm sure you could get a bed for the night, but I doubt it would be empty, if you take my meaning." Rhapsody shuddered. Achmed chuckled. "Of course, it's really up to you. I don't know how much you're craving a warm night."

"Not that much. What do you suggest?"

"Well," Grunthor began, "to the north, there are a number o' farms like this one. To the south the road comes to some kind o' village. It ain't exactly large, but it's pretty well built. Beyond that, the road goes on for some way.

"But Oi'll tell ya what—about 'alf a mile into the woods, just to the southeast, there's a nice lit'le dell, with a tree fallen over it. If we was to throw a few more branches on that tree, we could build a fire, and 'ave a cozy lit'le den that no one could see."

Achmed and Rhapsody stared at him for a moment. They looked at one another, then stared at the Sergeant again.

"Precisely how do you know this?" Achmed asked.

"Oi don't know. Oi just do. Oi got a feelin'."

"I see. Well, let's see how right your feeling is."

17

Grunthor's "feeling" turned out to be as accurate as a map, or a skilled guide. He seemed to know the terrain and the structures that touched it naturally, as if the Earth had been whispering her secrets in his ear as he slept. He gave them a list of its traits: the land they were now in was a series of hills, made from limestone and clay, pushed together by great underground pressure from the south.

For miles around and as far as he could sense, the land was completely wooded. None of the people who lived on the land had cleared it; instead they kept small subsistence gardens to feed themselves, sometimes trading their wares with each other. Their livestock were forest cattle, and served as barter for the other things they needed; he surmised this by the frequent patterns of transport of the animals to market. There was a small town farther east with no defenses to speak of. It and all the farms had been laid out willy-nilly with no eye to fortification. And there was the Tree.

"The Tree?" Rhapsody asked, unable to contain her excitement. "The Root Twin?"

The Sergeant shrugged. "Oi guess. It's not far from 'ere, a lit'le to the south. It's like the great Lirin Tree we came through, only it roots are everywhere. It's like the 'ole forest is part of it."

Rhapsody drew her sword and held it over an armload of wet kindling she had gathered in the hope of drying it out. "My mother used to say the same thing about Sagia. She called it the Oak of Deep Roots—I had no idea how true a name that was. The Lirin believed Sagia was tied to every living thing. If this is the Root Twin of that tree, I'm sure it's the same."

"Oi don't know about that, but this tree 'ere certainly is tied to all the forest. It was like Oi was standin' in a wide plain, and Oi could see this thing at the edge o' my vision, even though Oi didn't know it was there, ya know?"

"Not really," Rhapsody admitted, setting the fire alight with her sword. The wood blazed up immediately, consuming the wet wood as though it were dry and seasoned.

"I do," Achmed said. "When you see the world vibrationally you can't see forever, but some things stand out like beacons, things of great power."

Grunthor sat up, a look of interest on his face. "You think Oi can see vibrational-like?"

"No, not from your description. It sounds more like an elemental bond. Like you're one with the Earth. Like you know what it knows."

"Yeah, like that."

Achmed tossed a handful of dried burrs onto the fire. "The Ancient Seren, the first people of the Island, were like that. They were each bound to one of the five elements: earth, air, water, fire, or ether, the element they believed the stars were made of."

"Lore," Rhapsody said. "Ancient powers, the elements' stories."

Achmed nodded. "Perhaps by passing along the Root, each of us came to be bound to one of the elements. That would explain my sudden ability with paths and trails. As I found the right path to take, I gradually began to gain the ability to see down those paths to their terminus. I have kept that ability, but now it works not just with roots, but with any path I set my mind to."

"Or perhaps being in the presence of so much power just brought forth natural ties you already had," said Rhapsody, standing more wood up to dry by the fire. "Both of these newfound abilities seem to be based in the earth, which is, after all, where the Firbolg come from, isn't it?"

"Yes."

"I think it's more likely that. I haven't been tied to anything."

Achmed chuckled. "Actually, Rhapsody, I think you've been affected the most of all of us." He stretched out his legs before the bristling fire to warm.

"How so?"

"Well, in case you'd forgotten, you've taken to warming Grunthor's chest at night with your body to stave off your nightmares. They're dreams of the Past and the Future, aren't they?"

"Some," she admitted, "but that's nothing new. I've always had dreams like that." She pulled her knees up to her chest and rested her chin on her arms to keep warm.

"They certainly seemed more intense on the Root, miss, than out in the field when we first got you," Grunthor said.

"Perhaps, but that may have had something to do with the place we were trapped within, and the company, no offense."

"That gift, that lore, if you will, is called prescience, the ability to see the Future, or the Past, and to absorb images and memories from objects or places. You've had it happen once or twice, if I'm not mistaken."

"Yes, but Namers have the ability to do that, too, in a way. We can attune ourselves to a specific note that picks up vibrations, at least occasionally anyway. It's a skill."

Achmed smiled. "Well, that may be, but it doesn't explain the fire."

Rhapsody looked up at him from her curled position. "What about the fire?"

"You haven't noticed the fire?"

She was beginning to grow irritated. "Of course I have; I built it, you numbskull."

Achmed rose and held out his hand to her. "Come here."

Reluctantly she gave him her hand and allowed him to pull her to her feet. He led her several yards away, then pointed at a large flat stone that jutted up at an angle from the snow.

"Take off your scabbard and leave it there," he said.

Rhapsody unbelted the thin stone sheath that held Daystar Clarion and placed it carefully down on the stone, then turned to face the Dhracian, trying to contain her annoyance. "There. So what?"

"Now have a look at the fire."

"I see it," she said. The wood had caught fairly well, and was burning quietly, snapping occasionally as a wet ember splintered in the heat.

"Good. Now walk slowly toward it."

Curiosity was beginning to replace her displeasure. She made her way carefully back to the camp, watching as the fire grew in intensity, rising as if to greet her. The emerald eyes opened in amazement; the flames leapt, roaring higher. Rhapsody backed away, and they settled down again.

"Gods," she whispered as her heart began to race, "what's happening?"

"It's you, miss," said Grunthor.

At his words she panicked, and the fire burst from its circle and crackled skyward, roaring to the height of the branches some ten feet above. The wood she had fed it a moment before dissolved into white hot ash.

The giant laughed aloud. "See? But if you don't stop it, you're gonna burn up my lit'le den 'ere, maybe set the whole forest ablaze."

Rhapsody glanced at him, and then at the bonfire that was flaming in front of her. "Calm down," she directed, but the fire only grew more intense, reflecting her excitement. She took a deep breath and concentrated as she did before attempting something with her music. The fire responded immediately, settling down into a merry blaze again.

Rhapsody closed her eyes and focused her mind on calm thoughts. A moment later she opened them to find that the campfire had diminished to a flicker no brighter than candlelight. She broke her concentration and set the fire free, watching it climb back to the level of a normal campfire, then tossed another pile of wood onto it to replace the fuel that had burned into dust a moment before. Rhapsody turned to Achmed again.

"Do you think this is a factor of the sword?" she asked.

"No, but it may be why the sword started to blaze when you touched it."

"The sword was glowing before I touched it. It almost blinded Grunthor."

Grunthor patted her back. "That might be because it was callin' you, miss; it recognized its own element in you."

Rhapsody was beginning to tremble, partly from the significance of what they were saying, partly because, in her heart, she knew they were right. "And you think the sword tied me to the element of fire?"

"I don't know," Achmed said. "I don't know enough about this sword. I still don't understand what it's doing here on this side of the world. And I don't know what causes it to burn as it does. When I knew of it, it glowed with starlight, but not flames. I'm fairly certain your tie to fire came when you sang us through the inferno at the Earth's core. I think that's when each of us changed. Certainly our bodies did."

"Maybe the fire just prepared us for the change," Rhapsody suggested. "Or maybe it was from eating the Root; I often wondered if it was a good idea to be ingesting something so powerful. It's possible that it changed us, made us susceptible to these elements. Perhaps you gained this—this path lore, or whatever it's called, when you sought out the way along the Root. And Grunthor tied himself to the element of earth when he threw himself into smashing through the rock, and me when I picked up the sword."

"No," Achmed said. "As soon as you stepped back through that fire you had changed. It was clearly visible, you had changed physically."

" 'E's right, miss," Grunthor agreed. "You sure look different than when we first met you."

The conversation was causing Rhapsody's head to pound. She looked around at the coming night, inhaling the sharp scent of the fire inside the shelter Grunthor had built. "Well, being unable to bathe for what seems like years, wallowing in the mudfilth, has not exactly made any of us more alluring. Trust me, you two don't want to be presented at court any time soon."

"But that's just it," said Achmed, growing impatient, "you *do* appear more alluring, more intense. You radiate something that captures the attention." He turned to the Bolg Sergeant. "Do you still have that signaling mirror?"

Grunthor sat up straight, pulled his pack over, and began rummaging through it. "O' course, sir, but don't kid yourself. 'Taint for signaling. Oi only carries it so Oi can do my 'air."

Rhapsody laughed. Achmed took the small piece of silvered metal from Grunthor and handed it to her.

"Here," he said. "Take a look."

Rhapsody took the jagged metal scrap carefully. As with almost everything Grunthor owned, it had been sharpened to an edge that could be utilized as a razor.

In the fading light of the sky she saw her image dimly

reflected in the mirror, smeared with dried mud, clumps of dirt in her hair, which had darkened slightly, as it generally did in winter. Her lips looked chapped and sore from the bitter wind they had been walking into. She handed the mirror back in disgust.

"Very funny."

Achmed left the glass in her hand. "I'm serious, Rhapsody; look again."

She sighed aloud, then gave it a final attempt. The detail available from the crude mirror in the dark was negligible. She could see a redness in her cheeks, but little else. Rhapsody shrugged, and gave the mirror to Grunthor. Then a smile of understanding came over her face.

"I've got it now," she said, humor returning to her voice. "No wonder you think I'm more attractive. I look like a Firbolg."

Achmed and Grunthor looked at one another, one thought passing unspoken between them. *She has no understanding— it's beyond her.* Grunthor shrugged.

Rhapsody scraped some of the dirt off her cheek with her fingernail. "I think I'll melt some snow and try to wash my face tomorrow, and at least get one or two layers of grime off."

"Get some sleep," Achmed said. A smile slipped across his uneven mouth as she settled into the back of the den for the night. She would have to learn the same way she had about the fire. She would have to see the results for herself. There was no question that, sooner or later, she would.

𝒯he following morning found the three of them lurking in a well-hidden copse of trees, spying on the villagers in the nearest settlement. The day was warm for winter, perhaps portending a thaw, and the farmers seemed out in force, exchanging conversation and sacks of grain and roots. Rhapsody remembered how temperate weather had brought the farmers of the villages around Easton into town more for human contact than commerce. This seemed to be the case here, as well.

To their surprise they found that many common words, notably *tree*, *grain*, and *marriage*, were the same as the words' counterparts in their own tongue. Rhapsody seemed to pick up the rhythms of the language, growing more excited the longer she listened. By the time noon had arrived, Achmed and Grunthor drew her away into a more distant thicket and conferred with her for fear she would give them away.

"It's a form of our language, I'm sure of it," she said when they were far enough away and certain there was no one nearby. "The main rhythms and cadences are exactly the same, and the word patterns are very similar."

"Well, Serenne is a ship-trade language. I guess it's not surprising that they speak it here as well. Or perhaps the farmers here are descended of settlers from a colony that had its roots on the same mainland as the people who colonized Serendair in the Second Age."

Rhapsody nodded. "Whatever the reason, we should look on this as a blessing. It means we may have a chance to understand the language eventually."

𝒯he chance came on their fifth day out of the Root. Grunthor and Achmed had gone about the task of procuring food, often by outright theft, and seeking information about the layout of the village and the surrounding settlements. While they were gone, Rhapsody had positioned herself in a hidden place on the outskirts of the town where she could hear the conversations of the travelers coming and going. On this particular morning, in addition to a few farmers consulting about their tactics in an upcoming haggle and a few women gossiping and cursing, she heard a song.

It was by no means the first song she had heard in this place; the farmers commonly sang as a method of herding cattle or to make long, mind-numbing tasks seem to go more quickly. But this day the singer was a child, a young boy who was walking home with a stick in his hand, dragging it so that it drew a line in the snow. It was a simple country folktune, sung slightly off-key, but the melody struck her immediately, because it was the same song that she and countless other children in Serendair had sung in their youth.

She listened intently, her stomach growing cold. The words of his song were about a milkweed seed from which the clouds had grown, just as they had been when she sang it as a child. The lyrics were in a strange but recognizable dialect, and as she listened to him sing, like breaking a code, she now understood the mutations and patterns of the language.

Keeping to the tree line, Rhapsody shadowed the boy until he met up with a woman on the road, then listened to their conversation, understanding almost all of it. Her palms grew moist with excitement. She listened as long as she dared, then ran back to camp to tell Achmed and Grunthor.

The next day the two Bolg joined her at the listening post, acquiring a little of the tongue under her tutelage. She translated three conversations before Achmed nodded in the direction of their shelter. They made for the camp with haste.

"So what do you want to do, Rhapsody?" Achmed asked. "I can see you're up to something."

"I think it's time I met one or two and tried to talk to them. There's no way to find a city unless we get directions. We can lurk in the woods forever, but if I don't find a port city, I'll never get home."

"The ramifications of a possible mistake are deadly for the two of us."

The winter wind blew the hair from her eyes, and Rhapsody nodded. "I know," she said. "So you two remain hidden, follow me, and I'll report back to you if I can."

"And 'ow are we supposed to get you out o' there if somethin' 'appens?" asked Grunthor. He was growing visibly upset.

"You aren't," she said simply. "It's a matter of survival now. I know this isn't the best way for the two of you, but we have different goals. You plan to stay in this place; I don't. I want to go home, and I'm willing to risk everything for that, but I don't expect you to. Either way, the two of you should be all right. If there are no problems, we will meet up and I can pass what I've learned on to you. And if something happens, well, break camp and get out of here. Drink a toast to me every now and then, if you care to."

"Naw," Grunthor muttered, "too risky. Can you speak that language, Duchess?"

"Not yet," Rhapsody admitted, "but I should be able to get by for a while until I pick it up."

"Just don't slip and talk to them in Bolgish," Achmed

warned. "You want to learn about them, not for them to learn about us."

"Right." She smiled at Grunthor, who was still shaking his head. "You realize it might take a while to get the information we need."

Achmed nodded. "Once we assess that you're safe we'll do some broader scouting, get some real information about this place."

"How will we get back together?" Rhapsody asked.

"We set a time and place. If you're not there, we go looking for you."

"And where would we meet? Here?"

"No. I don't want anyone trailing us back to the Root. Closed or not, I don't want anyone knowing where we came from. Agreed?"

Rhapsody rose in the darkness and came to Grunthor. She sat on his knee and wrapped an arm around his massive neck. "Agreed. We'll pick a place near the next village along the road, and, if you decide it's safe to leave, set up to meet in a few weeks. But don't go leaving me until I give you a sign that I think it's safe, too. I don't want to be counting on you to come and rescue me to find that you're twenty leagues away."

Grunthor sighed reluctantly. "All right, that makes sense. What's the sign?"

Rhapsody whistled a simple trill, and the two Bolg smiled. It was a tune she had hummed when they were able to walk upright in the tunnel, a sign that her mood had improved, if only for a while. "That's the all-clear. Now, if you hear this—" She whistled again, an unmistakable sound of distress, couched in the tones of a larksong. "—it means come if you can and help me."

"Got it, miss."

They laid their plans late into the night. Morning would find them on the road to the next village, a place the two Bolg had determined in their scouting to be larger and more central.

They blazed a marker that was clear and hard to miss, no matter what the weather brought. It would point to their meeting place. Then they settled in to wait. Rhapsody would approach a likely individual and try to make contact while the others watched for a few days or more. If they determined it was safe to leave her, they would meet in a little more than two months' time, under the full moon.

"You realize this is very dangerous," Achmed said as she bade them goodbye. Once she had identified her contact, she would not come back.

Rhapsody turned around and regarded them seriously. "I once was trapped with Michael, the Waste of Breath, for a fortnight, completely at his mercy and unable to escape. I survived that. This is nothing."

Achmed and Grunthor both nodded. They had known Michael. She was not exaggerating.

18

The thaw had progressed to a stage where the scents of the earth were hinted at in the air again. The snowpack was still deep, and showed little sign of abating, but the wind was a little warmer, and around the bases of the trees a thin ring of ground could be seen. Children were out more frequently, and the townsfolk of the villages along the road could be found making repairs to cottages and barns or gathering additional stores of wood in the forest before the return of bitter weather. The forays of the villagers into the woods made hiding more difficult.

The three travelers stood in a shaded vale, obscured by thick vines that would be impenetrable in summer when in leaf, not far from the village entrance on the road. Grunthor had pointed out a number of children who were alone at times, but Rhapsody was uncomfortable approaching any of them for fear she might bring punishment on them. Finally, toward noon, a group of farmers congregated on the road, awaiting something coming from the west. The three moved closer to observe.

As the sun crested the apex of the sky, one of the men looked down the road and pointed. The person approaching on a silver-gray horse was an older man, tall and barrel-chested, with a large, pocked nose and reddish-brown beard that was streaked with white. As he came into view more of the villagers assembled, some running forth to meet him, others hanging back to wait.

The man was dressed in woolen robes that had been dyed the color of earth, probably with butternut hulls, Rhapsody noted. He carried a knotted wooden staff, and each person who greeted him did so with reverence, most of them bowing their heads as his hand came to rest on them. His arrival had generated a mild excitement that was tempered with warmth and respect; obviously the farmers knew him well. He dismounted slowly, showing some of the signs of age.

It was clear from the brief benedictions he spoke and the blessings he conferred that this man was some sort of priest. His simple clothes and lack of adornment in Serendair would have indicated a cleric of lowly rank, but Rhapsody noted that the deference shown him was more on the level that would be offered to an abbot or another high-ranking clergyman. Her eyes sparkled excitedly.

"He's the one," she whispered to the two Firbolg.

"No," said Achmed. "Listen."

Rhapsody strained to hear the conversation between the wandering priest and one of the men. It was about snowfall levels and augury of forest animals in predicting the growing season; the signs seemed to indicate that winter would return soon, and with a vengeance in a month or so. They also exchanged a few words about a diseased cow and an injury that the farmer's son had sustained.

Then the priest laid his hand on the farmer's head, and spoke his blessing. Rhapsody's mouth dropped open. Unlike the language they had exchanged in their conversation, the same vernacular she had been hearing all along, the benediction was in the tongue of the Island of Serendair, word for word. It was spoken with a strange accent, with the staccato breaks of a man not using his mother tongue, but speaking clearly and correctly.

"Gods," she said, swallowing hard.

"I don't like it." Achmed's bony hand encircled her upper arm, drawing her back into the thicket.

Rhapsody turned to him in surprise. "Why not? Who would be better to talk to? He speaks our language."

"Perhaps, but I don't want him to know that we do, remember? Bolgish. We speak Bolgish. He's a priest. I don't trust priests."

Rhapsody slid her arm out of his grasp. "Perhaps you've just known bad ones; dark priests, evil gods. One of my favorite people in all the world was a priest, and I knew several kind ones in Easton."

Achmed looked at her in disgust. "First off, all priests have a plan, a design, sometimes their own, sometimes their god's. I am not serving any god's design. Second, how do you know this man *isn't* a dark priest?"

Rhapsody blinked in astonishment. "Look at him, for goodness' sake—he's blessing children."

The Dhracian's expression melted into amusement. "And you think evil priests walk the land randomly throwing curses around and smiting waifs with their walking sticks? Evil priests do the same things that regular priests do. It's the price that's different, and the tender it's paid in, that's all."

"Well, I think this is the best chance I'm going to get to meet someone who might be able to get me to port. I'm going to risk it."

This time Grunthor took her arm. "Don't take a chance, Duchess."

Rhapsody smiled at the giant. "He looks like a nature priest, Grunthor. What does your tie to the Earth say about him?"

Grunthor looked back through the thicket and closed his eyes. A moment later he opened them with a sigh.

" 'E's tied to it, too, in a big way. 'E cares for it, knows about it. You're right, miss, 'e's a nature priest o' some sort."

Rhapsody patted the enormous hand and slid free again. "I've got to chance it. If anything happens, and you can't intervene, I'll understand, and I won't give you away."

Achmed exhaled. "All right. I guess this is as good a time as any. Be careful."

Khaddyr spoke to the head farmer with as much patience as he could muster. "Now, Severhalt, I know poor old Fawn is getting on in years, but surely she is still performing her religious duties to your community." The look in his eye had a tinge of annoyance to it, but his voice was gentle.

The man's hands came to rest on his hips, and he looked down at the ground. "Services, yes, Father, but we're not gettin' the kind of support we need with the animals anymore. We need someone younger, someone who can handle the winter."

Khaddyr sighed. "Well, I certainly understand your frustration, my son, but these are difficult times. I know Fawn isn't as hale as she once was, but she still performs the rites for the congregation, doesn't she?"

"Yes, Father."

"And your village and homesteads are very near the Tree; there are certainly more than enough Filids there to aid you in times of great need if Fawn cannot. The Circle is in a bit of a bind, and unable to spare a new priest at this time. And I'm afraid Llauron granted Fawn the privilege of keeping her congregation here, in proximity to the Tree, as a boon for her years of faithful service. He wants to see her final years be holy ones. You can understand that, can't you?"

Severhalt sighed. "Yes, Father."

Khaddyr smiled. "Let's talk about this again in the spring. I have some acolytes who are spending the winter studying medicine with me. They should, by rights, go on to Gavin to train as foresters next, but perhaps we can reroute them here for a few months to assist with planting and the birthing of the calves. How does that sound?"

The faces of the men who had clustered around lit up, as did Severhalt's. "Wonderful, Father, thank ya. Can ya come in for a spot of supper—Father?" The delight on the farmer's face disappeared, replaced by concern. The Filidic priest was staring into the forest, his face drained of color.

A woman had walked out of the woods, appearing as if from nowhere. For a moment Khaddyr was not sure whether he was imagining her or not. She was caked in long-dried mud and clothed in filthy rags, but she was without question at the same time the most beautiful thing he had ever seen.

The hair beneath the clots of clay was as brilliant as the sun, and glistened in the filtered light of the gloomy afternoon. She was slight, but long of line, and walked with a grace that belied her unkempt state. Her eyes, even as far away as she was, were visibly green, deep and dark as a forest glade in the height of summer.

Then she smiled, and it was as if the clouds had cleared suddenly. The warmth in the look she gave him radiated into the coldest places of his heart. Khaddyr feared he might cry for want of her. He instantly began chanting under his breath, throwing himself into his rote religious rituals to ward off whatever spell she had cast on him.

As she approached his heart began to pound, and he leaned on the knotted staff to steady himself. She stopped at a respectful distance and opened her hands in a peaceful gesture of greeting. It was only then that Khaddyr noticed she was armed; a thin, rough-hewn scabbard, seemingly carved from rock, adorned her side. It seemed more decorative than utilitarian, and she was hardly threatening, even equipped as she was.

It took him more than a few moments to find his voice. The farmers with whom he had been conferring were staring, slack-jawed, as well.

"What are you?" he asked. His voice broke, and he cleared his throat in embarrassment. "What are you?" he repeated gruffly. The woman merely blinked. "Can you understand me?" She nodded. "But you don't speak?" She smiled uncomfortably, and shrugged.

Khaddyr's eyes ran up and down her exquisite, if unbathed, figure, causing his breath to come out more shallowly. Until this moment his vow of celibacy, a pledge not required of any Filid priest but him, had seemed an easy sacrifice in exchange for being sworn as Llauron's Tanist, the ancient leader's religious successor. Suddenly, the privilege of being named Invoker himself one day paled in importance. He cleared his throat again.

"I am Khaddyr. I am a Filidic priest and the Tanist of Llauron, the Invoker." *What is this?* he wondered. *A wood nymph? A tree spirit? A dryad?* He had heard the legends of forest creatures but did not believe them, at least until now.

The dazzling woman bowed her head. *Well*, Khaddyr noted, *she's respectful, whatever she is*. Something else that made her attractive.

"Well," he said finally, "I'm afraid you're a bit beyond my

powers of understanding. I have no idea who or what you are, so I suppose I shall have to take you to Llauron and let him have a look at you. Don't be afraid; the Invoker is a kind man. Will you come with me, please?"

The strange woman nodded, and smiled at him again. He held out his hand and allowed it to come to rest, trembling slightly, on her upper arm. Beneath the rotten fabric of the tattered shirt, her skin was deliciously warm. Khaddyr left his hand there long enough to turn her in the appropriate direction, then quickly dropped it down to his side. He turned west himself as well, only to find a wall of blank-faced townspeople blocking their path back to the Tree.

"I say," he growled, "do clear the path, please." The farmers didn't move. "Ahem," he repeated, glaring at them, "get out of the way."

The woman looked at him, then back at the people obstructing the path, and took a step toward them. Instantly they scattered like leaves, retreating to a safe distance, and continued to stare at her. Khaddyr didn't know how long they would stay at bay, so he took her arm again and led her to the silver-gray horse, lifting her easily off the ground and mounting behind her. He rode away just as the townspeople seemed to recover their wits. A shout went up as a few ran to their own stables, determined to follow him.

Khaddyr was becoming anxious. At each small village or large homestead along the roadway his unintentional caravan had taken on riders and followers on foot, creating crowds that blocked the forest road.

Farmers on the outskirts of the towns along the road had stopped and stared as they rode by. Villagers had swarmed to see the strange, beautiful creature riding before him in the saddle. There were scores of them now, perhaps hundreds, men and women alike, and a fair number of children, all clamoring to see or touch this filthy dryad with the dazzling green eyes.

He fully understood their unnatural desire to do so. Even the continual state of consternation he had been in since leaving Tref-Y-Gwartheg had done little to arrest the light-headedness he was experiencing.

Initially he had ascribed it to trepidation over what Llauron was going to say about the chaos of the surrounding villages and the arrival of some of their occupants on his lands near the Great Tree. After hours had passed, however, and the feeling had not abated, he began to realize that his anxiety about the Invoker's potential displeasure had little to do with it.

It was the giddy sensation of inhaling the surprisingly sweet scent of the filthy creature whose back occasionally pressed up against his chest, causing dark and lascivious thoughts unsuited in a celibate man of the cloth. At one point, to his great embarrassment, she had taken his hand and removed it gently from her breast, not bothering to turn around to face or glare at him. He felt humiliated; he had not even known it was there.

Finally he lost the half-dozen or so determined men who had continued to follow him after he had guided the horse past the crowds. Since the same problem was arising in each village, Khaddyr decided to abandon the road and take the narrower forest trails in the hope of avoiding further difficulty.

At the peak of the afternoon they arrived at their lodging for the night, the hostel of the forester Gavin. One of the same order as Khaddyr himself, Gavin kept the barracks on the eastern border of the deep forest, training the Filidic acolytes in the art of forestry. Upon completion of Gavin's training they served three years as pilgrimage guides, escorting the faithful from their villages to the Tree for holy-day celebrations and religious rites, though these days they had been more often utilized to defend the forest outposts against attack. *War is brewing*, Khaddyr thought. There was no doubt about it.

Khaddyr brought the horse to a stop outside the main cottage, reserved for the use of Gavin and other senior Filids. The Filidic religion was one of service to nature, and as such did not require its priests to remain celibate, except for him. Most of the Filids, men and women, were married, although acolytes usually refrained from matrimonial ties until their training and forestry service were finished. As a result, many of them lived within the villages that were their congregations or in the main settlements closer to the Tree. He expected the cottage would be empty, and it appeared that he was correct.

His enchanting passenger was looking around, taking in the sights with obvious interest. Khaddyr dismounted, finding some relief in his groin area, which had been experiencing considerable discomfort during their ride. He put his hands up to the strange creature to assist her down from the horse, but she shook her head and dismounted by herself. Swallowing his disappointment, he tied the horse to a slender sapling and nodded curtly to the hut. She followed him inside.

The hut had two low wooden beds topped with stuffed sackcloth mattresses filled with sweet hay and covered with blankets of undyed wool, as well as a sizable wooden table. None of the foodstuffs had been left in the cottage; they would have to eat what he could find out in the root cellar or share his meager dinner, which had gone uneaten in all the excitement. He turned to his odd guest and pointed outside.

"I'm going to see what I can find for us to eat," he said in a slow, exaggerated tone. "Will you be all right in here alone for a few moments?"

The woman smiled and nodded. Khaddyr felt the unwelcome rush of heat and blood again. He took hold of the cord that served as the door's handle.

"Good. Now, make yourself comfortable. I'll be back in a bit." He pointed to one of the two beds and left the hut hurriedly.

When he returned a few moments later, an armload of roots and winter apples in hand, the woman was sound asleep in the bed he had indicated, smiling as if in paradise.

Rhapsody woke to the warmth of a cracking fire burning peacefully in the small fireplace. She sat up with a start, disoriented in the dark, to see the man who had introduced himself as Khaddyr watching her intently from across the room. Night had fallen while she slept. She had no idea how much time had passed since she had slipped, gratefully, into the first bed she had occupied since the night before the world had been turned upside down an eternity ago in Easton.

The man smiled at her doubtfully. She returned the smile, hoping to assuage whatever concern was plaguing him. He

seemed intent on treating her kindly. By now Achmed and
Grunthor had undoubtedly caught up with them and were sta-
tioned somewhere nearby, or so she hoped. She felt around
beneath the blanket and sighed in relief. The sword was still
there where she had hidden it.

"Are you hungry?" Khaddyr asked. He had laid a plain
meal on the table, one bowl of which had already been eaten.
She nodded and rose from the bed, taking the chair opposite
him.

The hut itself was simple in its construction, better built
than the ones she had seen on the Island, with stone walls
and a thatched roof. As they had approached she had seen
something resembling barracks off in the near distance, long,
thatched buildings with wattle-and-daub walls cased with
skins and woven mats of forest brush. The buildings, for all
their simplicity, seemed surprisingly solid, and reflected careful thought in their design. The Filids, whoever they were,
must have some architectural or engineering knowledge not
often seen in farming communities.

Khaddyr watched her as she ate; it made her self-conscious.
When she had finished she pointed to the empty bowl and
gestured her thanks. The man's forehead wrinkled as he
watched her in the firelight.

"What sort of creature are you?" he asked her again, as he
had when she first emerged from the forest. Rhapsody had
no idea what to say, so she shrugged. She tried to formulate
a way to explain that she was a person—perhaps Khaddyr
had never seen someone of Lirin extraction—but was blocked
in her attempt by a sudden sound of shouting and commotion.
The crowd had finally caught up with them.

Khaddyr rose from his seat in consternation, and went to
one of the two cottage windows. Even in the light of the
waning moon Rhapsody could see his face grow pale. The
hunting party of determined villagers must have grown larger
in the course of following them.

The priest hurried to the coat pegs near the door. On each
of them hung a soft gray forester's cape with a hood and
caplet. On a man the size of an average villager it would hang
to the top of the thigh. Khaddyr draped it around Rhapsody
and exhaled in relief when he saw that it only brushed the

backs of her calves. He pulled the hood up over her filthy hair.

"Come with me," he said, urgency in his voice. "We can cut through the woods here to Llauron's." He seized his own staff and cape and held open the back door, which led out to the root cellar. Rhapsody followed him out into the darkness, running from the throng like a fox before the approaching hounds.

19

𝔍t took three days' travel to reach the place in the deep forest to which Khaddyr had been referring. The towns along the main roadway, though seeming to be in a wooded land when she had first seen them, were out in the open compared with the place through which they now traveled.

The forest to the west was virgin, primeval, and thick with stands of dark evergreens that blotted out the light and returned some of the green of the warmer months to the otherwise unbroken blanket of snow.

Their pace was slower than hers had been with the two Bolg. Khaddyr was a much older and fatter man than either Achmed or Grunthor, and so had to rest more frequently, but he had an innate knowledge of the terrain. The forest seemed to welcome him, easing his passage through the heavy underbrush.

More than once Rhapsody had looked off into the distance and caught a glimpse of a dark cape or a large shadow, and sighed in relief. Achmed and Grunthor had caught up and were making that known to her. Though she and Khaddyr seemed to have lost the mass of townspeople for the moment, the presence of the Bolg served to reassure her even as she followed the priest through the deepening woods.

Each morning Rhapsody would wait until Khaddyr had disappeared into a copse of trees to attend to the call of nature before finding a spot from which to sing her dawn devotions. Out of deference to Achmed's concern about revealing their history, she sang wordlessly, maintaining only a melody line

without the Ancient Lirin verse. On more than one occasion
she had turned around after finishing to find the Filidic priest
staring at her as if she were a mythical beast.

At night Khaddyr built a small fire, from which she maintained a respectable distance. Given the way fire often reacted
to her, she thought it wise to keep away from it. She could
see that her withdrawal from the proximity of the fire caused
Khaddyr to assume she had an aversion to it and to make
note of this fact. He had ceased trying to question her about
what she was, and instead spoke to her only when giving
directions.

Finally on the third day they came to a place in the deep
woods that appeared to be a large clearing. Dispersed
throughout the area were many cottages and huts, some of
stone and others of earth with turf roofs, or the wattle-and-
daub walls that she had seen in the farming communities. In
addition they passed a few very large buildings made of
wood, with heavy doors and conical thatched roofs. Smoke
rose placidly from the hearths of the buildings.

Above the doors of the huts and cottages were hex signs,
similar to the one she had seen back on the road but in far
more complex and colorful patterns. Most of the dwellings
had sizable gardens or kraals, and had been whitewashed or
faced with stone as ornamentation.

The people who milled about did not dress as the farmers
and villagers had, but rather were attired in robes of wool
similar to Khaddyr's, some dyed with indigo or goldenrod or
engilder leaves to bring forth hues of blue or yellow or green.
Others, as Khaddyr's, had been soaked in butternut shells or
heather, producing tones more earthy, shades of dismal brown
and somber gray. Often these robes had cowls like Khaddyr's,
which seemed to signify greater rank among the people of
this forest community.

In addition to the robed clergy were armed men, carrying
bows, spears, axes, and other weaponry of foresters and
scouts, and attired in leather armor. These men were often
haggard or injured, showing the signs of many months of
travel or battle, and their appearance made Rhapsody wonder
what might have attacked them in this seemingly peaceful
place.

The prospect of war made her stomach twist in anxiety. War had been in the wind back in Easton, and it meant the restriction of travel. If this place was at war or preparing for one, it would complicate her getting to a port and passage home. After coming this far, she was unwilling to face that prospect.

In the late afternoon she heard it, a song deeper and richer than any but one she had ever heard. It was the song of the Tree, Sagia's Root Twin. They must be coming closer to it.

As the sun was beginning to set they came to a vast meadow in the forest and she saw it, its trunk whiter than the snow, with great ivory branches that spread like immense fingers to the darkening sky.

Rhapsody stopped and stared in wonder. The Tree was easily fifty feet across at the base, and the first major limb was more than a hundred feet from the ground, leading up to more branches that formed a expansive canopy she wished she could see in leaf. The last rays of the winter sun glimmered on its bark, giving it an almost ethereal glow.

Around its base, set back a hundred yards from where its great roots pierced the earth, had been planted a ring of trees, one of each species Rhapsody had ever heard of, and many she had not. It resonated a song of ancient power, different from Sagia's but with the same depth and magic. Rhapsody's eyes glistened with tears that did not fall.

Khaddyr was watching her face carefully. He stared at her silently for a long time, then seemed to shake his head as if waking. Finally he spoke to her.

"You respect the Tree?" he asked. Rhapsody nodded, still not taking her eyes off it. Khaddyr smiled. "Well, then, you will be welcome here. Llauron will be very interested to meet you. Come; we are almost to his house." He led her through the meadow, past the outside of the tree ring and beneath the outstretched branches that blocked the sky above them.

On the other side of the meadow stood a great copse of ancient trees, vastly tall and broad, though no match for the Great White Tree in height or breadth. Built throughout and around this grove of trees was a large, beautiful house, simple yet breathtaking in design.

It was set at many odd angles, with sections placed high

in the trees or on stilts with windows that faced the Tree. Intricate woodwork dressed the exterior, in particular the large section with a tower that reached high above the forest canopy.

A great stone wall, lined with sleeping gardens, led up to a section on the side of the smaller wing, where a heavy wooden door was guarded by soldiers similar to the ones she had seen before. She turned to Khaddyr and pointed at the house questioningly. The hawk-nosed man smiled.

"This is Llauron's keep, where the Invoker lives. Not much of a rectory for someone of his religious and family stature, but he's comfortable here. Come; I will bring you to him." He led her through the winding gardens and up to the door, nodding to the staring guards, who moved aside as they passed.

From within the branches of their hiding place Achmed and Grunthor watched as the man knocked and a woman opened the door. After a moment's discussion with the priest she stepped aside and he led Rhapsody into the strange, angular house. The servant shut the door behind them.

Achmed closed his eyes and leaned back against the trunk of a white alder. The taste of the wind was thin and sweet, the silence deafening. The rhythm of Rhapsody's heart was becoming softer the farther into the house she went, leaving only Grunthor's and his own resonating in his skin. *This must be what peace feels like*, he thought. He was not sure he liked it.

Then, at the edge of his consciousness, he felt another rhythm, and then another, pulsing in the distance, unfamiliar, but not unknown. There were other heartbeats that he could still feel on the wind, but they were very far away. A vague thudding here, a whispering flicker there; somewhere out in the wide world there were still a few hearts whose rhythms registered on his skin, in his blood. Perhaps he was not as severed from his gift as he had believed. He had no idea how this could be, and whether is was a blessing or a curse. He shook off the thought and concentrated on Rhapsody. The other heartbeats fell silent.

They waited longer than planned, wanting to be assured

that whoever lived in the strange, angular house would not harm her. Achmed had tracked her heartbeat from the moment she had left; it had been clear and strong in his ears until she entered the woodland keep with the nature priest. Though it was muted, he could still feel it distantly, could still read what it was telling him.

She was nervous, anxious even. After a few moments he felt her initial unease flare into something approaching panic, but it did not seem in response to an attack. Had it been, they would have found a way to intervene, but such action did not prove necessary.

" 'Ow long ya want to wait, sir?"

"One more night. Then we'll go."

*H*er nightmares must have been especially intense. During the night he could feel her pulse begin to quicken from its slow, steady sleeping rhythm, the pattern he had learned over the vast amount of time they had spent in the Root. He was used to the crescendo that her heartbeat reached in the throes of her bad dreams, but this was worse by half again.

When dawn came he felt her leave the keep and walk to the base of the Great White Tree, where she sang her morning devotions. The wind carried the gentle vibrations across the wide field to where they washed over him, soothing his skin. The song was as it always was, though there was a melancholy air he had not heard since the Root, a deep sadness in the tone he could not fathom. But she was not hurt, or in danger. She was all right.

A moment later, he heard the whistled song, the all-clear sign. The tune was shaky, indicating that she was still upset from whatever had distressed her before, but confident enough to let them go. Achmed smiled.

He opened his mouth and let the frosty air whistle in and through it. There was no hideous taste of the demon on the wind, no odious smell; it was one of the first things he had looked for. In the silence all around him was the feel of absolution, of a new beginning, free from the old life and its horrors. They had made it. They had successfully managed to escape. The new challenge of survival paled in the face of what they had left behind.

The sting of the snow on his raggedly soled feet roused him from his musings. He caught Grunthor's eye, now almost open as he woke.

"We'd better find some clothing, then food. Can't eat the Root anymore; need to reprovision. After that, we'll scout around, see where the wind takes us. Maybe we can find Rhapsody her path to the sea."

20

$\mathcal{B}$y nightfall the two Firbolg had found their way out of the thickest part of the forest and were heading west to the sea. Achmed could taste the salt in the air, though it was still many miles away, like distant tears on the wind.

They found an abandoned barn not far from a small farming settlement and made camp there. Despite being a roof over their heads, the ramshackle shelter provided little comfort, as they decided they couldn't risk a fire. The floor was strewn with hay, packed and moldy, lying undisturbed for years, and they burrowed beneath it, seeking warmth and finding very little.

Grunthor had gathered fallen branches of cherry and black fritten wood and spent the better part of the evening sharpening them into arrows to replace the ones he had spent in the fields so long ago and during his time within the Earth. More than once Achmed caught him humming one of the melodies Rhapsody sang to herself while they traveled, gruesomely off-key.

The next morning they set off to scout the village and outlying farmhouses, returning with a handful of eggs and winter roots from a variety of storage sheds, several horse blankets, and some clothes that looked as if they would fit Achmed. They had ranged far and wide, trying to steal only a little in each place to avoid being noticed.

"My, you look lovely, sir," Grunthor joked, watching Achmed's face as he discovered that the tunic he had stolen was actually a dress. He slashed a hole in one of the horse blankets to fashion himself a rough vest. "But you won't be givin' 'Er

Ladyship any competition with the young bucks any time soon, Oi'm afraid."

Achmed ripped the bottom of the skirt off, shortening the garment to the length of a long shirt.

"Unless I miss my guess, I doubt the collective charm of every occupant of Madame Parri's Pleasure Palace could compete with her now," he said, donning his new clothes. "Whatever that fire did to her has had a powerful effect; it may prove a valuable tool one day. I was initially concerned that the priest would attempt to compromise her, but he was too intimidated to try anything."

"Ah, yes, Ol' Madame Parri's. Oi ain't thought about them in years. Wonder 'ow ol' Brenda and Suzie are doin'."

Achmed chuckled. "Grunthor, I'm sure they miss you still. I doubt anyone they've come across since has measured up." He tossed the giant a winter apple. "Come on. Let's have a look around."

The makeshift clothes, added to the tatters of their original garments, provided some protection against the frosty air. They had also stolen a few discarded reins and harnesses and had used the leather to patch their boots the best they could, though in this effort they were less successful. The snow still crept into their footgear, making their toes sting and cramp with cold.

A few miles to the west the settlement grew denser and the forest thinner until it could almost be seen as a village. Achmed and Grunthor found thickets to hide in, heavy with blackthorn brambles and scrub, and watched the comings and goings of the villagers, listening as best they could from far away.

Though not as proficient with the language as Rhapsody had been, they could understand enough of it to catch the occasional word or phrase. One word, *Avonderre*, seemed to be repeated often, usually with some sort of southwesterly directional reference. The Bolg decided that this must be the name of the neighboring area, though whether it was a village, a city, a province, or a nation all its own was unclear.

They had circled the whole of the settlement by mid-afternoon, and were preparing to move on, when a distant vibration on the forest road caught Achmed's attention.

From his hiding place in a copse of silver-barked trees not found on Serendair he closed his eyes and concentrated on the road out of the village. It was no more than a beaten path, scarred with the ruts of wagons and hoofprints, muddy from the mild weather and melting snow. Rhapsody's voice spoke softly in his memory.

Unerring tracker. The pathfinder.

He swallowed and held on to the nearest tree trunk, then loosed his mind. His vision of the road surged, then sped forward, following the sloppy path into the distance at a sickening rate.

Racing over the lightly forested path, his mind's eye hurried along until it came upon the sight of horsemen, armed and drawn, galloping toward the village. There were a dozen or so of them, clad in greenish-black leather and riding roans, red-brown forest horses.

With a lurch the vision came to an end, but not before Achmed had a chance to make note of two things. First: even more noticeable than the strange armor and horses were the shape and coloring of the riders' faces. High cheekbones below large, wide eyes, tapering to chins as severe as their blank expressions. Tones of skin and hair the color of the earth and its flora. Lirin.

Second: they were carrying torches.

Achmed uttered a Bolgish curse and turned to Grunthor.

"Lirin soldiers, armed with fire, heading this way."

Grunthor stared at him blankly.

"Lirin? With fire? Are you sure, sir?"

Achmed nodded as he extricated himself from the underbrush, understanding the Sergeant's bewilderment. Lirin had a natural aversion to fire, particularly the Liringlas, owing to the hazard it posed to their lands. With the exception of Lirinpan, the strain of the race that were city dwellers, Lirin tended to reside in places of forest brush and open field, where wildfires could easily destroy their settlements. Seeing a troop of them wielding fire as a weapon was a disturbing contradiction. But there was no time to ponder it now.

"Come on," he whispered.

Hurriedly they moved through the bracken, taking care to

remain hidden, in an arc to the southwest. When they came to a place where the woods were thick with evergreen growth, Achmed scaled a tall pine and hid within its branches, ten or so feet off the ground. Grunthor settled into the underbrush. When Achmed looked down again, he could barely see him.

They had just enough time to settle out of sight when the troop came riding into view. Screams rent the air as farmers and townspeople panicked, scurrying out of the road, dragging children with them. They scattered like a flock of birds before the oncoming mayhem.

Achmed watched, sickened, as the first few soldiers rode past the villagers still within reach, leaving them to their companions in the ranks behind, who clubbed them where they stood. The men in the forefront rode instead to the nearest buildings and torched them, setting the village ablaze within moments.

A few of the farmers fought back with whatever tools or weapons they had been able to lay hands on, but they had no chance against the horsemen. One of the men-at-arms bringing up the rear rode mercilessly down on a villager, the impact sending the child fleeing with him flying onto the roadside near their hiding place where she lay, limp and not moving.

Achmed was staring as the soldier stopped and turned, then started for the child when an arrow whistled near his ear, piercing the Lirin's neck. The horse rode out from under the man as he fell, lifeless, to the ground.

He turned to Grunthor to find the giant nocking two more arrows, the Sergeant's face as grim and resolute as he had ever seen it. Grunthor drew back and let fly again, and another soldier fell into the burning thatch of the roof he was igniting.

A birdcall went up from one of the remaining men-at-arms, and the horsemen stopped in the road. Words were shouted in the calm voice of command, and the soldiers turned and left the village, riding over the body of one of their fallen comrades as they went, without stopping.

Silence fell over the tiny hamlet. Then, as if something shattered, cries and moans rent the air. A sobbing woman ran to the child in the brush and gathered her up, laughing and crying in relief as the little girl opened her eyes, too distracted to notice the face of the Firbolg giant a few inches from her.

When she was gone, Grunthor lowered his bow and leaned forward to get a better look through the thick black smoke that was now beginning to waft their way. He shook his head in amazement.

"What in the name of all that is good was that?" he asked, incredulous.

Achmed shrugged. "Your guess is as good as mine. Maybe all those stories they told us as children about people on the other side of the world walking upside down on their heads were true. If you had told me when we got up this morning that we would witness a Lirindarc slaying party, armed with fire, torching a village in a forest, and leaving behind the bodies of their fallen in the process, I would have told you your brain had curdled." Grunthor nodded in agreement.

They climbed down amid the acrid stench of burning thatch and the sounds of wailing from the village behind them, then carefully made their way through the patchy woods to the west. The smoke billowed over their heads in the wind, covering their exit as they left the scene of the carnage behind.

By the end of the eighth day of their scouting mission, they were all but certain their brains had not only curdled, but had fermented. In place after place, senseless and inexplicable violence erupted.

Sometimes the participants were Lirin, but more often it was humans savaging their fellow humans. The Firbolg were beginning to wonder if they had lost their place as monsters in common belief, to be replaced by those who used to relegate them there.

Equally inexplicable was the aftermath of some of the attacks. In one town on the border of the forest and the open lands beyond it they observed in amazement the pillagers of the town return to their barracks just around the bend of the road, half a league away. A few of the soldiers from the same quarters even came to help tend to the wounded.

"What is goin' on in this place?" Grunthor asked indignantly as they watched the cleanup from their hiding place behind the granary. "Don't make no sense a'tall."

Achmed shook his head but remained silent. He could handle war as long as he could tell what the sides, the motives, and the players would be. Here he knew none of these things.

21

As they came closer to the sea, the thinning snowpack disappeared altogether, leaving brown grass and bare trees in the grip of an icy wind that showed less mercy than the soldiers did. Achmed and Grunthor kept a wider barrier between themselves and any sign of civilization in order to be able to sleep near a sheltered campfire without fear of being spotted. They only approached empty houses or barns when they were acquiring supplies.

They were in Avonderre now. They had overheard enough conversation to deduce that it was the name of the province, and that it bordered the sea. The scent of salt in the air was now strong enough for Grunthor to detect it, and they followed their noses, moving closer to the ocean day by day, week after week, remaining always at the outskirts, avoiding any contact with the inhabitants of this new land.

The settlements and towns had become larger and closer as they approached the port city, eventually beginning to blend in with the wide expanse of buildings that lined the horizon. Where huts and kraals had once housed the populace, now homes fashioned of mud- or fire-formed brick appeared, with doors carved from heavy wood and roofs of clay or sealed thatch.

The roadways widened into roads, and eventually streets, lined with ancient stone and cobbled. Grunthor had whistled at the expense that must have been incurred; back home cobblestone streets were only seen in the wealthiest sections of the largest cities, and then only in front of public buildings and temples. Here it appeared that each street of this sprawling city, at least three times the size of Easton, was paved.

Avonderre's wharf was even bigger, stretching north-south

along the coastline for as far as the eye could see. Fishing
villages made up the extreme edges. Closer in were the docks,
designed and built from gleaming stone and wood, with slips
and moorings of shining metal. And in the dead center was
the sheltered harbor, a colossal port with more ships than
Achmed or Grunthor could count.

"Would ya just look at that?" the Sergeant murmured as
they watched from a distance the off-loading of a hundred
merchant vessels at a time, barrels and crates and horses and
wagons working with the precision of an anthill.

"No," Achmed said, tapping his friend on the shoulder and
pointing skyward. "*You* look at *that*."

Grunthor glanced up from the pile of oilcloth and lump
coal he had been pilfering from behind a blacksmith's shop,
the most distant building on the city's outer fringe. The sun
was going down, and was taking the last of the unbroken sky
with it, leaving in its place ominous storm clouds racing to
the horizon, swollen with rain and charged with lightning. A
moment later the wind picked up in the face of the oncoming
storm.

"Blimey. Better get out o' 'ere, then."

Achmed had already scrambled over the low wall behind
the smithy, heading north away from the wharf.

"There're some rocky outcroppings at the outskirts of town.
That'll be a decent place to hide and find shelter at the same
time. Come on. It's going to be a rough one when it hits."

𝕿hey made their way beneath an angry sky, buffeted by
the wind, to the guardian rocks that loomed forbiddingly up
from the shore. The waves crashed and roared back into the
wind, sending salt spray into the faces of the two men.

Darkness blanketed the sky all the way to the horizon, with
rare breaks in the clouds allowing the light of the full moon
a moment's glory, then squelching it back again.

"Shall we find ourselves a cave, sir?"

Achmed squinted in the dark, but saw very little except the
rocky crags and the roaring waves. Firbolg eyes were suited
to the darkness within the Earth, not above the ground.

"Perhaps on the other side of that cliff," he suggested.

Grunthor shook his head, spattering salt water and sweat.

"Naw. Nothin' there—solid rockwalls for a few miles. But down near the shore is an enormous shelter o' some kind."

"You can feel all this through the Earth?"

"Yeah."

Slowly Achmed and Grunthor climbed down until they finally reached the sand of the shoreline. Then both men broke into a run. Drops of rain had started to fall intermittently, stinging their eyes and skin like icy needles from the sky. The beach wound around a large bluff to the north, following an inlet that opened into a small lagoon; they had seen it from afar when they were still up on the precipice. The guardian rocks stretched up endlessly into the black wind above them, like mountain crags.

As they came around the cliff they saw a monstrous edifice surrounded distantly by four other buildings. In the dark and the whipping wind it was almost impossible to see its outline.

"It's a temple," Achmed shouted to Grunthor. "What kind of idiot builds a temple on *sand*?"

The Sergeant barely heard him above the noise of the wind. "And so close to the water's edge. Strange, eh? Want to look into it?" His heavy hair, blackened with spray from the pounding surf, hung wet in his eyes.

Achmed hesitated. Temples meant priests; he hated priests. But the towering building alone was dark. There were lights burning in the four more distant ones, undoubtedly the rectories where the clergy lived or places where supplies were stored. They would run less of a risk of being spotted in the basilica itself.

"All right," he muttered, pulling the ragged edges of his hood closer to his face. "But any priest I run into better be able to swim."

Until they came around the northern side of the rocky crags, neither of the men could see anything more than a vast expanse of stone towering in the air above the shoreline. Once on the other side, however, they stopped in their tracks involuntarily, oblivious of the rain.

The temple rose out of the darkness of the crashing wind and surf, its oddly angled spire pointing away from the sea. The base of the structure was formed from enormous blocks of quarried stone, gleaming gray and black in the shadows of the moon, irregular and purposefully shaped, mortared together around tall beams of ancient wood. Carefully tended walkways, formed by great slabs of polished rock embedded in the sand, led up to the front doors.

A shattering breeze ripped through, flapping their makeshift clothing. The rain clouds overhead whisked away from the face of the moon for a moment, and its light came to rest on the structure, illuminating the whole of the building.

The temple had been designed to resemble the bow of a great wrecked ship, jutting from the craggy rocks and sand of the beach at an ominous angle. The immense entrance doors, fashioned from planks of varying lengths with a jagged notched pattern at the top, appeared to depict a vast hole torn in what would have been the keel. The crazily angled spire was the representation of a mast. The colossal ship had been rendered accurately, down to the last nautical apparatus. The moorings and riggings, detailed in exquisitely carved marble, were a half-dozen times their normal size.

Farther off shore was another part of the temple, an annex connected to the main building by a plank walkway. Like much of the annex, the walkway was only visible at low tide, submerging into the sea when the tide came back in. This additional part of the temple evoked the wreckage of the stern. A gigantic anchor, lying aslant on the sandbar between the two buildings, served as its threshold.

Despite the architectural care that had been taken to elicit the feeling of an off-balance wreck unevenly resting on the sand, it was obvious that the enormous edifice was sound and solidly built. It stood, undisturbed, amid the churning waves of the raging sea. Grunthor let out a long, low whistle.

"Criton. What ya make o' that, guv?"

Achmed was struggling to contain the dislike he felt for the water. In the old days, the sea could mask the heartbeats of his prey with its conundrum of conflicting vibrations and colossal power. It was the only place a victim could hide from him.

"Couldn't say. Perhaps the local worshippers are merchants, or fishermen. Very rich fishermen; its design is superior to anything I've ever seen, and building it must have been a huge undertaking. It certainly took a fair amount of complicated construction. The event it is commemorating must have been very traumatic to have inspired such a monstrosity. Too bad Rhapsody's not here; it might make more sense to her."

"Yeah, Oi think 'er family must of been sailors or worked the wharves in Easton. One night in the Root she was mutterin' about wantin' to see the ocean."

Achmed shook his head. "I doubt Rhapsody was born in Easton, or any other city. She may have picked up the skills to survive in the taverns and alleyways of Easton, but she's not a child of the streets. I suspect she grew up in a farm village or settlement, probably poor, but not destitute. She doesn't have the whetted edge she would if she had been born a guttersnipe." The wind caught the sand from the beach and blasted it across their faces.

"Ya think she's all right?"

Achmed began tying up the ends of his cloak. "Yes. Come on. Low tide won't last long. I want to see what's in the building farther out."

'Ere comes the rain."

They waited long enough to be sure no guards or worshippers came to the temple. After a few moments it was obvious that the darkness and the approaching storm would keep away anyone who might discover them.

The shrieking of the wind grew louder as sheets of rain began to fall, drenching both men to the skin. The ocean waves, even in ebb, crashed violently against the shoreline, frothing over the rocks at the temple's base.

The light of the moon was now completely gone, replaced by black, racing clouds that muted the sky. Achmed and Grunthor scaled the guardian rocks and ran up the pathway leading to the huge doors of the temple. The tall hooded torches that flanked the entranceway had long since been extinguished by the wind.

Grunthor grasped the great brass handles and pulled; the left door opened without resistance. The men hurried inside, quickly hauling the heavy door closed behind them.

Dripping wet, they took in the cavernous basilica. Its ceiling towered above them, the distant walls arching up to meet it. Great fractured timbers of myriad lengths and breadths were set within the dark stone. It looked a little like the fragmented skeleton of a giant beast, lying on its back, its spine the long aisle that led up forward, ancient ribs reaching brokenly, helplessly upward into the darkness above.

Round windows in the design of portholes were set high in the walls, affording the temple light by day. A single line of translucent glass blocks of great heft and thickness had been inlaid in the walls, about knee-height on Grunthor. The churning sea was diffusely visible through them, bathing the interior of the basilica in a greenish glow. In daylight it would be magnificent; by night, in a storm, there was little Achmed could do to shake off the eerie feeling that had drenched him even more deeply than the rain had.

Grunthor shook his head, spattering the water from his dripping hair onto the floor. There were no benches or seats of any kind, except for a wide circle of marble blocks near the middle of the temple. Despite its proximity to the water and at least part of the floor and lower walls being actually built below water level, the temple was surprisingly dry. They noticed, however, that the surface of the stone that had been used to construct the floor was rough in texture, allowing for better purchase when wet.

Achmed nodded forward, and the two Firbolg started down the aisle, looking around and above them all the while. The immense timbers, though carefully preserved, had been worn and weathered in their previous life, undoubtedly when they were part of the hulls of ships. The variation in the color and condition of the wood seemed to indicate that it had been gathered from many different vessels.

At the midpoint of the aisle the ceiling opened into a tall shaft, a broad tunnel of blackness with small slits cut into the distant top of it. The wind and salt spray whistled through the slits and down the shaft, its howl echoing within the temple.

"Must be the mast," Grunthor noted. Achmed nodded in agreement.

Beneath the opening in the center of the circular stone benches was a small, round fountain carved from blue-veined marble, with several larger basins of the same stone opening into ever-wider circles around it to catch its overflow. A pulsing stream of water bubbled from the font, spraying suddenly in the air, then subsiding again in rhythm with the pounding waves. Occasionally a violent jet would spurt forth, dousing the floor, but far enough from the stone benches for them to remain dry.

At the far end of the great building was another set of doors, wrought in copper and inscribed with patterns too distant to see. The Bolg circumvented the fountain and went to the back of the temple, their footsteps swallowed by the sound of the waves outside the walls.

Two wall sconces flanked the copper doors, their glass domes surrounding a wick of twisted metal. As they approached the door, they could see it was inscribed with runes, writing Achmed couldn't read but in which he thought he recognized a few symbols. They were vaguely similar to the those in the written language of Serendair.

A raised relief of a sword had been wrought into the copper of each door, one pointing up, the other down. Scrolled designs ran down the blades, similar to ocean waves, and the points were flared in a similar pattern.

The background of the relief gave Achmed pause. It was an engraving of a winged lion, a crest he had seen before. It took him a moment to place it.

"This is the coat-of-arms of MacQuieth's family," he said, more to himself than to Grunthor, though the Sergeant had also known of the legendary warrior, the champion of Serendair's king. "What's it doing here, half a world away?"

Grunthor rubbed his chin and stared at the etching on the doors.

"Oi believe MacQuieth came from elsewhere. Didn't they use to call 'im Nagall, the Stranger? Seems to me 'e sailed from some far-off place to come to the Island when 'e was young. Maybe this is where 'is family's from."

Achmed nodded, annoyed with himself. The churning frenzy of the waves around them was muddling his mind, keeping him from thinking clearly.

"Well, that may tell us where we are. I believe he came from Monodiere." He grasped the handle of the left door and pulled, but it was wedged shut. He tried the other, to no avail.

"These must be the doors to the annex," he said, rubbing his hand on his cloak to clear the moisture.

"Allow me," said Grunthor, bowing politely. He spat into his palm and grasped the handle, wrenching the door open with one smooth tug. He stepped back quickly as the salt spray slapped his face.

On the other side of the door, its outer copper surface turned green-blue and corroded from the salt, was a wide stone step that led to the plank walkway. Already the path was beginning to be touched by puddles swelling before the returning tide.

The men shielded their eyes with their forearms and stepped into the gale, Grunthor's hand locked on to Achmed's shoulder. The walkway was long and narrow, crossing the sandbar, and littered with seaweed and the debris left behind when the tide ebbed.

They crossed as quickly as they could, struggling to remain upright in the whipping wind. Grunthor stopped long enough to extricate a large, oddly shaped shell that had gotten itself stuck in the rough wood of the planks.

As they approached the annex they could see it had no door of its own, but rather just a rough archway that left the annex's hollow chamber open to the ravages of the sea and the air. When the tide returned, much of the annex would submerge again, the water high enough to crest Achmed's head. In the sand before the archway lay an immense anchor, rusted and pocked, which served as the doorstep.

When they reached the archway they stepped over the anchor and hurried inside before looking around, then stared at what they saw.

Unlike the temple, which was an edifice built to look like a ship, the annex was a piece of a real one, wedged upright, bow skyward and aslant, in the sand. The ship had been a sizable one, judging by its wreckage, which appeared to be the better part of the stern and midship. Its deck had been stripped away, leaving nothing but the hull, which now formed the walls of the annex. Upon closer inspection, it was evident that the ship had been built of something other than ordinary timber, but the material was not something either of them had seen before.

Also wedged into the sand in the center of the annex was a stone table, a block of solid obsidian, gleaming smooth beneath the pools of water that danced across it with each gust of the wind. Two brace restraints of a metal neither man recognized were embedded in the stone, their clasps open and empty. There was not a trace of rust on either one.

The surface of the stone had at one time been inscribed with deep runes that had been worn away over time by the insistent hand of the ocean. Now it was smooth, with only a bleached shadow marring the obsidian where the inscription once had been.

Attached to the front of the stone was a plaque, with raised runes similar to the ones they had seen in the copper doors. Like the braces on its horizontal surface, the marker was un-affected by the scouring waves.

"This looks a little like the written language of Serendair, but only a little," Achmed said, bending to examine the marker. "I wish Rhapsody were here."

"That's twice in ten minutes you said that," Grunthor an-swered, grinning, "and Oi'm gonna tell 'er."

"She won't believe you, or she'll think I wanted to pitch her into the sea," Achmed said, rising and slinging his pack off his shoulder onto the stone block. Quickly he took out the oilcloth and lump coal they had stolen and stretched the cloth over the runes. Then, with the coal, he made a quick rubbing of the plaque and returned both to his pack. "See—we didn't need her after all. We'd better get out of here, the tide is coming in."

Grunthor nodded. The water was up above his ankles now, which meant the sandbar would soon be barely visible.

Achmed shouldered his pack. As he did, his hand brushed the stone block, and his fingers vibrated gently. He crouched down once more, examining the stone itself. It was plain black obsidian, a slab of impressive size, but otherwise quite unremarkable. Nonetheless there was a hum to it when he touched it, a vibration that was both utterly unknown and oddly familiar. He looked up at Grunthor.

"Does this feel strange when you touch it?"

The Sergeant rested his palm on the stone, considering. A moment later he shook his head.

"Naw. Feels cold, like marble. Smooth from the sea 'ittin' it all the time."

Achmed took his hand away. The vibration ceased, leaving him feeling both relieved and strangely bereft. But there was no time to ponder the meaning of it; the tide was coming in.

They stepped into the screaming wind and waded back through the knee-deep water to the temple. Once inside, Grunthor shoved the copper door back into place. He sighed and looked at his friend.

"Well, whaddaya make o' that?"

Achmed shook his head.

"No idea, but perhaps—" His words choked off and he glared, angry at himself.

Grunthor snorted with laughter. "All right, you don't gotta say it, sir. Per'aps she'll know."

"We best be getting back there, anyway," Achmed said, brushing the water off his shoulders as they walked back through the basilica. "We have a date to meet up with her. With all those strange attacks between here and there, the journey may take longer than it should."

22

The front door of the Invoker's keep was ancient and thick, with deeply carved designs that somehow reminded Rhapsody strongly of home.

It had at one time been gilded with a gold-leaf image, which had faded and peeled with age, in the vague shape of a dragon or other mythical beast. It bore the signs of salt spray that had worn some of the surface down to a smooth finish, made even balder by time. It was also marked in the upper right corner with a hex sign unlike any she had seen, a circle formed from a spiral.

Khaddyr rapped loudly on the door with his walking stick.

He waited a moment and was about to knock again when suddenly the door opened.

In the entranceway stood a middle-aged woman of mixed blood, a half-caste Lirin like Rhapsody herself, though her coloring was more like that of the forest Lirin from the Island. Her skin was dark and sallow, and her eyes and hair the color of the bark of the chestnut tree. Her temples bore a touch of gray.

She wore a robe of undyed wool, similar to the others Rhapsody had seen, and nodded deferentially to Khaddyr, then turned to look at his guest. Her mouth fell open and she stared blankly. Rhapsody blushed. *I must be a horrific sight*, she thought, her throat tightening in embarrassment.

Khaddyr's eyes darkened in annoyance. "Ahem," he said, clearing his throat, "Good evening to you, too, Gwen. Is His Grace in?"

The woman blinked, then colored in abashment. "Forgive me, Father, and you as well, miss; I don't know what's come over me. Please come in." She stepped aside from the door and Khaddyr entered the house, taking Rhapsody by the elbow and leading her inside.

They followed Gwen through a hallway crafted from polished wood and adorned with carvings and variegated stone floors. At the last door before a spindled stairway Gwen stopped and knocked politely, then opened the door slightly and called inside.

"Your Grace?"

"Yes?" The voice that answered was a smooth, cultured baritone.

"You have guests, sir." Her eyes returned to Rhapsody.

"It's I, Your Grace," said Khaddyr. He glared at Gwen. "Stop gawking; you're being rude." The woman turned hastily away.

The door opened a moment later and Khaddyr led Rhapsody inside. She looked around at the cozy room, a surprisingly small study with a large, whole-wall hearth on which a fire was burning quietly. As she entered the room the flames blazed in greeting, then settled back down into a steady, insistent incandescence.

The room was filled with odd objects, maps and scrolls, and bookshelves that lined the three remaining walls. There were several comfortable chairs clustered around a low, round table made from a center slice of a wide tree that had been struck by lightning, a liquor chest, and other pieces of furniture that were hidden in the shadows of the firelight.

The door closed quietly behind them. Standing there was a thin, elderly man dressed in simple gray robes. His face was kind and wrinkled, with a good many lines around his eyes, his hair silver and white with heavy brows and a matching mustache, neatly trimmed. His build was tall and somewhat slight, though he appeared in good health. The old man's skin had the weathered look of someone who spent most of his time outdoors.

"Well, well," the man said softly. "What have we here?"

"Your Grace, this woman came to me from out of the forest of Tref-Y-Gwartheg," Khaddyr answered respectfully. "She doesn't speak the language, though she seems to understand it somewhat. She sings to the sunrise as well, though she has placed no words to these songs; her voice is otherworldly in its beauty. I thought perhaps she would interest you, as I am at a loss to define what she is. It occurred to me that she might be a dryad or sylph or some other nature spirit with whom you might be familiar, if anyone was."

Rhapsody stared at Khaddyr in surprise. Initially it was the name of the town that had caught her interest; Tref-Y-Gwartheg, in the tongue of the Island, meant simply Cattletown.

It was his final comment, however, that caused her some shock. She had thought when the townspeople first started swarming about her that they had never seen a Lirin woman before, but Gwen was proof that her theory there was incorrect. Why would the priest think she was a nature spirit? Was it her wild appearance, or something more? She thought back to Achmed and Grunthor's awkward attempts to explain the way the fire had changed the way she looked. Apparently it made her look freakish.

The old man smiled in amusement. "Thank you, Khaddyr." He came a few steps closer to her and looked into her face.

"My name is Llauron," he said, directly and pleasantly. "What may I call you, my dear?"

"Rhapsody," she answered. Khaddyr jumped at the sound of her voice.

"I didn't know she could speak," he said.

"Sometimes it's just a matter of asking questions that one can answer, isn't it, Rhapsody?" His voice, rich and distinguished, had a gentle, disarming tone to it. She couldn't help but smile in return.

"Yes."

"Where are you from?"

Rhapsody's brows drew together as she puzzled over how to answer him. She had agreed not to give much information away, and yet she didn't want to lie, on top of which she was uncertain of her ability to communicate accurately in the dialect. "I don't know what you would call it," she said carefully. "It is far away."

"Yes, I can imagine," the Invoker said. "Well, not to worry. Can I get you something to eat, or perhaps a bath?"

Her face lit up, and with it, the fire; the flames roared in delight. "Yes, a bath would be wonderful," she said slowly. The desire to be clean outweighed all caution.

Llauron opened the door of the study. "Gwen?"

The half-Lirin woman appeared again. "Yes, Your Grace?"

"This is Rhapsody. She is to be our guest, at least for this evening. Please draw her a nice, hot bath with plenty of soap, and set Vera to preparing a supper tray for her." The woman nodded and left. Llauron turned back to them again. "Now, while that is being undertaken, would the two of you like some tea?"

"Yes, thank you," Rhapsody said.

"I would as well, Your Grace."

Llauron gestured to the chairs while he prepared the tea, hanging a pot of water on the hearth. He took three cups out of a cabinet near one of the glass windows and set them before his guests. When the water had boiled he removed it from the fire and poured it into a china teapot with some tea leaves to steep. Then he sat in the chair opposite her.

"Well, Rhapsody, I do hope Khaddyr has been a good host, aside from failing to offer you a bath."

Khaddyr was mortified. "I am sorry, miss," he said to her in embarrassment, "but I didn't want to offend any custom your people might have."

Llauron looked amused. "Come now, Your Grace, surely you've met enough Lirin to know that they bathe." He poured the tea into the cups and offered them the small honey server.

"Lirin?" Khaddyr asked in astonishment.

"Half-Lirin, I would guess. Is that correct, my dear? One of your parents was Liringlas?"

Rhapsody nodded. "My mother." She sipped the tea, reveling in its warmth.

"I thought as much."

A knock sounded on the door, then it opened. "The bath is ready, Your Grace."

Llauron rose. "I imagine that's the thing you desire most in the world right now, isn't it, my dear?"

"Yes." The great exhale of breath in her answer made the Invoker chuckle.

"Well, enjoy your soak. Gwen, please get her anything she needs, and wash her clothes for her while she bathes. I'm sure you can come up with a new robe for her as well, yes?"

"Yes, Your Grace."

"Excellent."

Rhapsody followed Gwen from the room. As they stepped out into the hall and climbed the stairs she could hear the men continuing their conversation.

"A dryad?" Llauron's voice barely contained his mirth. "Really, now."

"I've never seen a Lirin like that," she heard Khaddyr say defensively.

"Apparently not, but I'm sorry to say there are no more nature spirits; the last of them perished with the Island centuries ago—"

The sound of his voice was cut off as Gwen closed the bathroom door.

𝕿he bathroom contained a great porcelain tub which had been filled with steaming water and scented with herbs; *fennel and lemon verbena*, Rhapsody thought with a sigh. She turned to see Gwen watching her, with no apparent intention of leaving.

Self-consciously Rhapsody removed her filthy clothing, leaving the locket around her neck, and eased herself into the tub, feeling an ecstatic rush as the heat of the water closed around her body. She looked up to see Gwen bundle her rags and leave the room, closing the door behind her.

With a deep sigh she slipped even further down into the water, feeling the blissful sensation of shedding the mud that had soaked into the pores of her skin, allowing it to breathe for the first time in as long as she could remember. As she scrubbed the muck from her hair and skin the water lost none of its heat, even as it turned a repulsive gray color. It was as if the tension of the endless time spent in travel was melting off her along with the dirt. She could not bring herself to imagine what the tub would look like when she was finished.

She was drying herself with one of the thick sheets of cloth that had been left beside the tub when Gwen came back, carrying a white wool robe similar to the ones she had seen among the Filids in the forest glen. The servant left the room, and Rhapsody donned the robe, enjoying the feel of a whole garment on her skin. Then she looked down at the sword; it seemed ludicrous to belt it onto the robe, so she decided to carry it in her hand. There was no place to hide it, anyway.

She waited for a few moments, but Gwen did not return. Rhapsody opened the door and peered down the corridor. There was no one in sight. She went down the stairs slowly, her eyes taking in all the angles and details of the marvelous house, from its glowing woodwork to the odd pieces of art that adorned the walls.

The door to the study was open, and she leaned into the doorway. "Hello?" she called.

Llauron's voice answered her, but seemed distant. "Ah, you're done. Come in, my dear."

Rhapsody walked into the study to find the room empty. On the wall that abutted the fireplace was a door she had not seen, standing open. She crossed the room, noting the embers on the hearth leaping in greeting as she walked past, and went into the adjoining room.

It was very similar to the study except for the central piece of furniture. A messy, ornate desk took up much of the room, covered with papers and scrolls that seemed piled randomly on it. Another hearth, a smaller one, was visible between two paned windows. Glass was a luxury that Rhapsody had seen only rarely in the old world and only in this house since arriving in the new one. Llauron rose from the large chair behind the desk and smiled at her.

"Well, now, are you feeling better?" She nodded. "Good, good. Did you recognize the herbs?"

Rhapsody thought for a moment. She did—lavender, fennel, rynlet, lemon verbena, and rosemary—but she was unsure how to say the words in this dialect, and didn't want to speak them in the old language. "Yes," she said.

The Invoker laughed. "Very good. You're something of an herbalist, then?"

She shook her head. "No, I know a little about plants, but not much."

"Well, if you are interested in learning more, this is the place to do it. Our chief herbalist, Lark, is Lirin also, though not Liringlas."

"Perhaps. I'm sure it would be very interesting."

"Indeed. Customarily I have Gwen put rock salt in the bath as well. It soothes sore muscles, or at least I hope it did."

Rhapsody smiled. "Yes, thank you. I feel worlds better."

Llauron opened his hand in the direction of a soft-looking chair. "Khaddyr made his apologies; he is needed at the hospice. Perhaps you'd like to ask me some of the thousand questions you must have, and I admit I have a few of my own. Have a seat by the fire, my dear, and help yourself to the supper tray."

Rhapsody complied, breathing deeply to keep the fire from reacting to her nervousness. It was of little use; the flames leapt to life as she sat in the chair. Llauron didn't seem to notice.

"What is this place?" she asked carefully, trying to keep within the dialect.

Llauron smiled. "You are in the home, the keep, of the Invoker—that's me, of course—of the Filids, the religious order that worships the One-God, the Life-Giver, by tending to the various aspects of nature. My home is at the crest of the Circle, the community where our order lives, trains, and tends the Great White Tree—I imagine you saw it on your way here, it's difficult to miss." Rhapsody nodded. "The name of the holy forest in which it grows, and we live, and you presently are, is Gwynwood."

Rhapsody sat back in her chair. She had never heard the names of any of those places or things before.

Llauron saw her disappointment. "Can you read maps?"

"Fairly well. Mostly sea charts."

"Excellent. Then come over here." The old man rose and led her to a strange orb in the corner suspended from a hinged floorstand. On the orb a map had been painted, showing the landmasses of the known world. He took the round map in his hands and spun it, locating a northern continent with a long, irregular western seacoast.

"This is where we are," Llauron said, pointing slightly inland from the coast. Rhapsody blinked but said nothing. She had seen this landmass before in her studies, but it was thought to be uninhabited.

The Island of Serendair was in the southern hemisphere on the other side of the world. Though she had anticipated this possibility, her throat tightened nonetheless. She was much farther from home than she had hoped.

"May I see the round map?" she asked hesitantly. Her vocabulary was failing her occasionally.

"Certainly. It's called a globe." Llauron swung it over to her on the stand.

Rhapsody turned the globe slowly, making note of some of the places she had seen before, and many more that she hadn't. Carefully she examined each part of the world, trying not to be obvious, her heart pounding. The language with which it was labeled was similar to that of her homeland, but with a few characters she didn't recognize. Finally she was able to turn it to the place where Serendair was, and found the Island in the correct place, on the opposite side of the Earth and sea. But instead of being labeled by its actual name, it was rendered in gray and annotated as *The Lost Island*.

Her hands grew cold. The Lost Island? It didn't surprise her that the mapmakers of this place were unfamiliar with the geography on the other side of the world, just as the Seren cartographers had been unaware that this place was inhabited. But why call it lost?

Her eyes scanned the globe quickly. She noticed that in addition to its strange appellation, Serendair was also the only landmass colored in gray. She swung the map back to the place Llauron had indicated they now were.

The Invoker was watching her in interest. "Here, let me show you a little of the geography." He went to the high pile of maps on the sideboard and rummaged through them until he came to the one he was looking for, unrolling it for her to see.

"The Tree is here, in the central forest region near the southeastern border of the forest. Gwynwood itself is a religious state, and as such is not aligned with Roland, our neighbor on the southern and eastern sides."

Rhapsody followed his finger, and saw that the seaside province to the south of the forest was labeled *Avonderre*, and the eastern one *Navarne*. Across the wide ocean to the left was an area depicted in green, as the areas he was now showing her all were. Part of the mainland across the sea, the other green area was labeled *Manosse*.

"Avonderre and Navarne are part of Roland?"

"Yes, as are the provinces of Canderre, to the northeast, Yarim, east of that, Bethany, due east of Navarne, which is the Regency seat, and Bethe Corbair, east of Bethany."

Rhapsody studied the map with interest. Avonderre, Navarne, Bethany, Canderre, Yarim, and Bethe Corbair were the provinces of the country of Roland, but were not the only lands depicted in green. The color was used only in the section of the world Llauron was indicating, and nowhere else on the globe.

From the map it appeared that Roland encompassed part of the western seacoast, great rolling hills to the south of Gwynwood, and spread eastward into a vast, wide plain that was labeled *The Orlandan Plateau*.

It stretched further eastward to the foothills of a sharply broken mountain range, cut by a deep valley. The mountain range was labeled *The Manteids*. At one time the land around the Manteids had been noted as *Canrif*, but that had been neatly crossed out and replaced by the hand-written word *Firbolg*. Rhapsody swallowed hard upon reading the word.

She pointed to a country to the south that bordered on Bethany and Bethe Corbair. It seemed to be mostly composed of the same mountain chain as the Manteids, stretching south into a wide, high desert. This land was also depicted in green. "Is this part of Roland, too?"

"That's Sorbold. It is not part of Roland, but a nation unto itself."

"And this?" She indicated the area labeled *Firbolg*.

Llauron laughed. "Goodness, no. Those are the Firbolg lands. That's a dark and treacherous place, if ever there was one."

Rhapsody nodded; she could believe that of a land occupied by Firbolg. Her finger traced along the southern edge of the country of Roland, the final area shaded green, unlabeled. "Why does this area seem to have no name?"

Llauron uncurled a corner of the map as it rolled closed. "These are the nonaligned states that were once part of the Cymrian lands." His voice was matter-of-fact, but he watched her intently as he said the word.

Rhapsody's face was blank. The word meant nothing to her. "Cymrian lands? The green ones?"

"Yes, all of Roland and Sorbold, as well as those states that are currently nonaligned, Manosse, on the other continent, and the Firbolg Waste were once part of the lands settled by the Cymrians, spelled with a 'y,' though pronounced as a 'u.' "

"Who were the Cymrians?"

A flicker of surprise crossed Llauron's face. "You've never heard of the Cymrians?"

"No." Her hands began to tremble slightly. Llauron noticed, and patted one comfortingly.

"The Cymrians were the refugees who fled the Island of Serendair prior to its destruction."

23

Rhapsody heard the words Llauron had spoken: *the Island of Serendair prior to its destruction.* They slowly took up residence in her brain, settling in her mind like music from a distant orchestra. *Its destruction.*

A sense of calm descended on her; it was the physical reaction that occurred in her in the advent of great danger or panic. She fought to keep her face placid as the blood rushed from her head, cramping her stomach and leaving her feeling mortally weak.

With a practiced hand she picked up the map and carried it over to the chair she had occupied, and sat down again, balancing the scabbard across her knees and letting the fire warm her suddenly pale face.

"I'd like to hear more about the Cymrians, but will you explain two more lands to me?" she asked, her voice sounding exaggerated in her own ears.

Llauron sat in the chair opposite her. "Of course."

She forced her eyes to focus on a land depicted in yellow to the south of Gwynwood and its southern neighbor, Avonderre. The land seemed to be part of the same enormous forest but, aside from being shown in a different color, was labeled *Realmalir.* "What is this?"

A smile flickered across the Invoker's elderly face. "Those are the Lirin lands, the Great Forest of Tyrian. The word is Old Cymrian for 'the Lirin kingdom.' The Lirin were indigenous to this land. They were here when the Cymrians landed, and they are here still."

"But not part of Roland?"

"No. During the Cymrian Age the Lirin were allies of the Cymrians, but the Great War changed that."

"Great War?"

Llauron took a deep breath. "When you say you are from far away, I see you are not exaggerating. What is the other land you wanted to ask about?"

Rhapsody pointed numbly to the white lands to the north of Gwynwood and Roland. "What is this?"

"That is the Hintervold. It comprises all the lands to the north and east past the old Cymrian realm. I have some maps if you'd like to see them."

She was beginning to grow nauseated. "Some other time, if you don't mind. Tell me more about the Cymrians, please."

Llauron glanced out the window into the darkness. "Well, I can tell you a little, but it's a rather long story.

"A very long time ago, the last of the Seren kings, whose name was Gwylliam, made the discovery that the island nation of which he was the rightful ruler was doomed to dissolve in fire. The ancient manuscripts I've studied are not clear on how he came to know this, but kings of Serendair were often gifted with foresight, and knew a great many things indisputably." Numbness tingled at Rhapsody's temples. She had never heard of Gwylliam.

"Centuries before, the Island had sustained widespread damage when a star fell from the sky into the sea," Llauron continued. "It caused a great deluge which split the island and buried much of it beneath the waves. It was not hard to believe that something such as that could happen again."

Rhapsody struggled to breathe normally. She was familiar with the legend of the Sleeping Child, the story Llauron was now telling her.

Her mother had told her the Lirin tale of two stars that were sisters, Melita and Oelendra; how Melita had fallen from the sky and into the sea at the land's edge, settling below the waves but still churning with unspent fire. Islands to the north of Serendair, formerly mountaintops, became tropical from the heat, and the seas between them raged, making it treacherous for ships to sail near them.

The star at the bottom of the sea became known as the Sleeping Child. The Lirin believed that one day it might awaken and rise again, taking the rest of the island to the depths with it when it did. The sister star, Oelendra, was said to have fallen in despair, leaving its light still burning in the sky even after its death. She had thought the stories to be myths.

Llauron's voice came back to her as if through a fog. "Gwylliam was, by nature and training, an architect, an engineer, a smith. He refused to accept his kingdom's death knell, and instead decided to find a way to preserve the culture that his royal line had fought so hard to protect.

"He undertook great plans to evacuate the Island, although some of his subjects, notably from the older races, such as the Liringlas, chose to stay behind rather than leave, even in the face of impending disaster. Others chose to travel to nearby landmasses within the shipping lanes that had been plied by Seren sailors for centuries.

"But Gwylliam was not satisfied with either of those alternatives. He wanted to find a place where the Seren culture of all its races could be preserved, a sanctuary for his subjects where they could rebuild their civilization. To that end he chose a sailor, a man of Ancient Seren stock, who was called Merithyn the Explorer. He was sent out in a small ship, alone, to find a suitable place to relocate the Seren who wanted to flee.

"By the way, let me clarify the difference between *Seren* and *Ancient Seren*. Any citizen of what was at the time modern Serendair, regardless of race, was Seren, though since they came here they have been referred to exclusively as Cymrians. The Ancient Seren were a particular race, tall, gold-skinned people from long before the races of man colonized Serendair. They died out, for the most part, well prior to the era I am telling you about." Rhapsody, herself Seren, nodded numbly.

"Eventually Merithyn came to this place, which at the time was the impenetrable realm of a dragon named Elynsynos; that's much too long a story to get into tonight, but if you stay for a while, I will be more than happy to relate it to you.

"At any rate, Elynsynos took to him, and sympathized with the plight of his nation, so she invited them to come and live within her lands, the places you now see, for the most part, in green on the map. Merithyn returned with the news happily, and the Seren came to this land in three fleets of ships.

"Eight hundred and seventy-six ships set out, though considerably fewer landed, and they sailed in three Waves, which all left and landed at different times and in different places.

It was harrowing, and difficult, but they survived, and eventually met up again, banding together to form the greatest nation this land has ever seen, and ushered in the most enlightened Age it has ever known. But that civilization has been gone for a very long time."

Rhapsody tried to maintain her composure. "I still don't understand why they were called Cymrians. Didn't you say they were from Serendair?"

The Invoker stood up again and stretched, then crossed the room to a case where a strange, rocklike object was displayed under glass. Rhapsody followed him, fighting rising hysteria. He pointed at the rock, into which runes had been carved. She stared down at the words through the glass.

Cyme we inne friđ, fram the grip of deap to lif inne đis smylte land

"Can you read this, my dear?"

Rhapsody nodded. It was written in a combination of what Llauron had referred to as Old Cymrian, the language of her father, the common tongue of her homeland, and the strange language of sailors and merchants that was universally used in shipping trade.

"Come we in peace, from the grip of death to life in this fair land."

Llauron smiled approvingly. "Very good. This was Gwylliam's command to Merithyn, the salutation with which he was to greet anyone in the new land he might find.

"Gwylliam translated it into a universal tongue, to expand its chance of being recognized somewhere in the world. They were Merithyn's first words to Elynsynos, words he carved upon her lair, with her permission, of course, as a signpost to any who might come after him.

"When the Cymrians arrived, each fleet having landed in a different place, they left markers along the way as they traveled to find each other again and make their settlements. Those historical paths are called the Cymrian Trails, and they were the origin of the name *Cymrian*.

"The indigenous people of the land, like the Lirin of the Great Forest of Tyrian, saw the words on the signposts or were greeted with the words upon meeting these refugees, and began to refer to them as Cymrians, which is why their appellation sounds like 'come.' So it has come to mean the people of the Lost Island, and their descendants, without regard to race or class, for all were represented on the ships."

"I see," said Rhapsody politely, but inside she was feeling the world spin. "How long ago was this?"

"Well, the fleets departed just shy of fourteen centuries ago."

Rhapsody gasped in spite of herself. "What?"

Llauron smiled. "Yes, it may seem hard to believe, but fourteen centuries ago a civilization lived here that gave us many of our greatest inventions and contributions to our culture. They were, in some ways, even more advanced than we are now. It was the war that changed it, the war that ended the Cymrian Age and set us back many centuries. Are you all right, my dear? You look pale."

"I—I'm really very tired," Rhapsody said, her voice barely above a whisper.

"Of course you are; how thoughtless of me." Llauron went to the door and called into the study. "Gwen? Is our guest's room ready?"

A moment later Gwen came into the office. "All ready, Your Grace. The bed has been turned down."

"Good, good," said the Invoker. "Why don't you head up with Gwen, my dear? Have a good night's rest and sleep in late. I'm sure you could use it after your long journey."

Rhapsody nodded as if in a trance. She made a slight bow in Llauron's direction. "Good night, and thank you."

"Not at all. Sleep well." His eyes twinkled merrily in the firelight as she left the room and followed Gwen up the stairs again, clutching the railing.

*H*er room was at the end of a long, crooked hallway. Gwen not only had turned down the blankets but had slid several warm stones under them to drive the chill from the sheets.

The room itself was simple and neat, with a chest, chair, and looking glass in addition to the bed, as well as a coat peg and sword rack. A small glass window looked out a different side of the house than she had seen, though nothing was visible in the dark. The woolen blankets on the bed had been woven with hex signs for protection from nightmares. Rhapsody wondered ruefully how potent they were. To spare her from her dreams would require nothing short of a miracle.

As the door closed behind her she sat down on the bed numbly, unable to allow the thoughts to come through sensibly. *The Island of Serendair prior to its destruction.*

Llauron had said that Gwylliam had foreseen its ruin, but perhaps that had not occurred. Prophets made predictions all the time that never came to pass, like the soothsayer in the Thieves' Market in Easton. Then she thought back to her nightmare on the Root, the image of the star falling into the sea, the burning walls of water enveloping the land, and knew that it had come to pass. It was a premonition; Serendair was gone.

Even if they had survived the catastrophe, even if they had been among the refugees who survived the voyage, no one she had ever known or loved would still be alive. Her heart twisted in misery at the thought of her parents and her brothers. Her father was definitely gone, dead for centuries, more than a millennium, if Llauron was to be believed. Her mother was Lirin, and therefore by race blessed with a longer life span; some Lirin had been known to live as long as five hundred years. But almost three times that length of time had passed. She was gone as well, and her brothers, too. Rhapsody felt her heart shatter under the weight of the agony.

She crawled into the bed and curled up like a baby in the womb, trying to remember her life before the nightmare of the Root. It would be easy to curse Achmed now, but it was really her own fault.

She had been headstrong and thoughtless as a young girl, running away from home. Some of the price of her foolishness she had paid herself; life on the street had been unspeakable in its horror for a while. But the worst part was knowing the pain she had caused her family, the despair they must have felt, wondering what had happened to her. The only salvation from the crushing guilt had been the intention and the knowledge that someday she would find a way to go home. And now that was gone, too.

One by one her brothers' faces came into her memory, smiling and laughing. She could almost feel her father's strong embrace, her mother's gentle caress. All gone now. She'd never see any of them again, never fall asleep to the sound of her mother singing. Never feel truly safe again.

A lump of anguish took hold in her throat. The Past was too painful to contemplate, the Future more so. Exhausted and overwrought, Rhapsody fell into a troubled sleep.

Her dreams were even more terrifying than they normally were, visions of great walls of water crushing children beneath them as they consumed the land, tall golden people immolated by a bursting star, Sagia sinking slowly beneath the waves with the Lirin in its arms.

In the last of her dreams, she stood in a village consumed by black fire, while soldiers rode through the streets, slaying everyone in sight. In the distance at the edge of the horizon she saw eyes, tinged in red, laughing at her. And then, as a bloodstained warrior rode down on her like a man possessed, she was lifted up in the air in the claw of a great copper dragon.

Rhapsody woke, gasping for breath. She reached out for Grunthor, who had been her source of comfort from the nightmares, but the grinning green face was nowhere to be found. The room and the bed had grown cold while she slept, but as she came to consciousness her anguish roared back, and the fire within her raised the temperature of the air around her immediately.

It was almost morning. Gray light was filling the sky outside her window, signaling the approach of another dawn. Somehow the world seemed different today, although nothing had occurred in the night. The changes were centuries ago; the world had been inexorably altered while she was crawling within it. A great deal of time had passed. What she didn't understand was how it had managed to miss her. She looked into the mirror to find a face not vastly older from when she had left, at least to her view.

Rhapsody went to the window and looked out into the wakening sky. Dawn would be coming soon; she needed to sing her morning devotions, wanted the comfort of the memory of her mother teaching them to her beneath the sky half a world away. She was afraid of being alone with the knowledge of the Island's death, but had no one to share it with—no one living, at least.

Even if she could find Achmed and Grunthor, who were undoubtedly far away by now, neither of them would feel moved to any sadness at the loss. Achmed, in fact, having been hunted, would probably celebrate, and that would be more than she could bear. She made the bed, then walked to the coat peg and took down the hooded cape Khaddyr had given her.

Rhapsody made her way quietly down the stairs so as not to disturb the Invoker and his staff. She opened the heavy door slowly and nodded to the guards, who stared at her. They said nothing, so she passed between them, then through the snow-covered garden and over the fields to the Tree.

The dawn was just beginning to break as she arrived at the edge of the meadow. Rhapsody walked between a stately maple and a towering elm in the circle of guardian trees and came, for the first time, within clear sight of the trunk. The bark of the Great White Tree caught the first ray of the sun and glimmered in the morning air, heavy with fog. As the light touched it, the song of the Tree deepened, then soared, as if it too was greeting the dawn with music.

Rhapsody closed her eyes, feeling the tones of the Tree rumble through her. For the first time in as long as she could remember she felt small, insignificant in the presence of so much magnificence, of such inestimable power.

But there was also a familiarity to the lifesong that was humming within her. The melody of the Great White Tree was very much the same as the song of Sagia, a deep, abiding presence that spoke to her soul. It was a part of her; it would sustain her through her loss, even though her heart would never heal.

Softly she sang her morning aubade and, when the devotions were finished, whistled the all-clear, the signal for which Achmed was waiting. Then she left the ring of guardian trees and hurried back to the house.

She exited the tree-circle from a different place, taking the path between an enormous holly-berry bush and an engilder, a slender, silvery tree she had known from the old land. From where she now stood she could see a different side of Llauron's keep, a winding side garden that led around behind the house.

In the distance she could hear the sound of the Filids beginning their day, tending to their labors. Still seeing no one in the meadow, she walked around to the back of the keep and found herself in expansive gardens for as far as the eye could see.

Llauron's lands reached out to the forest again a mile or more away. In between the house and the woods were trees and ponds that dotted the landscape, around which beds of herbs and flowers had been built. Here and there marble benches stood where the leaves of the trees would cast shade in summer. The garden slept now in the depth of winter, the beds mulched and packed with snow.

Near the back of the house stood a young ash tree, tall and vigorous, beneath which grew a small sheltered herb garden. Llauron was sitting on the ground next to the tree, tending the plants in the beds, singing in a mellow baritone that sent shivers up her back. It was not the beauty of his voice that made her tremble, but the vibrations issuing forth from it.

He was using musical lore, the skills of a Singer, though it was clear from the occasional vocal wobble and the incorrect phrasing that he was not one himself. The song was a simple one, though she did not recognize the language. She opened her mouth to offer a few simple changes that would make the song work better; it was a song of warmth and healing, obviously meant to sustain the plants through the winter. She closed it again rapidly as Achmed's words came ringing back to her.

And when we do make contact, let's keep as much information as possible among ourselves until we agree to share any of it. It's safer for all of us that way.

As she approached, the Invoker stopped singing and turned to meet her. A smile lit up the wrinkled face.

"Well, well, good morning, my dear. I trust you slept well?"

Rhapsody thought back to the terrifying nightmares. "Thank you for the use of such a lovely room," she said.

"Not at all. I hope you will be staying for a while." He began to get up.

Rhapsody came to him, forestalling his attempt to stand, and sat on the bench beneath the ash tree. The stone was cold, causing a shiver to race through her. "What was the song you were singing?"

"Ah, that. It's a healing song intended for the plants, a piece of lore passed down from the Filids of Serendair. I use it to help some of my medicine garden through the nastier weather, keep it healthy. The more fragile plants I keep inside, of course, but there is only so much room, after all. Besides, Mahb here likes the music, too." He patted the ash tree beside him.

"Mahb?" It sounded like the Serenne word for *son*.

"Yes, yes, he looks after the garden, keeps away any man or beast or malevolent spirit that might bring it harm, don't you, old boy?" Llauron looked the young tree up and down, then leaned forward conspiratorially. "Confidentially, I don't think he likes Khaddyr much," he said, his eyes twinkling. Rhapsody smiled wanly. "Now, perhaps I could impose on you to add your lovely voice to my own, and do the plants some real benefit."

Rhapsody looked surprised. "Excuse me?"

"Now, my dear, don't be modest. I can tell you are a Singer of great skill, perhaps even a Namer, yes?" She blinked; the chilly wind blew over her body, suddenly moist with sweat, causing her to shiver. "When you speak, you make the day a little brighter by the sound of your voice. It's really quite beautiful, my dear. I can only imagine how you sound when you sing. I hope you will not leave me guessing much longer. Come, favor my plants with a song."

The dilemma of what to do next tied a substantial knot in her stomach. Llauron had already guessed something critically important about her. To deny it would be to lie, to dodge, to be rude. She sighed silently.

"If you'd like," she said at last. "But I don't know the song you were singing. Why don't you begin, and I'll join in when I have learned it."

"Fine." Llauron went back to his work, singing the odd song again. The pattern became obvious to her after a few bars, and tentatively she began to sing along, correcting the flaws in his musical line. As he noted the changes Llauron matched her, and when he was carrying the melody correctly, she threw in a harmonic line for good measure. When she looked back down at the medicine garden the plants appeared somewhat healthier, though the exact nature of the change was hard to detect.

Llauron nodded approvingly. "Excellent! I was right, wasn't I, my dear? You are a Namer."

Rhapsody looked off into the distance to avoid meeting his eyes. They were bright blue, with a sharp edge to them, and she knew if she wasn't careful he would size her up even further. "I did achieve that status, yes."

"I thought as much. Well, thank you. That should keep the garden quite nicely, at least until the end of this thaw. Come, let's go inside. You're cold, and I'm finished here anyway." He rose with more agility than his age suggested and led her into the house through a back door.

The door opened into a vast kitchen, with an enormous hearth and brick ovens enough to feed an entire farm's hands easily. A copper hook hung over the fire with a kettle steaming away. Llauron warmed his hands in the steam and then swung the kettle out, removing it from the hook with a thick, clean rag.

"I was expecting you might want some tea," he said, filling a china pot that had been left on a central table. "Are you still feeling worn out from your journey?"

"A little."

The Invoker smiled. "Well, then, we'll just mix you a tea with some properties to revive you a bit. Have you ever taken mim's lace internally?"

Rhapsody shook her head. "I've never heard of it."

Llauron turned away and walked to a large storage cabinet, pulling forth many small sacks of loosely woven burlap. "I'm not surprised; it's indigenous to this area. What about spring saffron?"

It suddenly occurred to her that Llauron might be using his tea inventory to isolate the place from which she had come by her knowledge of the herbs. "Whatever you're having is fine, I'm sure," she said hastily.

"Well, then, I think we shall mix some of that with dried orange blossoms, sweet fern, and raspberry leaves."

"You have raspberry leaves in winter?"

"Yes, in the glass garden. Would you like to see it?"

"Yes, indeed. This smells wonderful, by the way." She picked up the steaming cup Llauron set before her and followed him through a door in the kitchen into a structure that adjoined it.

Three walls of the room were made of glass, with a strange hearth in the center. The bottom of the hearth was filled with stones that glowed red with heat, over which two large copper kettles hung, filling the air with steam.

Between the kettles was a large iron brazier filled with granite-like stones, also heated red-hot. A metal cone hung from the ceiling above, dripping water slowly onto the coals, where it hissed into vapor. As a result, the room was heavy with warm moisture, which served to keep alive the thriving plants that filled the glass garden in rows, one on top of the other.

Rhapsody walked between the crowded banks of plants, enjoying the sense of false summer. She looked up at the dripping machine that was spattering droplets of moisture into the air. "What a fascinating device."

"Oh, you like that, do you? Rather ingenious, I would say. I wish I could take credit for it, but it was my father who designed and built it as a gift for my mother. She loved orchids and other hothouse flowers."

"You have some very interesting plants in here."

"Well, as I said before, you're more than welcome to stay here and learn the lore of the Filids, if you wish. There are many aspects of nature worship that I think you might enjoy, having a propensity for some of them already. I will tend to many of your lessons myself; it will be a nice break from my work."

"I don't want to take you away from your duties, Your Grace."

The Invoker smiled. "Nonsense, my dear. The nice thing about being in charge is that you get to say when you can leave. And do call me Llauron, you're making me feel old.

So, what will it be? Can you stay? Or do you have somewhere else you need to be?"

Rhapsody looked up into the twinkling blue eyes that were watching her intently. An uneasy feeling came over her; it was as if Llauron could see inside her. Even the scholars at the music academy were not able to tell a Namer from his or her speaking voice. That this pleasant, elderly man seemed to know things about her that he shouldn't made her feel even more vulnerable than she had that morning under the Tree. Still, she was here to learn more. She might as well be gracious about it.

"No," she said finally. "There's nowhere else I need to be, not for a while, at least."

24

After breaking fast with the repast Vera had left out for them, Rhapsody and Llauron walked out through the gardens and across the wide field behind the keep to the stable where the Invoker kept his horses.

Gwen had arrived prior to their leaving the house, with a new pair of leather boots and soft woolen leggings for Rhapsody. They were a little large, but wrapped her feet in warmth and kept them dry, and she thanked the house servant gratefully.

As best as she could tell, despite the size of the house and the importance of his position, the Invoker only had the two women servants aside from the guards. Rhapsody had known minor nobles in Serendair who had kept far more than that, and it made her think well of him. Llauron looked after himself, for the most part, a unique and pleasing trait in the head of a religious order.

The stables were cleaner than most houses, with cobbled floors lined in thick straw and old rugs. It was easy to see why; Llauron's steeds were among the most magnificent she had ever seen. Some were war horses, sleek and rippled in their musculature, while others had been bred according to their breed and their bloodlines, making fine riders and dray horses. Rhapsody walked up and down between the stalls, clicking to them the way her father had to his horses, and finding Llauron's steeds to be equally responsive to the soft sound.

"Do you see one you like, my dear?" Llauron asked with an approving smile.

"I like them all."

"Yes, but you can only ride one of them. If you'd like to meet Lark, we'll have to travel a bit. The herbery is on the other side of the forest clearing, several leagues from here. What about the strawberry bay? He's gentle."

Rhapsody nodded, and Llauron signaled to the stablehand. "Saddle him up, please, Norma, and Eliseus as well; we'll be heading out shortly." He took Rhapsody by the elbow and led her back out of the stable into the biting wind.

While they waited for the horses, Llauron raised the hood on Rhapsody's cloak as if she were a child. "It's probably best for you to keep this up, my dear, the wind is brisk." He followed suit with his own, then turned as the door to the stable opened and Norma came out, leading the bay and a roan with glossy mane, neatly plaited.

"Ah, there's my boy now; good morning, Eliseus." The horse snorted as if in reply, thick vapor issuing forth from his nostrils in the cold wind. "Well, then, Rhapsody, let's be off to the herbery." They mounted and rode off, Rhapsody following him over the fields to the woodlands.

𝕿his is where the herb gardens are maintained," Llauron said as they approached a wide meadow, visible past the glade through which they had ridden. "As nature priests we practice a good deal of herb lore, both in medicinal and spiritual uses. Oh, and cooking; I despise bland food."

Rhapsody chuckled and slowed the bay to a plodding walk next to Llauron. Riding through the forest had been pleasant, primarily owing to Llauron's knowledge of the terrain and the well-maintained forest paths that scored the ground, even in the snow. It seemed as if they had traveled the distance in no time.

The Invoker stopped before a large brick cottage with a thatched roof on the edge of the meadow. He dismounted and held out his hands to Rhapsody, but she shook her head politely and stepped down without help.

"This is where Lark lives, the herbalist who is responsible for maintaining the order's herb stores and gardens," Llauron said. He knocked briskly on the door. There was no answer. A moment later a voice called out from across the field near an area gated off with a large wooden fence.

"Your Grace! We're out here." Rhapsody turned to see a tall woman, dressed in thick trousers and a tunic-like shirt, waving to Llauron. Llauron raised his hand in acknowledgment.

"That's Ilyana. She's in charge of planting and training the acolytes in farm lore. Shall we go and meet them?"

"By all means."

They stepped carefully around the sleeping beds of herbs that lined the fields for miles around until they found the cobbled path, buried in the snow. As they approached the fenced area two women came around from behind it.

One was Ilyana, whom she had seen a moment before. The other was a slight woman, with a long dark braid down her back, held in place by a kerchief. Her face bore the signs of middle age and a life lived outdoors, and something else: she was Lirin.

Unlike Rhapsody's mother, who had been a Skysinger, of the Liringlas, a people noted for their blond or silvery hair and rosy complexions, Lark was Lirindarc, like those who had lived in Sagia's wood, a dark, leather-skinned people with the same slim build and angular faces as the Liringlas, but with black or brown eyes better suited to the filtered forest light.

Rhapsody's throat tightened at the sight of her, as it had earlier when she had seen Gwen. There were Lirin here; Llauron had made reference to their existence the night before in a place the Cymrians had called Realmalir, now known as Tyrian. She was not alone in her race.

Llauron stretched out his hand and brought it to rest on the woman's shoulder. "Lark, this is Rhapsody. She's my guest for a while, and a bit of an herbalist herself."

Rhapsody flushed at his words. "Oh, not really. I know a

little bit about plants, that's all." Lark nodded, her face passive.

The tall human woman put out her hand. "Nice to meet you. I'm Ilyana." Rhapsody shook hands with her and smiled, noting that a moment later an odd look crossed the woman's face.

"I'd like Rhapsody to study a bit with both of you, primarily you, Lark," Llauron said. "She's interested in horticulture, and I plan to give her a few lessons myself."

"Is she an acolyte?" Lark asked, her face still unresponsive.

"No, just a visitor. I trust you will treat her with all due respect." Lark nodded again. "Good, good. Well, please find a place for her and some work clothes. You're not afraid to get your hands dirty, are you, my dear?"

"You did see me when I came in last night, didn't you?"

Llauron laughed. "Good point. Very well, if that's clear, I'll leave you in capable hands, Rhapsody. I'll be back for you at sunset."

"She's not staying in the barracks?" Lark asked.

"No. As I believe I've already noted, she is my guest." Llauron's voice was gentle, but his eyes glinted in a manner that made Rhapsody momentarily uneasy. "I expect you know that I would not waste your time with anyone who might not be a friend to our cause, Mother." Lark nodded again, stone-faced.

"Cause?" Rhapsody asked uneasily.

Llauron and Lark exchanged a glance; then the Invoker turned to Rhapsody and smiled.

"The preservation of the forest and the Earth, the care of the Great White Tree. I have not characterized you unfairly, have I, my dear? You do respect nature, do you not?"

"Yes, indeed."

"Good, then all is as it should be. Goodbye, Mother; you as well, Ilyana. Enjoy your studies, my dear." Llauron walked back down the path to his horse, mounted, and rode off, waving.

The three women watched him until he reached the forest and had ridden out of sight. Then Ilyana put an arm around Rhapsody.

"You came last night?"

"Yes."

The two Filids looked at each other. "Then it must have been you that all the commotion was about," Ilyana said. Lark turned around and headed back to the fenced area.

"Commotion?" Rhapsody asked, her stomach going suddenly cold.

"Yes, scores of villagers from the east showed up in a rabble at the foot of the holy forest last night. Llauron had to address them all in the middle of the night and send them home. I had no idea what to make of it. Apparently they were seeking the return of someone they felt had been taken from them."

Icy claws clutched Rhapsody's stomach. What did the villagers think she had done that made them chase her this way? She hadn't been there long enough to do anything but meet Khaddyr before he whisked her away. Surely they couldn't be blaming her for any crime that had occurred.

Then she remembered her horrific appearance when she had come out of the forest. Perhaps they thought she was some kind of evil spirit, responsible for someone's death or illness, or farming woes. She pulled her cloak a little tighter about herself.

Ilyana saw her nervousness and drew her closer to her side. "Don't worry, darling, they're gone. And they won't be back. It's clear Llauron plans to protect you, and if that's the case, you can be certain you'll be safe. Come on, you can help us rake over the compost heap."

For more than a week Rhapsody came each day to study with Lark. The herbalist rarely spoke, unless she was talking about plants. It took some time for Rhapsody to realize that she was innately shy.

When she was pointing out herbs or methods to care for them, however, Lark became animated, a growing excitement entering her voice. She was a wealth of knowledge on the subject, and Rhapsody took copious notes, scribing Lark's teachings onto parchment that Ilyana had provided.

They generally spent the hours when the sun was directly overhead, or days when the weather was too rough to brave the gardens, in Lark's cottage, drying herbs and blending them together for medicinal uses and sweet-smelling sachets. The scent of the cottage was heavenly, and Rhapsody did not mind the long hours of painstaking work, enjoying the opportunity to absorb the lore. Occasionally she sang for Lark, Lirin songs that her mother had taught her, though Lark did not understand the tongue.

After ten days, Ilyana had claimed her, taking her on long rides over the vast fields in which the Filids toiled, even in winter, preparing them for spring planting. The faithful to which the Filids ministered were largely farming communities, and Ilyana had told her that the religion encompassed more than half a million known followers in the western part of the continent, a number Rhapsody found staggering.

By far the most interesting were the planting and harvesting rituals, rites that blessed the newly tilled ground and the fruit of the farmers' labor prior to it being gathered. The ceremonies that the Filidic acolytes studied were in the language of her homeland, the tongue Rhapsody had spoken as a child. The Filids called the language Old Cymrian, a thought that filled her with ironic sadness. Did that make her, and Achmed and Grunthor, Old Cymrians?

The thought gave birth immediately to an even more desolate one. They were not, in fact, Old Cymrians, but their *ancestors*. Given how long ago in the history of this place the Cymrian Age had been, it seemed as if Time had forgotten all about the three of them. When it remembered, it would undoubtedly be back to claim them.

At the end of the first month Rhapsody was handed over to Khaddyr again. The priest was the master of the healing arts, a talent he seldom let anyone forget, and though he could be somewhat pompous, Rhapsody found him to be a clear and skillful teacher, imparting his wisdom in a way that she could assimilate easily and practice immediately.

After two weeks of tending to the patients in the hospices that Khaddyr managed, she went on to Brother Aldo, who was also a Filidic healer, but of animals. She enjoyed learning from him; he was gentle and soft-spoken, and had a manner that quieted even the wild animals in his care.

Finally, she was sent to Gavin, the somber, silent chief of the foresters and scouts, the armed men she had seen when Khaddyr first brought her to the Tree. These men traveled the wide land, sometimes serving as guides to the faithful along the Cymrian Trails, two series of markers that commemorated the journeys of the First and Third Cymrian Fleets after they landed, which Llauron had referred to on her first night with him. Apparently very few people followed the Trails now; instead, the pilgrims came to worship at the Tree.

Rhapsody could see that the majority of the scouts and foresters were not escorting pilgrims, but were traveling the lands of the holy forest, engaging occasionally in combat. Many of the patients in Khaddyr's hospice were men such as these, coming in haggard and worn, and often injured. Apparently this was not particularly unusual; Khaddyr and his acolytes tended to the men without any obvious surprise.

Late each afternoon Rhapsody returned to the Invoker's house. Llauron would be finishing up the duties of his office as leader of the Filids—a substantial job, from what Rhapsody could tell.

Each town had a Filid assigned to it to assist with crops and animals, and to help maintain a balance between nature and agriculture. In addition to providing guides to the religion's spiritual sites, it also fell to Llauron's office to maintain the hostels along the way. He did not object to these tasks, but early on he had confided to her how much he missed the days of his youth, when he had roamed the wild seas and wandered the forests of the world, free from administrative duties.

His way of recapturing those lost days was by taking her with him on long walks, where he would instruct her on the balance of nature and various aspects of the forest and the world around them. He knew every animal, and roughly how many of them lived in the wood, as well as each plant and tree, knowledge that he imparted to her in his light, pleasant voice.

It was almost like listening to a song, and she strolled with him, fascinated, as he told her of trees, how the oaks were strong and sacred, how ash trees were close to the spiritual world and so their branches were often used for wands and ritual magic. He said that willows were greedy, maples were leaders, and evergreens were adventurous. He told her of the woodland plants, of mistletoe and holly, which held spiritual properties of life, of ferns and mints and countless others. Occasionally he would sing sea chanteys for her as they walked.

Llauron walked with a young man's pace and a vigor in his step; Rhapsody had known men half his age whose pace was half that of the Invoker. On their outings he carried a staff made of white wood and topped with a gleaming golden oak leaf, which he swung to keep pace rather than to bear his weight.

It had been made from a branch of the Great White Tree that had fallen ages ago during a storm and had been given to Ulbren the Younger, the Invoker of the Filids who had come from Serendair, bringing with him the religion they now practiced. It was considered the symbol of his office, but Llauron carried it as if it were an ordinary stick, pointing out birds and rapping on the trunks of ancient trees to sound their health.

Each evening their walks would end at sundown beneath the branches of the Great Tree, in time for Rhapsody to sing her twilight vespers. She had determined that Llauron had known the customs of the Liringlas prior to her arrival, and would expect her to sing her salutations to the rising sun and the stars, and so she did not attempt to hide the ritual from him, though Achmed's voice nagged in her head. The Invoker always stood beneath the Tree with her as she sang, smiling to himself, but never sharing whatever thoughts occurred to him during these times.

They would share an evening meal together, often talking late into the night about the forest and its creatures, or the Cymrian Age and all its wonder. In particular they discussed the Cymrian Council, an annual meeting of all the refugees of Serendair, held in something called the Great Moot. It was the intent of the council to maintain peace among all the diverse races that had fled the doomed Island, to keep communication channels open, a worthy aspiration that had died on the battlefields of the Cymrian War.

Llauron was of the belief that the fragmented nations that

had once been part of the Cymrian empire, Sorbold and Roland and the lands now occupied by the Firbolg, would only be able to maintain peace and resist war again if they were reunited into a common land. Rhapsody had noticed one realm missing in his discourse.

"What about the Lirin?" she asked, looking up over her sweet-fern tea.

"The Lirin were never part of the Cymrian realm. They were here first, after all, and resisted becoming part of it. But they were allies, and good friends to the First Generation, the refugees who had actually made the voyage and landed here. It was unfortunate that they ultimately got drawn into the war, which devastated much of Tyrian. And on top of that, it fragmented their society as well. Now even the Lirin are divided among themselves. A shame." Rhapsody nodded as Llauron fell silent.

"I will need to be going soon," she said as he stared into the fire. The Invoker's eyes turned back on her immediately, but she saw no sign of the glint that came into them occasionally when he was annoyed.

"Oh, dear, what a pity. I knew this day would come eventually, but I have to admit I've been dreading it, my dear. We've all grown to love you around here, Gwen and Vera and I. And I'm sure your instructors will be sorry to see you go."

"I'll be sorry to leave everyone as well," she replied sincerely. "And I've learned so much from all of you." A thought occurred to her when he mentioned the teachers. "May I ask you something about the Filidic instructors?"

"Certainly."

"The religion does not ascribe celibacy to its priests, does it?"

"No, we leave that unnatural state to the Patriarchal religion of Sepulvarta, to the Patriarch and his benisons—those are his version of our high priests, the next rank below him in the hierarchy of that faith. Benisons are sometimes also known as Blessers when it is a specific title, such as the Blesser of Avonderre. Why do you ask?"

"Well, I thought it interesting that none of the high priests of Gwynwood are married."

Llauron sat back in his chair and touched his fingertips together. "No, none of them are at that, are they?" he mused. "Well, Ilyana was married, but her husband was killed in a border incursion ten or so years back.

"Lark has never married, but then, as you know, she is very shy, as is Brother Aldo. He prefers the company of beasts to that of women, though I certainly could introduce him to some that qualify as both." Rhapsody laughed. "Gavin isn't here often or long enough to marry; he is constantly on the forest path somewhere. And Khaddyr, well, actually, he is proscribed from marriage and progeny as my Tanist."

Rhapsody blinked. "Your what?"

"The Filids now use the laws of Tanistry to select a successor to the Invoker instead of some of the uglier rituals they once practiced, which generally involved fighting to the death."

"Oh, yes, Khaddyr did tell me something about that, but he said those rituals had not been practiced in a very long time, and you had not ascended through them."

"That is correct," Llauron said. "Tanistry dictates that the religious order pick its successor, generally someone hale and hearty and likely to survive the leader." He leaned forward conspiratorially. "Frankly, I think I am much younger in body than Khaddyr, poor fellow. I doubt he'll outlive me."

She laughed again, feeling a little guilty. "I agree."

"In fact, I think that when the Circle elders meet, it's possible they will remove the title from him and make Gavin my Tanist. He has a better chance of surviving me, and is a very wise man. Not that Khaddyr isn't as well, of course. Khaddyr is one of the kindest men I know, and I think that's what makes him such a singular healer." Rhapsody nodded.

"But a Tanist vows celibacy because the whole point of having one is to avoid the problems of succession and family lineage. If the Tanist were to have children before he or she became Invoker, it would complicate things, make him less likely to have a successor named. It's an awful system; it allows the Invoker to marry eventually if he so chooses, but usually by the time he takes the office he is a brittle old man like me, having waited for his predecessor to die. Silly, isn't it?"

Exhaustion was descending on Rhapsody. "I guess so. If you'll forgive me, Llauron, I think it's time for me to retire for the evening."

Llauron stood as she did and walked her to the door of the study. "Yes, my dear, get some sleep. You have a busy day ahead of you." He touched her arm. "And you're more than welcome to invite your two companions to come back here for a visit, too. I would most enjoy meeting them, I'm sure."

Rhapsody's arm trembled beneath his touch. She had never spoken of her Firbolg friends. She looked into the blue eyes and found them twinkling in the reflected firelight.

"Excuse me?"

"Come now, my dear. These are my lands. Did you think I wouldn't recognize something foreign when it came onto them? At first I believed it might have been a Firbolg incursion, but that is most unlikely. The Firbolg lands are very far away, and two of them traveling alone would doubtless have run into one of my scouts between here and Canrif.

"No, I assumed they were waiting for you, since they have been watching this place. I long to hear the story of how you ended up in their company, but that can wait until another time. Why don't you invite them back for a visit?"

Rhapsody's entire body was trembling. "I—I don't think that would be a good idea," she whispered, her voice betraying her. "They're a little—well, antisocial."

Llauron nodded. "Well, I don't blame them a bit. Firbolg are often treated as less than human. How about a compromise? I will come to them. Ask them if they're willing to meet me, how's that? I will come to their camp instead, and come alone. It would be most enlightening; I've never met a Firbolg before."

Rhapsody's head was spinning. "All right," she said finally. "I can ask them."

The elderly face broke into a broad smile. "Very good. I will look forward to the meeting. Good night, my dear."

"Good night." She left the study quickly and wandered, as if in a daze, up the stairs and to her room. She undressed quickly and slid beneath the covers, pondering how she was going to explain this to Achmed, given his dislike of strangers and priests. Every answer she came up with was inadequate, so she closed her eyes at last and fell into an anxious sleep. Her dreams of disaster shifted from the sinking of the Island to the reaction of her friends when they learned how many of their secrets were out.

25

The light of the full moon overhead cast strange white shadows on the melting snow. The winter wind was high, and blew the cloak Rhapsody wore behind her as she rode the strawberry bay into the darkness of the forest road.

Once she came to the spot where she and the Firbolg had parted, near Tref-Y-Gwartheg, Rhapsody tied the horse to a bare-branched sycamore tree, leaving him with a feed bag of oats. Then she struggled through the mud of the forest floor to the clearing where she had agreed to meet Achmed and Grunthor.

It was easy to find the spot for two reasons, the first being that she had trained with Gavin. He had taken her through this area several times, and each time it had been effortless for her to find the spot Achmed had blazed as a waymarker.

The second reason for her ready location of the meeting place was that two shadows, one enormous, were already waiting for her there.

Until she saw her two Firbolg companions in the glen, she had not realized the depths to which she had missed both of them. The feeling was not a surprising one where Grunthor was concerned. What did cause her a moment's astonishment was that she found herself feeling the same way about Achmed. For a considerable amount of time along the Root she had hated him, blamed him for bringing this nightmare on her. Even after the passage of endless time it had not been an easy relationship to convert to the status of friendship.

But now, seeing his shadow in the moonlight beneath the branches of the forest canopy, she realized he was far more dear to her than she ever would have believed. Perhaps it was the passage of time and the natural outcome of growing accustomed to him. Perhaps it was more that he was one of only two people in the entire world who had known her in her other life.

She threw herself into Grunthor's waiting arms, struggling to ignore the hideous odor that had remained on his body from the Root. Unlike herself, the two Firbolg had not found the opportunity to wash well in the intervening two months; it was amazing that they had remained undetected all this time. She could smell them from a good distance away.

"Oi was worried, Duchess, but you're a sight for sore eyes," the Sergeant said, a slight catch in his voice.

"I can't tell you how glad I am to see you," she said, hugging him tightly. When he put her down she turned to Achmed and opened her arms as well. She thought she saw a flicker of a smile cross his face in the moonlit shadow; then he returned her embrace quickly and led her over to a sheltered copse of trees where they could confer out of the wind.

Once they had reached the hidden glen they sat on a frozen log facing each other, to keep the distance between their spoken words short.

"Did they treat you well? Were you abused in any way?" Achmed asked, tapping his gloved fingers together.

"No, not at all. Did you find out anything interesting?"

"Quite a bit. Most important where you're concerned, we explored the principality to the south of here, a place called Avonderre, and found the main trade route to the seaport. It shouldn't be too difficult to get you there undetected, and then you can secure passage home."

Rhapsody's mouth went dry, and she fought back the tears the Dhracian had forbidden so long ago. "No point in that now," she said, her voice breaking.

A look of puzzlement came into the mismatched eyes. "What? Why not?"

"Because home has been gone fourteen hundred years now."

𝒜fter she regained her composure, the two Firbolg questioned Rhapsody intently about what she had learned during her time at Llauron's, particularly the information that had pertained to Serendair.

She went over everything she knew, in some cases several

times, outlining Llauron's story of Gwylliam, the last of the Seren high kings, and his forewarning of the Island's doom. She explained the arrival of the Cymrians and their assimilation into the culture of this land, and how the Age they had brought and the realm they had founded had disappeared in the smoke and devastation of a great war centuries ago.

Achmed had asked her many questions she had been unable to answer, notably exactly how the Island had really met its doom, and how long it had been between their leaving the Island through the Root, and when the Cymrian ships had sailed. Rhapsody found the questions tiresome.

"Look, I didn't think it was wise to ask that," she said, somewhat testily. "What did you expect me to say—'Hey, Llauron, I've never heard of Gwylliam before, he must have come after Trinian, who was the crown prince when I lived there. How many years or kings after him was Gwylliam?' "

Beneath his tattered hood Achmed smiled slightly. "I suppose you have a point. I was just hoping to know how things worked out there, if anything that was being planned when we left came to pass."

"I have no idea. I don't even know if Gwylliam was of Trinian's line, or if Trinian even ascended the throne. For all I know, Gwylliam or one of his predecessors usurped the throne from the rightful heirs."

"You have no idea what a real possibility that is."

"And I don't care!" she shouted. Grunthor quickly put his hand to her lips, covering much of her face.

She lowered her voice, but the anger was still there. "Don't you see? It doesn't make a damned bit of difference. Everyone and everything I've ever loved is *dead*, and has been for more than a millennium; do you think I care what the lineage of the king was? Whether your hunters lived a year, or ten, or a hundred? They're dead, too. So celebrate; you've lost your enemies. Just don't expect me to join you."

Achmed and Grunthor exchanged a glance. "Oi 'ope you're right, miss," Grunthor said at last.

"Of course I'm right. Didn't you hear what I said? *Fourteen centuries.*"

"It's not a given, Rhapsody," Achmed said tersely. "There are some evils for which time is not a barrier or a limitation."

"Well, Achmed, you can have a go at asking Llauron yourself. He wants to meet you both."

Achmed recoiled like the spring of his cwellan. "What?"

Rhapsody withered under the icy stare. "He knows you're here; he told me so last night. I didn't give you away; I swear. He is the supreme head of his religion, the Filids; each of them knows the forest intimately, and these are his lands. He could feel you on them. He said he would like to meet you, and would come to you, if you were uncomfortable coming to him."

Grunthor looked dismayed, and Achmed buried his head in his hands. "Gods. Well, I suppose it was to be expected. This is a very strange place; what we saw made no sense, wherever we went."

"How so?"

"Everywhere we scouted there seemed to be peculiar border incursions, and random raids on villages that were totally unarmed and unprepared, though it is obvious the people of this region have come to expect this, in a way.

"At first we thought the Lirin lands to the south and this area were at war, but there are no other signs of it. Just pointless pillaging and looting, destruction of property and slaughter for no apparent reason.

"The raiders are from different places each time, and they don't seem to be after anything but destruction and terror. We watched huge stacks of valuables seized in one of the attacks piled into a village square and burned, instead of being taken and sold.

"Once we tracked a raiding party that had destroyed a town in Avonderre and saw it return to the guard barracks of the very town it had attacked. We could have written it off to treachery, but then within a few days the town came under attack again, and this time the same guards defended it with their lives.

"Something evil, diabolical even, is going on in this place. War is the end result of actions like this, particularly when racial hatred is involved. It's only a matter of time before the Lirin lands and some of the central principalities of Roland are in all-out combat."

Rhapsody sighed. "Wonderful. Is it too late to go back and live on the Root?"

Grunthor chuckled. "Sorry, Yer Ladyship, the tavern is closed."

"Perhaps meeting this priest might give us some answers at that," Achmed said as if musing aloud. He grimaced. "I hate the clergy, but I suppose I could hold my nose long enough to talk to him for a few hours."

Rhapsody laughed. "No offense, brother dear, but I don't think you're the one who will be needing to hold his nose."

Despite the distance Grunthor was maintaining, Rhapsody could tell the strawberry bay was nervous. She could feel the trembling muscles of its flanks beneath her legs.

"I'll be back in the morning," she said, running her hand comfortingly down the animal's neck. "Once I've given Llauron the message I'll come back and stay with you until he comes." She took the reins in hand.

"Hold up," Achmed said. He reached into the pocket of his makeshift cloak and pulled out the oilcloth rubbing. "Can you read this?"

Rhapsody took it and held it up to her face in the darkness, trying to illuminate it with the moonlight. A moment later a tiny flame sparked, and Achmed held a wick from the tinderbox over it.

Her brow furrowed. "What is this?"

"It's a rubbing we took off the plaque we told you about in that ship-temple."

"Hmmm. It's not very clear. These symbols on the top spell out *Kirsdirke*—no, *Kirsdarke*. There are too many parts down below it that are smudged or missing to get a real sense of what the text says. Something about Kirsdarke being committed unto the sea and the hand of All-God, probably 'the Creator,' Abbat—Father—something that begins with 'M'; I can't tell. This part says something about the altar stone of the All-God's temple."

"The plaque was on the front of an obsidian block."

"Maybe that was the altar stone. It mentions Serendair here, I think, at least I can make out several letters in the right places to spell *Serendair*. It could be something else. It also mentions something about Kirsdarke being borne by someone named Ma—gint, maybe, Monodiere."

"MacQuieth? MacQuieth Monodiere?"

Rhapsody nodded. "Perhaps. It could be, I can't tell. Was that *the* MacQuieth? The hero from home?"

"Yes. We thought perhaps this place was Monodiere, but I guess we're farther away from Serendair even than that."

"You're right," Rhapsody agreed. "Monodiere was on the mainland of a landmass that Serendair traded with, and was commonly known to cartographers. This place was uncharted, at least in detail, thought to be uninhabited when we—" Her voice broke.

"It must have been difficult trying to adjust to the knowledge of how far out of time we are, all alone these past few months," Achmed said, his voice uncharacteristically gentle. "It will get easier."

Rhapsody tried to smile, but the attempt was feeble. "Perhaps for you," she said. "I'll be back." She clicked to the horse and rode off into the night.

*L*lauron came to the clearing in the woods two nights later. A fire had been laid, and logs set around it to sit on, better to facilitate what Rhapsody expected to be a difficult conversation. Achmed was fully robed and hooded, with only his eyes showing. Grunthor, on the other hand, had opted to be comfortable and had removed his spiked helmet, under the assumption that he would be rather discernible no matter what he did.

The Invoker came dressed as he usually was, in the plain gray robes of his order, a simple hemp rope tied as a belt around the waist. He maintained a respectful distance from the fire until invited nearer, and then sat and chatted pleasantly while he opened the sack he had brought with him and offered the others fruit, bread and cheese, and a stout bottle of brandy, for which he had brought silver snifters.

"It's a pleasure to meet you both at last," he said as he poured a generous splash into Grunthor's glass. "Any friend of this lady is welcome in these woods and in my home. Perhaps after we've had a chance to get to know one another a bit, you might do me the favor of taking advantage of my hospitality for a while. The house is simple, but the beds are comfortable and the food is wholesome. And we can see about reoutfitting you." A shower of sparks from the fire broke into the air and was extinguished on the wind.

"We'll see," said Achmed noncommittally.

"I was hoping you might tell us a story, Llauron, perhaps of the history of this place. I've told Grunthor and Achmed what a wonderful storyteller you are," Rhapsody said.

The blazing firelight reflected off the kindly face. "Of course; I'd be delighted." He leaned forward, resting his elbows on his knees, and touched the fingertips of his folded hands to his lips for a moment. His eyes glittered in the dark.

"Long ago, more years than even He-Who-Counts can remember, an ancient copper dragon lived at the foot of the Great White Tree, though it was but a sapling in those days of the Earth's childhood. These were her lands, from the northern fringe of the Lirin realm in the south to the edge of the Hintervold in the north, and she lived here alone, for she was suspicious of outsiders, and humans in particular.

"Because her power over the Earth was so great, no human was able to broach her domain, and so this place was one of mystery to the world of men. The Lirin she trusted, for though their race was not as ancient as her own, they were one with the land, much as she was, and they lived peaceably as neighbors. The dragon's name was Elynsynos.

"One day the dragon looked out over the sea and saw a light on the waves unlike any she had ever seen before. It was a fire burning within water, and held within a tiny crystal globe, serving as a candle on the water, a mariner's marker in times of darkness or shipwreck, a beacon in the dark. The melding of the two opposing elements, fire and water, fascinated Elynsynos, and she took it as a sign that change was in the wind.

"Not long afterward a sailor touched the shore of her realm. He was a tall man, golden of skin, one of the race known as the Ancient Seren, the indigenous people of the Island of Serendair, the land on the other side of the world from which he had come. The dragon grew even more excited, because she recognized his race as one of the Firstborn, the five strains of beings that were created first when the world was new. She knew this because, like the Ancient Seren, dragons are also a firstborn race."

"What are the others?" Grunthor asked.

"Each of the five elements, ether, water, wind, earth, and fire, was the parent of a race. The Seren were the oldest, born of ether, the matter that makes up the stars. The children of water were called Mythlin. Those born of the wind were known as the Kith. The dragons were the offspring of the Earth itself. Lastly, the race given birth to by the rashest of all the elements, fire, was called F'dor. But that's a different story, one better suited to the light of day.

"The sailor's name was Merithyn. He was an explorer, sent out in the service of his sovereign, Gwylliam, the last of the Seren high kings, to find a suitable place for his people to colonize. Gwylliam knew that their homeland was about to be destroyed in fire, and he wanted to save his people and their culture, though I suspect there might also have been the desire to maintain his rulership as well. He had sent Merithyn forth to find that suitable place.

"Eventually Merithyn came to the borders of Elynsynos's realm but, unlike the other men, he was able to cross them without trouble. Perhaps this is because, as a member of a firstborn race older than Elynsynos herself, his bond to the elements was stronger than hers. Or, more likely, it was because she wanted him to come to her. In her fascination she had assumed a human form, one like that of his own race, designing it to be what she perceived he would find attractive. Apparently she chose well, for, upon seeing her, Merithyn fell in love with her.

"Elynsynos lost her heart to the wayfarer as well. When he explained his mission she decided the best way to solve his dilemma and to keep him with her always was to offer his people haven within her lands.

"Merithyn was overjoyed, and returned to Serendair to issue the invitation to Gwylliam and prepare the refugees for the voyage. He promised to return and, as a token of his pledge, he gave her the gift of Crynella's candle, the distress beacon of melded fire and water she had first seen him by, named for the Seren queen who made it for her own seafaring lover.

"Gwylliam was delighted with the news. In Merithyn's absence he had been preparing for the evacuation, and so now three fleets of vessels, almost a thousand in total, were being readied. Gwylliam had waited until he had word of their destination before choosing the final makeup of the fleets, whom he planned to send in three waves to ensure the greatest possibility of survival.

"Upon discovering that the new land was uninhabited, he determined that the army did not need to be in the First Wave. Instead, he sent the people who would design and build the new world, the engineers and the architects, the healers and the farmers, the masons and the carpenters, the physicians, the scholars, and the Filids. While all races were represented, about half of the First Fleet were Lirin, because of the presence of that race in the new world. To protect the First Fleet he sent the Lirin champion, a Lirin woman named Oelendra, who was the Iliachenva'ar, and a few of her retinue."

"The what?" Rhapsody interjected.

"Iliachenva'ar. The word, loosely translated, means 'bearer of the sword of light,' a weapon known as Daystar Clarion. It was a fiery blade, consecrated to the elements of fire and the stars, known as ether, or *seren*, in their language."

Achmed nodded, but said nothing. So that was how the Seren sword had come to this place.

"At any rate," Llauron continued, "with Merithyn to guide them to the new land, and Oelendra to protect them, the First Fleet was well prepared to sail across the world and survive in the dragon's lands.

"The Second Fleet, made up largely of the same types of people, but with more military might, would set sail a few weeks behind them.

"The Third, and final, Fleet would be delayed until the very end. It was the last chance for people to evacuate, and the army would travel in that Wave to guard their exit. It was with this fleet that Gwylliam himself sailed, having remained behind to encourage as many stragglers to leave as he could. He stayed until the last ship of the last fleet was ready to sail, and then boarded, watching the Island that had been his birthright disappear over the horizon for the last time.

"They say the voyage was dangerous and difficult. Halfway across the ocean a great storm came up, a hurricane the like of which had never been seen before. The legends say that at its eye was a demon of supreme evil, a monster who had caused the storm for the purpose of destroying the fleets." Llauron's face lost for a moment the rapt expression it had held since the tale had begun, and a mischievous look twinkled in his eye. "Of course, if you learn more about the Cymrians, you will see that they suffered from an inflated idea of self-importance. A natural disaster could only have been meant for them, despite all the other innocents who suffered because of it.

"Back to the tale. Merithyn's ship went down. There are accounts that say he died sacrificing himself to the demon at the center of the storm, saving the First Fleet in the process, but more likely he was merely a victim of the hurricane, since his ship broke apart in the storm and went to the bottom with all hands. A few other ships were lost as well.

"Without Merithyn to guide them, the task fell to Oelendra, the Iliachenva'ar, to lead these refugees onward to a place she had never been before. The flaming sword of the stars served as a beacon in the raging tempest, keeping the flotilla together, until they finally made it out of the storm's clutches and to shore.

"The First Fleet landed on the coast of Avonderre, miraculously near where Merithyn himself had dropped anchor. Once they had regrouped, and determined that no other ships from their Wave were coming, Oelendra led them into the lands of the dragon, their host, who had invited them to come. There were two problems, however."

The story, one which Llauron had never related before, had intrigued Rhapsody. "And what were they?" she asked, trying not to seem overly interested.

"Well, obviously, Elynsynos was extremely upset that Merithyn had not returned. It was her interest in him personally that had led her to open her lands for the first time to men other than the indigenous Lirin. To say that she was disappointed in his absence is a bit of an understatement.

"In addition, she did not know what had happened to him, and felt betrayed. She went on a terrible rampage, abandoned the Tree and her lands and retreated to her cave in the northern wastes, the place where Merithyn had carved Gwylliam's missive: *Cyme we inne firð, fram the grip of deaþ to lif inne ðis smylte land.*"

"Meaning what?" Achmed asked. His tone was surly.

Llauron smiled. "Of course, how rude of me not to translate. In the Old Cymrian and Universal Ship's Cant it meant 'Come we in peace, from the grip of death to life in this fair land.' Perhaps a better translation of *smylte* would be *serene*. It was this phrase that earned the refugees of Serendair the name 'Cymrians' with the people they eventually met here, since that was the first thing the refugees always said upon meeting someone.

"One of the tragedies of this tale, of which there are many, of course, is that if Merithyn had not loved Elynsynos as well, she would have known what befell him. He had given her Crynella's candle, his distress beacon. It was a small item, but a powerful one, because it contained the blending of two opposing elements, fire and water. Had it been with him when his ship went down, she would have seen him, and perhaps might even have been able to rescue him. But he had left it with her to comfort her, as a sign of his commitment. Alas, such it is with many good intentions. And now it only serves as the key ring of an old man."

With that he reached into the pocket of his robe and drew forth a small crystal globe the size of a chestnut. The tiny glowing light inside it pierced the darkness, illuminating the Invoker in a circle of radiance that outshone the fire at his feet.

Rhapsody's mouth opened in awe, despite her best efforts to remain disinterested. "That's it? That's Crynella's candle?"

Llauron chuckled. "Yes, or a good copy. You can never trust antiquities merchants entirely, after all."

"You bought it? An ancient artifact?"

"Yes; paid quite a sum for it, actually."

"You said there were two problems." Achmed's distinctive

voice cut through the reverie that the glow of the candle seemed to have caused. "What was the other?"

Llauron's wrinkled face lost its smile. "What Merithyn did not know was that, when he left, Elynsynos was with child."

26

"With child? The dragon was pregnant?"

Llauron laughed at the look on Rhapsody's face. "It does make a rather amusing mental picture, doesn't it?"

"Not to me," she said. "I find it very sad. I'm sure she was terrified, as well as lonely and devastated at what she thought was betrayal, especially if she was trapped in a form that was not her own." The Singer grew silent, and the firelight dimmed noticeably.

"Indeed, which is probably what led her to do what she did."

"Which was—?" Achmed prompted, annoyed at the storyteller's tactics.

"When she saw that Merithyn was not among the First Fleet, Elynsynos abandoned the children at the foot of the Tree and left."

"Children?" Grunthor asked. His voice caused Rhapsody to jump a little; he had been silent for almost the entire tale. "More than one?"

"Yes, she had given birth to three girls, triplets, though not identical. As she was an egg-layer in her natural form, a multiple birth was hardly unexpected. When the Cymrians came to the Tree they met the women there; they had grown quickly in the absence of a nurturing mother. Dragons are very resilient, I've been told.

"The women resembled their father, in that they were tall and golden-skinned, as he had been, though they all had features of their mother as well. Because they had the appearance of Ancient Seren, the First Fleet immediately felt a kinship with them.

"The women were blessed with unusual powers, as you can imagine would come from the union of two firstborn races.

Because their father had sailed back and forth across the Prime Meridian, they were tied to Time as well as to the other elements. They were Seers, oracles who could look beyond the moment and into other places in Time. Unfortunately, as a result of this gift they were all insane, though to varying degrees.

"The youngest, Manwyn, was the Oracle of the Future. She was said to have been the most mad of the three, because the knowledge of the Future is the most powerful and the most threatening. The legends say she was often delusional and spent most of her time muttering to herself. And though her gift held great power, it was also, in a way, useless, for it was impossible to distinguish the true prophecies from the mad-woman's ravings.

"The middle sister, Rhonwyn, was the Seer of the Present. It was said that she was kind and lucid, but only in the mo-ment, having no memory of her thoughts a moment later when the Present became the Past.

"Of the three, only the eldest, Anwyn, was able to greet the refugees. She held the secrets of the Past, knowledge that was less volatile and dangerous to possess than that of her youngest sibling, and more coherent and meaningful than that of the middle child. As a result, she knew who the Cymrians were, and why they had come, and made them welcome in the lands that had belonged to her mother.

"So the Cymrians of the First Fleet, recognizing her as the living bond between the old world of her father and the new world which was her mother's, made her their lady, and set-tled into a harmonious union with these western lands and the Lirin of Realmalir.

"Now, to the Second Fleet. Unlike the First Fleet, who caught the brunt of the hurricane, the Second Fleet saw it approaching, being some distance behind the others. As a re-sult they were able to avoid major damage from it, though a few ships were lost, but were instead blown off course by it.

"When the storm abated, they were too far from the course to correct it, especially since once they crossed the Prime Meridian they were forced back again. Land came in sight shortly thereafter, and rather than trying to find Merithyn's paradise, their leader, the great warrior MacQuieth, decided to land there, in the inhabited country of Manosse. They and their descendants are there to this day."

At the name, each of the three companions felt their palms go dry. Nearly everyone in Serendair had heard of Mac-Quieth, though the Firbolg knew more of him than Rhapsody did.

"MacQuieth was the Kirsdarkenvar, the bearer of Kirs-darke, the legendary sword of water. He was also said to be the master of that element; perhaps that is why his passage on the sea was safe. And of course he was a great hero, the king's champion, the man who slew Tsoltan, the enemy leader in the Great War. He—"

"Llauron, hold up a moment, please," Rhapsody interrupted nervously. Achmed's face twisted into a scowl, and he exhaled in quiet frustration.

She did not see his irritation. "Could you explain what you just said about Manosse?" she asked. "*They* and their descendants? I don't understand. You said that was fourteen centuries ago. Surely the First Generation Cymrians are all long dead."

Llauron laughed. "One might feel confident in such an assertion, but one might be wrong. Singers; the guardians of accurate details. All right, let me elaborate.

"The First Generation had come from one of the five places where time began, the Island of Serendair. They crossed the Prime Meridian, which is the place the Earth demarks Time, and came to another place, where Time began—this land, the birthplace of the race of dragons—although the Second Fleet landed elsewhere.

"As a result, Time seemed to have no hold on them, and they did not grow old as other mortals did, but remained at the physical age they had been at the time of crossing over the Meridian. The exceptions were the children. They slowly continued to grow and age until they reached adulthood, and then remained there eternally."

"Are you one of them?" asked Achmed bluntly.

Llauron laughed aloud. "Goodness, no, though I wish I could have the longevity and the power sometimes. You must think me very well preserved, young man. No, I'm afraid I'm not. Just an interested student of them.

"If you'll bear with me, I'm almost done with the Second Fleet. A few of the ships, most notably those whose passengers were Ancient Seren and other firstborn races, traveled farther east, not wishing to be part of the western landmass that MacQuieth had chosen. They found instead a small, uninhabited island between the two continents, blessed with fair weather and temperate breezes from the trade winds and a warm sea current. It was a true paradise, and they chose to stay there and make their colony alone, separated from their countrymen. Their land is Gaematria, generally called the Isle of the Sea Mages.

"That leaves only the Third Fleet. Gwylliam's Wave of ships waited until there was no one left on Serendair who was willing to be saved, then sailed into the east wind northward. But they landed well to the south of where Merithyn and the First Fleet had, along the southern coast of what are now the nonaligned states and the country of Sorbold.

"Unlike this rich and primeval forest, kept undisturbed from man for millennia by the dragon who ruled it, the places that the Third Fleet landed were hostile and unforgiving. Most of Sorbold is arid, and that which is not is mountainous or grassland steppes. In addition, those lands were inhabited by people who did not especially appreciate the presence of the Cymrians, and oftentimes sought to drive them back into the sea. The Third Fleet had to struggle to survive, always fighting for what they needed.

"They had two advantages, however. The first was Gwylliam himself. He was a practical man and a resourceful leader, skilled in the sciences, by nature and training a talented architect and engineer. Many of his clever inventions, coupled with his battle tactics, were the only things that allowed the outnumbered fleet to survive.

"The second was the choice Gwylliam had made to keep the army back until the last. This was fortuitous for several reasons: it had allowed the First Fleet to be seen by the dragon not as hostile invaders but as invited guests, it added to the security of the Island in its last days, and it gave Gwylliam a fighting force on the most difficult of the three Cymrian fronts. It was Gwylliam's responsibility to see to the safety of the fleets, and he did as well as any man could. If evil followed them, there was no way he could have prevented it."

"And did it?" Achmed sat forward in the firelight as he asked his question.

Llauron looked away for a moment. When he looked back his face was grave. "It may have; there was a prophecy to that effect."

"A prophecy?"

The old man smiled reassuringly at Rhapsody, whose brow was furrowed. "Yes, there was a time in the Cymrian Age, before the Great War, when Manwyn, the Oracle of the Future, would occasionally spout predictions, oftentimes at meetings of the Cymrian Council. One of them was recorded after a long argument at one such council. Of course, I can only read the history, so I don't know how accurate it is, but I memorized it long ago. Would you like to hear it?"

"Yes," Rhapsody answered, feeling a sudden chill in the wind.

"Well, I'm afraid I've gotten a little ahead of myself. Let me retrench for a moment.

"Eventually the Third Wave Cymrians battled their way across the landscape, sometimes subduing their attackers, until they came to the mountains at the north edge of the Sorboldian desert. That mountain range was vast and forbidding, dividing the lands past it from the rest of the known world.

"Those lands were separated from the mountains by a deep canyon, but past it was a vast and fertile heath, and a hidden realm rich in soil and the treasures of the Earth. It was also uninhabited, and for many of the reasons I just stated, Gwylliam decided that this would be the place the Third Fleet would settle. He named it Canrif, the Cymrian word for *century,* because it was said that within one hundred years it would be the greatest civilization the world had ever seen.

"And, arguably, he accomplished the task. The fleet had contained immigrants of many different races, with many different needs, and Gwylliam met them all. The earth dwellers, the Nain and the Gwadd, made their homes within the endless tunnels of the mountains. Men found fields and meadows to live within and to farm on the Blasted Heath, and deeper within the Hidden Realm. The Lirin who had traveled with him set up villages within a dark forest they had discovered.

"In addition, Gwylliam built a vast and glorious city within the mountains themselves, devising great machines that filled the underground caverns with fresh air, as well as warmth in the winter. He and the Nain built giant forges that burned continuously, hammering out the steel for constructing his empire and the weapons to defend it."

"Where are these mountains?" Achmed asked. "What are they called?"

"They lie to the east of the province of Bethe Corbair, the easternmost border of Roland. They also border Sorbold's northern rim. The Cymrians called them the Manteids, but the Firbolg, who now live within them, call them the Teeth."

"The Teeth?" Rhapsody asked incredulously.

"Yes, and should you ever see them, you'll understand why. It is an accurate description. What was once the glory of Canrif is now the domain of the Firbolg; it is a dark and forbidding place."

Grunthor looked unimpressed. "Oi would certainly 'ope so."

Llauron smiled and took a sip from his silver snifter.

"Then one day, fifty years or so after they had landed, the First and the Third Fleets met up again. There was great rejoicing, and great confusion. The members of the First Fleet, many of them formerly Gwylliam's subjects, and their descendants, had sworn fealty to Anwyn, who had now been their lady for half a century. With the Second Fleet off in Manosse, still unaccounted for, it left a dilemma about what to do next.

"The Cymrians wished to be one people again, both for the sake of their original quest, the survival of their culture, and the new prospect of land domination. For between them, Gwylliam and Anwyn ruled all the lands of Roland and Sorbold, as well as Canrif. The Lirin were still apart, though they were Anwyn's allies.

"Fortunately, a peaceful solution was reached. All the Cymrians met in a great council, the first of such meetings, and chose the two of them, Anwyn and Gwylliam, to rule the newly united realm as their lord and lady. Recognizing the possibility of dynastic power, the two decided to formalize their union and marry."

"Did they love each other?" Rhapsody asked.

The Invoker looked at her oddly for a moment, the wind blowing the gray strands of his hair stiffly. "The writings do not mention that," he said finally. "But between them they ushered in the Cymrian Age, the greatest time this land has ever known. And they reigned in peace and prosperity for more than three hundred years."

"What about the prophecy?" Achmed asked.

"Oh, yes. I believe I've mentioned Oelendra to you. She had a tendency to be a bit paranoid, from what the writings say. Perhaps this was because she had not expected to shoulder the leadership of the First Fleet but was forced to do so when Merithyn died. She was convinced a great evil had followed on Gwylliam's ship, and at the council, when the lord and lady announced their engagement, she asked Manwyn before the assemblage if her suspicions were true. Manwyn's answer was this prophecy:

Among the last to leave, among the first to come,
Seeking a new host, uninvited, in a new place.
The power gained being the first,
Was lost in being the last.
Hosts shall nurture it, unknowing,
Like the guest wreathed in smiles
While secretly poisoning the larder
Jealously guarded of its own power
Ne'er has, nor ever shall its host bear or sire children,
Yet ever it seeks to procreate.

Silence fell as the four contemplated the augury. Finally Grunthor spoke.

"Oi've no idea what that means, Yer Excellency. Ya gonna give us a clue?"

Llauron smiled. "I have no idea either, my friend. As I said before, Manwyn was insane and sometimes muttered strange things. No one paid much attention to it at the time, but in hindsight, it may have been a prediction that an evil had come from the Island, one of ancient lineage—that's the 'among the first to come' part, I think—and, though powerless upon arrival, would grow in strength until it took over the land."

Rhapsody's hands went suddenly cold. "And did that happen?"

The elderly face grew sad. "That's hard to say, my dear. Ultimately it was Gwylliam and Anwyn themselves that brought an end to the Cymrian Age, raining death and devastation down on their own people."

"How?" Achmed asked.

"I don't know if there had been problems between them prior to the event which sparked it; I assume there were, as these things rarely come out of nowhere. Simply put, and without a lot of fanfare, Gwylliam struck her. History has never recorded why, but it is insignificant in the wake of the disaster that ensued. It has become known only as the Grievous Blow, more for the grief it brought to the Cymrian people than to either the lord or lady.

"Anwyn, furious, returned to her lands in the west and rallied her original subjects, the members of the First Fleet, to defend her honor. This represented an irrevocable tear in the nation, because the First Generation Cymrians and generations of their descendants had come to see themselves as a united people, loyal to both the lord and lady. But Anwyn was wyrmkin, meaning there was dragon's blood in her veins, and she was not to be appeased by anything but Gwylliam's death.

"In turn, when Anwyn's army began attacking his strongholds, Gwylliam became blinded by hatred as well, and set out to destroy his estranged wife and her allies. It would be impossible to describe the seven hundred years of bloodshed that followed; you haven't the time, and I haven't the stomach. It would suffice to say that, as glorious as the birth and life of the Cymrian Age had been, its death was equally hideous.

"Gwylliam's general was a brilliant, sometimes cruel man named Anborn. Anborn's victories against the First Fleet and subsequently the Lirin, whom Anwyn had managed to convince to join her, made his name the most hated word in their language.

"And Anwyn's army was responsible for the deaths of countless members of the Third Fleet, though the lines had blurred to the point where no one could tell who was winning, just who was dying. It would suffice to say that it was no one's finest hour, and is why the distant descendants of the Cymrians who still live in these divided realms tend not to make their lineage public."

Achmed broke into a smile. "So you're saying that around here, the word *Cymrian* is synonymous with *arse-rag*?"

Rhapsody jabbed him viciously in the ribs, but Llauron merely smiled.

"To many, yes. Time has a way of blurring the memory, however, and there are those who know mostly of the great power the Cymrians wielded, and little of the destruction they wreaked upon the land. In some ways they are revered, probably because most of the Orlandan provinces—the provinces of Roland—as well as Manosse, and the Isle of the Sea Mages, are all ruled by descendants of Cymrian stock."

"So 'oo won?" Grunthor asked.

"Well, no one, really. Anwyn killed Gwylliam, that much is known, or at least she claimed to have, and no one ever saw him again, so they tended to believe her. It would have taken someone of her power to do it, because of one important factor: Gwylliam was basically immortal, even more than the Cymrians themselves were.

"Unlike his subjects, who did not age or become ill, but could bleed as well as the next man, Gwylliam was impervious to damage in the new world. The writings speculate that this might have been because he had stayed to guard the retreat, had been the last to leave, the last to cross the Prime Meridian, and so the new world held no threat to him. The real reason is hard to say.

"Anwyn returned, triumphant, to the council, claiming victory and sole rulership of the Cymrians and their lands. To her shock the council cast her out and drove her from their realm. So, though she won the seven hundred years' war, and destroyed her hated husband, in the end she was left with nothing. A colossal waste, wouldn't you say?"

"Yes," said Rhapsody resoundingly. "What happened to her? Where is Anwyn now?"

Llauron drank the rest of his brandy and tossed the snifter back into the sack. "The writings say she retreated to a mountainous lair high in the crags of the White Peaks in the Hintervold, well beyond her former lands. Occasionally some poor unfortunate makes his way to see her, to gain knowledge of the Past; she was, after all, first and foremost gifted as a Seer. Whether they ever find her I do not know."

"So where do things stand now?" Achmed asked.

"Well, the Cymrians, even after the war was over, were so damaged by it that they never really healed. It has been almost four hundred years, and the rift was never mended. Instead, they assimilated into the lesser cultures around them; a pity, really.

"The ties they had to the elements and to Time were the secret to their tremendous advances as a civilization. Without that, the realm has become divided, uneasy, and has regressed from its days of splendor in science and scholarship, the arts and international trade, architecture and medicine. We are a more primitive people as a result.

"Even the religions are divided. Where once we were of one faith, now the areas that most commonly allied with the First Fleet are the faithful of my theology, the belief system of the Filids, the stewards of nature. Most of Roland, however, are adherents to the religion of the All-God, sometimes called the Creator. The head of that church is the Patriarch, whose basilica is in the holy city of Sepulvarta, to the south near Sorbold. Another pity. We both worship a single God; it seems a shame that even in this we are divided.

"And war will come again. Since the Great War ended there has been serious unrest, and though on the surface things are peaceful currently, that will eventually change. The last several decades have seen endless border skirmishes, incursions for no reason into villages and towns that result in horrendous destruction. Racial tensions are growing, and no one seems to know why these acts of terror occur, even, sometimes, those caught committing them. It's all quite frightening."

"What do you think can mend the rift, keep the war from escalating?" Rhapsody asked.

Llauron sighed. "I don't know if anything can, my dear.

When all this was laid at Anwyn's feet, just before she was cast out of the council, her sister Manwyn tried to intervene, promising that there was hope for the eventual healing of the rift and for peace to·come. But no one believed her; they knew she was trying to spare her sister from being disowned by her subjects."

"What was this prophecy?" Achmed asked. Llauron closed his eyes, thinking. Then he spoke.

> *The Three shall come, leaving early, arriving late,*
> *The lifestages of all men:*
> *Child of Blood, Child of Earth, Child of the Sky.*
> *Each man, formed in blood and born in it,*
> *Walks the Earth and sustained by it,*
> *Reaching to the sky, and sheltered beneath it,*
> *He ascends there only in his ending, becoming part of the stars.*
> *Blood gives new beginning, Earth gives sustenance,*
> *The Sky gives dreams in life—eternity in death.*
> *Thus shall the Three be, one to the other.*

The Invoker gathered the rest of his belongings and the remains of the meal. When he was finished he looked at them again.

"This made as little sense to the council as it does, no doubt, to you. It was clear that these three saviors were Anwyn and her sisters, which was why the council suspected that it was a ruse to spare the Lady Cymrian from being ousted. Anborn, Gwylliam's general, asked Manwyn in an ugly manner what it all meant, how the Three, as she called them, would be able to mend so great a rift. He got gibberish for an answer.

> *As each life begins, Blood is joined, but is spilled as well; it divides*
> *   too easily to heal the rift.*
> *The Earth is shared by all, but it too is divided, generation into*
> *   generation.*
> *Only the Sky encompasses all, and the sky cannot be divided;*
> *   thus shall it be the means by which peace and unity will come.*
> *If you seek to mend the rift, General, guard the Sky, lest it fall.*

"The great general cursed her then, shouting that she should keep her useless prophecies to herself. Manwyn left the council, to follow Anwyn, I suppose, but turned before she left and issued one last prophecy to Anborn.

" 'General,' she said, 'first you must heal the rift within yourself. With Gwylliam's death you now are the king of soldiers, but until you find the slightest of your kinsmen and protect that helpless one, you are unworthy of forgiveness. And so it shall be until you either are redeemed, or die unabsolved."

"And did he?"

"I've no idea. That was between him and his Creator. Well, gentlemen, as I told your friend, you are more than welcome to stay at my home for a day or so, or more, if you're not headed anywhere. I can offer you a bed and a chance to bathe, as well as some new clothes; Gwen has already outfitted Rhapsody quite nicely."

Rhapsody and Grunthor both looked at Achmed, who nodded after a moment. Grunthor broke into a pleased grin.

"Well, that's mighty kind o' you, Yer Excellency."

Rhapsody tapped him on the arm as the three companions followed Llauron out of the glade.

"Grunthor, generally the title of address granted to Invokers, the Patriarch, benisons, the Filidic high priests and other high-ranking clergy is 'Your Grace,' not 'Your Excellency.' "

The giant Bolg grabbed her hand. "And if we don't 'urry and catch up to 'im, *your* title is gonna be 'You're Lost.' "

27

Unlike the first part of her visit with Llauron, the time Rhapsody spent in the house of the Invoker with the Firbolg bristled with uneasiness. Neither Achmed nor Grunthor wished to be seen by any of the faithful who were constantly in proximity to the Tree.

Gwen and Vera were terrified of the two men, particularly Gwen, who was given the unwelcome task of making their new clothes. After one fitting with Grunthor, Rhapsody was able to employ the new medical skills she had learned from Khaddyr to help Llauron's housekeeper over her palpitations.

As soon as they were outfitted and provisioned again, they made ready to take their leave. Llauron seemed genuinely sorry to see them go.

"Where will you be heading now, my dear?" he asked Rhapsody, who was watching the men pack the satchels for traveling.

"East," she said simply. She knew better than to tell him that Achmed and Grunthor wanted to find the Teeth and the realm of the Firbolg; the prospect was not one she relished.

The three companions had talked long into each night, discussing their next moves, though Achmed had refused to give her the reasons for his plans, saying that they would discuss it once they were off Llauron's lands.

They had agreed, after some hot debate, to stay together until they got a better feel for the lay of the land, at which time they would determine where Rhapsody would live. Having spent so long in the hope of returning to the Island, she had not yet fully absorbed the thought of staying permanently in the new world.

Llauron looked back over his shoulder at the Firbolg. "East, hmmm. Well, if that's the case, why don't I give you a letter of introduction to my dear friend, Lord Stephen Navarne. He is the regent of the province due east of here, the duke, actually; quite a nice chap. I think you'll like him. And I know he'll enjoy you as well."

His eyes glittered momentarily; there was a subtext to his statement that Rhapsody was not sure she liked, but decided to ignore. "All three of you," Llauron added, as if reading her mind.

Rhapsody looked uncomfortable. "A duke? You want me—*us*—to drop in on a duke?"

"Yes; why?"

A crimson glow crept through her cheeks. "Llauron, for what possible reason would a duke even allow a person of my station through the door? I'm not exactly royalty." Dread wound its way through her stomach much as the blood was making its way through her face. She hoped Llauron had not guessed her history as a former courtesan, though the restoration of her virginity from her walk through the fire might confuse him a bit. The Invoker seemed to know things about her that she barely knew herself.

Llauron's smile was fatherly. "Stephen's not concerned with the trappings of family lineage. In addition to being a pleasant fellow, he is also a bit of an historian. If you're interested in any more of the Cymrian history, he would be the man to see. In his keep is the Cymrian museum. I know he would be delighted to show it to you. I doubt he has many requests to do so anymore."

"Really?" Rhapsody asked absently. She was preoccupied watching her friends. While Achmed was making more disks for his cwellan, Grunthor had apparently obtained some new weapons from Gavin, most notably a long curved sword he called a snickersnee. He was busy adding his latest acquisitions to the array of blades that protruded from behind his pack, making him resemble an evil flower with deadly petals.

She turned her attention back to the Invoker and smiled. "That would be very nice, I'm sure. How far is it from here?"

"Three to four days' walk." The elderly man took her by the shoulders. "Now, Rhapsody, I hope you have enjoyed your stay here. I've loved having you."

"It's been wonderful," she said sincerely, pulling up the wide hood of her new cloak, "and I've learned so much. Is there anything I can do to repay your kindness?"

"Actually, yes," the Invoker said, growing serious. "When you reach Lord Stephen's, give him my letter. In it I will ask him to lend you the manuscript on the Ancient Serenne language. As a Namer, you pick up foreign tongues easily, I'm sure, and its linguistic basis is musical. You should have no problem learning it.

"I want you to do so, my dear, that we might communicate in it. Now that you've learned about the Cymrians, and the growing unrest that threatens to sunder this land again, I hope you will agree to help me by being my eyes and ears out in the world, and report back what you see."

Rhapsody looked at him in surprise. Llauron had thousands of scouts and foresters in his service. She could not imagine what value her efforts might be.

"I'll be glad to help you, Llauron, but—"

"Good, good. And remember, Rhapsody, though you are a commoner, you can still be useful in a royal cause."

"That would be the preservation of nature and the Great White Tree?"

"Well, yes, and its political aspects."

"I don't understand."

Llauron's eyes glinted with impatience, though his voice was soothing. "The reunification of the Cymrians. I thought I had been clear. In my view, nothing is going to spare us from ultimate destruction, with these unexplained uprisings and acts of terror, except to reunite the Cymrian factions, Roland and Sorbold, and possibly even the Bolglands, again, under a new lord and lady of that lineage.

"The time is almost here. And though you are a peasant— please don't take offense, most of my following are peasants—you have a pretty face and a persuasive voice. You could be of great assistance to me in bringing this about."

Rhapsody was dumbfounded. "Me? I don't know anyone— I mean, as you know, we're not from this place. Who would listen to me? I'd never heard of the Cymrians until I met you, Llauron."

The Invoker took her hand and patted it comfortingly. "Anyone who looks at you will have no choice, my dear; you're pleasant to behold. Now, please, say you will do as I've asked. You do want to see peace come to this land, do you not?"

"Yes," she said, uncertain why she was suddenly trembling.

"And the violence which is presently killing and maiming many innocent women and children—that is something you'd like to see ended?"

"Of course, I just don't—"

"All right, Yer Ladyship, we're ready," Grunthor called. Achmed gave her a curt nod as he shouldered his pack.

Rhapsody looked back to Llauron once more. "Who are you planning to install as lord?" she asked.

"No one; that's for the council to decide. Remember the tales I have told you of the Cymrian philosophy, of their way of life. The lord and lady were chosen for their ability to rule, and though that means a certain amount of nobility is necessary, it is not in the lineage of one particular family, as it is in other nations.

"Just remember what I told you about the negative feelings that some people have about the Cymrians, so be discreet in your inquiries. Those who are of Cymrian lineage rarely speak of it. And those who are not will see it as I do, a philosophical lifestyle that would well serve to bring the fragmented nations of this land back together again, now that Anwyn and Gwylliam are no more. Keep me informed of your progress."

"I'm still not sure exactly what it is you want me to do."

"We're leaving now," Achmed shouted.

Llauron smiled broadly. "Always the well-mannered guest, isn't he? Well, let us get you to him so I can say my good-byes. Travel well, my dear; if you will give me a moment I will get you that letter."

The forest to the east of Llauron's was thinner and younger than the deep primeval woods that surrounded the Great White Tree. For a while they were retracing their steps, traveling down the forest roadway past the village of Tref-Y-Gwartheg and turning northeast in the attempt to avoid contact with the inhabitants as much as possible.

Rhapsody had discovered in her time at Llauron's, particularly on her sojourns with Gavin, that the forest was the size of the eastern half of the Island of her homeland, and that the Lirin woods to the south were three times the size of this one.

Though she had heard tales in her youth about forests the size of nations, she had never been within one until now. Somehow it seemed ironic that she be surrounded eternally by trees, since it was a Root that had brought her here in the first place.

It took them the better part of two days to locate the north forest road that ran from the upper part of Gwynwood to the province of Navarne, a partially wooded land with sparser forest than she was used to.

Soon the unrelenting grip of the woods gave way to patches of rolling farmland and small towns, built with the same ingenuity and frugality of material that was the hallmark of the subsistence farms in Gwynwood. Navarne was a more densely populated area, and the road was far more heavily used, with foot traffic interspersed with oxcarts and the occasional haywagon pulled by dray horses.

As the woods thinned out, it became increasingly difficult for the companions to remain hidden. Finally they decided to walk where possible in the disappearing brush and occasional copse of trees, and take to the road when no cover was present.

A few miles into Navarne, while they were still within the cover of the meager woods along the roadside, they came upon a group of peasant children playing on the forest road. Rhapsody moved closer, watching intently, while Grunthor and Achmed receded into the underbrush.

The children, oblivious of their observers, laughed and ran about in the road, playing a game that seemed to be a form of tag. Around them farmers and carts passed through the mud of the forest road, occasionally spraying the children with filth, making them screech gleefully.

A smile spread slowly over Rhapsody's face as she watched the farm children playing in the winter sun. There was something in their merriment that reached down into her atrophied heart and loosed it a little, making it ache and breathe easier at the same time.

There was an innocence to them, a carefree celebration of the ordinary occurrence of the thaw, that rang in her memory. As they scooped the mud from the quagmire that the road had become and pelted each other with it, she longed to run and join them. The grief that had been stifled so long ago by Achmed's order squeezed her heart, then dissipated on the warm, sweet wind.

At the edge of her consciousness and vision to the west she heard the sound of a horse's hooves, their thunder muted by the soggy earth. Rhapsody looked in the direction of the commotion to see the few travelers on the road staring in the same direction at the oncoming stallion, a black-barded war horse that was galloping down the forest road.

The children did not notice immediately, so intent were they at their game, until a gasp of horror erupted from two of the women who were riding in a haywagon. The man who was leading the dray team gestured frantically to the children, who stood, statue-still, in the middle of the road. The rider of the charger showed no sign of slowing.

Before Grunthor could restrain her, Rhapsody bolted from her hiding place into the muddy roadway, scattering the children like pinecones and interposing herself in the path of the oncoming steed. An equine scream and the rumbling of horseflesh roared over her, and instinctively she covered her head and neck, anticipating the impact.

In a swirl of violent motion the rider brought the panicked animal under control, muttering foul curses. When the horse came to a dancing halt, he glared down at her with azure eyes that burned like a raging fire.

"Bloody *shit*, woman!" he bellowed at her from above. "I'd run you down right now if I knew it wouldn't lame the horse."

Slowly Rhapsody rose to a stand and looked up at the horse's rider. The eyes beneath her own hood were scorching with a similar fire, turning them green as meadow grass in the height of summer. For a moment it seemed that the rider's face, contorted in anger, slackened a moment, as if he was surprised by the intensity of her reaction. Ugly words from her days on the street spilled out of her mouth.

"If buggering you twice a day hasn't killed that horse, it can take anything," she snarled, glaring back at him.

The man's face registered shock, then, slowly, amusement. The visor of his helmet was up, but he removed it anyway, and stared down at the small woman before him in the road.

His face was one of a middle-aged man, though his muscular body belied it; his hair and beard, black as night with streaks of silver, seemed undecided. His forehead and facial structure were broad, with features that seemed oddly familiar, despite the fact that Rhapsody was certain she had never seen him before. He wore a black mail shirt, its dark rings interlaced with bands of gleaming silver, and beautifully crafted steel epaulets from which a heavy black cloak flowed behind him.

"Tsk, tsk, such language from a *lady*," he said in a tone of condescending sarcasm. "I, madam, am appalled."

"No. You, sir, are appalling," Rhapsody retorted, straightening her shoulders. "Apparently you are also blind; didn't you see that there were children in the road?"

"I did." The soldier sat back a bit in his saddle, his smile widening. It did not appear to be an expression he wore very often.

Rhapsody's anger burned into a deeper rage. "And I don't suppose it occurred to you to slow down, or perhaps try to avoid them?"

"Actually, no, it didn't. In my experience they generally move out of the way of a charging horse. It's a good lesson to instill early."

"And what if they didn't, or couldn't?" she shouted. "What if you trampled them?"

The soldier shrugged. "Obstacles that small generally won't harm the horse if it rides over them. I should have kept that in mind for you; you don't seem too big yourself."

A screech of wrath preceded the handful of mud that spattered across his face and chest. "Come down here and I'll correct your impression," she bellowed, her hand on her sword.

"Yeah, and if there's anythin' left when you're through with 'im, Duchess, we can 'ave supper," came an angry rumble from the forest's edge.

The soldier turned and looked to see the giant Firbolg rise out of the brush, his hands clenched at his sides. The dray horses attached to the haywagon screamed in panic, as did one of the women, and the farmer hurried off in a dead run with them down the muddy road; the children had fled long before.

The soldier threw back his head and laughed. "Well, well, look at this, Paradise and Perdition, traveling companions. Fascinating. The least you could do is take down your hood, madam; I have. Or are you afraid to show your face?" He wiped the mud from his own.

With an angry tug Rhapsody pulled the hood off her head. The rider's eyes widened almost imperceptibly.

"Ah, now I know who you are; you're Rhapsody, aren't you?"

Her rage dimmed in the shock that followed his words. "How did you know that?"

The soldier shook his helmet and smoothed out the flaps, brushing the mess from them in preparation for putting it back on. "You've been studying with Gavin, and word of you has spread. From the descriptions of the foresters, you could only be the one of which they spoke."

Rhapsody felt a shuddering cold run through her as her body cooled from the fire that had blazed within her a moment before. "Why is that?"

He put his helmet back on, ignoring Grunthor. "There could only be one such freak of nature. Move out of the way, unless you want to see my horse's new shoes close up."

"Really? And just who are you? I don't know your name."

The soldier took hold of the reins again. "No, you don't," he said flatly. He clicked to the horse and then rode off in a wild gallop. She had just enough time to leap out of the way, and was spattered by the mud from the horse's wake.

Well, that was amusin', miss," said Grunthor in annoyance. "Come on, now, we need to be on our way."

Rhapsody wiped the mud from her cloak and nodded. As she crossed the road, following him back into the brush, she heard a small voice in the scrub at her feet.

"Miss?"

Rhapsody caught her breath and looked down to see a young boy, perhaps seven, hiding in the dead weeds at the edge of the road. She bent down to him and touched his face in alarm.

"Are you all right? Are you hurt?"

"Yes, miss, I mean, no, miss; I'm fine."

She helped the child to stand. "What's your name?"

The boy looked up at Grunthor and grinned. "Robin." The giant grinned back.

Rhapsody felt a lump rise in her throat. That had been the name of one of her brothers. The boy looked back at her.

"An' I know that man's name too."

"Really? What is it?"

The child smiled with an air of importance. "Why, miss, that's Anborn."

28

The head guard at the gate of Haguefort, Lord Stephen Navarne's keep, had called the chamberlain to make a judgment. Gerald Owen had served the duke for over twenty years, coming into his employ when Lord Stephen was still just a young man, and had seen many strange sights in his time on the job. Nothing could have prepared him for what stood before him now, he was certain.

Two of the three travelers, a small woman of elegant build with enchanting green eyes, and a wiry man a head taller than she, were cloaked and hooded. In her case, it gave him cause for some disappointment; on a deep level he longed to see her unveiled. In the instance of the man, however, he believed the concealment to be a blessing.

Standing with them was a monster of grotesque proportions, well over seven feet tall and on his way to eight. The sight of the tusklike teeth that protruded from his jutting jaw had set Owen's heart to pounding wildly.

"Uh, yes, well, everything does seem to be in order," he stammered, examining the letter from Llauron the Invoker once again; this made the fifth time he had read it. "Uh, please come in." He opened the gate and nodded to the guards, who left their posts and followed the strange retinue into the keep.

The castle itself was a beautiful one, of classic design with touches of artistry, crafted from a rosy brown stone. Climbing ivy, brown and dead in grip of winter, scaled the walls, undoubtedly making for a verdant tapestry in summer. Around the perimeter of the courtyard stood high-edged gardens, pooling with water from the melting snow.

When they reached the large front door, heavily carved in black mahogany, Gerald Owen paused. "If you'll wait here, I'll tell Lord Stephen of your arrival." He bowed, then opened the door and hurried inside, closing it behind him.

While they waited, Rhapsody turned in a circle, taking in the sights around her. Stephen Navarne's keep was situated on a gently sloping hill, with a wide view of the rolling countryside that surrounded it on three sides and the forest behind it. Grunthor had commented on their way up to the gate about the many hidden defenses the keep employed. Despite its beautiful architecture and peaceful appearance, in his assessment the castle was well fortified in the event of attack. Rhapsody could see that the intelligence of the fortifications had impressed both of her friends, at least a little.

The chamberlain had left the heavy door slightly ajar, undoubtedly to avoid insulting them completely by shutting it in their faces. Achmed now leaned back against it casually, nodding politely to the guards. The door swung open a little, as was his intent. Within the echoing foyer of the keep a rich tenor voice could be heard.

"And she's in the company of a giant *what*, did you say?"

Gerald Owen's uncomfortable reply was clearly audible.

"I believe it's a Firbolg, m'lord."

"A Firbolg? Splendid! I imagine I'll be the only one at the Lord Regent's meeting next month who has ever lunched with a Firbolg. Show them in, with full hospitality."

There was a pause. "Yes, m'lord."

"Oh, move out of the way, Owen. I'll greet them myself."

Footsteps could be heard approaching, and a moment later the heavy mahogany door swung open. Behind it stood a smiling man about Achmed's height. He was young and seemed full of energy, with just the beginning touches of white creeping into his otherwise blond hair.

As with Anborn a few days before, the occasional line or wrinkle on his face seemed in opposition to the youth apparent in his physique. Rhapsody wondered if this could be a Cymrian trait, an indication of the great longevity their voyage across Time had granted them and their progeny. As Lord Stephen was the Cymrian historian, it made sense that he might be one.

The young duke bowed politely. "Welcome! I am Stephen Navarne; please, come in." He looked at his chamberlain, who still seemed in a mild state of shock, and nodded curtly. Gerald Owen blinked, and then swung the great door open wider.

Rhapsody and Grunthor bowed politely; Achmed nodded slightly.

"Thank you, m'lord," Rhapsody said, and came into the

keep, followed by the two Firbolg a moment later. "I hope we didn't come at a bad time."

"Certainly not," said Stephen. His eyes, blue-green as highland cornflowers, smiled as he did. "And please, call me Stephen. I'm delighted you came. I will have to thank Llauron for thinking of sending you to see me. Was your journey uneventful?" As he spoke he took Rhapsody's hand and bowed over it.

The three looked at each other. "For the most part," Achmed said, forestalling Rhapsody's more candid answer. Lord Stephen looked over at him in surprise at the sound of the fricative voice. He turned and began walking away, gesturing for them to follow.

"Are you hungry? We'll be having lunch shortly, but I could scare up something for you in the meantime."

"No, thank you, that won't be necessary," Rhapsody said, hurrying to keep up with him in his excitement.

$\mathcal{T}$he noontime meal was served in a stately dining room at a table long enough to accommodate a legion of guests. At the southern end of the room was an enormous leaded-glass window, flanked by two banks of rectangular panes, that looked out over Lord Stephen's lands and the courtyard below. The opposite wall held a hearth wide enough, Grunthor observed aloud, to roast an ox whole, a comment that drew a gale of agreeable laughter from master of the house.

"What a marvelous thought! We shall have to try it at Melly's birthday; it coincides with the first day of spring, so we customarily celebrate with a big feast."

" 'Oo's Melly?"

The duke rubbed his hands together, then pointed to a large portrait, done in oils and bordered in an ornate gilt frame, hanging over the fireplace. It held the likenesses of a woman and two children, a boy and an infant girl. The woman was slender and dark, with rich brown eyes and a shy smile.

By her side stood a lad of about seven, with his father's snapping blue-green eyes and his mother's mahogany-colored hair. His baby sister, perched on the woman's lap, was his opposite, crowned with a sunshower of yellow curls above eyes as black as midnight.

"Melly—Melisande, actually—is my daughter. That's her as an infant, with my wife, Lydia, and Gwydion, our son."

Rhapsody was looking out the bank of windows with Achmed. At Lord Stephen's words she turned and smiled.

"And might we meet your family later?"

The duke returned her smile. "My children will be delighted to meet all of you. As for my wife, I'm afraid that I am a widower."

Grunthor watched the smile melt from Rhapsody's face. "Sorry to 'ear that, guv," he said, clapping Lord Stephen roughly on the back. The duke lurched forward under the well-meaning blow, then stood straight with a laugh.

"Thank you," he said, noticing that the door to the kitchen had opened and the cooks were carrying in the luncheon trays. "It's been four years now. Gwydion seems to have adjusted, and of course Melisande doesn't remember her mother at all. Come, I see Hilde bringing our meal. Gentlemen, if you'll have a seat, I'll assist the lady."

𝕴t took four more trays of additional helpings before Grunthor had eaten his fill of ham and roasted grouse. The china bowls that held the sweet yams and braised potatoes were emptied two or three times more than necessary to mortify Rhapsody completely.

Lord Stephen ignored her embarrassment and called for more food each time, seeming to delight in watching the giant enjoy his kitchen's hospitality. Finally, after consuming enough food to feed most of Lord Stephen's army, Grunthor declared himself full.

"Couldn't eat another bite, guv; delicious," he said, wiping his gargantuan maw with a dainty linen napkin. "Nice meal." Achmed nodded in agreement while Rhapsody covered her face with her hand and smiled.

Stephen rose from the table with a bounce. "Good! I'm so glad you liked it. Now, can I interest you all in a small glass of Canderian brandy in my study? Llauron's letter says you're interested in the museum, and it's a bit of a walk in the frigid air, so a little fortification might be in order, eh?"

"By all means," said Achmed.

Rhapsody looked up in surprise; the Dhracian rarely spoke

around people he had just met. And for him, the comment seemed almost jovial. She could tell that he liked Lord Stephen better than any of the people she had seen him meet thus far in the new world.

She agreed with his assessment. There was an openness to the young duke that she had not seen up to now, and, despite some sad events in his life, he seemed full of energy and vigor. There was an excitement in just being around him, an intensity in virtually everything he said, as if he found life profoundly interesting all the time.

Lord Stephen helped her with the chair and offered her his arm. Then he looked to the Firbolg. "It's this way," he said, turning and walking toward the door on the other side of the hearth from the kitchen. The leather soles of his boots clacked resoundingly on the polished marble floor as he led them from the dining room.

$\mathcal{L}$lauron says you are aware of the border incursions and attacks we have been suffering," Stephen said as he handed Achmed a snifter of brandy.

As before, the Dhracian was standing at the largest window in the room, this one on the eastern end of the keep, also overlooking the rolling hills of Navarne and the courtyard below. In the cobbled area two children chased each other, laughing. A broad smile crossed the duke's face when he saw them.

"Gwydion and Melisande," he said to Rhapsody as he nodded downward. She came to the window as well.

"He told us a little, nothing substantial," replied Achmed casually. He pointed over the farmlands to a thick, high stone wall, partially finished, that stretched to the north for as far as he could see. He did not mention his and Grunthor's firsthand observations. "Is that the reason for the ramparts being built?"

Stephen gave Grunthor, who had stretched out on a large leather-covered couch with his feet on the table in front of him, a glass of the rich-colored liquid as well, then joined the other two at the window.

"Yes, in a word," he said matter-of-factly. "Navarne has the disadvantage of being settled primarily in small villages and communities of two or three large farms together, and it is several days' ride from my holdings to the capital city. As a result, its inhabitants are more vulnerable than most to these kinds of attacks. When the nearest military post is at least two days away, a small village or farming community can be devastated, and no one even hears of it for weeks. We've had our share of brutal raids and incursions.

"At first I tried posting scouts and soldiers in or near as many settlements as I could, but it was to no avail. So I decided to enclose as much of the local acreage within a walled fortress as possible, in the hope that it will better protect the people and their land. I've invited as many as are willing to come and live within the new fortress, and some have agreed.

"Some would rather take their chances and keep the lands that are their legacy, and I can respect that. Eventually the land within the wall will become a heavily populated village, which will destroy the tranquillity of my holdings and the keep, but it's a small price to pay if it keeps more of them safe. Truthfully, I have no idea if even that will help, but while I am still breathing I have to try every option open to me."

"That's the sign of a good leader," said Rhapsody, watching the workmen in the distance as they mortared stones into the wall. Gauging from their height as they stood near it, she estimated the wall to be more than twelve feet high. Whatever Lord Stephen sought to keep out must have made a serious impression.

Lord Stephen's face grew grave for the first time since they had met him. "I have a personal reason in addition to that duty. You see, two of the casualties of these raids were my wife and her sister." He looked out into the courtyard where the children were playing in the frosty air, the snow gone with the thaw. Their shrieks of merry laughter rang suddenly hollow.

Rhapsody's heart filled with pain at his words, but they were spoken simply, without regret, and carried only a wistful sense of loss.

"I'm very sorry," she said.

Lord Stephen took a deep swallow from his glass.

"Thank you. It was four years ago. Melisande had just begun to walk, and Lydia had traveled into the city of Navarne to purchase some shoes for her, sturdy enough to support her little feet. She and my sister-in-law enjoyed traveling into the city; it gave them time to visit together and talk.

"The baby had come down with a cold. I suppose we were lucky she had taken ill, or else she'd have likely been with her mother. On the way home they and the rest of their caravan were accosted by a raiding party of Lirin soldiers. I'll spare you the details except to tell you that when I found her she was still clutching the shoes. Of course, we couldn't use them. The bloodstains didn't come out."

His words turned Rhapsody's stomach, but Achmed and Grunthor merely nodded politely. This was certainly not the worst they had ever heard.

"The strange part of it all is that, to a man, the Lirin raiders captured at the scene denied being involved in the massacre. There could be no doubt as to their guilt; they were caught in the act. Yet each man went to his death swearing that he knew nothing of the raid.

"It was extremely odd. I have known Lirin all my life, living so close to their lands, and they tend to be one of the more honorable races, in my experience. It is out of character for them not to take responsibility for their actions. I think watching the executions took some of the hate out of me; they seemed, more than anything else, perplexed, each one of them. Very strange."

The Bolg exchanged a look. "Indeed. Is it only Lirin that have attacked your villages and towns?" Achmed asked.

"No, that's also part of the peculiar nature of these incursions. There have been incidents involving other men from Roland. In fact, even soldiers from Navarne have been caught in other provinces and Tyrian, committing similar atrocities. I swear on the lives of my children that I have ordered no such raids. I have no idea where this is coming from.

"Worst of all, the new target seems to be the children of Navarne." He opened the window and leaned out, calling to his son and daughter in the courtyard below.

"Gwydion, Melisande, come in now, please."

The children looked up from their game, and exchanged a

glance and sighed before complying. Stephen waited until they had reached the door, held open by the chamberlain who had been watching them, and then turned to his guests again. "I'm sorry. These are days of paranoia and little restful sleep.

"Almost a score of the children of our province are missing, some taken in raids, others stolen from their own backyards. Their bodies are not found at the sites of the fighting, so we can only assume they have been kidnapped or taken to be sold.

"Only one has been recovered, when the child's father and uncle rode down the abductors, who were also from Navarne. The same strange circumstances; the captors swore they had no idea where the children had been taken from, despite having them in their custody. It's like the entire continent is suffering from collective amnesia."

His tale at an end, Lord Stephen drained his glass and set it down on his desk, then walked past the fireplace to the door, where he pulled a bellcord. A moment later the door opened, and a woman entered.

"Yes, m'lord?"

"Rosella, please get the children bathed and changed, and give them their tea, then bring them to meet our guests." The woman nodded and left, casting a look askance at the giant monster with his feet on her master's table.

An hour or so later the door burst open and the children ran in, dashing to their father. Stephen bent down on one knee and opened his arms, hugging the two of them together and rocking them wildly, causing them to giggle ridiculously.

In the midst of the laughter the little girl caught sight of Rhapsody. She stopped laughing during her father's roughhousing and stared. Rhapsody smiled, hoping to put her at ease, but the child broke free from her father's embrace and pointed at her.

"Daddy, who's that?"

Stephen and his son stopped their play and looked to where she was indicating. He took his daughter's arm and pushed it down.

"Well, that was rude," he said. His tone was exactly like the one Rhapsody's own father had used, and she covered her smile; some things apparently transcended social status. "These are our guests. I invited you in here to meet them. This lady's name is Rhapsody, and I expect you have something you want to say to her now."

The child continued to stare, as did her brother. Stephen's face clouded with mild paternal chagrin. "Well, Melly? What do you say?"

"You're *beautiful*," the child said, her voice filled with awe. Stephen flushed in embarrassment.

"Well, that's certainly true, but it's not exactly what I had in mind," he said.

"But it will do nicely," Rhapsody said breezily. Grunthor and Achmed exchanged a glance; perhaps she would believe it now that she had heard it from a child. A moment's further study indicated that the hope was unrealistic.

She came to where the children stood and smiled at them, first down at Melisande, then on eye level with Gwydion, who was almost as tall as she was.

"It's very nice to meet you both, Melisande and Gwydion. May I present my two friends, Achmed and Grunthor?" Melisande's gaze remained fixed on Rhapsody's face, but Gwydion looked over at the two Firbolg and broke into a wide grin.

"Hello," he said, extending a hand and walking to where Grunthor stood. The giant Firbolg clicked his heels, shaking the young man's hand with his enormous one, taking care to avoid scratching him with his claws. Gwydion then proceeded to the window, where he bowed slightly and extended his hand to Achmed as well.

"Are you going to be my new mother?" the little girl asked Rhapsody. This time the Singer's face matched Lord Stephen's, which had turned crimson to the scalp.

Across the room Grunthor laughed out loud. "There ya go, guv; my ol' man always said that children are the only thing that keeps a man from livin' forever, because they make 'im want to die o' mortification at least once a day."

"Well, if that were the case you could be visiting me in the cemetery about now," said the duke with a laugh. "I apologize for my daughter, m'lady."

Rhapsody crouched down in front of the child. "Please

don't," she said to Stephen, never taking her eyes off Melisande. "She's lovely. How old are you, Melisande?"

"Five," Melisande said. "Wouldn't you like to have a little girl?"

Lord Stephen reached for the child's shoulders, but Rhapsody waved him away and took Melisande's tiny hands in her own. There was a loneliness in the black eyes, deep as the sea, and it reached down in Rhapsody's heart, choking it. She knew exactly how the motherless child felt.

"Yes," she said simply. "But only if that little girl was as special as you."

"Don't you like boys?" Gwydion asked from across the room. Achmed grinned in spite of himself.

"If anyone needs me, I'll be in the Great Hall, jumping off the balcony," Lord Stephen said.

Rhapsody swiveled to look at the boy, a thoughtful expression on her face. "Yes, I like boys very much," she said seriously.

"Made a lot o' money provin' it, too," muttered Grunthor merrily under his breath.

Her common status notwithstanding, Rhapsody felt the need to soothe the pain in the lonely royal children. "In fact, if your father would agree, I would like to adopt you both," she said, flashing Grunthor an ugly look.

Stephen opened his mouth to speak, but Rhapsody rushed ahead before he could. She turned back to Melisande.

"You see, I'm traveling quite a bit, and I'm never in one place very long, so it's not a very good idea for me to be anyone's mother right now. But I could be your honorary grandmother."

"Grandmother?" said Gwydion doubtfully. "You're not old enough."

Rhapsody smiled ruefully. "Oh, yes I am," she said. "You see, I'm part Lirin, and we age differently than other people. Trust me, I am sufficiently old enough."

"What would it entail?" Gwydion asked, rubbing his hairless chin with his thumb and forefinger in the exact manner Lord Stephen did when considering something.

Rhapsody stood and let one of Melisande's hands drop, retaining hold of the other as she walked across the room to meet him. She sat in Lord Stephen's desk chair and pulled the little girl into her lap, reaching out her hand to Gwydion. He came over to her and took it. Rhapsody seemed to be considering the question solemnly.

"Well, first and foremost, I would never adopt any grandchild that I didn't think was special in a way that no one else in the world was, so it would mean that you would be dear to me in a way that no one else in the world is," she said.

"Next, each night when I say my prayers, I would think of you, and it would be like you were with me. I do that every evening when the stars come out, and each morning as the sun rises, so every day you would know that I was thinking about you at those times. I sing my prayers to the sky, so maybe you would even hear me, since we'd be under the same one; who knows?

"Whenever you're feeling lonely, you'd know that you only have to wait for the sun to come up or the stars to come out to have someone who loves you thinking about you, and maybe it might make you feel a little better."

"You would love us?" Melisande asked, tears glittering in her eyes.

Rhapsody fought back the ones forming in her own. "Yes," she said softly. "I already do."

"You do?" asked Gwydion incredulously.

She looked him deep in the eyes, and drew on her lore as a Namer, speaking truly. "Yes," she said again. She shifted her gaze to the little girl. "Yes, I do. Who wouldn't? I would never lie to you, especially about that."

She looked up at Stephen, who was staring at her in wonder, then quickly back at the children, the sin of overstepping her position beginning to twist her stomach.

"I will try to visit you if I can, and send you gifts and letters from time to time, but mostly it would be in here." She tapped her heart, then each of their chests. "So, how about it? Would you like to be my very first grandchildren?"

"Yes!" said Gwydion. Melisande nodded, too excited to speak.

Rhapsody looked up at Lord Stephen, who still looked amazed. She felt suddenly awkward, knowing she had not only overstepped the boundaries of social status, but of politeness and good manners.

"That is, if your father agrees."

"Of course," Lord Stephen said quickly, forestalling his children's clamoring. "Thank you." He allowed himself to look her over once more, wishing she would consider Melisande's first request, before turning to Achmed.

"Well, it's time for these two to be heading to bed. Shall we go have a look at the museum?"

29

The Cymrian museum was housed in a small building crafted of the same rosy-brown stone as the rest of Lord Stephen's keep. Unlike the other buildings on the castle's grounds, it had no torches burning in the exterior holders and sat, unnoticed, in the dark, locked and bolted.

Twilight was descending, wrapped in flurries of snow as they left the castle and crossed the courtyard toward the tiny, dark building.

Rhapsody had stopped long enough to sing her vespers, with the undesired result of causing everyone else in the keep to cease whatever they were doing to listen to her. Melisande and Gwydion, who had been watching them from the balcony, broke into applause when she finished, which made her laugh and turn red with embarrassment at the same time.

Lord Stephen smiled. "Go to bed!" he shouted gruffly up at the balcony, then chuckled as the two figures dashed indoors. He offered Rhapsody his arm, holding a torch to light their way in his other hand.

When they came to the brass-bound door he let her hand go with a small sigh and reached into the pocket of his cloak, pulling forth an enormous brass key with odd scrolling on it. He fitted it to the lock and turned it with some difficulty; it was apparent that the museum had not been visited recently. Grunthor helped him pull the door open with a grinding screech, and they went inside.

In the light of the single torch, the stone depository more closely resembled a mausoleum, with frowning statues and exhibits that had been lovingly displayed for no one to see. Lord Stephen's face glowed ghostly white in the light of the torch as he went about the small room, lighting a series of curved glass sconces with a long wick held by a brass lamplighter's stem. Once he was finished, the museum brightened noticeably, the light being enough to read comfortably by.

"That's impressive," Rhapsody noted. "Those sconces certainly give off a lot of light."

"An invention of the leader of the Cymrians, Lord Gwylliam ap Rendlar ap Evander tuatha Gwylliam, sometimes called Gwylliam the Visionary. He was an inventor and engineer, among other things, and is credited with many fascinating designs," said Lord Stephen. "These sconces are made from convex glass that was heated and then twisted along a curved piece of metal, so that the light reflects off the shiny surface and is magnified by the glass."

"I've heard of Lord Gwylliam," Rhapsody said as Achmed and Grunthor strolled about the room, examining the exhibits, paintings, and statuary. Grunthor stopped before a narrow stone stairway and looked up into the stairwell, as if gauging his ability to fit through, before continuing on his tour. "But those other words are unfamiliar. Was that part of his name?"

"Yes," Stephen said, warming to the subject excitedly. "When the First and Third Fleets met up after fifty years of separate existence, and then decided, with the Second Fleet, to become a united people, it caused no end of problems denoting lineage, particularly since many of the Cymrian races each had a separate genealogy practice and nomenclature.

"Simply put, they didn't know what to call themselves, or whether they should be known by the fleet they traveled with, or their family, or their race. So they devised a simple system they could all use.

"Each person's first name was stated, then the next two ancestors back of the same gender, followed by the name of the First Generationer from whom they had descended. Lord Gwylliam's father was King Rendlar, his grandfather, King Evander, and he himself was the First Generationer."

"I see," said Rhapsody, feeling a chill in her bones suddenly. Lord Stephen had just answered a part of another question that Achmed had been asking—how long had it been between their exodus through the Root and the sailing of the fleets. Although the historian had not quoted a number of years, it was apparent now that there had been at least several generations of kings between Trinian, the monarch-to-be at the time they had left, and Gwylliam. They had been gone even longer than they had thought.

Rhapsody turned to see if Achmed was listening. She was sure he had been, but he gave no sign of it as he examined a thick volume of Gwylliam's drawings and intricately rendered architectural plans.

"That's a reproduction, by the way," Lord Stephen told him as he leafed gently through the pages. "Obviously the actual ones decayed and crumbled long ago. Each successive generation has had an historian whose job includes recopying them to preserve them. Naturally, something gets lost in the translation, I'm afraid."

"How many generations have there been since they landed?" Achmed asked absently, studying a drawing of a ventilation system.

Lord Stephen was looking through a series of manuscripts neatly shelved on one of the bookcases. "Fifty-three," he said.

He pulled out a thin manuscript bound in leather, blew the dust off it, and handed it to Rhapsody.

"Here is that text Llauron asked about, the Ancient Serenne linguistics chart and dictionary."

"Thank you," Rhapsody said, coughing. "This is it?"

"Yes. I'm afraid it's not complete; not very much is known about the tongue."

"I see. Well, thank you."

" 'Oo are these ugly people?" Grunthor asked, pointing at the small statues.

Lord Stephen chuckled and came over beside him.

"These three are the Manteids, the Seers, Manwyn, Rhonwyn, and Anwyn, who you also see in this sculpture with her husband, Gwylliam. They were an odd blend of bloodlines. Their father was an Ancient Seren, who were tall, thin, gold-skinned people. Their mother was a copper dragon. You should see the paintings; they're even uglier. Manwyn's hair is flaming red, and her eyes are like mirrors."

"Are?" Rhapsody asked. "She's still alive?"

"Yes, she's the Oracle in the city of Yarim. Her temple is there, unless it has crumbled around her."

" 'Ow old are you?" asked Grunthor bluntly. "Are you one o' them First Generationers?"

Stephen laughed. "Hardly. I'm fifty-six years old, and a third of the way through my life, by my reckoning, a relative baby compared to those people."

His face grew somber. "By the way, I'd be happy to answer any question you might have, but please be aware that almost no other Cymrian or Cymrian descendant would. They're a secretive people, in many ways ashamed of their heritage. I suppose that's not surprising, given the history, and despite the fact that each of the dukes of Roland and many of the benisons are of that line. We're a strange, confused lot."

"What's upstairs?" Achmed asked.

Stephen walked to the stairs; his natural exuberance coupled with his interest in the topic made him seem as if he were running. "Come, and I'll show you."

$\mathcal{A}$t the top of the small stairway was a sizable statue of a great copper dragon rendered in jewels and giltwork, tarnished from neglect. Rhapsody eased by it carefully; the dragon seemed very lifelike, with cruel-looking claws and fangs, and rippling muscles. The expression in its eyes was fierce, and it was coiled to strike.

"This is the mighty wyrm Elynsynos, who held all these lands before the Cymrians came," Stephen said as he passed the statue. "She was apparently quite ferocious, and had successfully kept the humans from her lands from the beginning of Time, until Merithyn the Explorer came."

He led them to the back wall, where a series of portraits hung in pairs or triads, one on the end having been painted a long time before the others. An oil rendering of himself, somewhat younger, was displayed below one of them, another painting which depicted a sharp-faced man in a miter, wearing an amulet around his neck.

Rhapsody and the Firbolg examined the pictures. Each of

the men in the upper row was wearing a similar headpiece with robes that resembled those of the first man. She turned to Lord Stephen.

"Who are these?"

"The men in the top row are the Patriarch—he's the one on the end, alone—and the five benisons who serve him. At least that's what he looked like as a young man; he's quite aged now, I understand.

"In the bottom row, roughly corresponding, are the various dukes who rule the lands in which the benisons have their Sees. Except for him." He pointed to an auburn-haired man somewhat older than himself, with the same blue eyes. "That's Tristan Steward, who is not only the Lord Regent of Roland, but also the Prince of Bethany, which is the capital seat.

"Although each of our states is technically sovereign, he controls the central army and the largest area of land, and makes laws the rest of us abide by. There isn't usually a problem; most of us are related. Tristan and I are cousins."

Rhapsody nodded. "Why are the royalty displayed below the clergy?"

Lord Stephen laughed. "An astute question. Well, it's a traditional conflict, you know, the struggle between the church and the state. Ultimately, it puts the poor citizen in the middle, having to choose loyalty to the All-God or to his sovereign. Of course, only Cymrian royalty would have the temerity to think there should be a choice."

Rhapsody laughed. There was an irreverent twinkle in Lord Stephen's eye that was reinforced by the amusement in his voice.

"This, of course, is not true in my case, as the benison of this province is also the Blesser of Avonderre. His See is arguably the most powerful, certainly within Roland, but potentially on the continent as well.

"His only rival, and it is an active rivalry, is the Blesser of Sorbold, as he is the head of the Church for an entire country, not just a pair of provincial states like Avonderre-Navarne. They hate each other with a fury. Only the All-God knows what will happen when the current Patriarch dies.

"As a result, the Blesser of Avonderre-Navarne doesn't interfere too much with politics here, for which I am eternally grateful. He's after bigger quarry. There are renderings under glass over here of their respective basilicas. Have a look; the basilicas are the best examples of Cymrian architecture still standing.

"The mountain city of Canrif was far more impressive, but of course that was destroyed when the Bolg took over Gwylliam's lands—no offense meant, Grunthor."

"None taken," said the huge Firbolg absently; he was studying the dragon sculpture. Rhapsody thought it was interesting that Lord Stephen seemed unaware that Achmed was Firbolg as well, but was not surprised. She, after all, had not realized it either. She followed Stephen to the display he was indicating.

"This is a good example of Cymrian ingenuity and culture meeting up with a deep religious philosophy. The ancient Cymrians believed that the five elements of nature were sacred, the source of all power in the universe, and so each of the basilicas that they built in some way honors a specific element and makes use of that element to sanctify its ground."

Rhapsody looked with interest at the pen-and-ink etchings. They were all drawn by the same artist, and showed in minute detail the architectural features of the basilicas, some of them down to the individual stones from which they were built.

Most fascinating was one labeled *Avonderre*. It was an apparently immense structure fashioned in the shape of the prow of a great ship breaking forth from enormous rocks at the shore of the ocean. A second rendering showed more of the basilica, that part which apparently was only visible at low tide. Achmed had mentioned seeing something like this, and surely there could only be one.

Lord Stephen noticed her interest and smiled.

"That is the basilica our citizens attend services in, the great seaside church of Lord All-God, Master of the Sea. In the ancient language it is called Abbat Mythlinis."

Rhapsody returned his smile. Lord Stephen's grasp of the language was marginal. *Abbat Mythlinis* meant Father of the Ocean-born, a primordial race of people known in the old world as Mythlin. She glanced back at Achmed and Grunthor, hoping they would not correct him, but they were examining other exhibits, betraying no trace of amusement.

"This basilica was built largely from the wood of the great ships that carried the Cymrians from the Island before it sank," Stephen continued. "It was dedicated to the element of water, obviously, and the constant churning of the ocean waves reblesses it with each tide, keeping its ground holy.

"Finding holy ground was important to the Cymrians. As strangers in this land they needed a place for sanctuary at each of their outposts, where evil could not enter. That's why the basilicas were the first permanent structures that they built, after their guard towers. Avonderre is the coastal province where the first of the Cymrian waves landed. Except where Merithyn came ashore, we guard the oldest landfall of the Cymrian migration."

Rhapsody nodded and looked back to the gallery of paintings, her eyes scanning the portraits of the five benisons again. The Blesser of Avonderre was depicted in robes of green-blue silk, and the talisman around his neck was shaped like a drop of water.

The vestry pattern was repeated in the other portraits, with robes and talismans evoking the other four elements. The Patriarch was robed in gold, an amulet shaped like a silver star hanging from a chain around his neck.

It was easy to discern the benisons whose basilicas were dedicated to fire and earth, as well. The first was robed in flame-colored vestments and a matching horned miter. A golden talisman hung around his neck in the shape the sun with a spiral of red jewels in the center. The second wore robes in the colors of earth, with an amulet that resembled the globe Llauron had shown her. The last two benisons, however, were robed in white, and only one wore a neck chain, with no amulet on the end.

"What are the others? What about this one?" Rhapsody pointed to a rendering that was shown from two perspectives, straight on and from above.

This basilica, labeled *Bethany*, was round in shape, fashioned from what appeared to be marble, and consisted of several levels of circular outer walls that held seating for the faithful around the central core. Within the courtyard that surrounded the basilica were inlaid great flame-shaped mosaics, giving the impression when viewed from above of the sun in full splendor.

"That is the church of Lord All-God, Fire of the Universe, or, in Old Cymrian, Vrackna."

Rhapsody blanched; in Old Cymrian, that word was actually the name of the evil fire god from the days of polytheism. Lord Stephen didn't seem to notice.

"It is, of course, also consecrated to the All-God, but is dedicated to the element of fire. An eternal flame burns at the very center, powered by a deep well of fire that comes from the very heart of the Earth, which, of course, keeps the ground holy."

"And is this the Patriarch's basilica, since it's in Bethany, the, ah, capital seat?"

"No, Bethany is the political capital of Roland, but the religious capital is the sovereign city-state of Sepulvarta. That is where the Patriarch lives, and where the Citadel of the Star is. Only the Patriarch worships in that basilica, although the faithful come to attend services."

"I don't understand. What's the difference between worship and attending services?"

"Direct prayer. In our religion, only the Patriarch prays directly to the All-God."

"Why?"

"He is the only one deemed worthy to communicate directly with the Creator."

Rhapsody's brows drew together, but she did not give voice to her first thought. "To whom do the rest of you pray?"

"To the Patriarch. We celebrate the rituals of the faith, and pose our petitions to the lesser clergy, known collectively as the Ordinate, who pray for us. The Patriarch receives our intentions from the clergy and poses them to the All-God. By the time each prayer is elevated to the level of the Patriarch, it has the power of all the souls of the faith behind it."

"I see," said Rhapsody pleasantly. Nothing could be further from her own belief system, so she turned to the rendering of the Patriarch's basilica at Sepulvarta. "This is interesting."

Stephen beamed with obvious pride. "This is the Citadel of the Star, which I was just mentioning to you. The basilica itself is the church of Lord All-God, Light of the World, Lianta'ar in Old Cymrian."

He's closer, thought Rhapsody. *Lianta'ar* meant bearer of light.

"It sits outside the holy city-state of Sepulvarta, high on a hill. It's quite beautiful, as you can see; the rotunda of the basilica is the largest known structure of its kind, and it is beautifully appointed inside, being the seat of the Patriarch. But I'm more fond of this aspect of Sepulvarta."

He pointed to a separate part of the drawing, a rendering of an enormous pointed minaret that towered high in the air from the middle of the city.

"This is the Spire, an true architectural miracle, if I do say so myself. It is immodest to do so, as my great-grandfather was the architect and builder of it." Rhapsody made the appropriate noises to show she was impressed.

"The Spire reaches a thousand feet in the air, and can be seen from miles around. It is crowned with a single glowing star, the symbol of the Patriarchy. It is said that the Spire is the Patriarch's direct channel of communication with the All-God. The light that shines from the Spire is directed from the stars themselves, thus reconsecrating the ground each night."

"What about on nights when the sky isn't clear?" asked Achmed from across the room, still examining other museum pieces. Rhapsody started; she hadn't realized he was listening.

"Just because one can't see the stars doesn't mean they're not there," said Stephen simply. "And the Spire itself is illuminated by a piece of an actual star, the element known as ether."

"Fascinating," said Rhapsody. "And the others?"

"The basilica in Bethe Corbair is dedicated to the wind, the church of Lord All-God, Spirit of the Air, or Ryles Cedelian."

Breath of life, thought Rhapsody, and looked at Achmed. He was examining a piece of driftwood under glass.

"The special attribute of that basilica is a central bell tower with eight hundred and seventy-six bells hung within it, one for each of the ships that left Serendair, carrying the Cymrians to safety. It is set on a rise in the center of the capital city where it catches the west wind, and the breeze blows through the hollow tower, acting as a sort of carillon. The music is exquisite; you really must go and hear it, Rhapsody, being a Skysinger.

"As a part of the consecration of the basilica, the bells were rung for the same number of days as ships that set sail. Their ringing is what keeps the ground of the basilica holy, and makes the city of Bethe Corbair such a pleasant one; everywhere you go you can hear the sweet music of the bells."

"I shall make a point of visiting there," she said, smiling. "Which benison is the Blesser of Bethe Corbair?"

Lord Stephen pointed to one of the two men in white, with the silver chain around his neck.

"Lanacan Orlando. The other benison is Colin Abernathy, whose See is the nonaligned states to the south. As with Sorbold, that area is not part of Roland, and of course there is no basilica as a result."

"And the last basilica?"

Stephen pointed to a somber structure which appeared to be hewn from the side of a mountain. "This is the only non-Orlandan basilica, the church of Lord All-God, King of the Earth, or Terreanfor." Rhapsody nodded. This was the only completely literal translation of the lot.

"The basilica is carved into the face of the Night Mountain, making it a place where no light touches, even in the middle of the day. Sorbold is an arid, dusty place, a realm of sun, and so the Night Mountain is a place of deep reverence.

"There is a hint of the old pagan days in Sorboldian religion, even though they worship the All-God and are a See of our religion. They believe that parts of the earth, the ground itself, that is, are still alive from when the world was made, and the Night Mountain is one of these places of Living Stone. So the turning of the Earth itself resanctifies the ground within the basilica. Having been there, I think the people of Sorbold are right. It is a deeply magical place."

"Well, thank you very much for the wonderful explanation," Rhapsody said. "I must visit each of these places now."

"What's this?" Grunthor asked from across the room. He was standing in front of a small alcove in the corner, with a rack of votive candles in front of it.

Rhapsody came to where he stood and examined the display. The table that formed the base of it was covered with a lovingly embroidered cloth, much like she had seen on temple altars.

On the table lay a gold signet ring, a battered dagger, and a bracelet of interwoven leather braids, torn open on one side. Attached to the wall behind the display was a brass plate, intricately carved and inscribed.

She leaned forward to read it, but the tarnish that had developed in the tomblike museum was too heavy. Unlike the scholarly exhibits of jeweled circlets and ancient artifacts, this display seemed more suitable to a church than to a historical depository.

She reached into her pack and pulled out her handkerchief and a small flask, then held it up for Stephen. "Witch hazel and extract of lime," she said. "It should clear the tarnish. May I?" Stephen nodded, the look on his face becoming somber.

Rhapsody uncorked the flask and poured its pungent-smelling contents onto the center of the cloth, then stood on her toes to reach over the display and wipe the plaque clean. The tarnish rubbed off onto the handkerchief, leaving the few engraved words visible.

Gwydion of Manosse, it said.

Rhapsody turned back to Lord Stephen, whose face was now masklike. "What is this?" she asked.

Stephen looked away. "It's all that remains of my best friend, dead these last twenty years," he said.

30

 I'm very sorry," Rhapsody said. "Was he another victim of these unexplained hostilities?"

Lord Stephen carefully brushed the dust off the display with the hand of one who had lovingly cared for many fragile exhibits. "I would venture to say that Gwydion was the first of them," he said, putting the signet ring and the battered knife back on the cloth.

"Dead twenty years?" Achmed asked. "The incursions have been going on that long?"

Lord Stephen smiled and leaned on the wall next to the shrine. "I'm sure I don't have to tell you that brigands and thugs have been killing innocent travelers and attacking and looting villages since well before recorded history," he said. "But Gwydion's murder was different. He was a man of superior strength and swiftness, and well armed. His wounds defied description. Whatever killed him must have been ferocious and powerful beyond imagination."

"Was it a beast o' some sort?" Grunthor asked.

Lord Stephen shrugged, then sighed. "I don't know," he said. "Possibly, from the look of it. I was the one who found him first. I suppose I knew from the moment I saw him that he was dying; his heart was exposed and bleeding into the earth." Rhapsody touched his arm, and he smiled briefly at her before his eyes clouded over with the memory again.

"I was afraid to move him. It was as if the ground was all that was keeping his organs from falling out of his chest. I bound him up and threw my cloak on him, then ran for his father. He knew from my description where to find Gwydion and ran to him, sending me off on horseback to fetch the great Filidic healer, Khaddyr.

"By the time I returned with the priest, Gwydion had been dead for two days. He must have died just after I left him. I suppose I should be grateful that I had the chance to say goodbye to him as he left this Earth. Fate wasn't as kind with Lydia." He looked away, his jaw clenched. "I'm sorry. You would think by now I would have gotten better at this."

Rhapsody ran her hand up and down his arm in a gesture of comfort. "There is no set time limit on grief, Lord Stephen. Healing takes as long as it takes; you can't rush it."

Lord Stephen covered her hand with his own and sighed again. "No, I suppose not," he said. "In a way, I think the shock of Gwydion's death made it easier for me to accept Lydia's all those years later.

"He and I had been friends since childhood, when we met in Manosse. He was living there—that was where his mother was from—and I was visiting with my father. Eventually we both came back here, he to live with his father, and I to assume the responsibilities of the duchy when mine passed away. We were closer than brothers. My son would have been his godchild; instead he's his namesake. And his death served as a warning for what was coming, but we have been unable to stop it."

"Only now you say the marauders seem to be concentrating on children," Achmed said.

"Mostly, yes, at least here in Navarne and, from what I can glean, in the Lirin lands. My scouts tell me that there are incursions and raids from here to the Bolglands, south through Sorbold and the nonaligned states, north to the Hintervold. Whether the patterns in all those places match our own is impossible to say."

He flipped the end of the lamplighter's tool to the snuffer. "Well, unless there is something else you want to see, we should probably extinguish the lamps and go back now."

While the men set about quenching the flames, Rhapsody lingered a moment longer at the display, running her fingers along the little altar cloth. Carefully she picked up the signet ring and turned it over in her palm, then held it to her cheek.

There was something comforting about the feel of the cool metal on her face, something she had no explanation for. She looked down at the flat surface and examined the crest. It was a rendering of a tree with a dragon coiled around the base, a symbol common throughout this museum, though nowhere else she had seen since arriving in this strange land.

Memories are the first stories you learn. They are your own lore.

Rhapsody blinked at the sound of the voice in her mind. *A strange thought*, she mused. Obviously there were no memories of her own here; she had never seen the ring, or even heard the name Gwydion of Manosse before. Perhaps the thought referred to the power of Stephen's remembrances of his friend.

She hummed a soft note, a pitch that sometimes helped discern vibrations on objects, the signatures of their owners. Her mind filled for a split second with the hazy image of a man in darkness, drowning in unquenchable pain. It was a vision she had had on the Root. She dropped the ring.

The men had begun to troop down the stairs. Grunthor

stopped at the top of stairwell and looked back at her.

"Comin', Duchess?"

Rhapsody nodded. She turned and came to the staircase, waiting until Grunthor had descended with the torch, watching the jeweled eyes of the dragon statue glitter ominously in the vanishing light. She looked back at the corner where the shrine was now enveloped in darkness.

"I wish I could have been there for you," she whispered.

One by one the lights in the tower of the keep went out. The rosy glow of the stone settled back into the shadows of night, brown and flat in the dark.

Achmed watched from the window until the only light that remained was the flickering reflection of the torch flames. The lamplighters had finished their work long before; now the courtyard below was silent, filling with mist.

He crossed to the door and listened for a moment, then opened it slowly, taking great pains to be quiet about it. Satisfied the hall was empty, he returned and sat down in the chair next to Grunthor's bed.

"This was a lot easier when I still had a million heartbeats in my head," he said wryly, pouring himself a snifter of Stephen's best brandy. "Now I never know who's lurking about."

Grunthor untied the legging cords and unwrapped the cloth that served as his inner boot. When he looked up the expression in his eyes was direct, intense.

"It's 'ere, ain't it?"

Achmed swallowed and leaned forward, cradling the glass in both hands. When he spoke his words were soft.

"I don't know. I suspect something's here, at least in this part of the world. I don't know if it's the same or not."

A massive boot dropped to the polished floor. "Oi assume you saw the amulet?"

Achmed nodded. "It was very similar, yes. But Llauron said that MacQuieth killed Tsoltan. Anyone else might have botched it, might have killed the human and left the demon loose, looking for another host. But not MacQuieth—at least I'd like to hope not."

"So what next?"

The Dhracian leaned so close that even someone standing

in the room next to him would not have overheard.

"Nothing changes. We still need to go to Canrif; that's where it would have gone. That's where the power was, where the Cymrians were. Where the Bolg are now. If there are any answers to be had, I'm betting we'll find them there. But we need to go by way of Bethany. That's where the basilica dedicated to fire is. Perhaps there's something to be gleaned there as well."

Grunthor nodded. "And the Duchess?" Achmed looked away. The Sergeant sat up straighter and took hold of the Dhracian's shoulder. "Oi say we leave 'er 'ere. There's no need to be draggin' 'er into this anymore."

"She's safer with us. Trust me about this."

The Sergeant released his shoulder with a curt shove. "Says 'oo? 'Ad it occurred to you that maybe she's better off with someone like ol' Lord Steve? 'E seems smitten with the Duchess; 'e'd look after 'er. She likes 'is kids. Oi say we let 'er stay 'ere with 'im."

Sparks shot from Achmed's eyes like disks from the cwellan.

"And what if it *is* him? What kind of perversions do you think he'll subject her to if we leave her in his care? You want to be responsible for making her wish she was back in the clutches of the Waste of Breath? It'd be kinder if you just make good on all your threats and eat her for breakfast, alive. She'd suffer less."

Grunthor sat back, stung. Achmed sighed, and when he spoke again his voice was gentle.

"I know only a few things for certain anymore, Grunthor. It's not you; it's not me. After that things become cloudy. I'm fairly sure it isn't Rhapsody, but not entirely. Wouldn't that have been rich? For all I know she was bait waiting for us in the backstreets of Easton."

"That's loony."

"Perhaps. Perhaps not. Bear in mind she might not even know it. She was alone at Llauron's for a long time. But except for us, and possibly for her, there is nothing else we know for certain; am I right?"

Grunthor stared at him for a moment longer, then nodded reluctantly.

With a sigh, Achmed set the snifter down, empty.

"Look, how's this: we'll take her with us to Bethany. Once I've seen the basilica I should have a few more clues as to whether or not that bloody Seer was right. And then I'll tell her everything. If she wants to go back to Stephen, we'll make sure she gets here safely. Fair enough?"

Grunthor lay back and stretched out, pulling the covers up to his shoulder.

"One thing Oi've learned in my time with you, sir; Nothin' is ever fair enough."

𝕿he following morning Rhapsody had breakfast with her new grandchildren and went for a long walk in the forest with them and their father while the two Firbolg packed and provisioned for their journey. She sang the children songs of the woodlands, some in Lirin, some that she had learned at Llauron's in the common vernacular known as Orlandan.

While they strolled along she composed a tune that described them both in music, and watched as both children recognized themselves in the song. Melisande hung on to her, refusing to release her hand for even a moment, while Gwydion ran ahead, eager to show off his forestry skills and emerging talent as an archer. Lord Stephen said little, but just listened, smiling.

In their short time together she had already learned much about the individual natures of her new grandchildren. The haunted loneliness in Melisande's eyes was gone, replaced by her father's mirth and zest for life. She sang along with Rhapsody as they walked, oblivious of any need to know the song, and danced through puddles of mud, splashing and squealing with joy. It was as if all she had needed was permission to be happy again.

Gwydion, on the other hand, though blessed with a confident bearing, was clearly more introspective. Every now and then when he didn't know she was watching, she would see his face turn melancholy, his eyes darkening, reflecting his cloud-filled soul. There was a depth to him that his easy manner belied, but she could see it nonetheless.

Finally, when they returned to the courtyard of the keep, she bade the children goodbye so they could return to their lessons. She knelt and drew Melisande into her arms, holding her for a very long time, then released her gently and pulled back to look her in the face.

"I will think of you every day," she said, running her fingers through a twisted lock of curling gold hair, smoothing out the tangles. "You won't forget me, will you?"

"Of course not," said the little girl indignantly. Her heart-shaped face softened. "Will you ever come back?"

"Yes," said Rhapsody, brushing a kiss on her cheek, "if I can." As much as she knew the child was looking for assurance, she was unwilling to lie to her, especially given what had happened to her mother. With each passing day, she became more aware of her own vulnerability, and of the likelihood that she herself would meet a similar fate before the silent war was over. "I don't know when that will be. But I will write to you as soon as I come to a place I can write from."

"Are you still planning to head east?" asked Lord Stephen, looking at the ground with his hands on his hips.

She shaded her eyes from the glare of the winter sun. "I believe so; I'm not the navigator."

"Well, southeast of here a few days out is the House of Remembrance, an old Cymrian fortress and watchtower from the earliest days of the First Fleet. It's the oldest standing Cymrian site by far, and once held an impressive library.

"As a person of Lirin descent you might be interested in the tree there. A sapling of the mighty oak Sagia was brought by the First Fleet to plant in the new land, a blending of the sacred trees from both sides of the world. They planted it within the courtyard of the House of Remembrance.

"It's really a fascinating historical site, and I'm ashamed to say I haven't done much to keep it up; the building of Navarne's wall has kept me close to home this past year. The ugly reality is that protection of the Future has to outweigh preservation of the Past sometimes."

"Indeed." She kissed Melisande again, then turned to her grandson. "Goodbye, Gwydion. I'll miss you, and will be thinking of you. If I find any interesting arrows or tools for woodcraft, I'll send them to you."

"Thank you," the boy said. "And maybe you can show me

more of that lore about herbs and roots when you come back next time. I'll be taller than you then."

"You almost are now," she laughed.

"Next year, when I turn thirteen," Gwydion said. Rhapsody stood and opened her arms to him. He came into her embrace and lingered a moment, then pulled away. He took his sister's hand.

"Come on, Melly," he said. The little girl waved a last time, then went off with her brother into the keep.

Stephen watched his children walk away. When he had assured himself that they were within the walls of the keep and safely in the care of Rosella, he turned once more to Rhapsody.

"You're welcome to stay, you know. The children would love for you to visit longer."

She smiled, and Stephen's knees grew weak. "Thank you. I wish I could. In fact, I'm sure that would be a much more pleasant prospect than wherever it is we are going."

"Then don't go," he said abruptly; a moment later his face colored as if exerted from the speed of his reaction. He looked down at the ground awkwardly. "Sorry. I didn't mean to be rude."

Rhapsody laid her hand on his arm, causing his heart to race faster and the floridity of his face to deepen. "How can an offer of welcome be rude?" She sighed deeply; it was as if the wind sighed with her. "The truth is, Lord Stephen, wherever I am for a while, I'll still be lost. With any luck, by the time I come back this way, I'll have found me."

"Well, just remember you always have a home here," Lord Stephen said. "After all, now you're part of the family, Grandma." They both laughed.

The duke took her hand and kissed it gently, then pulled it into the crook of his arm, walking her back to her two Firbolg friends.

"Besides," he whispered, "you must come back, if only to relate the tale of how you ended up with those two."

31

From their conversations with Stephen Navarne the companions had gleaned that they had exited from the Root more or less immediately after the onset of real winter.

In western Roland traditionally the snow came almost immediately at the turning of the season, accompanied by a startling drop in temperature, then began an irritating dance of thawing and storming over its first two months, returning with a vengeance during its second half. By their calculations they were nearing the end of the thaw. There were signs that winter would take back its dominion soon.

Those signs were not in evidence as they set forth from Haguefort and followed the precise directions Stephen had given them to intersect with the House of Remembrance. The day was cold and clear, with a bright sun stinging their eyes and the occasional fall of melting snow from the bare tree branches as they passed beneath.

At first the Firbolg had little interest in going to the House, but had changed their minds when told that it had been the first military outpost of the First Wave. Achmed was certain he could analyze the construction and installation of the fort to determine some of the conditions that had been in place at the time right after the Cymrians landed.

"What's the need in that?" Rhapsody asked sullenly. She was feeling the emptiness of her palm where a small hand had clung all morning.

"It might give us a better idea of what, if anything, followed them," Achmed said.

The Singer stopped abruptly in her tracks and grabbed him by the elbow. "Are you saying you think something did?"

Achmed turned to face her. The expression on his face was even, measured.

"Sounds like a possibility, especially after the story of Stephen's dead friend."

Rhapsody looked around her. The silent wood, which just a moment before had seemed utterly peaceful, now held a threat, a feeling of dread. She looked back to find two sets of piercing eyes watching her from the faces of her friends.

"What is it, Duchess? What's the matter?"

She took a deep breath. "Is it possible that Lord Stephen's friend isn't dead?"

Both of the Firbolg blinked. "Anything's possible, but it sounds rather unlikely," Achmed said. "Why? Did you hear something I missed?"

"No," she admitted. "It's just a feeling, and not a clear one, as if perhaps only part of him is alive. I can't really explain it."

"Well, I'm unlikely to discount your feeling out of hand, as you have exhibited some signs of prescience, but I would think that both Stephen and Khaddyr are familiar enough with death to be able to diagnose it properly."

"I suppose," she said, and returned to walking. Sometimes it seemed as if she was to spend her life traveling endlessly, reaching each destination, only to be told that it was time to move on. In a way, this new land, the deep, silent forest, was just the Root in disguise.

The stars above her seemed so close she could almost touch them. Gladly reaching her hands skyward.

The brightest star trembling, shivering in the wind as if cold. Then, one by one, each star falling, not streaking blindly through the sky, but gently, wafting down on the warm night wind like shiny snowflakes.

Catch them! Hold them fast.

The wind whispering across her open hands. The electric thrill of the tiny stars touching her fingers, her palms. Her fingers closing.

I've got them! I've got them!

Radiant light pulsing from between her fingers. Her skin, translucent in the glow. The ecstasy.

Then the burning in her palms, the sudden darkness between her fingers.

Opening her hands. The scorching holes in the palms, the smell of withering flesh.

No. No, gods, no. Please.

A glimmer of light below. The undulating surface of the

water. The stars shining up at her in a circle around a long, dark crevasse. The sizzle of the embers burning out in the meadow stream. Then darkness again.

Rhapsody woke in the night, sobbing. It was an old dream, from the sad time; she had almost forgotten it. *Why now?* she thought miserably, hiccoughing as quietly as she could in an attempt not to disturb the men. She rolled onto her stomach, burying her face in her bedroll.

A moment later she felt thick fingers brushing back her hair, surprisingly gentle for their size.

"Duchess? Ya 'wake?"

She nodded, still facedown. Once Grunthor had ascertained that she was all right, perhaps he would leave her alone and go back to sleep.

"Oi got somethin' for you. Sit up, now."

Rhapsody let loose a weary sigh and turned her tearstained face to see the Sergeant smiling down at her in the dark. The grin was infectious and irresistible now, though it had taken some getting used to. She smiled wanly in return.

"Sorry, Grunthor."

He snorted. "No need to be, miss; Oi thought you knew that by now. Give me your 'and."

Reluctantly she obeyed, wishing as he pulled her up that she could just go back to sleep. She ran her fingers through the hair that hung in front of her face and pulled it back absently as Grunthor put something in her lap.

It was oddly shaped and hard, but smooth as silk. She lifted it up to look at it; it was a seashell.

"They say them things sing, but Oi don't 'ear it. Just sounds 'ollow to me. Put it to your ear."

"Where ever did you get this?" Rhapsody asked, wonder in her voice as she turned it over repeatedly, examining it from every side.

The giant Bolg settled back again. "By the sea. 'Twas jammed in the sand between them shipwrecks we told you about. Thought o' you and that you might like it, 'specially when the dreams are too strong."

Tears glinted in her eyes again. "You are the most wonderful Bolg that ever lived, did you know that?"

You are the most wonderful girl in the world.

"Damn right," said Grunthor smugly. Rhapsody laughed, blinking away the tears. "Now, put your 'ead back down and cover your up-ear with it. Maybe it'll sing you to sleep."

"Thank you; I'll do that. Good night."

"Good night, miss. Oi'd wish you pleasant dreams, but—"

Rhapsody laughed again, then settled back to sleep, listening to the shell's roar. Her dreams were filled with the sound of the waves crashing over the shore, the crying of seagulls, and the distant image of a long, dark crevasse, the serpentine pupil of one solitary eye.

After three days they began to come across more of the landmarks that Stephen had mentioned, confirming that they were indeed heading in the direction of the House of Remembrance. The woods themselves seemed somehow different, the trees cleared along old pathways which gave no sign of recent travel.

Gradually the ancient forest began to give way to younger trees. Poplars, pines, and birches sprang up, choking out the older oaks, ashes, and maples. The patches of white snow seemed to match the patterns of peeling bark on the white birches, adding a hollow, haunted feel to the air.

The melted snow had frozen in the night, forming a glossy layer of ice on the top. With each step Rhapsody and Grunthor broke through the thin crust of the snow, their footsteps crunching in marked contrast to Achmed's all-but-silent passage. The air grew colder the farther they traveled along the path, and soon Rhapsody could see the mist of her breath forming before her. It was as if the thaw that blanketed the rest of the land had yet to come to the deep forest around the House.

Rhapsody whistled softly as they walked, the rhythm of her tune matching the pace they set. Dawn had come up on the wings of a brisk wind, and she matched her melody to it, trying to dispel the gloom of the overcast sky.

The striking contrast of the white snow and the dark trees gave her the feeling of stark but ominous beauty, one that held something hidden within itself. She cursed herself for asking her friends about Gwydion; their obsessive caution was spoiling an otherwise peaceful walk.

Every now and then Grunthor slowed his pace and looked around, tilting his head as if hearing distant noises. He nodded to Achmed, who listened as well, then shrugged. The giant sighed, then quickened his pace again. Each time they stopped Rhapsody ceased her whistling. And each time she resumed it, the tune lost a little more of its sprightly tone, settling into a slower, more haunting melody.

Finally Grunthor came to a dead stop. He looked around the woods, and then glared directly ahead.

"Somethin's wrong 'ere."

"What do you mean?" Rhapsody asked. Achmed's cwellan was already in his hands.

The giant squinted in the sun. "Oi don't know, miss, but somethin's wrong. It feels tainted, and it's worse up there." He nodded down the path they were following. All three looked in that direction.

"What is it—men? Animals?" Achmed looked over his shoulder.

"Oi don't know," Grunthor replied. "It's like the ground is sick."

"Bend down here a minute." Rhapsody ran her hand over the giant's brow. It was hot and moist with fever. "It's not the earth that's sick, Grunthor, it's you."

"Perhaps it's both," Achmed said, swiveling around and listening again. Nothing but the silence of the forest answered him. "Grunthor is tied to the earth; we've seen it, remember? And if there's something here that's poisoning the ground, it's not surprising that it's affecting him. Get that steel torch of yours ready."

Rhapsody nodded and loosed the tie to the scabbard, but did not draw the sword. Grunthor shifted his grip on the poleax he was carrying.

Achmed closed his eyes and concentrated, focusing his thoughts on the road as once he had focused on human targets. In his mind's eye he could see the three of them, as if from above, and the world around them, tipping at an odd angle.

The path stretched before them, choked with branches and

brambles hanging amid the shadows cast by the forest light. Then, as he had on the Root, he loosed the lore he had gained in the Earth's belly. His vision raced along with the speed of one of his cwellan's projectiles, the trees becoming a blur of motion as the image passed them.

His course zigzagged with dizzying speed as his second sight raced along every turn of the road, under one fallen tree, and over another. Suddenly the picture turned to a clearing where a large house with a tower in one corner stood. On either side of its doors was a heavily armed and well-armored man. The vision stopped, but the image did not fade. Instead as he watched the picture it became awash in red light, and the guards that he had seen seemed to wither into nothing more than shadows.

Achmed felt his pulse increase as his own heart began to match the beating of another. In his ears he could feel the pressure of his blood rise, hearing the rhythm of this alien pulse.

For most of his life he had known this feeling, and long before his name had been taken he made his trade by it. He was sensing his bond to blood, the bond he had lost when passing through the fires of their rebirth along the Root. It was not quite the same as it had been, but similar; the bond was coming alive again. As the vision drowned in the dark red that filled his mind, his head began to ache and his stomach to knot in fear.

Grunthor was right; whatever lay beyond the door was twisted, evil. With some effort he drove the image from his mind and ripped his senses back into his own body. Suddenly disoriented, he stumbled, feeling the bile rise in his throat. He fell to the earth, retching.

At once Rhapsody was by his side, her hands on his shoulders. She gasped as the first splattering stained the pristine snow blood-red. Achmed coughed, then breathed heavily, shaking the last vestiges of the vision from his head. He looked up into the Singer's worried face.

"Are you all right?"

"I think I'll live," he said, swallowing hard

"What happened? What did you see?"

"Well, the House is indeed in that direction, and Grunthor

is right, something's fundamentally wrong there." Grunthor offered his hand to Achmed, pulling him to his feet. The Dhracian bent over from the waist and took several deep breaths, then stood up again. "Everything along the path seemed normal, but when I saw the House, my vision was clouded with blood, and a pulse. Almost like what I used to sense back on the Island."

"But I thought you said you had lost your contact with blood," Rhapsody said.

"I did. I had. This wasn't the same."

"Maybe this is the way you sense things through blood in the new world," Grunthor suggested.

"Because it's the new world, I shouldn't be able to sense *anything* through blood. Do you ever remember me vomiting before?" The Sergeant shook his head.

A cold wind whipped a spray of ice crystals into Rhapsody's eyes. There was something deeply frightening about seeing the two Bolg, who had seemed indestructible for so long, trembling and sick. She took a few measured breaths in the hope that the thunderous pounding of her heart would slow at least a little. Still, deep within her she knew they had to go forward, to discover what lay within the ancient house.

"Perhaps once we get closer we'll be able to tell what's going on," she said.

Grunthor wiped the sweat from his forehead and fixed his gaze on her. "Excuse me, Yer Ladyship, but why would we want to? Oi mean, after all, Oi don't mind a bit o' trouble, but Oi don't see no reason to go lookin' for it."

"No, she's right," Achmed said. He ran a thin, trembling hand through his unkempt hair.

"I never expected to hear you say that," Rhapsody admitted.

"Don't let it go to your head," Achmed said. "We need to know why I suddenly was drawn back into my blood lore, and what made you sick, Grunthor. We need to be certain that it isn't an old problem, come back to haunt us in a new place. The only way to find out is to investigate."

Rhapsody was rummaging through her pack. "I have some wintergreen leaves; they might settle your stomachs. And if you'll wait a moment, I'll give you each a wet handkerchief to sponge off with." She dipped two linen squares into the snow, then held them in her hands, concentrating on the fire within herself. An instant later the snow had melted, soaking the cloths, which she then handed to the two Bolg.

Even in the grip of nausea, Achmed forced a smile. "I see you're getting a little more comfortable with the idea of your new lore," he said. "I knew you'd see it eventually."

Rhapsody smiled back at him and handed him a wintergreen leaf. "Suck on this. You were right. Don't let it go to your head."

"Right then, let's get goin'," Grunthor said, wiping his forehead and cheeks.

"There are two guards at the gate who will need to be dealt with," Achmed added.

"Wait; what does that mean?" Rhapsody asked nervously. Grunthor and Achmed looked at her incredulously. "What if they're not responsible for the taint, haven't done anything wrong?" The two continued to stare at her. "We can't go killing innocent people just because they're in the way."

"Well, miss, that never sto—" Grunthor started, but stopped with a quick look from Achmed.

"Listen," Achmed said impatiently, "you seemed to like Stephen. He didn't mention any guards at this memorial, did he?"

"No." The hand that rested on the hilt of her sword began to tremble.

"What does that tell you?"

"Nothing conclusive," she said quickly. "They could be investigating the place, just like we are. What if they serve someone important? Do you really want to have gone through everything we have just to end up being hunted again?"

Achmed sighed in annoyance. "What do you suggest, then, O Wise One?"

"We could try talking to them."

Grunthor opened his mouth to object, but Achmed forestalled him.

He studied her face for a moment, the green eyes matching the boughs of the evergreen trees, glistening like the branches heavy with ice crystals. The rose-petal upper lip was set bravely, but the flawless forehead gave away the anxiety within her in each of its furrows. Normally it was an enchanting countenance, but with the added attraction of worry bubbling below the smooth surface, it was absolutely hypnotic. This would be a good test of its power.

"Are you willing to be the one doing the talking?" he asked at last. "Grunthor and I don't generally get the best of receptions when we knock on doors."

"Yes."

The Dhracian looked back at Grunthor once more. The Sergeant wore a decided look of disapproval, but said nothing.

"Very well, we'll try it your way," Achmed finally muttered. "We'll stand in the brush and cover you."

Rhapsody smiled unconvincingly.

"Fair enough," she said.

32

The gray day began to give way to a dim twilight. The forest had gone deathly silent long before the light had left the sky. No winterbird song could be heard, nor the rustling of any living thing. Even the wind was quiet. The only noise to break the stillness was the creaking of the white branches under the weight of the snow, the occasional crash of a limb giving way under the icy burden that bent it.

Finally they came to a clearing, the edge of which was choked by thick, thorny underbrush. Rhapsody noted absently that the brambles were blackberries, though they bore no sign of fruit on their sharp branches, and from the look of them, she doubted they ever would. Beyond the scrub they could see a shape, a house, it seemed, though at first it was difficult to tell through the brush.

They moved forward slowly, creeping along the edge of the road, until at last they could see beyond the brush. There they saw a large house in the clearing, too large to be mistaken for anything but the place they sought. In one corner was a tower, built of ancient stone and overlooking a square courtyard. It was protected on all four sides with walls guarded by sentries.

In this courtyard was a leafless tree, which from a distance looked dead rather than dormant to Rhapsody. Her time at Llauron's had given her ample schooling and opportunity to gauge tree health, and this one to her seemed choked with disease.

The walls of the courtyard were whitewashed, with many years' growth of moss and lichen clinging to them. The roof was made of slate, and a large front door was left partially ajar, almost as if someone was expecting visitors.

Achmed and Grunthor split to either side and began circling the house through the forest cover. It never ceased to amaze Rhapsody how silent they were in heavy brush, and how hard to discern, especially given Grunthor's gargantuan proportions. She looked around, praying desperately that they would not be seen while on their maneuvers out of her sight. She looked back at the house.

The door was guarded on either side by men holding long spears, clad in leather-backed ring mail. No candles could be seen in the open-paned windows in the growing dusk. The only sound came from the scratching of the long white limbs of the birch trees reaching out from the forest edge to tap gently on the windows, walls, and roof of the House of Remembrance. Rhapsody thought she heard a muffled wail, but decided after a moment's pause that it was the wind.

"Are you ready? Try to stay where we can see you." Achmed's whispered voice seemed to be next to her ear, though he stood a few feet behind her, obviously having returned from his circumspection of the outpost. She nodded, and he slipped into the shadows again, moving to the far side of the road. Grunthor readied the poleax for a charge. Rhapsody took a deep breath, then stepped out of the underbrush and walked toward the front door.

Instantly the guards leveled their spears. Rhapsody felt almost giddy as nervousness swept through her. She smiled at them and a disengaged calm came over her. She thought, distantly, that she smelled the odor of rotting meat.

"Hello," she said pleasantly. The effect on the guards was immediately obvious: their grip on their spears loosened, and Rhapsody thought she could see one of them tremble visibly, seeming entranced. "Could you tell me, is this the House of Remembrance?"

One guard nodded dumbly. She noted that the second man was not so quick to drop his guard. In him she sensed a stronger, almost consuming desire that set her ill at ease.

"Well, that was easy," she said, smiling brightly. The second guard's hands were now trembling, too. *Whatever transformation I underwent in the Great Fire must have left me frightening to behold*, she thought in amazement. Surely these guards were not intimidated by her small stature.

"I'm supposed to meet some friends here. Have you seen them?" Rhapsody chose her words carefully, thinking she might be able to tell if Grunthor and Achmed had been spotted during their scouting a few moments before.

"Will—will you marry me?" the first guard stammered.

Rhapsody blinked, then laughed. She thought about what Grunthor's reaction might have been to the comment if he had been close enough to hear it.

"You know," she said, leaning forward confidentially, "I don't think my friend would particularly like you joking with me about that. He's rather protective and can be quite ferocious if he thinks I'm being insulted."

Panic seized the guard's face. "No, miss, I—"

"Anyway, have you seen him? I'm sure you would know him if you had, he's rather—well, frightening."

The two guards looked at each other, and Rhapsody saw a look of fear pass between them. Her words had some meaning to these men that she had not intended.

The second guard summoned the courage to speak. "You're here to see *him*, then? No, he's not here, miss, but he's expected later today. Please come in and wait in the warmth; my friend didn't mean no insult."

The first guard stumbled backward, pushing the door open, and then held it for her. Rhapsody looked behind her, but saw nothing where Grunthor and Achmed had been.

A shouted warning went up from the sentries which appeared to have been directed to the others about her. She could almost hear the curses Achmed was undoubtedly directing her way under his breath.

Placing her hand casually on the hilt of the sword, she followed the first guard across the threshold. They entered a darkened foyer with heavy doors to either side and an open portal in front of them that led into a large garden. Rhapsody stopped and gasped in horror.

The first thing that hit her was the stench of decay. An almost visible cloud of overwhelmingly thick and sickly-sweet air tainted with the sour stench of fouled meat assaulted her nose. Rhapsody choked on the odor as the color drained from her face. She forced down the bile that rose from her stomach. The smell was nothing compared with what she saw.

The garden in the central courtyard was large, the dead tree in its center. The snow had been stained red, making it look like a rosy-hued blanket. Set in the center of the courtyard were two large wooden frames, the kind Rhapsody was accustomed to seeing used to slaughter swine.

Between them stood a large, dark-stained stone altar. A channel had been carved into the foot of the altar leading to an intricately designed trough that joined with two other troughs, each one coming from beneath the slaughter frames, where large vats had been built.

Together the three canals made an interweaving pattern leading in and out until at last they fed into a large brass brazier charred black from fire. Each of these canals was encrusted with dark stains, and in each of the basins were thick pools of a black, viscous liquid.

The source and nature of this liquid was not left for Rhapsody to guess. On the altar, and hanging upside down above each of the basins, was the body of a child. The children that hung from the frames had had their throats and wrists sliced open, and had been left to drain of their blood. The world swam suddenly before her eyes as she was overcome with nausea.

Her reaction was apparently not what the guards expected. The first turned to her with a questioning look. Behind her she could hear the other soldier shift position quickly, as if readying to attack. Then she heard the soft hiss of projectiles from Achmed's weapon, and the instant collapse of the guard behind her.

She drew Daystar Clarion at once, and the sound of the longsword as it emerged from its scabbard was like the winding of a melodic horn. The blade flamed to life, burning brighter than she had seen it before.

As she drew the sword the remaining guard tried a desperate and ill-balanced attack. The flames of Daystar Clarion swelled and billowed in her hand.

"Drop your spear!" she ordered, her voice harsh with fear and anger.

The guard charged. Rhapsody sidestepped the poorly aimed spear thrust and lunged, just as Grunthor has taught her to. Daystar Clarion slipped neatly into his chest, encountering only the slightest resistance as it sliced through his rib cage. The sickly-sweet smell of burning flesh filled the rancid air.

The man's eyes widened in surprise. He opened his mouth as if to scream, but all that escaped was a whimpering gasp as his lungs instantly blistered and seared in the white-hot fires of the elemental sword.

Rhapsody grabbed him and eased his fall to the floor as his face contorted in agony and confusion. His eyes, already looking beyond this world, fearfully searched her face, and in her mind she could read the question that filled his last thoughts: *What's happening?*

The same question was wrenching its way through her own mind. By the time he touched the ground his body had gone limp, and his wound was smoldering. She suddenly became aware of a slight sizzling noise as her blade cooked the meat of his body, and with a growing horror she quickly withdrew the blade and dropped it, even though the hilt was still cool to the touch. She stared at the body on the ground before her as the world began to spin.

"What's the matter?" Achmed whispered from behind her. She had not heard him approach. She turned to see him looking around the garden, Grunthor by his side.

"He's dead," Rhapsody answered, her voice shaking.

"Yes. Your sword skills are getting better."

"I've never killed a man before."

"Now you have," Achmed replied. "Let's get on with this." Rhapsody drew a breath and nodded. It had to be done;

keep going, she thought as her gaze returned to the macabre scene in the garden. Achmed motioned for her to pick up the sword.

"Any sign of anyone else?"

"No, but there are others here, at least one, and more people are expected," she said. She touched the cool steel of the blade, which showed no blood, and sheathed the weapon in its rock-scabbard with a shudder.

"Well, we can put a stop ta that," Grunthor said. He closed the front door behind him and barred it with the large bracing beam that stood next to it. "Well, sir, Oi guess we know why your blood sense came alive."

"Let's find out who else is here," Achmed said as he looked around the scene of the slaughter. He turned to the side door and gestured for them to enter.

Rhapsody stood on one side of the door, Grunthor on the other. At Achmed's signal, Grunthor slammed the door with his hand. The sound of splintering wood and the crash of the door as it was torn off its hinges filled the air. Achmed held his fire. They looked into an empty room.

It was a long hall, with smoothly polished wooden furniture that seemed almost organic in its design. A large woven rug covered the center of the floor, one corner and the wood about it marred by a dark stain. A long series of windows looked out onto the central courtyard, where they could see melting snow touched with pink.

Achmed crossed the room to the dark stain on the rug and bent to touch it. It was long dried, perhaps years so, but he knew at once it was blood. A person had been killed here, the blood draining freely from the body before it had been moved.

Grunthor stood by the door, wishing that there was room enough to use his poleax, but knowing it was safer to keep his snickersnee in hand as long as they were indoors. In the pit of his stomach he felt a knot that tightened to a deep nausea on looking out the window, even though he was used to ignoring such feelings.

Rhapsody moved to the next door, listening, guarding it. After a moment she shook her head.

"Nothing. What next?"

"Come on," Achmed said after a moment, and stood before the next door. The others took their positions as before and they repeated their procedure. The door opened toward a blank wall, and they had to enter the room to see it clearly.

They had come upon the Great Hall of the House, a room that stretched back to the main tower of the structure. Along one wall was a series of large windows which opened into the courtyard, on the other tapestries whose intricate patterns had faded and been defiled by excrement.

The far end of the hall was part of the tower, and a grand staircase led up to what had probably once been part of the defenses, but now was just an open doorway. The other wall was a series of glass-paned doors that were open into the courtyard.

Along the base of the tapestried wall stood a throne made from bones. Femurs, rib cages, long bones, and vertebrae had been crossed, stitched, and nailed together to form a gruesome chair browed by seven skulls, and a soft red velvet cushion had been placed on its seat.

In the center of the room sat, crouched, and lay a group of children, staring in fear at the trio who had just broken their way into the room. Like a pack of starving, beaten wolves, their eyes glittered in the half-light.

They were a mixture of humans and Lirin of varying ages and clad in clothes in successive states of disrepair. Iron manacles were bound to their ankles, and each child was linked to the others by heavy chains.

Their faces and bodies were covered with bruises and cuts, their eyes dulled with the look of those who had seen horror that no mortal should. They shivered with the cold of the winter air as it blew in through the wide curtains and open doors. None of them spoke or even cried as their eyes darted between Rhapsody and the two who flanked her. The children of Navarne.

33

Sorrow filled Rhapsody's eyes at the sight of the small faces frozen in an expression between horror and hope. To a one, the little captives had begun to tremble when the three companions broke into the room where they were imprisoned, a forest of human leaves in a high wind.

Aside from their involuntary shivering, the children remained motionless with the exception of one slightly older girl, perhaps sixteen years of age, bound hand and foot in the middle of the group. She struggled for a moment, glaring furiously at the door, then blinked as shock descended.

"Don't worry, we're here to help you." Rhapsody gave them her gentlest smile as Grunthor and Achmed moved quickly through the room toward the far door. "We're going to get you out of here and take you back to your homes." The children stared at her blankly.

Rhapsody turned to Achmed. "Were there keys on either of the guards?"

"No time for that now. Let's find whoever is running this little house of fun."

"There are at least nine of them." The comment came from one of the captives in the center of the room. It was the girl whose hands were bound. She looked uneasy as she spoke.

"Do you know where they are?" Rhapsody asked.

"No," the girl answered. "But they come through that door." She nodded toward the end of the hall the trio had not yet examined. Grunthor put down his poleax and drew his massive snickersnee. The two Bolg made ready to open the door.

"Thank you, and don't worry," Rhapsody said. "We'll release you when we get back." She gave the whole group another encouraging smile.

"Just don't tell them who talked if you get captured," the girl said acidly.

Rhapsody nodded in the direction of the two Bolg. "I

wouldn't worry about that too much. What's your name, dear?"

"We're ready," Achmed called from the door.

"Well, it's not *dear*," the girl said with a glint of defiance in her eye.

"It's Jo!" said a pretty girl of no more than six. "She told them when they started twisting her toes. I'm Lizette."

Jo looked disapprovingly at the child, but the little girl did not notice. She seemed enraptured with Rhapsody, unable to take her eyes off the Lirin Singer.

"Are you finished?" Achmed asked.

"We'll be back," Rhapsody said to the children. She was using the Naming technique of speaking truly. After a moment she saw belief creep back into their eyes somewhat. She blew them a kiss and went to join her companions. The older girl muttered something under her breath, but Rhapsody could not hear it.

Her attention was now drawn to the sounds of shouting and the pounding of footsteps coming from the next room. She quickly took her place by the door, and within seconds it burst open. Two men armed with spears raced into the room to find themselves faced with Achmed and the cwellan.

Rhapsody heard the now-familiar hiss of the weapon firing, and out of the corner of her eye she saw the silver streak of tiny disks as they flew past the men in the doorway and beyond.

He's shooting at people in the next room, she thought in distracted admiration; the speed and sureness of Achmed's hands as he reloaded never ceased to amaze her. What had once been a blur was now slightly more visible to her.

She lunged as the guard on her side swung at Achmed, driving the burning blade of Daystar Clarion through the man's back. He fell, writhing, pulling himself free of Rhapsody's blade as he did. Grunthor's great two-handed swing was but a moment behind her own, and his five-foot blade cleanly cut off the other man's head. Rhapsody struggled to stay focused; the nightmare of what was happening had caused reality to recede into the distance, making her feel like a spectator in the fight.

Achmed ripped open the door. "Go," he ordered. There was a moment where she and Grunthor nearly collided while both trying to enter the room, but she managed to dodge out of the giant Bolg's way just ahead of being trampled.

Inside was another scene of carnage, but this time it was of their own making. Six bodies were strewn across the floor.

In the center of the room stood a woman, dressed in white, desperately shouting orders to a handful of men who were running down a great stone staircase, the only other entrance in the room. The room was massive and built completely of stone, its walls lined with book-and-scroll-filled shelves. Armchairs and a few large desks were placed with care about the room.

Rhapsody and Grunthor rushed into the room, making certain to keep clear of the line of fire from the door. It took five strides for Grunthor to reach the center, bellowing at the top of his lungs. At the sight and sound of the screaming giant, the soldiers within the library froze in terror.

Rhapsody ran at the woman in white. The woman's eyes were quickly torn from Grunthor and sighted onto her, glaring with a furious hatred.

The woman drew the only weapon she seemed to carry, a long, cruel-looking obsidian dagger, and took up a fighting stance. Rhapsody recognized the weapon as an implement of sacrifice, a tool used in the rituals of evil. Her own eyes took on a similar hateful fury as she realized this woman must have been the one who had mutilated the children in the courtyard.

Rhapsody swung her sword with all the rage that had built up within her, a strong swift swing that Grunthor would have been proud of. The woman sidestepped it and lunged with her own dagger.

Pulled off balance by the wildness of her own blow, Rhapsody could not dodge, and felt a sharp pain as the dagger pierced her left shoulder. She winced, and drew a painful breath, then struck with the flaming sword again. The woman did not have time to scream before Rhapsody drove the blade through her heart. Once more the air was filled with the acrid smell of burning flesh, but no blood fell to the floor. The wounds were instantly cauterized even before the woman's life had fled her body.

Rhapsody followed in Grunthor's wake and moved sharply to the side as more disks slid through the air, too close for comfort. She did not spare the woman a glance, instead looking up to see how her companions fared. They were fine; none of their opponents were left alive.

The human debris scattered about the bottom of that stair showed that Grunthor had killed at least two more of the guards. Other bodies bore the cleaner wounds of the cwellan. With a quick glance she counted fifteen and wondered if any others remained.

Grunthor stood at the bottom of the stairs, his eyes fixed at the top, waiting with grim determination for more to appear there. He had drawn a hand ax, almost the size of a battle-ax for most men, a weapon that Rhapsody had seen him hurl at vermin with deadly force before.

"I guess we won't be questioning her," Achmed said, looking down at the body of the woman.

Shame suddenly flushed Rhapsody's face. "I'm sorry," she said.

"What are you sorry about?" Achmed said, annoyed. "Who knows who or what she was; she had to be taken down. You did it. It would have been handy to torture a few answers out of her, but sometimes you just have to address the situation as it happens. Is it serious?"

"What?" Rhapsody asked, confused by the question.

"Your shoulder—is the wound serious?"

"Hmm? Oh. No, it's not deep." Rhapsody looked down at the gash. "It can wait."

"Poison?" Achmed moved close enough to smell the wound.

"I don't think so."

"All right, let's see if there's any more company," Achmed said. He lifted the crossbeam that leaned against the wall and barred the door to the room before heading to the stairs. "Just to be sure any unexpected guests have to knock first."

They searched the rest of the tower, climbing the stairs quickly and quietly, but found no sign of any other occupants.

The higher rooms were where the soldiers they had fought had quartered themselves, and on the top floor was a large suite which had undoubtedly been the home to the woman in white, though there were signs that a man also had been there.

In that room they found a small chest, securely bound, which they took downstairs to examine when they were certain the rest of the House of Remembrance was clear. A quick search of the rest of the structure revealed a series of cloisterlike rooms that had not been occupied, and a kitchen that had been used recently.

Rhapsody started looking for a key with which to open the children's manacles, finally discovering one on a chain around the dead woman's neck. She hurried back to the hall where they were imprisoned and quickly began unlocking them, speaking to them in low, comforting tones.

In the absence of the two Bolg the children seemed to warm to her quickly, except for the girl named Jo, who continued to eye her with suspicion. Rhapsody went from child to child, speaking quietly to them and humming, comforting them as best she could for the moment. It seemed to work, and eventually even Jo seemed to relax a bit.

Meanwhile, Achmed deftly picked the locks on the small chest they had found in the rooms above. In it he found a few baubles, which he passed to Grunthor, who kept their supply of tender and coinage; a small notebook; a sealed scroll; and a large brass key with four blades and strange teeth.

Carefully he opened the scroll and saw that it was written in an ancient script which he could not read, but its form and format was clear and familiar to him. It was a contract. He called to Rhapsody.

She entered the room with a long trail of children behind her. There were fifteen in all, mostly under the age of twelve. The youngest of them clung to her, and on entering the tower library hid behind her from the two large monsters that had been their rescuers.

"It's all right, Feldin," Jo said to a Lirin boy of about seven. "They may be ugly as shit, but they set us free. They can't possibly do anything worse to us than was planned." Grunthor snickered.

"We won't do anything to you except return you home," Rhapsody said with a smile. Looking into her radiant face, the quivering children believed her.

"Look at this," Achmed said, walking over to Rhapsody. The children cleared out of his way quickly.

Rhapsody took the scroll and studied it for a moment. A frown came over her face, but it passed quickly.

"This is in Ancient Serenne," she said. "Isn't that odd? This is the tongue Llauron wanted me to learn; I didn't bother to tell him I already knew a little of it. It's a dead language. I mean, it was a dead language even when we left the Island. It was the tongue of the Firstborn, the Ancient Seren, the original inhabitants of the Island. But look at this scroll, the vellum is not really very old."

"Can you read it?" Achmed asked.

"I think so," Rhapsody said. "It's a musical language, and my mentor taught me most of the fundamentals—wait. I was wrong. The letters are the old script, but it's written in the language of men—I mean the common tongue of the people of these lands. Just give me a minute and I'll read it through."

Rhapsody walked over to one of the desks, sat down, and positioned two books to hold open the scroll. She took off her own pack, pulled out a piece of poorly tanned hide, and began jotting down notes on it.

As she did, the children swarmed around her, except for Jo, who moved over to the pile of bodies that Grunthor was quickly stacking in one corner of the room. Noticing this, Rhapsody considered moving the children into a different room, but quickly realized that, at least from this room, the bodies of the slaughtered children were not as visible as they were from some of the other rooms.

Only a day before, the greatest sorrow she had tried to assuage in a small child was the loss of the mother of Lord Stephen's children. Now she had in her care children who had suffered unimaginable trauma. She swallowed the lump in her throat, hoping she would be up to the task of helping them heal once they were free of this place.

Achmed leafed quickly through the small notebook. Unlike the other, it seemed to be written in the common tongue of this land. The letters were similar to those he knew, and so with some difficulty he began to skim through it.

It appeared to be a journal, like the kind scholars and scribes used while jotting down notes. Its text was about a lost city, though he was uncertain he was reading it correctly. He was more interested in the map that had been sketched in the book, and the reference to the brass key.

A smile crawled across his face when he recognized the name *Gwylliam*, and saw a marker on the map in an area distinctly denoted as *Firbolg lands*. Canrif. They had a map.

"Achmed, Grunthor, I've got it," Rhapsody said, holding up the sheepskin translation. "It's a contact. It was signed in the first hour of the Equinox, in the one-thousand-three-hundred-and-ninety-sixth year since the arrival of the fleet; I'm not sure which one that means, probably the First Wave, I would guess.

"The parties involved are Cifiona—I guess that would be the woman with the big dagger—and someone called the Rakshas, and through him his master. That's strange; his master is not referred to by name.

"She is apparently to receive, for services rendered, 'life unending.' I wonder if this really means immortality." She looked up at her friends, and the expression in her eyes matched theirs; the nature of the contract and its participants was becoming clearer. "Apparently she also agrees to be bound to the master; maybe this is a sort of marriage contract."

"I doubt it," said Achmed. He had been the unwilling party of a contract like this once.

Rhapsody's face was twisted in disgust. Grunthor was growing impatient.

"Well, miss? What else does it say?"

" 'Among those services shall be counted the commitment of the blood sacrifice of thirty-three persons of innocent heart and untouched body of human descent, and an equal number of Lirin or half-Lirin origins,' " Rhapsody read. She looked at Achmed. "I saw three in the courtyard. Do you think there were others?"

"No, I don't think so," he replied. "The amount of dried blood indicates the equipment is fairly new; I'd say this was the first round." He watched her sigh in relief and go back to reading, ignoring Grunthor's look of doubt.

"It has some nonsense about a particular undertaking, but doesn't explain what that is, except that it's what the blood is to be used for. I think this word is 'sustenance.' Then it sets the date of completion of service as the time of the Patriarch Rite of the following year, and the venue to be the House of Remembrance, of which this 'the Rakshas' person is apparently now considered Master. That's nice; I wonder what those First Generation Cymrians would think of that."

"Well, speakin' as one myself, Oi can't say Oi'm too pleased about it."

"And here below it is signed: Cifiona—something—I can't tell, and then simply 'Rakshas,' with these symbols next to it."

Rhapsody showed them the two signs, the first of which appeared to be a character in an unknown language, which neither Achmed or Grunthor recognized.

"I think I've seen this one before," Rhapsody said, pointing to the second symbol, a circle formed from a spiraling line.

"Where?" demanded Achmed. The sudden fury in his voice made her jump.

"It's a hex sign on Llauron's front door, or something like it."

The sight of the second symbol had clearly unnerved the assassin. He took the document and placed it back in the small chest. Rhapsody tossed her translation in as well.

"Let's get out of here," Achmed said.

"Wait, there's something I have to do," Rhapsody said, pulling out her higen and a small bag that Llauron had given her.

"What, you're going to compose a song about the beautiful things we've seen today?"

"No," Rhapsody said with a touch of impatience. "I'm going to see if I can heal that tree."

"Why?" Achmed's tone was tinged with irritation.

"Because it is a Sagian Oak, or hadn't you noticed? To me it's sacred. Lord Stephen said it was planted from a sapling brought by the Cymrians from Serendair. That means it is a sapling of Sagia. Even though I have regrets about leaving the Island, I am grateful to the Tree that let us escape the death that came after. The least I can do is try to heal its child."

"Not to be disrespectful, miss, but it's *not* a child, it's just a tree."

"No," Achmed said, looking in the direction of the garden. "Go ahead."

"Thank you," Rhapsody said, surprised at his willingness. "Just look after the children for a moment and I'll be right back."

"Excuse me?"

"Well, I can't very well take them into the garden, can I?" Rhapsody whispered. "I don't even want to go there myself; there are dead children in there."

"That's all right, miss; we'll look after them."

Achmed glared at Grunthor, but he did not disagree. As Rhapsody left the room, he sat on the edge of one of the desks and returned to reading the small black notebook. Grunthor continued to rifle the bodies for valuables and stack them in a pile in the corner. All the children, aside from the oldest girl, stayed together, anxiously watching the door through which the Singer had left.

ℜhapsody had to fight down her rising gorge as she rapidly made her way across the garden to the diseased tree at its center. Even in its withered state, the silvery-white bark was unmistakable. She blinked back tears at the memory of the one and only time she had ever seen Sagia, this tree's mother, whose story she had learned from her own.

When she reached the large oak she looked over its bark and the tips of its branches. Using the lore taught to her by Llauron as well as the knowledge from her own life, she quickly realized the tree was not dead, and began humming a tuneless song, its melody matching the whispers of a song that still reverberated from its ailing heart. It was the same familiar tune that had run through her soul all the while she had traveled along the Root. She opened the bag she had been given in Gwynwood and pulled out a tiny tube of ointment, then began to care for the dying oak.

Running her hands over the tree, Rhapsody uncovered three of the larger root trunks, and followed them down to smaller branchings, looking for the ends. Steeling her nerve, she crossed much of the garden, trying to avoid looking at the grisly sights, until she found some of the tiniest filamental roots. She coated the hair-thin strands with ointment, soaking the soil around them.

By the time she had anointed the first root, her song had gained a rhythm and a tune; when she had finished the third, her voice was strong and she was singing in a mixture of Old Cymrian, the language of her father, and the tongue of the men she had faced this day.

Devli protar hin elenin, *Hope is a safe anchor,*
Long was your journey at sea
Vidsuol hin yl gornit marbeth, *Time is the best healer,*
And whole once more now you will be

Calenda o skidoaun, Calenda o verdig, *A year of snow, a
year of plenty,*
You've suffered the cold and the gloom
Ovidae tullhin kaf san; ni wyn bael faerbon, *Sometimes
there's no summer, but always there's spring,*
And in the spring you shall bloom

A fynno daelik, gernal federant, *He who would be
healthy, let him be cheerful,*
So hold this song in your soul
Yl airen er iachâd daelikint, *A song of joyous healing,*
Sing it until you are whole.

Rhapsody had never written an original song of healing before, and inwardly she cringed at the poor verse. She had used for the main lyric adages from the old world, words of wisdom spoken by the people who had come here, part of their folklore, and somehow the music spoke to the tree. The song seemed to flow through its roots, moving up through the trunk and branches until it touched the leafless twigs.

Still humming the tune, she picked up the higen and ran

her fingers along its curved wood frame. The higen was her greatest treasure; it was the first instrument she mastered, and it had helped her learn the science of Naming. It was fashioned from wood from the old world, like the tree itself.

Rhapsody began to play an accompaniment to her song on the higen. The tune remained simple and clear as the notes leapt from her fingers, and slowly the tree began to respond. She could almost feel the sap move through its branches, restoring life where death had been lurking. The vibration of the song reached the smallest twigs, causing them to bring forth tiny green buds, the precursor of leaves that would come in the spring.

Rhapsody took the higen and set it in the highest crotch she could reach, right above the first hollow of the trunk. It continued to play, fueled by the tree itself singing the song in response. She smiled as the tree returned to life, then turned and headed back to her friends and the children.

On her way back through the garden Rhapsody passed a long, flat table, largely hidden beneath a blanket of snow. When she had hurried past it on the way to the tree she had presumed it was a garden bench of some kind, but now she felt compelled to stop and look at it again. As she did, an image formed, unbidden, in her head.

Her body began to shake as the snow melted away in her mind's eye, leaving the stone table black and gleaming in the ominous light of a full moon. On the table was the body of a man, lying still as death, looking as if it were formed from the ice left behind in the melting snow's wake. She could discern no particular features; in the moonlight, the body barely seemed human.

Within the darkness above the lifeless form she could discern movement, and concentrated as best she could to see it in her trance. Disembodied hands, their owner obscured from her view, gestured within the air, seemingly in the performance of a religious ceremony. They folded together, as if in prayer, then opened as if in blessing. Blood poured from between them into the lifeless form, staining it red as it filled.

Words, spoken as if in her ear, sounded in the darkness, absent of any voice.

Child of my blood.

Rhapsody watched, feeling nothing in the detachment of the trance, as a small glowing object appeared in the hands, pulsing with a light that twinkled almost like a star. It burned so intensely that she blinked, trying to shield her eyes from the pain.

With great care the hands placed the shining object gently into the blood-form that lay on the table. The body gleamed for a moment, then began to glow brightly, light surrounding it, swallowing the hands that had hovered above it.

Now shall the prophecy be broken. From this child will come forth my children.

The light began to fade, and as it diminished, the figure began to become solid, distinct.

The thunderous sound of horses hooves shattered the trance. Rhapsody's legs gave out and she fell to her knees in the pink-stained snow, shuddering from the sudden loss of the vision. Her heart pounding in revulsion, she leapt from the ground, ran to the garden wall, and looked down into the courtyard below.

Achmed looked up from the notebook as the music began to resound from the garden. He returned almost immediately to his reading; the book was proving quite useful.

According to the carefully graphed script, Canrif, the city of Gwylliam, capital of the Third Cymrian Fleet, had been abandoned after the death of the Lord Cymrian due to the alarming increase in Firbolg raids and the havoc that the war had played with the Cymrians' resources and ability to organize.

They had been unable to hold the city as the barbarian assaults intensified, and so with much regret they had sealed those parts they could and left it in hopes that they might one day return. Apparently they never had, and now this city, with its treasures and library locked away, was deep within the heart of the Bolglands.

What was more, the key to Gwylliam's vault had been left

in the House of Remembrance by Anborn, the general who had evacuated the mountain. A few notes seemed to indicate that regents of Roland, the ancestors of Lord Stephen and his fellow dukes, were Cymrian generals from the First and Third Waves, but Achmed was uncertain he was reading the fragmented annotations correctly. He would have to have Rhapsody read these parts.

His attention was drawn from the book when he noticed the older girl captive in the process of secreting away a dagger from one of the dead guards. She was nimble, good enough that Grunthor, who was watching the children, had not noticed. Achmed made a soft clicking noise, drawing Grunthor's immediate eye. A quick nod in the direction of the girl sent Grunthor ambling over to her.

" 'Ey, what you got there, lit'le miss?" the giant asked.

"Nothin'," the girl responded, looking away and shuffling her feet.

Achmed smiled. Her movements, intended to look like a coy, frightened or bashful reaction, had in fact been a ruse to hide the weapon within her clothing. It was well done enough that the assassin wondered if she had succeeded in fooling Grunthor. She hadn't.

"Well, what's this, then?" the Sergeant asked.

His enormous hand reached behind her back and plucked out the small dagger. The girl was surprised by the giant's speed, her expression quickly melting into one of fear. She had been caught, not just stealing a weapon, but lying about it. Her eyes quickly darted toward the door, looking, Achmed assumed, for the potential protection of Rhapsody.

"Um—it looks a lot like a knife," the girl answered.

"Now, what would a girl like you want with somethin' like this?" Grunthor asked, disdain on his face. He quickly drew a longer, nastier-looking blade from his own hoard of weapons, and smiled. "If you're gonna use a blade, make sure it's a good one. 'Ere, now this is a dirk worth carryin'." He handed his blade over to the girl, who took it with a questioning stare.

"Now, see, this knife 'as a real good edge to it, and see that bronze ridge along the top? It's perfect for parryin' the other guy's slashes. Once you do that, you can slice 'is wrist with the recurved bit on the front, see?"

"Yeah," the girl said. A wary smile appeared.

"Now, you practice that—a block and a twist, got it?" Grunthor said, demonstrating the movement with the small dagger he had taken from her. The girl nodded. Grunthor backed up two steps and watched her appreciatively before turning to go back to looting the dead. As he did, he noticed Achmed's look of disbelief.

"What?" Grunthor held his hands out in bewilderment. The Dhracian nodded at the girl, and the giant shrugged. "Oh. What's the 'arm, eh?"

Achmed merely shook his head and returned to the book. He read two sentences more before Rhapsody returned to the room, panting from running. Her eyes were dark with concern.

"There's a troop of men approaching," she said.

34

"They're moving quickly; they are almost to the door."

"What?" Achmed's unpleasant face went blank with surprise. He ran to the door of the library and through the glass windows of the connecting hall. From that vantage point he could see ten men entering the garden, walking gingerly through the bloody snow.

Leading them was a man in a heavy gray hooded mantle, flanked on either side by white wolves. When he reached the tree in the garden's center he stopped and looked up at it, then walked around it with interest.

Upon seeing the leader, a faint buzzing filled Achmed's inner ears; he was unsure if he heard it, or merely felt it. He ducked back through the door and, with an agile shrug, swung the cwellan from his back and into his hands.

Even back inside the tower, behind the solid wall, he could feel the vibration rattling in his skull, emanating from where the man in the gray cloak stood. He felt the pounding of blood in his ears, and the buzzing noise grew louder. Achmed quickly closed the door.

"Did they see you?" he asked Rhapsody.

"No," Rhapsody said, "at least I don't think so. I just caught a glimpse of them coming before I came to warn you. What do you think they want? Are they in league with Cifiona, or are they here to find the children?"

"If they're here for the children, it's not to help them," Achmed said. "I got the same sick feeling when I saw their leader that I had when I saw the House back on the trail."

"Oh, lovely," Grunthor said. He held his snickersnee at the ready. Suddenly a look of concern swept over his face. "Oh, son of a whore—Oi left my poleax out there."

"I don't think there's enough room for you to use it in here, anyway," Rhapsody said.

"It's not that, miss. When the bastards see it they'll know we're still around."

"Marvelous," Achmed sighed. "Rhapsody, take the brats upstairs. Grunthor, get your bow out and barricade this door as soon as I'm through it."

"You're not going out there alone, are you?" Rhapsody put her arm around a small boy who was beginning to sob in fright.

"I'm at my best when I'm alone. Now get them upstairs."

Achmed cracked open the door. The guards had not yet entered the hall where the children had been kept. Quickly he slipped through the door and Grunthor closed it behind him. The giant slid the crossbar in place before going to the library desks and quietly stacking them on their sides to form a barricade near the stairs.

Rhapsody gently ushered the children up the steps. Despite her best efforts, she could not hide the concern in her voice.

Slinking through the shadows like a cat, Achmed traversed the long hall unseen, even though some of the brigands entered the room before he had finished. The men carried themselves with the gait of the well-trained and were well armed. All but their leader wore ring mail, and several carried crossbows.

Crouching in the corner, all but invisible, Achmed closed

his eyes and listened. He counted fifteen soldiers, not including the nine who had been left outside the main door, and their leader. He cursed himself for letting Rhapsody and the children get caught in the tower, but it had been the preferable option. At least while they were there Grunthor could hold their attackers at bay for a long time while he picked them off slowly from outside.

Achmed decided to get a start on that. He crept through the door Grunthor had smashed from its hinges, into the long, bloodstained hall, and through the outer windows that lined it. The nine men outside the House died before their leader had left the garden.

Inside, Grunthor waited patiently behind his makeshift fortress of desks. He kept an arrow nocked to his long recurved bow, and had stuck the tip of his snickersnee in the floorboards near him. After a moment, he heard a slight rattling of the door, then a series of thuds, like a man trying to shoulder his way in.

Grunthor smiled. This door was thick, and even he would have had serious trouble smashing it in without the aid of a log. Then they heard a light noise, as if someone was knocking.

"Hello? Is anyone home?" It was a man's voice, warm and pleasant, tinged with humor. "It isn't very nice of you to lock me out of my house, you know. Let's be reasonable, shall we?—let me in. I know you're in there."

"BUGGER OFF!" Grunthor roared.

Suddenly the door burst apart in an explosion of dark fire. Burning splinters flew across the room, flames burned in black hues, and smoke filled the air.

Six or seven soldiers ran into the room. Grunthor began loosing his yard-long arrows. He heard the distinctive thud of crossbow bolts embedding in the heavy oak desks, and returned fire. One crossbowman was down; his other shots had missed the two who had leapt for cover.

Of more immediate concern were the three swordsmen who charged across the room toward his makeshift barricade. He managed to down one of them with an arrow in the thigh before the other two jumped the desks. More followed from the door. The first met with an arrow driven by Grunthor's hand into his chest; the second managed to get to his feet before the huge fist of the Bolg smashed into his face, crushing the front of his skull.

Grunthor grabbed his snickersnee as four ran around the sides of the barricade. The giant had to stay on his knees to avoid the crossbow bolts that were slamming into the staircase and the desks in front of him. With a quick lunge and a thrust, he dispatched the first, but he knew he would momentarily be flanked and outnumbered.

The Sergeant parried the blow of the next and turned to defend against the third, only to find the man spinning to the ground with a smoldering wound in his forehead.

A lithe form sped across his field of vision as Rhapsody left her victim and engaged the other man who had made it past the barricade. Grunthor smiled as he turned his own attentions on the soldier who was attacking him. He was surprised when the man was able to parry his blow without losing his grip on his sword. Grunthor lunged, thrust, and slashed, with little effect, receiving a deep cut to his forearm before dispatching the well-trained guard.

"Nice form, soldier," he said to the corpse in admiration.

He turned to assist Rhapsody just in time to see her knocked down by a kick to her knees. He cleaved her opponent in two and Rhapsody quickly regained her feet.

"Oi'm quite glad to see you, miss."

Rhapsody smiled. "The feeling's mutual," she said.

They turned to face any new adversaries about to rush them when they were knocked off their feet by another sudden explosion of dark fire that set the countless bookshelves aflame.

As Achmed slipped behind the altar in the garden, he saw the man with the wolves raise his hand. A blast of black fire sprang forth from his palm, blowing the heavy tower door into pieces. At once a number of his troops rushed the door.

Achmed flexed his hand, then raised his cwellan to his eyes to sight his targets with care. The first to fall were the two guards who stood by the doors to the garden. The next shot was aimed at the man in the gray hooded cloak.

The leader turned as the silver disks approached his head, but the missiles never hit their mark. Instead, the shining projectiles flared suddenly and burned away within inches of the man's eyes. He smiled as he raised his hand.

At once a ball of ebony flame sailed through the air and exploded at the base of the stone altar. The ground shook slightly, the frames that held the dead children collapsed to the ground, and the stone altar cracked, but Achmed backed away, uninjured.

As he heard the footfalls of soldiers rush into the garden, Achmed sprang once more into action, loosing a deadly hail of disks into the eyes and throats of the brigands, but their commander was out of his line of fire. At the entrance to the hall, a wall of dark flames had risen to block his way. Achmed swore, and moved swiftly to the main door, the only other route he knew to the tower. Silently he cursed the fact that the fires were black; obviously the lore of such dark power had not been lost with the Island.

Grunthor and Rhapsody rolled quickly to their feet as the fire spread and the smoke choked the air. In the doorway they could see the silhouette of a man. Grunthor grabbed one of the hand axes from his weapons belt and hurled it at the figure. The twirling hatchet never reached its mark, vanishing in a dark flash.

"Come now," the voice said, "you're trapped here—throw down your weapons and I will let the fires fall. Refuse, and I shall be forced to let you burn to death."

The voice in the shadow of the flames was sweet and rich, like honey on a warm day. Something in the words made her think back to their time after exiting the Root.

And then there's the fire.

What about the fire?

Come here. Take off your scabbard and leave it there.

There. So what?

Now have a look at the fire.

I see it.

Good; now walk slowly toward it.

Gods, what's happening?

It's you, miss. See? But if you don't stop it, you're gonna burn up my lit'le den 'ere, maybe set the whole forest ablaze.

Rhapsody closed her eyes, and calmed her spirit. She concentrated on the fire.

"Be at peace," she said.

At once the flames responded, the bonfire fed by the books and scrolls died down to flickering embers.

From the door she heard cursing and within her heart she felt a tug at the edge of her perceptions. At once the fires began to rise back to life.

Panic shot through her, and in response the flames burst forth even higher. She realized her mistake and quelled the flames once more, but she felt effort in the act, as if another will was struggling with hers. She gripped the sword tightly and tried to channel her thoughts and feelings through the blade. The effect was immediate. The fires were snuffed out, and a howl of frustration and pain came from the doorway.

Rhapsody moved in front of the barricade to face the enemy who had brought forth the black fire. Through the billowing smoke all she could see was an indistinct outline. It paused for a moment and then was gone. She doubted he could have gotten any clearer view of her than she had of him, though her hood had fallen back, revealing her face and hair, shining in the light of the diminished fire. She expected that the sight of the sword had something to do with his hasty exit. She and Grunthor raced to the door, but the shadowy figure was nowhere in sight. Upstairs she heard the children wailing.

Achmed had gotten as far as the long hall before he saw the gray-cloaked man racing toward him. The approaching figure's left hand held a black longsword, with a single distinctive white stripe down its blade. He felt a tingle of power from the sword, and a wave of nausea from the figure.

The man stopped long enough to look the Dhracian over quickly. Achmed could not make out much of the man's features beneath the war helm and cloak, but he could clearly see startling blue eyes and an insolent smile.

With a single motion Achmed shouldered his cwellan and drew the long, thin blade that he carried. He seldom used it, seldom had the need, but the complete failure of the cwellan to strike its target made him decide not to risk wasting time with another missile attack. The commander of the now-dead troop smiled more broadly, nodded, and jumped through the outer window.

Dropping his sword, Achmed shrugged, bringing his cwellan back into his hands, and ran at once to the shattered pane. The man was rolling to his feet. Achmed took aim, but the sudden appearance of the white wolves in the hall turned his attention to his own defense. The great beasts ran at him, but neither had a chance to leap to the attack before Achmed downed them with the weapon of his own invention.

When he turned back to the windows, the man with the great gray mantle was gone.

35

The three companions sat around the low-burning campfire, waiting in silence for the children to nod off. They had decided to chance sleeping in the woods at night rather than risking the man in gray returning with reinforcements.

Grunthor had gathered a number of blankets, which Rhapsody wrapped around the children. The strange group then headed immediately back toward Haguefort, Stephen Navarne's keep.

They traveled well after dark, until at last they realized that the youngest of the children could no longer continue. It was only then they made camp, gathering around two small fires that Rhapsody made. Soon the children, tired and bewildered, fell off to sleep, five of them in Rhapsody's lap or clinging to her sides.

Finally, after she was sure the last child was asleep, Rhapsody looked at Achmed.

"We're not going to make it back," she said. "With the children, we don't have a chance in these woods in the snow. It's only a matter of time before he hunts us down."

"I know."

"We're going to have to find a sheltered place to hide them, and one of us will have to go back alone."

"There's an abandoned bear den not too far from 'ere, north by northwest, a league and an 'alf," commented Grunthor. "It's big enough, and dry."

A moment of puzzlement, then delight shone on her face in the firelight. "Oh, that's right! I'd forgotten about your Earth lore. I'm sorry, Grunthor." She thought back to the scene at the House of Remembrance, and the destruction the hooded man had wreaked. "That bastard had fire lore, a lot of it."

"I noticed," Achmed said.

" 'Is troops was pretty well trained, too," Grunthor added, "not just a bunch o' brigands, you know. They was professionals."

"I noticed that, too."

"I think he was the person referred to in that contract. I think he was the Rakshas," Rhapsody said reflectively. The fire crackled and simmered down to match the quieting of her mood.

"Why?"

"Well, to begin with, he referred to the house as being his. In the contract it mentioned that the Rakshas was now the Master of the house. I got the impression from the contract that whatever the Rakshas and its master were, they were somehow demonic. The fire he threw at us felt twisted, evil."

"That wasn't the only thing that felt twisted," Achmed said. "I felt the same sense of evil when I saw him through whatever lore let me see the House. Besides, that was black fire. How many times have you seen black fire, Grunthor?"

The Bolg looked at Achmed silently for a moment, and then turned away, shaking his head slowly. Rhapsody looked from one to the other.

"What? What is it?" she asked nervously.

"Just that you're right," Achmed answered. "Black fire is associated with denizens of the Underworld. When I saw that *thing* we are calling the Rakshas, I felt sick—not before. I didn't sense it from a distance, only when I looked into its face. I think that if it were a demon, I would have felt its presence earlier, but it definitely is somehow touched by demonic forces. I'm not certain how yet, though. I would have to see it again."

"Let's try to avoid that, eh?" Grunthor suggested. Achmed nodded.

"But what's to stop it from doing the same thing again?" Rhapsody patted one of the children in her lap who had begun moaning in her sleep.

"Not us. We'll leave that to Lord Stephen's army. At least we can tell them who—what—to look for now."

The emerald eyes that looked up in surprise caught the firelight and refracted it like gemstones. "Couldn't you try to track it?"

"I did. I got nothing. I couldn't follow its path. So even if we wanted to go searching for it, it's gone now. Besides, we have fifteen kids with us. Do you want to bring them along on this little hunt?"

Rhapsody fell silent. They continued to stare into the flames for a few moments longer. A rustling noise could be heard on the other side of the fire as one of the children turned over.

She thought about the children and what they had endured. She hoped that they had prevented it from occurring again, but she somehow doubted it. Still, Achmed was right; their first task was to return the children to their homes, or at least to Navarne, where Lord Stephen could be responsible for them.

Achmed passed the journal he had been reading to Rhapsody for her opinion. She caressed the hair of the child who clung to her, his head on her shoulder, as she read. Finally she looked up.

"This is the post-evacuation report, from when the Firbolg overran Canrif at the end of the Cymrian War four hundred years ago."

"Yes."

The glittering green eyes looked him up and down. "So?" she asked, her brows drawing together. Achmed said nothing, but rose and stirred the fire. "What, Achmed?" When he still didn't respond, understanding came into those eyes. "Oh, tell me no. You want to go there, don't you?"

The look that met hers was piercing. "I believe that's been the understanding all along, hasn't it?"

"I suppose," she admitted grudgingly. "But now that we

know these people have the same map and the same idea, I'm not so sure it's a good idea anymore."

"Anymore? You never thought it was a good idea. But let's think clearly; these bastards *aren't* in Canrif, they're here—"

"Who said they aren't there, too?" she interrupted.

"—and, unlike us, they aren't Bolg."

"Speak for yourself. I'm not Bolg, either."

"And as a result there are any number of places you can choose to live and be welcome. There is only one such place for us, and that's Canrif. Grunthor and I are getting mighty sick of having to hide and skulk around these human lands. The Bolg will accept you far more easily than your kind will accept us."

"Of course they will," Rhapsody said nervously. "As supper."

"Look," Achmed said impatiently, "have you got somewhere better to go? I told you I'd take you to the Lirin land, Tyrian, but you decided to come with us. Have you changed your mind? If you have, I'll point the way and you and the brats can head out now. Bring her down, Grunthor."

Rhapsody stared at him, not comprehending the last comment. The giant Bolg leapt nimbly to his feet and darted out of the firelight, returning a moment later with a squirming bundle under one arm.

It was the teenager named Jo, caught on the brink of escape and swearing in language that both impressed and shocked the Singer. It was the cant of the street, gutter-talk; she had used it herself from time to time at Jo's age. The girl must be a street child. It explained the attitude.

Grunthor plopped Jo, backside first, into a large snowbank and regarded her in amusement. "Now, then, lit'le miss, where you be off to? You late for the royal ball?"

The girl struggled to get up, but the huge hand that came to rest on her head prevented it. She slapped at Grunthor's paw and glared at him.

"I'm not going back there," she snarled.

"Where, Jo?" Rhapsody asked.

"Navarne. I heard you talkin' about it. I'm not going back there. Let me up."

Rhapsody gently disengaged herself from her clinging sleepers and made certain they were warmly covered. Then she rose and came to where Grunthor was sitting, his hand on the pale blond hair of the flailing teenager's head.

She looked the girl over. The teenager was plain of face, thin and gangly, with a full bosom and angular chin, easily a hand's breadth taller than herself. Jo's eyes were pale, watery blue, but they had depth. Rhapsody felt as if she was looking at herself many years before, in those unhappy days alone on the street. She felt her heart swell with a fondness beyond reason.

"You have no parents, do you?"

"No," said the girl defiantly. "Let me up, you big, ugly swine."

Grunthor slapped his chest and laughed aloud. "Ow, you cut me to the 'eart," he said merrily.

"Don't make fun of her. Let her up," Rhapsody said. When the girl was free she turned the daggers in her gaze toward the Singer, then her face went slack, and she said nothing. Rhapsody bent down beside her.

"Why don't you want to go back to Navarne?"

"Because I'm wanted for theft, and I don't want to lose my hand."

Rhapsody blinked in astonishment. "Lose your hand? Have you ever seen anyone lose their hand in Navarne for theft?"

The street child's mouth opened defiantly, then snapped shut rapidly. "No, but everyone knows that's the punishment."

The Singer smiled. "Ah, yes, good old Everyone, the world's wisest man. I don't believe Lord Stephen would allow a law like that in his realm."

"Yes he would. He's an arse-rag."

This time all three laughed. "I'm sure your assessment of him is very astute, given what intimate friends the two of you are," Rhapsody said. Her face grew serious, seeing the panic that was creeping into Jo's. Despite her defiance, Rhapsody knew she was terrified.

"I'll tell you what, Jo; how about if I tell Lord Stephen that you're my sister? His children and I are quite fond of each other, and I think that would be sufficient for him to spare your hand."

The girl stared at her. "You'd do that?"

"Well, only if it's true. I can't lie, I'm afraid; against my profession."

Jo scowled. "What's that supposed to mean?"

"It means I'll adopt you as my sister, if you're willing, and then it'll be true, and Lord Stephen will overlook your crime."

"Gods," muttered Achmed.

"Is this an 'abit you forgot to mention?" Grunthor asked.

"Yes, I guess it is a habit of sorts," Rhapsody said to the giant, grinning broadly. "It's a good thing I adopted the two of you. The only people in the whole world I would ever put up with this much abuse from are my brothers."

"Well, Oi always thought there was a physical resemblance, particularly between you and me, Yer Ladyship."

"What do you say, Jo?" Rhapsody was growing excited. "Want to be my sister? I've always wanted one, and never had one before. We even look alike."

Jo snorted. "You must be joking."

The Singer was taken aback. "Well, no, actually. We're both blond and light-eyed."

"Yeah, you could be twins," said Grunthor, laughing.

"Shut up," Jo said to him. Grunthor's eyes twinkled affectionately.

"Actually, lit'le miss, you *do* remind me a great deal o' the Duchess 'ere. You got a mouth on ya. Oi suggest you take 'Er Ladyship up on 'er offer: otherwise, it's back to Navarne with you."

"Hey, sis," said Jo hastily.

Rhapsody clapped her hands in delight. "Marvelous. Well, it probably couldn't hurt to tell you my name is Rhapsody. What's yours?"

The girl looked at her as if she were an idiot. "Jo," she said, her voice dripping with disgust.

"Jo what? Is Jo short for something? Do you have a last name?"

The girl wrapped her arms around herself and glared defiantly at her.

"Bugger off."

"Jo Bugger-Off. An odd name."

"It suits you," Achmed said to the girl. The defiant glare faded somewhat beneath an unwilling smile.

"That's it," said Grunthor approvingly. "She's got a sense o' 'umor. You'll fit in with us just fine, darlin'."

In the morning they found the bear den Grunthor had mentioned, a hidden hole in a thicket of brambles that opened into a surprisingly large cave. Achmed had gone in first to make sure it was unoccupied and sound. After determining that it was, Rhapsody and Jo led the children inside and began preparing for the long wait. Achmed delayed his exit until he was sure they would be safe.

"Use up the supplies. I'm sure Stephen will reprovision us when we return with whoever he sends to pick up the brats," he said.

Rhapsody looked nervously around the silent forest. The temperature had dropped in the night, freezing the snow into a sharp crust and stinging the exposed extremities of the children. Each of the three had given their gloves to one of the little ones, but most of the children were still suffering the effects of the cold.

"Please hurry," she said, knowing the exhortation was unnecessary. "I'd hate to have rescued them just to have them die of frostbite or exposure to the elements."

"I'm not too concerned about that," Achmed said with a slight smile. "I imagine you'll find a way to keep them warm—rocks are a good conductor of heat—and you have shelter here. I'm more worried about predators, one in particular. Try and keep out of sight. I'll create some diversionary tracks to draw him away from you. Grunthor will stand guard."

Rhapsody looked into the unusual face and smiled. "I know. Be careful yourself." She embraced him, then turned to go back into the cave.

"Rhapsody?"

"Yes?"

"We need to talk about this girl when I get back."

Rhapsody turned around and stood directly in front of him. "Let's talk about it now."

The Dhracian shook his head. "There isn't time. I have to get to Stephen's as quickly as possible."

"Then there's nothing to talk about," Rhapsody said. "I know what you're going to say—that I shouldn't have adopted her, that you don't trust her."

Achmed nodded. "That's about it."

"Well, then, it seems to me that I've made my choice, now you need to make yours. Jo and I are a set. If you want us to leave when you get back, we will find our own way."

Achmed breathed deeply, trying to contain his fury. "It might have been nice for you to consult us before making this decision."

Rhapsody exhaled as well. "I know," she said softly. "You're right, and I'm sorry. I couldn't help it. It just seemed the right thing to do."

"I guess that depends on what you define as 'right.' You've just compromised our chances of survival, Rhapsody, whether you know it or not."

"How can you say that, especially after what we've just seen in that house?" Rhapsody spat. "You, who can take out a field of soldiers in a heartbeat? She's a child, Achmed. And, unlike those other poor children who, if they live until you get back, have families waiting to celebrate their return, Jo has nothing, no one. You might as well have left her there, for all *her* chances of survival without us."

"And when did this become your bloody responsibility?" Rhapsody's voice dropped to a murderous whisper.

"*I made it* my bloody responsibility. Believe it or not, I actually have some choices in life, despite your proclivity for making my decisions for me. This is one of them. She stays, or we both go. I'm not abandoning her."

"Oi like 'er, if that counts for anythin'," added Grunthor. His face was somber.

The Dhracian turned in his direction, his expression changing. He thought for a long moment.

"Are you willing to have her with us, to be responsible for her?"

"Sure, why not? It worked with 'Er Ladyship 'ere."

"It's hardly the same."

"Why?" Rhapsody asked. "I see no difference. You wanted to help me; now I want to help her."

Achmed stifled a laugh. "You think we were looking to *help* you?"

Rhapsody blinked. "Yes; well, at the moment we met, anyway. And you did, even if I didn't appreciate being dragged off-Island at the time."

Achmed's face twisted in amusement. "And it never occurred to you that we might have taken you along as insurance—"

"Or a food source?" added Grunthor playfully.

"Of course it did, but time has proven otherwise. Come on, you two, she needs us. She won't be any problem—well, no more a problem than I was."

"Uh-oh, now that you put it like that—"

"She's damaged goods," said Achmed impatiently.

The jovial look in Rhapsody's eyes vanished and was replaced with something darker. She cast a glance in the direction of the cave to be sure Jo could not hear them.

"Pardon me," she said acidly, "but in case you hadn't noticed, we're *all* damaged goods in some way."

" 'Ey, speak for yourself," said Grunthor.

"I am. This girl needs me, needs us. And I need her. I'll be responsible for her. If you don't want us with you any longer, that's fine. But I'm not leaving her."

Achmed exhaled angrily. "All right, she can come. But she needs to understand that she is responsible to all of us, not just you. We can't have a member of this team we can't trust. You can tell her where we're going, but nothing about our past. Are we agreed?"

Rhapsody threw her arms around him, knocking him off balance. "Yes. Thank you." She released him quickly and straightened his askew cloak. "Now hurry. Be careful, and tell Lord Stephen to send medical supplies, too."

For more than a week the strange group stayed within the cave, waiting for Achmed to return. Rhapsody kept the children warm with her fire lore, heating the rocks as Achmed had suggested, until the cave was as cozy as a house with a roaring hearth.

Food was plentiful; Grunthor had been provisioned for several weeks' journey, and one day's food rations for him fed all of the children with some to spare. With no need to have a fire for warmth they avoided having one, keeping the air of the cave fresh and leaving no trail of smoke by which to be spotted.

The absence of light initially frightened the children, so Rhapsody drew Daystar Clarion and stuck it, tip first, into the soft ground in a corner of the cave. Its flames gave off no smoke, and licked quietly up the blade, illuminating the cave and filling it with a warm glow, made sweeter by the quiet songs she sang to keep the children amused. With the herbs from her pack she treated their wounds and kept them tranquil, trying to avoid making any noise that would draw attention to their hidden den.

She softly maintained her morning and evening devotions, however. As she sang, the faces of her newly adopted grandchildren, Gwydion and Melisande, rose up in her heart, smiling as they had when last they were together. The warm memory stood in stark contrast to the bleak, anxious countenances that stared back at her now. It made her frightened for all the children of Navarne.

Once, while she was staring at the small faces, the knots of worry barely eased in their sleep, memories of the old days flooded her mind. She thought back to Analise, the child she had saved from Michael, whom he had derisively called Petunia.

The day after Michael and his men had left on their assignment she had taken the child, under the protection of Nana's guards, to the Wide Meadows, the great open plain that surrounded Easton on three sides. Together they had searched out the leader of the Liringlas who made their home there.

The Lirin house had taken the child in warmly, and Rhapsody had long comforted herself with the image of Analise, sitting before the leader on her horse, waving goodbye and smiling for the first and only time she had seen. She had smiled and waved in return, knowing that Analise would be well cared for.

It was not until much later that the pain had come, loss

that was not eased with the knowledge that she had absolutely done what was right for the orphaned child. She missed her still, and wondered whether she had ever found happiness after the terror she had experienced at Michael's hands. Rhapsody had vowed to herself, from that time forward, that no child would ever be abused if she could prevent it, no matter the cost to herself. She caressed the tiny heads in the darkness, choking back the memory.

For several days a wild storm raged outside, howling around them like a pack of wolves at their concealed door. Rhapsody took comfort in the fact that the pounding wind and snow had undoubtedly covered their tracks by now, but it was hard to stop feeling uneasy.

The children screamed in terror at the first crash of a tree above them, and scurried to Rhapsody, trying to burrow beneath her arms and legs for cover. Some were frightened enough to seek solace in Grunthor, and found him to be a highly satisfactory refuge. He comforted them with repulsive jokes and had them laughing even as the thunder rumbled around them, shaking showers of dirt and rocks from the cave walls and roof. Eventually the storm abated, but the children remained, sleeping or playing near their new gigantic friend.

Grunthor kept watch by day until the supper hour, sleeping until midnight, when he took up the guard post again. Rhapsody and Jo stood guard together while he slept, but no one came to disturb their hiding place, not even woodland animals. The tainted evil of the forest had driven the wildlife away long ago.

It was during this time that she and Jo got better acquainted, and found themselves developing a fond liking for each other, though the teenager still refused each request to share more details of her name. They had similar senses of humor, and each often struggled to keep from laughing aloud at the other's observations, particularly about Grunthor.

It was hard not to think back on her own childhood when watching Jo, which always left her feeling morose. Jo's life on the street had been a result of unfortunate circumstance; Rhapsody's painful history was of her own making. Jo had no family; Rhapsody had thrown hers away, left behind people who had loved her, had protected and cherished her, and who had died, never knowing what became of her. The dreams that followed such waking thoughts were so torturous that they must, at least on some level, be penance for her crimes.

Rhapsody found herself wishing that she were taking the girl back to Navarne, to a safe place, instead of into the belly of the Bolglands. Eventually she shared this sentiment with Jo, who reminded her with a nod to the sleeping children that danger was everywhere these days; it was better not to be deluded into feeling safe.

Finally, after almost a week, Achmed returned with reinforcements. The caravan was audible from a great way off, with Grunthor having been alerted early on to its presence on the land through his Earth lore.

Rhapsody stumbled out into the painful brightness and shielded her eyes, searching the frost-covered branches of trees and forest brush for their rescuers.

In the distance she could hear the sound of horses and wagons, making slow progress through the thick woods along the path they had traveled on their fateful visit to the House of Remembrance.

Almost an hour after she had heard them, soldiers came into sight, more than two score of them, led by Achmed and Lord Stephen himself on horseback. When Achmed came within range she rose and waved, bringing a smile to the face of the duke. Stephen dismounted and ran to the cave, sweeping her into a frenzied embrace.

"Sweet All-God the Creator, Rhapsody, are you all right? I've been worried sick about you ever since Achmed arrived." He pulled away and looked at her intently, then cleared his throat as color flooded his face along with obvious relief.

Rhapsody patted his shoulder reassuringly. "We're all fine, Lord Stephen, thank you. The children are inside the cave with Grunthor."

"Well, haul them out of there, and let's see who we've got," he said, bending and peering into the entrance of the den.

At the sight of Stephen's face, Grunthor marshaled the small troops. "All right, ya bloomin' skels, 'op to it and line up," he ordered. At the command the children leapt to attention and formed a wiggling line, chattering with excitement, the first jollity they had been allowed in a very long while.

One by one Grunthor handed the children up to Rhapsody, who passed them to Lord Stephen. The duke spoke reassuringly to each child, recognizing some, questioning others, until fourteen of the children had emerged and had been handed over to the care of the soldiers near the wagon. Finally, Jo appeared, walking ahead of a strong push by Grunthor. Rhapsody took the girl's thin, pale hand; it was trembling.

"Lord Stephen, may I present my sister, Jo?" She gave the girl an encouraging smile, then looked back at the Duke of Navarne.

Stephen stared at Jo for a moment, then turned to Rhapsody, whose smile grew noticeably brighter. "How do you do, Jo?" he said a moment later. "It's an honor to meet a member of Rhapsody's family. I'm sorry we didn't meet earlier."

"I'm not," muttered Jo under her breath.

"Was that all the children, then?" Lord Stephen asked.

Rhapsody's smile faded. "I'm afraid so," she said sadly. "I wish there had been more. We searched the House of Remembrance thoroughly, but we didn't find anyone else." *Not alive, at least,* she thought grimly.

Lord Stephen took her gently by the shoulders. "I'm grateful to all of you for finding these," he said. "There are many grieving parents and relatives who will be celebrating at week's end when we return."

"I only wish there could be more," she said, thinking back to the small lifeless bodies strung hideously from the slaughter altars. "I hope you sent troops with strong stomachs and no children of their own." She turned and watched Grunthor handing the children up to the soldiers in the wagon, then looked back into the young duke's smiling face. She regarded him seriously.

"Please go home with these children," she said gravely. "You've already suffered enough. It's better that you leave the cleanup of the House to others, m'lord."

Lord Stephen looked at the ground. "It's Stephen," he said. "And I will abide by your counsel."

"We're ready, m'lord," called the captain of the regiment.

Rhapsody and the duke looked at each other a moment longer, then Stephen reluctantly released her shoulders.

Once free, she trotted to the wagon and bade the children goodbye, blowing them kisses. The small faces looked back, some blankly, some smiling; the trauma would take a long time to heal. The driver of the wagon clicked to the horses and the cart lurched forward, flanked by mounted soldiers, and slowly made its way back down the forest road.

Lord Stephen stepped over several fallen logs and went up to the two Bolg. He extended his hand to each of them.

"Thank you," he said. "You have the gratitude of Navarne, and my family, always. I've provisioned four horses for you, and have included a letter of introduction under my signet if there is anyone to whom you think it might be useful. Know that you are welcome in my home at all times."

"Thanks, guv," said Grunthor, wringing the young man's hand.

"Where are you headed next?" the duke asked Achmed, absently rubbing his shoulder.

The mismatched eyes studied the royal face. "Canrif," Achmed said finally, "but I'd prefer you to be the only person who knows it for the time being."

"Done. I'd suggest you head north to the Orlandan Plateau and follow the main road through Bethany to Bethe Corbair; that's the last province of Roland before the Bolglands." Achmed nodded in agreement. That was the route sketched out in the notebook.

"Once you get to the province of Bethe Corbair, at the place where the rolling hills flatten into the Krevensfield Plain, travel southeast and approach the city from the south; it's safer. And if you get into trouble in Bethe Corbair, ask to see the duke, Quentin Baldasarre, or, failing that, sue for religious asylum and see the benison, Lanacan Orlando. He is a very kind man. Show him my letter, and I'm sure he will aid you in any way he can."

Rhapsody had joined the group with Jo. "Thank you," she said. "And may I suggest you have your soldiers who are going on to the House take whatever scrolls or items you wish to save. The perpetrator of these crimes considers that house his own, and may be back." Lord Stephen nodded.

"I've already briefed him extensively, Rhapsody," said Achmed, "and we're going to lose the light if we don't leave now."

"Goodbye, m'lord," Rhapsody said to Stephen. "Please give my love to my grandchildren." He took her hand and kissed it, then tried to do the same to Jo, who snatched her hand away and glared at him hostilely. Grunthor and Achmed walked the duke back to his steed and bade him goodbye as he mounted and rode off after one more backward look.

"Well, these 'orses ain't too bad," said Grunthor to Rhapsody, who was still watching long after Stephen had ridden out of sight. " 'Oo gets the big one?"

Rhapsody turned and looked in the direction of the giant. Three of the four horses were of muscular riding stock, while the last, roughly half again the size of the others, was a full-breed war horse.

"I think you should ride the mare, Grunthor," said Rhapsody, pointing to the most delicate of the four.

Grunthor was about to throw back a humorous answer when a choked voice spoke up.

"I can't ride." Jo sounded as if she were strangling.

Rhapsody took her hand. "Just because you never have doesn't mean you can't. You can ride with me."

Achmed nodded. "We can put the heaviest supplies on the fourth horse, and travel faster that way."

After a little repacking by Achmed and Grunthor, and much wheedling, reassuring, and coaxing of Jo by Rhapsody, the four finally saddled up and rode off to the northeast, across the provinces of Navarne and Bethany, south through the Krevensfield plain toward the capital city of Bethe Corbair, the gateway to the dark realm of the Firbolg.

36

What do you mean, I can't go into the city? I've ridden this bloody horse for a week, and now I can't go into the city? You're a fornicating pig, Achmed. I hope you get the pox. It couldn't make your face any uglier than it is."

Achmed cast a glance at Rhapsody, who had turned away quickly, trying to contain her laughter. Then he dismounted with an annoyed sigh.

"Remind me again why I allow you to share our food with her," he asked, tossing the reins over the horse's back, ignoring Jo utterly.

"Because you like her," Rhapsody answered, her green eyes twinkling affectionately.

"Hmmm. Well, perhaps you had best go over the plan with her again. Explain to her that we can't risk her walking the streets of Bethany lest she be snapped up by the local charm school as an etiquette instructor."

Rhapsody pulled her saddlebag down and carried it to the copse of trees where Grunthor had laid camp. Jo trailed behind her, arguing the entire way. Finally she turned back to the whining teenager.

"All right, look. Achmed and I are making a quick foray into Bethany. Bethany is the capital seat of Roland, and there are three times the number of soldiers and guards as there are in Navarne." She chuckled silently as the color drained from Jo's face.

"We need to be in and out as rapidly as possible. But our next stop is the province of Bethe Corbair's capital city. We're going to do some provision shopping there, and some scouting. You'll get a chance to go into the city then, if you behave yourself."

"All right," Jo said sullenly.

"Look, I'm sorry this isn't as exciting as your life on the streets, but it's safer, believe me," Rhapsody said, untangling a snarl in Jo's stringy blond hair.

"Not necessarily," said Grunthor. He was stretched out under a leaf-bare tree, hands behind his head. "If you want the lit'le miss to still be 'ere when you get back, make sure to leave the food behind when you go."

"You always say that, but when was the last time you actually ate someone?" asked Jo, still not mollified.

"Dead or alive?"

Rhapsody shuddered. "All right, we're going now. Goodbye, Jo." She held out her arms, but Jo just nodded. The

Singer turned instead to the Firbolg giant, who leapt to his feet and swept her up in a warm embrace.

"You be careful," he warned as he put her back down.

"We expect to be back by morning," Achmed said to Grunthor under his breath. Frost hung in the air between them, like frozen words hovering for effect. "Give us a day or two slip factor. After that, you and Jo are on your own." He signaled to Rhapsody and shouldered his pack. A hint of a smile crossed his face.

"And for that possibility I apologize most sincerely."

$\mathcal{B}$ethany was a round city, two or three times the size of Easton by Rhapsody's estimate, with a wide ring of settlements and villages outside its ramparts. From a distance it appeared to be almost dome-shaped, with the tallest buildings in the center, tapering down to those of lesser heights at the perimeter walls. The battlements within the circular walls looked out in all directions, the sweeping panoramic defense of a spherical city, in the middle of the province, at approximately the midpoint of the nation of Roland.

Their initial reconnaissance of Bethany had included a ride around the entire perimeter, keeping a respectable distance, back before they parted company with Jo and Grunthor. Achmed had determined early on that the number of soldiers and defenses, visible and otherwise, made anything but entering on foot in the guise of humble peasants impossible.

So now Rhapsody and Achmed stood, robed and hooded in the simple garments they had been given at Llauron's, outside Bethany's southeastern gate, one of only eight entrances they had seen during their scouting.

While Navarne had been a province primarily of scattered farms and villages broken by the large land holdings of its nobles and a small, charming capital city, Bethany appeared to have been designed from the very beginning to be a cultural center, the epitome of an Age now long gone.

Even at the city's outskirts the streets were paved, with small shops, inns, and taverns interspersed with rows of buildings that each seemed to house several families. Within the city proper every street was lined with more lanternposts than

Rhapsody had ever seen, glass domes covering the wicks atop gleaming brass poles. Watering troughs for horses as well as hitching racks appeared at the same place in each street.

By law all cattle and other animals of trade could only enter the city by certain gates, demarking Bethany into different districts. Markets and mercantile areas were limited to the eastern and western sections, while museums and the public gardens were located to the north and south. The basilica of fire and the castle of Tristan Steward, the Lord Regent and Prince of Bethany, the two most elevated of Bethany's structures, stood near each other in the heart of the city. Only the barracks of Bethany's soldiers could be found in all directions.

It seemed appropriate that the basilica dedicated to the element of fire had been built in the direct center of the city, an echo of the fire at the heart of the Earth. From far away Rhapsody had been able to feel the well spring, a pulsing flame that called to the fire within her. Even though the fire source was just a shadow of the real conflagration through which the three of them had walked, there was an authenticity to it that told her its genesis was the same inferno; it was genuine, a pure elemental fountainhead.

"Keep your hood up and your head down," Achmed advised softly as yet another troop of guards passed, prodding the occasional citizen to move along. "Just keep walking toward the fire. I'll be right behind you. You don't need to look back."

Rhapsody nodded and concentrated on the song of the flame in the distance, pushing her feelings of unease into the corners of her mind. For all its beauty, Bethany seemed a town without mercy or a sense of humor. The neatly manicured gardens appeared almost too perfect, the buildings too elegant, too architecturally commanding. There was a decided absence of poor people or beggars. And the soldiers were everywhere. *But*, she reminded herself, *it is the capital, after all*. Some higher level of security was to be expected.

After almost two hours they finally located the basilica. Long before it had come into view they had seen evidence of its proximity in the street below their feet.

Rhapsody had noticed that the cobblestones in one roadway

had been gilded in gold leaf and positioned in the pattern of a flame, stretching outward toward the east. The closer they came to the temple, the more raylike patterns appeared in the streets. She stopped and waited for Achmed to follow her lead.

"Remember those etchings in Lord Stephen's museum?" she whispered. A hand came to rest gently on her upper arm, moving her forward; a town guard had made note of her coming to a halt, and Achmed wanted her to keep walking. When the guard's attention was drawn elsewhere, he released his hold on her.

"Yes."

"The exterior of the basilica was a courtyard inlaid with flame-colored mosaics. They would look something like this up close. We must be in the outer courtyard."

A moment's walking proved her correct. As they came around the corner the enormous basilica came into view. It was a circular structure, grand and imposing, rising to a great height above the other buildings and built of polished white marble with gold flecks running through it in veins.

The inner courtyard was a great mosaic, neatly bordered by topiary hedges in the shape of tongues of flame. The floor of the courtyard was inlaid with stones the color of fire in patterns that suggested the sun's rays. The rays were trimmed with lapis and other precious gems, which evoked an incandescent glimmer when the sunlight hit them. Vast gardens stretched out to the foot of the elevated palace to the north, brown and dry in the death grip of winter.

The structure of the basilica itself was composed of several huge concentric circles, each a layer of elevated hewn-marble seating, all facing toward the center, where a wide golden brazier could be seen. A few faithful sat or knelt in the various levels of seating, praying or meditating silently while two robed ordinates walked about, tending to the basilica.

Leaping from the brazier was a flame of intense light, crimson and orange with twisting ribbons of blue, burning intensely, silently. The same power, the same pure light and heat, it evoked deep memories of the wall of flame they had passed through so long ago, back on the other side of Time. It was all Rhapsody could do to keep back tears at the recollection of the fire's embrace, the all-consuming acceptance she had felt at the Earth's heart as it surrounded her.

She could have stayed for a long time, staring rapturously at the brazier, but her reverie was interrupted by the thin, strong fingers encircling her upper arm again.

"Come on," Achmed whispered, shattering her trance of memory. "He looks like a good candidate."

He nodded slightly toward a nearby ordinate, a man of late middle years with a shiny bald head. The man was wearing a brown robe with a stylized image of the sun emblazoned on the chest, its center a curling red spiral. It was similar to the amulet they had seen in the portrait of the Blesser of Canderre-Yarim, Bethany's benison, in the Cymrian museum.

Rhapsody flexed the muscle in her upper arm to signal her understanding. It had been decided beforehand that she would seek to learn as much of the basilica's lore, and the stories that those who tended it imparted to the faithful, as she could while Achmed sought out the less public aspects.

When the grip released she made her way to the clergyman and stopped at a respectful distance. The ordinate was crouched over, polishing a brass railing that separated the first layer of seating from the one after it. Without looking up he waved a dismissive hand at her.

"Peasantry in the last Ring only."

When he went back to his task, puffing slightly, Rhapsody looked back to Achmed, already a fair distance away. He touched his hood, signaling for her to remove her own. She did, then turned back to the ordinate.

"Ordinate?"

The bald man sat back on his haunches and glared up at her. Then, an instant later, his face slackened and his mouth fell open, a look approximating horror filling his now-round eyes.

"Sweet Creator. Now?" he whispered, dropping the polishing cloth.

Simon had been cleaning the basilica all morning, preparing for the benison's service on the high day of the week. Despite the winter chill, the work was exhausting, and he had been sweating for the better part of an hour.

Humility, he kept reminding himself, one of the seven vows of the ordinariate. Again, for the fourth time that morning, he began to recite his prayer. But despite his rote repetition of the rite of humility, jealousy bordering on anger still permeated his pores, oozing out with the sweat, leaving him nauseous with it. He had, in fact, been feeling sick and weak all day.

Once again Dartralen had been given hospice duty by the Abbot when the wounded soldiers arrived. And once again, despite his seniority, and his age, and his skill at healing, Simon had been relegated to the rites of preparation—also known as housecleaning—while Dartralen smugly tended to the injured, that clumsy butcher.

He was struggling to put the malicious thought out of his mind when the peasant woman approached him. Simon pointed the way to her proper place, the outer Ring, but she had apparently not heard him.

"Ordinate?" The voice was soft and warm, like the breath of the fire itself.

When he looked up his heart lurched into his throat.

Standing before him, clothed in the brown sackcloth of a peasant, was Beauty itself, a woman with eyes as deep and green as the emerald depths of the sea, and hair the color of the sun, glistening in the winter wind. A warmth radiated from her; he had been around the Holy Brazier long enough to recognize its source. This must be the Fire Spirit, the harbinger of death in the Ancient Lores, now come for him. The exertion of cleaning must have been greater than he thought.

And when this angelic escort had come for him, he was thinking jealous thoughts, arrogant thoughts. His heart sank into the Earth. He was damned.

"Sweet Creator. Now?" he asked, his voice tremulous.

The beautiful apparition blinked. "Are you unwell?"

Simon struggled to rise. "Ah, forgive me. I—I mistook you for someone else." He closed his eyes, praying that mistaking her for a peasant would not make his punishment in the Afterlife even more painful.

The vision bowed respectfully. "I was wondering if I might impose upon you to instruct me in the lore of this basilica? I am from far away."

Simon's trembling grew more violent. *Ah, that's it*, he thought, his eyes casting about wildly to see if anyone else was witnessing his imminent demise. *I'm being tested.* Only a few of the faithful were scattered in the Rings, lost in prayer or meditation. Another hooded peasant was wandering the basilica, making note of the frescoes and mosaics on the walls and floor.

Well, he thought grimly, *my place in the Afterlife depends on this moment. I am being judged on my priestly comportment, and how well I am versed in religious ritual and rite. I may as well expend every effort of which I'm capable.*

"It would be my pleasure," he said, making the attempt to smile benevolently, choking back his fluttering heart as it tried to escape through his throat. "This way."

"Thank you," Rhapsody said, folding her hands inside the sleeves of her robes as the ordinate did. This was much easier than she had expected, especially after his initial reaction.

The look of utter terror on the ordinate's face when he first looked up had made her stomach clench in cold nausea. It was a reaction she had seen a few times before, in Stephen's servants, in the guards at the House of Remembrance, among Llauron's followers. It was Anborn, the great Cymrian general, who had summed it up most succinctly.

Ah, now I know who you are; you're Rhapsody, aren't you?
How did you know that?
There could only be one such freak of nature.

Even Khaddyr, who as a healer had seen people in all degrees of illness and decay, had stared at her.

I thought perhaps she would interest you, as I am at a loss to define what she is. I've never seen a Lirin like that.

Whether it was her Liringlas appearance, or something that had happened to her in her walk through the fire that had made her appear freakish, she seemed to evoke responses that she did not recognize.

Occasionally she saw something that almost resembled awe, an emotion she had seen in another form back in the brothel. Either way, she would need to learn to live with it, probably much the way Achmed did—by remaining hidden.

Rhapsody pulled her hood back up and followed the sweating ordinate.

He began by leading her directly to the brazier.

"This is the holy flame-well of Vrackna, Lord All-God, Fire of the Universe," he said carefully.

Against her will Rhapsody went pale, then swallowed, an action that caused the nervous ordinate even more consternation. She had forgotten the misuse the Cymrians had made of the ancient evil fire god's name. The ordinate struggled to regain his composure.

"The—the basilica—is, of course, consecrated to the Creator. It is unique in that it is dedicated to one of His five children, the element of fire. The flame within this Brazier comes directly from the heart of the Earth, the fire at the core of the world."

Rhapsody smiled but did not look at the fire for fear she would begin to weep or stare, entranced by the leaping colors. Instead she nodded to Achmed, who hovered nearby.

"This is my associate," she said, gesturing to the Dhracian to join them. "I believe he is interested in what you have to say as well."

A beneficent smile now frozen firmly in place, the ordinate turned to greet Achmed, who dropped the veil from in front of his face and grinned. Rhapsody had just enough time to grab the cleric's arm as his eyes rolled back and he lurched forward.

𝒟eath's angel had apparently not come alone.

"This is my associate," the apparition said softly. "I believe he is interested in what you have to say as well."

Simon had steeled himself, expecting another vision of supernatural countenance, perhaps a lesser spirit of the fire. Instead the face that stared back at him, silhouetted against the Brazier's leaping flames, was a face born of nightmares. The eyes, piercing with the look of the Soul-stealer, stared into his own. The mouth, a twisted line in the pocked skin's surface, contorted into a leer in greeting.

As the world grew dark around him, Simon knew that this was his fate if he failed, the demonic other side of the angelic coin. Instead of ascending to the Afterlife in the arms of the Fire Spirit, he would be choked in the clutches of this denizen of the Underworld who laughed at him now. Good and evil, battling for his soul where he stood.

With his last clear thought, he wished desperately that he had paid more attention to the lessons of the Ancient Lore, now no longer part of the dogma. Simon began to tremble violently, then pitched forward as the blood rushed from his head.

A strong, warm hand gripped his forearm, and he was uplifted again. As Simon raised his head he inhaled the fragrant scent of the Fire Spirit's hair, and found himself staring into the hypnotic eyes, green and verdant with life.

"Ordinate?" The smile she gave him had a ring of encouragement to it, and he took heart. Perhaps she was not dissatisfied with his answers after all.

She leaned closer, the sweet scent of her skin making his head feel light again. "You needn't fear him," she whispered. *A blessing*, Simon thought gratefully. *My faith, and the All-God's harbinger, will protect me.*

He struggled to a stand. "I'm fine. I'm sorry. Now, where was I? Yes, of course. The faithful of the See of Bethany attend services here, using this gift of the Creator to center their thoughts, to purify them, to make their prayers worthy of offering up to the Patriarch."

The Fire Spirit nodded. "And these?" She extended a graceful arm and pointed to the frescoes and mosaics that decorated the basilica's walls.

Simon summoned the strength to stand alone. He pointed to the fresco of a young man in red robes and a horned miter painted on the northern wall of the innermost Ring.

"That is a portrait of His Grace, Ian Steward, the Blesser of Canderre-Yarim. He is the benison of the See for which this is the basilica."

"Tristan's brother?" asked the demon. His voice was as dry as black fire, with a haughty undertone to it.

Simon shuddered. He did not want to be responsible for aiding in the damnation of his sovereign in any way, though it was of little surprise to him that the demon was intimately acquainted with the prince.

Simon cast a glance around for Brentel, the other ordinate assigned to preparation duty, but he had disappeared, probably into the reliquary or the vestry. He looked back to the Fire Spirit, who was, by her expression, also anticipating his reply.

"Ye—yes," he stammered. The angel nodded, as if pleased; it gave him a sudden jolt of courage. He turned to the other mosaics.

These are artistic representations of the birth of Fire," the ordinate said, nervously wiping the sweat from his shining pate.

Rhapsody followed his outstretched arm. A series of mosaic images graced the other three walls of the basilica's Innermost Ring. In the first, on the eastern wall, an image of the sun appeared in the distance behind a shooting star, blazing across the black tiles that represented the void of the universe. The globe burned brightly, flames dancing across its surface.

"The Earth was formed when a piece of the star that is our sun broke off and streaked across the void, coming to rest in orbit about its mother," the ordinate intoned. His eyes sought hers anxiously, and though she had no idea why he was seeking her validation, she smiled and nodded. He relaxed visibly and turned to the south.

"Fire burned, unchecked, on the Earth's surface. In the absence of ethereal fuel, however, Fire could not sustain itself and sank into the Earth, forming its core, where it burns to this day in the purest of its forms." The mosaic captured, in tens of thousands of tiny tiles, the image of the Earth, now dark at the surface, a red spiral leading down to the center, where it glowed intensely.

Achmed and Rhapsody followed the ordinate to the last of the picture-walls, the stylized image of the sun with the coiled red center from the amulet, the image he himself wore on his chest.

"This is the symbol of the F'dor, the primordial race that existed long before the birth of mankind. They were the children of fire, the ancient culture that it originated, that sprang from it.

"It was the F'dor that tamed fire, at least a little, and gave it to mankind for its use in protection, in the warming of homes in winter, in the forging of weapons. The F'dor, now long deceased, were the forefathers of steel, of hearths, of every way in which we now make use of this holy and powerful element, one of the original gifts of the All-God."

The ordinate's words ground to a halt as he caught the expression on Achmed's face. He quickly looked back at Rhapsody, who smiled again.

She extended a hand to the cleric, who took it, still shaking. "Thank you. I think we should be going now."

The ordinate collapsed in a faint. Rhapsody barely had time to stop him from slamming his head into the paved mosaic of the basilica floor.

"What on Earth is the matter with this man?" she asked as they propped him against the inner wall of the basilica beneath the F'dor symbol.

"Nothing," Achmed answered, casting a glance above him at the mosaic. *It's something* within *the Earth*, he thought.

Rhapsody was uncorking her flask of brandy. She held it to the unconscious man's lips and poured a little down his throat. The ordinate sputtered, spilling a little of the flask's contents down the front of his robe, but did not regain consciousness. She gave him a little more, then recapped the flask.

"There; I hope that helps," she said.

"Well, it might temporarily," Achmed said with a smirk. "Clerics who tend shrines of fire are generally forsworn from alcohol, for obvious reasons. I imagine he will have a hard time explaining the reek of brandy on his clothes when he wakes up."

He saw concern cloud her eyes, darkening them. "Let's go," he said impatiently, forestalling Rhapsody from any further attempt to wake him. "Don't worry about him, he'll come up with something. These people are almost as good at self-delusion as you are." He pulled her to a stand.

"What's that supposed to mean?" she demanded.

"Come with me now, and I'll tell you once we're outside the city walls," he said. He gave her hand another tug, and together they bolted from the basilica, walking quickly away and blending into the crowded streets.

Simon fought to waken, and lost. In his few fragmented moments of awareness he could recall the scent of the Fire Spirit's sweet skin, and the warmth of her hands as she tilted his head back.

He had seen the moment of his own death. The Fire Spirit had taken his hand. *Thank you*, she had said. *I think we should be going now*. At least she had chosen him; he had won salvation, not the damnation of the demon with the nightmare face. The world had gone dark.

Then his head was in her hands, and the burning liquid ripped down his throat, searing him with molten fire. He had gasped, had tried to fight it, only to find that her ministrations had filled him with a sense of well-being, a warmth that lulled him to sleep, easing his fear and his distress.

At least it had until the Abbot found him.

37

"Hurry up," Achmed muttered. He was standing beneath the eaves of a harper's shop at the edge of town, waiting for Rhapsody to return.

The sound of delight she had made when she first sighted the shop could have come from a two-year-old, it was so full of childlike joy. The sound had a music that stopped him in his tracks, had made her pleading impossible to resist. It was a dangerous sound, one that he would be wary of from now on.

I want to send some gifts to my grandchildren, and I deserve a new harp, she had said, *I keep leaving all my stringed instruments behind.*

It had taken an inordinately long period of time for her to choose another, however. The noise of the street, and the vibrations that the foot and cart traffic were generating, made his head throb. He was preparing to go into the shop himself to drag her out when she appeared at the door, disheveled and flustered, a decided look of anger in her eye.

"Bastard," she muttered, handing him the three-stringed instrument she was lugging.

"Excuse me?"

"Not you, him," she spat, gesturing at the shop door, then smoothing her hair back under the hood again.

"What happened?"

"Apparently harps aren't the only things his fingers want to pluck," she said angrily as they walked away from shop, joining the flow of human traffic again.

Achmed snickered as he passed the instrument back to her. "How did you react?"

"I tried to think about what Grunthor would do, and did my best imitation of it," she said, slinging the package back under her robe. "Only I used the blunt end of my dagger; Grunthor wouldn't have. So the arse-rag's singing a soprano accompaniment to the organ, rather than missing one."

"Must be descended from the Cymrians," Achmed said wryly.

Rhapsody's mood lifted a little with the joke. "Well, I certainly knew a lot of them in the old land who qualified as arse-rags. I can't believe you said that to Llauron, though."

"What did you buy?" Achmed asked.

"It's a physician's lyre; it's supposed to help in songs of healing. Khaddyr had one, but he didn't know how to play it very well. It only has three strings, and I've never actually used one before, so it may take a while to pick up. The instruments of this land are very different from home."

He took her shoulder to navigate her away from a passel of soldiers standing on a street corner near the southeastern gate, laughing amongst themselves.

"Rhapsody, I hate to keep breaking it to you, but *this* is home now."

He watched as she continued to walk, staring at the ground as though lost in thought. When they had exited the gate, she looked up at him.

"Perhaps for you," she said. She looked back at the ground and kept walking.

* * *

Deep in the village at the outskirts of the city Rhapsody turned suddenly and grabbed Achmed's arm.

"Are we being followed?"

The Dhracian nodded and continued to walk, dodging a stream of scurrying children and circumventing the acrid smoke of a barrel fire outside a shack where haunches of meat were being dried. He almost had to shout to be heard above the din of the crowd milling around them, the people who would never be allowed to walk the pristine streets of the city proper in Bethany.

"It's Grunthor. He's been shadowing us for a while."

"Why? And where's Jo?" Rhapsody craned her neck to see if she could catch sight of the large shadow again, but it was gone.

"Because I asked him to. Probably with him; we're not far from camp."

A piercing shriek rose over the cacophony; it carried with it the pain of a child in distress. Rhapsody turned to see a small boy on the ground, cowering, with his hands over his head. He was curled into a ball, trying to shield himself from the savage kick being aimed at him by a man with a grizzled black beard.

Rhapsody bolted forward, only to be hauled back by a tug on her arm born of Achmed's superior speed.

"Don't intervene," he warned, watching the black fury on her face fade to gray shock at his words. "This is the way these people live, the way most people live. Look around you."

Indeed, the passersby were milling past the child and his attacker, avoiding the scene or even oblivious of it. Rhapsody struggled to break away again. Achmed tightened his grip.

"Think about the beating that child will get later on if you get involved in this, Rhapsody. And you can't adopt another one; if you try, I'll abandon you and Jo here, in Bethany." The child cried out again as another kick connected.

"Let go," she snarled. The black fury had returned.

Reluctantly Achmed released her arm and faded back angrily. She charged across the street, head down, crouched in the position Grunthor had taught her called the Battering Ram. The situation was unspooling wildly; there was nothing he could do now but watch.

She connected just below the chest of the furious man as his leg was on the upswing. Caught off guard by the momentum of her attack, he reeled backward, both of them toppling into a row of barrels and small logs.

As the man's head struck the ground Rhapsody drove the heel of her palm upward, breaking his nose. Blood sprayed the dirt of the roadway, leaving small dark stains on the cobblestones, now wide-spread and farther between as the street led away from the city.

The initial shock past, the man's eyes cleared, and he made a grab for her throat.

"Bitch," he panted, swinging his arm wildly at her. "What—"

Achmed sighed as he saw Rhapsody, now astride the peasant, pull back for her famous right cross, the blow Grunthor had commented on admiringly. She connected impressively, a direct impact to the man's bloody nose, snapping his head back with a resounding crack.

As the man lay sprawled on the street Rhapsody rose and wiped the spatters of his blood off her forehead. The passersby who had not stopped to notice the child being kicked were beginning to slow now, staring at the scene.

"Why were you kicking that child?" she demanded, panting.

The man blinked and squinted into the fading sun above him, then grimaced.

"He's—my son," he muttered, his words choked.

"Really?" Rhapsody asked sarcastically. "That's why? Glad you told me." She gave his testicles a savage stomp, causing him to curl into the same position his child had been in the moment before. A man watching nearby recoiled in horror.

"There; hopefully you won't have any more, then. You're obviously not fit to." She turned to the little boy, who was still curled up on the ground, and bent down to him.

Achmed's attention was drawn up the roadway to where another commotion was occurring. A team of soldiers on horseback had stopped in the midst of the traffic. One was bent forward, listening to a man who was gesticulating wildly, pointing in Rhapsody's direction. He looked back at her.

She was soothing the ragged child now, touching his face comfortingly, asking him if he was all right. The little boy was nodding, staring up into her hood, slack-jawed. Rhapsody turned back to his father.

"What's your name?" she demanded.

The man leaned up on one elbow, trying to stanch his bleeding nose.

"Styles Nielsen." The words were a whisper.

Rhapsody bent close to him. "Hear me, Styles Nielsen," she said, her voice low and musical. Even across the roadway Achmed recognized the tone; she was using her Naming lore.

"It is your life's mission from this moment on to protect this child, to raise him lovingly, to tend to his needs. When your actions are in keeping with that mission, you will feel pleasure. If you violate this edict in any way, if you hurt him, you will feel his pain tenfold. If you abuse him with words, it will feel like your skin is on fire; do you understand me?" The man nodded, staring into her hood the way his son had a moment before.

Achmed saw the guards move in a second too late, his attention diverted by the soldiers up the roadway. The first grabbed her by the arm and hauled her into the street, while the other pulled her hood down with a vicious tug. Achmed ran across the road.

Pandemonium broke loose. From up the street the soldiers were riding in, toppling the citizenry right and left before their horses. The crowd that had been hovering, watching the assault in horror, swelled forward, grabbing at Rhapsody, trying to touch her, hold on to her. Achmed pushed forward with them. He was almost within reach.

Her shining hair, once bound by its standard black ribbon, came billowing loose, streaming in the winter wind. The crowd gasped, then began grabbing for it. Achmed saw Rhapsody disappear beneath a sea of humanity, a multitude of hands and arms flailing around her. He ducked as another swell of people rushed in, trying to get nearer to the strange, compelling creature in their midst. The population of the village swirled in blind commotion like waves in the sea.

The soldiers on horseback rode into the throng, stopping next to the thickest part of the mayhem. One shoved a woman aside and began to dismount, a club in his hand.

Achmed struggled to remain upright. He reached through the morass of limbs, following the sound of Rhapsody's racing heart, the only pulse he could hear other than his own. He seized the tiny wrist just as the soldier was upon her.

Then the air and the frenzy around them was shattered by a familiar roar. An ear-rending scream of fury, it rumbled through the street, sending waves of panic through the crowd, beginning with the horses, both of which bolted in terror.

As the crowd swirled in fright, Achmed dragged Rhapsody through the chaos and ran, head down, toward the edge of town, shoving aside anything that got in his way. When he hit the first clear patch he stopped long enough to pull her hood up, then cast a glance behind them.

The hubbub was beginning to slow, as the villagers looked around them, trying to find the woman with the shining hair. The soldiers were still working to quiet their mounts, at the same time attempting to keep them from trampling anyone.

Achmed looked into Rhapsody's face. She was staring blindly ahead, looking back over her shoulder.

"Come on," he said, pulling her forward. Without another word they walked as quickly and inconspicuously as possible out of the roadway and away from the frenzy she had caused in the streets of Bethany.

Twilight came and settled over the fields of the Orlandan Plateau long before they stopped walking. Achmed had paused long enough for Rhapsody to sing her devotions, noting the same melancholy tone that had been present the morning after he had left her at Llauron's. There was pain in the music, deep as the sea, and it clarified many of the fragmented assumptions that had been running loose in his mind. He heard her whisper the names of Stephen's children into the darkness.

As the shadows grew longer they came to a sheltered knoll, where a deep swale in the field had been overgrown with trees and brush. Grunthor had suggested this area as one that was hidden largely from the paths of the wind. Now, upon seeing it for himself, and feeling the vibrations of the air abate a little around it, he concurred. This was the place.

He led Rhapsody inside the tree-shelter and brushed a pool of melting snow off an enormous fallen log.

"Have a seat," he said. "We need to talk."

Rhapsody sighed, a look of utter desolation in her eyes. "Please don't berate me now, Achmed. I know it was a stupid thing to do, but I didn't have an alternative. I just couldn't stand there while that man—"

"This is not the topic of the conversation I want to have now," Achmed said quietly. Rhapsody dissolved into astonished silence. "You were given a piece of false lore today, a polluted story of ancient origin. I want to help you purify the lore."

Her eyes opened wide. "What?"

Achmed sat down across from her and rested his elbows in his knees, his folded hands in front of his lips.

"Wait for the onset of night," he said, looking into the dusk at the last vestiges of day disappearing beyond the horizon. "It will be easier if we hold off until dark."

38

Gerald Owen burst through the door of Haguefort's library.

"M'lord—"

"I see them, Owen." Stephen Navarne was standing at the eastern window, staring ruefully out at the panoramic view of his lands coming to light with the dawn.

The newly built rampart was swarming with moving bodies, men locked in deadly conflict, under a banner of black smoke that rose eerily from behind the great stone wall.

From the shells of each guard tower, recently erected and not yet complete, hung at least one body, sometimes more, twisting endlessly in the wind generated by the attack. Lord Stephen watched, stone-faced, as a falling victim slammed into one of the hanged men, sending the corpse spinning into the wall.

"What in the name of the Creator is happening?"

Owen bent over at the waist, his hands on his knees, red-faced from the exertion of running.

"They attacked just—before dawn," he gasped. "Burned—three closest villages, and the eastern guard post. Got the—stables, too."

"And the soldiers? What happened to the eastern barracks?"

Owen's red face paled. "In flames, m'lord. No one—got out, best as we can tell."

"Sweet All-God." Lord Stephen strode out of the study and into the dining room, stopping before the southern window. The scene was much the same, though the wall seemed to have held better on this front. He glanced over his shoulder at the portrait of his family, then turned to Gerald Owen again.

"All right, Owen, pay close attention. I want you to take my entire personal guard retinue and get Melisande and Gwydion out of here. Go through the tunnels to the wine cellar and out through the western stables. Take Rosella with you, and try not to alarm them all unduly. Head for Llauron's; send word to Anborn on your way." Owen nodded and started for the door.

Lord Stephen leaned his head on his forearm, unable to look away from the scene of carnage.

"Owen?"

"Yes, m'lord?"

"One last thing before you go: summon the quartermaster and tell him to bring my gelding 'round. In the absence of the soldiers from the eastern barracks, I'm going to have to rally the villagers to their own defense."

Owen's words were filled with pain. "M'lord, the attackers *are* the villagers."

𝔚ell, you've finally seen fit to come and report, have you?"

Gittleson sat back, fascinated at the upcoming exchange, but afraid to draw undue attention to himself. It was dangerous enough being the only witness.

The man beneath the gray mantled cloak bowed stiffly, then took down his hood. A cocky smile wreathed the handsome face, blue eyes twinkling merrily.

"We've lost the House," he said cheerfully.

The air in the small room became suddenly warmer, and Gittleson found himself breathing shallowly, trying to escape notice.

The red-rimmed eyes of his master were firmly fixed on the smirking Rakshas, however. When he spoke, a moment later, his voice was measured, with a hint of threat below the surface.

"Despite your limited capacity to reason, I assume you know that this is a very bad setback," he said dryly. The Rakshas nodded, his red-gold curls catching the light. "Then why are you grinning like an idiot?"

The Rakshas dropped into a chair and swung his legs up over the arm. "Because of who we lost it to."

"Don't play games with me, toy. Who was it?"

"I have no idea." The Rakshas sat forward suddenly, a wild look in the crystalline blue eyes. "But there were three of them."

Gittleson recoiled as his master rose.

"What are you babbling about?" The cultured voice dropped to a menacing whisper.

The Rakshas's voice was warm and rich as honey. "Look, I may not be the most acute thinker, but even I can count. There were three of them, a woman and two men, I think, though I only got a glimpse of one close up. Ugly as sin. They drove us out of the House, took down my troops around me. And at least one of them seemed to have as much control over fire as I do."

"Impossible."

The Rakshas shrugged. "Suit yourself."

"Where are these three now?"

"Couldn't say exactly." The Rakshas stretched out, hands behind his head. "They were headed east last time I knew, towards the Krevensfield Plain."

"Canrif." The word was a whispered hiss. Gittleson, in his corner, shuddered at the sound. "They're heading to Canrif."

"Perhaps."

The red-rimmed eyes turned suddenly, fixing their gaze on Gittleson. He could feel the blood drain from his face.

"Gittleson, I may have need of your services shortly."

39

They sat in silence for a long time, listening to the wind in the distance, watching the darkening sky. Finally Achmed looked at Rhapsody. Her face was calm, but concern resonated in her eyes.

"Can you play that new instrument enough to have it cover the vibrations of what we are saying, so that they don't get onto the wind?"

She nodded and pulled out the physician's harp, loosing the ties that had held it under her robes. With a gentle tug she pulled off the soft cloth cover and ran her fingers over the strings.

"Any particular song?" she asked.

He shook his head. "Just something to distract the wind, keep it from carrying what we have to say anywhere else."

Rhapsody thought for a moment, then began to pluck out a tune, abstract and discordant. It had very little tonal variation or melody, and no obvious repeating pattern. She played for a few moments, then set the harp on the log next to her.

"*Samoht*," she said.

Achmed smiled wryly as the small harp began to play, repeating the unpleasant song. She had no idea how ironic her action was.

He caught her glance again and held it for a long moment. There was anticipation in her eyes, and trust, something he had rarely seen. And none of the revulsion he frequently did.

"Tell me the stories of the Ancient Lores, as much as you know."

Rhapsody blinked. "What do you mean?"

"We heard a little of the story of the birth of the world today."

"Yes."

"I want you to forget what that imbecile ordinate told you for a moment, and think back to what you learned from your mentor when you were studying. Those were undoubtedly the purest of conditions under which to learn lore, so he was probably the most reliable source we have."

"Yes." A tinge of confusion was beginning to gleam in her eyes.

"What *is* the story, as you know it? Tell me, as a Namer, Rhapsody. Do the most credible job you can. Believe me, nothing you have ever done in your profession has been more important, has been more critical to be done correctly, than what you are about to tell me."

"About the birth of the elements?"

"Yes." Achmed sat back in the dark, leaning against one of the shelter's slender trees.

"It's in Ancient Serenne, a language I don't speak well. I had to translate it from a lore scroll, so though the language might not be exact, the lore itself is."

"Do the best you can."

She took a deep breath, clearing her mind, and concentrated on the moment in her memory when she had learned the tales he wanted her to impart. When she had a firm fix on them, she began.

"In ancient days, in the Before-Time, the five elements were born. They came into being as the paints of He-Who-Created-the-Universe, the tools with which the cosmos was made. They are sometimes called the Children of the All-God, or the Five Gifts, because they were what He chose to create first."

She looked at Achmed, who was still leaning back, listening with his eyes closed. He nodded for her to continue.

"The first element to come into existence was ether, the matter which makes up the stars. It was believed to hold the very essence of time, of life, of power, of what some called magic. Ether existed before the birth of the world, and therefore contained the secrets of power that preceded worldly knowledge.

"The second element to be born was fire, and it was in the origination of this element that the world became an entity separate from the rest of the universe.

"The mythos says that the Earth itself was a piece of a star that had broken away and streaked across the black void, coming to rest in its orbit around the sun that was its mother. Fire burned on its surface, finally cooling in the absence of ethereal fuel and subsiding into the core of the world. But the fire was not satisfied being relegated to the darkness inside the world, and repeatedly attempted to escape through eruptions of volcanic lava."

Achmed smiled broadly, but did not open his eyes. "You'll notice our friend the priest left that little part of the mythos out."

Rhapsody's eyes kindled dark green in annoyance. "Shall I continue?"

"Yes."

"Then shut up; it's hard enough to concentrate on a translation from an ancient language. As the fire receded, the world was left covered with water, the next element in the mythos to be born. In water there was balance; it could be both destructive and healing.

"With the cooling of the world's surface in water came strong winds, so air is accorded the next rank in the order of the elements.

"As the wind swept the surface of the globe, blowing back the water, earth was revealed.

"This last, youngest element had none of the speed and elusiveness of the earlier ones, but was strong and steadfast, and in that enduring strength was its power. Just as the stars were the keepers of the knowledge and wisdom of the Before-Time, the era prior to the birth of the world, the Earth was the repository of all the knowledge of its history and its present." She took a deep breath.

"There. Now you know what I know."

Achmed chuckled. "Actually, I know a good deal more than you know, but that will come in a moment." He opened his eyes and leaned forward.

"Do you know anything about the Firstborn?" he asked.

Rhapsody hesitated. Achmed did have access to knowledge that only the great Namers should have.

"A little," she admitted reluctantly. "The Ancient Lores are one of the last things a Namer learns, Achmed. I had only begun to study them when Heiles disappeared."

He sat forward so quickly that she started and almost fell off the log.

"Think clearly. You need to remember that time as accurately as you can. What were you able to learn about the Firstborn before he vanished?"

"I'll just tell you what I remember, fragmented as it is. I know more about some than others. Long before the races of man, Lirin and human, Nain and the like, came to Serendair, there were older, primordial races of beings who sprang from the elements themselves, retaining some of the characteristics of those elements. These races were known as the Firstborn.

"The race born of ether was that of the Ancient Seren, tall, lithe people with golden skin and eyes. They were extremely long-lived and had an ageless, patient perspective; their tie to the matter of the stars attuned them to the rhythms of nature and of power.

"Their name, literally translated as *star*, was also given to the bright celestial object that was visible year-round over the Island. Serendair, literally *star-land*, was the place the race originated, and was therefore known as one of the five birthplaces of Time."

Achmed nodded. "What happened to the Ancient Seren?"

"They died off over time, or went to live within the Earth during the racial wars of the Second Age."

"And what about the races that came from the other elements? Do you know anything about them?"

Rhapsody swallowed, trying to remember the fragments of the lessons. "There were the Mythlin, the race descended from the element of water. That race lived within the seas that spanned the globe, almost indiscernible to human sight. Like the Ancient Seren race they held a long worldview, but generally were unconcerned with happenings outside their own domain.

"It was in Mythlin that humans were said to have their origin, that the human body was an evolutionary solidification of the salt water and translucent membranes that comprised the Mythlin physiology. This was offered as an explanation as to why men often felt drawn to the sea, and why human tears and blood are salty."

Achmed smirked. "Did you notice that Stephen thought *Abbat Mythlinis* meant Lord-God, King of the Sea, or something like that?"

Rhapsody laughed with him. "I was wondering if you were listening when he said that. I think it might have been *Master of the Sea*."

The face within the hood lost its smile. "You're about to see how dangerous the sloppy use of lore can be, Rhapsody. The Cymrians certainly have added their own beliefs, or polluted the originals, in many of their interpretations of the ancient stories."

"Everyone does, Achmed. Folktales and myths that get handed down over time change and evolve as they pass from one teller to another. That's why Singers and Namers exist; the science—well, perhaps it's more an art—was developed precisely to counter that tendency, to try and keep the history pure. To separate the lore from the folklore."

"And look how well it worked. Go on. What others do you know about?"

Rhapsody loosed the hastily tied ribbon and ran her fingers through the shining locks of her hair. "I know a bit about the Kith. They were the race believed to be born of the wind, beings with an innate knowledge of the currents of the air and the vibrations of the world. The Kith were people who looked to the sky for guidance. It is in their ancient teachings that the sciences of astronomy and meteorology have their basis.

"The Kith were the originators of music, and the forefathers of the Lirin race. The name *Lirin* comes from the Ancient Seren word for *singer*."

A look of amusement came into his eyes, evolving a moment later into something darker. "The Dhracians are descended of them as well. That's where we inherited our vibrational sensitivity."

Her face went blank. "Really? I didn't know that."

"How would you? Had you ever heard of Dhracians before we met?"

"No."

Achmed pulled his cloak closer around him as if cold. "There are a great many things that exist in the world that you don't know about, Rhapsody, that almost no one knows about," he said, his voice a little softer than it had been a moment before. "Just because no one knows about them doesn't mean they aren't there. And the Earth?"

"That primordial race was dragons, and we learned a little of their more modern lore, First and Second Age stuff, but nothing ancient."

Achmed nodded. "And now, the last. What about fire?"

She shook her head. "I only know what I heard today. You asked about Heiles. I'm fairly certain that this was the lesson we were about to study when he went away. He had laid out all the materials that he needed for the instruction. I know this, because I helped set it up the night before, just before I left him."

Achmed's glance grew cold and piercing. "What were they? Do you remember?"

Rhapsody shook her head. "Not really. A brazier of some kind, I think. Assorted herbs and roots, a few elixirs. He would have explained those to me during the lesson, but of course we didn't get that far. And there was the scroll. He had used it in the teaching of all the other lores."

"So the two of you made these preparations, and the next day he was gone."

"Yes. He sent me to gather some rare manuscripts and music. I never saw him again. I haven't thought about that lesson since, until today when the ordinate told us about the F'dor."

Achmed reached into his robe and pulled out a small folded cloth, which he tossed into her lap. Rhapsody opened the edges gingerly. It was an altar wiping cloth, the kind used for cleansing holy goblets or other small religious items, a piece of white fabric embroidered with the stylized image of the sun she had seen in the temple of Bethany. She let out a long whistle.

"Well, you certainly are brazen, stealing from a basilica in broad daylight."

"What do you think that symbol is?" Achmed asked.

Rhapsody tossed it back at him, irritation building in her features. "I'm getting really sick of this game, Achmed. I'm not deaf. I heard what he said. It's the symbol of the F'dor."

His face was in hers in the next second. "I misspoke. What

do you think the symbol represents, literally?" His voice was arid with intensity.

Rhapsody tried to shake off the sudden chill that gripped her. "The sun?"

Achmed shook his head slowly. "That's what you think, because that's what *they* think. I assure you, it's not. Or at least it wasn't when it was used in the old world."

She struggled to keep from giving in to the tremors that were now causing her to shake, like a brown leaf clinging to a bare tree in the winter wind. "What was it?"

Achmed opened the cloth again. He ran a long, bony finger around the golden circle gently, almost lovingly.

"The Cymrians must have thought it was the sun when they saw the old symbol. It looked much like this representation, but rougher. This," he said, touching the central circle, "is the Earth, and these rays were flames—the Earth, in flames. Not from the old times, when the fire was born, but the race's ultimate goal. *The Earth in flames.* Do you understand what I'm telling you, Rhapsody?"

She nodded, unable to speak.

"And this, this represents the means by which that goal would be achieved." His finger followed the red spiral up from the center of the design to the outside edge of the circle. "I assume you can figure out what that was supposed to represent, having seen a very small part of it with your own eyes."

Her voice came out in a whisper, barely audible above the jangling of the harp. "The wyrm."

"Indeed. Now, as far as I can tell, your lullabye worked. Serendair was destroyed in volcanic fire, the explosion of the Sleeping Child, not by the wyrm, as planned. But bear in mind it was the impact of that falling star that let the F'dor out of the Earth in the first place, so it's not impossible that one might have survived the cataclysm that took the Island down. And if even one of that race is still alive, it will seek to make good on that goal. And it will find the means."

"I don't know what you're talking about." Rhapsody pulled her hair back into the ribbon, tying it nervously.

Achmed sat back, his hands pressed together, the fingertips at his lips again.

"Perhaps we'd best begin over. Back in the Before-Time when they were born in fire, the F'dor were demonic spirits, twisted, dark beings with a jealous, avaricious nature, longing to consume the world around them, much like the fire from which they came. Their birthplace was the Fiery Rim, a ring of five active volcanic mountains submerged beneath the sea.

"Also like fire, F'dor have no corporeal form, but rather feed off a more solid host, the way fire grows by consuming fuel, destroying it in the process.

"Like fire, the second element, F'dor were the second race to be born. And while the F'dor were less powerful than the Ancient Seren race which preceded them, they were stronger than the others that came after them. Like their birth element, they retreated into the shadows, emerging occasionally; when they did, they were as destructive as their counterpart in nature.

"Fire itself eventually began to burn purely in the Earth's core, as you have seen. It would only occasionally erupt in ruin. F'dor, however, never underwent that cleansing transformation. If anything they became even more twisted, and thrived by using deception.

"They would attach themselves, spirits that they were, to a human host—or Lirin, or Nain—and feed off it, possessing it until it coexisted as two entities, one of them man, the other demon. They had tremendous power to hold their victims in thrall, to make them do their will. And they were almost impossible to discern, sometimes even to the person who was the host. Perhaps you might gain an inkling of insight now into why I don't appreciate you adopting everyone under the sun. For all I, or you, know, *you* could be one yourself now, or under its power, and not even know it."

"How do you know all this?" Rhapsody exploded. "Where did you get the ancient knowledge that only the greatest Namers are supposed to have?"

Achmed looked up into the darkness. The stars winked between the clouds that hung heavy in the air above. Mist was beginning to form on the ground, as if rising to meet its counterpart in the sky.

"I learned some of the secrets of the F'dor while in its employ."

"The demon that was your master? It was F'dor?"

"Yes. It had my name, was holding it captive, and could bend me to its will as a result. The F'dor's own name was Tsoltan; perhaps you've heard it before." He glanced at the harp, still grinding out its discordant song.

Rhapsody sought the answer in her memory, and found it a moment later. "Llauron said that the enemy of the king in the Great War that raged after we left the Island was named Tsoltan. Is that the one?"

Achmed nodded. "And just when he was telling us about him, you interrupted with something inane, though you didn't know better at the time."

"I could have, if you had told me about him earlier, instead of waiting until now."

"When? Would you have had me speak his name within the Earth? You, a Namer, should know more than anyone what might have happened." The anger in her eyes diminished, like an ember burning out, and she nodded.

Achmed's voice grew softer. "There is another reason I know of the F'dor. I'm part Dhracian. As a race, we loathe the F'dor with every fiber of our souls. I suppose part of our hatred stems from their indiscernibility; as a people sensitive to vibration it is particularly offensive for a Dhracian to know that the demons are there, but they can't be detected.

"Our history is one of racial conflicts, great crusades by the Dhracians against the F'dor. This is a long story, better suited to another night, but I will tell you just one fragment of the history.

"After the Dawn of Time, in that era sometimes known as the Day of the Gods, the primordial races you spoke of had their own difficulties with the F'dor. What eventually came to pass was an alliance of sorts, albeit a tentative one, between the Ancient Seren, the Mythlin, and the Kith—the dragons stayed out of it. It was the union of these three, working together, that drove the F'dor back into the Earth, containing them there, until they were released by chance.

"The falling star, the Sleeping Child, hit the Earth in the middle of the Second Age, millennia later. Its impact tore a hole in the fabric of the world, and some of the F'dor escaped from the core. I believe the spirit that eventually came to possess Tsoltan was one of them. Tsoltan was evil before the F'dor took him, a priest to the Goddess of Void, the Devourer. He was a perfect host for the F'dor."

"You're losing me."

"I'm sorry; I digress. In the battle in that First Age, when the F'dor were contained, it was the Kith, our ancestors, who found the F'dor, and held them in thrall by means of vibration. They were the assassins, the ones who had studied how to kill both the host and the demon. They bequeathed that ability to their descendants, the Dhracians.

"The Dhracians are an elder race, though not Firstborn, obviously. They came before the races of man. And for reasons too complicated to explain tonight, the Dhracians made it their lives' ambitions to destroy every last trace of the F'dor. So we have the ability to do it; it is our racial gift, our lore. Which is what made the fact that I was Tsoltan's thrall, his personal assassin, all the more perverse and nauseating.

"So it comes down to this, Rhapsody: our world, the world we knew, is gone. I need to find out if it took Tsoltan with it, either by MacQuieth's hand, or by death in the cataclysm.

"Most likely the F'dor died in the Great War. MacQuieth was the one non-Dhracian warrior that might have been able to kill both the demon and the human, but we don't know that for certain. Obviously the wyrm was not released, or we would not be out here, freezing our arses off in the middle of a winter's night half a world away from Serendair.

"But the possibility exists that the F'dor didn't die, as well. Something is definitely behind these strange incursions, and where there is unexplainable chaos, it is often a bellwether of F'dor. Of course, F'dor do not have exclusive rights to mayhem and aggression; man has been an active participant in that for centuries on his own.

"Obviously, the greatest fear is that a F'dor spirit escaped, and has come here. It would not have to be the same one I knew in order to wake the wyrm, assuming that monstrosity is still alive in the bowels of the Earth. And any F'dor would know of its existence; that's their lore. Any F'dor would seek its release. I need to know if the F'dor that I was enslaved to survived, but it is critical just to find out if any F'dor is here among us."

"Well, that's easy," Rhapsody said, rubbing her hands up and down her arms to dispel the chill. "Its temple is right here, in Bethany. They're worshiping it, in plain sight."

Achmed laughed. "Not necessarily. You have to remember, Rhapsody, if the legends are correct, the forces of the F'dor *lost* the Great War of Serendair. The loser's history isn't the one that is told and retold until it becomes legend. These poor fools, the descendants of the war's *victors*, probably only had crumbs of the truth, just another example of Cymrian self-delusion. They wanted to honor the elements, the five children of their Creator. They just didn't know the whole story."

"Is it possible that they are just evil, and sincerely worshiping it?" Rhapsody asked.

"Anything is possible, but let's assume for a moment those idiots in the basilica are innocent dupes. They seem too stupid to be evil. Besides, F'dor don't tend to reveal themselves, and their infrastructure, publicly. Their strength is in remaining hidden.

"So where did the Cymrians get this inaccurate story? Perhaps they came upon a painting of the symbol somewhere. Tsoltan used to wear an amulet depicting the Earth in flames, but it had an eye in the center. Maybe by the time they built the cathedrals, trying to commemorate their heritage, they had forgotten the origin of the fire symbol, or maybe they never knew it in the first place. That's one of the reasons I asked you how long it was between our leaving, and the Cymrian exodus.

"It doesn't matter. What they've done, however inadvertent, has exposed a large segment of the population in this place to the F'dor if it is here. By putting themselves in a worshipful mode, in the presence of an elemental well of fire from a vent in the Earth's heart, and by speaking of the F'dor as a beneficent force, they've handed this continent over to it, if it's here. They invited it here."

The winter chill had crept into Rhapsody's bones, along with something colder. "Then what do we do? How do we find something that can't be found, in a place we don't know, a thousand years out of our own time?"

"We start in Canrif," Achmed said. "It would have followed the Cymrians if it came with them. That was where the power was. It's where the Bolg are now, and even if it turns out that nothing evil followed the Cymrians, it will be worth the journey just to see Canrif, and the Firbolg that live there."

"And that's why this has been your plan all along, ever since you heard Llauron's tale?"

"Yes. And even more so since we met the Rakshas, and you told me of that vision you had near the altar in the garden. Though that was certainly demonic, it doesn't sound much like the work of F'dor. Truthfully, Rhapsody, if the religion of this place is struggling with its own demons, I say we leave them to it.

"I suspect the blood of those children is the source of sustenance for the Rakshas, keeps it alive. Stephen plans to set a trap for it. If his army, and the army of his cousins, can't destroy the Rakshas, we have no chance against it anyway. This problem is of their world; we need to find the answers to our own concerns. And the place to do it is Canrif."

Rhapsody sighed. "All right, then. I suppose there really is no alternative but to at least try and find out if something came with the fleets or not, and if it's what is causing all the strife. Can I just ask you one thing more?"

Achmed rose and stretched, gathering his robe around him. "Certainly."

"What are you going to do if it turns out to be what you fear it is?"

He looked up into the branches that arched above them, white bare arms gleaming in the dark, lost in thought for a long moment. "I don't know what I *can* do," he said at last. "Since we were remade in the fire, many things are different. I have powers and skills I never had before, and have lost some of those I used to count on. I'm not sure what weapons I still have to bring to bear against it."

"That's only part of the answer," Rhapsody said softly. "Maybe I should have asked what you're *willing* to do. I don't know how much you care about this place and its people. In the past you have seemed distant from both of them."

He stared at her, unblinking, then finally smiled. "I don't

know, either. Let's get back. Grunthor is probably sitting on Jo to keep her from eavesdropping." He took her hand and pulled her to a stand.

"All this talk of ancient races made me think of something," Rhapsody said, pulling up her hood. "Do you remember the prophecy of the Three? Child of Blood, Child of Earth, Child of the Sky?"

"Indeed."

"Could that have referred to those primordial races, the alliance of the Kith, the Mythlin, and the Ancient Seren, rather than Anwyn and her sisters, the Seers, like Llauron said?"

Achmed stared at her in disbelief. "Is that really who you think the prophecy is about?"

"I have no idea who the prophecy is about. I was just posing a suggestion."

Achmed smiled and pointed to the harp. "Get that thing and make it stop; it's addling your brain." *Children of the Sky must have air between the ears*, he thought. *Liringlas. Your own race, and you don't even recognize yourself. Or Grunthor and me.* "You definitely are a Cymrian, Rhapsody; your self-delusion exceeds even theirs, and that's a hefty accomplishment."

"What's that supposed to mean?" she demanded.

The mismatched eyes twinkled. "Nothing. Let me just tell you this: prophecy is clearest after the fact. I don't allow myself to be taken in or led astray by it. Overconfidence is often a result of trying to read signs you can't translate with certainty. After all, what has your prescience ever done for you? You dreamt of the Island's death—were you able to stop it?"

He pulled aside the branches of the thicket and started back to the camp. Rhapsody watched for a moment before following him.

When morning came, it was like the spell of the night before had been broken. The companions saddled up sullenly, preparing for their journey to Bethe Corbair, the last human stronghold before the Bolglands.

Once they came to the western edge of the Krevensfield Plain, the endless meadow that wrapped around the province of Bethe Corbair, Rhapsody tried once more to sound Achmed out, to see what he was thinking, to no avail. He had returned to his customary distance, resisting any overture she made with thorny silence. It was as if the conversation had never happened.

40

$\mathcal{H}$e was at the crest of a deep swale in the Krevensfield Plain when Ashe felt it. At the very edge of his awareness he sensed something alien, something his perceptions had never before come across, and it made him stop in the morning shadow he was walking behind, unseen.

Power, the dragon within his blood whispered. *Fascinating power. I want to touch it.*

The dragon was a source of constant struggle. It was part of him, a faction of his own nature that had a mind of its own, and though he was perennially in a state of vigilance to keep it under control, Ashe had grown used to it over the years.

He had come to appreciate its vast awareness. Because of that element in his makeup he was conscious of the infinitesimal details of the world around him; he could feel and sense every blade of grass in the field he now stood within if he gave the dragon the leeway to do so. But Ashe tried to avoid that sort of thing; the dragon was unpredictable, and wanted more freedom than he was willing to allow it.

Its senses were never wrong; there *was* something alien around here, something mystical and old and perverse and fascinating all at the same time. Something more than a source of power, but exactly what it was he was at a loss to determine. It took him a moment to locate where it was coming from, and when he did, he sighed in annoyance.

Bethe Corbair; it was coming from within the city. Ashe hated cities. He avoided them whenever possible, primarily because Ashe's life was a life of shadow and solitude; it was not a wise thing to put oneself around people when one was hunted.

Still, there was such a thing as being lost in a crowd. Ashe would have been known to have done that every now and then, if anyone had known anything about Ashe, but in truth no one really did. Though technically Ashe could be seen, he was generally overlooked. He lived his life shrouded in a cloak of mist, made from woolen cloth but powered by an elemental force of water beyond the comprehension of most.

Because of this, the signature of his heartbeat, his breath, his physical form and immortal soul were not discernible to the naked eye, or even to the devices that could read the vibrations in the wind. This was a good thing, for the pain he carried—constant, and excruciating to both body and soul—would have made him an obvious target were it not for his mist cloak. Ashe was a paradox: invisible to all, but aware of everything.

I want to touch this, the dragon insisted. Rather than pushing it back, as he generally did, Ashe was forced to agree. He needed to see what this new power in Bethe Corbair was. Silently he followed the moving shadow of the morning sun across the Krevensfield Plain until he reached the gates of Bethe Corbair, where he slipped in, unnoticed, and blended into the crowd.

Νο stealing."

Jo rolled her eyes. "Oh, brother."

Rhapsody shuddered and looked at Achmed, who smiled beneath his hood in spite of himself. "Careful," she said to Jo, "a phrase very similar to that once got me into unbelievable trouble."

Jo dodged out of the way of an enormous cart filled with baskets traveling the road on which they now stood, outside the entrance gates of Bethe Corbair. A sea of humanity swirled around the city walls, generating a humming rumble they had heard from miles away. There was excitement in the air, a tense, edgy energy that only a city on the fringe of the wilderness could sustain.

"We've been on the road for weeks. What's the point of

coming to the city if you're not going to loot a few pockets?" she demanded.

Rhapsody held up a small coin pouch. "How about actually paying for what you need?"

She received a surly glance in return. "That's *your* money."

"It's *our* money," Rhapsody corrected as she unwound the rawhide cord closure of the coin purse. "Sisters, remember?"

She took Jo's hand and opened it, then poured half of the contents into it. "Here's some 'walking-around money,' at least that's what my father used to call it. Be careful with it; it may be a while before we have money again."

"This is a city," said Achmed, looking around outside the gate. "For you, money is as close as the nearest street corner. You have earning talents the rest of us don't have."

Rhapsody glared at him. "I beg your pardon?"

"You're a musician," said Achmed in annoyance. "What did you think I meant?"

"I don't know if you make an effort to be offensive, or if you just come by it naturally, but you are very talented at it either way. Come on, Jo," she said, pulling up the hood of her cape. "We'll meet you by the basilica at noon, Achmed. I'm sure there will be someplace to eat in the center of town."

She took Jo's hand and followed the crowd into the city of Bethe Corbair, the last town before the Bolglands.

Grunthor and Achmed waited until the women were out of sight, then began to walk the perimeter of the city outside the wall, far enough away that they were inconspicuous.

After completing their reconnaissance of the entire perimeter they conferred at the city's northern edge. Although Bethe Corbair was a walled city, it had numerous scattered settlements at its outskirts ranging from rickety shacks to small villages.

It was a border town, a place that looked east to the mountains known as the Teeth with trepidation. There was no fresh evidence of a Bolg incursion; such raids left visible scars. Still, if the residents of the area felt the need to keep within sight of the city walls, the historical bloodletting must have been horrifying enough to convince them that isolated living was a bad idea.

"Scout farther, wider sweep," Achmed said. Grunthor nodded. "We'll meet at the eastern outskirts at sundown." The Dhracian watched as his enormous companion walked away and blended into the landscape, then turned and went into the city himself.

The city of Bethe Corbair was an old one, older than the capital at Navarne, though according to Stephen the areas were settled at about the same time. Rhapsody thought back to the history lessons she had learned from Llauron and Lord Stephen.

Navarne and Bethany had been settled by the First Fleet, the initial group of planners, architects, and builders that Gwylliam had sent forth to construct the Cymrians' new home. They built their guard towers and homesteads first, then took their time building the common areas. That explained the beauty of the cities, a sensibility of design coupled with artistry that endured, making them marvels to behold.

Bethe Corbair, by contrast, had been built by the Third Fleet, Gwylliam's own contingent. The Third Fleet had been made up of soldiers and peasants, merchants and unskilled laborers, and as a result bore the signs of a fortress mentality. The city walls were thick and high, the buildings utilitarian in their design and built to withstand attack. Time had eased the military feel somewhat, but the city still held the intrinsic attitude of wariness.

That attitude was not evidenced in the people, however. They seemed as any other populace, made up of a typical number of the courteous and the rude, the peasant and the aristocrat, the educated and the illiterate. It was a city without scars, unpretentious and unafraid. Its streets spread out within its walls, filled with noise and foot traffic, merchants, carts and animals and the stench of human residence.

What made Bethe Corbair unique was the music. Rhapsody walked the streets as if enchanted, listening to the airy random melodies played by the bells in the basilica tower. Their songs were subject to the will of the wind, and therefore carried a feeling of freedom and wildness that made her heart rise into her throat at the beauty of it.

The townspeople went about their business oblivious of the music, though when the bells were ringing in a high breeze it had an undeniably pleasant effect on their attitudes. Street merchants stopped haggling, fishwives bickered at lower volume, and children squabbling in the streets generally found reasons to resolve their differences. Rhapsody smiled as she observed the power of the music.

Jo was fairly dancing with impatience.

"This is boring," she whined when Rhapsody stopped at the table of a fabric merchant. "Please, my head is going to explode if I look at any more of this. I'm going to scout around."

"All right," Rhapsody said reluctantly. "We can meet at the basilica at noon; look for Achmed if you don't see me. And stay out of trouble. Remember, no stealing. I'd hate to see you lose your hand." She smiled as Jo shuddered visibly, then nodded and disappeared into the crowd.

Ashe glanced around the open-air market at the center of the city. The Krevensfield Plain lay to the south of Bethe Corbair, so he had entered through the southern gate, though the power he had felt lay somewhere to the east. Or at least part of it did; one element of it seemed to have split off and was now circling the city at the very edge of his dragon senses. It had different properties than the other did, and was so methodical in its movements that he was unable to tell whether it was a being or an object on a cart of some sort.

His inability to discern the power's nature bewildered Ashe. Generally he was able to accurately assess the properties of anything within his range, but for some reason this power was unknown to him even in the kind of form it was taking. The dragon was squirming impatiently; only the presence of the myriad items in the marketplace was able to distract it sufficiently to allow Ashe to remain in control.

He carefully sidestepped a swaggering buffoon, drunk with spirits and excitement about the warmth of the winter day. The man had been celebrating the temporary respite from the cold that the thaw had provided, and came within a few feet of driving an elbow into Ashe's chest, largely because the tipsy fellow had not seen him standing there. Ashe was nimble enough to avoid these encounters, but they played havoc with his concentration.

He turned his attention once again to the source of the power, but once again it had dispersed, as if dividing itself. He felt particularly attracted to one of the two aspects, the one that was somewhere nearby, radiating an irresistible warmth.

Ashe was immediately suspicious; servants of fire were the main hunters after him, and he had survived only by recognizing the potential for traps in every tantalizing situation. The source was around somewhere, and sooner or later it was bound to end up in the marketplace square. He resolved to hang back and wait.

In the meantime he was struggling with the dragon. Another reason he tried to avoid cities, particularly ones on a trade route like Bethe Corbair, was the fascination the dragon had with merchandise. The element of his nature had grown rampant as they passed a table of gems displayed under glass, whispering in his soul in excitement.

Pretties, it insisted. *I want to touch this.*

Ashe beat it back down again. *No.*

I want to touch this.

No. He walked away from the gem merchant, who had looked up a moment before as she became indistinctly aware of Ashe's presence, then looked back to her table, having not seen him as he passed by.

The dragon noticed the next table as well, spread with fine spices. *Peppercorns; I want to count them,* it whispered again as it made note of each grain, seed, bean, flake, and sprinkle.

Ashe willed it down again. *No.* He looked around for the source of the power.

Perfume and ambergris; it came from the vomit of a leviathan which had eaten seventeen mackerel, one hundred seventy —

Stop.

Look at the fabric; no silk today, just linen, cream velvet, and wool in thirteen textures. The wool is in shades of blue, azure, violet, indigo —

NO. Ashe turned around again; it was near. He sublimated the dragon with an intense effort and tried to clear his mind.

Across the street a commotion caught his attention. It seemed to be centered around a small woman in a gray cape and hood, not unlike his own. He moved closer, feeling the call of the power source.

Rhapsody had been struggling with her own personal dragon, the desire to run her hands over the exquisite fabrics on the table in front of her. The cream velvet was especially exquisite, but far outside her ability to pay. With a sigh she forced her hands back to her sides and moved on, looking at the other wares of the marketplace.

At the end of the street a table caught her eye; the items on it were pooled in clusters that sparkled in the sun like light on a moving stream. Her interest piqued, Rhapsody hurried down the street in the direction of the gleaming objects.

She stopped before the merchant's table. The sparkling pools turned out to be jewelry, mostly earrings, by and large tawdry merchandise, but there were a few things of value and craftsmanship, some of which were genuinely lovely. She had a weakness for beautiful clothes and baubles, though she would rather die than admit it to her Bolg companions, and so in their absence she allowed herself the secret pleasure of looking at the glistening trinkets, her eyes matching their glow and even exceeding it.

The merchant turned to her when he was finished with his other customer, checking the table before raising his eyes to her face. Rhapsody knew immediately he was unconsciously taking stock in case she had stolen or would try to steal something.

Her Lirin blood had elicited the same reaction in Easton, something she never really understood. Lirin had little use for material possessions, especially items as useless as adornments like earrings and necklaces, so why they were automatically suspected by shopkeepers and tradesmen was beyond her. She had written it off to racism and tried not to be offended, but each time it happened it made her blood boil. She swallowed hard and tried to maintain a pleasant expression as she turned away from the table, her interest gone.

"Miss?" The merchant's voice held a note of desperation.

Rhapsody innately held her hands up slightly, putting them into plain sight, in case he was about to accuse her of lifting something.

"Yes?" She did not turn back.

"Please, don't leave yet. Did you see anything you like?"

Rhapsody turned around again. The look on the merchant's face was utterly different than it had been a moment before when he was trying to wheedle a bald man into purchasing a matching pin for the ring he had just bought. His eyes were wide, as if amazed, and he was gripping the table in front of him so tightly his knuckles were turning white.

"Is something wrong?" Rhapsody asked, concerned. The merchant shook his head quickly, but did not release the table. "Yes, there are a lot of very nice things here. You have some lovely merchandise, but I was just looking." She turned once more to go.

"Miss?" The tone was even more urgent this time.

Rhapsody sighed, trying not to be visibly annoyed, and looked back at him again. His face was flushed and his hands were trembling.

"Are you ill?" Rhapsody asked in alarm. She was about to reach for her waterskin, but the man shook his head and pulled a linen handkerchief from his pocket, mopping his brow rapidly.

"No, thank you, miss. Please, take a minute. Is there anything you would like?"

"I just told you, I'm only—"

The man seized a pair of gold earrings from the table and held them in front of her eyes. "These match your locket perfect, miss. Why don't you try them on?"

Rhapsody looked at the earrings. They were one of the items she had identified as lovely, with a simple but elegant artistry that did, in fact, match the gold lavaliere she always wore. Undoubtedly they were far more than she could afford, but she couldn't resist a look.

The trinkets caught the sun and flashed, and the secret part of Rhapsody that coveted pretty things was delighted, even as her mind reminded her sternly that street hawks could sell seawater to a shipwrecked sailor. She had never been good at resisting, and so had avoided the Thieves' Market, as the bazaar in Easton was affectionately called, whenever possible.

"Please, miss. They were made for you. Try them on; I just want to see how they look on you. Please." His insistence seemed more than even the most fervent sidestreet pitch.

Rhapsody couldn't stand it anymore. "Oh, very well, as long as you understand I probably won't buy them." She took the jewelry the man proffered with an intense gleam in his eye, and pulled down her hood to try them on.

The gold was a different grade; she could see that even before they were attached to her earlobes, and it made her wistful for a moment. She remembered the pride on her mother's face as she had opened the box with the locket, and Rhapsody had known then, as she did now, how dearly it had cost her. Next to the earrings it looked less lustrous and rich, though its craftsmanship held up as a match.

A deafening screech, followed by a crash and the splintering of wood, erupted in the street behind her, and Rhapsody jumped.

She spun quickly around, dropping the earrings on the counter, and moved back; two oxcarts had smashed into each other. The first cart was unbalanced and about to tip over onto the table of the jeweler.

The animals snorted and screamed in panic as the drivers tried to get out of the way of the toppling cart. Rhapsody ducked under the table and pulled it back out of the fray, managing to keep most of the wares in place. The jeweler panicked, and would have abandoned his merchandise if there had been a place to run, but his exit was blocked.

After a precarious moment, the drivers sorted it out. Amid much cursing and recriminations the wagons were pulled apart, and Rhapsody busied herself helping the jeweler reset his table; it gave her a chance to experience the enjoyment of touching the baubles while helping him. He seemed to be in shock, so she passed him her waterskin while she worked. His wide eyes never left her face as he drank.

It only took a few minutes to set the bench to rights, and after making sure nothing was missing as far as she knew, she helped the man up, brushed him off, and gently retrieved her waterskin from his rigid grip.

Poor soul, Rhapsody thought with sympathy, *how terrified he is.* "Are you all right?" she asked, receiving only a glazed nod in answer. She was surprised that a merchant in a bazaar would have such a long recovery period. The ones she knew were amazingly fast on their feet, and probably wouldn't have let an event like this even slow, let alone stop, a sales pitch. But the jeweler was an older man, and this was a different world than she was used to. As she turned to go, once again, the man called after her.

"Miss?"

With a sigh, Rhapsody turned to face him for what she prayed was the last time. Nana had tried to teach her the fine art of walking away courteously, but she had never quite got it down. "Yes?"

The jeweler held the earrings out to her. "Please. With my thanks."

"No, thank you. I couldn't possibly accept."

"You must," he said, his voice louder than he meant it to be. "Please," he said, exhibiting more control.

The look in his eyes was so urgent that Rhapsody feared hurting his feelings. "Well, thank you," she said, giving in, and took the earrings from hands that trembled. She attached them to her ears again and swung her head slightly so that they caught the light. "How do they look?"

The man's mouth fell open, and he stuttered his answer. "Beautiful."

Rhapsody reached into her pack for her coin purse, but the man waved her hand away. "A gift. Please."

"All right; thank you," she said, smiling. "I hope you are feeling better soon." She put up her hood and walked away, leaving the jeweler, as well as the cart drivers and the witnesses to the accident, watching her in stunned silence.

41

From across the street Ashe watched the proceedings, first in amazement, then amusement. Whatever was beneath the hood of the remarkable creature in the gray mantle had clearly stunned the street merchant, but the woman had not seemed to notice.

The tradesman was standing, mouth agape, and staring intensely from the moment he had looked up inside her hood, while she continued about her business. Ashe's dragon senses wondered if she might be hideous, but he could make out no deformity or injury at this distance. He would have to see for himself what the commotion was about.

Whatever it was about, the commotion was growing. Ashe was not easily rattled, but he was somewhat taken aback when the two oxcarts slammed into each other. The drivers obviously had been able to see what their vehicles had obscured from him—she had pulled down her hood a few seconds before the accident occurred.

Whatever else she was, she was agile; a second after the moment of impact she was under the table, rescuing it and its owner from the collision, then helping set things to rights before ambling off again.

She made her way down the street, oblivious of the havoc she was causing, as tradesmen and soldiers, farmers and peasants, women and men alike stopped and stared after her, some of them dropping their belongings. Ashe's hand came to rest casually on the hilt of his sword as he turned to follow her with his eyes as long as possible, but all he could make out was a glint of sun-colored hair and—

A flash of agony shot through Ashe, twisting his stomach and nauseating him, originating at his scrotum, which had been violently wrenched to one side and had gone numb in preparation to experience excruciating pain.

In the moment of shock that preceded the wave of misery he knew was coming, his hand lashed out and seized the wrist of the young girl whose fingers still encircled his testicles. He felt the bones of her wrist grind as he squeezed with a crushing force, freeing his genitalia just before the incapacitating sensation coursed through him and made him gasp deeply.

The offending hand belonged to a young pickpocket, a girl of about sixteen, who had inadvertently mistaken his balls for a coin purse while attempting to raid his pocket.

Normally Ashe was immune to any sort of problem of this nature; between his dragon sense, his speed, and the near-invisibility afforded by his misty cloak, those who would bother him in any way would be unable to get within arm's reach of him. The depth to which he had been distracted by the strange vibrations of the gray-cloaked woman had allowed him to be vulnerable for the first time to this form of attack.

The girl cried out in pain as he gripped her wrist even tighter and dragged her back as she started to run, lifting her off the ground.

She was tall and thin, with long, unkempt hair the color of winter straw, and Ashe allowed himself the involuntary mental check he made unconsciously any time he was near a blond woman; he pulled her within visual range and looked down at her. Her eyes, staring up into his hood in abject terror, were a pale, watery blue, and he noted, as he always did, that this could not have been who he hoped.

An ugly, guttural snarl escaped him; it was the only noise he was capable of making at the moment, compromised as he was by her actions an instant before. The pallid eyes widened in fear, and Ashe felt his jaw clench in preparation of his utterance of vicious threats. But as he struggled to control his fury for fear he might kill the street wench, he felt pressure, this time of a different nature, against the wrist of his other hand.

"Kindly unhand my sister, or I will un-hand you."

For the second time that morning Ashe had been caught off guard, and it both astonished and infuriated him. The dagger blade that now lay along his wrist had been put there without his notice, mostly due to the throbbing pain that threatened to cause him to vomit. The knife was pressing deep enough to serve as a warning without drawing blood yet.

He turned in fury to the other assailant, and felt his mouth drop open like those of the people he had been watching on the street a moment before.

Beneath his swimming gaze was undeniably the most beautiful face he had ever seen, or even heard tale of. Most incredible among all its exquisite features were two emerald green eyes, kindling in anger to the color of pale spring grass, glaring at him with a fury that superseded his own. Framing the elegant face were tendrils of hair that gleamed like gold in a smelting fire; had it not been restrained within its hood it would likely have outshone the winter sun.

The dragon blood within him danced in excitement.

I want to touch this. Please; let me sense.

Ashe beat back the urge, but had to concentrate to force his mouth to close, and gave silent thanks for the anonymous cloak and hood that were both the bane of his existence and his saving grace, particularly in situations like this.

Realization that she couldn't see his face gave him sudden confidence, so he tempered what would have been his normal reaction and took a deep breath. When he did, he inhaled her scent, and felt his head grow weak with the pleasure of it. He struggled to keep his voice under control.

"I don't know why you are snarling at *me*," he said. "I'm not the one who transgressed."

"You are hurting my sister, and if you don't desist immediately I will return the favor." The blade of her dagger bit a little deeper, but still did not pierce his flesh.

Good pressure control, he thought with a tinge of admiration. He released the girl, who remained staring up into his hood. To remedy that situation he moved away slightly, closer to the beautiful woman. She removed her dagger from his wrist, but continued to glare at him.

"My, aren't you impressive," she said sarcastically. "Don't you have anything better to do than assault young girls in the street?"

Ashe's jaw dropped again. "Excuse me?"

She turned to the streetwench. "Are you all right, Jo?" The girl, still staring at him blankly, nodded. "It's a lucky thing for you she's not hurt."

Ashe could not believe this was happening. Never in his life had he felt at such a loss to control a situation; in fact, he was having a hard time forming a coherent sentence.

"Your sister—your—whatever she is, your friend, tried to pick my pocket."

The beautiful woman glared at the girl, but said nothing.

"And she *missed*," he said, punctuating the last word for emphasis. "She reached in and felt what she thought was a coin purse, then tugged on it most ungraciously—tried to yank it free from my trousers, in fact."

His ears began to burn; he could not believe he was having this conversation at all, let alone in the street and with a complete stranger. The otherworldly quality of the woman's gorgeous face had totally unhinged his tongue, and it was flapping as though in a high wind.

The woman cleared her throat, and when she removed her hand from her mouth a slight smile remained behind.

"Let me guess; it wasn't a coin purse."

"No." His tone was pointed.

She glared at the girl again, who seemed to wither at her glance. Then her gaze turned back to him, and she sighed. There was music in the exhalation of breath, a music that Ashe could feel in the tiniest hairs on the back of his forearms.

"I'm very sorry," she said, her emerald eyes twinkling with effort to remain serious. "I hope there was no major damage done."

"It's a little early to tell," he said ruefully, feeling the throbbing pain begin to subside and the nausea abate a little.

"Nonsense," the woman said mischievously. Her hand shot out like a flash into his cloak and cupped his testicles.

Ashe felt his mouth drop open. Normally someone would have gotten as far as the mere thought of doing what she had before his reaction stopped them; his agility was thus far unsurpassed by anyone he had encountered in his 154 years. But here she stood, this enchanting thing, with his balls in her hand, smiling up at him before he had a chance to take a second breath.

She gave his genitals a gentle pat, sending waves of frenetic, if pleasant, shock through his entire body, and blood to many places she could not currently see but might be aware of momentarily. Then she bounced them carefully in the palm of her hand, her face intent on the reaction of their elasticity; at least, he hoped that was what she was gauging.

He knew he should ferociously order her to stop; had it been anyone else there would have been no point in speaking, as the dead can't hear well. But again he said nothing, partly because he hadn't recovered yet from his abject state of surprise, partly because he didn't want her to.

Just as the reaction to her touch was beginning, she removed her hand. "They seem fine to me," she said, her eyes sparkling wickedly. "Is the feeling returning yet?"

"The feeling was never gone; that was not the problem,"

he said, attempting to match the humor in her tone. "But you could say that it has changed."

Arousal was coursing through him now. He was extraordinarily uncomfortable with all this taking place on the street, and in particular with his stupid, moonstruck reaction to it. Then words came forth from his mouth, unbidden—words that must have been spoken by someone else, for surely they never would have come from him.

"They really need a more thorough examination."

The beautiful woman laughed, and her laughter had the ring of wind chimes to it. The dragon's interest piqued again, and it fought to emerge.

Let me touch this. I want to touch this.

He struggled to hold it down, but for the first time since he had entered the bazaar the dragon wanted the same thing he did.

A cold sweat broke over him as he had a dual realization. First, he knew that the dragon's unpredictability and voracious appetite for whatever it desired made him dangerous at the moment. Before he might stop himself it was possible that he would take her right there in the street, which would surely be the death of both of them.

Second, and far more disturbing, he knew that he didn't care. He wanted to let his senses run rampant over her, learning, in the time it would take for her heart to beat twice, every intimate detail about her. It was becoming more clear that he was going to. He fought it, but his twin nature defeated him before he even put forth a half-hearted effort.

I want to touch this. I want this; so do you.

The magnificent face broke into a dazzling smile. "Well, I'm glad to see you've recovered your sense of humor, at least. With any luck the rest will return momentarily. I apologize to you, sir, on behalf of my sister, and ask your pardon. We'll be on our way and out of yours now. Come along, Jo." She wrapped a protective arm around the shoulders of the younger, taller girl and began to lead her away.

"Wait," he said. The word tore forth from his throat before he could stop it. She turned back to him.

As she turned her hair caught the light; even under the hooded cloak she wore the glint of gold was obvious. She blinked, and as the long black lashes touched the bottom of her deep green eyes, the dragon rushed forward again, straining against his will.

I want to touch this.

She could be a servant of the demon, Ashe thought, his resistance crumbling.

I want to touch this.

Yes, he thought silently, succumbing.

It began like a rapid boiling in the pit of his stomach, awareness rising with the temperature of his skin and the frequency of his respiration. Then, like the repercussion of a bowl of finest crystal falling onto cobbled stone, shattering in a final, terminal puff, clarity of sight and sound and mind followed, dilating his pupils and making his skin conduct electrical impulses of the tiniest frequency. His blood surged, primed for discovery, and his muscles knotted throughout his body to withstand the rush of his newly dominant nature.

The dragon roared forth, consuming him internally, taking the reins of control away. With a mind and sense born of the elements that made up the fabric of the universe, it expanded its awareness to the outward limits of its reach, making note of all things within a five-mile radius down to the most infinitesimal detail. The total number of lenses in the eyes of the ants within the cracks of the city streets was as evident to him as the state of the weather. That awareness then centered on the woman before him, to the exclusion of everything else.

First the dragon sought to find and define the source of the odd magic that emanated from her. It was singular, different from the two other sources, which were also unrecognized, and unique.

There was a music to her that touched every nerve in the dragon's mammoth network of senses, a song that came forth from her and was tied to the world around her; she must be a Singer of great power or potential, she might possibly even have attained Namer status. Though he himself knew nothing of the art of music and its use in other forms, he was fully cognizant of what power lay in it, and it made him crave to touch her more deeply, to learn this lore, to take it, even.

There was more to it, an exquisite blend of other elements.

He could sense she was out of time and space, but wasn't sure what that added up to. The concept excited him greatly; possibly she was only prescient, with the ability to see into the Future, but more than likely she was in fact Cymrian. There was a strong air of it about her, but that could be deceptive as well. There was more, but it was unknown to him; he assumed she was somehow tied to fire, the one element he couldn't recognize, being void of it himself.

Her physical form was a jubilee of observations. The outer edges of his senses swept over her, unabashedly drinking in all the information he could receive about her physical makeup. The heavy cloak by which she shielded her body from the eyes of the public was irrelevant to him, as were her clothes.

She was robustly healthy; the signature from her physical form swelled with life and energy and a surprising muscularity, given her size and stature. She was very small, even for a woman with Lirin blood, but her body was long and willowy, giving her a sense of height she did not merit. The lines of her figure were lithe; she was perfectly apportioned, with narrow shoulders, long arms, and longer, exquisite legs, the incredible beauty of which even the casual wool pants could not contain.

In addition to the sleek, long legs, her torso was long and slender, as was her beautiful neck. He found himself staring at the curving indentation at the hollow of her throat, imagining caressing it with lazy, warm kisses, breathing her in there.

That neck tapered down to a bosom that was in keeping with the rest of her, with breasts that were graceful and small, but perfectly formed. It was a good thing he could only sense their shape; he knew that the sight would reduce him to a quivering mass, mist cloak or no.

Her abdomen was slender and flat, and Ashe knew he could easily span her waist with both of his hands. She had the slim hips typical of the Lirin build. With great difficulty he stopped his physical assessment of her before his senses swung around behind her; he was afraid of what might happen if he allowed himself to continue.

Besides, the unpleasant side effect of such a search was

that the longing welled up in the corresponding places to those he had concentrated on; his lips were beginning to burn when he imagined kissing the hollow of her throat, his fingers stung at the thought of caressing her waist. Since the dragon required satisfaction to calm itself completely, he was buying a lifetime of permanent, though minor, discomfort if he never had the opportunity to touch her as he imagined. Given how well he was doing with her so far, he was unwilling to risk it, despite the fact it could never compare to the agony he carried anyway. For that reason, he forced the examination to stop here, before he turned to the shining hair that peeked out from under the hood. From what little he had seen already, he knew he would be helpless if he let himself think about it at all.

To keep himself from becoming even more entranced with her than he already was, the dragon searched for flaws, any imperfection that would prove she was real. Ashe found it on her fingers. They were well formed and soft, but the tips were hardened with dry calluses, owing to years of playing at least one stringed instrument. It was the only imperfection he could find.

The man, subservient by choice to his own dragon sense, shivered as the dragon's senses explored her more.

Her face was crafted as though by an expert sculptor lovingly working a lifetime on a masterpiece he would one day finish and commit to humankind. The features were all in perfect harmony with the possible exception of the large, deep-green eyes. They were fringed with thick black lashes and were intense in their colors, the whites very white against the dark green contrast. They sparkled with a light of their own; they were hypnotic, and even the dragon had a difficult time pulling away from them.

She's perfect, it said in ringing tones, inaudible to all but Ashe. *I want her.*

But behind the fascination of the dragon was the interest of the man. What appealed to him about her was altogether different. He could see that she was comfortable in her own skin, and confident, but if she had any idea as to the staggering nature of her own beauty it wasn't apparent in any of her outward signs.

She had a gentleness in her eyes that pulled him in, but only so far; there was pain there, too, pain the depth of which he could not even see a bottom to. He found himself wishing he knew what it was that troubled her so greatly, and knew he would go, without request, to the end of the Earth to find her the solution to it. When she laughed her eyes laughed first, and when she was angry, they were the bellwether of that emotion, too. Everything he was—secretive, solitary, hidden from sight—she was not. There was an openness to her that he envied, that he wanted to touch.

She is untouched, a virgin, whispered the dragon excitedly. *Perfect.* But within his subjugated awareness the man knew something more. There was a sensuality about her, too, an obvious knowledge of the charms of the flesh that bewildered him utterly. A virgin with the enchantments of a courtesan. It was too fascinating; she was a true paradox. He wanted to know more. His mind reached out to the Future.

As clearly as he saw her now, attired in traveling clothes and a soft gray hooded cloak and mantle, he could see her in her wedding gown, smiling at him, flowers in her hair. He allowed the fantasy to run further and pictured her in her wedding night peignoir, and could feel the heat rise to his face. He saw her cradling their child, and their grandchild. He could imagine her bent with age but unbowed, still beautiful; his throat tightened as he saw her in her shroud, white film netting covering the amazing eyes, closed now eternally.

The eyelashes returned to their open position.

"Yes?" she said. His dragon sense abated; his research was all accomplished in the blink of an eye, a verdant green eye.

"Why don't the two of you join me for lunch?" he said lightly. "Just to show there are no hard feelings."

The woman's eyes sparkled wickedly. "If there are no hard feelings, either I didn't do it right, or you are more grievously injured than I thought."

He laughed. "Maybe it's just because I didn't pay first."

The beautiful eyes opened in shock, then narrowed in anger. "Excuse me? What are you implying?"

Ashe knew immediately he had made a huge tactical error. "Nothing—I'm sorry, I was only kidding. I just think you're lovely enough to turn quite a profit as a courtesan." He winced; now the hole he was digging for himself was even bigger.

"You think I'm a courtesan?"

"No, not at all, I—"

"How dare you. Come along, Jo."

"Wait—I'm very sorry, please; don't stalk off."

"Stand aside."

"Look, really, I didn't mean to—"

"Get out of the way." The woman glared daggers at him, and guided the girl away and back toward the town square, keeping herself between them. He felt a wave of deep despair wash over him as they walked away, and whatever fear that she was a demonic minion that had remained vanished. He remembered that she had responded to humor, so he made a last-ditch effort.

"Does this mean we won't be having lunch?"

She whirled in the street. "Given the size of your coin purse, I doubt you would be able to treat both of us. In fact, you would be lucky to pay for yourself." She turned, and she and the girl disappeared into the crowd.

Ashe laughed aloud, causing a number of people around him to start in surprise; until they heard him, they had had no idea he was there.

42

"Don't say it; I know. I'm sorry."

"Are you insane? Losing your hand is looking more like a lucky option for you. You could have been killed."

Jo sighed. "I know."

Rhapsody came to an abrupt halt in the alley. "Why, Jo? I gave you money. Did you need more?"

"No." Jo reached into her pocket and drew forth the coins Rhapsody had given her. She held them out, as if to return them, but Rhapsody just stared at her hand. When she spoke again her tone was gentle.

"Tell me why, Jo."

Jo looked away. "I don't know."

Rhapsody reached up, grasped her face and turned it toward herself. Jo's expression was defiant, but in her eyes Rhapsody could see deep fear, and it went to her heart. It was a look she recognized, the street child's worry that she had alienated the only person in the world who cared about her. She loosened her grip on Jo's face, and caressed it gently.

"Well, at least you're all right. Let's go meet Achmed for lunch."

Jo's expression melted into astonishment. "That's it? You're not going to yell at me more than that?"

Rhapsody smiled. "Do you want me to? I'm not your mother, I'm your sister, and I've done more than my share of stupid things."

"Yeah? What kind of stupid things?"

"Didn't Achmed tell you anything about what happened in Bethany? Come on." She took Jo's hand and led her off through the streets toward the town square.

*A*chmed waited impatiently in front of the basilica at Bethe Corbair. It was noon; the sun had been directly overhead for a few minutes, and there was no sign of either of them. In the old world he could have sought their heartbeats to locate them and reassure himself of their safety, but things were different here; he had no power to find them.

Then he thought again. He had no power to find Jo, but Rhapsody was from the old world; he could still hear the sound of her heart. He would need a sheltered place to sit and concentrate.

Glancing around, Achmed located a small tavern with a few pine tables outside in the area near the street; the wood was wet from its covering of snow that had evidently melted with the thaw. He pulled out one of the benches under the table and brushed the pool of water off it, then sat down, grimacing.

He closed his eyes and tried to clear his mind of the noises around him in the street, in particular the bells of the basilica. Their sound was subject to the wind, and was unpredictable; they cluttered the vibrational landscape with inconsistent clamor.

Achmed opened his mouth slightly, allowing the icy wind

to fill it and whistle out again, as it would through a cave. His hands rested on the table in front of him; he raised one finger slightly, as if surreptitiously testing the breeze. This was the miniature version of his Hunting ritual, the means by which he had successfully plied his trade of assassination in the old land.

His Dhracian physiology blessed him with a skull structure of complex sinus cavities and long glands in the throat that vibrated with the rhythm of a particular pulse. He knew Rhapsody's heartbeat instinctively; he had walked, rested, crawled, fought, and slept beside it for what may have been centuries, if any of the history was to be believed. He could taste it on the wind.

She was nearby. He had found her heartbeat and now felt her approach. He started to close down his sensing when a foul taste filled his mouth, more sour than bile, more repulsive than vomit. It was a putrid taste with a stench of the grave to it; the taste of evil. And this time he was all but certain it had the stench of F'dor.

Rapidly he opened his eyes. Rhapsody and Jo were walking toward him on his left, coming from the southwest side of town. Achmed looked away from them for a moment, tracking the evil taint. It was coming from the north.

He turned to look as the sun crept behind the spire of the basilica with the passing of the hour of noon. In the momentary darkness that fell he saw a shadow in front of the basilica, but could place no pulse to it; it blended into the larger silhouette of the basilica itself. The air whistled through his mouth and nose again, taking the odor of evil with it as it left, cleansing his senses of the taint.

"Sorry we're late," Rhapsody said, shattering his concentration. She pulled out the bench opposite him. "Here, Jo, sit down. Have you been served yet, Achmed?"

Achmed looked back at her, swallowing his irritation. The sun crept out from behind the basilica, though it was behind him and he couldn't see it; he knew because a shaft of light fell on a lock Rhapsody's hair, making it gleam within her hood.

He turned around again to look for the shadow, but it was no longer in the same place. Instead he saw a man, someone it took several glances to discern, standing in the street before the basilica, looking their way.

Instantly his hackles went up; this was probably the shadow he had seen, but it gave off no signature that he could pick up on. The figure was cloaked and hooded, with his face completely hidden from view, and the sun as it appeared caught a thin veil of mist around him, almost as if steam was rising from him. Then, to his surprise and annoyance, the man began to walk toward them.

The tavernkeeper had opened the door and was carrying a rough-hewn tray of food to the customers who occupied another outside table. Achmed recognized the smell instantly: mutton. He hated mutton. His mood blackened visibly, causing the smile on Rhapsody's face to vanish abruptly, to be replaced with a look of concern.

"What's the matter?"

Jo leaned closer. "It's him. He's coming."

"Who?" Rhapsody craned her neck to look behind Achmed's shoulder.

"That man from the market." Jo flushed red, either from embarrassment or excitement; it was difficult to tell.

Rhapsody rose from the bench, looking annoyed. Out of the corner of her eye she saw Achmed return to his position facing her with his back to the approaching man; she saw him draw a dagger. The fact that she was able to see him do it was his way of telling her that he was armed and ready; she nodded imperceptibly as Grunthor would have. She was becoming accustomed to the silent language.

"What do you want?" she demanded. The man stopped in his tracks.

"Sorry," said the voice from within the hood. It was a pleasant baritone, with an interesting dryness to it. There also was a sweetness to the voice. "I came to apologize for my earlier rudeness."

"You did already; now please go away."

"I was hoping you would allow me to make up for my offensive comment by buying you both lunch." There was a pause as the man looked down at Achmed. "And your friend as well, of course."

Achmed said nothing; he watched Rhapsody's face, waiting

for his cue. She was thinking; she turned and looked at Jo, who could barely contain her excitement. Achmed saw Rhapsody's brows furrow in puzzlement as she surveyed her new sister, and then she turned back to face the man who stood behind him. Her glance moved down to Achmed.

"What do you think?"

"If he was rude to you, send him away," he said in an even tone. "He might do it again, and then I would have to kill him. I don't want to have to defend your honor before I've had lunch; it gives me indigestion."

The man behind him chuckled; it was all Achmed could do to remain seated. Rhapsody smiled.

"I think we can chance it," she said, turning to Jo again. "What do you think?"

"Yes, definitely," Jo said, the words tripping over themselves.

"Very well," Rhapsody said, pointing to the place next to Achmed, "why don't you sit there?"

"What's your name?" asked Jo, shifting eagerly in her seat.

"Ashe," said the stranger. He looked toward the inn; the tavernkeeper was approaching. "And yours?"

"Jo," she blurted excitedly. "And this is Rhapsody, and— ow!" Her words were choked off as her sister gave her a vicious pinch on the thigh.

"It's a pleasure to meet you, Jo," said the hooded man. He turned to Rhapsody, who was glaring at Jo. "Rhapsody. What a beautiful name. Are you a musician?"

"Yes, she—ow! Stop that!" Jo demanded as she moved her leg away.

The man coughed into his hand for a moment; Achmed was sure he could sense a smile beneath the hood. "Is Jo short for something else? Joanna? Joella?"

Jo turned red to the roots of her pale blond hair. "Josephine," she said, her voice cracking.

Rhapsody stared at her in amazement. She had been unable to coerce this information out of her newly adopted sister; now Jo was confiding it to a stranger.

"Also a lovely name, to be sure. And you, sir? What may I call you?"

Achmed turned for the first time to look at the man. He

could see the very tip of an unkempt beard, but nothing else. "I think 'sir' will do just fine."

"Don't be rude, Achmed," said Jo, an annoyed tone in her voice.

Achmed scowled at her. Her mouth was flapping, clearly unhinged from her brain. Jo understood the need to keep a name in reserve; she had done it herself. Before she could compromise them further, the tavernkeeper was at their table, asking what their pleasure was.

Jo ordered the mutton, Rhapsody plain bread and cheese. Achmed and Ashe both ordered stew simultaneously, then looked at each other as if reconsidering their choice. The tavernkeeper had jumped when Ashe spoke; he would have overlooked him completely had he not spoken up.

Achmed's final glower seemed to have gotten the message to Jo at last; she sat in sullen silence during much of the meal. Rhapsody attempted to make up for the awkwardness by chatting charmingly with the stranger, who had both women laughing by the end of lunch. Achmed listened to him carefully; he found the man's brand of easy banter annoying but without rancor or insistent prying. His stomach was roiling; the smell of Jo's mutton ruined the stew. He couldn't wait to be done.

Finally the meal was over. Ashe and the women had discussed the thaw in the weather, the bells of the basilica, and their impressions of the quality and availability of goods in the marketplace; nothing of substance. Achmed stood up, pushing the bench back from underneath himself and Ashe, nothing the lightning-quick response of the stranger, who managed to rise and be out of the way before the seat disappeared from under him.

"Where are you headed now?" Jo asked as the stranger pulled forth an oversized coin purse from the folds of his cloak; he held it up for a moment and Rhapsody laughed while Jo colored in embarrassment.

Ashe threw two silver coins on the table, sufficient to pay for their meal generously. "South. And yourselves?"

Before Rhapsody could stop her, Jo blurted again. "We're going to live in Canrif."

The stranger shuddered visibly; Achmed made note. "Why?"

"Well, I don't know that we're going to *live* there," Rhapsody corrected. "We're going to observe it. It seems an interesting place."

"That's one way of putting it," Ashe said dryly. "Do you expect to be there long?"

"She just told you we don't know," Achmed snapped.

"Why do you ask?" Rhapsody asked hurriedly.

"Well, if you will be there more than a few months, I will be back in that area again. Perhaps I will drop by and see how you're doing."

"Yes! You'd be welcome," said Jo, then she quickly became silent under the glance from Rhapsody and the glare from Achmed.

"We might be there still; it's hard to say," Rhapsody said, rising herself from the bench with Jo. "You're welcome to check, of course, if you're in the area anyway."

"I may do that. Well, good luck to all of you. I hope your journey is pleasant. Good day." Ashe bowed to the women, nodded to Achmed, then turned and started away into the town square. After a few feet he stopped and turned to Rhapsody once more.

"I hope I've made up for my rudeness in some small way. I apologize again."

"Accepted," she said, smiling. "Please don't think about it another moment." The stranger bowed again, then disappeared into the crowd and was gone.

Rhapsody turned to Jo and smiled. "See, things do turn around quickly, don't they? It's a good thing you didn't get away with stealing his purse, Jo; otherwise we would have to pay for lunch ourselves."

Achmed sat back down and pointed at the other bench, indicating he wanted the women to do so as well. "At least you might have had enough left over to buy some heavy, strong thread, the kind suitable for sewing lips shut." Jo flushed, looking mortified.

"Shut up," Rhapsody snapped. "Don't talk to her like that."

"Fine; then I'll pose my question to you. Who was that, and why did he follow you?"

The women sat back down, Rhapsody's brow furrowing in thought. "I don't know any more than you do now, Achmed. We came across him in the street and he invited us to lunch."

"What did he say to you? What was this rudeness he mentioned?"

Rhapsody looked at Jo, who appeared on the verge of tears. She took the girl's hand under the table and stroked it comfortingly, turning Achmed's question over in her mind, replaying their meeting point by point.

She thought back to the events leading up to the moment when his attributes were in her hand. She had given the area in question a playful squeeze. *They seem fine to me. Is the feeling returning yet?*

The feeling was never gone; that was not the problem. But you could say that it has changed. They really need a more thorough examination.

She had laughed, apologized and started to walk away with Jo.

Wait.

Yes? She had felt a tingle pass along her skin. When this would happen to her as a child, her father would say that a goose had walked over her grave. The strange cloaked man invited them to lunch, and then insulted her. He presumed she was a courtesan, and she had taken offense; she left with Jo in a huff.

"Nothing, really. He's a flirt, Achmed, and a bad one at that. I don't think there's any more to it. I didn't find his company unpleasant, even though you seem to have."

"And is he responsible for the earrings, too?"

Rhapsody flushed; she had forgotten about the jewelry. "No, they were a gift from the merchant for helping him spare his wares during a street mishap with some oxcarts."

"Hmm. Well, let's not belabor it. We have a few hours before we need to meet up with Grunthor. Let's explore the city. I think it may teach us a great deal about Canrif, since much of Bethe Corbair seems to have been built in response to fear of the Firbolg."

"I thought the Cymrians built Bethe Corbair," Rhapsody said, folding her napkin. "Lord Stephen said they built the basilica."

"The city proper, yes. But if you look carefully, you'll notice that, unlike the other provincial capitals in Roland we have seen, Bethe Corbair has an inner city, with fine architecture designed by artisans, and a newer, outer city, built almost entirely of stone and mortar, designed by soldiers as a livable barricade. There don't seem to be many farms or villages on the outskirts of the city; the few settlements that do exist are right outside the city walls. It's the outer city that should give us some answers."

"Sounds good. I'll be right back," Rhapsody said, rising once more. "I want to have a look at the bell tower before we go." She patted Jo's shoulder and trotted across the street to the southern side of the basilica.

Jo watched her cross, then turned to Achmed. "She caused that accident, you know."

He gave her a sharp glance. "What do you mean?"

"The oxcarts that ran into each other. I was across the street when it happened. People had been looking at her all morning, even with her hood up. Then she pulled it down to put the earrings on, and the drivers of those oxcarts stopped watching where they were going and smashed into each other. After that, men were dropping flowers in her path, trying to get her attention. She picked them up and handed them back, thinking the idiots had let them fall by accident. It was really strange."

Achmed nodded. He had seen the same thing ever since they had left the Root.

"And she has no idea," Jo said.

"No. And I doubt she ever will."

The three who had gone into the city met up with Grunthor as the sun was setting over the thatched fields on the outskirts of Bethe Corbair. They exchanged information and impressions, then took stock of their supplies, which they had replenished in the city.

"I'm now even more convinced a visit to Canrif is worthwhile," Achmed said as they ate their evening meal. "It sounds like a substantial power base, heavy with resources, but lacking organization. What they need is leadership. They're ripe for the picking, unless I miss my guess."

"What does that mean?" Rhapsody asked, wiping her mouth on her napkin.

Achmed looked up into the sky. Night was coming, heady with promise and excitement. "The Bolg need a king; I know one who might be willing to take the job."

"You?" Rhapsody asked incredulously.

Achmed looked at her. "What's wrong with me?" he asked in mock offense.

"I didn't realize you were of royal blood."

Both the Firbolg laughed aloud. "Only the races of men believe in that preordained, divine-right-of-kings nonsense," said Achmed. "Class structure means nothing among the Bolg. You rule when you're qualified to do so, either by strength, or by ingenuity. I hope to offer both."

Rhapsody stared into the campfire in silence. Though his words made sense to her, they clashed with a deeply ingrained belief in the limits of her own class. But then, even that was topsy-turvy now. Llauron had called her a peasant in the same breath he had sent her to meet the duke.

"I think it's likely we'll fit in very well there, even you two non-Bolg," Achmed said.

"Agreed," mumbled Grunthor, chewing on a pork shank. "Oi think we might find a place to establish your own outpost."

"Among the Firbolg?" Jo demanded. Her demeanor had returned to normal. "I don't want to be left alone among them. They're monsters."

"Let's see what it's like and give it a chance," said Rhapsody, watching her two companions from the old world. "There are a lot of myths about the Bolg that are greatly exaggerated. I'd be willing to wager they're not monsters at all. We might even get to like them."

Achmed and Grunthor merely smiled and finished their supper.

43

The four companions camped that night on the northern-most edge of the Krevensfield Plain, the wide-open lands that stretched as far as the eye could see between Bethe Corbair and the Teeth, the mountains that formed the fortress barrier of the Bolglands.

The field wrapped around the city on three sides, so the travelers headed east until Bethe Corbair and its surrounding settlements were no longer in sight. When the night came they were surrounded by an all-encompassing sphere of stars and darkness. It was a lonely sensation, as though they were the only living things in the world, and as a result they stayed up quite late, talking to each other as a means of warding off the desolation.

Wrapped in darkness as she was, Rhapsody thought back to the emptiness she had felt during the endless journey along the Root. While that had been a constant struggle, a fear of giving in to her own feelings of panic, now she felt utterly alone, vulnerable, lost here among the stars.

She drew her cloak around herself and thought of her grandchildren, as she often did when the night was loneliest. Were Gwydion and Melisande safe in their fortress of rosy brown stone, with their father's army to protect them? All their wealth and privilege had not kept them from devastating loss; perhaps nothing could protect anyone from it. Rhapsody reached out and gently brushed a lock of pale hair off Jo's forehead. Nothing.

The fire had died down, the hot embers casting flickering shadows on the sleeping faces of her companions, the only friends she now had in the world. Rhapsody sighed brokenly, painfully, and continued her watch, trying to avoid looking up into the eternal blackness above her.

The gray mist of dawn still found her solemn. Her companions rose sleepily, grumpy in the last vestiges of sleep. Rhapsody reached into the campfire, still merrily blazing.

"*Slypka*," she said, watching the fire snuff out in a thin

wisp of smoke that vanished almost as quickly. It was a word she had learned early on in Namer training, roughly translated as *extinguish*. It eliminated every trace of fire or mist, or anything that hung, vaporous, in the air. She often wished the word could be applied to other things, such as bad dreams or haunting memories.

When morning broke they started out as the snow began to fall again. Over the course of their journey the winter weather returned, making traveling difficult and tempers short. The howling wind was both a curse and a blessing; in addition to sparking some of their angry confrontations, it swallowed their verbal exchanges, sparing their friendships.

Four days passed, and the wide plain of Roland, known as the Orlandan Plateau, began to take on a hillier aspect, with attributes that were more akin to steppes than open fields. These rocky fields were the precursors to the foothills of the Teeth.

After more than a week the mountains themselves came into sight, rising above the steppes in the distance, jagged and sharp against the sky of the horizon. Gwylliam had called these crags the Manteids, the Seers, in honor of his wife and her sisters, but Time had erased that name, and now they were known across the land by their more fanglike description. It was an apt one.

It took another three days before they were in the foothills, the mountains growing closer all the time. When she first sighted them Rhapsody thought they were uniformly brown, dark reaches that rose threateningly skyward.

As they grew closer she could see that they were in fact a multiplicity of colors and hues, blends of black and purple, green and blue, stretching toward the clouds in many peaks and crags within each mountain. They were at once beautiful and forbidding, standing a silent watch between the world of men and the hidden realm of the Firbolg beyond.

Finally, after two more days, they came to the feet of the mountains. They had been in the steppes for half that time, semi-hills that undulated across the now-rocky plateau, with steep rises and deep swales spanning the landscape. At the top of a particularly tall rise Achmed stopped; the others followed his lead.

Below them, cloaked in snow, lay a great bowl-like amphitheater, cut into the earth by time and nature, enhanced, perhaps, by the work of men. It was vast in size and breadth, surrounded by rocky ledges and rimmed internally in gradated rings that leveled out onto a wide, flat floor, buried in snow and the debris from centuries of neglect. Rhapsody recognized it instantly from the writings in the notebook.

"This is Gwylliam's Great Moot," she told the others excitedly, her voice echoing off the sides and disappearing into the snowpack. "According to the writings, the Cymrians used to meet in council in times of need or celebration. The entire populace could fit within the Moot, which served as the meeting place. This is where Gwylliam and Anwyn held court with all their subjects in attendance."

"It's a *cwm*," said Grunthor, using the word from the old world for the crater formed by a glacier or volcano. He closed his eyes and inhaled the frosty air; it was snowing lightly, making it difficult to see. Through his feet he felt at one with the Earth here, even more than when he had just emerged from the Root. It was a place with layers of history, and the Earth whispered the secrets to him now in the silence of his heart.

The base was the ancient time, long ago, when the Bowl was formed. The great Moot had once been a glacial lake, dug by the freezing and thawing of ice on the mountain faces of the Teeth when they were young. The glacier had carved the Bowl of the Moot as a vessel for the melting tears of the great wall of moving ice. As the land warmed, the lake had sunk into the earth or sent its water skyward, dried by the sun, leaving the amphitheater hewn into the mountainside. That was the first layer.

Then came the layer of the old days, when man polished what Nature had carved into a gathering place for the people that came to live on the land. The power of the land, and the people who walked it, who gathered here, had melded, forming an Age the like of which the world had never seen, nor would it see again.

And there was now, the sleeping time, when it lay, forgotten and desolate beneath the shroud of snow. Even dormant, there was no mistaking its immense power. Grunthor opened his eyes, returning from his reverie, looking around for the others.

Achmed had located a pathway through the foothills, and was concentrating on finding the easiest route to where they wanted to go.

As his mind wandered over the terrain, he could see a series of passes in the mountains, larger than mountain-goat trails but smaller than roads, that crisscrossed the landscape, providing somewhat accessible paths from crag to crag and through the twisting hills.

Mountain to mountain and beyond, over the heath at the top of the world and deep into the Hidden Realm, hundreds of roadways and bridges scored the land. Some clearly traveled, others forgotten by time, the trails opened up the high country that Nature had never intended to be accessible. The system was an engineering marvel, and looked like the work of mountain dwellers, the Nain of the old land, earth-movers and miners of incomparable skill. *Gwylliam's handiwork*, he noted.

As his mind's eye wandered over the land, he could see them. In the distance of his second sight, tiny figures, black in the morning light, traveled the paths, hiding in the shadows. Kin that he had never known, and planned to one day rule.

"This is the place that Gwylliam called Canrif," he said to the others. "There are Firbolg scattered throughout the Teeth in roving packs; there seems little, if any, organization."

"And that's what you were hoping for, wasn't it?" Rhapsody asked. "Ripe for the picking, isn't that what you said?"

Achmed smiled. "Yes."

For a race of beings that had sprung up from the caves, the Firbolg seemed oddly reluctant to journey outside at night. The four companions watched from half a league away, noting their movements and counting the intrepid ones willing to venture outside the Teeth, looking for food or prey. When twilight came, however, the Bolg became fewer and farther between until finally an hour went by with none in sight.

"Night blindness," Achmed said; Grunthor nodded in agreement.

"How strange," Rhapsody murmured, straining to see the mountain passes as darkness took the Teeth. "You would think cave dwellers would be especially good at seeing in the dark."

"They are, underground, where there's no light at all, not even the glow we had on the Root. It's the darkness of the air in the world above that confounds their sight." Achmed looked around to ensure that Jo had not heard him.

Rhapsody shuddered at the memory of the Axis Mundi, then returned to her watch. "Yellow roots and green-leafed vegetables."

Grunthor gave her a strange look. "Eh?"

"Two of the cures for night blindness. One of the famous legends you learn when you study lore as a Singer tells of a great Lirin army that became invincible by changing its diet; it gained nightsight by eating certain foods. All its enemies were still night-blind, so the Lirin only attacked in the dark."

Achmed nodded, making note. "Are there any other remedies beside vegetables?"

"Liver," Rhapsody said. Jo made a gagging sound.

"Maybe they're not night-blind after all," said Grunthor. "The Bolg ought to get enough o' that just eatin' their enemies."

"What enemies?" Rhapsody asked, ignoring the cannibalistic comment. "Bethe Corbair is their nearest neighbor, and it doesn't look like there's been a raid there in the lifetime of anyone who lives there."

"No, it doesn't," Achmed agreed. "And from what Grunthor gleaned from his reconnaissance, Sorbold, the kingdom on the other side of that mountain range, is effectively kept out by the Teeth and the rough terrain in between. So there doesn't seem to be much external raiding. I imagine they prey on each other."

Rhapsody shuddered again. "Wonderful. Are you sure this is where you want to live?"

Achmed smiled. "It will be."

Snow had crept into the crevasses in the foothills and hardened, forming frosty stepping-stones on which it was difficult to maintain purchase. Jo had fallen half a dozen times, once almost tragically.

"How much farther?" Rhapsody shouted into the screaming wind. She stared down into the canyon below them, a sheer cliff stretching down several hundred feet to the floor of the steppes.

"Almost there," Achmed called back. Leaning at the waist on the rockwall, he hoisted himself up onto an rocky out-cropping, then crawled onto the ledge above. He lay flat and extended a hand to Rhapsody, hauling her easily over the ledge as well.

Rhapsody cast a glance around to be sure they were unob-served before joining him on the ground to help pull Jo up. She secured the rope while Achmed slid his hands under Jo's arms, dragging her up to safety. The teenager was trembling with exhaustion and cold. Once she was firmly on the flat surface Rhapsody wrapped her cloak around Jo and concen-trated on the fire within herself, trying to impart warmth to her sister.

A few moments later the spike on Grunthor's helmet ap-peared, and with a smooth motion he pulled himself onto the ledge.

"Well, that was fun," he said. "Ya all right, Duchess? Lit'le miss?"

"We need to get her to shelter, out of the wind," Rhapsody answered, her own teeth chattering. She could no longer feel her fingers or the tip of her nose.

Achmed was bending down near them both, and nodded. "Take just a moment, Rhapsody, and look up. See what our fellow Seren have wrought, and destroyed."

She turned and gazed around her. Rising out of the whirling snow was a mammoth stone edifice, carved into the very face of the mountain before them. It stood, black against the sky and nestled within the crags of the whole of the mountain range. Giant walls, hewn smooth and camouflaged to blend into the rock, led up to dark openings that appeared to be towers and ramparts, though of a size that was incomprehen-sible to her. Anything else they had seen since arriving in this land, the basilicas and cities, the keeps and castles, were dwarfed by comparison.

No wonder the populace thought of Gwylliam as a godlike figure, she thought, her eyes unable to take in all of the structure from her vantage point on the cliff. It was as though the hand of the Creator Himself had carved this out of the mountainside, this seemingly endless series of walls and crumbling bridges, barricades and roadways, tunnels and bulwarks stretching across the center of the mountain range and over the vast heath beyond. A city for giants, not men of Grunthor's size, but of titanic proportions, hidden from sight among the Teeth. Canrif.

"Is there a tunnel you think might be safe?" she shouted over the whine of the wind. "Jo's freezing."

"Can you walk?"

"Yes."

"All right, let Grunthor carry Jo, and you come with me. There's a cave not too far from here, blocked by a boulder I'm sure Grunthor and I can force out of the way. The Bolg won't go there. Take hold of my cloak so you don't get lost if the visibility gets worse."

Rhapsody nodded and grasped the edge of his cape, tucking her free hand inside her cloak, and grimly followed him out of the storm.

Once inside the tunnel, the howling wind diminished, leaving their stinging ears pulsing. Shards of falling rock and dust covered them, filling their eyes and nostrils, as Grunthor shoved the boulder back in place, leaving only the smallest of openings, so the Bolg would not detect their hiding place.

Rhapsody coughed and brushed the grit off her head and shoulders, then helped Jo do the same. The teenager was still bleary-eyed but coming around from the trauma of the climb.

"Where is this place, do you think?" she asked.

Achmed looked into the darkness of the huge tunnel. Smooth tiles lined the walls around and above, rectangles of ancient stone honed into perfect symmetry. Long trenches, probably gutters, scored each side of the tunnel, while a series of drainage holes were visible in the ceiling overhead, clogged now with centuries-old rust and debris.

"I'd guess it's part of the aqueduct, probably a drainage tunnel. There were dozens of them within Canrif itself, diverting the rainwater and runoff from the mountain springs through the general water system, and carrying off whatever excess remained into the canyon below. Since wells would have been impossible this far up in the mountain, it provided a ready supply of water for drinking and other uses, while preventing flooding. The sketches in the Cymrian museum were very detailed."

Rhapsody fumbled in her pack and pulled out the journal they had found in the House of Remembrance.

"This isn't much help," she said after a quick examination. "I wish I had paid more attention to what you were looking at in the museum."

Achmed chuckled. "You underestimate the scope of this place, Rhapsody. Canrif wasn't a mere citadel, or even a city in the mountains. It was a nation unto itself. The fortress within the Teeth is only a very small part of it. Beyond the canyon and the Blasted Heath is the bulk of it, forests and vineyards and mines and villages, cities and temples and universities, or at least that was what composed Canrif in the Cymrian days. I doubt the Bolg have kept it up, however.

"I wasn't able to see but a fraction of the plans. I could see there was a water system, and ventilation units to bring fresh air into the mountain, and great forges in the belly of the rock, whose residual heat they used for warmth. Whatever else Gwylliam was, he was a visionary, someone who could design and execute the building of a living, functioning world from nothing but solid rock and ingenuity. We could never have committed it all to memory if we had studied it for a month."

Rhapsody crouched near a pile of crumbled stone, recently fallen. She laid her hands on the rocks and felt the fire within her swell, then directed the heat into the stone. "So what's next?" she asked as the rocks began to glow red.

Achmed was dragging food supplies out of his pack. "After we've had something to eat, I'm going on a bit of a scouting expedition. Grunthor, you stay with them, and if I'm not back in a few days, take them back to Bethe Corbair."

"Had it occurred to you that we might actually deserve a say in where we go, especially in your absence?" Rhapsody asked angrily.

Achmed blinked. "All right; if I don't come back, where do you want be taken?"

Rhapsody and Jo looked at each other. "Probably Bethe Corbair."

The Dhracian laughed. "And they say Bolg are unnecessarily contentious. Don't worry, I'll be back. I just want to pay a little visit to my future subjects."

44

Contrary to the timetable in Cymrian legends, the Bolg had actually inhabited parts of the mountains long before Gwylliam's war ended. The Lord Cymrian had been too engaged to care that a ratty population of cave dwellers found its way across the eastern steppes and into some of the older sections of his vast labyrinth. The Bolg were aware of him, however, and quietly opened a hidden front inside Gwylliam's realm. Minor reports of lost Cymrian patrols or stores unaccounted for were hidden in the greater and bloodier balance sheets of the battles against Anwyn.

The Bolg were not heroes, or soldiers; they were cruel and considered anything they could catch worth eating. They had stolen fire and the concept of war, and they could live in any climate or terrain, though they were poor builders.

Centuries before, some distant warlord had enslaved several tribes of them and found them tractable when well fed, but upon his death, they destroyed his estate, stayed for a short time, then wandered somewhere else. His survivors theorized that, not unlike wolves, they obeyed him because they felt he was one of their own. That was a unique situation; most of mankind they viewed as prey, not partners.

The groups that inhabited Gwylliam's mountains were an unmatched lot of refugees and savages fleeing bad weather or poor hunting. Some had been chased out of their previous homes by greater strength. This faction of Bolg brought with them in retreat the weapons and harsh view they had of the world; encounters with them were uniformly unpleasant.

After Gwylliam discovered the Bolg, he made halfhearted

attempts to exterminate them. He set traps, sent contingents into their lairs, but that only served to weed out the stupid and the weak. It was Grunthor's observation that Gwylliam had perfected the Bolg. They had come to his forges flawed and he had made them sharp and hard. They were a weapon he never had a chance to use against Anwyn.

𝒯he day after the companions took up residence in a sealed-off drainpipe of the Canrif aqueduct, a party of ragged Bolg hunters cornered a subterranean wolf in the Killing Hall deep within the Teeth. The hall was the traditional spot to which game was lured, a killing ground for the larger animals or hominid intruders that were unfortunate enough to be chosen by the Firbolg for slaughter.

The Bolg had found the ancient corridor after the Cymrians had been routed and fled. It was massively long and twisting, with a heavy stone door at the end that they had been unable to unlock or pry open. So instead they trapped their victims there, though it was not always in their favor to do so.

It appeared to have been a mistake this time; the wolf was winning. Prehistoric mammals the size of a large bear, the subterranean variety of the species were ferocious creatures, solitary and vicious, with the musculature of an animal that survived and hunted in underground tunnels with the eyesight to match.

This one had already taken out one of its Firbolg predators and was chewing on an unfortunate second when the dark man came. He arrived without being noticed, managing to appear at the precise moment when the hunting party had determined itself outweighed and were tottering on the edge of flight.

At first they did not see him, his flowing black garments blending into the inky darkness around him. Instead, it was the voice they heard, sandy and full of snarling spit, speaking in a tongue that they recognized as an older version of their own.

"Down." The word bounced up and down the corridor like the green wood of the hunters' crude arrows against the stone.

The Bolg reacted as if they were travelers turning into a strong wind. One folded himself against the floor, others turned slowly toward the source of the word. What they saw froze them where they stood, making it impossible to obey the growled command.

The dark man's hood had fallen back as he drew his long, straight sword over his shoulder. The face was frightening, even to the Bolg, and unknown to them, but it held a kinship as well, a familiarity that made them realize that this was, in a very disturbing way, one of them.

The figure made a blurred movement and light whistled through the dark corridor. The slender sword spun end over end and pierced the throat of the rampant monster that had risen over the body of one of its victims. The fire was still in the wolf's eyes as its deep growl choked off and the beast fell.

The dark man was there as it did, moving to retrieve his sword with speed akin to that of the weapon's deadly flight. He stood in the midst of the hunting party; all were armed, but none made a move until he reached to pull his sword from the neck of the wolf.

As he touched the fur in which it was buried, the Bolg hunter who had fallen to the floor slashed at his legs with a wicked-looking hook that had been honed on the inside edge. The dark man broke the hunter's wrist with the first stamp of his heel, and then his neck with a fierce kick. He stood for a moment and met the gaze of each of the remaining hunters before reaching down again. This time there was only the feathery sound of the blade's exit from the tangled fur.

"Good hunting." The black-cloaked man turned and melted into the darkness.

Frint's pallid eyes glittered in the reflection from the embers of the small fire. He had barely touched the belly meat and shank of the wolf, accorded to him as the one who had brought the kill back to the clan.

"Man was like the night," he whispered to the others. The children, watching from behind their mothers with great interest, were pushed back, only to wriggle forward again to better hear the tale the great hunter was telling. "Did not see him come."

"What wanted he?" demanded Nug-Claw, the clan chieftain.

Frint shook his head. "Nothing. Killed wolf, and Ranik. Ranik tried to hook him. Man stamped him out like a firespark." He shuddered, and the children retreated a little.

"Took no meat?" Nug asked. Frint shook his head. "Said nothing?"

Frint thought for a moment. "Blessed the hunt."

Nug's eyes widened. "And?"

"After we left Killing Hall, found two goats and rat. Got all."

A murmur of fearful excitement swept through the clan. Nug's woman spoke.

"Maybe Night Man is god." Nug aimed a blow at her, but she dodged out of the way.

"Not god. Nug is clan-god. But we beware Night Man. Must warn all of Ylorc."

Frint blinked rapidly. "Maybe Night Man is all-Bolg-god."

In the shadows behind Nug, Achmed smiled and slipped away into the darkness.

𝕿he walls of Canrif's labyrinthine tunnels had crumbled somewhat over time, leaving uneven roadways where the detritus had eventually hardened into mounds and pits. The obstacles meant nothing to Achmed's ease of passage and silence, but left him feeling strangely sad at the neglect of what had once been a majestic fortress.

In Canrif's heyday the tunnels had each been wider than a city street and smooth, carved and polished painstakingly from the basalt of the mountain's interior, laid out with mathematical precision. Formidable and confusing from the exterior to thwart attackers, they were systematic and easy to predict from the inside. At one time they had been lined with sconces that had illuminated the great underground complex. Now all that remained were the broken bases, still attached to the walls, or holes where the sconces had been.

The enthusiastic pulsing of his own heart brought an awareness to Achmed of the secret delight he was taking in his mission. This sort of work brought him back to the old days, the era of his training, the time when the race of F'dor was engaging in a campaign of extermination against the Dhracians.

He had reveled in those journeyman days, before his invention of the cwellan, before his ascension to the rank of the world's foremost assassin, when he still had to make his reputation one killing at a time, letting his name slip on the wind ahead of him, leaving it behind like his signet.

He slid through the shadows now as the tunnel emptied into a wide, cavernlike room, something he recognized as a guard barracks by the contours of the floor and the stairs that had once been wall-mounted beams, the actual weapons racks and bunks long gone or decayed. Even the soldiers' quarters had at one time been beautifully appointed, with an elongated domed ceiling on which peeling frescoes of historic battle scenes could still be faintly seen, the paint cracked and marred with time.

Achmed stared up at the corroded figures, images of soldiers in combat, musing. The science of combat was dictated by the philosophy of connection, the art of making a deadly impact on one's opponent, clinging to the enemy, making contact over and over again until the enemy could no longer withstand the connection.

It was a rubric which worked very well in explaining the motives and actions of F'dor. The demonic spirits clung fast to their hosts by necessity; it was a fact of their existence. Connection was required of them in order to survive. It was little wonder, then, that F'dor hated the Dhracians.

Dhracians, unlike fighters of other races, subscribed not to the philosophy of connection but to one of separateness. Detachment from the fight meant a keener perspective into flaws and chinks in armor. It was the finding of places where the enemy's weapon was *not*, where the armor was *not*, that Dhracians relied upon to give them entrée into the places between the blows, below the armor. It was this detachment that made the Dhracians anathema to the F'dor, beings who had to cling by nature, had to be connected, or cease to exist.

It had occurred to Achmed back when he and Grunthor first observed the explosions of inexplicable violence that perhaps the violence itself was really the intention all along.

While Tsoltan had been a strategic thinker, with a long world-view, it was possible that whatever was now causing men to erupt in senseless mayhem did not need a master plan, or an end goal. Perhaps it was just the power, the friction caused by men connecting with each other through violence, that it sought, that gave it life, and strength.

His contemplation was interrupted by sounds of strife in the tunnel on the other side of the barracks. Achmed trotted across the vast room, taking care to remain within the shadows, and stopped at the tunnel entrance. He breathed deeply and let his mind follow the path through the tunnel to the source of the grim noise.

His second sight did not have to go far to find it. Ahead in the tunnel a ragtag crowd of Bolg was brawling, slashing at each other with fragments of spears and what may once have been swords. There were markings from two different clans, one sign etched in the faces of its members, the other inscribed on their forearms. A screaming female with an arm-sign was pinned to the ground by two from the face-marked clan, doubtless the prize for the victorious chieftain. Achmed unslung the cwellan.

The Night Reavers were on the brink of winning when lightning whistled through the tunnel, cutting down both chieftains. The Bolg stood stock-still, watching the bodies topple and fall, each with the same slash across the throat, front and back, where the shining blades had entered and exited, ripping through one on its way to the other. The partially detached heads wandered in and out of the rapidly forming pools of blood.

A man formed out of the darkness in the hallway before them. With little more than a whisper the blackness around him became robes and a hood, beneath which two piercing eyes could be seen, looking them up and down.

One of the Reavers had heard the stories from the Killing Hall.

"Night Man." The word carried with it a primal fear that was palpable.

The Night Man took a step forward, and the Bolg of both clans rushed to the walls. He bent to pick up a broken sword and tossed it to the woman, then turned back to the others.

"Run," he said. Even the Bolg could recognize the whisper of death in the colorless voice.

In a blind panic, the tunnel emptied of both clans, stumbling and tripping in their haste to obey. Only the woman hesitated for a moment, and so she alone caught a glimpse of the smile beneath the hood. Then she turned and followed her clansmen, leaving the darkness to swallow the Night Man again.

The four companions returned to the Killing Hall later that night. Achmed had led them through the easiest of the passes in the Teeth; the route was a little longer but avoided the interior tunnels as much as possible. Jo could not see well in the dark, and though Rhapsody had survived the dimness of their endless journey along the Root, becoming accustomed to the lack of light, she was uncomfortable within the Earth, at least initially.

They had been attacked twice on their way across the crags.

"Twice too often," said Rhapsody as they entered the caves.

"Half as much as we should o' been," said Grunthor, wiping off his snickersnee. "Pathe'ic. It's gonna take some real work to get these lads in shape."

"Well, not those lads," said Jo, looking back at the bodies from the unsuccessful ambush. Grunthor cuffed her playfully.

Achmed raised his hand, and the other three fell silent. They followed him down the twisting pathways, the stone cold and crumbling from neglect and time. Rhapsody shuddered. The desolation within the mountain was tangible; she could feel it in the air around her.

When they passed a large opening in the hallway, Rhapsody stopped for a moment and looked through the portal. She could see a ledge that led out above an enormous cavern. She turned questioningly to Achmed, who nodded.

Stepping past the opening, she looked over the rim of the ledge. In the colossal space that surrounded her a heavy wind blew, thick with dust, and none of the freshness of the air of the open world. She shielded her eyes and looked down into the blackness at her feet.

Below her spread a vast, ruined city, dark and silent. Streets and buildings, broken and decaying, stretched to the edges of her vision. She could see places where fountains and gardens had once been, now standing dead and quiet, the life in them long since dried up. Yet despite the squalor there was evidence of order and beauty in the design of it, architecture that in its lifetime had far outstripped that of Bethany or Navarne. Now fading into history, crumbling in a melancholy state of anonymous rot.

Gwylliam's great masterpiece, Rhapsody thought sadly. *Canrif*, the word meaning *century*. Surely just the carving of the cavern's great firmament that reached up into the peaks of the Teeth above them must have been the life's work of thousands of men. It still stood, a hollow testament to the hollow vision of a hollow genius, who had thrown it arrogantly away. Now it was nothing more than a hollow shell, sheltering packs of roving demi-humans who walked its crumbling tunnels, oblivious of the glory that had once been.

Achmed touched her shoulder. "The Killing Hall isn't far now," he said.

When they reached the point of the last curve before the straightaway section of the hall, Achmed nodded and Grunthor stopped. He and Jo took their positions just around the curve of the bend, guarding the hallway. Achmed and Rhapsody ventured down the remainder of the corridor until they came to the heavy stone door at its end.

"I expect this is the vault, Gwylliam's library," Achmed said softly. Rhapsody nodded in agreement. There had been no map or account of the interior of Canrif in the book they found in the House of Remembrance, but the description of the door was unmistakable. Deep within the stone face was a cracked inscription, a disintegrating artistic rendering of Gwylliam's aphorism.

Cyme we inne frið, fram the grip of deað to lif inne ðis smylte land

It was carved above a rusted metal plate and solid handle, beneath which had been bored a series of identical holes, approximately the diameter of an arrow shaft, arranged in symmetrical rows.

"It's a lock of some kind," Achmed said, running his thin, bony hand over the holes. Dust and fragments of rocks fell from the door's face as his fingers passed over it. "I'm sure that stupid motto of his has something to do with the key. That man was a one-stringed harp."

"Gwylliam was an engineer and a mathematician, so he must have somehow encoded the axiom into a number pattern corresponding to the holes," Rhapsody said, brushing the residual dirt from some of them. "There doesn't seem to be a correlation between these holes and the alphabet of the old Cymrian language, however."

"Could it have been in another language? Nain? Lirin?"

Rhapsody shrugged. "I don't know. That seems politically precarious, especially if others used the library. There would be a taint of favoritism to it. I don't think Gwylliam would have risked it."

She counted the holes again; they were set up in lines of six, with five rows in all. Her face clouded over as she thought. Then she broke into a smile; Achmed observed, even out of the corner of his eye, that it was as if the sun had suddenly risen in the tunnel.

"Of course! It's a musical lock. They only counted six notes back then, instead of the eight that Lirin Singers always had. When I was at Llauron's I discovered that the rest of the world now uses the eight-note scale as well. Back then they only commonly used five groupings, what we now call octaves."

"I hadn't realized Gwylliam was a musician."

"Gwylliam was an engineer and an architect. Music is a largely mathematic system; I'm not surprised." Rhapsody pulled an arrow from her quiver and snapped the point off. Slowly, painstakingly she inserted it into the hole that would have corresponded to the initial C in *Cyme*.

Deep within the stone they both heard an almost imperceptible click, a grinding sound that hummed for a moment and then fell silent. Rhapsody's face grew more excited, as did Achmed's.

"Easy; take your time," he admonished. "If you mess it up

you may fuse the locking mechanism, and then we'll never get it open."

"Sshh," she whispered, her eyes gleaming. Her brows knit with concentration as she counted off the letters, pushing each of them within the pattern of the words in the aphorism. She was on the second-to-last word when Jo appeared at the corner.

"Someone's coming; a whole bunch of them."

Achmed turned to Rhapsody. "Keep going; I'll help Grunthor. Don't hurry."

Rhapsody nodded and pressed in the next hole, exhaling in relief at the click as Achmed ran up the tunnel, exchanging places with Jo. The teenager looked over her shoulder at his retreat, then joined her adopted sister at the door.

"What are you doing?"

"Sshh," Rhapsody answered, trying to concentrate. "I'll tell you in a minute."

Sounds of strife issued from around the corner and echoed down the hall. To Rhapsody's dismay Jo turned and bolted down the corridor again.

"Jo, stop! Stay here." She turned around and made a grab for her.

Jo shook her off. "Are you insane? There are at least ten Bolg out there."

"Only ten? By the time you get there Achmed and Grunthor will have already looted the bodies and stacked them out of sight. Wait here and watch my back, please. I can't protect myself and work the lock at the same time."

Jo sighed, then agreed reluctantly. "You never let me have any fun."

Rhapsody hid her smile as she returned to the lock. "I let you fight in the passes on our way through the Teeth, didn't I?"

"Oh, that was a challenge," the teenager said sarcastically. "Slicing up night-blind mongrels armed with weapons made of sharpened rocks. As Grunthor would say, 'Pathe'ic.' "

"You'll get your chance; I imagine you'll see plenty of fighting. In fact, I'm going to attack you myself if you make another sound."

Rhapsody struggled with the last hole, scraping bits of de-

bris from the hole with her finger, rubbing the skin raw and
drawing blood. She shook her stinging hand, then slid the
arrow shaft in one more time. The hole clicked, and deep
within the rusted metal panel was a sound like a cymbal striking.

"Go get Achmed if it's clear; stay hidden and keep back if
the fighting's still going on," Rhapsody said to Jo, who could
barely contain her excitement. The younger woman nodded
and dashed up the hall, to return a few moments later with
their two Firbolg companions.

"Did you get it open?" Achmed asked, wiping his sword
on his cloak as he walked and returning it to his scabbard
without missing a step.

"I think so," Rhapsody answered, surveying the door. "It
tripped, or at least it sounded like it did. I didn't try to pull
it open until you got here, of course."

"Have at it, big fellow," Jo said to Grunthor, who smiled
down at her. Achmed nodded. Rhapsody drew forth her bow
and nocked an arrow onto the string. She was not entirely
certain she wanted to see what was behind the massive door
to the hidden vault.

Her reservations proved right a moment later. Grunthor
swung the immense slab of stone open and a hissing of air
issued forth, bringing with it the dusty stench of death. It was
an old smell, long contained within the huge room beyond
the opening, but putrid enough to cause Jo to retch where she
stood.

Rhapsody ran to her side and held her head while Achmed
looked within the vault. Grunthor took up a position between
the women and the hall to guard against any other Bolg that
might come down the tunnel. Jo's nausea cleared up quickly,
and after a few minutes she insisted she was able to investigate the cavernous room behind the door.

Gwylliam's vault opened above and around them, preserved as if Time had never touched it. The great cavern was
filled with documents, scrolls of parchment and bound manuscripts, maps and globes and charts enough to have kept an
army of scribes and sages working for centuries. Polished

shelves of immense height stood in rows, holding the remnants of Gwylliam's plans and serving as the repository of the knowledge of the Cymrian civilization in silent testimony to what had once been the pinnacle of the age.

Rhapsody looked around the vast room in amazement. The ceiling had been carved into a great smooth dome, which was painted the color of cobalt and dotted with silver-gilt stars in constellation patterns, set up in precise position to map the heavens above this land. The landmasses had been graphed in minute detail on the walls, and were annotated in the nomenclature of the time.

What were now the countries of Roland and Sorbold were jointly described as the Cymrian lands, while Tyrian was noted as Realmalir—the Lirin Realm. Other parts of the world were mapped as well, including the Lost Island that had once been their home, lovingly rendered in exquisite detail.

Sprawled across the great dome, in between the stars, was the enormous image of a dragon, its scales layered in red-gold leaf, each one inlaid individually within the beast's hide. Cruel talons, gleaming in silver gilding, stretched out over the lands to the west. The eyes had been set with clear gems, faceted into prisms, sparkling down into the darkness from the ceiling. Fresco flames of yellow and orange poured from its open maw.

In the center of the room was a large round table carved from black marble, its center covered with a clear dome. Several odd types of apparatus protruded from the floor next to it, and one strange fixture hung suspended from the ceiling above it. The metal from which it was wrought displayed no hint of rust or tarnish, even with the passing of centuries. Rhapsody would have liked to examine it further, but was held at bay by what lay on top of it and on the ground in front of it.

Slumped over the table was a mummified body dressed in robes. It had fallen on its back, a deep, cruel wound bisecting its chest. A simple gold crown lay balanced on its side next to the body's head; as Achmed approached it began to roll slightly back and forth on the table, glittering in the dark.

On the ground in front of the table lay another dried figure, a parchment-skinned skeleton with a broken neck. The skeleton was dressed in fine mail armor that had obviously not been sufficient to spare its owner his fate.

Grunthor closed the door after setting several stones in place to hold it ajar and determining that the handle worked from the inside. He looked over at Achmed, who stood above the bodies, arms crossed, looking down with a half-smile on an otherwise-serious face.

"Well, here's the great and mighty Gwylliam, I'll wager."

Rhapsody and Jo came forward slowly.

"Who is the other one?" the Singer asked.

Achmed looked in the direction of the other skeleton. "A guard, possibly. Strange; one would think there might be two of them. That was a hallmark of the Seren royal guard."

Rhapsody looked sharply at him. "How do you know that?"

Achmed ignored her question. "I would also hazard a guess that Gwylliam may have killed this one himself." Grunthor nodded in agreement; he had been examining the angle of trajectory at which the body had fallen and had come to the same conclusion.

Rhapsody looked puzzled. "I thought Llauron said Anwyn killed Gwylliam."

"So he did. Well, perhaps he doesn't know as much as he pretends to; wouldn't surprise me. I don't trust him."

"You don't trust anybody," said Jo absently. "Can I have the crown?"

"Hold off a bit, lit'le miss," said Grunthor gently. "Give us a chance to look around first, eh?"

Rhapsody walked around the table, giving the bodies a wide berth, and examined the dome in its center. It was outside the reach of her arms, though Achmed might have been able to touch it, and, despite being coated with dust, showed a high level of craftsmanship.

It appeared to be composed of a single, highly polished stone with a diameter longer than she was tall. The dome rested above what appeared to be a schematic of the labyrinth, interior and exterior views, which was intricately carved into the stone of the tabletop.

"All right, Achmed, what do you make of this?"

The Dhracian came over to the table and examined it, his

eyes flickering over the schematic and dome more rapidly than Rhapsody could follow. After a moment he reached out and touched the dome; as he did it glowed foggily beneath his fingertip. Parts of the map began to shimmer as well.

Achmed smiled. "I don't make anything of this. It will make something of me."

"And that is?"

"King."

45

Everything we need to conquer the Bolg is right here— everything. In a matter of a few weeks they will be a united kingdom for probably the first time in their history, on their way to becoming the greatest force to be reckoned with since the Cymrians invaded this land fourteen centuries ago."

Rhapsody looked askance at her friend. She was certain she had never seen Achmed this excited, and she didn't want to take away from it in any way, but what he was saying made no sense to her.

"Care to let us in on how you plan to accomplish this?"

Achmed pointed to the table. "I've seen this instrumentality, or one like it, before. It belonged to the Seren king in the old world; it was the way he determined the movements of troops and migrations of population centers. I'm not surprised Gwylliam brought it with him, or made a new one; it's a useful tool for a king to have. What?" he asked Rhapsody, who was staring at him strangely.

"I learn something new about you every day, Achmed. Here we've spent the last fourteen centuries together, and I never had any idea you were so well traveled in circles royal. How did you get a chance to hobnob with the blue bloods?"

" 'E was a bloody *assassin*; 'oo do you think 'ired him most often?"

Jo looked at Achmed in wonder. "You were an assassin?"

He ignored her and glared at Rhapsody. "This will give us the ability to determine where the largest groups of Bolg are, and how frequently they move. We'll start by recruiting a small, mobile tribe that can be trained as elite guard. The word will spread, after a few victories, that the earlier you come on board, the better your training and rank will be in the end."

"Victories? You make it sound so clean and simple. Aren't you talking about battles?"

Achmed snorted. "Hardly; skirmishes, really. Any race that has remained disparate after four centuries lacks the staying power to put up much of a fight.

"When I was scouting in Bethe Corbair, I heard some town guards make mention of an annual ritual called 'Spring Cleaning.' The soldiers of Roland, out of Bethany, ride down on the outlying Firbolg villages every year and destroy the inhabitants. They put the Bolg they can find to the sword, women and children included, and burn the crude huts." He ignored the expression of horror that washed over her face. "Now, what Bolg racial trait do you think is indicated by the fact that this happens, year after year?"

"Stupidity?"

"Not at all; it's actually rather clever. The Bolg have figured out that if they sacrifice a few of the weak and the sick they can keep the Orlandan army from coming further into their lands, which they call Ylorc, by the way. So they rebuild the same tattered village and stick a few unfortunates in it. The mighty men of Roland sweep through, setting the sham ablaze and butchering a few defenseless waifs, then ride back to Roland, having achieved orgasm as a result of their brave and manly actions."

"I assume you'll be putting a stop to that practice immediately," said Rhapsody, still pale.

"Of course."

"Bastards," muttered Jo. "Count me in when that happens. I'd be delighted to help you skin some Orlandan soldiers."

The look of shock returned to Rhapsody's face. "No, you won't. Achmed, you talk like the four of us are going to personally subdue hundreds of thousands of Bolg."

"Right."

"Wrong. I don't mind helping you, even though I think that a hundred thousand to four are suicidal odds. But it will have to be a hundred thousand to three, because Jo stays out of it. I didn't bring her along to get her killed."

"Who asked you?" spat Jo. Rhapsody turned to see her sister's sallow face florid with anger. "This mother-hen routine has got to stop, Rhaps. I'm a big girl and I've lived my entire life on the street. I can take care of myself, thank you very much. Now stop coddling me or I'll set your hair on fire."

"That won't work with 'er, you know she's got that strange thing with fire. But Oi can help you come up with somethin' else if she won't leave you alone," offered Grunthor, casting a playful look in Rhapsody's direction. "Come on, Yer Ladyship; she sounds an awful lot like another lit'le girl Oi use to know." He winked his large amber eye at her. Rhapsody laughed in spite of herself.

"Oh, all right," she said, giving Jo a hug. "I guess I can't keep you out of the fray forever. Where do we begin?"

"Well, Jo begins by handing over the crown, and any other valuables she looted from Gwylliam's body while we weren't looking."

"What?" Rhapsody pulled away and looked up into Jo's face; the expression on it was a mixture of defiance and sheepishness. The Singer looked over to the body that was sprawled backward on the table. The crown was indeed missing, and the corpse had been picked clean of every valuable, gem, ring, and button.

Grunthor stretched out his massive palm reproachfully, though Rhapsody thought she saw a twinkle in his eye, and Jo slowly returned the crown, looking humbly at the floor.

"Now let's 'ave the rest, lit'le miss," said the giant Firbolg. Jo looked up and, seeing the stern look that had replaced his smile, dug reluctantly into her pockets and handed over a fistful of jewelry and other trinkets.

"Is that all, now?"

The street wench nodded.

"Bad answer," said the silty voice from behind her. Quick as lightning, Achmed's hand shot out and tore the pocket off the vest Rhapsody had bought for Jo in Bethe Corbair. A shriek of protest caught in Rhapsody's throat as a golden ring tumbled out and fell to the stone floor, where it spun on its end in ever-smaller circles.

Achmed stooped to pick up the ring.

"You are a bad judge of value, Josephine," he said, using her hated given name. "This might have bought you a decent horse, or ten acres of land in Bethe Corbair, but it has cost you far more than it was worth. Your lie has been purchased at the price of my trust. No one here would deny you your fair share of treasure, but you must understand that the valuables, as well as the bodies, we find in this place, are artifacts, clues to the puzzle of our survival here.

"I admire your self-reliance, but it makes you dangerous to have on the team, and I can't risk that. Too much is at stake to take a chance on a disobedient brat who doesn't understand the rules. Tomorrow we will choose one of the horses to leave with you and take you back to the outskirts of Bethe Corbair."

"You had better choose two, then, because I'm going with her," said Rhapsody, battling to keep her temper in check. She looked up into her sister's face and grew even more furious at the sight of Jo struggling to keep up a brave front while fighting back tears. "And if that's the way you feel, you can speak to me from now until we leave in the morning. I don't want you to say another word to her."

Achmed regarded her coolly. "You wish to split up now? Leave us for her?"

"If necessary."

"Why?"

Rhapsody looked from the quivering girl to Achmed's blank face. "She needs me more than you do."

"Come on, sir, per'aps we can work out a compromise," offered Grunthor gently. "It's gonna take 'er a while to get use to bein' out of danger and off the street, eh, Jo? Oi'll vouch for the lit'tle miss; she won't do it again, will ya, darlin'?"

"And we can ban her from the library. She can stay in whatever home base we establish," Rhapsody said.

"I'm sorry," Jo whispered. The three looked at her in astonishment; it was the most unlikely thing they had ever heard her say.

"Well, Achmed? One more chance?"

"I can see I'm outvoted. Very well. I'll relent this last time, but I think it is a mistake. You're rash, Jo, and headstrong; it must be a family trait." He glanced at Rhapsody, who smiled at the floor. "I can't stress to you how serious I am about this being your final chance. We can't have a half-member of the team; either you're all the way with us, with full privileges, or you're out. I will not continue to jeopardize my life for your immaturity, nor the lives of Grunthor or Rhapsody. You're not worth it."

"That's enough," Rhapsody said bluntly. "She's got the message."

Achmed looked at the Singer and spoke one sentence in the Bolgish tongue.

"Mark my words; we will regret this."

"Strange words coming from someone who wants my help in pitting four people against an entire mountain range of monsters," Rhapsody retorted, wrapping a protective arm around Jo and leading her over to a chair. "Are you all right?"

Jo nodded; her jaw was clenched so firmly that a tiny muscle vibrated in her cheek.

"Just sit here for a few minutes and keep out of trouble. Achmed can seem harsh, but he's just trying to ensure our survival."

"I understand and accept what he's saying," muttered Jo. "It's you I can't stand at the moment. Please leave me alone."

Stung, Rhapsody walked away and back over to the two Firbolg, who were conferring by the stone table.

"The vaults are under 'ere," said Grunthor, pointing to the center of the table.

"How are we supposed to move this?"

"Let's worry about that in a moment. Watch this." Achmed rested his hand on the dome over the map and, as before, the crystal began to glow. Beneath the clear covering the table began to glisten in spots, glimmering for a moment and then moving to another area of the schematic nearby, then disappearing altogether to reappear a moment later on the other side of the table. The flickering lights meant next to nothing to Rhapsody, but Achmed and Grunthor seemed to understand them, and began conferring

Rhapsody glanced back at Jo, who was staring resolutely

at the floor, arms crossed tightly over her chest. When her attention returned to the two Bolg, they seemed to have reached consensus.

"We need to do some investigating," Achmed said, slipping on his gloves. "I suggest you and Jo wait here in the library and look around for whatever manuscripts you can find that might be useful. The Bolg have never opened this door, and so if we leave it barely propped, there is little likelihood that they will even notice it's been opened."

"And what if they do? What if we're trapped in here when they come?"

"Well, you have a pretty fair sword, and the kid has been longing for some battle action. Do the best you can."

"Your concern is overwhelming," Rhapsody replied sarcastically, glancing back over her shoulder at Jo again.

"We won't be that long. Grunthor has already made sure the door opens from the inside, so if we don't return after a day or so—"

"A *day* or so?"

"—wait until you are sure nothing's moving around and head back for Bethe Corbair. You should be comfortable there; they have a good-sized market for shopping."

"You're a pig, you know that?" she retorted, watching Grunthor smile out of the corner of her eye. The giant went over to the chair where Jo was glowering.

"Keep your nose clean, lit'le miss, and have a look around. See if you can find anythin' we can use, eh?"

"All right," Jo muttered. Grunthor patted her head encouragingly and gave Rhapsody a hug.

"See ya soon, Duchess," he said, then followed the shadow that had already slipped out of the great stone doorway without a sound.

Whispered words in the ancient corridors.

"Night Man. Killed Brax-Eye and Grak-Claw with sky-fire."

"Gave Grak's woman a slash-iron. Now she carries his child."

The Bolg glanced rapidly around, their eyes searching the black tunnels for movement.

"Maybe here now. Night Man's blood is darkness."

"Night man comes to kill Bolg?"

"No. Night Man is Bolg. Maybe Bolg-god."

"Maybe Night Man comes to challenge Fire-Eye. And the Ghost."

There was silence in the darkness. Then a sentiment that left each of the huddled Bolg nodding.

"Much blood spilled there will be."

While the two men were gone, Rhapsody, and eventually Jo, searched the library. They started with the maps and log-books of Gwylliam's journey from the Lost Island, which Rhapsody read aloud, translating from the Old Cymrian.

They then progressed throughout the repository as they figured out the organizational system. Everything seemed to be based on groupings of six; plans for buildings and base structures were hexagonal, following Gwylliam's belief that the six-sided construct was the most architecturally solid.

In addition, they found another door, this one unlocked, and after a good deal of debate decided to risk opening it without waiting for their companions to return.

With great effort they pried the heavy stone slab open to discover a tunnel that led to caverns filled with rusting machinery, great wheels and gears and pipes that ran vertically up the sides of the mountain. The mechanisms in the cavern were each large enough to have easily filled the town square in Bethe Corbair.

"What do you suppose all this is?" Jo whispered.

"I'm not sure," Rhapsody answered, paging carefully through a manuscript she had found in the repository. "I think it must have something to do with the ventilation system."

Jo had walked down a few of the stone steps that led down into the cavern, and was staring at the huge gearwheels above her. Each of the countless cogs was twice the size of her hand.

"The what?"

"This is the machinery, if I'm not mistaken, that managed the air within the mountain. As you can tell by the dankness of the tunnels, it doesn't work anymore."

Jo turned around, her eyes still transfixed by the mammoth pipes attached to the mountain's interior. "How'd it work?"

"I'm not exactly sure. One of the things Gwylliam brags the most about in his writings is his wonderful accomplishment of bringing fresh air and warmth into the mountain. The fortress here inside the Teeth was his headquarters, where he had his Great Hall, his throne room, and the various bulwarks that kept enemy armies at bay. I have to admit it was a brilliant system. The ventilation made the mountain inhabitable for the Cymrians who lived within the Teeth."

"I'm confused. I thought all Gwylliam's Cymrians lived within the Teeth."

"Most of the Cymrians who lived in Canrif actually lived past the canyon behind the Teeth, beyond what Gwylliam called the Blasted Heath, whatever that means. The lands are so vast it's indescribable, and it's impossible to tell from outside the Teeth, because all of them are shielded from sight by the mountains. I'll show you that manuscript when we go back."

"Won't do any good," Jo said, casting her gaze around the quiet stone and metal gears, still looking threatening in the dark, even in their silent state. "I can't read."

Rhapsody nodded. "I thought as much. I'd be happy to teach you. I taught Grunthor."

"Really." Jo started to walk farther down the stone steps hewn into the mountain along the cavern walls.

"Let's go back," said Rhapsody hurriedly. "I think we should wait for the other two to go exploring down here."

Jo sighed in annoyance but did not protest, following her sister back up into the library again.

𝒯he better part of a day had passed before Achmed and Grunthor returned, little the worse for wear. Grunthor had sustained a minor injury to his hand, which Rhapsody washed and bandaged over his protests of the wound's insignificance. Both seemed satisfied with the day's reconnaissance.

"We found a few in the crumbling city—by the way, their word for the Cymrians is *Willums*," Achmed related over supper.

"Interesting," Rhapsody said. "Well, at least someone remembers old Gwylliam fondly."

"I thought you might enjoy that, Rhapsody. Anyway, the tribes are dispersed throughout the Teeth and deep within the old Cymrian realm; we only saw a few groupings."

"Yeah, we saw a lot o' Claws and Eyes but no Guts," added Grunthor, chewing on his rations.

"Claws and eyes? Guts? What are you talking about?"

"That's one method by which these Bolg describe themselves. The Claws are the soldier types, the hunters and marauders. It's that kind of tribe that Roland generally gets to clean out every spring.

"The Eyes are the spies, obviously. They live on the mountaintops, facing the steppes, and on some of the higher slopes that look inward, facing the heath. They tend to be thinner of body, less muscular, and scavenge more than they raid.

"And the Guts live deep within the mountain and elsewhere in the hidden parts of the realm. I couldn't glean much about them except that they are some of the more feared tribes. Generally they keep to themselves, but when they spill out of their lands, there's havoc."

"Spilling Guts. That's precious," said Rhapsody.

"Their chieftains incorporate the type of clan they are into their names. Oh, by the way, we now own some Claws of our own, a small herd called the Night Reavers."

"Excuse me?"

Grunthor grinned, showing his carnivorous smile. "Yeah, the Warlord 'ere—that's what they call 'im—got 'is own personal 'onor contingent now."

"Warlord?" Rhapsody asked.

"Well, it's an improvement on 'the Night Man,' which is what they called me at first," Achmed said, chewing.

"I'm not callin' you no damn Warlord," Jo muttered into her mug. "Warthog, maybe."

Rhapsody hid her smile. "Where are these—these Night Reavers now?"

"Tied up in one of the lower hallways."

She dropped her bread in alarm. "Tied up? You left them tied up? Won't the other Bolg wandering by attack them?"

"Well, possibly, but the Night Reavers were considered the most fearsome of the groups we could find within a day's travel. I doubt the other Bolg would want to risk the wrath of anything that could subdue the Reavers and leave them trussed like turkeys in a hallway."

Achmed was correct; other tribes did wander by the captive Reavers, but did not seek to attack or loose them. They were able to see this on the great marble table beneath the dome. Achmed showed the women which lights represented his prisoners, and the flickering movements that indicated the visiting tribes.

Jo had made a remarkable discovery that went a long way toward redeeming her in Achmed's eyes. It was she who had determined the purpose of the apparatuses next to and above the stone table.

The pipe that hung from the ceiling above the table was a speaking tube, a form of acoustic address system that allowed for a speaker's voice to be transmitted throughout the mountain or to specific regions, depending on what had been selected on the table map. The apparatus that protruded from the floor was the opposite, a listening tube, that allowed the sounds from specific areas to be transmitted back to the library through the pipe structure.

Both of these apparatuses were tied into the duct and ventilation system that ran throughout the mountain, a complex series of tunnels and vents that drew air from the fierce winds that circled the mountaintop to cool and cleanse the air within the mountain fortress. When heat was needed in the cold months, the air could be diverted through Gwylliam's mighty forges, which now lay dormant in the depths of the Teeth.

At one time from those forges great vats of iron, steel, and bronze, as well as precious metals, had been poured and beaten into some of the finest weaponry and armor in the known world, as well as impressively crafted items of ornamentation.

Achmed had gathered a collection of weapons from the various display cases to analyze, and had spread them out on one of the long study tables. Rhapsody came upon Grunthor running his hands over one of the swords from the vault. There was a look of sadness on his face that reached down into her heart. She walked up to him and wound her arm through his.

"What are you thinking?" she asked.

Grunthor looked down at her as a smile crept over his face. "Oh, nothin', darlin'."

"Missing your troops?"

"Naw. Oi'll 'ave some new ones soon enough, Oi suspect. Oi was just thinkin' what a waste it all is."

Rhapsody sighed; she had been thinking much the same thing. It was painful to see what the Cymrians had been, their fellow Seren, their countrymen, perhaps even descendants of their loved ones.

In the artifacts left behind she could see the life's work of craftsmen, engineers, architects, draftsman, builders of intricate roadways and great machines that had outlived their civilization, men and women of great vision and the ability to bring it to life, now gone, crushed beneath the heel of senseless power-hunger.

"Cheer up, Grunthor," she said, forcing a smile. "Just think about how Gwylliam will spin in his grave, knowing all his sophisticated machinery and weaponry will soon be in the hands of the Bolg for use in building up their civilization."

The Sergeant chuckled. "Oi don't think the ol' boy 'ad a grave, if that's 'is body over there. But maybe if we get 'im to spin fast enough on the floor, 'e can get the machin'ry goin' again."

Achmed had selected his next tribe to recruit. The Dark Drinkers were an Eye tribe, a group of swift scavengers that used the shadows of the mountain to ambush solitary travelers or the weak among other Bolg clans.

This time all four of the companions took to the tunnels, lying in wait for those Bolg who relied on the element of surprise. The rout was messy, but thorough, and within an hour Achmed had a new group of loyal spies who would act as spokesmen for him.

"Go throughout the tunnels with this warning," the new Warlord instructed the survivors. "The King of Ylorc has come to the mountain. Those who wish to be part of the realm will gather in the canyon beyond the Teeth when the moon is full, ten days hence.

"In three days you will feel me inhale, cold as the winter wind; anyone I touch thus is summoned. The following day you will feel me exhale; the warmth of my breath will touch you again. You must come at full-moon's night to the canyon. Anyone who ignores my summons will be consumed in the fire of my belly on the eleventh day." The night eyes of the ragged cave dwellers blinked rapidly in the dark at the words.

$\mathcal{D}$eep within the Hidden Realm, the Bolg shaman woke in the darkness of his cave. His eyes, cracking open as sleep fled, stung around the edges, even bled a little as awareness slowly came back to him.

The vision was almost upon him. He had time to sit up and grasp his head before it broke across him like a strong wind.

Something had come to the mountain. There were whispers of it from the Eye clans, a low buzzing hum about a man who blended into the darkness, but they were only fragments of a story. The tale itself had not yet made its way here, to the Deep lands, far beyond the Teeth.

Saltar, whom the Bolg called Fire-Eye, rested his hand on his chest, concentrating on the vision, but it was still unclear. The images were strangely familiar, but far beyond his comprehension. He would wait, keeping watch, until the visions became clearer.

$\mathcal{B}$right of you to threaten to breathe on them without making sure the vents worked first," muttered Rhapsody. She sat atop Grunthor's shoulders, trying to pry loose one of the main gear levers.

They were deep in the belly of Gwylliam's ventilation system, having found the architectural drawings and notes indicating how the operations had been designed and implemented.

It had been an arduous process, trying to locate where the massive structures matched the drawings. Once they had figured that out, the task had become dangerous. More than once the men had needed to climb out to the exterior crags, digging loose centuries of rock and debris from the wind that clogged the outer vents. The wind howled around them, tearing at their clothes, all but pulling them into the canyons below.

The ventilation system had been built from the same strange metal Achmed and Grunthor had seen in the cathedral in Avonderre, and was seemingly impervious to rust, despite centuries of disuse. The machinery itself seemed to still be in working condition, but occasional fittings and levers were rotten with age or decay from exposure.

"Just because you open this once doesn't mean it will work when we need it to, Achmed," Rhapsody warned from her perch on the giant Firbolg. "There are so many pieces to this apparatus, and many of them are close to rotten or sticky from having sat so long untended." They had already had to reopen several passages which worked the first time, only to catch and jam shut the second time around.

"This is the last one. If you can open this area we will have cleared the system for all the tunnels within the Teeth; not bad for two days' work," said Achmed. He and Jo were oiling an enormous gearshaft next to a giant fan. He gave the securing chain one final pull, then turned to the other two again. "How's it coming?"

"Let's try it," Rhapsody said to Grunthor. The giant Bolg nodded and lifted her down from his shoulders, then gave the lever a firm tug. The grate it was attached to slid open with little resistance.

"Perfect; now close it up quickly," said Achmed. "Let's hold our 'breath' a little longer."

Rhapsody closed her eyes. She was already holding hers.

𝕿he next morning the sun rose over the Teeth in a deep fog. Just as it crested the horizon a terrible grating sound was heard within the mountains, a scraping sound like a sword against the grinder's wheel. Moments later the tunnels of Canrif were filled with an icy wind, whipping through the corridors with a ferocious whine, blasting the Bolg with gale-force intensity.

Even within the belly of the ventilation system Rhapsody could hear the cries of panic. She turned to the others with alarm on her face.

"Enough, Achmed; you'll freeze the children and the injured."

Achmed nodded, and Grunthor and Jo pulled the levers, shutting the outside vents. They went about closing down the rest of the system while Achmed and Rhapsody hurried up the stairs to the speaking tube.

As they climbed, Rhapsody grasped Achmed's elbow.

"It isn't always going to be that violent, is it? Canrif will be uninhabitable."

"Not once it's been running regularly. I think the air just needs to come into balance on both the inside and the outside of the mountain. And, by the way, we call the place *Ylorc* now. In case you hadn't noticed, Gwylliam's century is over by a millennium or so."

When they reached the stone table, Rhapsody drew forth her lark's flute. They had agreed the night before that Achmed's voice, while frightening in person largely because of the sandy quietness of it, was insufficiently frightening for an initial address. Rhapsody planned to compensate for that musically.

She started a discordant melody that served to pick up on the tones in the Dhracian's voice and exaggerate them, adding in the sounds of howling winds and voices that shrieked and moaned. Achmed cleared the speaking tube and delivered his message.

"Tomorrow I exhale, one breath, long enough for you to feel my heat without being ignited this time. Those who come to me in the canyon when the moon is full will be part of the new power of Ylorc. All others will perish under my heel." His voice reverberated in a monstrous echo. Achmed closed the speaking tube.

"Well, that was horrifying," said Rhapsody as she put her flute away. "Do you think we convinced them?"

"Some of them. Others will be convinced tomorrow. And some will remain defiant, preferring to pit themselves against a new warlord than take a position of secondary power."

"And what about them? What are you going to do to convince them?"

"Let's just say they won't live to regret their skepticism."

* * *

He breathed on us, the Fist-and-Fire spies were saying. *Cold, like the screaming wind.*

Saltar rubbed his eyes, trying to make the vision clearer, but he could hear nothing more. The sight that was his gift was not a sign from the Future, or a prediction. It was merely the ability to see something that was here, and inevitable, an eye with especially long vision.

The screaming wind. The words reverberated in his head.

The Spirit was always looking into the wind. Perhaps whatever was coming was what it sought.

46

"*T*his is never going to work."

"Don't be so negative, Duchess; give it a try."

Rhapsody turned to face the smiling giant. "You don't understand. Forges this size are stoked constantly for centuries. If we had a week we couldn't gather enough fuel to get this up to the point where it could melt ice, let alone steel again."

"It doesn't have to melt anything," said Achmed patiently. "All it has to do is be hot enough to heat the air. There's a warm spell on its way, I can tell by the clouds. Besides, if you think back to your fiery baptism and concentrate, I'm sure the forge fires will burn hot enough to convince the Bolg I'm breathing on them."

"If we could duplicate your real breath, they would surrender in a heartbeat," said Jo, who was working the bellows over the small fire that the others had built. "Perhaps we should throw some stinkweed in there."

Grunthor rubbed his chin. "Might not be a bad idea at that, sir."

"Not this time, but thanks for the suggestion, Jo," Achmed said. He turned to the Singer again. "Well? Come on, it's almost morning."

Rhapsody looked up at the giant copper-banded bellows, sagging and full of holes. The forges were deep in the belly of the mountain, reachable only through dark, forbidding caverns that crumbled as they descended. The sheer size of the forgeworks took her breath away. It must have taken a thousand men to run and maintain the equipment, night and day, feeding it constantly.

They had located a trove of hard coal, a black underground hill, around which had been scattered trowels, picks, and scuttles for transporting the lump fuel to the forges.

A number of skeletons lay nearby, the trapped workers who had never made it out again when Gwylliam's mountain had been overrun by the Firbolg. The bones had been the first fuel committed to the flames, with a dirge sung by Rhapsody, four hundred years too late. The skeletons were those of wide men with broad shoulders and rib cages—*Nain,* Achmed had noted, to Grunthor's agreement.

Taking a deep breath, she seized the side of the firepit and concentrated, clearing her mind of the doubts that had filled it since they had begun the conquest of the mountain.

She called on the fire within her soul and set a tone to it, humming with her mouth open, until the music swelled out of her being and filled the endless cavern. She could feel the flames roaring to life, shining on her face, heating the fabric of her shirt until it felt about to ignite.

In the distance she could hear the shouts of the others as they began to work the great bellows. She cleared the outside noises from her mind and concentrated once more on the burning coal in the pit below her.

The inferno in the forge crackled and roared, drowning out all other noise within the mountain. Rhapsody maintained her shuddering grip on the firepit while Grunthor and Jo continued to work the hole-filled bellows, itself screaming along in time to the cacophony that was blasting through the bowels of the Teeth.

The sound of the grates opening again shattered her concentration, and she fell back into strong, thin hands that steadied her and kept her from losing her balance on the edge of the pit. Again, deep in her ears she heard the cries of the Bolg within the mountain, but they seemed more of excitement than panic this time.

"That's enough; shut the vent," Achmed instructed Grunthor and Jo. "We don't want them to get used to the heat yet; it is winter for a few more weeks still." He turned to the panting Singer and patted her arm. "You did it."

She nodded between gasps for breath. "Yes, I did; may they one day forgive me. I'm not sure if I'll ever forgive myself."

Gurrn feared the Night Man more than he feared Hraggle, despite the fact that Hraggle was standing before him. As chieftain of the Bloody Fang clan, Hraggle took what he wanted, bullying and brutalizing the others, Gurrn among them.

The chieftain had survived the raids of the men of Roland, and even had a broken sword as a trophy; he was the most powerful Bolg on the western crag known as Grivven. Hraggle did not fear the Night Man, even when his voice and breath had come forth from the Earth itself.

Gurrn now stood in silent fury, watching Hraggle raid the supply of food he had set in store, rations that were intended to keep his family fed over the thin hunting season of winter.

The other members of the Bloody Fang clan eyed Hraggle as well. He had threatened Gurrn's woman and was holding their child under his arm, the boy screaming in protest, the woman in fear. Gurrn held her back; Hraggle would be satisfied with the food, and would leave the child when he left, unless he was feeling particularly cruel.

Then, suddenly, Hraggle stopped. He dropped the child and stood motionless, his hand at his throat, the same hand that moments before had been pilfering Gurrn's hoard. A narrow crimson line bisected Hraggle's neck, put there by thin white hands that had emerged from the darkness. The red line quickly spread into a wide, dark stain as Hraggle fell, lifeless.

Gurrn caught sight of strange eyes in the shadow behind the falling corpse. A vague outline surrounded the Night Man, who appeared as part of the darkness, formless as liquid night.

"Tomorrow." The voice had a dry whisper of death to it. The clan watched, wide-eyed, as the figure dissipated into the darkness again.

On the tenth day the Firbolg began to gather on the ledges facing the canyon at sunrise. Achmed had not been specific in his message as to the time of their summons, so over the course of the day they came, Eyes and Claws and Guts, the tribes of the mountains that served as the barrier reef of the Bolglands.

Beyond the canyon that separated their lands from those of the mountain dwellers, some of the deeper Firbolg watched, the tribes and clans that made their homes on the Heath or far within the Hidden Realm. Their curiosity was self-serving; they knew it was only a matter of time before this new warlord came for them as well.

The sinking sun had touched the tops of the tallest crags when a hush fell over the crowd. It had been a day of noise and violence, of positioning and brawls over proximity, but as the Bolg had no idea where this king would appear, it was impossible for them to be sure of where the site nearest his feet would be. It made for an unpleasant atmosphere.

The stillness that descended had been engineered; Rhapsody stood at the edge of the tunnel onto the ledge from which Achmed planned to speak and began to whisper the name of silence. It had echoed off the rockwalls and ledges, touching the crags and peaks with a heaviness that shut down the babbling below him. Achmed smiled; it looked as if almost all of them had come.

Noticeably absent were the Hill-Eye, the most bloodthirsty of the mountain dwellers. It had been Grunthor's assessment that this clan would withdraw deeper into the Hidden Realm and wait to be flushed out, or attack once the others had established peace. His guess seemed accurate; not one of their markings was visible.

Achmed surveyed the assemblage. There were perhaps thirty thousand of them, gathered in crags and standing on ledges, perched on high rocky outcroppings, staring down at him. Some were huddled in packs at the base of the foothills, backing up to the canyon's edge at the bottom of the ravine that rose up a thousand feet or more to the heath.

It was a heady, disturbing feeling to see them there, similar to the sensation of walking into a pit of scorpions. From every crevice and rise the Bolg stared down at him, a truly bastard race of near-men, of an elder origin that had been adulterated with the blood of every other race it had contacted.

There was a twisted beauty to them, this mutant strain, a

pollution that would appall men but that served to preserve their species; in all the worlds he had never seen another race as adaptable and diverse. No matter what condition they were subjected to they would survive and develop a response over time. And he was one of them.

It was a feeling similar to being among the wolf pack at rest, the chieftains of each tribe placed higher on the crags than the others, better to see their power fall.

Into each face, or, in some clans, every arm, was carved or burned the insignia of the clans. The Bloody Claw, the Fangs, the Shadow Stealers, each lineage was written in scar tissue. Clothing had been replaced in most cases with scraps of hide that passed for armor. Even the young had been out-fitted with an eye toward protective value rather than comfort, though this was largely illusory, since the few bits of useful armor had been torn and split among so many wearers that it wouldn't have shielded them from the wind.

Rhapsody was waiting behind him; he heard her catch her breath, and instantly knew why. The children had been placed forward, closest to the edges of the rock outcroppings, as if prepared for sacrifice. He saw her bite her lip; she was aware that this was not a culture she was akin to, nor one she understood at present. Then her face softened, and she smiled.

He followed the direction of her eyes to see what had initiated the change, and was not surprised to see her looking at a group of small, dark faces, grinning repulsively back at her. Children; Rhapsody was a soft touch when it came to any child. It was a weakness he liked in her in spite of, but that posed a threat he was unwilling to risk.

Grunthor was in place; it was time to begin.

Achmed took a deep breath. He had studied over the six intervening days since his summons with Rhapsody, practicing the musical cadence she had given him to compose the speech by which he would address his new subjects.

It was like a symphony, with an overture and movements, rising to a thunderous crescendo early on; he had melded his innate understanding of the rhythms of the Bolgish tongue with her composition skills, resulting in an address he hoped would serve in place of a bloody insurrection. He stared at the waiting Firbolg, meeting their eyes.

"I am your new king. You live in the mountain, and the mountain serves me, as soon the Heath will, and the canyon, and the Hidden Realm. Ylorc will rise in power again, in ways it never has before. No more will we live under the heel of Roland."

A great rasping roar issued forth from the assembled Bolg; it echoed off the mountain and spread down the canyon, vibrating through the Heath and into the deeper realms. Here and there rocks slid from the cliffs, and dust rose. Achmed smiled; the overture had gone well. Now he timed the opening movement to punctuate the rhythm of the echoes resounding off the canyon.

"Whatever you are now, you are but the splinters of a bone, perhaps once of one blood, but now without strength. When you move it causes pain, but comes to no purpose. Join me, and we will be as the mountain itself moving. I will not be a king like the one before, not a warlord like any you have known. We shall bring the mountain to life around us, and our enemies will come to our terms.

"Is there anyone who would deny me the crown?"

Achmed knew where to look; all afternoon they had been at the listening posts to get word of the possible strategies of the arriving Bolg. He knew that one Janthir Bonesplitter, a Claw chieftain who claimed to be descended of Gwylliam's line, had been calling himself Emperor of the Teeth. It would be a matter of honor for him to object. Many of the clans knew his name and his reputation for cruelty and his desire for more territory and more slaves.

Bonesplitter had positioned himself between two massive, waist-high boulders, perhaps to avoid arrow fire or to conceal his position until he chose his time to act. At Achmed's challenge he drew a heavy, ancient sword that still had some gleam to it in the glow of the bonfires that burned throughout the canyon.

With a roar, he moved out from between the rocks, raising his sword above his head. "I Emperor of the Teeth! And fire breath or ice breath I will wring from you, Usurper! This night, I swallow your eyes!"

The collective attention of the assemblage shifted toward

Achmed, who was much smaller and thinner than Janthir Bonesplitter. According to Firbolg custom, it was his turn for a boast or an acceptance of the challenge.

Achmed smiled condescendingly. "You have a strong back; perhaps you will be of use to me. If you are able to prove yourself worthy I might take you for a chieftain. I have already taken your lands. Swear fealty to me now and you may unspeak your threat."

The roar of fury that echoed in response conveyed Janthir's answer. As a stream of violent invectives rumbled across the canyon and up through the crags to the night sky, Achmed could feel Rhapsody shiver behind him, hidden in the shadows though she was.

"As you will," Achmed said patiently. His voice did not reveal even a hint of nervousness or anger. "I gave you the opportunity. I command the mountain, but even I cannot save a fool from himself. I told you the mountain serves me. Know my words to be true."

The Bolg spectators gasped collectively as one of the two massive rocks flanking Janthir unfolded itself smoothly, rose to a monstrous height, plucked the heavy sword from the upraised claw of the speechless Bonesplitter, and struck off his head. Even before the gasp resolved into a stifled scream from the nearby onlookers, the head rolled down off the ledge. The rock which had attacked Bonesplitter tossed the sword into the canyon, returning to its position again. The entire incident had taken less than half a minute.

Achmed waited until Grunthor had blended back into the rock ledge before addressing the assemblage again.

"Who else wishes to challenge me?"

No sound answered him except the howling of the wind through the canyon and the crackling of the roaring bonfires.

"Very well, then; this is what you will do. Each clan will send me their five best warriors and one child, with its mother. These groups of five shall be my chiefs and elite guard, and will receive my blessing and training superior to that of any army in Roland.

"Each child, if it passes a test, will be given a gift. Choose well. Send soon. You have three days. For any who would doubt my resolve, hear this: I come. You will be part of this body, or you will be cut off and the tribe you sprang from cauterized like a stump—in fire."

Achmed stared across the silent assemblage for a moment longer, smiling as he took in the sight of the frozen Bolg gazing down from their lofty perches. Then he turned on his heel and vanished from the ledge, pausing long enough in the tunnel to pluck the trembling Rhapsody from the shadows and take her back into the depths of Canrif with him.

𝔚ell, that may not have been the single most repulsive thing I have ever witnessed, but it certainly was up there."

Grunthor looked offended. "What are you talkin' about? It was great; no blood got spilt, and the Bolg are still out there now, pickin' their captains. We can start trainin' in the mornin'. Whaddaya mean, repulsive?"

"I think Janthir might take issue with your assessment of blood not being spilled," Rhapsody said as she and Jo rolled bandages and packed medical kits.

"Well, 'e might, but Oi don't think we'll 'ear the old boy too well, 'is mouth bein' down at the bottom of the canyon and all."

"I can't believe you wouldn't let me come and watch," Jo pouted. "It sounds like a great time."

Rhapsody started to answer, but reconsidered and said nothing. Both Achmed and Grunthor were reveling in their victory; it seemed unfair to deny them their celebration. "How long before we take the Heath?"

Achmed looked up from the map he was drawing. "I'd say within two weeks we'll be well set to consolidate the Heath and the outer sections of the Hidden Realm in time to have a united front for Spring Cleaning. The experience the army will gain there will make it easy to take whatever stragglers have not already joined forces afterward." Rhapsody nodded and returned her attention to the bandages.

𝔊altar closed his burning eyes as the cold mist descended on his face and shoulders.

The Spirit had come. He knew it would show up eventually, once he had heard about the new warlord's meeting in the canyon at the edge of the Heath.

What do you see?

"Nothing yet; still cloudy," Saltar said. As always, he heard the voice in his mind, the sensation akin to being violated.

Look harder. Search the wind for one who walks between the gusts of air.

Saltar closed his eyes, feeling the sting abate a little. He put his hand again to his chest, but saw no more clearly.

"Nothing yet," he repeated. "But he will come."

47

Keep your eyes closed, we're almost there."

Rhapsody tried to swallow her anxiety. The excitement in Achmed's voice, so wildly out of character, had a compelling effect on her; she couldn't resist dropping whatever she was doing to see his newest discovery or solution. It was not compelling enough, however, to drive from her mind the ever-present thought that the Bolg recruits would be arriving in the morning, and they had not finished their preparations.

"This is the last time I can do this, Achmed," she said, trying to keep from tripping on the uneven floor. Her head swam, knowing that when she opened her eyes, the darkness would still be there. The halls of Gwylliam's fortress conjured up too many memories of the Root. "I have to get the quarters finished."

Achmed chuckled. "All right, if you don't want to see the Great Hall, we can just go ba—"

"You found the Great Hall?" Rhapsody exclaimed, opening her eyes.

"And something possibly more interesting, but if you have a pressing need to get back—"

She grabbed his hand. "Show me. It can wait."

"Somehow I thought that would be your attitude. Follow me."

Rhapsody hurried behind him through the darkness. The

tunnels were beginning to open in width and height, until they were four times their normal dimensions. The corridor finally emptied into a large entryway, where fragments of gold leaf still clung to the marble walls.

Achmed rounded the corner, and stopped before an opening where two colossal doors had once been. One was there still, fashioned of hammered gold, embedded open in the wall next to it as if by the force of a violent storm. The other was missing.

"The Great Hall," he said, making a sweeping gesture toward the room beyond the doorway.

Rhapsody stepped over a pile of crumbled basalt and through the frame of the entrance. A round room stretched out before her, built in the same vast proportions as the rest of Canrif, with pillars of blue-black marble lining the white stone walls all around, leading up to a wide dais. The domed ceiling, though cracked and peeling, was an exquisite shade of blue, colored to resemble the sky.

Blocks of clear glass had been embedded in a full circle around the top of the round ceiling, allowing daylight to enter. Rhapsody could see a bit of the real sky, and the shadows of mountains through the glass, and deduced that the Great Hall had been built near the summit of one of the crags of the Teeth, hewn inside the mountaintop.

The floor, now littered with rubble, had once been patterned in colored marble as well, inlaid in huge designs of the Earth, sun, moon, and an enormous star. A chill ran through her; it was the symbol for Seren, her birth star.

"*Aria*," she whispered.

Unbidden, the voice welled up from her memory.

If you watch the sky and can find your guiding star, you will never be lost, never.

She choked back tears. A warm, strong hand gripped her shoulder.

"What's the matter?"

Rhapsody blinked rapidly and looked around again, stepping farther into the Great Hall. At the far end of the room, on the elevated dais, were two large chairs formed from the same polished marble, covered with grit from the cracked ceiling above. Blue and gold giltwork channels ran through each of them, up the arms to the backs, and ancient cushions still rested on the seats beneath the debris.

In the center of the symbol of Seren was a hole where a small door had once been hinged, now gone. Rhapsody bent down and looked inside. In the space below the floor was a long, deep cylinder, with a grate at the bottom where a fire had once burned, fairly regularly from the look of it. Above the grate were a number of circular metal frames that once had held mirrors, judging by the shards of glass scattered across the fire grate. The broken glass had long since melded to the floor of the hole.

"I've seen the drawings of this in the library," she said, half-aloud. She looked up at Achmed. "This is the device Gwylliam invented to both warm the floor of the Great Hall, and project light onto its ceiling. It gave the impression, if you want to take Gwylliam's word for it, of the sunrise, and the changing colors of the sky during the course of the day, fading, as the fire did, with the coming of night. He even had crystals inlaid in the ceiling to resemble stars; supposedly they glittered when the last of the light hit them. All controlled by the turning of the Earth. I wish I could have seen it in working order."

"You will," Achmed said, examining one of the pillars near the two thrones. "I'd like to see that manuscript when we get back. Any mention of the pillars? There's one for each hour of the day."

Rhapsody nodded, then stood and brushed the dust from her hands. "The design centered around the celestial observatory, which should have been directly above this part of Canrif. There was a spyglass of some size situated in the pinnacle of one of the tallest crags in the Teeth. The observatory was accessible from a stairway in one of the back rooms of the Great Hall." She pointed to doorways behind two of the pillars.

"If there was a stairway there once, it's now part of the rubble," Achmed said. "It will have to go on the list for rebuilding." He left the pillars and walked over to the thrones, stepping over the largest pieces of wreckage.

Rhapsody decided to join him. As she crossed the floor she came to the symbol of the sun and stopped. The room was suddenly warm, its heat rising to the surface of her skin, leaving her feeling light-headed.

"Achmed," she called, but her voice came out in a weak whisper. His back was to her still; he hadn't heard her.

The Great Hall seemed to sway a little as a tingle swelled through her. In her mind she recognized the physical feeling she was experiencing, but it made no sense. It was the sensation of passion.

Wet warmth pressed against her throat, the feeling of a lover's kiss, and slid lazily down her neck. Pressure, like the touch of fingers, surrounded her waist, moving slowly up to her breasts, where it began to circle. Rhapsody struggled to break the vision.

"Achmed, please," she called again. "Help." The sound of her own voice was very far away.

The world grew darker, warmer, and she felt herself sinking to the floor, supported by invisible hands. The air around her closed in, caressing her body insistently; she could feel the shirt being pulled from her waistband. Her mind tried to fight it, to bring her back to the Present, but it was a losing battle.

As much as her brain protested at what seemed a violation of her will, a stronger force, tied to the lore of Time that was part of the fabric of her soul, won out. Overwhelmed, her mind surrendered to the emotions of someone else, whomever's story it was that she was reliving. Instead of her own feelings she was momentarily consumed with lust, and passion. And anger, almost violent rage. Then, as suddenly as it came, the vision passed.

Her eyes cleared. She was looking up into Achmed's dark hood.

"Are you all right?" he asked, extending a hand. She took it, unsteady, and allowed him to pull her to her feet.

"I've had more than enough of this nonsense," she muttered, brushing off the debris and smoothing her hair. Her shirt, though loose, was still tucked in the waistband of her trousers. "I'd rather not know these pieces of lore, thank you."

"What did you see?"

Rhapsody's face, already warm from the vision, reddened

to an even deeper shade. "I didn't really see anything. It was more tactile than that."

"Well, what did you feel, then? It might be important." Achmed was growing annoyed.

"Let's just say I think this may have been the place where Anwyn and Gwylliam—er, consummated their union."

Achmed chuckled. "Lucky you."

"Excuse me?" The warmth of her face changed from embarrassment to fury.

"You're fortunate that Grunthor wasn't here. If he had been, you would never hear the end of it, though the comments would have been choice, I'm sure."

"Indeed. Does this mean I can count on you not to mention it again?"

"Maybe. Do you want to go to the bedroom now?"

Rhapsody felt her hands curl into fists, even as she reminded herself that Achmed's choices of words were often not the best. "By that do you mean that you found the royal chambers?"

"Yes."

She exhaled. "All right; let's get out of here before something like that happens again. Anwyn and Gwylliam were married an awfully long time. I'd prefer not to stay here if this is where they trysted after all the courtiers had gone home."

𝔚ell, if you want to avoid having another out-of-body sexual experience, it looks like Gwylliam and Anwyn's bedroom is the place to be."

Rhapsody couldn't help but agree. The bedchamber had been designed in the same outsize proportions as the rest of Canrif, but had been divided severely into two separate sets of quarters, both grandly appointed, but neither imparting the feel of any real warmth.

In one of the huge rooms an ornate fireplace and mantel had been carved into the stone of the mountain, its vents and the arched window above it in the same mountain wall as the outer side of the Great Hall. The window, filled with the same heavy glass as the apertures in the ceiling of the Great Hall, had grown cloudy and distorted with time, but was still intact, and offered what must have once been a magnificent view of the steppes leading to the Krevensfield Plain.

Above the fireplace was a stone relief of a family crest, rendered in painstaking detail. In the foreground a rampant lion and a griffin faced each other, a star shining over their heads. Behind them was an image of the Earth, an oak tree growing on it, with roots that pierced through the bottom. Rhapsody recognized it immediately; it had been minted onto the back of every coin she had ever seen in the old land.

"The coat-of-arms of the Seren royal family?"

Achmed nodded.

Rhapsody whistled. "It's becoming increasingly apparent to me why these people didn't get along."

"Oh? Why?"

She pointed to the crest. "Well, displaying the symbol of his dominion in the old land in prominent view of his marital bed does not seem to indicate that Gwylliam had much respect for Anwyn's heritage. Or much interest in putting her in a good mood."

"She's got her own crest above the fireplace in the room next door. A dragon at the edge of the world."

"And either way, if they were to share a bed, one would be winning, and the other would have to look at the evidence of it. So they probably didn't. I can't imagine, if I was a jealous half-dragon, not entirely comfortable in a human form in the first place, wanting to lie, night after night, beneath Gwylliam's sweating body as he pumped away, all the while being forced to stare at his family crest, knowing I was not a part of it."

Achmed smiled as he looked down at the floor, shaking his head, before he turned away from the fireplace.

"I'm very glad to know the experiences of your past have not soured your attitude toward sex, Rhapsody."

On the opposite wall, facing the fireplace, was an equally ornate headboard, carved from the same blue-black marble as in the Great Hall, veins of white and silver running through it like tiny rivers. A matching footboard lay on the floor atop a shallow pile of ancient mulch and a wide stain that had probably once been the bedclothes.

"Did the bed itself just decay here, do you think?" Rhapsody asked.

Achmed chuckled. "Well, according to you it would be unlikely that they set it afire in a fit of passionate humping, so I would guess that, yes, it rotted here. Why?"

She began to hum, trying to get a fix on the strange feeling she was picking up from the bed area. After a moment she gave him a direct look.

"Can you feel anything strange here?"

He concentrated for a moment, then shook his head. "No. What is it you feel?"

Rhapsody looked down again. "I think it's blood."

A dark expression crossed Achmed's face, but his voice did not change. "I don't sense anything."

"Do you want me to try?" she asked. Achmed nodded. "Then we have to agree now that if I seem unable to break the trance, or if I become agitated, you'll intervene and make it stop."

"I can carry you out. I'm not sure if that will bring you around, however."

Rhapsody's face hardened. "Drag me; you know how I hate to be carried."

"All right."

She closed her eyes again, concentrating on the discerning pitch, the same tone she had used to check the ring in the Cymrian museum. An image formed in her mind, the body of a man lying on the bed, his head and neck askew. As the vision cleared, she could see another man, gray-bearded, wearing linen robes painted with gold, sitting on the bed next to the corpse, his face buried in his hands.

Her skin grew clammy as she began to absorb the emotions of the scene—desolation, betrayal, guilt, anger, agony. One by one they washed over her, weaving a mantle of pain around her, until she could barely breathe for the sadness of it. Her heart thudded hollowly in her chest.

"We have to get out of this place," she said. "I don't know what happened here, or if we ever will know, but it's no surprise that the mountain itself reeks of devastation. Violent, passionate sex on the floor of the Great Hall, death in the bed of the king, the king himself rotting in the library—what kind of monsters were these people? It's not the Firbolg who make the place feel ravaged, it's whatever the Cymrians did."

Achmed laughed. "I could have told you that. Before we go, however, there's one more thing you might want to see."

$\mathcal{A}$nwyn's chamber was as huge and empty as Gwylliam's, except that the headboard of her bed had been wrought in gold and affixed to the wall. The footboard was missing, probably a casualty of looting after the Cymrians fled Canrif.

At one time the mantel around her fireplace had been gilt to match the bed, but now all that remained were a few flakes of gold leaf. Rhapsody stared up at the stone relief of the dragon sitting at the world's rim, the look in its eyes forbidding.

The loss of home crept up on her unexpectedly, and caught her off-guard. *What am I doing here?* she thought miserably, the ache of missing her family and her old life consuming her. *If I could have known that leaving Serendair would have meant ending up in this place of endless nightmares, might I have just surrendered to Michael?*

"Stop feeling sorry for yourself," Achmed said, reading her mind. His hand was on the door between the two chambers.

Rhapsody's mouth dropped open in surprise. "What? How do you know what I'm thinking?"

"You get the same pathetic look on your face every time, that's how. Perhaps one of the things your walk through the fire made you was transparent, although I seem to recall you've been that way all along. Come over here and have a look at this."

Rhapsody followed him to the door and looked through the opening. Instead of being a connecting portal, it led into another room, unlike anything she had ever seen.

The floor was tiled with small squares of polished blue marble, sanded roughly. Against the inner wall of the mountain was an enormous hexagonal vessel, much like the pool of a fountain but carved from marble as well. There were pipes that ran vertically up the wall, rusty and corroded, tapering down to a strange spout that was suspended over the pool.

On the other side of the room, against the same wall, was

a odd throne, carved from marble and attached to the same strange pipes. Its cushion had apparently been torn off or lost long before, leaving a substantial hole in the base of the chair, which was hollow. A thin tunnel no larger than a fox's den opened down below the base, bending out of sight.

The back of the throne was high and straight, and formed from the same gleaming metal that composed the ventilation system. A metal chain hung from the top of it.

"How strange," Rhapsody murmured. "Why on Earth would they need these things in their chambers? And why in a room by themselves?"

"What do you think they are?" Achmed asked, hiding a smile.

"I'm not sure. This looks like some kind of fountain, and this is a throne. Doesn't look particularly comfortable."

He laughed. "Do me one last favor, and use your discerning note on the throne, just to get an idea of what it was really used for."

"All right." Rhapsody closed her eyes and sought the right pitch, letting the image form her mind. A moment later, she turned red as the sunset.

"Gods," she said, her eyes full of embarrassment, "it's a privy. There are some very strong vibrational signatures associated with it. I never thought they'd build one indoors. How mortifying; I thought it was a throne."

"Don't be ashamed; from what we've learned so far, I'd say it would make a very appropriate throne for these people," Achmed said. "And I assume you've figured out that your fountain is a bathtub."

Rhapsody shrugged. "I've always bathed in a metal tub in front of a fire, in a stream or the public baths. I've never seen a bathtub that big, and with six sides."

"Well, Gwylliam was nothing if not redundant. Whenever he decided he liked something, whether it was that asinine saying about coming in peace, or six-sided construction, he used it at every possible opportunity, in case you hadn't noticed. The more I learn about these people, the less I'm impressed."

Rhapsody pulled the chain, and dry crumbs of rust fell into the base of the privy. "This used to have water in it?"

"Yes, and it will again when we figure out how to make the water system work. But for now that's a secondary project. The cisterns are full, so we can drink; the rest will have to wait until we subdue the first two phases and deal with Roland in the spring."

Rhapsody looked at Achmed carefully. He had the same quiet excitement in his eyes that was now always there when he spoke of his plans for the future. It was a tangible sense of purpose, of a higher aspiration. He was on the way to finding the answers to his questions, and to making a home.

How she envied him.

48

After that, it was a matter of steady progress and time. The Bolg from the Teeth had arrived the next day, the members of almost seven hundred clans, over four thousand hunter-warriors and children, some trembling in fear, others with excitement. With them had come many others, not selected by the clans as designated warriors, but intensely curious, wanting to be part of the new warlord's regime.

Achmed had turned to Rhapsody as the throng arrived, swelling the vast courtyards of the inner city.

"Laborers. Look on them well; these are the men and women with whose help we will rebuild Ylorc. In a way, their accomplishment will be even more historic than the Cymrians' was in the original building of it." Rhapsody gazed down in amazement at the sea of eager faces murmuring in the dark cavern.

"Careful, Achmed," she warned, "you're starting to sound a little like Gwylliam."

The Warlord turned to her after a moment's consideration. "No, actually, he and I are diametric opposites. We both are in the role of the swordsmith whetting a tool against a grindstone. The difference is that he saw his goal as using the tool in the honing of the stone into smoothness, while I seek to use the stone to make the tool sharper."

"Your imagery is lost on me, I'm sorry."

His eyes grew brighter in excitement. "To Gwylliam, the building of Canrif, the bending of the hostile mountain to his whim and control, was his objective. The workers were only there to provide the labor achieve his vision. They were the tool that honed his stone into smoothness.

"My goal is not the building up of the mountain, but rather the building up of the Bolg. They are like the tool, rough, needing to be sharpened. In the rebuilding of the mountain, which is their grindstone, they will learn to work as one people, will gain the destructive skills of war and the constructive skills of renovation. The mountain doesn't matter to me except as the means by which the Bolg will be united and advanced. What I seek is a sharper weapon, not a smoother stone."

A look of frank admiration had crept into her eyes, pushing aside the skepticism from a moment before. "An interesting analogy. The clever part is that, regardless of the intention, the stone gets shaped and the weapon gets sharpened either way, simultaneously."

"Yes."

Rhapsody looked back at the sea of Bolg swirling below her. They seemed somehow more fortunate than they had a moment before. "They're lucky to have you," she said. "Perhaps history granted Gwylliam's title of Visionary to the wrong Lord of the Mountain."

Achmed chuckled. "That remains to be seen. Come on; we need to wade into the fray."

The children and their mothers were immediately committed to Rhapsody's care. The warriors, meanwhile, were brought to the old guard barracks. Within a matter of a few months they were to be trained and turned into a ferocious fighting force under Grunthor's command.

The giant Sergeant Major had clearly missed his duties at the head of a regiment, and he threw himself into his new leadership role with relish. Rhapsody was occasionally awakened by the sound of trainees being marched past her chamber, singing cadences that would be awful if they weren't so funny.

Bugger you up, and bugger you down
Spread your legs akimbo,
Your time on your own is over and done,
You're mine forever, now, Jimbo.

Your nightmare is just about to begin,
And worlds of pain await you,
Pray to the gods with all your might
That the ol' drillmaster don't hate you.

So stick a cocklebur up your arse,
To get it good and ready.
It will be the sergeant's favorite home
If you hear him call you Betty.

Or Jo's favorite:

Stay in line, soldier-boy, keep with the bunch,
If you lag behind, you will be the Sergeant's lunch;
We count one-two, we count three-four,
We count it up to five;
You can't count any higher, you're the dumbest things
 alive.

Grunthor's ringing bass, answered by the raspy croaking of
the new Firbolg army, added a surreal quality to the already
nightmarish existence that Rhapsody was living in Ylorc.

At her request Achmed had closed off the corridors around
the Great Hall, and its surrounding chambers where Gwylliam
had held court.

Rhapsody and Jo were assigned rooms across from each
other on one of these protected halls, several doors down from
the new king's chambers, which were guarded day and night
by the most intelligent and trustworthy of Grunthor's recruits.
Grunthor kept quarters there as well, but had chosen to bunk
in with the army in the barracks. Achmed seemed pleased at
the speed at which the transition was progressing.

He had renamed the fortress complex the Cauldron, largely
owing to the heat produced by the forges once they were
primed and running. A thousand Bolg were put to work there,

mining the coal and feeding the mighty furnace, bringing it up to a heat level sufficient to forge weapons.

They had agreed that the development and manufacture of weapons was the crucial initial step, because it gave the Bolg the protection they would need, the tools to train the army with, and a source of income once trade agreements could be reached. Achmed had great skill in weapons design, having invented the cwellàn himself. He had adapted the other weapons in his and Grunthor's personal arsenals to complement their respective strengths while compensating for their weaker points.

He set up four large pieces of oilskin on stands in the chamber behind the Great Hall where the planning took place, labeled *weapons*, *clans (not aligned)*, *infrastructure*, and *social*.

"We've already had some of the Heath clans and the clans on the outer rim of the Hidden Realm come to us, asking to join forces," he reported, marking their names off the *clans* list with an inked quill.

"Oi expect no problems in convincin' those others to enlist, once my troops 'ave a chance to talk with 'em, sir," Grunthor added. Rhapsody shuddered; the army was growing every day, both in size and enthusiasm.

Achmed nodded. "That should give us about seventy percent of the population united. Once we've put Spring Cleaning behind us, we'll deal with the rest of them, the clans deep in the Hidden Realm, and the Hill-Eye."

"When can I get to the vineyards?" Rhapsody asked, looking at the notations under *infrastructure*. "The sooner I can see them myself, the better plan I can devise for their cultivation."

"Grunthor should have that area cleaned out—er, consolidated—before you leave on your diplomatic mission to Bethany."

Grunthor's brow darkened. "Oi still don't like the idea o' you goin' there, miss, especially alone."

Rhapsody smiled at the Sergeant. "I know, Grunthor, and I appreciate your concern, but we need to try to put a stop to the Spring Cleaning massacres by talking first."

"Why?"

"Because that's the way men do it," she replied. "Do we

want the Firbolg thought of as men, or monsters?"

"Actually," interjected the Warlord, "we want them seen as both."

A deep, annoyed sigh and a thudding sound issued forth from across the room. Jo had exempted herself from the discussions of the cultural structure of the future kingdom, announcing that the subject was boring and she would prefer to practice throwing knives.

Grunthor had set up a little hay target for her on the other side of the chamber. Often heated discussions were punctuated by the thud of Jo's missiles piercing their target. Achmed was particularly good at timing his remarks to coincide with the decisive sound.

Achmed smiled, then returned to the *weapons* chart. "The Bolg will need to be outfitted with crossbows, to maximize their range, as well as the swords they're learning to forge now. For purposes of trade we'll look to producing curved blades, and these."

He pulled forth one of the many sheaves of parchment on the table beside him and held it out for the others to see. On it was a drawing of a three-bladed throwing knife, made of steel and bound with leather at the grip. The blades curved like arms bent at the elbow, following in the same direction like a gearwheel.

"These throwing knives will be usable both in the open air and in the tunnels," Achmed explained. "They're sharp enough to be deadly in hand-to-hand situations. In flight they turn about the center of gravity, ensuring that they will cut or pierce at almost any attitude of impact."

"And will they be forged by the same method you were showing me earlier?" Rhapsody asked, still unsettled by the tour of the forges from the morning. Achmed had patiently explained the massive equipment, the vast presses that Gwylliam was still building when Canrif was overrun, but she had been too overwhelmed to follow the discussion.

"No; that's later, Stage Three. After we have one united land from the Teeth to the outer border of the Hidden Realm. Understand, Rhapsody, this is a lifetime's work. The Cymrians had master swordsmiths whose work with weapons was as impressive as the great harpers and instrument makers you sometimes speak of, each weapon so finely and carefully made as to be considered a work of art. It will take several generations for the Firbolg to get to that level. The equipment and the new forging process will help achieve it."

"Sounds like you're planning to live a long time," she said, smiling slightly.

Achmed didn't smile in return. "Forever," he said simply. "So how is the medical training going?"

"It would go better if I had some facilities. Did you plan those out yet?"

He located another set of scrolls and passed them to Rhapsody, showing her the elaborate schematic he had drawn. In addition to precise notes detailing his plans, scripted in his neat, spidery handwriting, Achmed had done a credible rendering of the internal workings of the mountain, showing the forges, the ventilation system, and the internal structure of the new city that would be rebuilt from Canrif. One small area was labeled *medical supplies*.

Rhapsody studied the plans intently, a frown drawing her brows together. Finally she looked back at Achmed.

"Where's the hospital? The hospice? We discussed this already; you should have included them in the plans."

"I did." Achmed rerolled the scroll and drew out a separate parchment document, folded in quarters. He opened this in sections and pulled out a field map. "Any immediate medical care can be provided by your trainees in the field. We will be forming a rear guard which will surround the medical station until the worst wounds have been addressed, and then the guard will advance."

"Doing what with the injured?"

"Leaving them there. We'll pick them up on the way back."

"Don't be ridiculous," Rhapsody said, annoyed. "You can't leave battle-wounded alone and untended. They'll die."

"Perhaps I need to remind you that these are Firbolg; they are not used to being pampered or coddled like Lirin and men, nor do they want to be."

"I'm not talking about coddling anyone. If they are wounded in the field, they will have to be transported to a place where they can receive care."

"I'm trying to explain that they would rather die in the field than have that happen."

Rhapsody struggled to remain calm. "These are your future subjects. It is you that keeps insisting they are not monsters, but people, and can achieve the greatness of Canrif and more. You can't have it both ways, Achmed. Either the Bolg are monsters, and if that is what you choose to rule over, by all means do so your way, but I have nothing to help you with; I have already acknowledge that I don't understand that mentality. Or they're people; primitive, brutish people to be sure, but children of the One-God, the Life-Giver, nonetheless. They are therefore entitled to same basic rights as other men.

"One of those basic rights is healing in sickness and care in dying. If that's your choice, I can help you, but I'll need facilities within the mountain, not just in war, while you're bringing them together, but always. People become ill and injured even in peacetime, and the old and sick need someone to tend to them. That requires space. Now, what's it going to be? Men or monsters?"

Achmed chuckled. There was something ironic and oddly touching about hearing her defend the monsters she had once believed the Firbolg to be. "Exactly how much space is the 'men' option going to cost me?"

"A lot. I'll need two full halls for the hospital and one for the hospice until the Heath and Hidden Realm are fully subdued." She pointed to two of the larger spaces on the barracks diagram. Achmed winced. "But here's the good news: once the kingdom is united, you can take back one of the hospital halls for barracks, and the hospice can split its hall with the orphanage."

"You may be underestimating the number of orphans."

"No, I have a plan for that. If you bless each of the orphans personally and mark him or her as special, then offer the child for adoption, the clans will vie to take them in, especially if there is some sort of long-term favor associated with doing so." Achmed nodded, and Rhapsody smiled. "See? I'm trying to be reasonable and practical."

"No doubt. All right, before I choose 'men or monsters,' I have one more question."

"Yes?"

"Can I count on your sword and musical skills in the sub-dual, assuming I'm willing to introduce this luxurious medical strategy?"

Rhapsody sighed. This had been a standard argument, and point of resistance on her part, since the planning had begun. She wanted nothing to do with the war; although she was willing to fight for defense and against what she perceived to be tyranny or evil, she was uncomfortable with the prospect of shedding blood, even Firbolg blood, just to take the mountain. Still, she acknowledged that Achmed's intentions were ultimately good ones, even if she did not like his means.

"All right," she said, acquiescing reluctantly. "I'll fight. Now, what's it to be?"

The hint of a smile came over the face of the new Firbolg Warlord.

"Men," he said. "Albeit monstrous men."

49

ℐ need to speak with you immediately."

From around the large circular table in the meeting room behind the Great Hall a dozen female faces looked up in surprise, all but one of them dark and hairy. The exception to the rule blinked in shock, then turned to the other women as she rose from her chair.

"Excuse me," Rhapsody said to the group, and hurried to the door that had only a moment before been flung open. Achmed suppressed a laugh; her use of idioms in the Bolgish language was still sporadically rough. She had just asked the group to spare her life.

"What's the matter?" she asked, her face filled with worry as she came alongside him.

"I need the brass key we found in the House of Remembrance. You had it last, I believe."

"Why? What's the emergency?"

"We just found an inner vault with the library." Achmed's strange eyes sparked with excitement. "I believe the key will open it."

Rhapsody's mouth dropped open in amazement. "That's it? You came roaring into my meeting with the midwives for that?"

Achmed's gaze returned to the group. The women, for the most part, were thin and wiry, with broad, masculine shoulders. They stared at him evenly, with no hint of the deference the other Bolg granted him as their new king.

Rhapsody had been amazed to discover these practitioners existed, and was delighted with what the fact indicated about the Bolg as a race. The warriors were expendable, given little care, even in the approach of death, even the most prized ones.

The race's infants and the mothers giving birth to them, however, had the best care the crude talents of the healers could give. The midwives were revered above even tribal leaders, and wielded a good deal of influence. Perhaps Rhapsody's idiom was not entirely misplaced.

"I need the key," he repeated impatiently.

Rhapsody took hold of the collar of his shirt and pulled his ear down to her lips.

"Listen to me," she said in a deadly tone, "do not speak to me like that again, *ever.* Especially not in front of the midwives. You lose nothing by being respectful to me; you are at the summit. But your rudeness puts me in a very precarious position. And yourself as well, because even if I don't lose face with these women, I may rip yours off just for good measure. Now try again, or go away." She pushed him back and glared at him, smoke rising from her green eyes.

Achmed smiled; she was learning the culture. In the weeks since the arrival of the first recruits she had come to understand virtually every aspect of Firbolg protocol, such as it was. He bowed deferentially from the waist.

"If it would not be too much trouble, would you please grant me this favor?" he asked loudly.

Rhapsody's face lost a little of its anger. "It's in my chamber."

"No, it's not."

She blinked again. "How do you know?"

"Because I've checked there already."

The facial thunderclouds rolled back in. "I beg your pardon? You ransacked my room?"

"I didn't want to disturb your meeting with the midwives," he said hastily.

"I don't suppose the concept of *waiting* ever occurred to you? Gwylliam's vault has been undisturbed for four centuries. You couldn't wait another half-hour?" She sighed in irritation. "It's in the chamber pot under the bed."

A look of disgust came over Achmed's face, making it comically hideous. "You have definitely been here too long already. That sounds like something Grunthor or I would do."

"I don't use it, you idiot; there's a privy in the room attached to mine. Next time, ask before you rifle my lingerie drawer."

"And deny Grunthor one of the few small pleasures in life? Selfish thing." Achmed turned to the midwives. "I apologize to all for disrupting your meeting with this urgent matter. Thank you for allowing me to consult my wise counselor." He turned away, rolled his eyes, and left the room.

Any word from Grunthor?" Rhapsody asked at supper that night, at the same table where she had met with the midwives.

Achmed shook his head, twisting a hard roll as he broke it in two. "He's left on maneuvers in the highlands past the Heath, the place we think is the abandoned vineyard. I don't expect to hear from him for at least four more days."

"And who are the lucky recipients of his attentions this time?"

"The Rippers. They're a Claw tribe that claims Gwylliam never died, and lives among their ranks."

"Maybe he does, and was just making a trip to the library to return a book when we found him," Jo suggested, picking her teeth with her dirk. "I guess the service is a little slow. Grunthor said I can go with him next time if you don't object, Rhaps. I assume you won't, will you?"

"No," said Rhapsody, laughing. "If anything, Grunthor is even more protective of you than I am. If he thinks it's safe enough to take you, I won't stand in your way."

"So what came out of your meeting?" Achmed asked, filling her glass and his own, then passing the pitcher to Jo.

"Quite a bit." The Singer sat forward, excitement lighting her face, and rose from the table. "Here, let me get the notes." She went over to the old sideboard near the wall below an ancient tapestry and shuffled through a pile of papers, finally finding what she sought. Her nose wrinkled in disgust as she returned to the table.

"Achmed, this place is a disgrace. Now that you're King of the Hill, how about getting rid of some of this garbage and redecorating? The tapestries stink."

"That's because they urinated and defecated behind them," said the Dhracian, taking a sip from his tankard. Rhapsody's face contorted in revulsion, and he laughed. "The Bolg *and* the Cymrians, both; I guess it took a while for the indoor privies to be built. Llauron may think they were a race of demi-gods, but you'd be surprised at the revolting things we've discovered about them."

"Unless it's critical to our survival, please spare me," Rhapsody said.

She unrolled the parchment pages. "All right, the midwives have agreed to take the medicinal skills I've taught them back to the various clans and train the most promising candidates, mostly female, so the next generation of midwives is taught at the same time. Then those medics will come back and staff the hospital and the hospice until the land is totally united."

Achmed nodded. "Good."

"In addition, we've laid out plans for the care of children which I'd like you to codify into law, making it a criminal offense to abuse or molest a child. The Bolg have an enlightened attitude about children already; this will be easier to peddle to them than it would be to some of the 'men' in Roland, who think children can be used as footstools and hitching posts."

Achmed smiled but said nothing. He thought about having to bail her out of the situation in Bethany where she had intervened on behalf of the boy who had been kicked several times in the marketplace by his father.

When she had attacked the man in the street, the crowd that formed was not trying to stop her, but had wanted to touch her and keep her for themselves, much the way the peasants of Gwynwood had. Rhapsody had not understood this, any more than she did all the other incidents of over-whelming attraction she had experienced.

What bothered him, then and now, was his uncertainty that he would have been able to save her alone. It was only by means of a diversionary roar from Grunthor that they had managed to escape. And shortly he would be sending her back to Bethany by herself. He shook his head to drive the prospect out of his mind.

"What about the products?" he asked.

"Wait a minute; I'll get to that. In addition to the child-protection law, we want you to mandate fair treatment of captives, healing of the injured when possible, and management of pain and death."

The new Firbolg king rolled his eyes. "The examination of laws and codes will happen after the word of the new order has reached Roland and Sorbold. I want to have conferred with whatever emissaries, if any, come, though I will be very surprised if anyone sends an ambassador before you have visited Roland about ending the Spring Cleaning ritual. Can we table this until then?"

"Yes, I'm just telling you now because you asked for an update. We also started planning for the school. The children you requested at the meeting are the first class, with eventual enrollment for all. By the way, you owe their parents armor, weapons, and food as a gift. That should be everything about the school—oh, and I have twelve new grandchildren."

"Ick," said Jo, picking up a hambone and biting on it with the same gusto Grunthor would.

"Is that in response to my grandchildren, or the meat?" Rhapsody asked humorously.

Jo chewed loudly and swallowed. "The meat's fine. I'm not crazy about kids. If you remember, I spent a good deal of time locked up with a bunch of them."

"That would make anyone crazy," Rhapsody agreed.

"They're Firbolg?" Achmed bit into the other half of the roll.

Rhapsody nodded. "Orphans. I really like them. They're a little rambunctious, but so was I when I was a kid."

"But I doubt you made a game out of catching rats and eating them alive, like they do."

"No, I'll give you that," said Rhapsody, smiling and shuddering at the same time. "But I love them anyway."

"If you're done waxing poetic about your new brats, can we discuss the plans for what we will be producing aside from weapons?"

"Certainly." Rhapsody drew forth a second large sheet of paper. "In addition to whatever weapons and armor the smiths turn out, by the end of the growing season we should have a pressing from the vineyard. It won't be spectacular, but I learned enough at Llauron's from Ilyana to produce a decent harvest.

"Once Grunthor has secured the lands past the Heath I'll go like I did after the canyon battles and gather the battle orphans, and while I'm there I'll say the Filidic blessing of the land and sing to the plants; it should help. The vines have been scavenged enough to keep the grapes healthy, and if they're left alone we should have a pressing with a high sugar content and a nice flavor. You can take a sample pressing this spring."

Achmed nodded, writing furiously. "What else?"

Rhapsody and Jo exchanged a glance. "We discovered something interesting about the wood from the tree limbs you brought me back from that dark forest beyond the Heath."

"What's that?"

Rhapsody nodded; Jo rose from the table and disappeared from the room. "Something happens to it when it's cured, like it would be in making furniture."

A moment later the girl returned, bearing a beveled spindle, and handed it to Achmed. It had a dark, rich color with a distinct bluish sheen to it. The blue color gave it a magnificent, royal look, like the tables in the Great Hall that had once belonged to Gwylliam and Anwyn, as well as other pieces they had found.

"So that's how they did it," he murmured, turning the spindle around in his hand.

"Jo's the one who figured it out," said Rhapsody proudly. "Nice work, Jo," Achmed said pleasantly. The girl flushed red to the roots of her pale blond hair and went back to eating in silence.

"And finally, my modest contribution. Do you remember those loathsome spiders that had filled six hallways with webs?"

"How could I forget? Your screams are still echoing in my ears."

Rhapsody snapped him with her napkin; it was made of heavy linen and had been found, along with intricately embroidered tablecloths, in a copper chest deep within the vault.

"Liar; I didn't scream. Anyway, their strands of gossamer, when blended with cotton fiber or wool, yield a stretchy, strong thread, suitable for weaving into lots of different items, particularly rope that is surprisingly light and tensile." She reached into her pocket and pulled out a small braid, which she tossed to him. Achmed gave it a sturdy pull, then bounced it in his hand.

"Excellent," he said.

"Glad you like it. It's also pretty because of its shine. Well, that's the end of my report. Did the key open the inner vault you found?"

Achmed drained his glass. "No," he said flatly.

Rhapsody smiled. "Pity. Well, at least it wasn't for nothing; Grunthor got to rummage my undergarment drawer without retaliation."

"Right. It's getting late," Achmed said, putting down the glass and casting a sideways glance at Jo.

"I can take a hint," said Jo. "Good night, Rhaps." She rose from the table and left the room. The Singer watched her go.

"What was that all about?" Rhapsody asked.

"She's probably tired," Achmed answered. He went to the odious tapestry, reached behind it, and pulled out a small, ornate chest and a heavy manuscript wrapped in leather and velvet. Rhapsody made a gagging sound.

"I can't believe you put anything you ever wanted to touch again back there, after what you said earlier," she said.

Achmed came back to the table. "This from the woman who kept the key to Gwylliam's reliquary in her chamber pot. I got the idea from you."

She opened her mouth to protest, then shut it abruptly. "The key to the reliquary? I thought you said it didn't fit."

"Jo was here, and I didn't want to discuss it in front of her."

"And she knew it, too." Her stomach knotted in sadness. "I can't believe you don't trust her. Why don't you like her?"

"I do like her," said the Firbolg king. "I just don't trust her. It's nothing personal. There are only two people in this world I do trust."

"Don't 'like' and 'trust' go hand in hand?"

"No." Achmed began unwrapping the book. "We can discuss that in a moment. I thought you might be interested to see this." He opened the ancient book and slid it carefully across the tabletop to her.

"What is it?" Rhapsody asked, looking down at the feathery script on the cracked pages, dried and worn with time despite their careful storage.

"It's one of Gwylliam's most valued manuscripts, the documents he considered most sacred," Achmed said, smiling slightly. "You should see the second library within the hidden vault. There are plans for parts of Canrif he wanted to build, and a few that he did that we haven't seen. Books brought from Serendair—a whole race's history. This seems to be a family registry, the royal annals of births and deaths, and family trees. It appears to be written in the same language as that contract was."

Rhapsody studied the frail page. "Actually, this is real Ancient Serenne, not just the script like that was."

"Can you make anything out?"

She turned the pages carefully, feeling pieces of the paper crumble beneath her fingers. Tracing carefully, she found the line of the royal family that she had known. Trinian, crown prince at the time of their leaving Serendair, had been four generations before Gwylliam. She passed this information on to Achmed, then turned the page, following the faded ink.

Suddenly her face went pale. Achmed noted the change in the light of the fire on the hearth, which suddenly leapt as if in panic.

"What's the matter?"

"Look where the line ends," she said, pointing to the last

entries on the page. "Gwylliam and Anwyn had two sons. The elder, and heir apparent, is listed as Edwyn Griffyth."

"And the younger?"

She looked up into his face, her emerald eyes wide in the light of the blazing fire.

"Llauron."

ou know, it's possible the name is the same for two different people," Achmed said as Rhapsody stared into the fire and drank the rest of the wine in her goblet. "What's the likelihood that either of Gwylliam's sons would have survived the war that killed their father, who was supposedly immortal?"

"Who knows?" Rhapsody said dully. "I suspect it is the Llauron we know, though."

"Any particular reason?"

"Little things. He had a fascinating device in his glass garden that provided the equivalent of summer rain indoors in the middle of winter. He said his father had built it for his mother."

"That would count against your theory, I would think; Gwylliam hated Anwyn."

Rhapsody opened the book again. "Not always. And stop it; you're baiting me. I know you think it's the same Llauron, too."

"You're right, I do. Gwylliam was, if nothing else, a visionary as an inventor; everything in Ylorc attests to that."

"And Llauron wants to see the Cymrians reunited. He said it was his hope for peace that made him believe in the need for the reunification, but now I wonder if it's just a lust for power."

The Warlord sat on the edge of the table. "This is the religious leader of more than half a million people, who lives like a well-paid gardener. Why would he be likely to want the trappings of royalty just because he was Gwylliam's heir, when he could have them now and doesn't bother?"

"I have no idea." She searched the book but could find no further entry. "It's hard for me to imagine this lovely man having any nefarious thoughts whatsoever. I mean, when I was brought to him I was totally at his mercy, and he showed me nothing but kindness. He reminds me of my grandfather. It turns out he is the son of this world's biggest bastard, with dragon blood to boot. Well, at least that explains how he knew things about me without asking; legends say dragons can sense things like that. I wonder what else he knows about us."

Achmed sighed and closed the book in front of her. "This dovetails nicely into our talk about Jo. By now you know Grunthor and I have both had some contact in the old world with demonic entities."

Rhapsody rolled her eyes. "Yes."

"Don't be rude to your sovereign; I'm not being sarcastic. Several types of demons—not just the ancient ones we have been discussing—are able to bind people to themselves, and their victims don't even know it. It's possible that anyone we meet here, if they have been in contact with such an entity, is working for an evil master, willingly or not. Trust me; I know what I am talking about here." He stared at her so intensely that she had to look away.

"And you think that's true of Jo?"

Achmed sighed. "No, not really. But I don't know that it *isn't* true, either. Rhapsody, you are too willing to trust, especially in the circumstances we find ourselves. You're busy adopting half the known world, trying to make up for what you've lost."

She looked back up at him and smiled, though her chin trembled slightly. "That may be true. But adopting one person as my brother saved my life."

It was Achmed's turn to look away to save her from seeing his own smile. "I know. What are the odds of good coming out of it again? Look, I have nothing against Jo, and Grunthor seems to like her, too. I think it's just better not to trust anyone but the three of us among ourselves."

"Better, or safer?"

"Same thing."

"Not for me," she said vehemently. "I don't want to live like that."

The Warlord shrugged. "Suit yourself. Behave as you have been, and you may *not* live like that. But remember, there are worse things than dying. If you are bound to a demonic spirit, particularly the kind from the ancient era, the time you spent with Michael, the Wind of Death, will seem like paradise, and will last for eternity."

Rhapsody shoved the book away and rose from the table. "I've had enough of this. I'm going to sing my patients to sleep."

Achmed swallowed his annoyance. If ever there was a waste of time, it was the hours she spent ministering to the wounds of the non-mortally injured Firbolg, dabbing them with herbal tonics for pain and singing to them to chase away their anxiety.

"Well, that's a useful investment of your evening. I'm sure the Firbolg are very appreciative, and will certainly reciprocate your ministrations if you should ever need something."

Rhapsody's brow furrowed, and she turned back to him. "What does that mean?" The light of the flickering fire caught in her eyes and hair, making them gleam intensely in the dark.

Achmed sighed. "I'm trying to tell you that you will never see any return for your efforts. When you are injured or in pain, who will sing for you, Rhapsody?"

She smiled knowingly. "Why, Achmed, you will."

The Firbolg king snorted. "Don't you want to see what's in the chest?"

She paused near the door. "Not particularly. And definitely not if it's going to make me find out that Lord Stephen is responsible for the sinking of the Island of Serendair and the Plague. A few more days like this and I'll be as paranoid as you."

Achmed ignored her words and opened the chest, pulling back the dry velvet covering. He lifted the contents aloft, and it caught the light of the fire; it was a horn.

Rhapsody stopped in spite of herself. "Is that the council horn? The instrument that calls the Cymrians together in council?"

"The very one."

She stared at it, dumbfounded, for a moment. Despite its centuries in the vault, the horn was shining as bright as a spring morning. There was good cheer in the air that clung to it, a sense of hope that only moments before had been driven utterly from the room.

"All right," she said at last, "so what are we going to do with it?"

Achmed shrugged. "Nothing at the moment. Maybe we'll fill it with wine to celebrate your successful trip to Roland next week. Or decorate your birthday cake with it. Or maybe Grunthor and I will get very drunk, use it to summon the surviving members of the council to the Moot outside the Teeth, and piss on them all. Who knows? I just thought you might want to know we have it."

Rhapsody laughed. "Thank you. Maybe you might learn how to play it, and then you can come accompany me on my nightly lullabye rounds."

Achmed set the horn back in the case. "Rhapsody, I can assure you, all of the things I just mentioned and more will happen before that does."

50

*T*ristan Steward, High Lord Regent of Roland and Prince of Bethany, stood at the window in his library, wondering if his counselors and his fellow regents, gathered in his keep for his annual meeting, had gone collectively mad.

From shortly after breakfast that morning to the present they had come, one by one, and had interrupted his work with insistent, if polite, suggestions that he entertain the uninvited guest that was waiting patiently in the foyer of his keep.

Tristan had refused each time, citing an overload of pressing grain treaties and a decided lack of protocol. Once he had been told the emissary was from the Bolglands he was even more unwilling to consider the possibility.

Yet here was Ivenstrand, Duke of Avonderre, second among his fellows only to Stephen Navarne, both in title and in the Lord Regent's estimation, tapping like a timid woodpecker on his door and peeking in like a chambermaid.

The Lord Roland sighed. "Gods, not you, too, Martin. First the chamberlain, then the High Counselors, and the other dukes, and now you? What is so bloody pressing that you keep me from my work?"

Ivenstrand cleared his throat. "Ah, Your Highness, I think perhaps this is a visitor you will want to meet. I took the liberty of bringing her to your office in case you decided to do so." He looked nervously at the Regent.

The Lord Roland slammed shut the atlas that he had been trying to study. "Fine. I can see I'll have no peace unless I do." With a glare he strode to the door and past Ivenstrand, only to stop and turn back again. "Did you say 'her'?"

"Yes, m'lord."

Roland shuddered. It was bad enough that the Bolg had sent an emissary to his keep; undoubtedly the place would need to be aired afterward. But a female one—the thought staggered him and pushed his irritation into the level past full-blown. He marched to his office in fury.

The chamberlain was standing at the rightmost of the double doors, averting his eyes. He had caught the expression on Roland's face and tried to slide closer to the wall as the Lord Regent approached. He opened the door for him and announced the guest.

"M'lord, the Lady Rhapsody, out of the lands of Ylorc."

"What? What nonsense is this?" demanded Roland of the chamberlain. "I've never heard of any such place. Stand aside."

He stalked into the library, bracing himself for the sight of the monstrous emissary. The new Firbolg warlord was either a coward or a genius for sending a Bolg female in the hopes that she would not be put to the sword immediately.

She was small for a Bolg. Her back was turned to the door as she stared up at the arched ceiling above her, admiring the ornate carving. The emissary was attired in a plain, unremarkable winter cape and hood, and appeared to be wearing trousers. Somehow the Lord Regent wasn't surprised by the lack of court clothing. As soon as she heard him enter the library she wheeled and dropped a low, elegant curtsy. Roland was taken aback, as he had not expected her to do much more than soil the floor with spittle.

"What is it? What do you want?"

The female looked up, and Roland was caught off-guard by the correction of his many wrong assumptions. That she was not Firbolg was surprise enough; her other attributes were cause for astonishment that he could not overcome.

Rhapsody smiled at the Lord Roland. "I'm here with a message from His Majesty, King Achmed of Ylorc." Her smiled broadened as she thought of the official Firbolg appellations she had left off—the Glowering Eye, the Earth-Swallower, the Merciless. "He has asked that I deliver it to you on his behalf, as you have not yet sent official ambassadors to his court."

Roland closed his mouth; he was unsure how long it had been hanging open. "You are not Firbolg."

"No. Should I be?"

Tristan Steward shook his head numbly. "Definitely not. I mean, no. No, you don't have to be." He cringed inwardly at how stupid he knew he sounded.

"Thank you." Rhapsody smiled respectfully, but Roland could see amusement glitter in her amazing green eyes. He took a deep breath and tried to recover his composure.

"Sit down. Please. Chamberlain, take this lady's cloak for her. Would you care for some refreshment?"

"Thank you. And no, thank you." Rhapsody sat in the curved walnut chair he pointed to after removing her cloak and handing it to the chamberlain, causing another moment of awkward silence. Finally, as though shaking off sleep, the chamberlain shook his head, took her cloak, and left, with a bow to the Regent.

The Lord Roland walked hurriedly behind his desk and sat down himself, hoping it would shield him somewhat from the pleasant effect she was having on his physiology. He was, after all, publicly betrothed.

"So, before you tell me your message, indulge me, if you will: where or what is Ylorc, and why do you come on behalf of the Firbolg warlord?"

Rhapsody folded her hands patiently. "Ylorc is the Firbolg name for the old Cymrian lands that were once called Canrif. I am here as his messenger, on behalf of my sovereign."

The Lord Roland swallowed, and Rhapsody tried not to laugh. She could read his thoughts plainly on his face: the idea of her being subservient to a Firbolg ruler was clearly disgusting to him. She decided not to let his prejudice bother her. Unconsciously she crossed her legs, and watched as his face turned magenta. When he came back to at least partial lucidity, he addressed her sternly.

"What is the message?"

"It involves the annual custom of Roland that your soldiers call 'Spring Cleaning,' the practice of ransacking Firbolg border villages and encampments."

"I know the practice; what of it?"

"It needs to cease, immediately and in perpetuity, beginning this year."

The Lord Roland snapped out of his reverie. "Really? That's interesting. And who does this warlord believe he is that he would make such a brash dictate to me?"

Rhapsody's voice was calm. "He knows who he is; if you had been listening, m'lord, you would know as well. He is the king and singular ruler of the Firbolg lands, and, as such, objects, along with his counselors, including myself, to the unwarranted and heinous slaughter of innocent Firbolg citizens."

The Regent looked at her as if she were insane. "Citizens? Are you daft? The Firbolg are monsters, and aggressive ones at that. The Spring Cleaning ritual is a defensive maneuver that has been practiced for centuries, ever since the mudspawn took over the old Cymrian lands. It eliminates the potential for the brutal raids and other border incursions that they are well known for."

The light in Rhapsody's eyes began to burn a little brighter, and the color of the irises began to kindle. "Really? When was the last of these brutal raids?"

Roland stared at her in silence; she met his gaze unblinkingly. Finally, he glanced about the room and looked back to her. Her eyes had not moved.

"Well, it would be difficult to cite you a specific raid. As I told you, the Spring Cleaning custom has been practiced for centuries, and has been very effective in keeping the violence at a minimum."

Rhapsody's face lost the last vestige of its smile. "Oh, I see. Now I understand. Violence is only violence if it is against your citizens, Lord Roland; the slaughter of the people of Ylorc doesn't matter."

The Regent's mouth fell open. "People? What people? The Firbolg are monsters."

"That's right, you did say that earlier, didn't you? Aggressive monsters, I believe. So, the army of Roland, under your direction, is responsible for a yearly raid that routinely destroys towns and shelters, leaving children dead and homeless. You cannot, on the other hand, name me one single example of a similar, even retaliatory raid on their part, in your lifetime, and probably not the lifetime of your grandfather. I am moved to ask, Lord Roland, since this is the case, who is it that qualifies as the aggressive monsters?"

Roland leapt to his feet. "How dare you? Who do you think you are, young woman, to address me in such an insolent manner?"

Rhapsody sighed. "Once again, my name is Rhapsody. I am an emissary from the court of Ylorc. I believe my answers have been consistent, and therefore bear out the fact that I do know who I am. I must say, m'lord, I'm not sure you can say the same thing."

His eyes began to smolder with rage. "Meaning what, exactly?"

"You see yourself as lord of a civilized and noble people, and, for the most part, you are probably right. But when a people such as yours deny the humanity of a race of individuals that builds homes and villages, makes tools and forms family groups, you are doing a far greater disservice to yourselves than you are to the innocents you kill; you become far worse monsters than you accuse them of being."

The Lord Roland slammed his hand down on his desk. "Enough! Get out. I cannot believe I have wasted my time being insulted by the likes of you. You are a very disturbed young woman. You may look more like the previous inhabitants of the Cymrian lands, but you have the manners and attitudes of the current population."

Rhapsody stood and stared him down. "Thank you. From what I understand of the Cymrians and their history, you have just delivered me a great compliment, however unintentional. I will leave posthaste, with two final comments."

"Make them quickly, before I call the chamberlain."

"That won't be necessary; as I said, I am going. First, the

other part of the message. King Achmed says to tell you that if you abide by his wishes and cease hostilities this year, he will guarantee no incursions into Roland by the Bolg."

"The Bolg are a loose collection of brainless beasts that know only animal instinct, and could not organize an official incursion any more than they could fly. In addition, I doubt that this warlord, if he is still alive when you return with my scoffing message of refusal to him, has any control or jurisdiction over what they do."

"Well, m'lord, you are certainly entitled to your opinion, however misinformed that may be. Allow me to pass on a bit of intelligence you might not have: the Bolg are now united, for the first time in their history, under their king. We are training them, and educating them, in many things, including the production of salable material goods for which we hope to have Roland as a trading partner."

"You are a very sick girl."

"Be that as it may, their first vintage will be available in the autumn, along with some credible weapons of a design I guarantee you have never seen before. In addition, if you are unwise enough to doubt what I've said about the king's resolve, your aggression will prove costly to you and your soldiers, mark my words."

"Get out."

Rhapsody turned her back on him and went to the door as he called for the chamberlain. She took her cloak from the man and turned to face the Regent again.

"Thank you for seeing me, Your Highness; I'm sorry what I had to say wasn't better received. If you wish to meet with me again I will be happy to do so, despite this conversation."

"Have no fear of that," the Lord Roland replied, his eyes glinting with anger. "You are a very beautiful woman, madam, but you haven't the sense the All-God gave a grasshopper. Please do not trouble me again. I will be instructing my counselors to turn you away if you should ever return to my domain."

Rhapsody smiled as she put on her cloak. "As you wish, m'lord. I hope you realize that this means when you want to meet with me you shall have to travel to the edge of my realm yourself now. Happy New Year." She nodded pleasantly at the chamberlain and left the hall, escorted by the guards outside the door. The High Lord Regent watched her go, then turned to the chamberlain himself.

"Get my counselors in here immediately."

"Yes, m'lord."

*L*ord Stephen Navarne listened as patiently as he could while the Lord Regent berated the other dukes. He had not been there that morning, had no hand in the matter of the ambassador about whom his cousin was bellowing, because he was attending to the return of those of Tristan's soldiers who had helped put down Navarne's most recent uprising. He had answered the Lord Regent's angry summons anyway; now he was especially glad he had come.

After the tirade was over, and the other dukes had been dismissed, Stephen hung back, seeking a private word with his cousin.

"There is something I'm not certain you're aware of, Tristan," he said pleasantly, trying to mask the concern he felt knotting his stomach. "The woman you are snarling about, and her Bolg companions, are the ones who rescued the House of Remembrance some time back."

The Lord Roland stared at him blankly. "Oh?"

"Yes, I'm afraid so. And, in fact, they are seen as local heroes of somewhat mammoth proportion in Navarne, as they also managed to return a sizable number of the missing children I had mentioned to you at our last session. They apparently took on the forces of a demon or something like it in doing so."

Tristan Steward said nothing for a moment and walked back to the window of his library as he had that morning. He poured himself a glass of port.

"Interesting," he said.

*W*hen Rhapsody returned to the Cauldron, Grunthor swept her into an enthusiastic embrace.

"Oi was worried," he said, looking into her face with relief.

Rhapsody smiled. She knew he meant it.

"I'm fine," she said, giving the enormous shoulder a pat, and turning to Jo.

"How'd it go?" asked Achmed, watching the girl run to her and hug her. His eyes met Rhapsody's and a smile passed between them. This was a first.

Rhapsody put an arm around Jo and followed her Bolg friends into the dreary hall, where a crude breakfast had been laid for her.

"Well, I have two observations."

"Yes?" Achmed crossed his arms and leaned against the wall as Grunthor held her chair for her.

"Well, are you sure you aren't the one who's prescient, Achmed? Everything went almost exactly as you said it would, word for word."

Achmed smirked. "That's not prescience, it's predictability."

"And two, given the reaction they had to me, you might as well have gone yourself; it couldn't have been any worse. Now I understand why you're so cranky all the time."

51

Deep within the old Cymrian lands, past the wide heath beyond the canyon and sheltered by a high inner ring of rock formations, was Kraldurge, the Realm of Ghosts. It was the only place the Bolg, without exception, did not go, a desolate, forbidding place from the look of its exterior structures.

What heinous tragedy had occurred here was unclear in the legends, but it had been devastating enough to scar the psyche of the Firbolg who lived in the mountains permanently. They spoke in reluctant whispers of fields of bones and wandering demons that consumed any creature unfortunate enough to cross their paths, of blood that seeped up from the ground and winds that ignited anyone caught on the plain.

Rhapsody had come upon the guardian hills quite by accident while scouting for battle orphans, and now she and Achmed made their way arduously back through the edge of the inner Teeth, trying to find the place again.

They had been searching for a time before Achmed's impatience got the better of him. He closed his eyes and concentrated on the hidden pass he had located in the rockwall. He loosed the lore he had gained in the Root and let his sight speed along the path, a narrow, overgrown hall in the mountain that had clearly seen no traffic in centuries.

At its terminus the pass opened into an uncovered meadow, thick and overgrown in high weeds from years of isolation. A hill-like mound rose in the center of the meadow; otherwise there was nothing remarkable in the hidden canyon-dell.

"Well, I hate to disappoint you, but I don't see a single demon, and there are no gushing geysers of blood."

Rhapsody sighed. "Good. I had more than enough of that at the House of Remembrance, thank you. But I'd still like to see this place; there must have been something there to inspire such hideous fear, even if it has been gone for centuries. Besides, I brought all these seeds; it would be a shame to have to cart them back to the Cauldron."

"Very well."

Achmed pulled his cwellan out and slipped between the rockwalls. Rhapsody never ceased to be amazed at the speed and silence with which he wielded the bulky weapon. She followed closely behind him, her bow out with an arrow on the string.

As they crept through the pass their footfalls sounded up the canyon walls, echoing at an enormous amplification, so that anything that might have been waiting for them would have had ample warning. Despite the noise they made, on entering the hidden meadow they found nothing different from what Achmed had described.

The canyon that hid the field was so tall that the wind rarely reached down into it; it howled around the top of the surrounding crags, creating a mournful wail. Achmed and Rhapsody smiled at each other. Even the bravest Bolg could mistake the noise for demonic shrieking. Despite the natural explanation for the sound, Rhapsody could sense an innate sadness to the place, a feeling of overwhelming grief and anger.

She bent and touched the earth but could discern nothing unusual; perhaps this was a forgotten burial ground from the earliest conflicts of the Cymrian War. There was no mention of it in the manuscripts they had found within Gwylliam's, but there probably wouldn't have been, anyway.

Achmed began to scout the perimeter of the internal canyon. The field was small enough to be seen in its entirely from the top of the mound, and it seemed completely enclosed, with the only egress being the pass through which they had come.

He gave Rhapsody a nod, by which she knew he meant for her to go about her business while he surveyed the terrain. When she reached the gentle summit of the central hill Rhapsody took from her pack a burlap sack full of seeds and her hand tools, as well as her flute. A harp would have served her purposes better, but she had left hers at the House of Remembrance in the crotch of the oak tree, playing its song of healing, protecting it from the corruption that had almost killed it.

She cast a glance over at Achmed, reassuring herself that she could still see him, then set about digging in the earth, taking a sample to determine the type of soil that lay beneath the grass. To her surprise the newly thawed ground, warm in the light of almost-spring, was loamlike and fertile beneath a thin layer of rocks, rich with nutrients. She had guessed the shelter from the wind and elements would have left it more barren. She was glad to be wrong.

Rhapsody touched a small patch of highgrass and called forth the fire she could feel in her soul. Instantly the brown weeds burst into flame at the base, burning out quickly under her hand.

She pulled the now-dead scrub out by the roots and dug into the earth, turning it to the depths the seeds would need for best planting. They were hear'sease, a flower she had loved in the old land that had been brought by the Cymrians to this one, its blossoms often given as a sign of condolence and planted on graves or battlefields in memory of loss. It had seemed the obvious choice. The plantings would grow to cover the mound by midsummer, and come back each spring until the whole of the canyon bloomed with it in a year or two.

The wind moaned again high above her as she opened the burlap sack and drew forth a handful of seeds. She sang along in tune with the wind as she planted them, a song of atonement and comfort, seeking to bring consolation to the wounded land.

When the earth was back in place she took the highgrass and covered the area to hold in the moisture from the rain and protect it from the wind. Then she moved a few feet away and repeated the process up and down the sides of the hill.

She had planted most of the mound when the trowel slipped from her hand and disappeared into the earth. Rhapsody was astonished; the hole she had dug was no deeper than her hand, and certainly could not have held the tool. Perhaps she had hit another hole or pit of some kind.

She called to Achmed and began moving more of the dirt away. By the time he had crested the hill she had located a small crack, about as wide as a string, with a larger hole in the middle big enough to have held the tool, but not deep enough to have swallowed it.

"Look at this," she said to Achmed as he put his weapon down. "It ate my trowel."

"It's been undisturbed for centuries; perhaps it's hungry."

Rhapsody peered down into the crack. "It looks hollow down here, but I can't see the bottom."

"Let me look." Achmed moved above the crack and stared down into the tiny hole. She was right; there was a depth past the surface of the soil. He closed his eyes again and made use of his path lore once more.

His mind raced through the hole and down through the crack in the earth. It was enormously deep and regular, almost cylindrical past the layer of rocks, becoming a tube of sorts in the ground.

A hundred or more feet down the tube widened out and emptied into a vast underground cavern, the firmament of which they were standing above. The dome of the firmament was several hundred feet above the bottom of the cavern, and the grotto was filled with water.

"It's an underground lake of sorts," Achmed said, standing erect again. "Shall we go exploring?"

"Yes, of course," Rhapsody answered excitedly. "Just let me finish up here; I'm almost done. Why don't you get out our noonmeal while I put these last few seeds in the ground?"

Achmed nodded and opened his pack, noticing that the

song of consolation she was singing had changed in tone to far more cheerful than it had been before.

When she finished she picked up her flute and sat down on top of the hill in a shaft of sunlight. She began to play the song she had sung; it blended with the wind and softened a little the discordant wail bellowing down from the peaks above. It had all the sorrow of a maypole dance; she was having a hard time containing her excitement at the thought of the upcoming adventure. He shook his head and smiled to himself as he began to eat.

After a brief search of the meadow they located the passage down. It was cleverly hidden in the darkest part of the canyon, in an alcove that always seemed touched by shadow. Achmed had not seen it when he was canvassing the place.

He led the way, while Rhapsody concentrated on not slipping on the lichenous path, overgrown with slime. She shuddered; the dank air reminded her of being on the Root, and it was all she could do to keep going as the tunnel turned and she could no longer see the light of the meadow.

"How deep do you think it is?"

"Three, four hundred feet, taller at the center. Maybe a thousand at the highest point."

They followed the path down for a long time. Just as Rhapsody's stomach had had all it could take, they came out into a huge grotto, a cavern that stretched out into seemingly endless darkness.

It was lighted from above by a series of tiny holes in the firmament like the one that had swallowed her tool, and the light was strong enough to have produced plant life all along the shores of the massive lake that filled the base of the cavern. The scent here was less dank and more fetid, like stagnant water from a swamp, even though there was a current in the lake.

Down at the water's edge was a copper structure, rectangular in shape and sealed with wax, its sides ornately engraved with intertwining patterns. Buried just beneath the surface of the sand before it lay the remains of a series of metal rollers, once held in place by an iron trackway. Time and water had fused this system into a mass of rust.

The front wall of the copper structure was hinged on the

bottom. After careful examination they determined it was a storage place for a rowboat that had once been moored nearby. The rusty iron mooring still stood in the sand, fragile and encrusted with algae.

Achmed pried the copper structure open and found the rowboat and a metal oar still inside, resting on a bed of rice. Rhapsody had initially thought the rice grains were vermin larvae and leapt away as they spilled out onto her feet. Achmed had taken great pleasure in her embarrassment and laughed for several minutes while he pulled the rowboat out of its drydock to examine it.

It was made from wood covered with thin hammered sheets of copper, which had turned green but had managed to preserve the boat's integrity over time. The vessel was free from holes, though the wood showed signs of dry rot, and he knocked on it several times to check the soundness of the floorboards. He must have deemed it seaworthy, because he turned it over again and shoved it into the lake.

"Can you swim?"

"Yes," Rhapsody answered. She glanced across the lake. In the distance she could see something, a structure of some sort, on the far shore. "Can you?"

"Somewhat. Enough, I suppose; it doesn't appear very deep." Rhapsody eyed him doubtfully. She would guess it to be at least seventy feet in the middle. "Are you game?"

"Of course," she retorted indignantly. "I'm the one who can swim. Let's go."

She climbed into the boat, and Achmed followed her after locating the other oar. It, like its twin, was made of a metal neither of them recognized, and was surprisingly light and free of rust or tarnish.

They rowed across the lake, taking turns at the oars. While Achmed rowed, Rhapsody looked all around her in amazement.

The dome above her was higher than she could see in the light that flooded down from it, much like looking up into a cloudy sky. The lake was clear and pure a few yards from shore, so that they could almost see the bottom, even in the middle. They were able to discern the movement of fish, and a wind was noticeable on the water, though nowhere near as strong as it would have been above ground.

Stalactites and stalagmites protruded from the ceiling and the floor of the cavern on the outskirts of the lake, glistening in crystal iridescence. Now and then one of the toothlike structures would catch a stray sunbeam and flash it over the surrounding walls and water, leaving gleaming patches of light that glittered for a moment, then were gone.

A waterfall was visible when they were almost over to the far shore, tumbling from a rock ledge that jutted near the top of the cavern where the grotto wall met the dome. It was roaring, swollen with the spring rains, and Rhapsody was enchanted with the music that it made as it fell into the lake and echoed in the cavern all around them.

"This place is beautiful," she said to Achmed. He raised an eyebrow, but said nothing.

Finally, as they approached the shore, the structure they had seen from across the lake came into view. It was a small cottage, centuries old, standing not far from the shore of what appeared to be an island. An equal expanse of water was visible behind the island, setting it almost exactly in the center of the lake. The house was dark, and stained by dusky patterns where ivy or something like it had once grown. It seemed structurally sound, but it was impossible to be sure from the boat.

Rhapsody wriggled with impatience as Achmed maneuvered the boat into its ancient dock; it was all she could do to keep from leaping from the craft and wading to shore. He had probably not had much experience piloting boats before, she realized in amusement. This was the first time she had seen him not the master of the task he was undertaking, and she was enjoying it. Apparently he was not.

"Make yourself useful—tie off the rope," he instructed through his teeth. Rhapsody hid her smile and complied. She climbed out of the boat after him and followed him up the shore.

52

At the top of the shoreline where the sand met dry grass they could see the whole of the island. In addition to the small cottage they found what once had been flower beds, now long dead, and a marble gazebo set a considerable way back from the house. The marble structure was solidly encrusted with centuries of grime, like the house, but also bore the ancient marks of fire damage, black stains that spread irregularly across one side of the gazebo.

From the moment they set foot on the island they could both feel it, a mournful, pulsing anger inherent in the place. It did not scream of evil, but rather of rage, and sorrow beyond measure. Rhapsody shuddered and moved closer to Achmed, but he seemed oblivious of the feeling. He had seen birthplaces of hatred before.

They did a quick reconnaissance of the island, but it was hardly necessary; the utter absence of any other living presence was obvious. Achmed looked carefully at the chimney, examining the bricks, which were still held in place by the ancient, crumbling mortar. He nodded toward the door of the cottage, and Rhapsody followed him inside.

The odor of lost time was heavy inside the place, the scent of mold and musty fabric, stale air and decay. Rhapsody drew her sword and held it like a torch in front of her, her eyes sparkling in wonder.

The parlor opened to the right, with a small staircase leading upstairs on the left across from the front door. Achmed let her pass ahead of him with the glowing sword, his eyes scanning the architecture. It bore many of the hallmarks of the Lost Island, as did some of the furniture. It was from the Cymrian era, though that had been obvious from the beginning—the Bolg certainly had never set foot here. He opened the front door as wide as it could be opened and added stale air to the dank place.

The parlor contained a fireplace on its outside wall, a beautifully carved mantel above it thick with dust. It probably had once been a cozy room, and it led into a kitchen area that spanned the entire back of the house.

Achmed examined the enormous hearth and food-storage areas with interest. The sophistication of the design was higher than was commonly in use in this land now, indeed, even more than in Canrif, with multiple depths in the hearth for different kinds of food preparation, and a dredge dug from the lake to cool the brick storage areas and pump water into the house. Pipes fashioned from copper ran through the ceiling into the area upstairs.

Rhapsody had circled around the back of the staircase and found herself in the dining room, furnished with a small oak table, still in beautiful condition, and four chairs. A huge window wall was fashioned out of blocks of glass, clear in the central panes, but the exterior ones had been carved like prisms.

This side of the house faced the waterfall, and doubtless the view was the reason for the window wall. It was also a western exposure, and Rhapsody speculated that light must come through at the junction of the rock crag and the dome of the firmament. No doubt the filtered light of the setting sun added to the atmosphere of an evening meal here, accentuated by the rainbows that the prisms must have cast around the room. She wished she could have seen it in its glory.

She walked through the doorway that led back into the front hall to find Achmed there, starting up the stairs. Rhapsody followed carefully, pulling the cobwebs away from the ceiling above the steps.

Once upstairs he had gone to the left and she stood in the doorway behind him. It was a small empty room, its only interesting feature the turret from a small tower she had failed to notice from outside, with a curved bank of windows and window seat. The fabric on the window seat had rotted beyond recognition, but the glass of the windows was intact. It was Rhapsody's impression that it had been a study, though there was no furnishing to confirm that belief.

Across the hall on the other side of the staircase was a larger room, its nature made obvious by the large bed against the staircase wall. The headboard was carved in dark wood, and even the years of dust could not obscure the masterly craftsmanship and beauty of it.

A fireplace took up the wall opposite it, sharing a chimney with the hearth in the parlor, the mantel a smaller version of the one downstairs. It had a window that looked out onto the lake, caked with grime and mildew. The floorboards had begun to rot, and Rhapsody walked carefully, fearful of crashing through the ceiling of the room below.

There were two additional doors in this room, one on the same wall as the headboard, leading to an area over the stairs, the other over the kitchen. The area over the stairs turned out to be a cedar closet with nothing in it but a small chest of carved mahogany. In it Rhapsody found a tiny gown of white lace and colorful embroidery, sized to fit a very young infant. She returned it carefully to the chest and left the closet.

Achmed had already opened the other door and was leaning on the frame. She came up behind him and peeked into the room beyond.

It was an indoor bathroom like the ones in the Cauldron, with a large tub, beautiful despite its centuries of tarnish and dust. The floor was made of marble tiles, and the copper pipes she had seen downstairs ran to the privy and the sink as well. Both the tub and sink had pumps beside them, and the basin and tub floor had discolored where the water had dripped for years.

"Seen enough?" Achmed's voice broke the age-old stillness, causing Rhapsody to jump.

"I guess so," she answered, reluctant to leave the fascinating house. She followed him down the stairs and out the front door, casting one last wistful glance around before closing the door again.

𝒯he small gardens had apparently gone largely untended even before they had been allowed to die, Rhapsody determined. The stains on the house and the ground suggested climbing roses in at least two places, vines that had been allowed to spread, unchecked and unpruned.

It seemed a shame to her; in her mind she was already imagining what the place could look like, covered in plantings, tended lovingly, with an eye toward balance and the strange light conditions beneath the ground. But even as she fantasized about the quintessential gardens, she knew that nothing could grow here now, anyway. There was something fundamentally wrong with the place, a disturbance in the very nature of it that would counteract anything growing or blooming, an anger that had penetrated the soil.

Achmed was already approaching the gazebo. It was situated on a small rise on the other end of the island, strategically placed, no doubt, but for what strategy he could not tell.

He walked around it, examining its placement on the ground. He determined it was probably carved on the spot where it stood, a fact that fascinated him. Its sculptor had been a master, with an eye for stone. Even an untrained eye could see that the original marble block had been positioned perfectly to allow for the accentuation of the stone's best features. It was smoothly hewn and polished, with delicate engravings along its roof and six columns supporting the dome.

Rhapsody wandered up one of the two sets of marble steps leading into the gazebo. Within it there were two semicircular benches facing one another in opposition, forming an S shape in the center of the rotunda. They were carved from the same stone as the gazebo itself; in fact, she thought perhaps they had been carved as part of it.

At the far end of the building was a battered birdcage lying on the gazebo floor, its door broken off, next to what must have been its stand. Both pieces were remarkable in design, and wrought from what looked like gold.

The stand was taller than Rhapsody herself, and the birdcage was big enough to hold a small child. It was black with tarnish and soot from whatever fire had coated the gazebo itself, but seemed more or less intact. She marveled at the craftsmanship of the cage, so strangely out of place in the Bolglands. Rhapsody reached over and touched the tiny door.

As she did she was blown backward by the force of the vision that overtook her. Time slowed to a torturous pace, and she saw the gazebo as it had been long ago, its columns gleaming white in the darkness of the garden.

Before her stood a man, human and full-bodied, with a thick gray beard and heavy, dark eyebrows. He wore robes of linen painted with gold, and his face was contorted with a rage that made his eyes smoke.

Slowly, second by second, she watched as he drew his arm back and swung, a powerful, grievous blow aimed squarely at her face. She felt the air around her shatter and pain wash over her, the force of which left her face stinging, as the columns of the gazebo swirled around her and tilted. And then the darkness of the vision dissipated and she was staring up at the cloudy firmament, her head in Achmed's hands.

A deep groan escaped her as Achmed helped her stand. He led her to one of the stone benches and she sat down, trying to make her world stop spinning. It took a long time for that to happen. Finally she spoke.

"Well, now I know why this place feels so angry."

"What did you see?"

She rubbed her temples. "I got the wonderful opportunity to see Gwylliam through what must have been Anwyn's eyes at the moment he struck her. Remember how Llauron said he had hit her?"

"Yes."

"Well, that's putting it nicely. He must have done some serious damage; my ears are still ringing."

"No wonder she tried to destroy him."

"Well, as bad as it was, I still think her reaction was a little extreme. I mean, I'd be furious too, but I don't think I'd lead an army of tens of thousands to their deaths over it. I probably would have just poisoned his porridge."

"Well, from what I've read, the First and Third Fleet Cymrians were looking for an excuse to beat on each other anyway. The Third Wave had the attitude that they had sacrificed the most, had stayed behind and held the beachhead while the others made a speedy retreat. They had a rough time when they landed, had to fight their way in while the First Fleet found no resistance and an easy life in the woods. Of course, what I've been reading is from his point of view. I'd say Gwylliam and Anwyn's little sparring match was just the spark that lit the conflict."

Rhapsody stood and looked around. "So this is where the war began. Right here on this island, in this gazebo. No wonder the place is haunted."

Achmed chuckled; it was a strange sound, and her eyes went immediately to his face. "Are you afraid of ghosts, too, Rhapsody?"

"Certainly not," she said, offended. "If anything, I'll bet they're afraid of me."

"Well, I can certainly see why they would be," the Firbolg king said sarcastically. "You are so very frightening, after all."

Rhapsody smiled knowingly and took out her flute again. She sat back on one of the benches and closed her eyes, listening to the listless wind over water.

She took in the sounds and vibrations of the grotto, searching for the discordant notes, and found them almost immediately. Rhapsody raised her flute to her lips and played a sweet note. It filled the air at once and amplified forth from the gazebo, echoing off the walls of the grotto and filling the cavern with its sound, hanging in the slow air until it dissipated a few moments later. She turned to Achmed in excitement.

"It all makes sense now!" she exclaimed, leaping to her feet. "The reason we couldn't find this place is that it is naturally hidden by layers of vibrations—the bowl of the canyon that the field lies within and the wind that rips around it, the water beneath the ground and the churning of the waterfall make a rising mist that shields the cavern.

"And the gazebo is like a megaphone of sorts. Sounds here are amplified because of where it is placed and what it is made from; it's like a natural podium if you want to have what you say heard everywhere. So the hatred that is ingrained in this place is being transmitted out through those layers, which is what scares the Firbolg, and why the ground feels so awful in the glen."

Achmed nodded but said nothing. It was also the reason he disliked the place. Water had always been his enemy when trying to find a vibrational path. The only place anyone had been able to hide from him in the old world was on, in, or near the sea.

"Well, now that your mystery is solved, let's go back."

"Wait; I have to try something else." Rhapsody ignored the ugly look he gave her and began to play the flute again. She concentrated on the painful notes, the dirge that the cavern contained, and matched each sorrowful tone with a brighter one, weaving a song of atonement and peace. The effect was not permanent, but she could feel a slight improvement when she was finished.

"Can I have this place for my own? Please?" She ignored his incredulous stare and pushed on. "I can restore the house; it just needs a little carpentry and a lot of cleaning. And I can work on the song of the place, make it healthy again, drive away the memories that Gwylliam and Anwyn left here to fester. Can this be my, well, my—"

"Your duchy?"

"My what?"

"Your duchy. Grunthor's always calling you Duchess or Your Ladyship; it seems appropriate that we make you one. Congratulations. You will be Firbolg royalty."

Rhapsody ignored the sarcasm. "Well, good. That way I can act as your ambassador and have a title to make me legitimate." She laughed as Achmed smirked. "Be that way. I've never had a place that was all mine; it was always owned by someone else."

"I will deed it to you in perpetuity, as long as we can leave now."

"Bargain." They shook hands, and Rhapsody ran for the boat.

𝒮o what are you going to call this place?" Achmed asked as he rowed back across the lake. Her excitement had sustained itself; they were moving much faster than they had on the voyage across.

"I've been thinking about that," she said, her eyes sparkling. "Let's name it something from the old world, something powerful and royal, so it takes on some of the traits. That seems appropriate, doesn't it?"

He sighed. "Whatever you want. It's your duchy. You will owe me taxes, by the way, on whatever goods you produce."

She knew he was joking, but she regarded him seriously. "Fair enough. I think you will have to take it in trade, however. I don't intend to sell it, it's better if it's just given to someone you love."

Achmed's eyebrows shot into his hairline. "Excuse me? I thought you had decided to be celibate."

Rhapsody glared at him. "Not that. Spices, herbs; maybe flowers. You can be a real pig, you know."

"It was a joke."

"I know. It's always a joke." She stared off into the distance at the disappearing waterfall, its music ebbing with her spirits.

Achmed regarded her sharply. "I'm sorry." She waved a dismissive hand at him. "Rhapsody, what's the matter?"

She didn't look at him, but continued to watch the island as it faded into the mists of the cave. "I don't know. Jealousy, probably. That's not exactly it, but I don't have a word that describes it better."

"You're jealous?" Achmed's brows furrowed. "Why?"

Finally the green eyes turned on him, absent their former sparkle. "All right, I'm not jealous, I'm lost. You have no regrets that keep you awake at night, Achmed, no losses in the old world to mourn. Here you have a reason for being, a place that needs you, and people who do, too; an opportunity to do something good on a historic scale. You have a new life."

He swallowed; he was not good at this. "You're a part of that life. You have a contribution to make to the same goal; it's your opportunity as well."

She shook her head. "Don't misunderstand, please. I want to help you, to help the Bolg, especially the children. But it's not my reason for being."

"So what is?"

Rhapsody shook her head sadly. "If I knew, I wouldn't feel lost." She took the oar from him and began to row.

"You know, my mother was always chiding me about leaving the door open. We lived on a wide-open plain, and the winds that tore through the rolling hills could be violent. I can still hear her—'Please close the door.' I never learned. And it's ironic; my past is a corridor of doors I left open, never meaning to close them. Except now, the house is gone, too, blown away by the wind.

"I guess I've never really accepted what I've lost. I don't know why; I try, but it keeps coming back to me, night after night, even after all this time. So now I have to come to terms with my loss and figure out what to do next.

"I need the things you have—a home, and a goal, and a chance to do something good of my own. And someone who needs me—Jo, my grandchildren, the Bolg, to a small degree, and maybe even you and Grunthor. Maybe having this place, this duchy of my own, is a start toward finding those things."

Achmed exhaled. The light was returning to her eyes a little, banishing the desolation he had felt a moment before, against his will, on her behalf. *What is this strange power the fire gave her?* he mused. It was even beginning to affect him.

"So what is the name of this new farm?" he asked.

She thought of the castle of the Seren high king, perched on a rocky face above the crashing sea.

"I think I'll call it Elysian," she said. It was a place she had never seen.

Ｃhree weeks later it was announced throughout the Bolg-lands that the new warlord king was making a trip to the demons in Kraldurge to offer sacrifice. An enormous wagon was loaded with gifts to the evil gods, tied with cloth to keep the sacrifice from the prying eyes of the Bolg, though none showed up to wish the king well. The gifts had been bought in Bethe Corbair and Sorbold from a list carefully prepared by the Singer, known throughout the Bolglands to be the king's First Woman.

Rhapsody had grown used to the necessity of the reference, though it still amused and annoyed her. *Anything to keep us safe here*, she had told Jo, herself known as the king's Second Woman. The Bolg would only bother those women who belonged to leaders they wanted to challenge, and thus far that meant no one came near either of them. She did not tell Jo about Elysian, keeping it a surprise for when the renovations were finished.

The enormous Cart of the Sacrifice set forth in the night toward the Inner Teeth, where it was swallowed up by dark-ness. The king and the Sergeant Major returned the next day, slightly tired from their meeting with the demons but none the worse for wear.

The demons had acknowledged the rulership of the king, the Sergeant had announced. They would not eat any more of his people on the condition that the Bolg continue to keep away from their lands. If the Bolg violated the agreement, however, the horrors of the tales of old would seem as nothing compared to the fate the intruders would suffer. Achmed smiled as he detected the collective shiver that ran through the assemblage as Grunthor finished.

Rhapsody remained in Elysian, delighted by her new furnishings. She had been thrilled when Achmed and Grunthor delivered her furniture and the material for her to make drapes and bedspreads, serving them dinner to express her thanks from the stores they had laid in the freshly scrubbed kitchen.

As they sat in the dining room enjoying the beauty of the sunset through the wavy panes, rainbows from the prismatic glass fell over each of them, illuminating their faces with colored light. She smiled; the song of peace was taking hold, her plantings were beginning to grow, and she had a place of her own to share with her friends.

She walked them down to the water's edge and waved as they climbed aboard one of her two new boats. Rhapsody watched until they had passed from her sight, then turned back to her house, where the smoke curled contentedly up from the chimney and the lights burned in the windows, a growing warmth in the darkness of the grotto.

Once inside, she gently closed the door.

53

Rosentharn, Knight Marshal of Bethany, cleared his throat and knocked nervously on the door.

After what seemed an eternity, the Lord Roland's voice answered.

"What? Who's there?"

"Rosentharn, m'lord." Even through the door he could hear the stream of muttered curses.

"What do you want? If it's another of those blasted border raids, I don't want to know about it unless they're sacking my own keep."

Rosentharn loosened his collar. "Nothing like that, sir. I just came from the northern gate, where news has come in that Lady Madeleine Canderre is on her way to Bethany."

The door opened a crack, and the Lord Roland's head emerged, his hair wildly tousled. "When?"

"She arrives sometime after dawn, m'lord."

Tristan Steward ran a hand over his unkempt locks. "Ahem, yes. Well, thank you, Rosentharn."

"My pleasure, m'lord." Rosentharn waited for the door to close before giving in to a wide smile. Then he turned on his heel and returned to his post.

Fornication!"

A throaty chuckle came from across the room.

"As you wish, m'lord. That's what I'm here for."

Tristan smiled and retied the belt of his dressing gown.

"Sorry, Pru; my fiancée's coming."

Prudence laughed. "If you get over here quickly, perhaps Madeleine might be able to make the same statement."

"You're so naughty. It's one of the things I like best about you."

Tristan turned to the mahogany sideboard, poured two glasses of port from a crystal decanter, and carried them back to the bed. He handed one to Prudence and raised the other to his lips, allowing his gaze to roam over her body. The rim of the glass hid the melancholy look brought to his face by what he saw.

Each time he looked at her it grew harder to believe that they had been born on the same day, minutes apart. Despite the difference in their social classes they had always been together as children, growing through each awkward stage as a pair, almost as if they shared a single soul. And while time had not yet ravaged his flesh, still bequeathing him the muscularity of youth for the moment, Prudence was beginning to show the signs of age, inevitable in those not born from the bloodline of the Cymrians.

It was something he had always known, but had never

thought about until recently. Perhaps his own impending marriage had made him take stock, caused him to try to account for the years that had flown by, leaving him unscathed, for now. Perhaps it was the fact that, when he was alone, lost in the solitude of his thoughts, he was not certain if there was anything to show for all that time.

Either way, it had made him look at her with new eyes, eyes that now saw the slight slackening of the dewy skin, the whisper-thin lines around her eyes and the corners of her mouth, the faint spots that dotted her hands, once as smooth and clear as alabaster. He swallowed, feeling the burn down his gullet.

Prudence pulled the comb from her hair and tossed her head, the long strawberry ringlets catching the light of the blazing fire on the hearth. In the fireshadows any hint of gray that Tristan thought he might have seen earlier was gone. She smiled knowingly at him and drew the satin counterpane up under her arms.

"What are you thinking, Tristan?"

The Lord Roland set his empty glass on the bedside table, and took back the one he had handed her a moment before. He sat down on the bed, facing her, and gently slid his hand up to the top edge of the counterpane, winding his fingers slowly over it, bringing them to rest at the base of her throat.

"I'm thinking that I hate her, Pru."

Prudence leaned back against the pillows, her smile fading to a serious expression. "I know; I know you do. I still don't understand why you chose Madeleine. I always thought you should propose to that nice girl from Yarim—what was her name?"

"Lydia."

"Yes, that's it. She was a pretty thing, and charming in a quiet way. Her father was well landed. Whatever happened to her?"

"She married Stephen; died a few years back in a Lirin raid."

"Oh yes, of course. I remember now." Prudence reached out and gently stroked the side of his face, his whiskers rough beneath her fingers.

Tristan's eyes met her gaze and held it while he pulled the

counterpane back. There was an understanding in her eyes, a depth that he could not even fathom, and it felt warm, surrounding him completely, like the hot spring they had once coupled in so many years ago. Their honesty was the only truly pure thing in his life. Prudence turned her face to the fire and closed her eyes.

From the crystal glass Tristan drew out a drop of the port, and dabbed it gently on her nipple. He felt the air come into her as she inhaled beneath his touch, the same way she had in their youth, on the night she deflowered him, and the arousal that had been eluding him began to build.

The skin of her breast had eased noticeably from the time he had first touched it thus. He closed his eyes and thought back to his first sight of it, firm with anticipation, warming to a deep rose color beneath his trembling hand. Now it was slack, loose, her breasts flecked with the same brown patches that marred the skin of her hands. Tristan lowered his lips and drank in the drop of port, trying to keep her from seeing the pain he knew was flickering across his face. He tugged the counterpane off her completely and dropped it to the floor.

Now laid bare, Prudence drew one knee up and began to untie his dressing gown. Her hands slid into his lap, stroking him gently.

"Why don't you tell me what's really bothering you, Tristan?"

His lips left her breast and slowly began to trace down to her abdomen.

"What makes you think anything is bothering me?"

Firmly she pushed him back and sat up against the headboard, pulling a pillow in front of her chest. Her eyes were angry.

"I was your father's courtesan, Tristan; I always thought that I was your friend."

The shock of her reaction snapped over him, shattering what little excitement he had felt. "Of course you are."

"Then don't play games with me. I'm too old for this nonsense. I can tell when something's on your mind—I know your moods better than you do. Usually you tell me everything. Why are you playing coy tonight? It's not very stimulating."

Tristan sighed; she had caught him. It was more than the melancholy he was battling, watching the unfair ravages of time on her, more than the sickening sense that the woman he loved, and bedded regularly, was beginning to resemble his mother. It was even more than the horrific reminder of what that aging would eventually lead to, a loss he was not willing to contemplate.

He was struggling with the memory of Rhapsody.

He had not been able to get her out of his thoughts since the moment she had walked out of the keep. And more than that, it was the thought of her, subservient by choice to a Bolg warlord, that had made his skin burn with frustration. The image of her in the arms of a subhuman mongrel had been almost as upsetting as the strength of his own reaction to her; for the few moments they had spent together, he should hardly have even remembered her name.

He looked back at Prudence and smiled, seeing the intensity of the look in her eyes.

"All right," he said. "I'll tell you, as long as you don't allow anything I say to interrupt our lovemaking. Madeleine will be here soon, and I want to have you as many times as I can before she arrives."

Prudence exhaled happily, and her hands returned to his lap. "As you wish, Your Highness."

Tristan looked up at the ceiling, waiting for the stimulation of her hands and his hidden thoughts to return him to his former state of arousal. It happened quickly.

"You know the lands where the Cymrians once ruled, Canrif?"

"Vaguely," Prudence said, massaging enthusiastically. "Somewhere in the mountains that lie to the east?"

"Yes, that's right. It's been overrun by Firbolg for four hundred years or so now."

Satisfied with the results of her efforts, Prudence released him and ran her hand up his chest to his dressing gown. She slid both hands beneath it and onto his shoulders.

"Who is Firbolg?"

Tristan chuckled. "Not who, what. They're monsters, humanoid beasts that eat rats and each other. And any human they can catch as well, by the way."

Prudence shuddered comically and pulled the dressing gown off him, exposing his chest to the light of the fire. Her smile of amusement resolved into something more real at the sight of the fireshadows licking his muscular arms and shoulders. He looked the same as he had so long ago, on the first night he had come to her.

"Sounds awful."

"They are, believe me. Every year I have to deal with them; the army goes and rounds up any we find marauding near Bethe Corbair. The time is approaching to do it again this year."

Prudence drew up her knees and rested the soles of both her feet against his chest. With a gentle shove she pushed him off the foot of the bed and onto his knees on the floor.

"So if you do this every year, and have been for the last ten or so—"

"Almost twenty now. It was Father's responsibility before that."

"—all right, twenty; if you've been doing this for so long, why is it troubling you tonight?"

Tristan reached out and grabbed both of her thighs, and dragged her on her back, laughing, to the edge of the bed. He parted her legs and leaned between them, his hands cradling her hips, made rounder than he remembered by the passage of time.

"They have a new warlord, apparently, though what that really means I have no idea. A while back he sent an emissary, a woman, who came and told me in a most rude and insubordinate way that we were to desist the centuries-old tradition of Spring Cleaning."

"That being the annual roundup of the marauders near Bethe Corbair?"

"Yes." Tristan ran his hands up her abdomen, over her waist, until they came to rest on her breasts. He closed his eyes and imagined them smaller, firmer, more perfectly shaped, above a slender waist, a small gold locket dangling between them. The image made the arousal he had attained more intense, and he leaned into the edge of the bed below Prudence, his hands gently cupping her flaccid breasts, caressing her.

Prudence arched into his palms, running her feet over the back of his legs. "So why is this a problem for them? If they want to avoid the soldiers, all they have to do is desist attacking Bethe Corbair, right?"

"Right."

"And you told the emissary this?"

"Yes—well, actually, I just sent her back to her warlord master, with a jeering message spurning his demands." Tristan's palms began to moisten as he remembered Rhapsody's face, the shining tendrils of golden hair framing her smooth, rosy skin, her eyes kindling to an even deeper green as she listened to him.

Prudence took hold of one of his hands and placed it between her legs. "Then why are you so upset, Tristan?"

Rhapsody's legs were impossibly beautiful, even swathed modestly in woolen trousers. He remembered the way she had crossed them, and his breathing became shallower. Tristan could feel his skin begin to burn and his hand trembled as he explored Prudence, guilt flashing intermittently for imagining her to be someone else.

"Because I don't trust the warlord. I—I think he's planning to attack this year, now that—now that the Bolg are—supposedly united."

Prudence sat up to meet him, pressing her sweat-shiny chest against his, and wound her arms around his torso. The moves she was making were all the ones she knew he liked; a lifetime's worth of practice and comfortable familiarity had made the act almost automatic. For some reason it was different tonight, more strained, with a darker passion bubbling beneath the surface.

Tristan's hands moved to her hair, something he rarely touched during lovemaking. His fingers entwined in her curls, running the length of the strands and wrapping them around his palms.

Like liquid sunlight, he was thinking. Bound in a simple ribbon, black velvet of modest manufacture. His fury at her words had been the only thing that kept him from vaulting across his desk and tearing it from Rhapsody's locks, pulling her golden tresses down with it.

"What are you going to do about it, then, Tristan?"

The Lord Roland couldn't stand it anymore. He grabbed Prudence's hips and pulled her onto him, shuddering as she wrapped her legs around his waist. In the heat that enclosed him he felt the fire he had seen in Rhapsody's eyes, her internal warmth, the warmth he had imagined in his hottest dreams.

"I'm going to rout them," he gasped. "I'm going to—send—every soldier I can spare and—and—destroy the bastard, and every—last—one of his—miserable kind." His mouth closed on hers, ardently, vehemently, stealing her breath.

As he plunged desperately, repeatedly into her, Prudence's lips broke with his, and went to his ear. She ran her hands through his glistening hair, damp with exertion and fury, then whispered as she clung to him as if for her life.

"Tristan?"

He could barely force the word out. "Mhhnmm—yes?"

"What is this woman's name?"

"Pru—" he panted.

"Her name, Tristan."

"Rhapsody," he moaned, the fire exploding inside him. "Rhapsody," he whispered again, as the thunder rose up and consumed him. He fell across Prudence, spent and ashamed.

He lay there until he returned to his senses, until he felt her body cool beneath him. When he couldn't avoid facing her any longer he pushed himself up on his arms, suspending himself over her, and looked down.

The expression on her face was not at all what he had expected. Where he had feared he might see rejection, and embarrassment, and hurt, there was calm understanding, and nothing more.

"I'm so sorry, Pru," he said softly, his face flushing.

Prudence kissed his cheek, then slid out from underneath him. "No need to be, dear," she said, picking her dressing gown up off the floor and wrapping it around herself.

"You're not angry?"

"Why would I be?"

Tristan ran a hand through his soggy hair. "How did you know?"

Prudence walked to the absurdly tall windows in the sitting

area, and pulled back the drape, looking into the vast, starry sky beyond. After a long moment she turned back to him, the expression on her face solemn.

"I've known you all my life, Tristan. That was me, if you recall, that urchin daughter of your scullery maid, hiding from your father with you in the pantry. I've had your hand up my skirt for almost forty years; I can tell when it's me you're groping, and when your mind is elsewhere.

"I know you love me, and you know I love you, too; I always will. You don't have to want me, Tristan; loving me is more than enough. In fact, these last few times when you've made love to me out of pity—"

"I have never done that, *never*," he interrupted angrily.

"All right; lie to yourself if you have to, but I won't. These last few times I've known there was someone else on your mind, and at least one other of your organs. You're more aroused in your sleep lately than you have been for the last ten years during sex. I'm just grateful to know it wasn't Madeleine you were dreaming about; I was beginning to think you'd lost your mind. She's a hag, by the way." Prudence smiled, and Tristan smiled with her in spite of himself.

At last she came away from the window and went to the dressing table, where she picked up her dress, and donned it quickly while he watched. She ran his platinum comb perfunctorily through her tangled locks, then turned and regarded him seriously.

"If you don't hear anything else I've said tonight, Tristan, hear this: whatever obsession you feel for this woman, whatever she makes your body long for, don't lose your head, or the hand that holds your scepter. I sense you are considering this escalation in violence out of lust, or anger, out of something that comes from between your legs, not out of anything from your brain. Forbear, Tristan. Wars started over women only lead to disaster."

Tristan's face fell. "I'm astounded that you would say that to me," he said in an injured tone. "Any commitment I make of Roland's soldiers is purely out of concern for the safety of the provinces and our subjects. I can't believe you think I would escalate a war to impress a woman."

"No? Perhaps it is to pay back her master, then, for winning, for being her choice over you. Even if it is neither of those things, if it is your pride that's injured, don't fall prey to it."

Tristan turned away, awash in angry emotions. It was painful to hear her say such demeaning things, and even more so to know she might be right.

"Prudence?"

When he looked back, she was gone.

54

The end of winter brought dread to the Bolglands each year, for a short time anyway. The annual thaw was the time of the Lottery, the means by which the most expendable citizens were chosen to be positioned in the artificial villages that were hastily constructed at the outskirts of the Teeth.

This yearly sacrifice to the bloodthirsty men of Roland, probably more than any other single factor, had convinced Achmed of the Bolg's sophistication when he initially assessed their development. That this cunning, if grisly, program could be designed and executed for centuries without the invaders catching on was impressive enough, he reasoned, but the weighing of impact, of loss versus gain, proved to him beyond a shadow of a doubt that they were a force to be reckoned with. Even the system's corruption by which it was regularly rigged pleased him.

All had been summoned to the canyon beyond the Teeth on the day following the first thaw. The Bolg were unusually silent when Achmed appeared on the heath above to address them; generally the strong and the influential were excused from the Lottery, and to have been called together without regard to crude social position was disturbing and insulting to the powerful among them. Their attitude changed quickly when he began to speak, however.

The Lottery had been abolished, he said; no more would they offer themselves as lambs for the slaughter to Roland. This year the ritual would be very different, and open to all who wanted to take part. When he explained the plan, there was none among them who would have sent his regrets had he known of the custom.

𝒯ristan Steward watched the troops assemble from the window of his study. Generally the recruits and noncommissioned forces assigned to the Spring Cleaning ritual met in the stable area; his Knight Marshal never sent more than three or four hundred. But since he himself had decreed that all available soldiers would take part this year, that place was far too small to assemble, so they were quartering here in the courtyard, making a tremendous racket. They numbered almost two thousand.

Stephen Navarne looked down into the throng uneasily. He had endeavored to persuade his cousin that this was inadvisable, but had been scoffed at, not only by Roland but by Quentin Baldasarre, the Regent of Bethe Corbair, as well. Ihrman Karsric, the Duke of Yarim, had kept his opinion to himself.

There was a knock on the study door, and Rosentharn, the Knight Marshal, entered the room.

"M'lord?"

"Yes?" The Lord Roland turned and eyed him in surprise; generally the soldier stayed with the troops until after the men had returned, and only came into the keep if there was something extraordinary to report, which there rarely was.

"If you would be so disposed, would you consider addressing the men, sir? There is some belief that this is a pejorative assignment, and morale is quite low; so low, in fact, I believe the success of the mission is in doubt."

"Really? And why would that be?"

The Knight Marshal coughed. "Well, sir, cleanup duty in the Bolglands is generally a task assigned to trainees and people under disciplinary action, so the other men, who have served this duty before, are wondering if they are being disciplined."

"Well, if they aren't, perhaps they should be," said the Duke of Bethe Corbair. "My army never feels the need to question the orders of its commander."

"Oh, shut up, Quentin," the Lord Roland snapped. "I'll thank you to keep your opinions to yourself. You haven't seen fit to commit any of your soldiers to this little undertaking, a rather strange position given that the monstrosity borders your lands. This is a nuisance for me; my soldiers are seven days' ride from the Bolglands. In fact, I am thinking of assessing you taxes annually from now on to help pay for this action which we have been undertaking on your behalf for centuries."

"Our taxes maintain that army of yours now," interjected the Duke of Yarim. "If you are going to assess on a mission basis, I say we look at the need to continue supporting it at all. My troops can easily take this task on if it proves to be necessary, or additionally costly."

"Perhaps we should be looking at the necessity angle, Tristan," said Stephen Navarne. "I have told you, the people you are going up against are not the Bolg leaders of old. They are exceptionally well trained, and very powerful. I again advise you against this invasion. Why would you not want to pursue a peace treaty instead? Perhaps it will open a new trading partnership."

The Lord Roland looked at his cousin incredulously. "Are you insane?" he asked, his voice indicating he had already determined the answer. "Trade with the Bolg? Sign a peace treaty? No wonder I had to bail you out of your own peasant revolt. Get out of my way." He swept his subregents aside and strode out of the room with the Knight Marshal.

Achmed watched them come—two thousand, by his guess, confirmed a moment later by Grunthor.

" 'E's sent a full brigade, three, maybe four cohorts, sir," the Bolg commander reported from the Cauldron lookout. "Oi think we ought to take it as a compliment."

"We must think of a very special way to say thank you, then," the king said. "Rhapsody, perhaps you and Jo had best stay out of this one."

"Not me," said Jo indignantly. "I've been practicing all week with boiling pitch. I'm really good at it now; don't you dare make me waste all that smelly training."

"Suit yourself," replied Achmed.

"Atta girl," Grunthor whispered approvingly.

Rhapsody sighed. "Gods, Roland, you fool. Well, I warned

him. I had the feeling he was none too bright when we met. It seems a shame all his soldiers are going to pay for his stupidity."

"It's an age-old shame," said Achmed. "Well, look on the bright side. If we're really convincing, perhaps he won't try next year, though that is probably giving him too much credit."

"And besides, it'll be great fun," added Grunthor. "My troops can't wait."

"Well, then, let's have at it," said Achmed. He spurred his horse and the others followed him over the battlements and down to the crags above the outer Firbolg villages.

The rout took less than an hour. Instead of the weak, infirm, and incompetent losers of the annual Lottery, the soldiers of Roland were greeted by the elite forces of the Bolg mountain guard, personally trained by Grunthor, lying in wait inside the empty huts.

The reckless soldiers had beheaded two mannequins and lost one horse and rider to a sinkhole of boiling pitch before the realization took hold that they had ridden into a trap. Retreat was not an option either, owing to the sudden, mammoth eruption of armed Bolg from beneath and behind every crag and rock formation. Like an avalanche they appeared on the ledges and hills above, grinning down into the canyon defiantly, then swarmed over the crags and onto the terrified army below them.

It began with a rain of fist- to head-sized stones, hurled from the mountaintops by the Ylorc army, which outnumbered the unfortunate Orlandan brigade almost five to one. In the chaos that ensued from the deadly hailstorm, the Bolg mountain guard, hiding within the makeshift huts of the sacrificial village, grabbed and pulled the trip wires that had been wound through the dust of the valley floor. Horses lurched and fell, or stumbled, throwing riders into the fray.

By then the tide of Bolg had reached that part of the army still standing amid the rubble and screaming horseflesh. The soldiers of Roland had frozen in place. A few scrambled to draw forth their bows, but most had come armed only with swords, clubs, and torches, weapons that were swept away from them in the initial moments of the Bolg flood.

A few at the outskirts sought to flee and were consumed in the inferno of boiling pitch, hurled by the four barrel-throwing catapults that had been erected at the mouth of the canyon to cover any attempt at retreat. Rhapsody stood with her arms wrapped around herself, shuddering at the sound of Jo's maniacal laugh blending with Grunthor's as she sliced through the trigger cords of the wooden launchers with her bronze-backed dirk.

She looked back at the Bolg, for centuries the victims in the annual sacrifice, moving quickly amid the turmoil, dispatching what remained of the Spring Cleaning force. They seemed infinite in number and intense in their concentration. Grunthor later observed he would be hard-pressed to recall a more efficient slaughter.

Rhapsody stared down at the desolate sight, the gruesome aftermath of the battle turning her stomach. She had not participated in the fighting, either with sword or musical accompaniment, and watched as Achmed's ragtag army methodically stripped the dead of their weapons and armor, then stacked the bodies near the pit of pitch.

"What an unholy mess," she said.

"Not to worry, Duchess; we always cleans up our messes," said Grunthor cheerfully. He was sparring with Jo, preventing her from joining in the looting.

"Yes; now that you mention it, perhaps this would be a good time for you and Jo to go back to the Cauldron," said Achmed. He was counting the casualties, making sure none had been dragged off as personal coup.

"What, no booty?" Jo demanded.

"Later, lit'le miss," said Grunthor affectionately. "We gets the pick o' the lot, and we'll share."

"Right. Come on, Jo," said Rhapsody, taking her elbow and leading her away. Something in Achmed's expression convinced her of the wisdom of a hasty return to the Teeth.

When the women were out of sight, Achmed turned to Grunthor and the generals, waiting at the scene below.

"The army will now feed," he said.

* * *

$\mathcal{L}$ate in the night a week later, the Lord Regent of Roland was in the midst of a nightmare when he awoke to strange clicking sound.

"Tsk, tsk." A dark figure stood near his bed, slowly turning Tristan's crown in its thin fingers. The light from the solitary candle on the bedside table caught the gold filigree and sent it intermittently around the room, flashing in spurts like blood from a pulsating wound.

Tristan Steward sat upright in bed, but the nightmare image did not fade into the darkness. Instead it tossed the crown to him, striking him lightly in the chest.

"If you cry out, it will be the last utterance of your life," said the cloaked figure. The Lord Roland could not have cried out, even if he had wanted to.

From within the shadow a tiny flame emerged. Aside from the fire and the darkness the only thing the prince could see were pale, thin hands as they set about lighting a few of the lamps in his chambers. He struggled to return to his wakening senses.

When the room began to take on more light, Achmed pulled back his hood and smiled in amusement as a look of fright came over the prince's face. He came closer and sat on the edge of the Lord Roland's massive bed, running his long fingers over the satin counterpane.

"Get up," he said absently. He pointed to the chairs in the small sitting area near the window.

Tristan Steward rose, shaking, and complied. Neither his bare feet nor the well-made boots of the hideous man made more than a whisper of sound as they crossed the stone floor to the dark seats with the starry night rising in the glass behind them.

As he took his chair the Lord Roland gripped the arms tightly, hoping the move would minimize the trembling in his hands. From the moment of his awakening, with the clarification of his senses had come the growing realization that he had more to fear with each passing second. He was grateful in the back reaches of his mind for the darkness, believing that the nightmarish visage of the man who sat across from him would be unbearable in full sun. He summoned his courage and concentrated on keeping his voice steady.

"Who are you? What do you want?"

"I'm the Eye, the Claw, the Heel, and the Stomach of the Mountain. I have come to tell you that your army is gone."

A gurgle of confusion issued forth from the prince in lieu of words that would not come.

"You sent two thousand men, but this is the only report you will ever get."

Disbelief, then panic took hold. "Where are the survivors? What have you done with them?"

"The Mountain fell on them. Now listen carefully. Assuming you live long enough to keep this meeting a secret, you have ten days to draft a trade agreement and to sue for peace. You will attend personally, since this parlay will be your idea.

"My emissary will be waiting at the present border of my realm and Bethe Corbair on the tenth day. On the eleventh day the border will begin to move closer, so as to facilitate our meeting. If the inclement weather discourages you from traveling, you can wait a fortnight and hold the meeting right here at the new border." The Regent's eyes widened, but he said nothing.

"This is the only offer you will receive, king to king, people to people. Ignore it, and you will see what monsters are made of. We have been getting lessons every spring." Achmed stood up to go.

"Oh, by the way," he said, "if it's any comfort to you, your men were sung an exquisite dirge by my Lirin Singer. It was really very touching. Rhapsody has grown quite proficient in requiems and laments, living in the Bolglands."

He smirked as the Regent's face turned scarlet at the mention of her name, and leaned forward conspiratorially. "Don't worry; she has no idea that she was the one who inspired their massacre. Of course, I do. Why do you think I sent her to you?"

Bile rose in Tristan Steward's throat. "It was a trap."

"Come now, Lord Regent, don't underestimate your part in it all. You are a man of free will. If you had genuinely desired peace, you would have greeted my offer, and my emissary, with open arms, no doubt."

His smile dwindled into a direct stare. "Any man, especially one who is betrothed, with less-than-honorable intentions toward a woman, would be untrustworthy as a neighbor as well. It's just as well that you threw two thousand lives away trying to win her attention now. You learned your lesson early. The cost would have been far greater later on." He turned and walked toward the door into the shadows.

"I'll leave you now to get ready," he said over his shoulder.

"Get ready for what?"

The Firbolg king looked back at the Lord of Roland and smiled. "The vigil you will no doubt want to hold for your men." The shadows of the room shifted and he was gone.

At dawn on the tenth day the party from Roland rode into sight on the steppes. Rhapsody and her honor guard were waiting. She had made sure that none of their horses had come from the Orlandan raiding party; *taste has its limits, after all*, she had told Achmed. She smiled as she recognized the Lord Roland himself and remembered their unpleasant exchange some weeks before.

The five men in the Regent's party were clad in plain garments and woolen cloaks, probably for the purposes of remaining as anonymous as possible. Rhapsody was attired similarly. She had debated the wisdom of Achmed's suggestion that she deck herself in her grandest finery, fearing that it would be unseemly. She had sighed when dressing simply in the early morning hours. *After all*, she thought, *how many chances do I get to dress nicely these days?*

Riding with Tristan Steward, in addition to two heavily armed guards, were his cousin, Stephen Navarne, who exchanged a smile with her as their eyes met, and another man who favored the Lord Regent facially, though was somewhat younger. He wore a horned helmet and a heavy gold amulet wrought in the image of the sun, with a gleaming ruby spiral in the center. It was the symbol of the benisonric of Bethany. This must be the benison whose See was the northern provinces of Canderre and Yarim, whose portrait graced the wall of the basilica of fire.

The Lord Roland pulled his chestnut gelding to a stop and dismounted quickly, eager to get this distasteful duty over with. He had considered every other possible option and had come to the distressing conclusion that this treaty was unavoidable, mostly from assessing the cool reaction his proposal of invasion had received from the other dukes.

The country of Sorbold, a peaceful rival and ally in trade and conflict had politely declined as well, citing their preexisting intentions of establishing trade with Ylorc and plans to offer the new warlord a place in their benison's See. The cords in Roland's neck had extended several inches outside his body at the ambassador's words; the news of the Orlandan army's defeat had convinced most of his allies that trade with the Bolg was an idea they had actually been toying with for centuries.

He watched the Bolg emissary dismount and approach. As he feared, and hoped, it was the woman he had banished from his keep some weeks back, whom he had not been able to banish from his thoughts. He steeled himself for what he knew would be a well-deserved jeer, but her face held no gloat, just a welcoming smile. He found himself staring at her, his thoughts not totally honorable.

"Welcome, m'lord," Rhapsody said, bowing to him. "We are honored by your presence." There was no sarcasm in her tone, and the Lord Roland found himself swimming in warm and lascivious feelings in spite of all that had happened; he shook himself roughly to bring his mind back to the task at hand.

"M'Lady Rhapsody, allow me to present my brother, His Grace, Ian Steward, the Blesser of Canderre-Yarim."

Rhapsody bowed over the ring he extended. "Your Grace."

"And I believe you know my cousin, Lord Stephen of Navarne."

"Yes. How are you, m'lord?"

"Very well, thank you, m'lady. Thank you for seeing us." Rhapsody smiled. "My pleasure."

She nodded to her honor guard, and two of the dozen soldiers dragged a wooden table forth and set up chairs around it. The Bolg guards smiled pleasantly at the Orlandan lords, causing a collective shudder to rumble through the men. Their reaction delighted the Bolg, who hurried back into position with the others.

Tristan Steward cleared his throat. "Well, now, here we have documents for your examination. First, an interprovince

trade agreement sanctioned by the dynastic seat of Roland—
Bethany—which allows for and encourages similar subagree-
ments for the exterior provinces. In it you will find generous
terms with the same tariffs we assess on our historic trading
partners, and, in fact, each other interprovincially."

"I'm afraid that is not satisfactory," Rhapsody said mildly.
"We ask a waiver of all tariffs for the first ten years, as a sign
of goodwill that Roland seeks to encourage the fledgling Firbolg economy, as well as in restitution for the centuries of
gratuitous destruction visited upon Ylorc by Roland under the
hand of Bethany."

Three mouths dropped open. Stephen's closed first into a
hidden smile, while the expression of the Regent and the benison curled into something less pleasant.

"Surely you are joking," said the Lord Roland. "Waiver of
tariff? What is the point in trade without tariff?"

"Trade without tariff is called commerce, m'lord," Rhapsody answered gently. "It is the fair exchange of goods for
other goods, services, or currency. It is the practice in its true
form before the tax collector became involved. King Achmed
refuses to pay the tariff that supports the armies which have
long abused his subjects. He would, however, see it as a gesture of real intention for peace should you agree to the
waiver."

"I, for one, would be willing to waive the tariff for Navarne," Lord Stephen added, ignoring vicious looks from the
two Orlandan brothers. "First, I think each province would be
free to set its tax rate as it is now, would it not, Tristan?"

"That is the current practice," said the Lord Roland.

"Well, Navarne owes the King of Ylorc a debt of gratitude
stemming from his participation in the rescue of the children
of its province. In addition, one would say that the Cymrian
line of Roland might have similar appreciation regarding the
liberation of the House of Remembrance, as well as the restoration of the Tree there." He winked surreptitiously at Rhapsody.

"So why don't you agree to the tax waiver for Bethany,
Tristan, and let the others do as they like? I would hazard a
guess that the other provinces would be willing to trade an
initial tariff just for a look at Firbolg-crafted weapons."

"Indeed. Well, I suppose there is no harm in that," said the Lord Roland testily.

"Excellent. Thank you," said Rhapsody. She smiled brightly, and bent to amend and sign the document, unaware of the stares of longing that entered the eyes of the men sitting opposite her. "Now, what's next?"

The Lord Regent unrolled another scroll. "In exchange for the promise of nonaggression and the return of the bodies of the casualties in the last raid, Roland agrees, as a united kingdom, to refrain from any unwarranted hostility against the lands of Ylorc."

Rhapsody shook her head, maintaining her pleasant expression.

"No, I can't agree to that," she said reluctantly. "First, there are no bodies to return. It is as if your army sank at sea without a trace, m'lord; commit their memory to history and forget about the mortal remains."

She leaned forward and spoke in a confidential whisper. "Between us, the battle was over in less than a quarter hour, although some residual action went on for a few more minutes. After that, it was as if nothing had ever happened.

"In addition, I'm afraid I don't like the term 'unwarranted.' What Roland had considered warranted for centuries is what brings us here today. No, I think this should be a standard nonaggression pact, signed between both rulers.

"King Achmed guarantees his citizens will not invade or aggress on the people of Roland, in exchange for which the Lord Roland will guarantee the same thing reciprocally. Any violation of the treaty is the breaking of the sovereign's oath, and will be considered an act of war, assuageable only by immediate deeding of land in the amount of ten percent of the aggressor's realm. How's that?" She stifled a laugh at the three shocked faces in front of her.

"Isn't that excessive?" asked the young benison of Canderre-Yarim. "Who would want ten percent of Ylorc?"

Rhapsody laughed merrily. Her mirth had the tone of chiming church bells.

"Why, Your Grace, how refreshing. An honest question, to be sure, but certainly not the proper and holy way to look at it. You see, if Roland's intentions are strictly honorable, as I'm sure they are, and the oath of the Lord Regent is as ironclad as I believe it to be, you could guarantee any price, because your honor as a people is at stake.

"And as to the value of Ylorc, I don't need to remind you that this was once the Cymrian seat of power, the place where your ancestors chose to rule. Don't judge things at their surface value, Your Grace. There are as many children of the All-God within those mountains as in all of your See, probably more. I'm sure to you that alone makes it worth protecting, am I right?"

"Ye-yes," the benison stuttered, withering under the thunderous look directed his way from the Lord Regent. "Well, she's right, Tristan. That seems a fair compromise, to be sure."

The Lord Roland seized the quill and scratched the terms into the parchment, quivering with rage. When he finished, Rhapsody took the pen from him to sign as well; her hand rested lightly on his for a moment. When it moved away, his fingers betrayed only the slightest tremor, the floridity of his face cooling immediately.

"That brings up my part," said the benison. He unrolled the last scroll and held the corners down for her examination.

"Bethe Corbair has always been the See within which the Bolglands belonged. This document is the inscription of the Blesser of Bethe Corbair, Lanacan Orlando, offering religious solace and membership within his See, at our request, for the—er—citizenry of Ylorc.

"The benison of Bethe Corbair has agreed to provide you with clergy, religious rites, and pilgrimage escort, as well as sanctuary and healing, with appropriate tithing, of course."

He looked nervously at the dukes; this was the most risky proposition. The Bolglands bordered on Sorbold as well, another benison's See loyal to the Patriarch. Should Ylorc choose Sorbold instead, it would be vastly unbalancing to the theocratic power of Roland.

Rhapsody smiled again. "Thank you, Your Grace. That is a matter I had not anticipated. The religious loyalty of the Firbolg is not something to which I feel qualified to speak.

They have their own shamen, and their own theology. Perhaps there is interest in your church, or the religion of Gwynwood. Either way, I cannot speak to it today.

"It would be best if you or the Blesser of Bethe Corbair himself sent an emissary to discuss this in depth with the king. He told me to relay to you that he will be receiving ambassadors after the first of the month."

The benison nodded numbly.

"Well, then, gentlemen, if that is all, I thank you most sincerely and bid you good morning." Rhapsody rose and motioned to the guards, who collected the table and the chairs before the Orlandan nobles were even fully standing. She tucked her copies of the documents into the pocket of her cloak.

"Wait," said Lord Stephen as she turned to go. "We have a few gifts for you. Mine are both tokens of appreciation from the people of Navarne and mementos from your grandchildren, including a small portrait of them."

Rhapsody grinned in delight. "My! Thank you! How are Gwydion and Melisande?"

"Very well, thank you. They send their love, and wish to express their gratitude for the flute and harp you sent them. They hope you will be by soon to see them."

"I hope so as well. Kiss them for me, will you, and tell them I think of them daily, as I promised? Perhaps they can come and visit me here one day."

"Perhaps," Stephen said, avoiding the incredulous glances of his cousins. "Stay well."

He stepped back to allow the guards to transfer the chests that the other two nobles had brought to Rhapsody's horses, then kissed her hand and took to the saddle. The others followed suit, and she waved as they rode off toward the west.

The Lord Roland paused at the edge of the field, a strange look on his face, then raised his hand. Rhapsody smiled and dropped him a deep, respectful curtsy as she had the first time they met. A broad smile broke over his face. He spurred his horse and galloped out of sight.

"Not bad for a peasant, eh, Llauron?" she said to herself as she returned to her mare. She slapped away the hands of the Bolg guard who was examining the gift chest. "Hey, keep your mitts off. That's my present."

$\mathcal{H}$ere, give me that; you're going to eat them all."

"What, you wanted to set them in store for winter? Besides, I've been sharing."

"Right. One for me, six for you, one for me, four for you—"

"Well, you're a tiny little runt. You need less food."

"Watch it," Rhapsody said, trying to look stern and failing miserably. "We'll go ten rounds with mace and chain and we'll see who's a tiny little runt."

Jo swallowed the bonbon and made a face. "Mace and chain?" she said in mock disgust, wiping the chocolate smear from her face with the back of her hand and snatching another sweet from the tin. "Firbolg toys. Give me a dagger any day."

Rhapsody smiled and made a grab for the last chocolate on the top layer. Jo snagged it and popped it into her mouth, grinning.

"Dagger is a weapon with more finesse, I agree," Rhapsody said, settling for a dried apple. "But it won't do you much good if you need to maintain some distance. What do you think of this candy?"

" 'Sss mgooddd," Jo answered, her mouth full. She swallowed and pulled out the empty divider, opening another layer of the box for exploration. She dove in, scattering comfits and sweetmeats onto the bed and floor around her, hooting with delight as she discovered more of her favorites, with an expression so gleeful that Rhapsody could not help but laugh in pleasure at the sight of her. "But I can still taste that shit you fed me to ward off poison. Honestly, who would put poison in a gift meant to curry favor with a king?"

Rhapsody gave her an amused look of disbelief. "This is Achmed we're talking about here. I'm amazed it wasn't full of acid."

"Is that the reason you refused to wear the lovely garnet earrings sent by the benison of Avonderre-Navarne?"

"No, I was afraid those would turn my ears green, the tawdry things. I have to admit I'm a jewelry snob. I don't wear much of it, but I like it to be nice."

Jo took a bite of another candy. "Except that one day in Bethe Corbair, I don't think I've ever seen you wear anything but that locket," she said, pointing to the gold lavaliere that dangled from Rhapsody's neck on its thin chain. Rhapsody took it in her hand and looked at it for a moment, but said nothing.

"Anyway, whoever this Lord MacAlwaen is, he has good taste in things that taste good," Jo said, unwrapping some caramelized nuts.

"He's a western baron; his lands are a little to the south of Sepulvarta," Rhapsody said, stretching out on the floor. "Be careful; those are harder than they look. I would guess his gifts are purely a courtesy; he's not particularly vulnerable to Ylorc."

"As if Achmed could be bought off with candy."

"Well, that's not all he sent. It's actually a pretty clever gift, because it tacitly recognizes that there is a new sophistication in the leadership of the Firbolg."

"Tacitly? I guess that sophistication doesn't include me. What in hairy balls is *tacitly*?"

"Sorry; it means basically, naturally, silently. Are there any more nougats?"

"Not anymore," Jo giggled, tossing the last in the air and catching it in her mouth. "They are *tacitly* gone."

"Wench." Rhapsody smiled at Jo; it was good to see her laugh. "I think I'm going to keep your present after all."

Jo rubbed her mouth with the back of her sleeve and sat up in interest. "Present? What present?"

"Well, I just thought with all these gifts of state pouring in for Achmed that you deserved a little something, too. But you've been such an unbelievable hog with that box of sweet-meats that—"

Jo's eyes widened. She quickly grabbed the first thing she could find in the box and offered it to Rhapsody with a comic sincerity. Rhapsody looked down; it was a prune. The two burst into gales of laughter.

"All right, all right," Rhapsody said, rising and shaking the chocolate crumbs off the long skirt of her nightgown. She went to the high wardrobe, brought by cart from Bethany, and hauled out a large wooden crate. She dragged it across to the bed, and with an elaborate curtsy presented it to Jo, who grabbed it and pulled the top off, spilling the wood chips used for packing all over Rhapsody's chamber.

Jo unwrapped the stiff paper at top of the box to find many small flat disks with metal spikes in the center. She looked at Rhapsody quizzically. "Oh, thank you," she said sweetly, "just what I wanted—cockroach traps."

Rhapsody laughed. "Keep going." She watched as Jo dug further and brought out a handful of candle tapers, both tall and short in multicolor hues. "I thought since you didn't have a fireplace in your room, you might like to have some warmth and light at night."

Jo looked amazed. "There must be a thousand in here." she said, examining one closely. "In all my life I only ever had one, and it was for emergency use only. Got it off a dead soldier." She carefully returned it to the box and looked up, a strange look in her eyes. "Thanks, Rhaps."

"You're more than welcome," Rhapsody said, touched by the expression on her face. It was like looking at herself a few years back. "Don't hoard them, use them. We can always get more. I mean to make your life a brighter place than it used to be."

"Which is why you brought me to live under a mountain surrounded by Firbolg." Jo smiled. "Let's go try them out." She pulled herself off the bed and lifted the large crate. Rhapsody opened the door, and they scurried across the hall to Jo's room, lugging the heavy box.

Rhapsody let out a little shriek as Jo opened the door. "Gods, what happened in here?" she said, surveying the mess. "Your room has been ransacked. I'll go tell Achmed and have him get the guards—"

"What are you talking about?" Jo asked incredulously. "It's fine—it's just the way I left it."

"You're kidding," said Rhapsody, looking at the clutter in bewilderment. "You did this on purpose?"

"Of course," answered Jo indignantly. "Don't you know anything about hiding stuff?"

"Apparently not."

"You've gotta do it in plain sight," said Jo, wading through the litter, pulling the crate with her. She sat down on the rumpled blankets of her unkempt bed. "That way nobody can find anything." She rummaged through the box again and pulled out a variety of candles, then began spearing them onto the metal candleholders.

"Including you," said Rhapsody, observing the disorder with a mixture of horror and amusement on her face. "You could get lost in here yourself, and we'd never find you, Jo." Gingerly she stepped over a pile of dirty clothes and around some debris from an in-room snack, to a small wooden chair onto which several pairs of shoes had been thrown. She removed the footwear and sat down cautiously.

"Don't be ridiculous," Jo retorted, tossing a few of the tapers at Rhapsody along with some of the disks. "I know where absolutely every last thing is. I'll prove it. Give me an example."

"Oh, Jo, I'd be afraid to ask."

"Go on, name something, and I'll tell you where it is."

Rhapsody cast a glance around the room, then set to work on the candles, hiding her smile. "All right, where are your wrist sheaths?"

Jo gave her a disgusted look and held up her wrists. "Ahem."

"You wear your daggers to bed?" Rhapsody asked in astonishment.

"Only two," Jo answered defensively, covering the sheaths with the sleeves of her nightgown again. "The rest I keep under the pillow."

"Gods. All right, where do you keep your money?"

Jo glared at her suspiciously.

"Never mind, bad choice. Let's see, how about that book I gave you to practice your letters in?"

"Ah-ha!" Jo crowed triumphantly. She shot out of the bed and bustled over to an enormous stack of crates, cloaks, and tins of dried meat. After shifting the equivalent of her own weight in garbage and rummaging through several cloth sacks, she finally held up a tattered bound manuscript. She blew the dust off and dropped it in Rhapsody's lap, a smug look of victory on her face.

"I can see you're studying hard," Rhapsody said in dismay.

"One more. Ask me another one."

"No, that's not necessary, Jo, I believe you."

"Come on, Rhaps. This was just getting good. Ask me another."

"Well, where do you keep your clean undergarments?"

Jo looked uncomfortable. "Define clean."

"Eweeeyuuu." Rhapsody looked sick. "What do you mean, define clean? There's clean; there's not clean. What else is there?"

"Well, there's sort of clean," Jo said, looking sheepish. "You know, stuff that's only been worn this month or last."

"Please, I beg you, don't tell me any more," Rhapsody said seriously. "You win, Jo. As soon as I go back to my room, I'll adopt your system. Just please, don't make me ask you anything else."

"Oh, who are you kidding?" Jo retorted, standing up with the candles in her hands. "If you don't have your clothes organized in order by color of the rainbow with matching accessories stored in attached bags you go into an apoplectic fit. Where do you think we should put these?"

Rhapsody looked around the room. "Didn't you used to have a dresser in here somewhere?"

Jo brightened. "Good idea," she said, and navigated over to an enormous mound decorated with clothes in all different states of soil. With a sweeping motion she shoved the clothing onto the floor, revealing the dresser, and began setting the candles carefully on it.

Rhapsody shuddered, lifted the hem of her nightgown, and picked her way through Jo's treasures until she made it to the other side of the room. She began surreptitiously straightening some of the area under the guise of setting up her candles on a large trunk.

"I'm not sure this is such a good idea, Jo. I would hate to see a fire in here."

"Don't worry," Jo said, rummaging through the dresser. "I'll move everything into one or two big piles in the middle of the floor; that ought to do it."

"Only if you then set them ablaze," said Rhapsody. She touched each taper and concentrated on the fire within her soul. The wicks glowed, then snapped with flame.

"Whoa," said Jo, watching from the other side of the room. "That's impressive. Where's your flint? I can't find my tinderbox."

Rhapsody rose and crossed the room again and stood next to Jo. Despite the girl's greater height she wrapped an arm around her shoulder and touched the second group of candles, setting each of them alight as before. Jo continued staring for a moment, then sat down on the bed once more.

The glow from the candles settled over the room, bringing a warmth and heat to the musty air. The mess retreated into the darkness and the chamber assumed a friendlier, more comfortable atmosphere. Rhapsody pulled her knees up in front of her on the chair, smiling at Jo from across the room.

"Well, how do you like it?" she asked, watching Jo's eyes in the candlelight.

Jo was silent for a moment, looking all around her in amazement.

"It's marvelous," she said, the hard edges of her face receding in the dark. "Light at night. I've never seen anything like this before, except where they light the lamps in Quimsley Garden, the rich section of Navarne. I tried to sleep there one night, but after the lamplighters make their rounds the town guard make theirs, and when they find you they make you more than willing to return to the darkness of the friendlier streets. Anyway, it really makes the room look nice."

"My mother used to say that the simplest house was a palace in candlelight," Rhapsody said, looking thoughtful. "Now I see what she meant."

"I'll bet she never imagined your house would be like this," Jo said, stretching out on the bed, her arms beneath her head. "She probably would have a fit if she saw you here."

"You'd be surprised," Rhapsody smiled. "My mother was hard to rattle. She lived through a lot of ugliness, but she never let it touch her. It was like she carried candles in her eyes that could weather anything without blowing out."

Jo was quiet again. Finally she pulled a dagger out from beneath her pillow and began balancing it, tip first, on the fingers of her outstretched hand. "You must have loved her a lot."

Rhapsody looked into the candles burning brightly near her. "Yes."

"And she probably loved you too, right? Well, didn't you just have the nicest life."

Rhapsody made note of the bitterness in her voice, and took no offense at her words. "Yes, Jo, I guess I did. But that didn't stop me from throwing it all away."

"Yeah? That sounds pretty stupid."

"It was," Rhapsody agreed.

"Then why did you?"

Rhapsody's hand came to rest on the locket at her throat again. She stared into the light of the new candles, trying to force the words out that had never been spoken to another soul.

"It was for a boy."

"Oh." Jo switched hands. "Was he your first?"

"Yes. And my last. I've never loved anyone like that since. I never will."

The dagger whirled between her fingers. "And you ran away with him?"

Rhapsody wrapped her arms more tightly around her knees, the shadows from the firelight dimming. "No. I ran away to find him. Never did. He got what he wanted from me, and then he was gone."

"Why didn't you just go back home?"

"That's a question I ask myself every day."

"And now you can't?"

"No. Now I can't."

Jo listened in silence, but her sister said nothing more. Rhapsody continued to watch the candleflames, lost in memory. Finally Jo sat up and began running the dagger along the edge of her boot.

"So what's it like? You know, the mother thing."

"Hmm? Oh. Wonderful. At least mine was. Some of my friends and their mothers hated each other; I'm convinced that was why so many of them married early, just to get away from home. But my mother was extraordinary. She had to be; she was the only one of her kind in the whole village."

"Kind?"

"Yes; she was Lirin, the only survivor of the destruction

of her longhouse. When she first married my father I'm sure she had to put up with a lot of nonsense, but she undoubtedly bore it as she did everything, with gentility and grace. I don't believe I ever heard her say anything unkind about anyone, even those who had been unkind to her. Indeed, when people were cruel to my brothers, she never let them give in to anger over it. By the time I came along—I was the sixth child and the only girl—everyone in the village loved her."

"She sounds special." Jo's voice was noncommittal.

"She was to me. The favorite memories of my whole life are of how we would sit, after dinner, in front of the fire, just she and I. She would brush my hair and sing me the old Lirin songs, and tell me the old tales so they wouldn't be forgotten when she was gone. We could talk about anything. I think of her now every time I sit in front of a fire; in a way, it comforts me. Of all the things I miss in my life, I think I miss her the most." Rhapsody fell silent, and around the room the candles flickered for a moment.

Jo stared at the wavering shadows on the ceiling. "Well, at least you had a mother who wanted you. It could have been worse."

Rhapsody came out of her reverie. "Tell me about your mother, Jo," she said gently.

"What's to tell? I never knew her." Jo manipulated the dagger over the back of the knuckles of one hand, then the other.

"So how do you know she didn't want you?"

Jo dropped the dagger on the floor, then bent to retrieve it.

"Is this a trick question? If she had wanted me, if she had loved me at all, don't you think I would at least be able to look all weepy like you and say nice things about her? Don't you think I'd at least be able to remember what she looked like?" With an angry stabbing motion she slid the dagger back under the pillow and lay down again, hands beneath her head once more.

Rhapsody rose and came across the room. She sat down on the bed at Jo's feet. "Not necessarily," she said, trying not to catch Jo's eye. "You have no idea why you were separated. Maybe she had no choice."

Jo sat bolt upright. "Or maybe I was more trouble than I

was worth to her; maybe she couldn't wait to be rid of me. You have no idea either, Rhapsody. It's great that you had a wonderful mother who loved you; I'm happy for you. But do me a favor—spare me the nice thoughts, all right? It doesn't help.

"Besides, it's easier to believe she didn't love me; then I can just hate her and not feel bad about it. What's the point of believing otherwise? One way or the other I've been alone as long as I can remember, and it's not going to change. In the end it doesn't make any difference whether she loved me or not." Angry tears spilled out of her eyes.

Rhapsody took Jo into her arms and cradled her as she wept, shuddering with painful, ugly sobs. She caressed her sister's hair as she cried, whispering a song of comfort so low that Jo couldn't hear it above the sound of her own misery.

After a moment the tune had its effect and Jo grew calm, but she left her face buried in Rhapsody's shoulder until the Singer pulled her away gently, and took her tearstained face in her hands.

"Now you listen to me, Josephine the Unnamed. It *has* changed; you are not alone, and you never will be again. I love you. We belong to each other now, and I am here to make it better for you."

Jo sniffed. "Make what better?"

"Anything. Everything. Whatever needs to be made better. And it *does* make a difference. Your mother loved you; how could she possibly help it? Who wouldn't? Go ahead, give me all the nasty faces you want; it doesn't change the truth. I can't explain it to you, but I am sure of it. She loved you. Now she's not the only one anymore."

Jo watched her a moment more, then smiled. She pulled Rhapsody's hands from her face and pushed back on the bed.

"Well, you certainly have a good opinion of yourself," she said jokingly. "I never said *nobody* loved me." A wicked smile crept over her face.

Interest came into Rhapsody's eyes. "Oh? And who might we be referring to, hmm? Is there something you haven't told me?"

"No," said Jo, sighing. "Not yet, at least. I'm hoping, though."

"And who might this lucky person be?"

Jo sat cross-legged, picked up a cushion and held it tight to her stomach. "Ashe."

"Who?"

"Ashe. You know. *Ashe*."

"Who's Ashe?"

"Gods, Rhapsody, are you dead or something? Ashe. You know, the one with the beautiful hair, from Bethe Corbair."

Rhapsody was utterly perplexed. "Jo, I have literally no idea who, or what, you're talking about. Who is Ashe?"

Jo rolled her eyes. "You know; the guy with the—well, you know—" Her face turned red with embarrassment.

Rhapsody looked at her quizzically again, and then the memory returned of their encounter with the cloaked stranger in the street market.

"Oh! Him." Amusement began to sparkle in her eyes, and she leaned forward and whispered in a conspiratorial tone. "Jo, I have it on pretty good authority that just about every man has 'you know.' "

"Brat." Jo belted her with the cushion, laughing, but still looking embarrassed. Rhapsody saw her begin to turn self-conscious, and she artlessly changed her tone from teasing to encouraging.

"How do you know he has beautiful hair?" she asked. "If I recall correctly, we didn't see his face at all; he had a hood on."

"*You* didn't see his face," Jo corrected. "My angle was a little different—"

"I'll say," laughed Rhapsody, earning herself another belt with the cushion.

"I caught a glimpse of him under his hood when he lifted me off the ground. His hair is the color of copper; not dull like copper coins, but like the shiny pots that hang in the tinker's booth in the market. And his eyes are the most incredible shade of blue. That's about all I saw, coppery hair and crystal-blue eyes, but it was enough." She let out an exaggerated sigh.

"Gods, Jo, what if that's all of him there is?" Rhapsody said in mock concern. "I mean, what if that's all there is under there—hair and eyes and nothing else? Bbbrrrrrr. Not a pleasant thought. Don't you think you ought to at least see all of him before you pick out your wedding china?"

Jo crossed her arms in annoyance and fell into a petulant silence. Rhapsody hastened to make peace.

"I'm sorry, Jo; I'm being ridiculous. I'm glad you met someone you like. But if I recall, wasn't he trying to cut your hand off?"

"No, you were trying to cut his hand off," Jo said, still annoyed. "He was nice to me, that's all. Let's just forget it, all right?"

Rhapsody sighed. "You really have been ill-used, my girl, if that's what you call someone being nice to you. But who knows; sometimes first impressions are the most accurate. So what do you think your chances are of ever meeting up with him again?"

"Probably none," said Jo, uncrossing her legs and putting her feet on the floor. "He did say he'd come to visit, though." She reached under the bed for the chamber pot.

Rhapsody took her cue. "We'll see," she said, rising from the bed and heading for the door. "You never know, Jo; stranger things have happened. In the meantime, get some sleep. Maybe this time if you're more rested you can actually pick his pocket successfully." She gave Jo a playful wink and opened the door.

"Good night, sis," Jo answered, laughing.

Rhapsody smiled and Jo felt warmth surround her, like an embrace. "Good night, Jo." She closed the door quietly, and leaned up against the wall, hugging herself with joy. After a moment, she returned to the darkness of her own chamber, made somehow brighter now.

56

They're coming.

"I know."

Saltar rose from his stone chair, running his fingers over the granite arms, worn smooth by centuries of hands other than his own gripping them. It was one of the treasures from the old time, grabbed when the great Willum village-beneath-the-ground had been conquered, along with other relics that remained locked within the depths of the Hidden Realm. But it was not the most significant one.

His army comes, but the one I seek is not with them.

Fire-Eye swallowed but said nothing. The Spirit had been of great assistance, had given him a terrifying invulnerability, an invaluable asset in his rise to power, but it was obsessed, not easily distracted.

He took the chain from around his neck, staring absently into the eye amid the golden fire, the symbol that had given him his shaman name. Fire-Eye. It was the name by which the Bolg called him, generally whispered when spoken.

The fire-eye had lain in the bottom of a great chest for centuries before him, the Bolg of the Hidden Realm too frightened to touch it, let alone put it on. Even the fiercest hunters in the Fist-and-Fire, his own clan, had shied away from it. Only he had been able to summon the courage to lift the golden symbol from its casket, to wear it on his chest. He reveled in watching the other Bolg of his clan recoil in abject fear.

It had never occurred to him to wonder why the Willums would have buried such a powerful item away, had left it under a pile of rags along with a small pair of alabaster lions and a brooch made of mother-of-pearl, baubles that no one had wanted to touch but that had instantly disappeared once he took the fire-eye out of the crate. Twenty season-cycles had passed since that day.

The Spirit had made itself known to him almost immediately. It had come to him in darkness, reflecting his own image back to him, frightening him into shaking fits. When it spoke its words were hard to hear clearly, though he had gotten more used to the silent voice over time. It had given him his name, Saltar.

Saltar?

Fire-Eye looked up again, searching the darkness for the all-but-invisible Ghost. That was what the other clans called the Spirit. They were almost as terrified of it as he was. It spoke to him now, just as it had then. A thought occurred to him.

"I know how to draw him out," he said to the air around him.

Silence.

"You must fight this time," Saltar said, fingering the fire-eye, then slipping the chain around his neck again. "Then he will come."

The air bristled, a whiff of heat rising in Saltar's dismal chamber.

Yes.

Emmy.

Tears welled beneath Rhapsody's eyelids at the sound of her mother's voice, a voice she heard in her heart. Dreaming, but still clinging to the last fragments of awareness, she struggled to keep the vision at bay. Too often the nightmares began like this, catching her off-guard and vulnerable.

"No," she whispered in her sleep. "Please."

A gentle hand came to rest on her head.

Don't cry, Emmy. Her mother's smiling face, swimming before her, blurred by her own tears.

She surrendered to sleep with one last sigh. "Mama."

I like your house, Emmy, especially the candles. Her mother's eyes cast an appreciative glance around at the tiny glimmering lights that appeared, as she spoke, in the darkness. *Even the simplest house is a palace in candlelight.*

"Mama—"

Come over here and let me brush your hair by the fire the way we once did.

Rhapsody felt the heat radiate over her face. She rose and followed her mother to the hearth. Flames twisted and danced, burning insistently.

The caress of smooth hands running down her hair, the bite of the comb.

Do you remember this, child?

"Yes," she whispered, choking on the tears. "Mama—"

Shhh. Her mother reached into the fire. *Here, child, put your hand in; I can't get it for you. It won't let me pick it up. You'll have to do it.*

She reached into the roaring flames, feeling their heat but no pain. Her hand grasped something smooth and cold, and she drew it forth from the fire. Instantly all the flames died away except for the ones licking up the blade of the sword in her hand.

"Daystar Clarion," she murmured.

As it was in the Past, before it was taken from our land, away from the light of Seren. See how it looked then.

Rhapsody turned the weapon over in her hands, running her fingers along the silvery blade.

"It looks the same."

Look harder.

She turned it over again. In the hilt, just above the tang, a small light burned blue-white, more brilliant than the sun, held in place by silvery prongs.

"This light isn't there anymore," Rhapsody said. "The prongs are empty now. What was it?"

It was a piece of the star, of Seren. A source of great power, of elemental magic, from the Before-Time. Your star, Emmy.

"*Aria*," she whispered. My guiding star.

Yes, her mother said. She pointed into the darkness above, where Seren gleamed, as it once had. *I told you this long ago, child: if you can find your guiding star, you will never be lost. You have forgotten this.*

"No, Mama, no. I remember." It was becoming difficult to breathe.

Then why are you lost?

"I—I lost the star, Mama. I lost Seren; Serendair is gone, dead a thousand years."

The land is gone; the star remains.

"Mama—"

Watch, child. Her mother pointed skyward. From Seren, high in the darkness above, a tiny piece broke off and streaked across the sky, an infinitesimal falling star. In her hand, the light in the sword's hilt winked out, its prongs empty once more.

Rhapsody followed her mother's finger; it almost seemed to be guiding the star in its descent.

In the darkness ahead of her she could see a table, or an altar of some kind, on which the body of a man rested. The figure was wreathed in darkness; she could see nothing but his outline. The tiny star fell onto the body, causing it to shine incandescently. The intense brightness gleamed for a moment, then resolved into a dim glow. Rhapsody went cold, remembering the vision from the House of Remembrance.

That is where the piece of your star went, child, for good or ill. If you can find your guiding star, you will never be lost. Never.

Even in her sleep, Rhapsody could tell that something about the vision was not right. Generally the lore related to her in her dreams by her parents or people from her past were tied to her memories, things that had happened while they were still alive. Visions of the Future were usually unconnected to anyone she loved who had died in the cataclysm. But here her mother was, imparting things that she could not possibly have known in her lifetime.

"How can you tell me these things, Mama?"

She felt the warmth of her mother's arms encircle her.

I can tell you because, just as I am, these are memories of yours. You just don't know them yet. If you can find your guiding star, you will never be lost. Never.

The glowing body on the altar faded into darkness and disappeared.

"I can't see him anymore, Mama. Why can't I see him?"

It's not what he is, it's what he wears.

Rhapsody turned over, tangling herself in the blankets. "I don't understand."

Look over your shoulder.

Rhapsody turned. Hovering in the darkness were three eyes. Two were placed in an otherwise dark face, their edges rimmed in the color of blood. The third hung suspended below them, set in the center of a blazing ball of flame. She began to tremble.

"Mama?"

Remember what I said, Emmy: It's not what he is, it's what he wears.

The flames from the ball began to expand until they filled all of her view. She looked back to see her mother, engulfed in the inferno. Rhapsody reached out her arms as horror swept through her.

"Mama!"

Her mother continued to smile as she withered to a dark ember, then was swallowed up in the flames.

Your family was destroyed in fire, Emmy.

"Mama!"

Fire is strong. But starfire was born first; it is the more powerful element. Use the fire of the stars to cleanse yourself, and the world, of the hatred that took us. Then I will rest in peace until you see me again.

"Mama, no! Please come back!"

It's not what he is, it's what he wears. The voice echoed softly as it died away.

"Rhaps?"

"No," Rhapsody moaned, reaching into the darkness, clawing desperately as the dream evaporated. Mama.

"Rhaps, are you all right?"

She sat up in bed, wiping away the tears that were pouring down her face with the sleeve of her nightgown. Jo's silhouette lingered in the doorway, casting a long shadow.

"Yes," she said quickly. "I'm sorry, honey; did I wake you?"

Jo came into the room and sat on her bed, giving her a quick hug.

"No, Grunthor did. They need you down at the hospital."

57

The Bolg medics were still bringing in the wounded when Rhapsody arrived with her medical bag, still in her dressing gown, her hair loose and wild around her shoulders. She ran to Grunthor, who was carrying one of his soldiers to a cot.

"Grunthor, are you all right? What happened?"

The Sergeant stripped off the leather breastplate, exposing a gruesome chest wound that bisected the man from his throat to his waist.

"Oi'm fine, darlin', but ol' Warty 'ere is in bad shape." The Sergeant's voice was anxious.

They switched places smoothly as Rhapsody opened her bag. This drill was becoming routine. There had never been such a tremendous number of casualties at once, however. Something must have gone terribly wrong.

"Clean compresses and pipsissewa, please," she said to Krinsel, a midwife hovering nearby, who nodded and disappeared.

Grunthor's face fell at her words. He recognized the herb she had asked for, used to ease the pain of the dying.

" 'E's a goner, then, Duchess?"

Rhapsody smiled at her friend sadly. "I'm afraid so, Grunthor, he's taken damage to his heart." She took the cloths the midwife handed her and tried to stanch the bleeding. "We'll try to make him comfortable while we're tending to the others."

"First Woman?" the Bolg lieutenant whispered.

Rhapsody ran her hand gently down the side of his face. "Yes?"

"Fire-Eye and his clan it was."

Rhapsody's eyes filled with sympathy, though she didn't comprehend what he meant. "Rest now," she said gently.

The dying Bolg blinked rapidly, trying to focus on her face. "Fire-Eye—Bolg—call him, but—Saltar his—name is."

She took the pipsissewa from the midwife. "I'll tell the king."

"First—Woman?"

She applied the herb. "Yes?" she said softly, watching the life begin to leave his face.

"Like—the sunrise—are you." The lieutenant's eyes went glassy.

Rhapsody's throat tightened. She leaned forward and kissed the sweaty forehead, feeling the contorted wrinkles ease a little. In his ear she softly sang the beginning of the Lirin Song of Passage, the traditional dirge sung at a funeral pyre, meant to loose the bonds of Earth and ease the journey of a soul to the light.

A violent swell of noise and screaming broke off her song in midnote. The hospital corridor burst into chaos as soldiers and medics swarmed in, dragging the wounded in a seemingly endless caravan, a ghastly parade of the dead and dying.

"Dear gods," Rhapsody gasped. There were hundreds, their life's blood gushing onto the floor, the hideous smell of burning flesh fouling the air. She leapt from the cot and ran into the center of the fray.

Achmed stood in the hallway, directing the still-ambulatory soldiers into the areas where the medics were caring for the worst injuries, checking each injured Bolg they carried to ascertain if he was still alive or not, and sending those with corpses out of the hospital area. The expression on his face was grim; he had not been at the scene of the battle.

Rhapsody took a badly injured Claw soldier out of the shaking grasp of another, also wounded, and pulled his arm around her neck. She dragged him to a clear area of the floor, out of the way of the roiling cacophony, signaling Grunthor to help his companion.

"What happened?" she asked the Sergeant again as she removed the Bolg's armor, wincing at the sight of what remained beneath it.

"We was on peaceful maneuvers," the giant Firbolg said, tying a tourniquet around his patient's leg.

"So I see."

"Oi'm serious, Duchess," the Sergeant snapped. "Standard procedure: recruit first, sack second. We was deep in the 'Idden Realm. Warty and Ringram took a party and went on ahead. You should o' seen the ones we couldn't get out o' there; this is just a few by comparison."

Rhapsody shuddered as she tied off the bandages.

"Rapz-dee?"

She looked up to see Krinsel standing over her, trembling. The sight caused her to go numb; Krinsel was one of the most stern-faced and unflappable of the midwives. Rhapsody had never seen a flicker of emotion on her face before. Now she was struggling to keep from dissolving into panic.

"Krinsel?" she asked, standing quickly, and taking her arm.

"Come."

Rhapsody and Grunthor followed her through the windstorm of casualties, stepping gingerly over the bodies of the wounded and the dead.

Krinsel led them to another group of bodies tucked away in a corner of the hospital. The reek of burning flesh was overpowering, and Rhapsody covered her face to shield her lungs from the stench.

Each victim had slashes, deep as sword wounds, scarring their torsos and abdomens, and occasionally their faces. Rhapsody eyes opened wide as she saw them.

"Achmed!" she shouted as she bent down, checking for heartbeats. Only one was alive, clinging to consciousness by a thread.

A moment later the king was beside her, watching as Grunthor turned the victims over, examining their injuries.

"Look at this," Rhapsody said, pointing to a gruesome gash across the back of the last living victim. Gently she traced the wound with a healing solution of thyme and clarified water. It was deep and wide, but limited by bloodless edges, as if it had been cauterized with a sharp branding iron. The wound was still smoldering.

Achmed bent down beside her. "What do you think did this?"

"I don't know, but this is what the wounds made by Daystar Clarion look like," she said, applying pressure elsewhere as the man began to gasp.

"Only deeper, and not as narrow," Achmed agreed.

"Looks like claws ta me," said Grunthor.

Rhapsody glanced up at Krinsel, who looked as if she was about to faint.

"Krinsel, what did this? Do you recognize what made these wounds?"

The Bolg woman nodded, her arms wrapped tightly around herself.

"Ghost it was. Fire-Eye's Ghost."

ℛhapsody finally left the hospital at sunset the following day. By then the bodies had been removed and taken to the crypt near the great forges, beds found for the wounded, all their injuries treated and bound at last. The Firbolg medics and the midwives moved silently among the victims, tending to them as ably as the Filids in Khaddyr's hospice at the Circle.

She had left Jo with Grunthor, who had lapsed into silence, refusing to leave his injured men. There was a look in the Sergeant's eye that she had seen before, although never so intensely, an expression that crept over his face when he used to speak of his troops long ago in the old world. She had tried to comfort him to no avail; the giant Bolg had only grown more somber and distant beneath her ministrations. At last she determined what he needed most was to be allowed to sit vigil, and so she gave him his solitude after asking Jo to keep an eye on him.

Though what she longed for more than anything was an extended soak in Anwyn's bathtub, she cinched the tie of her gore-soiled dressing gown tighter and headed for the tunnel that led to the Blasted Heath.

The night was coming. Darkness was encroaching on the pale sky, stained with fingers of red and crimson. The clouds swirled in a deepening spiral toward the horizon, mirroring the topsy-turvy angle that the world had assumed since she last slept. She sang her vespers woodenly, finding no solace in the ritual, trying to keep the anguish that she felt at bay. The Bolg had suffered so terribly.

Achmed was sitting exactly where she had expected to find him, at the mouth of the tunnel that overlooked the canyon and the heath beyond, the place he had first stood to face his subjects, where he had claimed dominion over them. His legs hung off the edge, dangling above the vast crevice a thousand feet below, his eyes fixed across the canyon and beyond the Blasted Heath.

Rhapsody sat down beside him and stared silently into the approaching darkness. They watched the sun as it slipped quickly over the edge of the world, as if ashamed to remain in the sky a moment longer than proscribed. With the onset of darkness came a chill wind, and it blew across their faces and through their hair as it shrieked and moaned through the canyon below.

Finally, when the shadows had reached completely across the vast Firbolg realm, Achmed spoke.

"Thank you for not trying to fill up the silence with well-meant words," he said. Rhapsody smiled slightly but said nothing. The Warlord let loose a deep, painful sigh. "Has Grunthor said anything yet?"

"No, not yet."

Achmed nodded distantly, his mind on the other side of

Time. "He's been through this before, and much worse. He'll be all right."

"No doubt," Rhapsody agreed. She watched his face, reading plainly on it deep concern and sorrow. And possibly even fear, though she wouldn't recognize it on him. "I was told something by one of his lieutenants before he died."

Achmed turned to hear what she had to say. "What was it?"

She brushed back a strand of hair that the moaning wind had swept into her eyes. "He told me Fire-Eye's name, his real name, I think." Achmed's glance became more piercing, but he said nothing. She coughed, and glanced around nervously. "He said his name is Saltar."

"Yes, I know."

"And does that sound in any way familiar to you, like any other name you've ever heard?"

"Yes. Tsoltan."

Rhapsody exhaled, her nervous excitement deflated. "All right, I guess I'm not surprised you knew."

"I didn't, not really. I've just been expecting it. I've been waiting for this day since we crawled out of the Root." He looked out over the heath, watching the distant meadow scrub bowing in the breeze. "The irony of the universe never fails to amaze me," he said, almost to himself. There was none of his customary sarcasm in his voice. He picked up a pebble from the tunnel floor and ran it absently between his fingers.

"Tell me what you mean," Rhapsody said gently.

Achmed looked into the distance again, as if trying to see into the Past.

"All my adult life I have been a predator, and a good one at that. I was raised as the answer to the relentless campaign of genocide the F'dor waged against my people, so I in turn by nature was relentless.

"I was given a gift at birth, a tie to blood that allowed me to be the Brother to all men. I used that gift in the name of Death, to walk alone and let that blood, rather than tie myself to others with it, to seek and find any heartbeat in our land and follow it, unerringly, until I found my prey. I was as unstoppable as the passage of time, Rhapsody. Unless my victims chose to hide in the sea, there was nowhere I couldn't find them. No one could run away from me forever.

"And now, here I am, on the other side of Time. I gave all that up, everything, every natural weapon I had, and ran, futilely trying to escape the one pursuer that I had no chance against—myself. Because that was what I was trying to outrun. It had my name. I was his accomplice in the hunt for me.

"Just as I never lost a quarry, the F'dor never loses, either. It will win the battle, or, in losing, take over the victor, making him its new host. So either way, it will win. The far better choice is to die at its hands than have it live on through you, but I'm not sure that I'm not already bound to it in either case. I should have known that this world was not a big enough place to hide from it, from myself. The avalanche is coming, and there is nothing I can do to stop it."

Rhapsody said nothing, but gently ran her fingers up his forearm until her hand came to rest in his. Achmed stared down at their joined hands.

"And then, Rhapsody, you came along and changed everything, addled my brain with your incessant babble, distracted me into believing that the F'dor's leash on me was broken, that I could somehow escape it, when I should have known better, having been myself the deliverer of the inescapable. It was only a matter of time before it found me again." He tossed the pebble into the canyon below.

"You don't know that it has," Rhapsody said quietly. "And perhaps you have it backward. Maybe you're still the predator, Achmed. Maybe you are destined to face it, and kill it. Perhaps it will be your final victim. But you're right about one thing: you can't run away anymore. If you do, it will find you sooner or later. If I were you I'd rather not have my back to it."

"The sanctimonious words of someone who has no idea what the consequences are for me," he scowled, snatching his hand away.

"Perhaps not. But I know what they are for me. I could lose the only family I have left in the world, in particular my irritating brother who is the opposite side of my coin." She saw his glare temper into something deeper. "You cannot possibly understand how deeply I fear that happening again. But whatever those consequences are, I will be facing them with you, as Grunthor has. That's what families do." She smiled, and Achmed felt his heart rise against his best effort to remain morose.

"Have you heard the Bolg talking about Fire-Eye's Ghost?" she asked.

"Yes."

"What do you suppose that is all about? If this is Tsoltan's demon-spirit, if it escaped from the destruction of Serendair and came here, clinging to one of the Cymrians on the last ship out, could they see it?"

Achmed shook his head. "I doubt it, though perhaps the first step in our plan is to acknowledge that the rules have changed, and what we knew for certain in the old life may not apply anymore. F'dor are generally indistinguishable when they are bound to a human host, though once in a great while you can catch a whiff of their putrid odor. But not often. That's what makes them so damned dangerous."

"Then what do you think it is?"

Achmed stood and brushed the sand of the tunnel out of his robes. "I've no idea. Whatever it is, it wields dark fire like a weapon; that's where those burn wounds came from. The Bolg think the Ghost is part of Saltar's magic, a mysterious defense that makes him indestructible, that always gives him the upper hand."

"Can we kill it, then? Are we fighting a man possessed by a demon?"

"I don't know." Achmed took her hand and helped her rise. "I don't plan to take any chances. I need to face Fire-Eye myself, Rhapsody. There is an ancient Dhracian ritual called the Thrall that holds the demon-spirit in place, prevents it from leaving its human host. That way, if Fire-Eye is the host of the F'dor, both man and demon will die. The tricky part is not killing him unless he is in Thrall. But if he's not the host of the F'dor, then obviously the ritual won't work."

"And can you find him?"

Achmed leaned against the tunnel wall and closed his eyes. His vision centered on the deep canyon below, and the wide space of air between the crag they sat within and the Heath on the other side. And then his second sight was off, racing over the crevice, speeding over the wide Heath, past the rock-walls of Kraldurge and the wide fields, waiting the plantings of spring.

It was a journey he knew well, having traveled extensively with Grunthor on the campaigns to recruit and subdue the Bolg. These lands were his now, were under his domain and subject to his will.

The vision flew over the ancient vineyards, wide slanted hills with a river between them, lined on both sides with vines awaiting the warmth of spring, tended carefully by the Bolg Rhapsody had trained as farmers. Through forest lands and the openings in the hillsides that had once been the realm of the Nain and Gwadd, the Cymrian races that had chosen to live within the Earth, he followed the path at a sickening rate of speed, past the deep woods where the Lirin loyal to Gwylliam had once built their homes.

Then into the Hidden Realm, past the decaying remains of Cymrian villages and cities, outposts that were now no more than stains on the ground and stone wreckage. The land here was rich, dark and undisturbed, its populace hidden within the labyrinthine network of tunnels stretching out endlessly within the far mountains.

His path lore sped between the mountain passes and into the tunnels, following their twists and turns into a colossal cavern with a large cave at its far end. His distant sight came to an abrupt halt before a Bolg figure, sleeping on a wide stone bed, the mattress gone for centuries. In the dark, the Bolg shaman's eyes opened and stared at him, rimmed in the color of blood. Then the vision faded and disappeared.

Achmed exhaled as the vision left and looked back at Rhapsody. He smiled involuntarily at the expression of anticipation on her face, her deep green eyes gleaming in the dark.

"I know exactly where he is," he said. "And now he can say the same thing about me."

58

"Did she give you any trouble, Yer Ladyship?"

Rhapsody struggled with the vambraces of the armor Achmed had given her.

"Not a bit," she said, twisting her arm around to try and cinch the closures, finally giving up and turning to Grunthor for help. "I made sure she got a good look at the bodies of the worst victims of Fire-Eye's Ghost. Jo was more than happy to stay behind and help in the hospital. In fact, she even volunteered to watch my grandchildren."

Grunthor smiled, his eyes absent of their normal sparkle of humor.

"Good. At least she'll be safe. Oi don't suppose you might change your mind as well, Duchess?"

She patted his arm, satisfied with the fit of the vambraces. "No."

"Well, then, Oi'll be grateful to have you along. Just remember what Oi taught ya."

"Of course. And Achmed's sage advice as well: tuck your chin, you're going to get hurt, so expect it and be ready, you may as well see it coming."

The Firbolg king smiled behind his veils. "Are you ready, then?"

Rhapsody came to the mouth of the tunnel and stood next to him. She looked down over the sea of Bolg that swelled in the canyon below. Tens of thousands of them, itching with anger, bristling to wreak vengeance. The noise was deafening.

The black mass of soldiers roiled with their martial preparations, their ugly shouts and outbreaks of violence audible even from a thousand feet below. The size of the convocation continued to grow as more fighters, men and women, joined with each passing moment.

"Are you sure they're going to remain in control?" she asked nervously.

"Nope," Grunthor replied, almost cheerfully. "But at least Oi know 'oo they'll take it out on if they lose it."

* * *

The horses were dancing in place, the nervousness rippling through their muscles. Rhapsody imagined she had the same wild look in her eyes as the animals did.

It had been frightening enough to observe the Bolg from the ledge a thousand feet above. Now, here in the belly of the canyon, it was like being in the unstable eye of a hurricane.

All around her was writhing humanity, or demihumanity, muscular movement laced with the stench of sweat and the excitement of war. She could see the battle frenzy building, glittering in tens of thousands of eyes, and it terrified her.

"Any sign of the Hill-Eye?" Achmed asked Grunthor, who was giving commands atop Rockslide, the massive war horse that Lord Stephen had given him.

"Nope. Oi don't think even they would be stupid enough to attack now." Grunthor cast a satisfied glance around the canyon, teeming from rim to rim with his army.

Rhapsody moved her leg out of the way of the Bolg quartermaster, who was checking her mare's barding.

"Are the Fist-and-Fire an Eye clan, or Guts?" she asked.

"Guts," Achmed and Grunthor answered in unison.

"Then why is their leader called Fire-Eye? Don't Bolg chieftains usually put their clan type into their own name?"

Achmed dismounted and came to the mare's side, rather than shout over the cacophony that blared all around them. She leaned down to hear him.

"Virtually every clan in the Hidden Realm is a Guts clan. This shaman's name undoubtedly refers to the bloody edges around his eyes. Occasionally you can catch a glimpse of a F'dor like that, but it's fleeting. You've seen them in your visions sometimes, haven't you?" Rhapsody nodded. "And it's also possible that it is using the same holy, er, unholy symbol, the representation we saw in the basilica at Bethany. That was Tsoltan's sign."

Rhapsody thought back to the vision of her mother, the last nightmare she had before reality turned into one. "I think he does; I believe I saw it in a vision."

"Well, I didn't when I looked, but he didn't have it embroidered on his blankets. Whether or not it is displayed on his ceremonial robes, if he even has any, I have no idea."

Achmed grabbed her bridle and dodged out of the way of a scuffle between three Bolg crossbowmen. Grunthor cuffed one and barked an order at the others, and they quickly moved back into the chaotic ranks.

"Remember what I said about the Thrall ritual. Don't strike him until you're sure he's entranced."

The noise was too loud to be heard, even if she shouted, so Rhapsody just nodded. Achmed patted her leg and went back to his mount.

𝒯he long ride to the Hidden Realm was harrowing. Rhapsody struggled to remain in her seat, gripping the horse with her knees and hanging on for her life.

They rode at the head of an endless column of Firbolg, their ranks expanding to the sides as well as behind them. From every hillside and crag of the deepest Teeth came more clans and families, hunters alone and soldiers in groups, fathers with one or more of their sons, swelling the horde until it seemed as if the mountains themselves were following Achmed. In her memory she heard his voice, brimming with excited energy, addressing his new subjects for the first time on a dark ledge overlooking the smoke from the bonfires in the canyon below him.

Whatever you are now, you are but the splinters of a bone, perhaps once of one blood, but now without strength. When you move it causes pain, but comes to no purpose. Join me, and we will be as the mountain itself moving.

It was coming to pass, just as he predicted.

To her left she heard the Sergeant's ringing bass begin a marching cadence.

Revenge I am told
Is a dish eaten cold
But me, I prefer my food warm
So when I come for you
The first thing I will do
Is to rip off and chew on your arm.

Thousands of voices immediately picked up the next verse, croaking in rasping tones.

> From your head to your feet
> I'll devour the meat
> But your bones I will just toss away
> And with any luck then
> Your kin and your friend
> Will pick someone else to betray.

Rhapsody clung to the saddle, struggling to remain upright in the vibrations of the echo that resounded off the Teeth. It was a ferocious sound, low and mighty, despite the ridiculous words. There was depth to the voices, pain still hovering at the surface, and she could feel the energy in it, bristling in the sound issuing forth from the throats of the Bolg.

She added her own voice to it, concentrating on amplifying the sound. Suddenly the song was even louder, and many more voices joined in, chanting their vengeance in march time.

A shiver of fear mingled with excitement ran through her, tingling from the base of her spine to her scalp. She glanced over at Achmed, who smiled at her, then back to Grunthor. The Sergeant was shifting into another song, this one a gruesome battle ode, his face intent, without the joy that singing cadences usually brought to it. He had taken the slaughter of his men very seriously, she knew, and planned to avenge them in ways she might be horrified by. She steeled herself for what was to come.

For the first three days of the journey the army continued to swell, new members joining as the colossal column marched by. From the fields and forests a sizable number had come, Claw and Eyes and even a few Guts clans eager to join once they determined that the shaking of the ground was the army passing, and not an earthquake.

They camped at night, those sitting watch tending massive bonfires, still singing the martial hymns. Rhapsody watched the enormous shadows from the fires light the hills at the edge of her vision, clouds of smoke billowing across the dark sky where it hovered among the stars.

Toward the end of the fourth day a few skirmishes had broken out. The Bolg now dashing from the hills or emerging from the broken ruins of abandoned Cymrian settlements were not intending to enlist, but rather to take out the fringes of the royal troops. Any such attempts didn't even make a ripple through the column, and were quashed without missing a note in the cadences.

On the fifth day everything changed.

Achmed had warned her the night before, in the light of the blazing bonfires, that they were now within the territory of the Fist-and-Fire. Though he suspected they would not be a match for an army of this size, they were a vast and vicious tribe, with an impressive ability to ambush.

They demonstrated that ability as the sun was rising. Achmed's troops, now fed a steady diet of roots and organ meat to improve their night vision, saw them coming, charging out of the foredawn mist, gray and lightless. Aligned in two waves, the outer force formed a wide ring around Achmed's army, stretching from end to end of what had once been a large city, now crumbled and decaying. The inner wave swarmed from all sides, emerging from tunnels throughout the ruin, swinging torches that burned with caustic fire.

"Enfilade!" roared Grunthor. Rhapsody reined her mare to a halt in horror as Achmed's forces split down the center and turned, firing their crossbows at the charging Fists. Up and down the charging line they sprayed, loosing bolts methodically into the oncoming attack.

From all around them flames roared skyward. The outer circle of enemy troops had set great fields of oil and pitch alight, clogging the air with rancid smoke and cutting off escape on all sides.

Grunthor turned to Rhapsody. "Sing!" he shouted.

Waving the fumes away, she began the war chant they had practiced, a song written to match the rhythms of Bolg hearts, enflaming their blood. A savage roar echoed across the plain, undulating through the dirty black smoke and the blinding heat. The royal forces, enraged and invigorated by the chant, fired again and then waded into the fray.

A patch of heavy vapor wafted near her knee and Achmed appeared at her side, his hands outstretched.

"Come on; leave the horse. We have to get into the cave before the fire rings us and the smoke cuts off our exit."

He pulled Rhapsody down and seized her hand. Together they ran through the melee, dodging the blows and bodies that were falling all around. A moment later Grunthor appeared, his nostrils flaring in fury, tossing soldiers of the Fist-and-Fire out of his way, slicing a path with Sal, his beloved poleax. He came alongside his companions and stopped, his weapon shielding Rhapsody from the blows falling around her.

"We goin' in now?" he panted.

Achmed pointed to a hole past the billowing inferno. "Over there. That's the entrance," he said.

$\mathcal{S}$altar's eyes were closed, but his hands twitched nervously.

"They're coming," he said.

The hall of the dark cave echoed his words, and then there was silence.

His red-rimmed eyes broke open in alarm.

"Did you hear me? I said they're coming."

A cold mist dampened his face, though he wasn't sure if it was from the Spirit or from his own sweat, now pouring from him.

He is not with them.

Fire-Eye grabbed the Willum sword that was his second-greatest treasure. He had not expected to need it.

"What do you mean? Of course he is! They're here, they're coming."

I do not see him. He I seek is not with them.

A string of curses, foul even by Bolg standards, roared forth from Saltar's mouth.

"You must help me," he said, his breath coming out rapidly. "You must fight."

Only the echo answered him.

$\mathcal{A}$chmed stopped at the fire's edge. Just past the conflagration a jagged line of Fist Bolg leered back at them, the vanguard left to protect the entrance. He pulled Rhapsody up to the boundary of flame.

Rhapsody took a deep breath and drew her sword. Daystar Clarion swept forth from its scabbard, a ringing call blasting across the tumult. She held the blade in front of her face. The last image she saw before she closed her eyes was the shocked panic that had replaced the cocky expressions the Fist had worn a moment earlier.

"*Slypka*," she said. *Extinguish*.

In a twinkling the wall of flame before them disappeared.

With a bellow Grunthor charged through, swinging Sal in broad, slashing blows in front of him. He made contact with a few of the unfortunates too slow to dash out of the way, screaming at the top of his lungs. The path to the entrance cleared immediately. Grunthor stopped long enough to extricate Sal's spearhead from the Bolg he had skewered on its point, then ran into the passageway, Achmed and Rhapsody close behind him.

Rhapsody slowed long enough to sheathe her sword. Behind her she could hear the echoing of feet pounding, soldiers following them into the cavern. She had no time to determine whether they were Bolg loyal to Achmed or not.

Before them was a cadre of guards, Fist Bolg armed with ancient swords and spears with antique heads. Achmed drew the long thin sword she had seen him use in the House of Remembrance. Rhapsody glanced behind her.

The tunnel was erupting now in hand-to-hand combat, Bolg against Bolg, their blood indistinguishable as it splattered the floor. When she looked back, the cadre of guards was on the floor, efficiently dispatched.

"Come on," Achmed said, grabbing her hand again.

They ran, Grunthor in the lead, deeper into the cavern, a place that had once been a city for the Cymrian earth dwellers. The pounding of their feet matched the pounding of her heart. Her breath was coming in short gasps from the smoke she had inhaled and the pace they were setting.

Her arm stung suddenly as Achmed jolted to a halt.

Standing before them was a Bolg of unimpressive size, about as tall as Achmed, a Cymrian sword in one long gangly arm. He was swathed in tattered robes, with hair as wild as if he had been standing in a high wind. From beneath his wrinkled brow, eyes rimmed in red stared at them. Rhapsody was convinced that in them she saw stark fear.

Achmed was standing directly in front of him. He closed his eyes and opened his mouth slightly. Rhapsody put her hand on the hilt of Daystar Clarion, while Grunthor dropped Sal and pulled out Lopper. Achmed was beginning the Thrall ritual.

From deep within Achmed's throat came four separate notes, held in a monotone; a fifth was channeled through his sinuses and nose. It sounded as if five different singers had simultaneously begun a chant. Then his tongue began to click rhythmically.

Fire-Eye blinked in amazement.

Achmed raised his right hand, palm open and rigid, a signal of halting. His left hand moved slowly out to his side and up, his fingers pulsing gently, seeking the strands of the F'dor's vibration, the ancient practice of the Dhracians. Then his eyes snapped open.

He felt nothing. There was nothing within the air. Not even a hint of F'dor.

Saltar's eyes cleared and his face contorted in fury. With a murderous snarl he leapt forward and swung the sword, a blow aimed directly at Achmed's unprotected neck. As the blow fell, Grunthor loosed a howl that sent waves of shock rippling over Rhapsody's skin. He shoved his king and dearest friend out of the way, the impact throwing Achmed to the ground, then interposed himself, catching Saltar's blow in the chest. Rhapsody gasped and drew her sword.

Saltar sliced again, then spun out of the way of Grunthor's return blow. The Sergeant's mouth dropped open. Fire-Eye had anticipated his move, one that should have been totally unexpected.

"Hold still, ya lit'le shit," he muttered, and swung again.

Saltar dodged and glanced another blow off the giant Bolg. Sweat poured from his face, mixing with bloody tears of exertion that were trickling from his eyes. He leapt back, foreseeing Grunthor's double-fisted pummel.

Grunthor snorted in rage. "The bastard knows what Oi'm gonna do before Oi do," he growled. He lifted his sword, knowing that Saltar would parry, then summoned all of his strength, bringing Lopper down on Saltar's blade. The weapon snapped under the impact. Saltar's red-rimmed eyes widened as the blade cleaved his head from his neck, sending it spinning onto the floor of the cavern.

Rhapsody stepped back, aghast. Saltar's body pitched forward, hitting the floor with a strange clanging sound. The head rolled a few times, then came to a stop. Its lifeless eyes, now absent their red tinge, stared blindly at the ceiling of the cavern, the light from Daystar Clarion flickering in their glassy lenses.

Achmed bent over the head. "Strange; the red is gone from his eyes."

Rhapsody was trembling. "The demon-spirit; where is it? Did you hold it in thrall?"

"There was nothing there, nothing I could grasp," Achmed said, studying the corpse's eyes.

Rhapsody looked down at her feet. From beneath the headless body's robes had fallen a gold talisman on a heavy-linked chain. She stooped to pick it up.

"Don't touch that!" Achmed shouted, his voice coming out in a shriek.

Grunthor gingerly slid the tip of Lopper under the talisman and flipped it over. The gold circle was licked by metal tongues of fire, wrought an Age ago to look like the Earth in flames. In the center of the circle a spiral of red stones traced down, ending in the center with one solitary eye. It glittered in the reflected flames from the sword.

Grunthor recoiled in horror. "That's *it*, sir! It's the one!"

Achmed took a further step away. Rhapsody looked quickly around, but saw nothing in the cavernous darkness. The Bolg in the entranceway still fought on, oblivious of the death of the shaman. Within the vast cave a cold mist descended, chilling the skin of their faces.

Suddenly Grunthor screamed, sending a bolt of terror through Rhapsody. It was not his war scream, the sound he made to frighten horses and men, or the uproarious laugh that issued forth when he was enjoying the mayhem he was wreaking.

It was a scream of agony.

He spun away from where he had been standing, a brutal, smoking slash across his eyes, delivered as if from the air itself. Rhapsody leapt to his aid and was hurled backward, as if by the force of the wind.

"Grunthor!"

The Sergeant lurched blindly backward, blood pouring from his eyes, his chest and shoulder bearing two more deep slashes. His cloak ignited, ripping into flame.

Achmed seized his friend's shoulders and pushed him to the ground, rolling him to snuff the flames as once Grunthor had done at the Earth's core for him. The Dhracian's neck snapped back with the force of the invisible blow that slashed across his chin, as the fire began to consume Grunthor.

Rhapsody struggled to her knees and held the sword before her, panting. She took in a deep breath and cleared her mind, then concentrated on making the fire vanish.

"*Slypka*," she whispered.

The flames disappeared. Grunthor's charred body, face down on the cavern floor, jerked again. A cruel wound ripped his back open from his waist to his neck. Rhapsody, staring in horror, gasped aloud.

"Achmed, look!"

In the light of the sword they could make out the shadow of something bending over Grunthor. All but invisible, it hovered above him, vaporous hooded robes hanging on skeletal arms with fiery claws at the ends. The silhouette glimmered in the darkness, barely there, whispering between the world of living men one moment and the spirit world the next. Within its hood was total darkness, glinting momentarily when it caught the light of the sword. Then it was gone.

Grunthor's body pulsed once more, then lay still. The flames from Daystar Clarion caught a shadow moving away, turning toward them.

"Shing," Achmed whispered, his voice choked. "Gods."

"Shing? What's that?" Rhapsody asked, her voice barely audible.

"An eye of the F'dor. And it's coming this way. Parry if you can. Back up slowly, then run. I'll hold it off as long as I can."

Still crouched, Rhapsody backed up. "The F'dor? You said there was nothing there."

"I couldn't find the vibration on him," Achmed muttered furiously, his eyes glancing around in panic. "But it's here. It's Tsoltan's servant. Saltar must have been the host; it must have been him."

It's not what he is, it's what he wears.

Rhapsody's back straightened. She could hear the words in her mind as clearly as if her mother had been standing beside her. She repeated them again.

"It's not what he is, it's what he wears."

Achmed's head snapped back, his shoulder slashed open, on fire. Grunthor moaned as his friend stumbled backward and fell, his huge hand flexing in agitation. It was the only movement he made.

It's not what he is, it's what he wears.

Her eyes went instantly to the amulet. Rhapsody reached out a trembling hand and grabbed the talisman.

"No," Achmed gasped, clutching his shoulder. "Don't touch it!"

Grunthor's body was flipped onto its back.

"Stop!" Rhapsody commanded, holding the amulet aloft.

From across the room, she heard the word in her mind. It was muffled, muted.

Tsoltan?

Rhapsody shook her head, trying to break free from the feeling that her mind was being prodded, violated.

Achmed raised himself up as much as he could.

"Rhapsody, run," he choked. "It will kill Grunthor, then start on me; it won't be diverted until it's sure its victim is dead. Get out of here." His face went slack with horror. "Gods, Rhapsody, your eyes!"

In the reflection of the amulet eye she could see her own green ones, now rimmed in the color of blood.

It's not what he is, it's what he wears.

"It's the amulet," she said softly. She turned and held it up again, looking in Grunthor's direction. "The Shing is not bound to the shaman. It's bound to the amulet."

She turned back to the hovering shadow, flitting from moment to moment in the darkness. "Get away from him," she ordered. A faint glimmer appeared above Grunthor's body. "What do you want?"

I seek the Brother.

"Did you hear that?" Rhapsody turned to Achmed, still propped on his elbow on the floor. He shook his head. "It seeks the Brother."

Shakily Achmed rose to a stand and picked up his sword. "Tell it," he said softly in Bolgish.

"No. It can't see you. You're Achmed the Snake now."

"Tell it," he repeated. "It'll return to Grunthor if you don't. It will kill you. Tell it."

"No."

Achmed clutched his shoulder and stumbled forward.

"*I'm* the Brother!" he screamed. "Me! I'm who you seek! Take me!"

"Achmed, no!"

Achmed's back straightened, his arms tight against his sides. Rhapsody watched in horror as he jolted, writhing in the grip of a glimmering shadow with flaming claws. The specter clutched him, pulling him off the ground. His body was lifted, then dragged, twitching, over to her, where it fell at her feet. Achmed lay there, not moving.

The Shing hovered in the air before her. Deep in her brain she could hear it speak again.

I have found the Brother. I have delivered him as commanded. Release me now.

Rhapsody clutched the chain of the amulet, the sweat from her hands making it slippery.

"Where are the other eyes? The rest of the Thousand?"

Gone, long dissipated on the wind in the heat of the Sleeping Child. I alone remained, having crossed the wide ocean in search of him. I alone succeeded. Release me now.

Achmed stirred, but didn't sit up. "Ask it about its Master."

"And he who called you forth? Where is he now?"

He is dead, man and spirit, his name all but forgotten. I was the last of his essence, of his fire. He is dead. Release me now. The voice was growing fainter.

Rhapsody looked down at Achmed. "It demands release."

Achmed nodded. She looked back to where she had seen it last.

"Show yourself fully, and I will release you."

A faint glimmer appeared. Rhapsody could see the outline of the hood and robes, its frail clawlike hands glowing feebly, no longer burning. The frame on which the robes hung was skeletal, brittle. No light at all was visible within the hood.

"Are there any other demon-spirits? Any other F'dor?"

The Shing grew fainter, its voice silent.

"*Slypka*," she said. *Extinguish*. The shimmering apparition vanished.

She bent and summarily checked Achmed, who waved her away, then ran to Grunthor. Tears poured down her cheeks, unnoticed, as she saw the hideous wounds that had mutilated his face and body. He was breathing shallowly, his tattered eyes glassy, staring at the ceiling above. The pallor of death was in his cheeks.

In a faltering voice she began to sing the difficult Bolgish name, with its whistling snarls and glottal stop. *Child of sand and open sky, son of the caves and lands of darkness*, she sang. Grunthor didn't move.

Bengard, Firbolg. The Sergeant Major. My trainer, my protector. The Lord of Deadly Weapons. She was starting to weep uncontrollably. *The Ultimate Authority, to Be Obeyed at All Costs. Grunthor, strong and reliable as the Earth itself. My friend; my dear, dear friend.*

Outside the cave, the sun was setting.

59

"Yer Ladyship?"

Throbbing pain across her eyes, a familiar voice in her ears. Swimming white circles in the blackness.

Rhapsody struggled to waken, but slipped instead back into the dream, a place where she could believe Grunthor was not dead. He smiled down at her, jostling her into awareness after a nightmare on the Root, comforting her as he had so many times.

"Take your time, darlin'." The gray-green face in her memory, grinning down at her. How many times had he said that to her, wanting her to be sure of her footing, not to fall? He had been so patient.

The voices seemed distant, hovering over her head.

" 'Ow long she been down?"

"Since dawn. She sang through the night until the sun came up; then she collapsed." Achmed's sandy voice was more brittle than last she had heard.

Her throat was full of pain. *Grunthor*, she whispered. The word was spoken in another's voice, the voice of an ancient man, a withered crone, a Firbolg.

"Oi'm 'ere, miss. Good as new."

Rhapsody fought to open her eyes, and succeeded with one. Swimming above her was the gray-green face, and it was grinning. She tried to speak, but only managed to move her lips soundlessly.

"Don't talk, Duchess. You fixed me up right nice, you did. Oi look a lot better than *you* do, you can be sure."

She swiveled her head to see what the pressure was beside her. Achmed sat next to her, bandaged and patched, but whole. From what little she could see, there was not a scratch on Grunthor.

From across the room she could hear Jo exhale in relief.

"She's awake? She's all right? Let me see her."

A moment later the teenager's tear-stained face appeared, hovering above her, her expression giddy and furious at the same time.

"Listen, you little runt—next time you go off on a fun expedition and leave me behind with your little brat grandchildren, I can guarantee you a severe thrashing when you get back. The little bastards tied me up and stole my stuff. If you hadn't come back when you did, I would have been the first human to practice cannibalism on a Bolg."

Rhapsody loosed a deep sigh, feeling the painful tightness in her chest ease a little.

"You're really—all right—Grun—"

"Stop," the Bolg commanded in a tone charged with ringing authority. "Don't speak, miss. Oi told you, Oi'm just ducky. Oi am most assuredly grateful, Oi 'ope you know. Oi guess you must know me pretty well, bringin' me back with a song, and me in such bad shape." A smile cracked his otherwise solemn expression.

"Well, I should hope I do, we been sleeping together and all," she rasped, then fell back into sleep to the sound of their laughter.

𝒯he wind whistled over the Blasted Heath, snapping their cloaks and hoods like sails on the high seas. Achmed and Grunthor were standing vigil in the wide field, waiting for Rhapsody to finish her study of the amulet. She had burned off an area of highgrass in a sheltered place, a rocky dell in which no wind was noticeable. The golden symbol lay on a slab of shale, its eye staring toward the dark sky.

The music she was humming had a high-pitched, fluctuating melody, a sound that set Achmed's teeth on edge.

"Grunthor, I've found a new method of torture," he said through gritted teeth. "No one could withstand that noise without cracking under the pressure. They'd tell even their deepest secret just to make her stop."

The giant Bolg laughed. "Oi think that's the idea, sir. She's gettin' the amulet to cough up its story."

The golden hair caught the light of the moon, turning it a pale silver. She had been at the task now for more than an hour, approaching two, singing into the windless dell. Finally she stood up, brushing her skirts clean, and returned to them, taking Achmed's arm as she walked.

"All right, this is the best I can determine. I've gleaned as many images as I can, using the musical vibrations of the amulet's lore, its story. It has seen some grisly things, believe me, and I have chosen not to go too far back into the Past. Aside from the time that I don't want to spend witnessing hideous memories, I'm not sure it wouldn't eventually have a detrimental effect on me.

"The amulet itself has no life of its own. It's just an object that once belonged to someone very powerful, with ties to the spirit world, so some vestigial power remains, linked to his memory, nothing more.

"Apparently what the Shing said was true. Tsoltan summoned the Thousand Eyes, a tremendous undertaking, and, in doing so, divided his demonic life force among them. They each took a little of his power, of his soul, if you will, with them. It was the energy that sustained them as they set out with one unwavering mission: to find the Brother, and bring him back.

"Because you had successfully escaped, the Shing continued to roam the world, searching for you. The one we encountered was the only survivor because, unlike the others, it left the Island and crossed the sea to find you. The others never returned to Tsoltan, still obsessed with their directive. They combed the world, looking for someone who was no longer there, at least not on its surface. Even if they had found you, they would not have recognized you any more than the one we met did, because you were renamed.

"So Tsoltan didn't have you captured and returned, and he couldn't recall the Shing. He lost the gamble. It left him weak, his demon side dissipated and committed elsewhere.

"When MacQuieth finally met up with him, it was really only the human side that remained. The power of the F'dor had been split up into a thousand pieces, all of them gone. So when MacQuieth killed the human host, there was nothing much left of the demon. It died with its host."

She began to shiver in the stiff wind, and Grunthor opened his greatcoat, wrapping it around her. Rhapsody chuckled from inside the deep garment.

"It's very strange to be interviewing a piece of jewelry; its perspective on life is a little skewed, to say the least. At any rate, it seems MacQuieth tore the amulet from the dying priest's neck and took it back to Elysian—the real one, the palace—with him, and presented it to the king as a trophy. I don't know which king that was, the amulet can't understand such things.

"For generations it hung on display in the royal museum. And like many relics and artifacts put on display, gradually people forgot its origin and its meaning, until it was just another gallery piece.

"Eventually the evacuation came, and when the Cymrians left, they packed the amulet in a box with other decorative treasures and carried it with them, as part of their cultural heritage. The box made it safely to Canrif, but never really was unpacked, its items left undisplayed. I guess there was more than enough grandeur and challenge in Gwylliam's life and the lives of his subjects not to need a forgotten symbol of a forgotten lore. And a rather ugly one at that, if I do say so; it didn't even have decorative value.

"So it lay in a box, gathering dust. Eventually the war began, and when Gwylliam died, the Bolg overran the mountain. They found the amulet in the ruins of a village, probably Lirin or Gwadd, deep within the Hidden Realm. But they were afraid of it, and left it to rot in the box until Saltar, or whatever his name was before he touched it, came along.

"Once the shaman worked up the courage to wear it, he found that it gave him power. I think initially that power was merely the fear the 'fire-eye' inspired in the other Bolg clans, and even among the Fist-and-Fire.

"But not long after he began wearing it, the Shing showed up. It had been searching for the Brother, but once the call of the amulet from which it had been originally summoned was on the wind, it came looking for Tsoltan, or whoever had replaced him. The Shing told Saltar how to use the eye to see at great distances, and how to foresee another's actions, like he did with you, Grunthor."

"Puny lit'le shit," the Sergeant muttered. "Oi would o' cleaved 'im right down the middle if he'd been without it."

"Undoubtedly. The amulet imparted that gift of sight, which caused the red eyes that Saltar had when he wore it, and I experienced when I was holding it. Anyway, I think that's the entire story, or at least as much of it as I was able to discern. There is one more interesting aspect, however, and it has to do with your name, Achmed—your old one, that is."

"Oh?"

Rhapsody fumbled in her pack and dug out a scrap of oilcloth with a smudged charcoal rubbing.

"Do you remember this?"

"Indeed." His strange eyes gleamed with intensity in the dark.

"You said the plaque you took this off of was adhered to a block of obsidian."

"Yeah, that's right," Grunthor interjected.

"And we postulated that it might be the altar stone of the

All-God's temple that the inscription refers to."

"Yes."

"The altar stone was captured when Tsoltan destroyed that temple in the name of his goddess, the Devourer, the deity of Void, long before he captured your name. He used the stone as an altar of blood sacrifice." Rhapsody examined his face, looking for indications of emotion, but none were apparent. "I believe it was within that stone that your name was once imprisoned."

"Makes sense."

"I assume this means that the victorious forces in the Seren War reclaimed the stone, and rededicated it to the God of Life, which I think was an earlier name of the All-God, though of course the amulet has no recollection of that. I did get a clear image of Tsoltan's panic when he discovered you had slipped the lead. I'm sorry I couldn't have shown it to you; it would have been a source of great amusement for you, I'm sure. Maybe someday I will write a comic ode about it. So, are we ready, then?"

The king and the Sergeant looked at each other, then nodded. Together the three walked back to the windy meadow where the amulet lay, staring blindly at the stars.

"Do you know what you're doin', Duchess?" Grunthor asked.

"Nope."

The giant Bolg blinked. "All right; Oi suppose there's somethin' to be said for wingin' it."

The Singer smiled. "I thought you might see it that way." As the wind settled on her she closed her eyes, then drew the sword from her belted scabbard, a steel sheath wrought in Achmed's forges and lined with the black stone stalactite in which she had found it. As Daystar Clarion came forth it sang with life, a sound that sent silver chills down each of their spines.

Rhapsody stood in the reflection of the flames licking the blade, gleaming below the fire with an ethereal light. She let its heat wash over her face, illuminating her hair until she glowed like a beacon in the dark meadow, shining at the crest of the mountains.

She matched her Naming note to the song of the sword

and felt its power fill her, rumbling through her soul like a glorious symphony. As the power of the fire rose in crescendo, she opened her eyes and searched the sky for the star she had found. It was the sailor's star, Maurinia, small and intensely blue, hovering above the Prime Meridian.

Once again as she had in her dream, she heard her mother's voice in her mind.

Fire is strong. But starfire was born first; it is the more powerful element. Use the fire of the stars to cleanse yourself, and the world, of the hatred that took us.

Rhapsody took a deep breath and raised her sword to the stars. She felt its music surge, ringing through her soul. She pointed the sword at Maurinia, and felt the voice of the star answer back, singing in exquisite harmony. She closed her eyes once more and called its name.

The crags of the mountains above and around them were suddenly illuminated by an ethereal light. It bathed the fields and canyon with silver splendor, making the darkness of night appear as bright as midday. Their three tiny shadows flickered black in the brilliance, then were utterly swallowed, making their bodies shine with a translucent radiance.

With an earsplitting roar, a searing flame descended, hotter than the fires from the Earth's core. It struck the golden amulet and the slab it lay upon, blasting the enormous rock into fragments of molten dust. The three shielded their eyes from the blinding light as it consumed the dell and everything within it. A moment later, it was gone, leaving nothing but the finest ash on the ground in the hidden place where the symbol had been.

Grunthor took hold of Rhapsody's shoulders.

"Ya all right, darlin'?"

She nodded imperceptibly. She was staring intently ahead, trying to capture the voice in her mind. It wafted on the wind, traveling away from her, whispering as it left.

Then I will rest in peace until you see me again.

"Rhapsody?"

She continued to watch, to listen with every fiber of her soul, until she could hear the voice no longer.

Grunthor's massive arms pulled her against him, wrapping comfortingly around her shoulders. Rhapsody blinked. It was as if she was saying goodbye to the last vestige of her dead family in the presence of the living one she still was part of. In the aftermath of the star-fire she felt morose, lost, as if the grief she was now left with was threatening to consume her. And it was held at bay only by the strong arms, and the comforting words, of her friends, these two she had adopted as brothers in a back alley a lifetime ago.

Rhapsody cleared her lungs with a deep, cleansing breath. Then she turned to the two Bolg, who were watching her with varying degrees of anxiety.

"Well, that's done. Now what?"

Beneath his hood, Achmed smiled.

"Back to work. Grunthor and I have a lot of clean up in the wake of our little excursion to the Hidden Realm. With the exception of the Hill-Eye, all the mountain clans, the clans of the Heath, and everyone throughout the Outer Teeth is united. Now it's just a matter of implementing the plan. Oh, and a rather large funeral."

She nodded. "Have you dug the graves?"

The king blinked. "I assumed we were going to commit them to the forge." He flinched at the look of revulsion that swept over her face.

"No. Definitely not," she said, shuddering. "With the exception of the Nain that died there, the bodies we found when we first discovered the forges, it's not suitable for any future cremations to take place there."

"Why not?"

"First, it's a place of building and creation now, and that would be an act of destruction, however necessary an act it may be. Second, and far more important, whereas Lirin commit the bodies of their race to the wind and stars through the fire of the funeral pyre, the Bolg are children of the Earth, not the sky. It is proper to bury them within the Earth that was their home in their lifetimes."

Achmed shrugged. "All right, I'll yield to your vastly superior knowledge of death rituals. The Bolg are lucky to have a Singer of their own to sing their dirges." He watched the clouds come back into her eyes again. "What's the matter?"

When she didn't answer, he took her by the arm.

"We're safe, Rhapsody. The amulet's gone, along with the

last of the Shing. We know that Tsoltan is dead, and it seems certain the F'dor spirit died with him after all. We can now go about the process of building up Ylorc without delay. The challenge stretches out before us, well within our grasp. We don't have to hide anymore, don't need to mourn. It's time to move on."

She looked up at him and smiled, a shadow of sadness unmistakable in her eyes.

"Perhaps for you," she said.

60

The afternoon sun glinted sporadically over the mountainside as Rhapsody climbed through the rock ledges that faced the Teeth to the heath at the top of the world.

Each morning she ran the steppes and the foothills with her sword across her back, training her body in stamina and speed, growing stronger and faster as she raced in the clear air of the Bolglands. She could feel herself improving; it was a heady feeling, though the regimen was tiring. Now she was seeking a place to run again, but this time, rather than running to new endurance and ability, she felt an overwhelming need to run away.

Achmed's new kingdom was a nightmarish place, and the dreams that haunted her sleep were growing stronger. Rhapsody could no longer bear the thought of going to bed at night. She had considered bunking in with Jo, but decided against it for fear her night terrors would frighten the girl.

Achmed and Grunthor were away from the Cauldron much of the time now, leaving her with little recourse but sleeping alone, either in the cold halls of the stony seat of power, or in Elysian. So, after dinner the thought had occurred to her that perhaps she could outrun the nightmares, force herself into a state of utter exhaustion and be too tired even to dream.

Standing on the heath now, though, it was difficult to remember that she was there because of any looming unpleasantness. The grassy meadow was awakening from the long sleep of winter, and the setting sun drenched the highgrass with a golden glow that made it seem touched by a divine hand.

The first flowers of spring were beginning to emerge, and their colors dotted the hillside like a shy rainbow waiting for an invitation to become glorious. Rhapsody bent and sang to them, giving them the beckoning they were awaiting. As the blossoms opened in response to her song, one that Llauron had taught her, she marveled at the beauty of these lands, wondering whether the Bolg ever stopped to appreciate it.

She stood up straight and spun around, her arms in the clear air above her, drinking in the sight of night coming to the Teeth and the surrounding fields. The world lay below at her feet, stretching out in a vast expanse for as far as she could see, butting up against the jagged peaks of the mountains that guarded the old Cymrian domain.

Rhapsody tried to imagine what this place had been like then, when the Firbolg still lived far away in the cavelands, and the people of her homeland tended this realm. How unlike Serendair this was, with its rocky steppes and mountainous fields of heather and scrub. Had the Cymrians felt at home here? she wondered, wishing she knew the secret if they had. Were they able to forget the home they had left, and console themselves in this new place, because they had brought their families with them?

A stabbing pain shot through Rhapsody's heart, and once more the reason for her climb came to mind. She needed to find a way to silence her nightmares.

She had taken to leaving Daystar Clarion out of its sheath, burning brightly in the corner of her chamber within the Cauldron, or her bedroom in Elysian. It provided a source of warmth and some minimal comfort when she woke in the night. That solace was offset by the guilt she felt over using an ancient weapon as nothing more than a night-light, like the candle her mother had left burning when in childhood she had suffered a bad dream. Then it had only been a rare occasion; now it occurred every night, without exception.

The dreams were now only rarely of Michael or his like. Instead, what tormented her sleep were images of home, and people now dead a thousand years or more. Sometimes she would hear them calling her, her parents or her brothers, waiting in endless sorrow for her to return.

Other nights she would dream of the Seren War, the destruction that came to her homeland just after she left, and wondered what had befallen her family. Had they lived to see its end, or had they fallen victim to it? What did her mother mean when she said the family was destroyed in fire? From these nightmares she would wake screaming, particularly when her imagination filled in the answers.

But worst of all were the nostalgic dreams, the ones so real she was sure she was home, that it was *this* place that was the phantasm, and she was safe within the bosom of her family and the life she had known.

Often in these dreams she spent a good deal of time convincing herself and those around her that her escape had really happened, that her new horrific life was real, begging them to hold her fast from having to come back to it, only to find herself alone and awake in the darkness of the Cauldron again. And then, against Achmed's direct command, she would dissolve into secret, forbidden tears of utter agony and despair.

Not tonight, she told herself grimly. *I will not go through this again tonight.* She surveyed the heath, watching the warm spring wind whip across it, billowing the new petals on the flowers, and she plotted a running path. She wished she had changed into her training clothes before she left the Great Hall; she was still attired in the soft gray gown that clung to her torso but flared at the sleeves and skirt. It was not really suitable for running, but it would do.

Rhapsody began to run. In blind, desperate abandon she fled into the wind, racing to nowhere in particular. She spread her arms wide and felt the wind catch her sleeves, snapping them out like the wings of a bird, rushing across her chest and through her hair.

The sensation was immensely freeing. She turned away from the wind and reached back, pulling out the ribbon that bound her tresses into her normal staid ponytail. The wind took her hair down gently, like a lover, and blew the strands all around her, catching the sunlight and reflecting it back to the sky.

She ran with the wind behind her, billowing her dress and hair, until she reached the southern end of the heath. Then she turned and ran back into it again, her hair streaming behind her like the flag on a high mast. She followed the sinking sun across the field, running west, dancing over clumps of grass and large stones. The wind danced with her, blowing her dress in patterns of gray waves on a storm-tossed sea.

Rhapsody twirled and leapt, feeling an inner grace guide her steps, hearing the innate music of the wind. It called to a place in her soul that felt tight, pinched in the effort to keep her heart from breaking. She loosed the bonds and that part of her soul broke free and joined the headlong plunge as she ran toward the night.

She ran around the perimeter of the wide heath, no longer dancing, but intent now on attaining speed. Her nearness to the edge of the chasm didn't bother her in the least; there were moments when she almost wished the wind would blow her off the plateau and into the crevice. She stood still, letting the disappearing sunlight bathe her face. She imagined herself falling through the Teeth, watching the sky grow farther and farther away from her as she soared to the ground. She ran the sun down, not letting up, as sweat poured from her and cooled when the wind hit her body, the breeze turning chilly with the coming of night.

After three score and twelve laps around the meadow Rhapsody felt she could run it with her eyes closed, and for several moments she did. She could see the shadows moving across the heath, growing longer as they touched the pointed outcroppings of the peaks that made up the Teeth.

Just as she felt the exhaustion that was her goal begin to come over her, she ran through a shadow and almost into an obelisk shape that had appeared in the field from nowhere; in the darkness she had to come to a stumbling halt to avoid colliding with it. Her arms spun wildly as she struggled to regain her balance. The shape reached out and grabbed her shoulders.

Rhapsody wrenched herself free and, with a fluid motion born of years in the street, flicked her dagger forward into her palm. She faced the gray figure with wide eyes, panting wildly, working to retain her composure.

"I'm very sorry," came a vaguely familiar voice. "I didn't mean to startle you."

"Who the—who are you?" she gasped between breaths.

"It's me, miss; Ashe," came the sheepish reply. "You know, from Bethe Corbair. We had lunch together, you may recall."

"Gods," she choked, trembling with exhaustion and the aftermath of panic. "Don't ever do that to me again. I might have cut your throat."

From within the hooded cloak she heard a chuckle. "I'll be more careful next time, I promise," Ashe said. Rhapsody could hear a smile in his voice, and it irritated her.

"What are you doing here? I'm amazed you got past the Bolg guards. Grunthor will be furious."

"Whoever he is, I hope he won't be too harsh with them," came the voice from the shadow, and it sounded sympathetic. "It's really not their fault. And besides, I'm here by invitation."

The shuddering chill of fear that had blasted through her, followed by a roaring heat of panic, left her weak and trembling. "Really? Whose?"

"Well, yours, I thought; at least that's what I assumed when Jo said I was welcome here. I'm sorry if I overstepped or misunderstood."

Rhapsody felt the trembling heat that had coursed through her a moment before begin to subside. "No, no, of course not," she said, her breath coming easier now. "It's I who must apologize; you are certainly welcome. I'm afraid you caught me when I was a little winded, and my brain was a bit addled."

"What are you running from?"

Rhapsody thought about how to answer, then decided it would be impossible, as well as unwise, to explain to this virtual stranger. "Nothing tangible," she said, mustering a slight smile.

"Really?"

"Yes," she said. "What are you hiding from?"

The hooded figure chuckled, then bowed in acquiescence to her point. "Also nothing tangible."

As the initial panic that had clutched her stomach unclenched, Rhapsody felt herself filling with other, darker emotions. The unexpected appearance of this stranger had set her pulse on fire. She had come to the meadow at the top of the world to run away from her nightmares, and instead she had run into something that was the stuff of one of them.

She struggled to remember the dream, the image she had seen twice. It was the vision of a body on a table in darkness, glowing, then disappearing.

I can't see him anymore, Mama. Why can't I see him?

It's not what he is, it's what he wears.

Rhapsody looked up into the wide hood, where not even a glimpse of his face could be seen. The fear she felt was tempered a little with sorrow; she, too, often needed to walk the world unseen. What was it that made Ashe feel the need to do so? Was his appearance, too, freakish in the eyes of the people of this land? Had he been scarred, or maimed? With all the violence in the countryside, perhaps he had fallen victim to something that had mutilated his face, had left him in pain.

Another image rose in her mind, leaving her trembling. It was the image of a man drowning in darkness, in unspeakable agony.

"Rhapsody? Are you all right?"

She felt her face, its muscles tight across her brow and cheeks. It was a face that conveyed her fear.

"Yes," she said shortly. "I'm fine. Why don't you come with me?" She smiled wanly, brushing her hair out of her eyes. "I'll take you to the Cauldron; Achmed will be glad to see you. He's king now, you know."

"The Cauldron?"

"Yes, that's what he calls his seat of power, the Great Hall and its surrounding area."

"Gods." She thought she felt a shudder from inside the cloak.

"Yes, well, these are Firbolg lands, after all. Come; allow me to show you some of our hospitality." She pulled her hair self-consciously back into its restraints, turned, and started back to the rock ledge.

The gray shape followed her easily across the heath, the wind whipping at the fringes of his cloak. "M'lady, believe me, I would follow you anywhere. I'm just not sure I would be able to keep up if you decided to run."

61

$\mathcal{A}$she had never been to Canrif before; it was a somber, astonishing sight. The passes in the Teeth were heavily guarded by Firbolg troops who were consistently, if sparingly, armed and armored. They held a watch as well as many of the soldiers of Sorbold, and better than those in Roland, whose armor some of them wore. Only the Lirin were better trained at this point; the concept was flabbergasting.

The last time he had come near the Bolglands was on his Spring Cleaning detail as a trainee in the army of Bethany, back in his other life, when he still had cause, and the ability, to walk openly in the world of men.

He had participated in the exercise with distaste but not malice, efficiently cleaning out the border towns and dispatching with alacrity and pragmatism the semi-human monsters who lived there.

It had bothered him a little at the time. It ate at him more now, seeing them as they really were: primitive and warlike, but people, not animals. And these two, Rhapsody and the man she called Achmed, had been able to harness the power the Bolg held, molding them into a formidable fighting force in almost no time. It was a significant piece of information, an indication of their power.

He had stood in the darkness of the heath and watched Rhapsody for a long time before he made himself known to her. At first he had no idea what she was doing, running into the wind, letting it billow her hair and dress about her like a sail on the high seas. After observing the intensity of her flight, the wildness of her dance, his throat tightened; she was trying to run away, but had nowhere to go. It made him want her even more.

Ashe tried to drive the thought from his mind as he followed her now, through the mountain passes and into the rocky halls, torch lit tunnels that led to the ancient Cymrian seat of power.

Canrif; it was legendary, the birthplace of the Cymrian Age, the best and brightest time in the history of the land, when systems of justice were formed and codified, great advances made in science, architecture, medicine, and art, the great basilicas and roadways built, and marvelous discoveries made. And all of it shattered by one blind moment of marital rage; a pity, really. Ashe looked around. It was like reliving history, walking these halls.

The ruins of the fortress were much as they undoubtedly had been left when the Cymrians fled: crumbling, dank with the odor of ancient pitch and smoke; the smell of grim defeat, still present four centuries later.

Gwylliam had been an engineer, a man who was responsible for some of the greatest structures in the known world, and Canrif was no exception. He had carved an almost unassailable stronghold out of an unwilling mountain, made sources for heat and light and ventilation, had found a realm in which the diverse population of races that had followed him on the last fleet out could live in familiar surroundings, and had held it together for three hundred years. It was a marvel to behold.

Rhapsody led him at last down a long corridor to what had once been the throne room, the Great Hall of Canrif, or Ylorc, as the Bolg called it. The two he had met in the market, the teenager, Jo, and the obnoxious man known as Achmed, were both there.

With them was an immense Bolg, obviously of mixed blood, whom Rhapsody introduced as Grunthor; this must be the captain of the guard she had referred to when he first arrived. The giant had clicked his heels and nodded, but said nothing. Jo was bustling with excitement, but had obviously received some sort of corrective lecture and therefore smiled brightly at him, but said nothing as well.

"What brings you here?" Achmed asked bluntly.

Ashe sighed inwardly; perhaps he shouldn't have come. Before he could answer, Rhapsody did it for him.

"We invited him, Achmed; you were there." She turned to Ashe and looked up into his hood, her glance not exactly in line with his eyes, but close. "We're very glad you came, aren't we, Jo?" She smiled, and Ashe felt his knees tremble a little.

"Yes," said Jo.

"When are you leaving?" Achmed asked.

"Achmed! Please forgive him, Ashe. What he meant to ask is how long can you stay? We'll need to ready accommodations for you." Rhapsody glared at Achmed and then smiled at Ashe again; he was finding it hard to break his gaze away from her, but it was necessary to keep alert about his surroundings.

"I'll stay as long as I'm welcome," said Ashe.

"Thanks for coming; it's been nice seeing you," said Achmed.

"Ignore him; he's trying to be funny, but he's not good at it," said Rhapsody, her face flushing with embarrassment and anger.

"I was about to say that I'll need to be on my way fairly soon anyway," said Ashe, amused by the kaleidoscope of Rhapsody's face; it kept turning from an expression of warm welcome to white fury and back again. It was a face he could spend a very long time watching without growing bored.

"We've been readying the ambassadorial quarters in expectation of the emissaries of the various lands and factions, now that we have signed a pact with Roland and Sorbold. You should be fairly comfortable there."

"Excuse me?" Ashe had heard about the rout of the army of Roland; it was impossible to escape the news. He had not heard that they had reached any kind of treaty; the three of them had only been in Ylorc for a few months. It seemed impossible that they could have even begun discussions, let alone signed a pact, when the peace treaty between Roland and Sorbold themselves had taken close to two hundred years to resolve. It was another cog in the wheel, another piece of the puzzle to the influence that these three had.

There were three; a significant number, though Ashe had no real belief in or fear of ancient prophecies. It was as obvious that they were not of this land as it was that Jo had been born here. Still, in the presence of such overwhelming and unique power one could be forgiven for giving in to the desire to believe again in hopes long abandoned.

Rhapsody laughed. "You needn't sound so surprised. A few weeks ago we signed a nonaggression pact and trade agreements with Roland, and a week later with Sorbold as well. The Bolg will be a force to be reckoned with again, but this time as an economic entity, not a marauding one."

As if to mock her words, in the distance a clamor went up, echoing through the rockwalls. Grunthor dashed from the room and into the hallway, followed by the others a moment later. They didn't need to go far; the messenger met them in the corridor outside the Great Hall. The Bolg guard was covered with blood.

Rhapsody pulled up short, listening to the exchange between Achmed, Grunthor, and the herald. She felt Ashe stop behind her.

"What's happening?"

"The Hill-Eye, the last of the renegade tribes, are attacking; idiots. Achmed has been working to bring them into the alliance, but they have resisted, and now they are burning some of the villages of the other tribes that have sworn allegiance to him."

"Hooray!" came Jo's voice from behind Ashe. "I've been in the mood for a good bloodletting since Spring Cleaning; it's been *so* boring around here. I'll get your bow for you, Rhaps." She took off at a sprint in the opposite direction toward their quarters.

Ashe touched Rhapsody's shoulder; she seemed distressed, but not afraid. "Is there anything I can do?"

"Well, you're welcome to pitch in if you'd like; at these times we can use all the help we can get. The Bolg are only recently organized and tend to panic and disperse when battle comes, especially with the Hill-Eye; they are the fiercest of the clans and bloodthirsty. It's in the master plan to spare the noncombatants, but it's not easy to get Grunthor to stick to that sometimes, especially if he's angry enough."

Ashe nodded. "I'll be glad to help you. Just point me in the right direction."

Rhapsody smiled. "Thanks. Follow me."

* * *

The fires that burned, lighting the exterior causeways of the Teeth, had been fed with rancid fat, contributing to the burning nausea Rhapsody felt encroaching on her lungs. She coughed, trying to clear the smoke from her sore eyes.

She had just delivered a swift, stinging blow to the thigh of the last Hill-Eye guard, knocking him to the ground, when a bony hand encircled her upper arm.

"Look," the sandy voice directed; even from just one word she sensed irritation.

She turned amid the diminishing mayhem to watch their guest in action. Even within the swirl of his cloak, the training and speed was undeniable.

He was standing alone, as he had been for most of the battle, knee-deep in casualties of his own making, sidestepping the awkward passes of the Hill-Eye with no apparent difficulty. It was almost as if he were trying to avoid killing them in the hope that refraining would be proper etiquette for a guest.

In a flurry of moves much too fast to follow with the eye, Ashe spun, his sword flashing blue in the dark. The remainder of the Bolg on him fell, one by one, like cards.

"He's good," Rhapsody murmured, watching him step artlessly in front of Jo, deflecting the blow that had been aimed at her. "I think he's almost as fast as you, Achmed. Hhmmm. I didn't think I'd ever see your match. What do you think, Grunthor?"

"Nice form," the Sergeant agreed. "What about you, sir? Whaddaya think?"

Achmed's brows drew together as they blackened with anger.

"I think he's a lot more dangerous than I originally gave him credit for."

The deepest part of the night had passed. Achmed sat alone in the dark, thinking.

The events of the day had been irritating and disturbing to him. It was not the failed assault on Canrif that bothered him; he had been anticipating the last-gasp attempt to drive him out. He was more troubled by the increasing revelations of the power of this stranger who was haunting their halls, following Rhapsody like a shadow.

He wondered if Ashe's arrival and the Hill-Eye's poorly planned raid were coincidental, especially given what he had seen in the lands around the White Tree and all the way from Navarne to Ylorc. Seemingly peaceful places erupted in strife and bloodshed out of nowhere, to return to foggy bewilderment as they tried to fathom the cause of the violence. The prospect that this danger had entered Ylorc angered him greatly. Far more upsetting, it worried him.

He and Grunthor had met after the assault was quelled. The Sergeant Major only had a short time to talk before he departed with the army to round up the Hill-Eye stragglers and subjugate the last renegade territory once and for all, but he and Achmed had been of one mind in their assessment of Ashe. Prior to seeing him in action, Achmed had written him off as a wastrel, a gadabout with delusions of gentlemanship. Generally his judgments did not prove so wrong.

Whatever else Ashe was, both Achmed and Grunthor agreed there was no doubt that this stranger was formidable. What Achmed couldn't understand was how he had missed this fact in the first place.

Certainly he had the capability to size up an opponent, to determine by the way one stood or moved what his abilities in combat were, at least. But there was something about Ashe that defied his capacity to do so. There was a haziness to him, a lack of definition or even visibility that made Achmed more uncomfortable than he had ever remembered being. That discomfort was heightened by Rhapsody's utter obliviousness of the stranger's odd vibrational cloaking.

Ashe had taken up arms willingly in defense of Canrif, slicing through the frontal assault on the halls of the Cauldron without help. Within a few moments after the fighting had begun, he had cleared the main hallway of half a dozen Hill-Eye infiltrators, then followed Grunthor out to the mountain passes in the Teeth.

He had served as Grunthor's cleanup man initially, dispatching the overflow the Sergeant allowed to pass, swinging with admirable sword technique in lightning-fast execution. His sword itself was hard to see, the blade appearing like a slash of blue in the darkness, sheathed quickly when not in use before it could be seen or examined carefully. He was well trained and obviously experienced. Achmed was more annoyed than ever, but at a loss to explain to himself why.

Ashe was also unassuming; he was easily directed and willing to fight on any front, including good-naturedly providing cover for Jo without being obvious about it to spare her feelings. And though it was apparent he enjoyed fighting beside Rhapsody he did not seem to seek to do so, but rather followed Grunthor's commands without question. He was personally responsible for taking out more than a captain's share of the rebellion. Even Grunthor was impressed.

Now Achmed sat alone, in the dim light of the Great Hall of the Cauldron, pondering what to do. He did not like the feelings he was experiencing; he was unable to recognize jealousy, as he had never encountered it before.

The rancid smell of the place was apparent to him for the first time since he had become Warlord; it caused a bitter taste in the back of his throat that made him choke. It was better to endure the presence of this man for the moment, he finally decided. Better to learn of him first than to drive him away, knowing all the while that he would be back. It was important to find out what it was Ashe really wanted there. Whatever it was, Achmed knew he wouldn't like it.

$\mathcal{R}$hapsody unlocked the heavy door and pushed it open, then moved back to allow Ashe to enter the guest chamber.

While he and Jo were at supper she had taken the opportunity to bathe and change clothes, cleansing and dressing a minor wound she had sustained at the hands of a Hill-Eye chieftain. Ashe had taken grim pleasure in beheading him for her as she fell back; it had impressed him that she recovered fast enough to counter her attacker's blow before the Bolg dropped.

His senses told him the wound was painful but minor as long as she tended to it properly to avoid infection, which she had, cleansing it with witch hazel and by applying plantain and thyme to it. As he passed her he inhaled her scent, fresh and unperfumed, with a hint of vanilla and soap to it, and it made him shiver.

He looked around the room in surprise. The chamber was scrubbed and whitewashed, with a cozy fireplace and a plaited rug to warm the room and floor. There was a bed with a packed-wool mattress and a blue quilted counterpane, a wash-stand with a basin and pitcher, and a chamber pot under the bed, as well as a coat tree in the corner. It was not what he expected in a guest chamber in the realm of the Firbolg, but then, neither was Rhapsody.

The fire was burning on the hearth with a merry crackling sound, almost as if it had been laced with green pine nuts. Ashe stretched out on the bed and settled back, waiting to see what she would do. He closed his eyes beneath his hood, enjoying the onset of the darkness while still feeling the heat from the fireplace on his eyelids. He opened them a crack. Rhapsody was still facing the door.

When she turned she was wearing the dazzling smile that had left him weak-kneed on more than one occasion, but there was something new in her eyes, something strange and won-derful and warm; they sparkled in the light of the fire as she looked across the room at him.

Without speaking, she gently placed her hands on her waist, then slid them slowly up her torso, over the prim blouse, caressing her breasts as they passed. They ended up at her neck, where the first of the laces that held the blouse together was carefully tied, and began to unthread it with delicate grace.

Ashe felt his breathing become shallow as she freed the lace from its closure and opened the top of her blouse, the light gleaming off the luminous skin at the hollow of her throat. His lips burned, as they always did when he thought of the lovely indentation of her neck.

One by one the other laces opened. As the closure of her blouse fell away her smile grew brighter until she stood, her breasts barely hidden by the fabric of her shirt. Then her hand moved around behind her head, causing the blouse to open and Ashe's heart to race faster as the arousal that was con-stantly there in her presence became even more intense. The fire on the hearth was cold by comparison to the heat in his blood.

With a gentle tug she loosed her hair from the black velvet

ribbon that customarily held it in place and shook her head. The waterfall of golden tresses spilled down over her shoulders and caught the light; Ashe felt his resolve, his requirement to remain hidden and alone, give way to a painful burning need that spread caustically through him. He began to breathe lightly through his mouth as the blouse slid from her arms over her waist to the floor, where it lay in a crumpled heap.

Now she stood at the door, the firelight flickering off her rosy-golden skin, looking for all the world like the legends of the goddess of morning. But it was night, and she was here, unclothed before him in the firelight.

Her smile broadened as she unlaced her skirt and slid it down over her hips, past the graceful legs that had made him tremble when he first had sensed her, even without actually seeing them. Then she came to him, and sat down beside him on the bed. He was afraid to sit up for fear of losing control.

That was apparently what she wanted. She reached out and took his hand with the grace of a woman who had been able to choose and capture the heart of any lover she had ever desired. His palm grew moist with the knowledge that her choice now was him.

With infinite patience she placed his trembling hand on her long, smooth thigh and gently drew it over her skin, moving upward toward her waist. She closed her eyes as his hand came to rest on one of her exquisite breasts; it fit perfectly within his palm.

Gently he traced the elegant nipple, feeling it harden beneath the callus of his fingertip. As he caressed her there she began to breathe lightly herself and took hold of his other hand, bringing it to rest on her leg again.

This time, however, rather than moving it up over her slim waist toward her heart, she parted her legs slightly and drew his hand over the silk of her inner thigh, breathing in a deep, musical pattern as he summoned his courage and moved to touch her intimately. The nervous moisture of his fingers met that of her desire; his hand turned to explore her more ardently, and as he did she looked deeply into his eyes, longing in her incredible green ones.

"I want to thank you for what you did for us today."

Ashe blinked. Rhapsody was still standing by the door, as she had been the moment before, fully clothed, her hair properly bound. His fantasy shattered and Ashe sat up, arousal still pounding through him. He gave silent thanks for the mist cloak; because of it alone she would be unable to discern the intensity of his stimulation.

"My pleasure," he said, smiling at the play on words; it could have served as his nickname for her. "You're quite a warrior, if you don't mind my saying so."

Rhapsody made a face. "Hardly."

"No, you really are," Ashe said, swinging his legs down to the floor and sitting up straighter. "You wreak a lot of havoc with that sword of yours."

"Well, there certainly was a lot of havoc wreaked today," she said, walking to the washstand and bending down before it. She drew forth a rough drying cloth from the lower shelf and draped it over the basin. "What an unholy mess that was. I have a serious dislike for untidiness."

Ashe chuckled. "You are an interesting woman, Rhapsody."

"Thank you. That's a little ironic coming from a man I've never seen because he never takes down his hood. Well, unless there is something else you need, I believe I will leave you to get some rest; you've certainly earned it."

Ashe thought back to his fantasy of the moment before. There was indeed something more he needed, but he was unwilling in the extreme to ask for it, at least at this point. "A song would be nice. Jo said you were a musician."

Rhapsody smiled. "Can it wait until tomorrow? I'm a little winded tonight, I'm afraid."

Beneath his hood Ashe winced; he had forgotten about her injury. "Of course. Does that mean I'm welcome here for another night?"

"You're welcome here for as long as you'd like to stay. We're grateful for everything you did to help in quelling the raid. And even if that hadn't occurred, you would have been welcome all the same."

"You're most kind. Then I suppose there is nothing more I need tonight."

Rhapsody nodded. "Well, good night, then," she said,

walking to the door and opening it. "Sleep well."

"I have no doubt I will." He watched as she closed the door behind her.

The agony he carried roared back, causing him to gasp deeply and clutch the bed. He breathed shallowly until it came slightly under control, then lay back and fell into an exhausted, troubled sleep.

62

"If you're really that lonely here among the Bolg, Rhapsody, I will get you a cat."

Rhapsody glared at him, and the light of the fire burning behind her intensified.

"And what exactly is *that* supposed to mean?"

Achmed sat forward quickly, the look in his eyes direct.

"It means that he has been here for a week now, and has shown no signs of leaving any time soon. He is wandering the halls of Ylorc with Jo, with no apparent restriction, despite what I thought was a rather clear directive to keep him away from any area that we might not want broached."

The hay target at the end of the meeting room exploded with a savage thud.

"*Excuse* me," Jo said icily, "who died and made you Supreme Ruler?"

Grunthor looked up from the field map he was studying.

"Oi think that would be Janthir Bonesplit'er, lit'le miss," he said, then returned to his reading.

"Maybe for the Bolg. I don't remember taking a loyalty oath." Jo pulled the dirk out of the remains of the target. "Look, I don't know what you're worried about. Ashe is a good sort. It's not his fault that you don't trust anybody, any more than it's mine."

"This is not a point you want to argue," Achmed said acidly. He turned to Rhapsody, who had put down the physician's lyre she had been attempting to study. "I want him out of here by morning."

Shock rippled across her exquisite face. "Why?"

"I don't want him here."

The shock waves were replaced with white anger.

"Really? I agree with Jo; I hadn't realized that yours was the only opinion that mattered. I thought we all lived here."

"All right, he can stay. Grunthor, kill him, please. Before supper."

"Wait," Rhapsody said, watching the Bolg put down his map. "That's not funny."

"I wasn't joking. Rhapsody, he's dangerous and secretive. I've told you this before. I don't want him here, but if you're loath to ask him to leave, bad manners and all, Grunthor and I can handle the social arrangements for you."

Rhapsody glanced between the two angriest sets of eyes in the room. Achmed was growing visibly more upset, but he would have a long way to go to catch up with Jo. Her sister's rage was only nominally contained. She stood, trembling with anger, fingering her dirk.

"All right, everyone calm down," she said, a Namer's tone in her voice. "First you, Achmed. I don't think secretive is necessarily a bad thing; you are the most secretive man I've ever met, including Ashe. Just because he doesn't show his face doesn't mean he's evil. Maybe he's scarred."

"I can't pick up any vibrations from him, Rhapsody. Whenever he's around it's like standing beside the ocean. You know how much I *love* the ocean."

It's not what he is, it's what he wears.

Rhapsody sat straight up at the sound of the voice in her memory. She listened intently, but no more words came.

"That may be nothing more than the function of something he's wearing," she said pragmatically. "What do you think, Grunthor? You've been fairly quiet."

The giant Bolg intertwined his fingers over his stomach.

"Oi agree with 'Is Majesty. Oi don' think we should let 'im out of our sight."

"Fine," said Jo quickly. "I won't leave him alone in any of the main rooms. I'll be with him whenever he's not asleep; how's that?"

"Fine with me," said Rhapsody. "He's leaving soon anyway. I just ask you to indulge me in one more thing, you two," she said to the men. "May I remind you that he helped quell the Hill-Eye rebellion, and did a credible job at it? He helped us when it was no business of his, without asking or expecting anything in return."

Achmed stood to leave. "Maybe he didn't need anything else in return," he said as he stalked to the door. "Maybe all the reward he needed was in causing the rebellion, himself, in the first place."

The heavy wooden door slammed shut with a sound like a thunderclap.

 The cool mist of Ashe's cloak settled on his face, diminishing the heat of his dream.

He turned over in the bed, shrugging away the garment that he wore at all times, night and day, with no exceptions. As he shifted beneath the blankets a pocket of steam rose from the cloak. There was comfort in the mist; it took a little of the edge off his pain. And it kept him safe, hidden from those who hunted him.

He had not been able to dream these twenty years, not since the night when his life had been torn asunder.

In younger days he had come to regard the time he spent dreaming as a blessing, the one chance he still had to be with the woman he loved, would always love, to the exclusion of any other. Her death had been the end of hope for him, or belief in the Future, but he still had his one and only memory of her in the Past. He had come to long for those rare nights when she graced his dreams, smiling in the darkness as she had so long ago.

When he's in port, it's actually very tiny—about as big as my hand. And he keeps it on his mantel, in a bottle.

His one and only memory. It had been enough.

And then, one night, even that solitary comfort was gone. Now his life was no longer his own; he was a shell, a pawn in an evil game. The pain he carried, day after day, moment by moment, was ever-present in his mind and body. It was an agony of the soul as well as the physical realm, a torture so complete that it required almost constant force of will to keep from giving in to it. The dream had vanished then, too holy and pure to be able to exist in the same mind that saw what he was forced to see, night after night, moment by moment.

But now something had changed. Ever since he had met her in the marketplace in Bethe Corbair, he had dreamt of Rhapsody. The guilt of the betrayal of Emily's memory had faded quickly, shoved aside by the ease that her voice brought to his pain, to the throbbing in his head and chest that he had been unable to escape before he met her.

Ashe sat up, untangling himself again from the blankets and the mist cloak. He closed his eyes and breathed shallowly, willing her to go away, to spare him the one thing he held holy. In body and soul, even in his memory, he had been unfalteringly loyal to the woman he had crossed Time to meet, if only for a moment.

There could be no other, he knew. Emily's place in his heart was a shrine.

So why was this woman there? Why couldn't he drive her out of it?

I'll be thinking about you every moment until I see you again.

63

As the days passed, Ashe became a fixture of sorts in Ylorc. Achmed had barred him, as he had Jo, from Gwylliam's vaults and the ancient library; only Rhapsody, Grunthor, and the king himself were allowed within those chambers. Ashe, of course, knew where they were anyway, owing to his dragon sense. But for some reason their contents were unclear to him; he was unable to make out the details from the restricted area, which was a rare occurrence.

It didn't matter. Rhapsody was generally more than willing to discuss the various artifacts they had discovered with him, and Achmed routinely read the manuscripts he found within the library in the evenings after supper, giving Ashe the opportunity to discern what they were then.

Once, as he was allowing his dragon sense to scan the

documents in the Firbolg king's hands, the scroll was abruptly rerolled. He opened his eyes to see Achmed staring at him from across the room. It was almost as if the Warlord could tell what he was doing, even beneath the misty hood. Perhaps it was a sign of his dominion over the land; Achmed held the law and lore of kingship and knew, innately, the minutiae of his kingdom, just as if he were a dragon himself. These were his lands; Ashe had no power here.

All the insults and restrictions were worth it, as it allowed him access to Rhapsody. She was a joy, there was no doubt about it. Her personality held myriad facets and contradictions; she was at once gentle and ferocious, depending on the circumstance, though she possessed a rare ability to laugh at herself and to graciously endure the sometimes brutal teasing of her friends. She was devoted to Jo, and kept after her like a mother hen, defending her chick in all confrontational situations with talons more akin to a raptor. And her intelligence and sense of humor were without peer.

Ashe knew he should be moving on; the one who was waiting for him would doubtless be growing annoyed by now, but he seemed powerless to leave her. He had established a casual, disinterested demeanor that had set well toward making Rhapsody comfortable around him; her guard was down, and she was growing to like him, or at least she seemed to be. *Just a few more days*, he told himself each night as he lay in bed, alone, wondering what she was dreaming about. Achmed's will had extended even into the stone walls, making it impossible to sense her when she was not in the same room. It was a disconcerting feeling.

Everything changed a few days later. Achmed and Grunthor had been gone for most of the day, exploring the caverns. Ashe had spent the morning teaching Jo to play mumblety-peg, a dexterity game he knew she would excel in, owing to her nimble fingers. She had mastered the technique quickly and was demonstrating it to Rhapsody when the two Bolg returned from the vaults, wrapped in an air of excitement.

"Wanna see what we found, Duchess?" said Grunthor, handing her a slim jeweled case. It was pristine, the outer box made from the dark, blue-toned wood of the hespera trees that grew deep within the Hidden Realm and from which much of the ancient furniture they had found had been crafted. The top was hinged with tiny golden braces, and the clasp had no lock.

"It was within many other layers of boxes and caskets, buried deep in the vault," said Achmed, pouring himself a glass from the decanter.

Rhapsody opened it carefully. Within it lay a flawed, curved dagger, the length of a short sword, made from bone or another inconsistent material. It was the color of rose-gold, the metal alloy formed when copper was mixed into a golden base.

"How very strange." She removed the dagger carefully from the box, turning it over in her hands. "Who would gild a weapon with red-gold? It's too soft for any battle use. And the craftsmanship isn't good; look how many defects there are in the surface."

"Perhaps it's ceremonial."

Rhapsody closed her eyes and listened, there was an intense hum in the air around the dagger. Then her eyes opened wide in alarm. "Gods; I think I know what this is," she said. Her face turned white and her voice dropped to a whisper.

"What?"

"It's a dragon's claw; look at it." She held it up at a curved angle; she was right. There was no mistaking it, or the extrapolation that the dragon it had come from had been immense.

"It'll make a great sword for the lit'le miss," said Grunthor.

"You're insane," Rhapsody snapped. Then regret flooded her face as Grunthor looked hurt. "I'm sorry, Grunthor," she said. "I just remember a little dragon lore from the old land. Dragons are particularly selfish creatures, and very jealous of their possessions. If the owner of this claw is still alive, it will know who has it, and may scour the countryside looking to get it back. I don't want Jo anywhere near this thing; in fact, I'm not so sure we want it anywhere within the mountain. We may have to take it back to her."

"Her?"

"Elynsynos, Anwyn's mother, remember? Llauron's grandmother. She's the only dragon I've ever heard of in this land."

"It's been fine here for centuries," said Achmed, annoyed. "Why do you think she will suddenly want it back?"

"Perhaps when it was in the sealed vault she didn't know where it was, but now that the air has reached it, its smell will be on the wind. I'm not kidding, Achmed; one of the first types of lore they teach you as a Singer is tales of dragons and others of the five firstborn races. Most of those stories have to do with the rampages the wyrms go on when a thief steals something from their hoard, or when it is taken inadvertently. We have to decide carefully what to do with this; it would be awful to wake up one night with fire raining from the sky."

Grunthor sighed. "Oi'm not showin' you nothin' from now on," he said.

"Perhaps she's right," Achmed said; the others looked up at him in surprise. He knew the tales as well, and darker ones. "But I'm not sure returning it is the answer. Perhaps we should just take it to the tallest of the Teeth and hurl it onto the plateau. If the dragon is still alive, she'll find it."

"Or someone else will," said Rhapsody indignantly. "Anyone could come across that box and open it; you'd be sentencing an innocent stranger to a horrible death. Besides, I don't think a dragon that would journey to Ylorc to retrieve something she thought was valuable would appreciate it being tossed from a mountain like so much garbage."

Jo had organized the Bolg children into crews that had cleaned up the centuries of filth and litter from the steppes. "Nobody better be throwing trash from the mountain," she said, then went back to her game.

"And how do you propose to return this to her?" Achmed asked.

"I'll go," Rhapsody said. "It will be interesting; perhaps I can learn some dragon lore firsthand."

"No."

"Excuse me?" Rhapsody's eyes narrowed; it was the first sign of anger brewing.

"I said *no*," Achmed repeated. "If I recall correctly, wasn't Elynsynos the dragon that rampaged when she found out that Merithyn didn't come back, and deserted her children as infants?"

"Yes," she admitted.

"And you want to seek her out and say, 'Here, we found this; I'll be on my way now'? I don't think so. Besides, you have no idea where to find her, do you?"

"I do," said Ashe quietly. He had been sitting by silently, observing the proceedings with interest and a touch of amusement. The women jumped when he spoke, having been lulled into forgetting he was there. "I could guide you there."

"No," Achmed repeated again, a snarl in his voice.

"Do you have a better idea?" Rhapsody asked, her annoyance growing.

Achmed sighed irritably and glanced in Ashe's direction. "Perhaps instead of *no* I should had said *not yet*. There may be some value in seeing what she might offer in return for it."

"You're going to ransom something to a dragon?" Ashe's voice contained a note of either disdain or amusement; Achmed couldn't decide which, but either one infuriated him.

"Don't be a jackass. I just want her to remember to whom she owes its return."

Rhapsody was becoming impatient. "I'm not willing to risk it," she said. "Ashe knows how to find her lair."

"Good; then he can draw us a map, assuming he's literate."

Ashe laughed. "I don't think so. If you're still interested in the morning, we can make plans for the journey. I think I will wish you all good night now."

Jo stood as well. "Me too. I'll walk you there." She kissed Rhapsody on the cheek, then followed the cloaked figure out of the room.

𝕽hapsody waited until she was sure the two could no longer hear their voices, then turned to Achmed again.

"Why are you doing this? What's the matter?"

"Nothing. It's not a case of something being 'the matter.' "

"Then what is it?"

"It's a case of being careful in unfamiliar territory."

Rhapsody's brows knit together. "It's not unfamiliar to Ashe, obviously."

"*Ashe* is unfamiliar territory. What's the matter with *you*, Rhapsody? You trip over this imbecile in the market; he calls you a whore and then buys you lunch to make up for it, and you forgive him, proving that, in a way, he was right. Then he shows up here, in my lands, unannounced and unwelcome, and worms his way into your good graces again. Are you so intolerant, is the company of Firbolg so repugnant to you that you crave the attentions of this useless idiot just to be around humans again?"

Rhapsody's eyes stung; Achmed had never been especially careful with her feelings, but even for him this was caustic. "What a horrible thing to say."

"Far less horrible than the things that could happen to you, alone and unprotected, with this man you barely know, outside the range of help. You know I can't leave Ylorc right now. This is not the time for me to go overland when the Bolg are finally united and the plans we put into place are beginning to bear fruit."

Rhapsody's eyes narrowed again. Grunthor caught a glimpse of them from across the room, burning like green fire; he knew that look. It was the warning of great wrath.

"And therefore I am required to stay in Ylorc as well, even though my part in your great unification plan is over," she said, her voice low with the effort to remain in control of her temper. "I have done my share in your effort, Achmed, at times even crossing the line of what I was willing to, all for you, because you said it was the right thing to do. What am I supposed to do here now?"

Achmed gripped the arm of his chair. "What about helping with the agricultural program? The hospital? The hospice? The education strategy?"

"Those things are done and in place."

"What about overseeing the production of the goods? The vineyards? Spring is coming; it will be time to plant soon. That's an important contribution to this land and these people you purport to care about."

"What about keeping them from frying in a wave of dragon's breath?" Rhapsody retorted. "Have you forgotten what this is really about? I think you are more bothered by who my guide would be than the prospect of what might happen if I don't go; not very good decision-making for a king, I would say."

"Oi could go with you," Grunthor offered.

Rhapsody smiled at the giant Sergeant. "No, you can't; in a way, your presence here is even more important than his is." Achmed nodded in agreement. She saw the light change in his eyes, but he said nothing. She went over and sat on the table in front of him, taking his hand.

"Aren't we old and good enough friends by now to say what we really mean? Why don't you just admit you're worried about me? That you're afraid the dragon will kill me, or hold me captive? That you don't trust Ashe alone with me, and that you're afraid if I leave here without one of you, I will not be able to protect myself?"

Achmed met her gaze. "Isn't that what I said?" She shook her head, smiling. "If you know that, why are you still considering going?"

Rhapsody sighed. "Because someone has to, and I am the obvious choice. My work here is at a stage where I can leave for a while without it coming to a halt. And I *can* take care of myself. You forget, I survived on the street for a long time before I met you two. I can handle it; really. And Ashe, too, should he try to take advantage of me. I have Daystar Clarion and the best training in the sword possible." She felt Grunthor smile, and turned to look at him. "Tell him, Grunthor; tell him I'll be all right."

"Oi can't, miss; you know Oi never lie to 'Is Majesty."

She sighed again. "Your faith in me is overwhelming. Look, do you remember what I told you that day on Elysian's lake? That I needed a goal, a chance to do something for the people I care about? This is my chance, Achmed. I'm needed in a way that I haven't been since I came to this place. This is my home now, too. Surely I should risk whatever I must to keep it safe. I can help the Bolg in a way you can't. It's important, to me, and, more critically, to them."

"Go then," said Achmed. "Take Jo with you. How long will you be gone?"

Rhapsody blinked. "Now you want me to go?"

He snorted in disgust. "Don't be an idiot. Obviously I don't want you to go. Just as obviously, you intend to. I've known you long enough to realize who is going to win here. So, since you've already made up your mind, what is left is to make sure you're provisioned well and the plans are sensible. Then we'll establish a date by which, if you have not returned, we'll divide up your belongings, give away your room, and forget about you."

Rhapsody ran a hand over her hair, trying to absorb the sudden shift. "All right," she said awkwardly. "But I can't take Jo; that would be a bad idea."

"She can watch your back. And she'll be out from under foot here."

"She'll be in danger, Achmed," Rhapsody said, annoyance in her voice. "I've finally got that girl to a place she might actually be safe, and you want me to drag her out across the continent again to a dragon's lair? I don't think so. Besides, you're the one who's always worried about her flapping tongue. She might tell Ashe or someone else more about what is going on here in the mountain than you want on the wind."

"Speakin' o' Ashe," said Grunthor seriously, "you might want to warn 'im that if anythin' bad befalls you, or you don't come back, Oi'm gonna track 'im down and kill 'im by several methods that'll get me enshrined in the Torture 'All o' Fame."

Rhapsody laughed. "I'll tell him." She leaned forward and kissed Achmed's cheek.

$\mathfrak{F}$ive days later she and Ashe set out, heading west again the way the four had come. She had spent much of the intervening time with Jo, who had desperately wanted to come as well, but had been finally convinced to stay by Grunthor.

"Oi'm gonna lose the Duchess and the lit'le miss, too? Naw. 'Ave an 'eart, Jo. Oi'll be so lonely Oi'll just curl up and die." The women had broken into laughter at the image.

"How could you possibly resist that plea?" said Rhapsody, hugging her sister. She pulled her closer, so only Jo could hear her whisper. "And look after the other one as well; he needs it even more." Jo had just nodded.

Jo's reluctant agreement had brought to light something odd, Rhapsody had noticed. It had been necessary for her to use many of the same arguments to dissuade Jo that the other two had tried, without success, on her. As a result, by the time Jo had finally acquiesced, Rhapsody was feeling far less certain of the wisdom of the undertaking than she had been, and more than a touch hypocritical.

The last day before their departure she spent with Achmed alone, going over plans and sitting in comfortable silence.

"Is there anything you especially want me not to tell him?" Rhapsody asked over the quiet dinner they shared in his chambers.

Achmed leveled a glance at her. "Everything." A smile crept over his face. "Tell him whatever you want."

Rhapsody was surprised. "Are you sure?"

"Yes. I expect you will be judicious and keep our shared information to yourself unless you need to do otherwise."

"Yes, I will. I'll also keep an eye out for those strange incursions and record what I find."

Achmed agreed. "Just be sure you stay out of harm's way. And you might want to watch for any link between those raids and Ashe; I have long suspected that they might be in some way connected."

Rhapsody looked startled. "What do you mean?"

"The Hill-Eye attacked just as he showed up. The last two incursions we've heard of from Roland were outside Bethe Corbair, just prior to us meeting him in the city, and shortly thereafter. Perhaps there's a tie."

She shuddered. "I hope you're wrong."

"So do I. It isn't too late to change your mind."

Rhapsody thought for a moment. "Better to take the risk now and influence the outcome than to hide and have it visited upon us," she said simply. Achmed nodded; he understood.

The three that remained behind had come to bid her farewell as she and Ashe left before dawn on the fifth day. She embraced and kissed each of them, her eyes dry, reassuring them as best she could that she would be back, well and safe. And then they were gone.

"She's never coming back, is she?" Jo asked tearfully as the two shadows disappeared over the far edge of the Teeth, too upset to maintain her normal disinterested demeanor.

"Now, there, lit'le miss, don't think that way," Grunthor said, draping an enormous arm around her thin shoulders.

"The Duchess is much tougher than she looks. You ought to know that by now."

Jo wiped her eyes fiercely. "She's gonna die, and then I'll be stuck here alone with you two. Wonderful."

Achmed smiled slightly. "Well, it will certainly improve your social position among the Bolg; you'll move up to First Woman, you can be the new Duchess of Elysian and take over the court role of Extraneous Blond Female, unless you have a better offer somewhere else. Then I suppose we can hold auditions."

"Bugger yourself," Jo scowled, and strode off.

Grunthor shielded his eyes from the rising morning sun, his expression dancing between thoughtful and worried. "Supposin' she does die, sir? 'Ow'll we know?"

Achmed shrugged, his hunter's eyes scanning the western horizon for a vestige of her shadow and not finding one. "We won't, though I suspect we might hear her last song on the wind; Lirin Namers have strange connections to music and death." He sighed silently. Or he might hear her heartbeat, a rhythmic, reassuring sound that soothed his sensitive skin, wink out like a candleflame in the distance. He shook off the thought. "Her work here is started and well in place. We'll live without her as best we can. Did you notice when she said she'd be fine her voice didn't have that Namer's ring to it?"

Grunthor nodded. "That's because she can only do it when she's sure she's tellin' the truth."

As she and Ashe reached the summit of the last of the crags before the foothills, Rhapsody turned and stared east into the rising sun, which had just begun to crest the horizon. She shaded her eyes, wondering if the long shadows were really the silhouettes of the three people she loved most dearly in the world, or only the hollow reflections of rock and chasm, reaching ominously skyward. She decided after a moment she had seen one of them wave. Whether or not she was right didn't matter, anyway.

There was something deeply poignant about looking back on the mountains as they receded into the distance, fissured crags pointing, fanglike, to the brightening sky. Rhapsody struggled to quell the sense of loss welling within her, her throat and chest tightening as it had one night long ago. *My family*, she thought miserably. *I'm leaving my family again.*

Somewhere within the multicolored mountains greatness was being born, a history was beginning. The people she had once thought of as monsters were rising out of the darkness as they had once crawled forth from the caves in ages past, coming together to forge a new era. Only this time the mountain would serve them; they would become sharp, honed by the grindstone, under the hand of a master swordsmith who was one of their own.

She no longer feared the Firbolg. She feared for them.

It was not just the bloodthirsty dragon lurking somewhere in the mists on the edge of the world that posed a threat to the primitive people under Achmed's hand. As different as the humans of this new land were from the ones she had lived among in Serendair, in one frightening way they were the same: they thought of the Bolg as monsters, just as she had. And they sought to destroy monsters.

The wind whipped through the Teeth and whirled up to the summit of the last crag, cold and sweet, clearing the morning mist from her eyes and the doubt from her mind. A fondness beyond all reason surged through her, looking back at this place where her friends remained, where the Bolg were just beginning to awake.

Once she had hidden in the highgrass, not knowing with which of two sides to ally herself—the men who had pulled her out of harm's way, or the people of her mother's blood. There was no longer a dilemma.

Her father's voice whispered in her ear, carried by the morning wind.

When you find the one thing in your life you believe in above anything else, you owe it to yourself to stand by it—it will never come again, child. And if you believe in it unwaveringly, the world has no other choice but to see it as you do, eventually. For who knows it better than you? Don't be afraid to take a difficult stand, darling. Find the one thing that matters—everything else will resolve itself.

Wherever she might eventually come to live one day, the Bolg, and those that ruled them, would always have her allegiance. Any risk, any loss was worth the undertaking to keep them safe.

"Look," said Ashe, his pleasant baritone shattering her reverie. Rhapsody turned and let her gaze follow his outstretched finger in the direction of another line of shadows, miles off, at the edge of the steppes where the lowlands and the rockier plains met.

"What are they?"

"Looks like a convocation of some sort, humans, undoubtedly," he said after a moment.

Rhapsody nodded. "Ambassadors," she said softly. "They're coming to pay court to Achmed."

Ashe shuddered; the tremor was visible, even beneath his cloak of mist. "I don't envy them," he said humorously. "That ought to shake up their notions of protocol."

Rhapsody looked up into the darkness of his hood, seeing nothing but a thin trace of vapor. The edges of her scalp hummed for a moment as she sought in vain for eyes in which to gauge an expression. Ashe had seemed at ease among the Bolg, a polite, nonjudgmental visitor, but that was only the most ephemeral of indicators. The hood could be hiding something far more sinister. And even if she could see his face, she would not be able to look into his heart.

He was her guide, the one who might be able to lead her to the dragon's lair, a necessary undertaking if she was to ensure the safety of the Bolglands. Whether or not she would make it there remained to be seen. But in any case, she would have to be wary of Ashe, for the sake of the ones she was leaving behind.

Ashe took up his walking stick again.

"Shall we?"

He looked off to the west, over the thawing valley and the wide plain past the foothills below them.

Rhapsody looked back at the panorama of the Teeth for a moment longer, then turned her eyes toward the west as well. A slice of the sun had risen behind them, casting a shaft of golden light into the gray mist of the world that stretched out below them. By contrast, the distant line of black figures moved through a jagged shadow.

"Yes," she said, shifting her pack. "I'm ready." Without

looking back she followed him down the western side of the last crag, beginning the long journey to the dragon's lair.

In the distance, a figure of a man touched by a darker, unseen shadow stopped for a moment, gazed up into the hills, then continued on its way to the realm of the Firbolg.

With a smoldering screech, the Time-strand broke and ignited, snapping off the spool. The projection on the viewing screen went blank as smoke began to rise from the lamp. A burning length of fragile film fell to the floor.

Meridion bolted forward and seized the spinning reel, patting out the gleaming sparks that clung to its broken edge. Quickly he passed a hand over the instrument panel of the Time Editor, and exhaled as it went dark, idle for the moment. Then he scooped up the strand of film from the floor and turned it over in his hands in dismay. Without even looking he knew the thread was irretrievably broken.

He sat back in the chair again, disconsolate, staring at the film fragment. Then he lifted it to the light.

He could almost make them out, tiny images of the small, slender woman with the gleaming hair tied back in a black ribbon, the hooded man in the gray mantle. Facing each other on the summit of the last of the crags before the foothills, illuminated by the rays of the rising sun.

Meridion sighed. How painfully ironic it was to leave them, frozen at the crest of a breathtaking valley, much as he had seen them that night in the Patchworks. At least he had brought them together again, on the same side of Time. Their souls were so scarred by its ravages that they didn't recognize each other. But they would. They had to.

Meridion waved his hand over the instrument panel again, and the Editor roared with light once more. Gently he slid the burnt edge under the lens. He patiently adjusted the eyepiece, moving it up and down, trying to bring the crisp cinder where the film had snapped into focus.

Finally he gave up, exhausted and distressed. The image was now permanently shrouded in darkness, burnt beyond recognition. He hoped fervently there wasn't something on those frames he had needed to see, an image that would have provided a clue to the F'dor's identity. Without it, he wouldn't be able to intervene again. They would be as much in the dark as the charred film of their lore-strand. Their story had been tragic enough. Without the clue he had been seeking, it was bound to only get worse.

He turned off the Editor again and sat back in the darkness to think.

The image within the burnt edge of the film, crisp with carbon ash, was shrouded in darkness as well.

Night was falling, but it didn't matter. Darkness was a friend to him, his eyes accustomed to the absence of light, having come long ago from the realm of black fire.

The rims of the whites of those eyes, indistinguishable from any other man's by day, now began to gleam with the tinge of blood. Had anyone been there to observe, they would have seen them darken at the edges to a scarlet hue. But, of course, no one was there. He was careful to hide his other side; it would not do to be unmasked now that he was so close to his goal.

In the distance he could see the ambassador coming, and he settled back in his chair and sighed. Finally, after all this time, the Three had come, he was certain of it.

The strange rumblings in Canrif, the whispered tales of the new Firbolg king and the advances of the monstrous population there, could only be evidence that his assessment was correct. Even the mighty Gwylliam had not been able to tame the Bolg. The question that now remained was what to do about it.

Things were going well, too well to be allowed to go awry now. Enough of the seeds of discord had been sewn to ensure the uprising at hand. The loss of the House of Remembrance had been a serious blow, but nothing that couldn't be dealt with.

More critical to his plan was the upcoming interruption of the Patriarchal rite. Whether this new power in the land posed a threat to that or not was uncertain. If that power was ensconced in Canrif now, concerning itself with greedy conquest and the militarization of monsters, it would be too far away to intervene. This was important; too much depended on the assassination in Sepulvarta to allow it to fail.

He closed his eyes and tasted the death that hung, heavy with ripe anticipation, on the wind. The time was coming, and with it the sickening, thudding excitement that built, like a marching cadence, into the frenzy of war. It was the rhythm of growing hatred, determined and unstoppable, sounding in the distance as it came. It would be here soon, all in good time.

The knock on the door shattered his pleasant musings. He rose slowly and went to admit the ambassador, one of only two in the world he could entrust with the most critical tasks. This first task was assessing Canrif and its new sovereign. The second was assuring that the Three remained in the Hidden Realm of the Bolg and out of his way while he tended to more important matters.

After his emissary had left for the court of the Firbolg king, he settled back into his chair again.

"We shall soon see who really deserves to be called the Child of Blood," he said, smiling to himself.

Only the darkness heard him.